We Speak No Treason

Rosemary Hawley Jarman

POPULAR LIBRARY • NEW YORK

DEDICATION:
For My Mother Who Told Me the Truth

WE SPEAK NO TREASON

Copyright © 1971 by Rosemary Hawley Jarman

Published by Popular Library, a unit of CBS Publications, the
Consumer Publishing Division of CBS Inc. by arrangement
with Little, Brown & Company, Inc.

ISBN: 0-445-08199-6

PRINTED IN THE UNITED STATES OF AMERICA

12   11   10   9   8   7   6   5   4   3

Foreword

Although this is a work of fiction, the principal characters therein actually existed as part of the vast and complex fifteenth-century society and had their recognized roles in history, sparsely documented though these may be.

I have therefore built around the lives of my narrators. They were all real people whose destiny was in various ways closely interwoven with that of the last Plantagenet king. I have endeavoured to adhere strictly to the date of actual occurrences, and none of the events described is beyond the realms of probability. Conversations are of necessity invented, but a proportion of King Richard's words are his own as recorded by contemporaries.

The tomb at Greyfriars, Leicester, was sacked during the Disolution of the Monasteries by Henry VIII. The remains were disinterred and thrown into the River Soar.

R.H.J.

Gloucester: You may partake of any thing we say;
We speak no treason, man; we say the King
Is wise and virtuous . . .

Shakespeare: Richard III: Act I, Sc. I.

PART ONE

THE MAIDEN

The maidens came
When I was in my mother's bower;
I had all that I would.
The bailey beareth the bell away;
The lily, the rose, the rose I lay.

The silver is white, red is the gold;
The robes they lay in fold.
The bailey beareth the lull away;
The lily, the rose, the rose I lay.

And thro' the glass window shines the sun.
How should I love, and I so young?
The bailey beareth the lull away;
The lily, the rose, the rose I lay.

                              XVth Century: *Anon.*

Gardening is all of my pleasure. It was ever more of a joy than a duty, to watch the tender shoots burst forth in spring, and to know that I had a part of them, in the cold season. When the scent of rose and gillyflower rises to mingle with the pungent breath of thyme and rosemary, chervil, basil and rue, I can close my eyes for a sinful instant, and be young again. Not old, and witless, and shattered by rheumatism like an oak after the lightning; but brimming with promise, as a fresh field awaiting the sower's careful hand. Like the good earth of England, made rich by the blood of strong men, slumbering in moist quietness yet, beneath, a moil of passionate life. Like my garden. I call it mine, but in secret; for nuns have no possessions, only their thoughts, and should the bishop and priest have power to read my mind, they might find me exceedingly worldly still. And I do not care. Sorrow is a sharper blade than penitence, and when a creature is bared to the bone she sees life as one might through a slanted glass, some of it faded, some of it out of true, some sharp and clear. I am very old. They say the old remember childhood best of all, and they do not lie, though this is a world of liars.

I have been thinking today about Elizabeth. Dame Elizabeth Grey, who was our Queen. I knew well that Elizabeth. I lived in her house, on the manor of Grafton Regis, when I was young, and reckoned myself so full of guile and cunning, and know now that I was not. Another Elizabeth is our Queen, and they say that she is ailing. May Our Lady of Sorrows have mercy upon her and guide her where I long to be. Though I have never seen her, I know that she is fair, like her mother; her mother of the herb garden. That brings me again to the flowers, and the neat rows of spices and the weeds which spread even unto the cloister with its tomb. Gardening too has its moments of truth, for a grave needs to be weeded, like everything else, and this is the grave of my beloved.

They buried him here, for there was nowhere else for them to lay him, in spite of the fact that he should have been entombed at Westminster, not only for the good he wrought but because he came of the old royal line. No ordinary man was he; neither knight nor squire nor honest yeoman, but one possessed of such extraordinary strength and compassion that you would think he would ever be loved and revered. Mine is a strange, barren story: more joy, more sorrow, than is the lot of most. Yet the sorrow is sometimes almost forgotten and the joy, which supported me through the years while he lived, was such to make me smile and dream, refusing the knights who would have married me, and being content with the memory of a few hours. It is no heresy to love, and be mad. And there are times when, hearing the things now shouted about him whom I knew to be a good man, I wonder myself if I were once bewitched by the bright fiends of Fotheringhay.

I say the sorrow is almost forgotten, yet days come when an old woman has to look anxiously for the comforting Eye of God, in the mote of a sunbeam, in the passing glint of a chantry window, all the while cursing her frail tools and her weak hands. And I have betrayed my secret, an open secret these days, and one which I could mouth with pride. Yet had he been the lowest of the commonalty I would have run gladly towards the love we loved together. Daily the shouts of calumny and disfavour reach my ears; the shouts that once were whispers. I can but smile and shake my head for, being what they deem a witless old nun, my testimony is useless.

Always was he all my joy. And I first heard his name at the manor of Grafton Regis, when I was twelve years old.

A king once loved me.

Two little boys played naked under an April sun. I leaned from the upper window, laughing at them. Tom, the elder, who was taller by a hair than Dick, had set up the quintain for lance-practice. It was a fearful Saracen's head, carved from wood and painted, and balanced so that the lightest thrust would send it spinning, arms opened wide to fell the jouster. Adding to the hazard was a bucket of water placed atop the Saracen. As I looked, little Dick, raising his weapon to shoulder height, made a charge untimely and unskilled. The infidel swung round. I heard a thud, saw the sparkling cascade then, howling, Dick sprawled on the sodden lawn, while his brother roared in triumph.

'They'll catch a chill.' Behind me came the grumbling voice of their nurse. 'Lord, Lord, what will their mother say?'

Say? Why, she will say naught, I thought to myself. She is too preoccupied these fair spring days. But I merely smiled at the nurse. I kept this secret as I kept my admiration for the absent Dame Elizabeth, for she was beautiful, my mistress. Tall and gilt-haired, with a small pouting mouth and heavy, mysterious eyes. I knew that, uncaring, she would let her boys run bare beneath the grudging sun, when they should be at their lessons. I imagined she had much on her mind.

So I said: 'They are hardy,' and went on watching them.

'Tchah!' said their nurse.

'Lady Grey approves of their sport,' I murmured. 'She says it will harden them for battle.'

And she had gone out riding, this day. Riding in Whittlebury Forest, where once she had met the man; the man with hair like the sun, and a body like a slim oak tree. I often wished that I were fair as Dame Elizabeth.

'Battle!' said the nurse.

' 'Twill be a long time yet,' I said comfortingly.

'Will it, in truth?' she answered crossly. 'I'm not so sure.'

Her wrinkled eye was upon me and I searched my mind for a task undone, a duty neglected. I had been beaten once already that day; thus was I standing to watch Dick and Thomas Grey from the window. I could not sit down easily.

'From what I just heard,' she went on, 'babes and sucklings ride to battle.'

I was dying to know what the courier had said. From the moment of watching him ride through the crumbling courtyard an hour ago, I had been a-boil of curiosity. It was unusual enough, even in these days of fretful peace, to have such a messenger visit Grafton Regis. A real royal courier, with the *rose en soleil* shimmering on his surcote. There were so many things I was hot to know. He might even be able to tell the name of my lady's handsome stranger, the sun-haired knight. So I laid my cheek against the nurse's sleeve, fawningly.

'What said he, sweet dame?'

'He talked of the King's brothers,' she said grudgingly. 'One of them leads the levies to join the royal army. Like a real captain and he only twelve years old. They are encamped at Leicester.'

Ah, Leicester. This gave me a pang. For it was at Leicester that I had been reared, in a nunnery, under the most virtuous Prioress that ever drew breath. Through war and peace and changing monarchs, in riches and penury, Leicester had been my home, both physical and spiritual. There I had lived with my mother until her death, and there had my father, dying, willed me to Grafton Regis and the service of Sir Richard Woodville's widowed daughter, Dame Elizabeth Grey.

'To my mind, it's shameful,' said the nurse, looking dolefully at the drenched boys. 'Nowadays, knaves are men before they're out of swaddling bands. Look at those two! And as for little Gloucester, I doubt he'll stand the journey.'

I knew hazily of King Edward's two brothers; there was George of Clarence, and this other, younger one, whom few had seen, who led an army, and who was of scant interest to me.

'Why did he not send my lord of Clarence instead?' I said. 'If this Gloucester is so young and weak besides . . .'

'George was appointed no commissions, the courier told me,' she replied. 'And the King thought it would be good for Richard. To give him confidence, courage.'

I dismissed this with a yawn. Then, eagerly, longingly, asked:

'Did the man . . . did he know aught of my lady's leman? The most handsome man, the hottest in love, for that he must be. Did he . . .'

Without warning, she boxed my ear. The wide sleeves of her worsted flew about.

'Leman! Lover!' she growled wrathfully. 'Cease this shameful talk! Remember always, there's none more chaste than Lady Grey!'

Had I been older, I might have mistrusted this fire-hot defence of virtue, and been wrong, for all that. Had I not witnessed a certain scene with my own eyes, I might have wondered on it. But, enthralled, scarcely comprehending, and a little afraid, I had seen the evidence of Dame Grey's incorruptible virtue. What I saw occurred not long after her first meeting with the great golden knight; a meeting which, in itself, had seemed a strange, oddly predestined thing. Elizabeth had gone out into Whittlebury one day, on foot, and unescorted save for the two little boys—and very sweet they looked, if a little ill-nourished and pale—hanging on her either hand. We had feared for her; the royal hunt was reputed to be about, and there was the hazard of her being trampled in the chase. Yet she returned at dusk, smiling, softly flushed, no harm having come to her save that the horse of a young nobleman had splashed her with some mire. It was soon after this that this man, terrifyingly handsome, like a saint or a sun-god, had begun to visit Grafton Regis. I did not know his name, though I strongly suspected that others in the household did. He often called himself 'Ned'— sometimes 'poor Ned'—this with a rich laugh—or 'lovelorn Ned' in songs he composed himself and accompanied on the lute. My awe of him was great. For one thing he was so tall his golden head seemed to graze the clouds. That he came to Grafton at all was a kind of miracle; so might a saint step down from heaven, or the sun itself swing low for a brief space to bless our days. Young and sturdy, he had a happy voice and a purseful of gold angels ready to drop at any small favour done him. Once, he pinched my cheek. I blushed and shrank; he called me 'hinny'. Then, Lady Grey entered—he forgot me and grew pale with longing.

And my days were filled with pleasant duty, brushing out Elizabeth's long hair of spun silver, bathing and perfuming that white body. It grieved her that she had but a handful of dresses in which to receive her splendid guest, so that I was forever refurbishing them, taking the tassels from one, the gold passement from another, to make of a third a thing of beauty. We were poor at Grafton. Poor by any standards, for Sir John Grey, while he lived, had fought for Lancaster, and most of his estates had been forfeit to the Crown. I think this

13

saddened Elizabeth; she had a passing tragic look at times, enhanced by the widow's barbe and wimple custom bade her wear. All her lovely hair was hidden, save for one little love-lock, a gilded promise that surmounted the broad brow, full lips and pointed chin. Lovesome was she, yet while she laughed gracefully and drank wine with the fair nobleman, she kept about her a cloak of chaste piety which might, I thought, have chilled his ardour. It did not; he was mad for her, as rams are mad in spring.

I rubbed my smarting ear and thought of the day I went to the herb garden on an errand for Elizabeth's mother. The old Duchess of Bedford, who lived with us at Grafton, kept her own small knot garden behind the long yew hedge next to the stables. A clipped, neat sward of lawn lay between beds which themselves were filled with strange plants and stranger fungi, most of whose names I did not know. Once, Jacquetta of Bedford had been as fair as her daughter, and now she spent hours brewing skin salves, or potions to revive her thinning hair. On this occasion she had sent me only for a few sprigs of rosemary and some cherry-blossom, should it be flowering yet. So I went down and the rich borders welcomed me with a joyous waft of perfume, so intense and inviting that my latest worry, the need of a new gown, fled from my mind, and I lay down, stretched out along the edge of the flowerbed, hidden by the bushes, watching a beetle stag-gering through the grasses, breathing thyme and sweet gale and pennyroyal, thoughtless and content. So their voices star-tled me, when Lady Grey and her tall young suitor came slowly down the lawn between the rectangles of raised shrubs. His velvet cap was tucked beneath one arm. With the bright light circling his head, he looked like the spirit of the sun. Yet he seemed ill-pleased about something, and a petu-lant smile lay on his mouth. Elizabeth's eyes were demurely downcast; as she walked she plucked a flower-head, a prim-rose growing in moss halfway up the garden wall. She held it for an instant to her lips. Instantly he snatched it from her, quite roughly, thrusting it deep into the breast of his dou-blet as one might plunge a sword into the heart. He took her hand. Their footsteps slowed. They stopped a few paces from where I lay; I dared not move or make a sound.

'Lady, be kind,' I heard him say. Then, desperately: 'Sweet Bess, why do you torment me so? I pray you, be kind. 'Tis lit-tle to you, and the whole world to me.'

She murmured something, low as her downcast eyes. She began to walk on, but he sprang, clasping her in his arms.

14

She made no move to evade him; she merely stood, smiling that same, faint smile, and looking at the ground.

'Flesh and blood, Madame?' he asked gratingly. 'Or stone, Madame?' Then it was I became uneasy, frightened. He was so changed, so fierce. With a sharp movement of his great hands he tore the wimple from Elizabeth's head. Her silvery hair spilled over his arms. Bending, he crushed his face into her throat, while she stood, motionless. I gripped a bunch of rosemary and prayed they would not see me. Lying there, afraid, I thought I heard the pounding of their hearts.

'Yield to me, Elizabeth!' he said in a terrible voice.

I could not hear her reply, it was so soft. Sunlight stabbed at the blade of a drawn dagger, and jewels burned at its hilt. He was holding the knife to her throat, the white throat bruised by kisses.

'Yield, Madame,' he said, like a madman. 'Or, by God's Blessed Lady, none other shall possess you. Bess, Bess,' he said, like a child, 'would you have me insane?'

Standing bravely, she said, calm and pleasant: 'Sir, I am too good to be your leman. Too good, Ned, to lie, even with you, in sin.'

Fierce colour mottled his face. He cursed and swore. He threw the knife, its hilt a jewelled rainbow, to the farthest end of the garden. Then he turned and strode, all swift anger, towards the house. For a moment Elizabeth stood musing, then coiled her hair deftly, rearranged her wimple and followed him, without haste, stopping only to pick up the dagger that quivered in the soft lawn. I rose and ran in the opposite direction, still clutching the bunch of rosemary for my lady of Bedford.

At one time I did wonder whether they were perchance enacting a scene from a play, or rehearsing some new disguising, some foolish romance, and that this was all in sport. Her calmness made me wonder thus. Yet I thought on it, and pondering, knew it had been no game. And so I learned of Elizabeth's stern chastity. He did not come again for some weeks; Elizabeth showed no sign of missing him, but her mother fell in a black fury, out of all proportion to the case. Her body-servant, Agnes, who was my dear friend, suffered the lash of Jacquetta's tongue, and nightly in whispers she and I surmised the reason for this wrath. We reached the conclusion that the old woman was in love herself with Elizabeth's suitor, and forgot our bruises in stifled mirth. But when he came again, all smiles and sweetness and contrition, we saw no signs of such a passion; in truth, Jacquetta withdrew into

15

her private solar, and mixed more herbals. Agnes swore she was at work on an elixir to make her young again.

The pain in my ear was fading. I sought to placate the nurse.

'Is the courier still here, sweet dame?'

'Aye, he is,' she said gruffly. 'His horse cast a shoe, and that's why.'

I was disappointed. No news of battles, then. Not that I wanted a battle, God forbear. No summons to the Court of King Edward, either, for any of us. That had ever been a lackwit dream of mine. I had heard that the King, whose deeds of courage were legion, was wonderful to behold, and his court a splendour. But the nurse was babbling again of the King's brothers.

'Such a babe to lead an army,' she mused. 'So they say. And so frail. Unlike his brothers, I have learned. While both his Grace and George of Clarence are ruddy and fair, Richard is small, low statured. Blue eyes, nearly black. His hair is very dark. Almost that colour.' She touched the oak settle. 'Wistful of mien, not given to smiling.'

He sounded a passing dull fellow. 'Is he to fight already, this Richard?' I asked mockingly. "And who's the foe?"

'He's only leading the levies,' she replied with restrained patience. 'Though, mark you, he could fight. They say he was trained in arms by the Earl of Warwick, at Middleham Castle in the north parts. And the King dotes on him.' She looked tenderly out of the window at Dick and Thomas Grey. 'Babes in harness,' she said. 'Certes, these are terrible days.'

'One king is the same as any other': I had heard it many times, until the sack of Ludlow, when we at the nunnery had been so terribly afraid. It was Queen Margaret, the French vixen, who had bred in us this chilling fear. She had let her men pillage and burn and ravish; it was only King Edward Fourth who had put a stop to it. As for her spouse, the old Lancastrian king, Henry—folk said he had been mad for years. My own father had fought for Lancaster, and those days had been far more terrible than now. We were at peace, and King Edward, from all accounts, was a good king. It was what a man was by instinct, blood and loyalties, not what his policy made him, as the Prioress at Leicester—the Mother whom I still missed—used often to tell me.

'Have you naught to do, child?' the nurse said, suddenly sharp. 'What of my lady's mending? Her shifts are in ribbons. And there is work aplenty in the stillroom for those idle, lady-hands of yours.'

'Is the courier well-favoured? May I go down and see him?'

Gaze fixed again on the boys, she was not listening. They ran and leaped, the sun shifting on their pallid bodies. Thomas had captured the large black cat which belonged to the Duchess of Bedford. He was tying a rusty spur to its tail.

'Lord!' mourned the nurse. 'Dame Grey sets great store by those young knaves. But my lady Jacquetta loves her cat equally. Should I go down and chide them, I wonder?'

She looked at me stupidly; she was a stupid woman. Often she berated me, often she sought my counsel. The cat whimpered and squalled. Dick sat down heavily astride its twitching back.

'I'll go,' I said. 'They'll be killing it soon.' Her protests floated after me down the stairs.

It was a good excuse to escape her vigilant eyes. At any moment she would find me another piece of tiresome labour and I was weary from a morning laundering Dame Grey's delicate linen. My hands looked red and would have been redder still save for the application of rose-water cream filched from my lady's vial. (I think that was my only dishonesty. I always salved my conscience with the thought that, as she used it so lavishly, she must have a little to spare for those more needy.) In any event I misliked to see animals maltreated.

It was warm in the garden among the sheltering yews. Patches of violets edged the lawn. Like wicked frogs, Thomas and Dick grinned up at me. I rescued the struggling cat and smoothed its fur. Maddened to ingratitude, it sought to nip me.

'Poor Gyb is not a horse,' I said sternly.

'In faith, he did not mind being ridden,' little Dick argued, sucking a scratched wrist.

'Set up the quintain again,' I said.

Thomas heaved a great sigh. 'I am aweary of that game.' He gave me his sly smile. 'Play Hoodman Blind! You never play with us now!'

Summoning my new dignity, I said: 'Well, I'm a child no longer, sirs,' and was glad of it. Their play was rough, and sometimes they would treat me with a thin contempt, aping great lords. Once, Tom, in temper, had reminded me that my father had been but a landless knight. Now, at twelve, I was a woman, and the gulf between was almost absolute, but on that occasion I had been a crying child, reminding them that that same landless knight had died of wounds taken in the

17

Lancastrian cause and the service of their own grandsire, Sir Richard Woodville.

'Put on your clothes,' I told them. 'You're wanton. Dick, get dressed.'

'I have no bonnet,' he said, grinning. 'Lend me yours, lady.' Swift as a bat, he seized my dangling veil. My short black hennin with its tarnished gold braid was tweaked from my head, and my hair fell down, a life-time's heavy growth. It covered me like a cloak; the sun felt unfamiliar on my brow.

'Wanton! Wanton!' mimicked Thomas, and they were off, flat-footedly racing, bearing my bonnet like a battle trophy. I was left with the echo of their floating laughter, and the slitted eyes of the cat, watching. It dabbed its coat with a quick tongue, then gazed at me again. Small boys were cruel, yet I felt a strange distaste for this particular beast, and marvelled that Jacquetta of Bedford should love it so. It slept in her bed all night. Its eyes were lines of amber, that looked on me with hate. Suddenly I clapped my hands.

"Shoo! Cursed Gyb!'

I know not why I called it cursed. It skipped, arching, behind the hedge. I walked on slowly. For a brief space I was free. At any time my mistress might return from her ride but, until then, I was at large to peek and glimpse, with fortune, a real royal courier. I tried to braid my hair. I loved my hair; it was long as Dame Grey's, and thicker, but a strange colour, seen by few, kept as it was in a great coil under my little blunt-pointed hat. Think of a fox, a chestnut, the setting sun on wine, a dying leaf. Those were the colours of my hair, and many more besides. I gave up trying to plait—it was too thick. I twisted it in a knot; it poured sleekly through my fingers like molten metal. I let it hang, and it waved and lifted about me as I walked, like the blown garment of an autumn tree.

I stepped into the kitchen and there was the courier. A courier off duty, by my faith, for he lay comfortably in a chair by the hearth, with its dusty andirons and smouldering peat, his boots extended to the warmth, while fat Agace, the cook, filled his tankard from the day's brewing. The blazing rose of York shone from his garment. He was laughing and, though he was past his youth, being at least eight-and-twenty, I thought him well-favoured; he lacked no teeth and his eye had an easy glint. He looked up when I entered, a little cautiously, as if unsure of whom he was about to see. Then he rose; he bowed. I found delight in that courtly bow. Agace, however, bustled over to me, proud and as insolent as she dared, full of outraged whispers. This was her kingdom, the scullions her subjects, my disarray her great displeasure.

'Bind your hair, mistress!' she growled. 'What will the gentleman think of us? My lady out riding, and you strutting like a wanton quean!'

The esquire caught her last words. He could scarcely help it. He said gently:

'Nay, nay, good cook. Like . . . a bride, I fancy. Yea, a bride.'

I felt the warm wash of pleasure. The dim kitchen seemed to glow.

'John Skelton, mistress,' he said, bowing again. 'At the service of Lady Grey's fair daughter, of whose existence I vow I did not know.'

Here was confusion. He had called me fair; yet Lady Grey had no daughter. I opened my mouth, foolishly, and heard Agace swiftly acquainting him of my life's history in one pompous breath. The kitchen was ordinary once more. I looked up at him, sadly spreading my hands. I was the child of charity, and fair no longer. Here the game must end.

'There you have my story, sir,' I said. 'Save that—' with an angry look at Agace—'my father was knighted ere he died.'

But he only smiled, gently. 'A tale of honourable misfortune,' he said. Then, half to himself: 'Mother of God, what a colour!'

He was gazing at my hair. I was little, I was unimportant, but he found me pleasant to look upon. I closed my ears to the scullions' giggling, and to Agace's disapproving sniff. I smiled into John Skelton's eyes, straightening my back. I liked the way he looked at me, though there was something oddly disturbing in it. Like finding a new, mysterious plant, lovely but unknown, in the herb garden.

'I have been in Calais, in Burgundy,' he said softly. 'Never did I see its like. By my soul, the Flemish artists would lose their wits over that hair. They would go mad while they mixed their paints. What is it? A bay horse's hide has it, and a beech leaf, but there's pure gold there, and red fire. Come to the light, child, that I may judge it better.' He drew me to the window.

Behind me, I heard Agace say, low-voiced: 'Court flattery. Certes, a right courtier!'

One of the stable-boys lurched in through the open door. 'Horse is ready, master,' he muttered. His tatters were shown

19

up cruelly by John Skelton's bright robes. I went with him to the stable, while the boy slouched ahead, kicking pebbles. We walked through the herb garden, and I feigned in secret that the esquire was my leman, begging me to yield at dagger point. But he was old enough to have fathered me. I kept eyes downcast, as Elizabeth did.

'Are you betrothed?' he asked. I shook my head. My face must have expressed some hidden shame, for he tipped up my chin with a kindly finger.

'But you're still young,' he said. 'That hair! It would be shame to hide that hair in cloister.'

My spirit drooped. I thought, yes, a nunnery! The only alternative. Having no husband, to be exalted to Christ's Bride. What better fate? But he had called me fair.

'When Dame Grey comes to court,' he went on, 'I doubt not she will bring you also, and her other maidens to attend her.'

I stopped dead in the middle of the lawn. Even the trees held their breath, and the flowers.

'She is to go to court?' I whispered. And then, forgetting all warnings, said loudly: 'How her lover will miss her! Oh, Master Skelton, he's the handsomest man in the world.'

Now it was his turn to stop. He caught my hand and held it tight.

'Jesu,' he said quietly. 'She has a lover? What is his name?'

I described him, babbling of his beauty. I said his name was Ned, and that was all I knew. I never saw a man laugh so lustily as did John Skelton then. He clasped his own waist and leaned this way and that. I said stiffly:

'I think you mock me, sir. You asked, I answered. Now, is it true my lady is for London?'

He ceased laughing, and gave me the strangest look, saying quickly: 'Nay, put it from your mind absolutely. I did jest with you indeed. Forgive me.'

Being very cross, I grew even more polite than usual. Looking straight ahead, I asked him:

'You say that you have been abroad? Tell me of the fashions, if you please. I hear that in France and in Burgundy ladies no longer wear the tall hennin but a little cone-shaped hat, trimmed at the crown with braid. Is this but another rumour?'

He said again, very humbly: 'Forgive me. Yes, I have been to France, where the ladies can't hold a candle to our English maids, but I fear I've no eye for fashion. And as for Burgundy . . . by God! My last voyage there still gives me bad

20

dreams. The most important commission of my life. And the most dangerous.'

His voice told me that this subject held neither flattery nor false rumour. His eyes were far-off, grey as the sea.

I said, 'Tell me.'

He looked down at me again, as if he had forgotten who I was. With sad face, he asked: 'Don't you recall the doings at Wakefield?' Then: 'Ah, certes, you would be but a young child.'

Seven years old, and in the nunnery. I remembered how the news came to us at Leicester. My mother had prayed for Lancaster, but the Mother of Leicester, the Prioress, had prayed for both Lancaster and York. 'Tell me then, Master Skelton,' I said. 'Tell me the truth of Wakefield.'

'It was to be the final triumph for the House of York,' Skelton said slowly. 'The Duke of York, King Edward's father, his young son, Edmund of Rutland, and the Earl of Salisbury, marched for Yorkshire in hopes of defeating the French Queen at last. My lord of York had already claimed the throne by right of blood. He had been hailed Protector of the Realm in Westminster. But he had reckoned without the Scots and the men of the North—all of them heathens and hot for the Frenchwoman. When he halted at his castle at Sandal, it was Christmas, and both sides declared a truce for the holy season. Alas! the Lancastrians enjoyed their feast and their disguisings right speedily, for on the last day of December they fell upon the castle, where York lay unprepared. He and many of his followers were slain in a matter of moments. They lay with the remnants of their gaiety around them, the holly and mistletoe boughs all spattered with their blood. Salisbury was taken and beheaded at once. Young Edmund of Rutland fled to Wakefield, where the battle raged, and there Clifford, the Lancastrian lord near his own age, cut him down as he cried for mercy. "Your father slew mine, and so shall I slay you and all your kin".'

We stood quiet together, our feet damp with the lawn's dew. From the hedge a bird sang mournfully.

'He was seventeen,' said John Skelton. 'And they took his head, together with that of his father and Lord Salisbury, and exposed them to the people of York, speared on pikes at the Micklegate Bar, with paper crowns about their brows to mock their aspiration.'

'Yet we are at peace,' I said softly.

'Through Edward, gallant Edward. He was spared that disgrace and death. Eighteen years old, and chosen by God.

21

Earl of March he was then . . . you heard of the vision he had at Mortimer's Cross? His Grace, rising on the battle morning, perceived not one sun in the sky, but three! Three suns! It was the sign, the Sun in Splendour!' He clapped a hand over the royal emblem on his heart, the fiery sun. 'I swear, I know, that God Himself gave him the victory. St Michael shielded him. Through Mortimer's Cross, through Towton Field—where the worst snowstorm ever known soaked up men's blood—Edward triumphed.'

'And you?'

'He had a task for me. The whole country was in uproar—churches were pillaged, children murdered—women were raped as though they were heathen women—men mad with looting-lust . . .'

'We prayed,' I told him. 'We prayed day-long, with the nuns. My knees were raw from the chapel stones.'

'Yes, the convent was safe for some. But not for those of the blood royal. It was January when the King sent for me at night, to escort his young brothers to Philip of Burgundy, where they would be best preserved. A risky adventure; I confess to being afraid. And, what was worse, the boys had been roused by the commotion and crept on to the gallery. They overheard our talk in the great Hall. I had hoped to bear them swiftly aboard ship without their knowing why, but Richard and George heard us speak of their father's and brother's deaths, and how their heads wept blood on Micklegate.'

I thought on my mother, slipping away in peaceful sleep; of my father, wounded and shriven, providing for me in death. To a Lancastrian household, Lancastrians, who had done these fearful things. But a Lancastrian household no more, since the King's pardon arrived last year. I thought: Death is a part of life, and a part of me. Held by John Skelton's story, it made me no less sad.

'Which is the right course, the right way?' I said. He did not hear me.

'The young princes had scarcely time to receive their mother's blessing. They call her the "Rose of Raby", that proud, brave woman. I saw her fighting her grief as she flung together a few necessaries for their journey . . . warm clothes, a missal, a jewelled dagger . . . She put little Richard in my arms. He was stiff with shock, like one dead. Jesu! How he favoured his father in face; he still does. When she kissed him I turned my head away—she knew not if she would see him

22

again. The rebels were everywhere. London was in madness. Even the 'prentices were armed with clubs. Mayor Lee donned mail; the city flew to hide behind him. They said that the Frenchwoman's army was sweeping down like plague to murder us all, and that London was doomed. Many repented of their sins, that night.'

He was silent, thoughtful. 'Where did you take ship?' I asked.

'At Billingsgate, on a Flemish merchantman. Days and nights we tossed on the North Sea. George enjoyed it. He harassed me with questions while I nursed Richard, whom grief had thrown into a sharp fever. He moaned for hours, his flesh on fire. He was a frail child at the best of times; through his infancy men marvelled daily that he lived. So off the tortured sea came we to Duke Philip. Young Richard lives yet. Praise God.'

'Amen,' I said, out of customary politeness.

'Now,' he said, smiling, 'he is Knight of the Garter, Admiral of England, Ireland and Aquitaine. The King is proud of him. He is having him trained in arms under Warwick himself. At Middleham in the North. And Warwick is the most powerful knight in the world.' Even I knew of Warwick; the man who made kings great, by sword and by will.

Just then Dick and Thomas Grey came into view, sparring out on to the lawn with their wooden weapons. I was glad to see that they were dressed. Dick was wearing my hennin; he had torn its veil. A look of amiable scorn crossed John Skelton's face as he watched them. He said:

'I saw Richard of Gloucester training just lately. He fights like a man. He is so frail and weak it seems he would drive himself twice as hard as any of the other henchmen, to prove his worth to King Edward. All the young knights cry quarter . . .'

'Tell of Burgundy,' I begged. 'The court of Duke Philip . . .'

He smiled. 'We were royally welcomed, exiles though we were, and regaled with strong pleasures. Mistress, you would have loved a sight of Master Caxton's library. You know of Caxton?' I shook my head. 'A worthy mercer, friend of King Edward. In Bruges, he has hundreds of manuscripts, illuminated in the colours of the rainbow, their bindings crusted with gems. And at Duke Philip's manor at Hesdin, there is naught but engines of most cunning trickery—books which, when opened, blow dust into your face; a great hall where

23

lightning shoots from the ceiling and thunder rolls overhead; marvellous birds and beasts, and bridges which collapse midway and tumble the unwary into a stream below.'

We had reached the stables by this time. I was about to ask more questions, when suddenly through the archway leading from the courtyard came the sound of hooves. Lady Grey was returning. Behind me, I heard a window in the east gable fly open. The Duchess of Bedford was on watch. I had wasted an hour.

'Farewell, sir,' I said at once. I gave him a curtsey, down to the ground. He laughed, tipped up my chin again.

'A kiss,' he said. I looked away, confused. ' 'Tis a courtly custom,' he said. 'Ned would tell you. Ned!' and laughed again, kissing me lightly on the laugh.

I might have been a whit enamoured of John Skelton. But he had told me naught of the court, naught of my lady's lover, had prattled only of King Edward's weakling brother.

He mounted and sat his horse, an ordinary enough man yet to me the emblem of glamour, with the *rose en soleil* shining from his breast. He smiled at me; the beast curvetted and sprang forward. I felt my hair whipping about my face, and his eyes upon it. Then he was gone, and a little space after, Lady Grey rode in, riding side-saddle, in the Bohemian fashion, her face fair and serene and haloed by the shabby wimple. Beside her rode an elegant figure. It was her brother, Anthony Lord Rivers. So he had come to visit us again. He frightened me.

Behind them came a scattering of ragtag henchmen and a man I had never seen before; a holy man, a black-robed clerk, with a wild, rolling eye and face the colour of whey.

I dreamed often of a knight, one whose countenance was never visible to me. Neither fair nor dark, pure nor swarthy, he would appear in dreams, mounted and armed, at the edge of a green meadow. The horse's legs were clothed in mist to the pastern, the rider's armour wore a sheen of fog. Always his visor was closed, but I would know that he watched me, with a deep, mailed look through his eye-slits, while I stared and stared, trying to penetrate that steely mist, in vain. Long after he had faded his essence remained, always a mystery. I told none of this dream; I knew it for what it was, a longing. Yet for what I longed, I had no knowledge. Once, the rider came close, and I touched the burning mail of his hand. The touch brought fear.

On the evening which changed my destiny I thought on him, my faceless knight. May Eve it was; I stood at the same window with which I began my tale, late and long past bedtime, a weird and weary hour, waiting to undress my lady when she rose from the parlour where she and her mother kept company with the pallid clerk. Agnes and I had discovered his name. This was his third visit to Grafton in as many weeks; from Stoke Newerne he came, a half-hour's ride off, and they called him Master Thomas Daunger. This night he had dined with them, and now it seemed that he would never leave. I left the window and crossed the landing to the stairhead, where I seated myself, yawning and shivering, upon the topmost stair. Below, the great curved balustrade disappeared where the motley-coloured tiles of the hall were lost in shadow. A thin line of candlelight licked under the parlour door; there was the constant low sound of voices, murmuring. I could distinguish Elizabeth's, now and again the harsh high rasp of her mother, and very occasionally the clerk's quavering tones. His voice, fit mate for his countenance, was milky and sour.

In contrast to the dim stillness of the house, the night outside blazed with life. A moon like a white, perfect fruit hung in a lattice of oak leaves, the humpbacked yews trembled as I watched from my vantage point near to a deep recessed window, and across the lawn long shadows flung their sleeping arms. A nightingale was singing, over and over the same careless tune, and was joined by another and another, until the fluid melody filled the night. From the border herb-scents rose, strong as incense in the Mass. Between the house's quietness and the perfumed song, I sat clasping knees on the top step, my thoughts wandering; no doubt looking ridiculously small-statured, and wishing Agnes would come to me. I had not seen her since before supper, and on this, the last day of April, she had made me a promise.

Folk said it only worked on May Eve: the hawthorn-spray trick, that was. I had given mine to Agnes, and she had vowed it would be dropped at the nearest crossroads, where the wind should take it. And down whichever way the breeze snatched my spray, thence should my true love come. Agnes had no need to toss a thorn twig; she was already betrothed, to a silversmith's 'prentice in the south, and when he had made his masterpiece they would be wed and she would leave Grafton. I felt sad at this; I should be lonely. I wondered if my lady Elizabeth had ever used a hawthorn spray. But then, she needed to even less than Agnes. Her own love

25

had already come a-riding. Nay, she did not need it, any more than the face balms, the potions her mother made to beauty's cause. This set me thinking of the Duchess of Bedford's skilled alchemies, and the last time tall Ned had come to call. I had been very close to him that day; in truth, the Duchess asked my help in a small work, to please our guest. She had let me pour him a flagon of wine. But before pouring, she had taken a little vial from her pouch, filled with dark liquid fresh and sharp-smelling like the earth at night. I had to mix this with the wine, stirring in a special way: six times to the left, five to the right. A little strand of the herb clung on the tankard's lip, and she brushed it off. It looked like the five-leaf grass, ruled by Jupiter for strength, a flower whose purpose I did not know.

'Our guest is weary,' she said. 'Stir strong; that is good! He has a melancholy. Men mislike to be cosseted. So let this be a secret work, for his well-being.'

Then, of all things, she asked if I were virgin. Truly I thought she wandered in her mind, but gave her fair answer, and she nodded, with folds of skin over her small bright eyes, and seemed well pleased. She gave me a thrust toward the chamber where they sat. He did not seem melancholy to me, only with love. He sprawled, long and sturdy, and listened to Elizabeth playing her little harp, with his chin propped on one hand and his eyes making their slow hot journey over her body. I poured his wine, as the Duchess of Bedford had told me, and those love-lorn eyes, with the pupils large and lambent, like the middle of two blue flowers, never left my Lady Elizabeth, not even while he drained the cup as if he drank her lips. Later the Duchess prepared him a special supper, a rare mushroom with a sharp sauce. Sometimes, if they had some unusual delicacy, Agnes and I were allowed to share the remains. On this occasion, however, Agnes had tried to taste the mushroom on its way to the table and had been rewarded by the Duchess with a blow on the neck. After he had eaten, Ned fell quiet and muttered to himself, while Elizabeth knelt before him, stroking his lax hand. When I bent to fill his cup again, I stole another glance at his careless eyes, and saw that their blue flowers had folded inwards, and were tiny, like the eyes of a bird.

Now I am wise, and skilled in herbal knowledge, I know that dish was of the *Amanita muscaria*, the most wicked fruit ever to foul God's earth. But then, being innocent, ignorant beyond thought, I reckoned naught of it and recalled the in-

26

cident with pleasure, for he seemed utterly content, and I had poured his wine.

I sat thinking forward to the morrow. Last year, and the year before that, neither Agnes nor I had been allowed to go to the Maying. In every part of England I knew they would be raising the great striped pole; there would be music, itinerant trinket-sellers, jugglers and the like. Gay clothes, strange faces, excitement. A country court in truth, just for one day, and, for both of us, forbidden. We could not be spared from duty. In a corner of my awakening judgement I knew this unfair—even the villeins and yeomen hirelings all around Grafton would be early on the road for Stoney Stratford tomorrow. 'They come home a disgrace, penniless and drunk,' fat Agace had told me tartly. Yet there was that in her face which told me she, withal her disdain, would gladly go, given the chance. Therefore I put it away from my mind, as a lost thing, and wondered for comfort about the destiny of my hawthorn twig, and where Agnes had got to.

I conjured her up, or so it seemed. In the next instant she was at my side, the flaring moonlight stroking the curve of her round face. Her hair escaped its kerchief in wisps. She sat down beside me on the step. I felt for her rough warm hand. Its touch comforted me.

'Oh, Agnes! You scared me,' I said.

'Lord Jesu! I lust for my bed!' she answered swiftly, squeezing my fingers. 'Why, you're nervous tonight! Are they still employed down below? Chatter, chatter. My lady will not be up to hear Mass in the morning. As for her mother, two hours I've waited to put her to bed. The warming-pan's cold. Such an evening I've had. Jesu! I mislike the looks of that fellow!'

'The clerk?'

'Yes, Master Daunger. When I was handing him his meat, he gave me such a look from those drooping lids I well-nigh dropped the salver. Like a black-beetle. Why does he come here, know you?'

'Maybe he's giving my lady spiritual instruction,' I murmured.

Agnes laughed shrilly. 'I would say rather she could instruct *him*. She's that pious . . . nay, sweeting, her drift tonight was something odd. As if a torch were lit inside her. And ill at ease. She knocked the chess-board off the table, and when I got down to pick the pieces up, that foul beast, Gyb, bit me.' She pulled up her skirt. On her moonlit flesh a

27

neat set of fangs showed black. I rose and leaned on the window sill.

'Did you take my thorn twig?'

She came to stand by me. 'What a moon for May Eve!' she said softly. ''Tis like the sun. Nay, Jankin took it. He had to go to the maltster's.'

'Tell me,' I said eagerly.

'Well, mine blew southerly, as usual. But yours! It did but lie sorrowfully in the dust, and never moved.'

I whispered: 'Jankin speaks false.' Agnes often teased me but this time I was unsure. She should not jest about this anyway; it was a heathen practice, frowned on by the priests. Then she pinched me, and laughed, and said:

''Tis I who's false, sweeting. All's well. Your true love will come from the north. The wind took it a little way north, then it caught in the hedge.' I knew no one in the north. None save the nuns at Leicester.

'Mayhap a Scotsman!' whispered Agnes gleefully. 'Yelling heathen foreign oaths, soaked in his foes' blood.'

I stared hard at the moonlit lawn, so as not to mind. Gyb's figure played in and out of the shadows, tossing up in his paws some luckless small beast. Only a little cat in the distance—I could hold him in my palm. He seemed unreal. At that moment I felt as I often did: something part of the moon and trees, intangible. One whose destiny was ordered, like my hawthorn spray, by the dictating breeze of others. Something that was shadow and not substance . . .

The parlour door opened abruptly. A voice said: ''Tis best he does not lie under our roof tonight.' And I heard the clerk answer: 'There is wisdom. Goodnight, my dames.'

'Till the morrow,' said the Duchess of Bedford. 'Speed our endeavour.'

'To our good fortunes.' Master Daunger was kissing hands in the doorway. Someone held up a light. His chalky face blazed in it; he looked like someone in Hell, like the pictures in my missal. Elizabeth said, very quietly: 'You are sure?'

'It cannot fail,' said Daunger. 'Do this night what I have said . . .' The tail of his words was swallowed up. They walked across the hall and went out.

'God be praised,' yawned Agnes. 'Now my lady will retire, and I can rest. If Gyb lets me. Last night he clawed me, even in sleep.' She ran upstairs, lighting her candle-end. She slept at the foot of the Duchess's bed, as I did with Elizabeth, in case they should wake in the night for food or drink or cosseting.

28

Lady Elizabeth came to the stairfoot, holding up the torch. The light fell about, casting quivering darknesses. Descending, I stole a look at her face; pale and marble-smooth, the blue eyes fire-bright, the lips like petals set firm. Demure and unyielding, and cool as spring water she was, but beautiful. I looked at her, marvelling; she was at least thirty years old and the mother of two great boys, but she had a maid's body, an angel's face. Yes, she was beautiful, that night.

'Who's there?' she asked sharply. 'Oh, 'tis you, wench. Where are the others? What's o'clock?'

'Nigh midnight, Madame, and everyone else is abed,' I said timorously. Then, 'It's May Eve, lady.'

In her hand the flame lurched suddenly. I wanted to explain: all I meant was—May Eve, the harbinger of May Day, when people pleasured themselves, and why not we? But I knew it to be useless. I stared at her like a moon-calf; she was tall and slender in the blue silk dress, a passing pretty gown, into which she had to be sewn. It had an intricate plastron under the kirtle, and she despised it as old-fashioned. She beckoned me with a long white finger. 'Why say you this?' she demanded. Saying naught, I looked at the floor, where fire and moonlight made patterns. She was ill-ease, in truth. I feared her swift temper. Then she said, quite kindly: 'How small you are, child,' and 'Get you to bed.'

'I'm ready to attend you, Madame.' I took the heavy torch in my hand. Its flame blew a hot breath.

'Go up,' she answered. 'I'll not need you.' She waved her long hand, a careless gesture. The wavering light etched hollows beneath her eyes. She went before me to the stairs, and the leaping darkness followed.

'I'll lie alone,' she said. 'I may spend the night in prayer. My mother likewise. Tell Agnes. She can sleep with you tonight.'

Something like joy ran through me, and I thought how pleased Agnes would be to be rid for a space of the Duchess's demands, of the fretting claws of Gyb. Neither did I think aught strange of my lady's whim; for I would rather share a truckle-bed with Agnes than snatch my rest at Elizabeth's feet. For the last two or three months she had kept me awake with her tossing and mutters, disturbing my own sweet mysterious dream; parting me from my fair faceless knight. He whose harness gleamed, who wore my favour in the tournament. She left me at the head of the stairs and went towards her little chapel. As she passed I noticed that her shoulder came level with my brow. How small you are, child! she had said. Shadow and not substance, that was I.

Agnes was sitting dolefully on a chest in the Duchess of Bedford's room. For moments I teased her, hinting at a treat, and got her to beg my pardon for jesting about the hawthorn twig.

'Ah! God be praised!' she cried when I told her. 'Maiden, let us to bed right lively before they change their minds.'

We ran tiptoeing to the attic. From next door, fat Agace's snores already shook the plaster. The moonlight mottled Agnes's lily flesh. 'There's a flea in this bed,' she complained, but was stripped and beneath the covers before I had unfastened my kirtle, throwing her clothes at the candle and leaving me to undress in gloom.

'Perchance they will even let us go a-Maying,' she said, while I struggled with my houpeland. 'You should have asked her, wench, while she was so full of charity.'

'And what should I wear, if they did?' I asked bitterly. 'I've no gowns fit to be seen. My best has a great rent where I tore it on a thorn. I should have all the knaves mocking me for a bawd, going naked in such fashion. And the one my lady gave me—why, I vow she wore it when she was great with young Dick—it swamps me, it's too long. I should be flat on my face in two paces.'

'I've made it to fit you,' Agnes said, in a little voice. 'While I was waiting for my lady. I'm sorry I vexed you over the hawthorn spell, sweeting.'

I flew to the bed and kissed her. 'Dear, kind Agnes!'

'Now, your Grace,' she said, mocking again, 'I'll help you disrobe. By the Rood, what fine jewels! I'll lay them in this coffer to be safe. There's a knot in your laces,' she said, fumbling. 'I'll have to cut you loose.'

I wrenched away. 'Oh, Jesu!' I whispered. 'My Lady Elizabeth!'

A trivial thing, so completely forgotten. A trivial thing, enough to change my whole life.

'Now what's to do?' she said crossly. 'Is there no peace in this dwelling? Come to bed.'

Naught really, yet it loomed like the shadows. My lady was wearing her blue gown, the dress despised for its ancient cut, into whose intricacies she had to be sewn, and further, unsewn at bedtime. Elizabeth's possessions were jealousy loved, none the less. In my mind I saw her careless disrobing, heard the split of cloth. She would burst from the plastron like the flesh of a ripened grape, with swift, high anger.

'I must find my lady,' I said wildly. 'I shall be sore beaten.'
Groaning, Agnes pulled the covers over her head.

I ran downstairs, under the bright latticed moon. I knew
my mistress. Useless to say she had dismissed me; useless to
plead that she herself had vowed no need of me; I saw only
her fury as I ran through the midnight house, now dark, now
bright. She was not in the chapel, and her bedroom was deserted, save for the little dog snug-curled in the centre of the
bed. I went next to the chamber of Jacquetta of Bedford,
hoping Elizabeth might have tarried to bid goodnight. Only
a candle burned there, slow and lonely. My hand slid like silk
on the banister. Small and demented, I reached the hall. The
parlour was unoccupied. More candles whispered there, softened tallow dropping like gentle tears.

I could have crept back to my bed. Years later, with all the
mists gone from my eyes, I wished I had done that very
thing, knowing that a thousand beatings would have been
small sacrifice and, but for my witless pursuit of a duty, my
whole existence changed.

I spun on my heel, shaking, as a sharp noise brought the
blood to my face. I was unquiet, prowling the manor at this
hour. Ghosts and demons rushed about me, catching at my
breath, then the sound came again: a rough, grating buffet,
and I knew it as the outer door swinging on its hinge. So,
angry at my own dread, I went firm and resolute to make it
fast. Even as I reached for the latch, it blew open again, and
I saw my lady and her mother, limned clear upon the shining
lawn. I opened my mouth to call to them and in that instant
saw what they were about. My mouth stayed open. Unbeliev-
ingly, I watched the Duchess raising both hands to the
moon's blank face. In one of them a small object gleamed. I
put my foot over the doorsill to see better. It looked like a
small manikin, a baby such as cottars' children play with,
rough-cut from wood, or wrought in some fast-hardening substance. The Duchess leaned towards her daughter. Her voice
came clearly through the soft white night.

'Have you his hair?'

Elizabeth scratched in the beaded pouch that never left
her waist.

'Yes, Madame—I took three strands last time, but it grows
less easy . . . I pray God . . .'

The Duchess hissed like a snake.

'Woman! Do not invoke *that Name* at this late hour in our

31

work! Know you not that all power lies close . . . Our task is nearly done. Be still.'

'All power!' repeated Elizabeth. She looked about fretfully. I shrank back into the dark porch.

'Yea! All richness, all knowledge, all might! From the moment of your birth, all was written, and shall be. Give me the hair, then. I have his blood, mixed in the image. His blood; where his hand was torn upon your brooch.'

'Madame,' I heard Elizabeth say uneasily, 'is there still need for this? Is not the prize gained already, I ask you?'

Heedlessly, her mother stretched bony arms to the sky.

'Mithras attend me,' she said devoutly.

'Fortune defend me,' cried Elizabeth. Then: 'But all is arranged—he will be here tomorrow, and were we caught at this craft . . . ah, Jesu! we should lose everything!'

I saw the Duchess's snarling teeth, like an animal's.

'Men are fickle, daughter, fickle, fickle!' she crooned. 'Let's leave naught to chance. Forget not the other! Had she slipped your mind?'

'Nay,' said Elizabeth, twisting her hands together. 'But he's mad for *me!*'

Jacquetta of Bedford was busy with the manikin, binding something about its head. From her pouch Elizabeth took another small figure, one that had breasts and was crowned with a gilded wisp.

'Shall they embrace?' she asked, bringing the thing close to the larger one. As she spoke, a black shape trotted over the lawn with a little lilting noise. The Duchess stooped and lifted it in her arms.

'Ah, Gyb, my sweet!' she cried softly. 'See, daughter, I did not need to call him. Now he can bind the charm. Yea, place them together, so . . .' and I saw my lady mould the little dolls as one . . . 'And the pelt of a black beast can seal the matter.'

She rubbed the entwined manikins swiftly over Gyb's arched back. He let out a high hoarse cry and leapt from Jacquetta's grasp into the shadows. The Duchess laughed, a pleased noise, and muttering, elevated both figures towards the moon.

'Attend me, Mithras,' said Elizabeth, kneeling. 'And send me my heart's desire.'

A terrifying little wind arose. It swayed the dark massed yews and ruffled the pale flowerheads sleeping against the stone house wall. It passed curiously through my hiding-place, and with cold mocking fingers lifted my hair. A drum throbbed fiercely. I touched my breast with the Blessed Sign; I touched the drum; it was my heart. For a further instant I stood motionless, staring to where the Duchess held the figures high, like a priest raising the Eucharist to heaven. The wind dropped, leaving me more afraid than ever in my life. Even when Elizabeth and her mother began to cross the lawn towards me, I could not move. Then, at the last second I ran back; I slid into a little closet before they reached the door. In the passage without, a candle bloomed. I heard a man's voice, a deep, soft chuckle. So Anthony Woodville had also left his bed.

'Is it done?'

'Aye, my lord. I'm drained of strength.'

He laughed again, unquietly. 'May our lady mother's wiles bring fruit, sweet sister. Yet I doubt not that yours would have sufficed.'

'It will be a rich harvest, my son,' said the Duchess wearily. She said again: 'All is written.'

'It's heresy.' This, with a trace of fear. 'Remember Eleanor Cobham!'

'Bah!' said the Duchess scornfully. 'She grew careless. And this is worth any hazard. You will see, a year hence. Come, Gyb!'

Calling him softly, she went away. I stayed in the closet. A quivering ran up and down my sides, as if I were being stroked with feathers. Then I felt a soft nudging round my legs. A roaring purr filled the chamber, and I knew it to be, not the foul fiend, but Gyb. I dared not even shove him away with my foot. The Duchess was returning.

'To bed, Mother, I pray you.' Elizabeth's voice was alarmingly close. 'I'll need you in the morning, fresh and bright.'

'I can't find my sweeting,' said the Duchess petulantly. 'Puss? Where are you, poppet?'

'I will find the creature, Madame,' said Anthony Woodville easily. 'Go now. I'll bring him to your chamber.'

Lady Elizabeth soothed her mother away. As their slow steps faded, I stood, frantically plotting escape. There was no way out other than by the door into the passage. I heard Anthony Woodville calling the cat. Fiend that he was, Gyb yelled in answer. He pressed against my legs, uttering pleased chirps and a long, wise wail. The candlelight grew brighter. Filled with terror, I closed my eyes. A drop of hot wax fell on my neck. My eyes flew open: Anthony Woodville,

33

tall, slender, elegant, looked musingly down at me. Gyb sprang to him, rubbing and roaring. Gently, he was pushed aside.

'Away, Gyb!' he said, just as if I were not trembling there in the flickering light. 'You are a plaguey monster. You have put hairs upon my new hose.'

His voice did not hold the anger I dreaded.

'Well, maiden?' he said. 'Why do you dawdle here? I was about to make fast the doors. We are late tonight.'

I swallowed. My throat was dry as old bread.

'Speak!' he said, more sternly. 'Are you moonstruck?'

I found my voice; I begged his pardon. I was but looking for my lady, I said—I was passing sorry. In my sight, his features looked long and thin. Sharp.

'Did you find her?' he said. His voice was gentle again.

'She was without.' I pointed to the door. I trembled. Then I heard him whisper a quiet oath, bitten off midway.

'Tell me, good maid,' he said, in the same even tone, 'how long were you here? You surely saw my sister and my mother in the garden—why did you not go out to them?'

Then, he needed no answer. My chattering teeth, my face, sufficed to inform him that I had seen something not for my eyes, bewildering and wholly bad, yet not altogether understood. I felt his long fingers on my arm. They gripped tight.

'What saw you, maiden?'

'They were playing with the cat.'

'What more?' His fingers bit my bones.

Suddenly something made me wise, more than I deserved. 'Naught else, my lord,' I said steadily.

He remained silent. I made a tiny flurried motion towards escape. His hand stayed firm. 'Do you dream o' nights?' he asked.

'Yes, sir, but why . . .'

'And your dreams are passing real, I doubt not,' he broke in. My arm was beginning to ache. 'So real, so true, that when you wake, you vow the dream was part of life. Is't so?'

'Yea.' My trembling stirred the candle flame. He smiled. His grasp relented. I rubbed my shoulder with an icy hand, my eyes fixed on his face.

'I've hurt you,' he said wonderingly. With great delicacy he drew aside the collar of my gown. 'How easy it is to bruise young flesh!' he murmured. 'Last week in London I saw a wench flogged at the cart's tail. The poor wretch had stolen a trifle of her mistress's beauty salve. And, though this good dame was fond of the child, she had no choice but to watch

34

her punished. Unfair, think you? I vow there's no maid alive who does not snatch a morsel of this cream and that lotion, especially if the mistress be old and ugly, the maiden fair. Is it not fitting for hands that prepare the bath to take a little healing balm to cheer their soreness? Or perfume to lighten a weary heart?'

In his eyes I saw myself, a tiny, wavering figure. He knew about the rose-water cream. 'My lady is not old and ugly, sir,' I whispered. Through my lashes I saw on his face a look that reminded me of Gyb, after devouring a bird.

'Yes, whipped at the cart's tail,' he said, musing. 'Jesu! how that poor damsel's back was bloody! A pretty skin. But that was at the start of her journey.'

My stomach began to churn and plunge, like the courier's horse. I began to cry. Anthony Woodville lifted my face with one finger.

'Do not weep,' he said. 'All shall be well, if you are wise. What saw you this night?'

'Naught, my lord,' I sobbed, and this time I myself believed it.

He smiled. 'You had a dream,' he said, and his eyes were large and sharp, eyes from a dream. 'Back to your bed. Tomorrow, you shall bring in the May.'

Agnes wondered why I wept. She held me in her arms and nursed me sleepily. But I would not tell her. I would tell no one of the dark and hateful things—then I had no wish to speak of them. And strangely, all was as my lord had said. The night faded, in the space of my drying tears, as if it had never been.

We were waked by a merry sun, and fat Agace banging on the door, dressed already in her scarlet kirtle, with glowing face to match—through joy, for we were to go a-Maying, all of us down to the smallest scullion; all of us, without exception.

'They will have to get their own dinner,' snickered Agnes. For a league she jested, making me laugh with images of my Lady Elizabeth's cherished hands cooking mutton, of her mother washing platters. I sat behind her astride the spavined palfrey, treading the road-ruts to Stoney Stratford. The day was merry. Great swathes of persil foamed in the ditches, the may-bloom hung low, and my heart lifted, through laced branches, to meet the blossom, its delicate cream and pale rose and its nested harvest of small birds, singing.

My head was bare, save for a chaplet of primroses, for
Agnes said it was right seemly for a feast-day maid to go
thus, and bother the priests! The sun turned my hair to gold,
to fire; I saw it, falling so bright and sheen below the palfrey's dusty sides. My lady's cast-off gown fit snugly, slashed
a thigh's length to reveal, under its gay russet, a glimpse of
tender green silk. The neck was low; Agnes had pouched and
padded my bosom to show it off. The sleeves were slit in
twenty tiny fronds. Five years from fashion it might have
been, but I was sore enamoured of it. And I had washed my
face in May dew; nay, I had rolled in it naked, so that every
limb had danced and tingled with the soft gay tears of spring.
Then I had made my lady Elizabeth ready for the day. Still
pale, but with a hidden glow, like a may-bud, she had tossed
aside the dark dress I offered her. 'Away with the old black
gowns!' I dared not ask her reason, either for this or for her
sudden disdain of the widow's headgear; her choice was a
small gold hennin with a high veil to match a dress, shimmering and dawn-rosy, that I had not seen before. I merely knelt
to straighten the long skirt and attach the broad gold cincture
about my lady's weasel-waist. Before the sun was clear of the
great oak's topmost bough, she drove me from the chamber.

'Lady Elizabeth gave me some money.' I stretched my arm
past Agnes's cheek, to show the half-angel in my palm. 'And
wished me good fortune at the fair.'

'The Duchess gave me a beating,' she answered tartly. 'Because I was not spry enough dressing her. Jesu, what masters!
I must find me a great lord who will burn Grafton about their
heads. There's a love-spell I wished I'd tried now. I'm sick of
being whipped, and cursed, and virgin.'

'Don't, Agnes,' I whispered.

'Don't what?'

'Talk of spells, love-craft. I would not see you damned.'

She reined in to laugh like a woodpecker. 'Well, Mistress
Pope-Holy!' she cried. 'And what's amiss? A little flower, a
straw in the wind—all good customs, to hurt man nor beast.
Hawthorn-wench, you're as guilty as I!'

Yea, my true love would come from the north. It was then
that I began to hate the hawthorn, for, after what I had seen
last night, which, though sunk deep in my mind's pit still
brought unease, my little wistful ruse ranked itself with the
worst spells of all.

'A great lord, then, Agnes?' I asked, for diversion. The
pony grazed. 'Would you desert Master Silversmith?'

She half-turned. 'How should I do that?' she demanded.

36

'I'm his by troth-plight—no other marriage would be valid.' The sunlight caught her dimples. 'Besides, I lust for Master Jack right well. He's a strong leg, a lickerish eye . . .'

The groom escorting Dick and Thomas Grey ahead, came trotting back.

'Would to God you wenches would cease chattering,' he said discourteously. 'We'll not make Stoney Stratford before noon.'

'Bite your tongue,' said Agnes. 'Why all the haste? You're like my lady. She chivvied me out of the house an it were on fire.'

'Yea, they seemed passing anxious to see our backs,' muttered the groom, hauling the pony's head out of the succulent ditch.

'Why, here's another in a hurry!' cried Agnes, staring up the road. Towards us rode a horseman. A black cloak flew behind him like a dusty sail. His mount's hide boiled with sweat. He rode without skill; as he reached us, his horse swerved blindly and struck the groom's beast, sending horse and rider plunging towards the hedge. He stopped to ask no pardon, but spurred on hotly and galloped off the way we had come. The groom struggled out of the ditch, shaking off broken blossoms.

'Pox take you!' he yelled after the departing figure.

Agnes said wonderingly: 'Was that not Master Daunger?'

Yes, 'twas Daunger. He had swivelled his chalky whey-face and hanging lip towards us for an instant. Daunger, a dangerous name. Do-this-night-as-I-have-said Daunger. I kept silent.

'Is the clerk for Grafton again, then?' Agnes murmured. 'More pious instruction for my lady?'

'Not today,' I only whispered. She had been like a spray of may-bloom, ready to flower. Could the clerk be her lover? I did not know what it was that lovers did that was so pleasant and nice and full of sin. Yet whatever it was I knew that chaste Elizabeth did it not. Agnes stood in the stirrups and clapped her hands, and I forgot all about Master Daunger, and cried with her: 'Look! the May Pole!'

Stoney Stratford opened to us round a bend in the road. Every house door stood wide. More hawthorn, scattered with blossoms, stood in great branches at every porch. Garlands of meadow-sweet and cowslips hung from window and door-frame. Folk thronged the narrow street, laughing, singing, crowned with flowers, with periwinkle, wild rose and young ivy; and in the square, with a breeze lifting its twelve gaudy streamers, the great ash-pole grew upwards to the sky.

Dressed from tip to ground with wreaths of marsh-marigold, primroses and may, it stood winking in the sun. On its head lay a ring of royal lilies. 'Worship me,' it said.

Children ran to meet us. One pushed a nosegay into my hand, violets clustered with harebell and eglantine, still dew-damp.

'Oh, Agnes,' I said, lost in delight. 'Look, Agnes!'

Agnes's eyes darted about. She flirted her lashes at an elderly merchant, pursed her lips as a band of young clerks rolled by, arms linked. Flushed with ale, they bawled a chant far from holy. 'How wicked the world is!' she said, with dancing eyes.

We halted on the green, where there seemed to have congregated a host of young men. As we dismounted one fell in courtly pose upon his knee, clutched his heart and feigned a swoon. At the comical look on his face I burst out laughing. Agnes swept by with a hauteur worthy of the Duchess. I looked up at the ring of faces. A youth in a blue doublet held a buttercup under my chin and guffawed. I heard: 'Great Jesu, that maiden's hair!' and 'But maiden-hair's a herb, Will, and she's a flower, yea, by the Rood.' 'Deflower, say you?' A great burst of mirth, and Agnes's cross, seizing hand. 'Stay close.' I caught the tail of a voice, strange and yearning, like the look in John Skelton's eyes. 'Little and young, I grant you. But by my mother's soul, she lights my fire!'

So I was conscious of the hot stares of men. Their looks were like lances, to prick and delve, to consume me. I knew the object of their joy. It rippled about me, hued like autumn fire, cloth of gold, a beech-nut, taking the colour from the flowers, laughing back at the sun. I say this in no conceit, for from my hair's lustre came more fear than pride, that day.

Agnes whispered: 'Come! We'll lose the others, or we'll be put in charge of Tom and Dick!' and tugged me, squirming, through the crowd to the far side of the green, where men were shooting at the butts and slender wands, and the sweet-meat booths were set up cheek by jowl with the ale-wagons.

'We'll have wine,' she decided. I bought honey cakes to go with the thin sour brew. I watched Agnes drinking, her full creamy throat tipped back. Pink drops escaped the flagon's lip and trickled on her white bosom. I told her she was fair and she laughed.

'There's your great lord, Agnes.' I pointed towards a corpulent squire of sixty. 'Or him, look!' turning to a man who, skinny as a thong, contorted his body into horrible shapes before an admiring crowd.

'Nay, sweeting, he'd make too restless a bedfellow.' She pulled me on. A juggler threw up coloured platters. Two bold-faced women balanced themselves upside down on sword-points, their skirts falling about naked thighs. A group of 'prentices stood over-close, gibing shrilly. 'Flemish whores,' Agnes muttered.

Lovers there were, too. Walking close-twined, sitting lip-to-lip on benches. And from the depths of a scented bush came a rustling and a soft cry. At the entrance to a side street, I saw two soldiers gazing at the Fair. Their stare was a mixture of longing and feigned disinterest.

We sat down to watch the mummers. First the Green Giant, then Robin! I sat with hands clasped, loving him. In his suit of Kendal Green, he strutted and bragged, showing his prowess in archery. Maid Marian, a pretty boy with long golden hair, piped of her love. She followed him languidly, all over the green. Wherever he went, so did she. Robin sprang into easy attitudes; Marian tripped on her gown. They performed a courtly dance, and one of Marian's false breasts crept round the back of her waist. She fell prey to the Sheriff; Robin hammered with his broadsword, and the pair were united by Friar Tuck, much the worse for ale. Agnes and I shared a bench with four 'prentices, who leaped to their feet every minute to whistle and shoot peas at Maid Marian. Once, they upset the seat completely and began fighting amongst themselves. As Robin bore off his bride, the crowd bawled and chanted for more. A troupe of bagpipers who came next were hounded from the green in fury.

A strange creature capered into view. Clad in sparkling motley, one leg red, the other yellow, he frisked around the hem of the watching circle, tweaking the noses of the men, patting the women's cheeks. He had a face so comical that even had he not pulled it into hideous grimaces, men would have smiled at him. He rolled his eyes so high that only the whites showed, and pulled down his nose with his tongue.

'Certes! 'Tis the King's fool!' said a low voice behind me. 'Poor Patch. The richest man at court.'

'Edward must be hereabouts.'

'Leicester,' said the first voice cryptically. 'Ah, Jesu!' liquid with laughter. 'Will you look! He does my soul good!'

He was not a tall man, this jester; only about a head higher than I, and Agnes would have dwarfed him standing. Neither was he old, he was lithe and supple, but his face was patterned with lines, like a withered fruit. He came skipping, and stood before us, duck-fashion; he pinned the pike of one shoe to the ground with the other, scratching his head; he looked mournfully about, cried: 'Succour!' bent bow-legged and, agile as a monkey, seized the offending foot and tossed a backward somersault.

'Ah, bravely done!' cried Agnes.

The fool's head turned. Unerringly, he pranced over to Agnes, and grasped her hand. He pressed a lingering kiss into the palm, gazing into her face, with lifted, mocking brows. I stared at the fretted cheeks, the temples with the heavy painted lines from each eyelid, the curling mouth, still kiss-puckered. The eyes were a clear dove-grey, and shrewd. He took my hand next. I felt his teeth nip my thumb.

'You're gallant, Sir Fool,' I said shyly.

The fool gave a great cry of passion and clasped his breast. 'Beauty has spoken soft words,' he declared. Everyone watched, grinning. 'Madame, my heart is yours. Keep it.' He delved in his overlarge scrip and drew out the glistening, blood-clotted heart of some animal, sheep or calf, or man! I know not what it was, save that it made me scream. The men roared. I felt sick, as the horrid thing dripped before my face. And he knew it instantly—no fool, this fool—for he dropped the offal on the grass and bent close, asking: 'What ails the little maid?' his voice deeper than the high whine he gave his audience.

'It's a weakness,' Agnes sounded vexed. 'A certain delicacy.' They were giving me wine. 'And she hates cock-fights. And bear-baiting.'

We had already passed the bear, with his poor burned feet, stamping a chained, ceaseless circle. And that was only a dancer.

'Strange, but forgive me,' said the fool. ' 'Twas a crude jest. Am I pardoned, fair one?' This in a loud whine; the crowd was impatient for him to continue. I looked in his grey eyes, saw tenderness, touched his gay shoulder with a trembling hand. He sprang away, tipping himself on to his hands, and sped thus around the eager circle. The hobby-horse, gaudy-ribboned, chased the fool across the green as the Moorish dancers ran before us in a straggling file. They wore green and red fustian, dagged sleeves, bells. 'Clack!' went their staves as they feinted in the dance. The smell of trodden grass rose sweet and sour. But my joy in it was dulled by the fool's nasty jest. Though I had forgiven him, the bad taste of it lay heavy in my mouth, and when he bounded back to us I looked upon him without pleasure. He had a bauble on a stick, a monstrous moon-face, gilded with a smile on one side, a frown on the other.

'Ladies, follow me!' he pleaded, and Agnes rose from the bench. The fool's eyes travelled up her height.

'By the Rood, maiden, you are lofty,' he remarked.

' 'Tis you that is low,' she said haughtily, but I could see he charmed her in the same way as did the young birds, the flowers. He stretched out a hand to me, as I sat motionless.

'Marry! the little maid's still wroth,' he said. 'Come, my honeycomb. We'll find a friend of mine.'

He skipped ahead, Agnes admonishing him, but smiling, for as he went he sang about a lustful friar, and most of the words were nonsense. I lagged behind; Agnes nudged me on, like a dog herding sheep. Patch prodded a passing belly with his bauble; an important, a fine belly at that, clothed in murrey and fur with a broad gold pouch. And the belly's owner merely loosed a great guffaw and slapped Patch round the shoulders.

'Jesu, Agnes!' said I. 'He's bold.'

She gave a knowing little grin. 'Well 'tis the King's fool, forget it not,' she said; and I ran after him, eager at last, wanting to ask about the King, the unknown magnificences that were his daily fare. He threaded through the revellers, supple and broad in his motley, and once he turned with a grimace like some evil sprite leading me on to danger. I ran beneath the sun. Red and yellow, the day.

I thought he might be taking us to meet a courtier, but he halted at an old man's bench. Despite the fierce heat, this man was cowled to the ears in threadbare wool so that little of his face was visible. Across his knees he cradled a harp of most ancient design. Pale as lilies, his hands were translucent and veined. The fool stretched out a hand to pluck one string of the lyre. The sound was a drop of silver rain falling.

'Old friend, how goes it?' he said softly.

The minstrel opened eyes clear as water. ' 'Tis you, rascal,' he murmured. 'Methought I felt a cold wind blowing then.'

'Aged blood runs thin,' said Patch cheerily. 'How many summers, old one?'

With a twitching smile, he said: 'I know not. Yet I remember the second Richard, and the day Wat Tyler rode on London. Richard saved that day of blood. Sweet Richard, they called him.'

This is truth: I felt a strange little pang. It would be easy for me to seek sensation, to say that in an instant the future showed itself to me, but it was naught like that . . . Only something in me which heard those words, and moved to tenderness.

Patch pulled off his tight scarlet cap, and I saw that he was indeed young, no more than eighteen. Tight buttery curls covered his head. He said: 'I've brought you two fair maids. To mind you of other May Days!' and laughed, a whit churlishly, and nudged the minstrel with his elbow. The hood fell back. I felt the clear wise eyes upon my face. Thin he was, and passing frail. Any lusty wind could have taken him up like a puffball. One hand left the harp and beckoned to me.

'He has written a fair ballad,' Patch breathed in my ear. 'The ending troubles him. Is it finished, master?' he bawled.

'Sit by me, little maid,' said the minstrel. 'I have a song in mind, certes, it has lived in me for months. A tale of lovers. The knight, I know him well, child of my mind as he is. But the woman . . .' his head drooped, wearily.

'Is she a good maid?' I asked.

He said, with eyes closed: 'I am deathly sick.' Then: 'Yea, she is one who loved so true that she followed her love into the wilds and the desolate places. I knew such a one, once . . .'

Patch spat delicately. 'Nay, master!' he said challengingly. 'These creatures are things of song and romance. Angels, to haunt the imaginings of men—in truth I vow they're wayward harlots to draw a man's soul from his body. Then they depart, leaving him sick from lust and longing.'

'If only I could complete it,' said the old man, uncaring. 'The maiden's name escapes me . . . I cannot see her. The Forest Maid,' he murmured. 'The Faithful Maid. The Lily Maid . . . nay, nay!' he twanged his harp, vexed. 'Lilies are cold and holy—this maid is warm.'

Suddenly, Patch crouched close to me.

'Look, master!' he whispered. 'Look at her hair! Does *this* not inspire you?'

The veined hand stretched out. Taking a lock of my hair in his fingers, the old man gazed as it lay like a live thing, shining and reddening in his palm.

'Aye,' he said, after a long space. 'Nut-brown hair! A Nut-Brown Maid. Brown eyes, brown hair, sheen as a fairy woman's, and a heart faithful to death. Is that your nature?' he asked sharply. 'Before the dedication, I must know. Are you a true maid to your lover?'

'I have no lover,' I said. He smiled, a kind, veiled smile. 'Only a dream of one, to which I'm true.'

'A fair answer.' Sweet uneven chords issued from the harp. Patch cried: 'Sing! Make her immortal!'

'Cynical Sir Fool,' murmured the minstrel. 'My first verse then, shall echo your philosophy.'

> 'Be it right or wrong, these men among
> On women do complain,
> Affirming this, how that it is
> A labour spent in vain
> To love them well, for never a dele
> They love a man again;
> For let a man do what he can
> Their favour to attain,
> Yet if a new to them pursue,
> Their first true lover then
> Laboureth for naught; for from her thought
> He is a banished man.'

I felt Patch stroking my hair, gently.

'We will have it in two voices,' said the rhymer. 'That first shall be sung by the man, in his ignorance. Now the damsel sets him right.'

> 'I say not nay, but that all day
> It is both written and said
> That woman's faith is, as who saith,
> All utterly decayed.
> But nevertheless, right good witness
> In this case might be laid . . .'

His strange acute gaze fell on me, sweeping my hair, my face, my body. 'Can you write?' he asked. Someone thrust pen and paper before me. 'Set this down,' he said. 'I have but a little time.'

> 'That they love true and continue:
> Record the Nut Brown Maid,
> Which, when her love came her to prove,
> To her to make his moan,
> Would not depart, for in her heart
> She loved but him alone.'

A circle of listeners formed about us. They were quiet. The slow voice's tune was passing soft. The verses flowed by. I wrote feverishly, knowing my spelling poor. I blessed the nuns of Leicester, who had taught me my letters.

43

'It standeth so: a deed is do
Whereof great harm shall grow;
My destiny is for to die
A shameful death, I trow.
Or else to flee. The t'one must be:
None other way I know
But to withdraw as an outlaw
And take me to my bow.

Wherefore adieu, my own heart true!
None other rede I can;
For I must to the greenwood go,
Alone, a banished man.'

' 'Tis Robin Hood!' mocked Patch. His nose was out of joint by the attention the crowd was giving to the old ballad-maker, who only smiled.

'This is an allegory,' he said softly. 'Know you not that every tale can have two, three, an hundred meanings?'

'Are we not in the greenwood?' demanded Patch.

'Your mind is no sharper than it seems,' said the harpist. 'The greenwood can be the battlefield; the tomb, even. He of whom I sing, simple or noble. Construe it as you will.'

He struck a chord, I gripped the quill. Three or four filled sheets already lay on the grass. I found myself trembling at the words' beauty, glad that I should have aided their birth, if this was indeed truth and not the guile of a cunning show-man. Then, glancing at the white fingers like crabbed stalks, I knew him too kindly, too much upon the next world's threshold to be counterfeit.

'Now sith that ye have showed to me
The secret of your mind,
I shall be plain to you again,
Like as ye shall me find.
Sith it is so that ye will go,
I will not leave behind.
Shall never be said the Nut-Brown Maid
Was to her love unkind.
Make you ready, for so am I,
Although it were anone,
For in my mind, of all mankind
I love but you alone.'

'Yea, that I do,' said Patch suddenly, close.
Rhyme snapped at the heels of rhyme. Frantic, I wrote.

'By Venus and St Valentine, I love thee, maiden,' he said, whispering.

'What next, what next?' chanted the crowd, as the ballad-maker paused.

'Good people, give me space to wet my throat,' he said wearily.

'I do not speak false,' muttered Patch. 'You've robbed me of wit. I think you even rob me of my soul. I love you.'

'Peace, Sir Fool,' I said, full of impatience. 'I cannot hear the minstrel's words. I'll laugh at your clowning later.'

But he leaped from the grass with an oath and swung away, broke through the crowd and was gone. A few turned to look after him, with little interest.

> 'I counsel you, remember how
> It is no maiden's law
> Nothing to doubt, but to run out
> To wood with an outlaw.
> For ye must there in your hand bear
> A bow ready to draw;
> And as a thief thus must you live
> Ever in dread and awe;
> Whereby to you great harm might grow:
> Yet had I liever than
> That had I to the greenwood go,
> Alone, a banished man.'

The tale of the Nut-Brown Maid leaped lightly from the ballad-maker's tongue, across the strings like sparkling rain, grew strong, sweet under my pen. She was constant and true, as I would be. She would cut her hair off by her ear, her kirtle at her knee, and so would I. The sheets of verse lay scattered like flowers. Now the lover tested his maid, tempered her steel with sorrow.

> 'If that ye went, ye should repent;
> For in the forest now
> I have purveyed me of a maid
> Whom I love more than you;
> Another more fair than ever ye were
> I dare it well avow,
> And of you both each should be wroth
> With other, as I trow;
> It were mine ease to live in peace
> So will I, if I can;

45

> Wherefore I to the wood will go,
>   Alone, a banished man.'

Someone cried: 'Shame!' I set down my pen. 'Master, I am unworthy of the song,' I said. 'I think I could not brook such a betrayal.'

The ancient eyes scanned my face.

'Yea,' he said, softly, smiling. 'Yea. You could, you will. A loving woman does not cease to love. Child, so will it be, even though your tears flow; flow like wine on a feast day.'

I thought: how should he know? And then: I must strive to be the brave maid of his dreaming. I thought on my petty failings, and was ashamed.

'But a happy ending, I pray,' I breathed.

His mouth quirked on a smile. 'How fortunate that we can shape our romances to fit our will!'

> 'Though in the wood I understood
>   Ye had a paramour,
> All this may nought remove my thought,
>   But that I will be your.
> And she shall find me soft and kind
>   And courteous every hour;
> Glad to fulfil all that she will
>   Command me, to my power:
> For had ye, lo, an hundred mo',
>   Yet would I be that one,
> For in my mind, of all mankind
>   I love but you alone.
>
> Mine own dear love, I see the prove
>   That ye be kind and true;
> Of maid, of wife, in all my life,
>   The best that ever I knew.
> Be merry and glad, be no more sad,
>   The case is changèd new,
> For it were ruth that for your truth
>   Ye should have cause to rue.
> Be not dismayed, whatsoever I said
>   To you when I began:
> I will not to the greenwood go,
>   I am no banished man.'

Fainter, the minstrel's words murmured on.

> '. . . I will you bring, and with a ring
>   By way of marriage

46

I will you take, and lady make,
As shortly as I can:
Thus have you won an Earles son,
And not a banished man . . .'

His hand crept to his breast, as if it sought something long-lost. The wan face grew paler. I touched the hand gently.

'Are we finished?' I asked. Before my eyes, he was fading. Shrinking into the coarse cloth of his habit.

'The heavenly dedication,' he whispered. 'One verse more . . .' I could scarcely catch the words.

'Here may ye see that women be
In love meek, kind and stable,
Let never man reprove them than
Or call them variable;
But rather pray God that we may
To them be comfortable,
Which sometime proveth such as He loveth,
If they be charitable.
For sith men would that woman should
Be meek to them each one;
Much more ought they to God obey,
And serve but Him alone.'

His head bowed low. Two men with fiddles stepped up.

'Give us the air again, master,' they said. 'We have two here to do your ballad justice.'

A boy and a girl stood behind them, she with a chaplet of lilies on her head, he swarthy, eager. 'Bring wine for our poet, fellows!' they cried. 'The best there is, and we will pay!'

He was so still. I crept kneeling and touched his cheek with fingers soft as butterfly. The heavy head fell on my breast, the frail weight into my arms.

'The song is ended,' Agnes said sadly.

A priest came near, his sombre cloth ill-tuned with the flowers, the sunshine, and the cups of wine. He knelt by the silent form on the grass. Awkwardly, men doffed their caps, shuffled their feet, uneasy in the presence of this unseen, unbidden May Day guest. I turned away. I wept a little.

Agnes and I went together across the green. I looked up at the sky where the sun was tipping rosily towards the west. The minstrel seemed a good old man; I wondered if he were there already, young and strong again, playing a better lyre, smiling with those loved years ago. He, who had called me his Nut-Brown Maid, and dedicated a bright song, not to some great lord, but to me. Me, and none other.

Then Patch came running, catching at my hand, his words stumbling, and a different emotion for each of the comic lines on his face; humble and repentant and mocking and mischievous, and with an odd sad desperate gleam, like that in John Skelton's eyes, and the yearning voices of the men in the crowd who had touched my face and hair. Yea, he would be my lover, he said, and do me solemn duty, yet he begged my pardon for his churlishness and for speaking in an ill-advised, goatish way. Was he, once more, forgiven?

Again I had to say I was not offended, which was true, for at no time had I paid him much heed, being caught up with the joyous song and sorrow of the day, and I said, sadly:

'Your old friend died. Why do men die?'

He could not answer this, the silliest question in the world, but dropped his jaw and hung his head; then asked: 'May we still be dear friends?'

'I'll look for you next May Day.'

He shook his head. 'My life hangs on the King's whim,' he answered. 'This time next year I could be in France, or Byzantium. I ride for London tomorrow.'

'Back to court,' I said wistfully. 'Well, good fortune, Sir Fool. I doubt not with your skill his Grace is pleased to employ you. But we shall never meet, and that is truth. Never in a thousand years will I come to London. I am bound to serve at Grafton Regis with the Lady Grey.'

The fool's eyes narrowed. 'Elizabeth Woodville?' he said wonderingly. 'The widow with the virgin's face?' He began to laugh. 'Be not so sure, sweeting, you will never come to court!'

'Another jest?' I asked. A good one by the look of it; he rolled about and bounced off the palfrey which Jankin was holding for me to mount and go home on while the sky was still blue and gold.

'The King's Grey Mare!' he said, and seized me round the waist, laughing like a jaybird.

'I don't understand,' I said, dizzy.

'A jape, a folly!' he cried. 'Ah, maiden, I love you. Forget me not!' With a frisk, he was gone, bright red and yellow bird, plunging across the meadow.

'I mistrust that fellow,' said Agnes, glaring after him.

'He would have loved me,' I said, feeling foolish.

'Yea, to some tune.' Agnes slipped her foot in Jankin's hand and swung astride the palfrey. She pulled me up behind her, asking Jankin how he had fared. Quite well, said he. He had tried his skill in the archery and come second.

'I would not have been beat,' he said indignantly, 'had not one of the King's archers, a great lummox, sneaked in and hit the highest score before my eyes! I complained to the arbiters, saying that he should be on duty and had no business with May-games, but they would not have it, and he got the prize. A cask of Rhenish, it was.'

'You should have challenged him for it.'

'Well, the knave was courteous enough to give me a drink,' said Jankin, wiping dirt off his doublet. 'I asked him why he was not with his fellows at Leicester, and he said they would have been, had not the King halted at Stoney Stratford.'

'I did not see *him* at the Maying,' sighed Agnes covetously.

'Nay,' said Jankin. 'For he had taken a fancy to go hunting, the man-at-arms told me. They thought it strange, in the midst of an array, but off he rode, leaving his company blunting their weapons on apples among the village folk.'

'No royal whim is strange,' reproved Agnes.

'Jankin,' I said proudly, 'I have had a song written for me today. In praise of my nut-brown hair. What think you of that?'

We rode homeward in an untidy line, I loitering with my thoughts as dusk fell. In a senseless way I thought that the old ballad-maker's death was my fault. I managed to dismiss this, by thinking quite kindly of Patch. He would have loved me, despite what Agnes said. Several men would have loved me that day. I pulled off my garland and breathed its dying sweetness. Behind me I could hear the sounds of horseplay, snatches of song mingled with the blackbird's bedtime twittering, and I mused on love, wondering at its essence. Men had found me fair—that was enough. For I suspected there was something a whit frightening in this business of love. One could die of love; that I knew well.

When we came again to Grafton Regis, the sober house was lit as for a festival. Lady Elizabeth wore her dazzling gown and a smile like the crown jewels; and my lady of Bedford had been giving her cat wine, for he lay in the hearth, dead drunk.

Even then, they contrived to keep it from us for the best part of the summer, what had happened on May Day when we had all been chivvied out into the morning, and sent safely far from home. There had been a wedding at Grafton, most secretly celebrated, the bride my Lady Elizabeth, and the groom none other than tall Ned, twenty-one years of age, comely and omnipotent. King Edward the Fourth himself, besotted and bewitched and driven to the brink of madness by my lady and her scheming mother.

Certes, she wrought a fierce work that day, did Elizabeth. A seduction which, in twenty years, was to cause the ruin of one more precious than my own soul. For this I cannot forgive her, and I never shall.

> Then between us let us discuss
> What was all the manere
> Between them two; we will also
> Tell all the pain in fere
> That she was in. Now I begin,
> So that ye me answere;
> Wherefore all ye that present be,
> I pray you, give an ear.
> I am the Knight. I come by night,
> As secret as I can,
> Saying, Alas! thus standeth the case,
> I am a banished man.
>
> (The Nut-Brown Maid)

Agace the cook, as I have said, was an insolent old dame, stout and proud. She considered herself accomplished; she could recite the feast days and the Saints' Days without hesitation when she was in a good humour. As she had known me many years and had seen me beaten on more than one occasion, she afforded me scant respect. Our conversation was therefore akin to the parry-and-thrust of swordsmen.

I went often to her kitchen, that December of 1468. Four years I had languished at Grafton Regis after Elizabeth's departure. And I was still not resigned to the fact that she had left me behind. Even her sisters, gathered up from the length and breadth of England, had gone with her to court. The Duchess of Bedford and her husband Richard Woodville, and Anthony Woodville, Lord Rivers (or Lord Scales, as he was sometimes called) were firmly ensconced there. So we heard, in fleeting spasms of news. In this bitterly cold manor I was sick with ennui. Dispirited, too. My dearest friend had left me: Agnes was in Kent, a respectable matron helping in Jack's silversmithy. Thomas and Dick were gone with their mother the Queen, to be trained at court. Their old nurse was dead. It seemed therefore that Agace and I were the last survivors of the Grafton we had known.

But this Christmastide Jacquetta of Bedford had come back. It was at least a familiar face, someone to whisper about. She had broken her journey at Grafton halfway through December, bringing an entourage of about twenty fashionable females, and complaining of the grippe. Straight to bed had she gone, and I remember it was I who had to fly around airing and sweetening chambers for the pack of them. As I stood by Agace's kitchen fire trying to keep warm, I thought I heard Jacquetta complaining from her bedroom aloft.

Stirring vigorously at a pan of food, Agace sweated and swore.

'By God's bones, let us hope this dish will pleasure my lady.' She ladled the egg mess on to soft toast. Herbelettes, she called it. The smell of the ginger and galyngale rose deliciously.

'I know not why she doesn't return to court,' I said.

The cook laughed derisively. 'Ha! I know why. This at least is her own domain. Despised, yet useful. Here she can be Queen in her own right. I trow my lady is still offended by the treatment she got two years ago!'

I thought on this for a moment. True, after the birth of the Princess Elizabeth, Jacquetta had come back to Grafton in a fine fury, swearing that she had not expected the Queen to use her thus. 'She babbled some wild talk that it was through her that Elizabeth was Queen at all, and now she must bid her aged mother do her obeisance like the humblest vassal,' said Agace, arraying a salver with the meal.

'And did she?' I wiped the foul table with a cloth.

'Oh, heard you not the tale? After the Queen's churching in Westminster, there was a banquet at the Palace like men have not seen in years, with four halls crammed with guests. The Queen sat in a separate chamber on a golden chair, while Margaret, the King's sister, and my lady of Bedford attended her. They dare not speak, and when Elizabeth addressed them, they must kneel. When the board had been cleared for revelry, my lady Jacquetta must kneel again, and she vowed that her gizzard has never been right since, for all the dust that the dancers kicked up. Princess Margaret, they say, was bidden to curtsey each time she passed the Queen's chair, even in the dance. This she did. She's a lovely wench. But her Grace's mother was far from pleased by her evening's entertainment.'

I choked on laughter. I pictured the old woman glowering on her knees, while Elizabeth, regal in her chair of estate,

51

looked loftily over her head. There was probably a grain of truth in what Agace said. Although her husband was Constable of England, and, it was said, a bounty of treasure flowed constantly into her children's lap, Jacquetta still occasionally would rule a smaller realm. I took the tray in my hands.

'Yes, you bear it up to my lady,' said Agace, turning to warm her rump. 'Great idle wench,' she said, not unkindly. 'Sixteen, are you? And not betrothed? You should be professed as a nun.'

'What?' I said, lusting to kick her fat legs. 'This minute? While my lady of Bedford still needs me?'

'Yea,' she said grudgingly, 'she seems to like your touch with her hair and finery. Outrageous vanities, she has.' She pursed a pious mouth.

'She minds me of our one-time mistress,' I said, 'when she was awaiting a visit from Ned . . . from the King.'

Agace tittered coarsely. 'Mayhap she has thoughts of a leman, too. To while away time while the Earl is busy with affairs of state.'

Once I would have laughed. Now I was shocked.

'Jesu, mercy!' I cried. 'At her age? 'Twould be a shameful thing!'

'Seemingly not.' Agace winked. 'The Queen's brother John wed the Dowager Duchess of Norfolk, and she is nigh eighty years, and he nineteen. They call it the devil's marriage.'

'He cannot love her,' I said, sickened at the thought.

'I always vowed you were lack-wit,' said Agace with contempt. 'What has love to do with it, I ask you? Or with any of the marriages of the Queen's kin? The Duchess of Norfolk is passing rich, and of ancient line. Likewise the Duke of Exeter's daughter, lately wedded to young Thomas.'

Little Tom, who played with me, Hoodman Blind. A wedded husband.

'I trow my lord of Warwick was ill-pleased with that,' Agace went on cunningly. 'The maid was promised to his nephew.'

Here was a name to play soldiers with. The great Warwick. The man who had saved England by the sword. The King's strongest ally, who had set him on the throne.

'Yea, Warwick,' said Agace, watching me. 'He who roasts six oxen for a breakfast, then throws his doors wide to all. Did you know? He welcomes men, strangers and knaves from off the street, to take as much meat as their dagger can bear away.'

She laid a spoon beside the platter. 'Now, carry this up to my lady, and pray it's to her taste!'

What should I call her, I wondered, mounting the draughty stairs. Countess? Dowager Duchess? Among all the riches Edward had showered on his Queen's kin lay an earldom for her father, Sir Richard Woodville. I tapped and entered Jacquetta's chamber. The air was pungent from reeking herbal potions. Gyb, white-muzzled now, added his rank odour from the centre of the bed.

'Try to take a little, Madame,' I said, proffering the meal.

The Dowager Duchess sneezed, and glared at me.

'Her Grace was right,' she croaked. 'This is a plaguey chill place for such as I to spend the holy season of Christmas.'

I made her a curtsey, looking under my lashes at the ill-tempered old face. White bristles, like those of Gyb, sprouted on her chin.

'The court would be warmer, Madame,' I agreed. I picked up her satin robe from the floor and hung it on a hook. I waited patiently while she spooned a mouthful of Agace's egg dish between her lips. As I expected, she spat it out into the bowl, like a cross-grained infant.

'I cannot eat this pap,' she declared.

Fighting an urge to throw the tray, I sympathetically smiled.

'They have wondrous cooks at court, have they not, my lady?' I murmured. 'I hear that the subtleties are fashioned so cunningly that one can hardly bear to eat them. Yet when they are tasted one cannot leave their enjoyment.'

'Yes, yes, it's as you say.' She nodded grudgingly. 'Men gorge themselves on forty, fifty courses, and think naught of it.'

'I fear Agace cannot attain such heights,' I said. 'Will the Earl be here for Christmas? We must order more provisions.'

She shook her head. 'I know not what his plans are. Her Grace begs me to come to court for Yule.' (She gave the holy season its ancient name.) 'But I fear with this malaise I'll be unfit for the journey.'

A strategy so beautiful that it made me tremble began to form in my mind.

'I will have you well, Madame, I promise,' I murmured tenderly. Gyb stretched out a paw, talons spread, as I tucked the covers about his mistress. 'I will prepare you a posset myself. And I swear you will be recovered. Right speedily.'

The old eyes flickered in my direction. She looked surprised, and in my conceit, I thought, gratified. 'You are a good child,' she said, not for the last time.

Returning to the kitchen, I rudely pushed Agace away from the fire.

'Give me room, dame,' I said. 'I am to brew a simple to have my lady on her legs again before Christmas.'

The cook gave me a shove equally strong.

'What are you meddling with?' she demanded. 'I don't want her up! Certes, we have more peace while she's abed.'

'You will have peace aplenty, Agace,' I said, smiling a secret smile. I crushed herbs between my fingers. Already I knew what would cure a chest cough and the sniffles. I had some powdered dandelion, too, for her lost appetite. The cook peered slyly into my face.

'By the look of you, you're brewing more besides a posset,' she said. 'And it's no secret how you lust after the court. I've not forgotten how you bawled when the Queen left you behind! And she gave you all her old dresses!' she added enviously.

I stirred away, red-faced from the fire. 'I had liefer gone to court in my shift than remain in this place with a score of dresses.'

My thoughts turned round and round with the ladle. Tangy as the smell of boiled dandelion, they rose and hung above me in a secret cloud. Though I had never been an actual cozen of the Duchess, at no time had she shown signs of dislike. Now here she was, under our roof again, her will doubtless low-ebbed from sickness. Mine to approach in servitude, but in a servitude passing kind. I thought of my destiny as a ship, drifting anchorless. But if I, through stealth, could blow a strong breeze, hold back the tide, bend the gale —then might I come into the slack water of my heart's desire, and sail towards London, the city of gold.

'All the sisters went to court,' I said, half to myself. 'The cousins, and their cousins' cousins, a legion. And they went in a gilt coach. I would go in a cart.'

'Mistress,' said Agace slyly, 'you aren't the Queen's kin.'

'Is it my fault,' I demanded, 'that I have no royal blood?'

Agace had one black tooth-stump. It showed as she howled with laughter.

'Christ in Glory!' she said, wiping her eyes. 'Have *they?* Better than you or I, mistress, but common, none the less, common as English earth. Hence there's so many ducal tempers aflame!'

I knew naught of ducal tempers. I knew only that the

54

Woodvilles were apart from me now, by reason of rank and greatness; aeons distant. Yet there was one close at hand, growling with the grippe, one who would like to be petted; that I knew well. I drained the posset into a jug.

'I will go up, Agace,' I said.

'Coddle her well,' the cook mocked me.

At the door I said: 'I did but think Bess Woodville would go to court as the King's leman. Not as Queen of England.'

'So did we all, mistress.' She started to laugh again. 'I can read you like a pack of cards. Do you have your way, speak, I pray you, for me also, and the stable churls. For it's as likely I should dance with the Duke of Clarence in Greenwich Great Hall, as you should accompany the Duchess to court.'

'Save my supper,' I said, closing the door.

But I got no supper that night. For from the moment I stepped into the bedchamber again, with my healing draught and words of honey, the breeze blew strong and my ship began to turn on to its course. I got no rest either, for from the instant I began to brush Jacquetta's hair, and held up the mirror with the murmured words: 'A queenly face, my lady, a right queenly face,' she would have the service of none other but me. I brushed and brushed her scanty hair, and at the right moment when she looked down to see the tress laid over her shoulder I whispered: 'Madame, it has the touch of gold.' Lie was it none; a strand of my own lay beneath it.

As we left the snowbound fields and came down Watling Street into Chepeside, I could no longer contain my excitement and started to ask questions, my voice raised through necessity over the bawling of the 'prentices—'Come buy! What d'ye lack!' and the constant clamour of church bells—the deep song of the Jesus Bells in their fat stone tower, the sweeter burden of St Paul's near by; the yells of the chestnut and apple sellers touting for custom and the cries of the cook-knaves at each shop door. Even while we approached through the milling street past the goldsmiths and silversmiths with the banners of their gilds and patrons in lavish display over the entrance, we caught the sharp strong odour of pigmeat and brawn, spiced venison and game, an advancing gale, pungent to the nose, weighty on the stomach. St Paul's steeple towered to half a thousand feet, monarch over the hundred other spires that pointed to Paradise. Houses huddled together, leaning dizzily, gilded and painted and bulging into the street, and the buzz of close life from

55

within them dazzled the crisp urgent air. Shouts of song came from the taverns, the Mermaid, the Mitre, the King's Head, while the gay signs that hung outside, blazing blues and reds and gold, had been framed overnight by an angel with frosty fingers. Down along Chepe we came, and the dwellings leaned close and hugged each other lovingly, and my joy made me believe that they, too, wished one another fair Yuletide greetings, and that in all the world, every face smiled. One great mansion soared high above the rest; in the distance I could see its mighty roofs, silvered by snow and sun. I turned eagerly to the woman at my side. All the Dowager Duchess's ladies seemed to be larger than I, and in the swaying litter I was crushed in the corner, the end of a fur rug wrapped about my knees.

'What is that building—where is it?' I cried.

'Guess,' she said teasingly, addressing a bumpkin.

'Is it . . . her Grace's residence, Ormond's Inn?' I asked wildly. I had heard of the magnificence of the Queen's town house, with its hangings of French cloth of gold, exquisite ornaments, where her wards were trained, and scores of retainers awaited her occasional visits.

She burst out laughing. 'That is at Smithfield!' she cried, and I felt foolish. Then, more kindly, she said: 'Nay, over there is Bishopsgate, and the high building, Crosby's Place.'

'Crosby's Place,' I repeated. A fleeting disappointment rose in me. The name said little.

' 'Tis Sir John Crosby's home,' she said reprovingly. 'He's a very important man.'

Still it meant naught, and how was I, no soothsayer, to know its very name would one day warm my cold blood?

A wintry wind blew off the Thames as we approached London Bridge and, to our left, saw the chalky pinnacles of the Tower. A few kites mingled with the seagulls, swooping and tearing at objects that were spiked upon the gates of the Bridge. I looked up in interest to see what it was they attacked so merrily, and looked hastily down again in the next instant. For they were the heads of what had once been men, empty-eyed skulls with tattered hair, whipped by the wind. A bird flew carelessly past our litter, a large piece of pallid flesh in its beak. 'Pirates,' said the woman next to me, and yawned. Still I gazed at my lap until the sight should be gone. Pirates, felons, thieves, they might have been, but once they were men, and mayhap well-favoured, and sometime loved.

The deep boom from Westminster Clock House calling the hour struck at my ears. The mighty river, choked with merchant galleys, rich barges, wherries and flotsam flowed strongly. A swift tide was running. Giant cranes lined the docks. Petermen offered penny-passage over the icy waters, their voices hoarse and salty. And on the crowded frosty river rode a thousand swans, like brave white blossoms fighting the swell. Our litter ventured cautiously towards the Bridge, for the road was foul with great wounds to catch at the horses' legs. I looked up at the score of arches formed by the joined house gables under which we were to pass, and was marvelling again, when we halted abruptly. The little brachet bitch on the lap of the lady opposite fell to the floor and set up a sharp yapping. Gently I picked it up, returning it with the sweet and docile smile which I had worn for days. I was thankful we had not brought Gyb. All the ladies seemed bored; they had made this journey before, and the Dowager Duchess was dozing in her corner. But I quivered like a lute when played by the master, and struggled to peer out of the side of the carriage.

'God's curse on this delay,' said one of the women languidly. 'What, is London drawbridge up at this hour? Why have we halted?'

Swaying gently, the litter waited. I could hear the shouts of men, the crisping of hooves on the snow, and as I looked out I saw a great body of horse advancing over the bridge. They will pass very close, I thought; there was small room for two such cavalcades and a crowd had suddenly gathered to swell the confusion. People lined the street: merchants, pedlars, monks, women with young children, ragged beggars, red-nosed with the cold—all pointing, gabbling in low excited voices. A milkmaid set down her pails in the dirty road, to arrange her gown in a becoming fashion. A father raised his infant high the better to see. What, is the King coming? I thought. The very air was alive. The King is coming to meet the Duchess, I thought, and was about to give my mind a voice, when a great roar went up from the people, a shouting tumult to make the heart beat fast.

'Warwick! Warwick!' they cried, like thunder. The echo rolled off the house gables and curled about our litter like a lash.

'Warwick! Warwick!' they roared, and the name was an anthem of praise.

All the gentlewomen lay back on their cushions, assuming disdain. I cared naught for their strange disinterest. I craned to see who rode towards us.

Had I not known the King by sight I would have hailed

this one as his Grace, so royal was he, both of countenance and bearing. Astride a great black horse he came in magnificence. The beast was housed to the knee in cloth of silver, the bit and bridle and stirrups fashioned of gold and studded with pearls and diamonds. A score of archers on foot surrounded horse and man. They walked as one man who wears one badge, and that emblem, the snarling Bear and Ragged Staff, was painted clear and bold upon the banners waving above them. A score of noblemen, sumptuously clad, surrounded Richard Neville, Earl of Warwick, and none heeded them, for all eyes were on their master. He wore a long gown of dark blue velvet, the sleeves rich with ermine, over which, slung carelessly, lay a wide gold chain heavy with sapphires. A vast diamond flamed in his velvet bonnet. His eyes were a keen clear grey in his square dark face, and his hair fell in black curls to his jewelled collar.

For all his greatness, he halted to pinch the cheek of the waving child, doffed his cap in honour of the milkmaid, bowed to the priests and the merchants, and threw a fistful of gold among the beggars. His swift gaze swept our entourage, and in a flash the benign eyes changed. A cold look of contempt, a thin veil as of snow over black ice, entered them. He bowed to the Dowager Duchess's litter, spurred his horse through the narrow way and rode quickly past with his train, leaving the townsfolk in a turmoil of excitement. I sank back, trembling, and thought with admiration and wonder of the noble Earl right up unto Greenwich, where the King and Queen kept court for the holy season.

Dimly, I heard the women talking, fierce icy voices. 'Devil damn the popinjay!' said one. 'To make my lady wait!' The Duchess waked from her half-doze, chuckled and snarled, and I smiled at her. I knew and cared for naught, save that I was in London. I was too stupid to be afraid, and God guards fools, that I am sure; thus might I have thought had I thought at all, springing to the side of my lady as we ascended the Palace steps. Some of the gentlewomen's looks were like half-sheathed daggers, but I stayed milk-mild, taking from Jacquetta's limp hand the musk-ball she had carried against the stink of London, giving her the ivory cane with the jewelled handle. I whispered sweetly in her ear, ever solicitous for her comfort. False, was I? Nay, at that instant I was a true maid, for I could almost love the old woman for bringing me to this place, this glory. I wore the Queen's old gown, but I was in the Queen's household, for good or ill.

Agace had warned me, before I left:

'Guard well your tongue, mistress, and your ways. For I hear the court is not all you would have it be; trust few, for there's envy and hatred there. Let no fickle knight or false nobleman weasel into your bed. Without it be the King, of course.' I had scoffed: 'Peace, old dame!' in a flurry of preparation. She had said, to my amazement, for we had had many sharp words: 'St Catherine keep you.' I thanked her for her blessing, but tossed her counsel aside as an empty nutshell, for I believed in Providence and the armour of my own keen wit.

So, of this mind, I came to court, and never shall I forget that first evening, with its disappointment and its drama, its joy and disillusion. With a throng of gentlewomen, I was swept up a twisted staircase into the Duchess's apartments which, within minutes, became a bedlam of bright plumage and chatter, spilt vials of perfume and barking dogs. Women were delving into trunks and coffers, drawing out dresses, yelling for the laundry-pages. Harassed servants kindled the fire, smoothed damask sheets upon the Duchess's bed, hung wreaths of herbs around the curtained gardrobe, lest a stink should creep through heavy velvet to annoy my lady's nose. I stood alone, my back to a great tapestry, its threads grazing my hand. For something to do, I turned and studied this rich arras, and found it more beautiful than belief. Worked on red cloth of gold, each figure sprang to life in silver thread, real pearls, with here and there a diamond's gleam. Ruby blood spouted from the wounds of golden knights. All along one wall of the chamber the tapestry shook, a shimmering blaze of beauty. I had heard of the phrase 'a king's ransom'. This was it, in truth.

The Duchess was surrounded by chattering, ministering women. So I stayed, lonely and ill-ease, backed by beauty, and wondering how to occupy myself. Then a voice fragrant with a foreign accent spoke in my ear, a cool hand touched my wrist, and I turned to look into eyes so like Gyb's that I almost laughed. For how could a cat's eyes live in a woman's face? Yet they were shaped like Gyb's, uptilted, a sparkling hazel green; and so kindly that I could have wept at their kindness.

'Child,' said the soft voice, 'the Dowager Duchess needs you now. I'm right joyous to see her well again. We've missed her sorely at court. Come, sweet, she would have you dress her hair for the evening's revels.'

I went gladly. The rest of the women faded into an antechamber. I lifted the Duchess's hennin and lovingly began to pluck the stray hairs from her forehead to give it the noble height she needed, while the fair, cat-eyed lady knelt beside us.

'Fetch me a gown, Elysande,' the Duchess told her. 'There'll be dancing.' She shrugged under my touch. 'Make the brow right clean, child. By my faith! I can scarcely feel you. You're more skilled than those squawking abigails!' I could hear them, laughing in the antechamber as they dressed each other for the evening. My gladness grew, excitement began to ferment in me. When Elysande returned with a crimson gown I whispered: 'Shall we be dancing, too?' and could not believe it when she, smiling, shook her head.

The lady Elysande sat with her arm lightly through mine. An hour earlier the Duchess had descended to the Great Hall with a stout train of attendant ladies, most of them ill-favoured, some of them downright ugly. In the antechamber full of truckle-beds, half a dozen of us were left; Elysande and I, and four stolid Flemish women who had shared the supper brought up to us by pages and who now slept resignedly on the floor, their backs against a linen-coffer. I was full of rich food and bad humour. Had it not been for Elysande's kind company, I might well have shed tears.

'Banquets are not for you and me,' she had said, giving me a quick kiss. 'We are *valetti* to her Grace. Is it not an honour to be left to guard her possessions while she adorns the court?'

Below, I could hear the sounds of music and laughter drifting from the direction of the Great Hall. 'They have started the dancing,' I murmured.

'You don't want to dance!' said Elysande lightly. 'Think how wearisome it would be with all those clodpoll knights, and the women with claws out, each striving to outdo the other! You and I will dance together on the gallery, if you wish. That is a beauteous gown.'

She smiled. In many ways she minded me of Agnes: soft-voiced, but without Agnes's coarseness.

'Sweet Elysande, you lie,' I said. 'This gown is one the Queen gave me when she left Grafton, and it's four years out of style.'

My eyes wandered again to the great tapestry. I stretched out my fingers to touch it. In the candlelight the gold threads held mystery, you could almost step into the picture, and the rubies were real drops of blood.

'That's the Siege of Jerusalem,' said Elysande. 'It was a gift from Sir Richard Woodville to his wife.'

One of the Flemish women woke up. Suddenly I had the feeling she had not been asleep at all.

'So highly prized, so easy gained,' she remarked. I looked enquiringly. Elysande was silent.

'Yea,' pursued the woman. 'That arras was despoiled from the manor of Sir Thomas Cook, he that was lately Mayor of this city, on Woodville's orders. There was talk that he had Lancastrian sympathies—and the King was persuaded by the Earl of his guilt. The Duchess lusted for this arras, certes—and it was while the Earl and Sir John Fogge sought treason in Cook's house, they saw it there and seized it for my lady's pleasure! Then, on mere hearsay, the Earl had Sir Tom cast into jail and fined eight thousand pounds! Queen's gold, they call it, a fancy name for thievery!'

Elysande took a little tablet from her pouch, wrote something upon it, looking hard at the Flemish woman, then hid the writing away and smiled at me.

'Poor Gerta has been drinking deep. She lusts to lose her tongue,' she said, her voice so sweet that its message was blown away, like chaff in a breeze. She rose, retrieved a torn dress from the floor, swept some spilled face-paint up, snuffed a candle, and, as another great roar of laughter reached us from below, looked at my downcast face.

'That will be the King's fool,' she murmured. 'They say he is the finest fool ever at court. Mine eyes have wept at his joculing.'

The thin savage note of the fiddles rose; if music has a taste, that was honey.

'They will be at it till dawn,' said Elysande. 'And I doubt not there will be some sore heads tomorrow at Mass. How my lord of Clarence does guzzle wine! I vow, down there, 'tis like the high days of ancient Rome!'

I could bear it no longer, and went and opened the door into the passage. Elysande came, and took my hand.

'Would you watch the gaiety, then?' she asked. ' 'Tis all artifice. But come with me. Soft, for God's love.'

It was cold on the gallery, and the stones were like ice as I touched them, to guide myself along the dark ways, for Elysande went ahead like a ghost. 'Stand well back,' her warm breath whispered, as we reached a little opening, a stone niche, with a torchlit embrasure through which I could peer. And down there was another world, which I surveyed as a fallen angel might look on Paradise. There, in a blaze of colour and light, gambolled the royal court, its laughter high and loud. Along each wall a painted tapestry danced, aping the courtiers who moved and swirled on scented rushes, their feet crushing the petals of late white roses.

'Where's the fool?' I asked softly. 'I know him. His name is Patch.'

'He makes his exit,' said Elysande, pointing. 'Too late, but he'll be back, with a new jape. Now they dance again.' She shivered.

The music took hold of me by the bones. There was something older than Christian in the thump of the tabor, the rebec's jewelled wailing. Yet it had all the holy season in it too, with its passion and promise. I looked down at the joy, standing close to Elysande and thought: So might Salisbury, in his doomed Castle of Sandal, have heard such music with a weary smile. The cries of the dying would have sounded in its shrillness, and in the wind beating without the walls. So would Salisbury have listened that Christmas, while his unknowing minstrels played through the hours to defeat and death.

I searched the room for the King, while the sweet high strains whirled about my head. Below, the dancers cavorted. In their leaping wind the painted knights upon the arras shuddered too, in a mocking fashion as of ghosts. Two pages with clarions blew a fanfare. From behind the great door I heard the rumbling wheels and grew rigid with sudden fear. For my thoughts were still with Lord Salisbury and that Christmas invasion. Elysande looked down at me and laughed.

'Watch the Storming of Troy!' she whispered.

There entered a walled city on wheels; a most wondrous sight, pushed by an hundred sweating yeomen. Banners fluttered from its heights. Women, clothed in flimsy stuffs of gold and peach and crimson, sat atop the battlements. In the wall nearest the royal dais was set a door fashioned from beaten brass, studded with bright beads and wide enough to admit a small army. Then slowly the candles around the outer edges of the hall were dimmed, bringing darkness broken only by the occasional flash of eyes, or the glitter of a jewel, so I could no longer see the vibrant, hot-breathing press of lords with their dragonfly ladies. Invisible were they, as were the butlers and guards, and waiting, quaffing unseen goblets, whispering in expectancy as through the great door, with only a faint rattle of pulley and chain, rolled the great Horse of Troy. Painted gold and white, garlanded with flowers and blowing real fire down its nostrils, it was, Elysande whispered, full of murdering Greeks.

'The King likes well this disguising,' she murmured. Pinching my arm gently: 'Jesu! It's cold in this place. I'm going back.'

She slid into the darkness and I was left alone, staring till my eyeballs ached at the mummery below. Though the whole court was mad with enthusiasm, smiting the tables with their hanaps and roaring bravos, I was not sorry to see the bloody battle finish. It was, after all, a man's sport, and I would liefer watch the dancing again, gazing at the rich gowns, the gracious gestures, jealous and a little sad.

Suddenly I saw Patch. He came riding a donkey, bringing light into the gloom with a blazing torch held high. His mount was caparisoned in red cloth of gold. Peacock feathers waved on his head and a blackamoor child ran at his stirrup like a hound. He circled the Hall smartly. As he passed below me I saw his face. Patch indeed, Patch, untrimmed by the years, still wrinkled and smiling wickedly, oddly dear to my sight. And the Hall was bright again, and I drank eagerly of the company, my eyes seeking first the royal chair of estate, beneath whose great broidered canopy King Edward lolled. His hair was ruffled, but he was more well-favoured than ever. His fine teeth showed in his laugh, he was tall as an oak, fair-skinned and straight of limb, with diamonds flashing on his doublet. Behind his head, thirty yards in measure, hung the royal dorsal with the leopards and lilies of England, watching with tapestry eyes the fickle splendour of their court.

Beside the King, Madonna-like, sat my late mistress, Elizabeth. Elizabeth the Queen, whose ivory face betrayed neither joy nor distaste for the scene under her eyes. The King drank, held his goblet to her lips, which pouted, smiled, declined. He dangled a bunch of grapes before her, made some jest, at which she smiled again, with downcast look. She took one grape, kissed it, and popped it into Edward's mouth.

Swiftly I scanned the others round the royal dais. I saw Earl Rivers, flushed and heavy faced, leaning close, talking earnestly in the King's ear. Anthony Woodville also bent his handsome head near the dais, smiling unceasingly. The torchlight flamed up and caught the coldness in his eyes for an instant. I remembered those eyes, how they had terrified me once as a foolish child. Never again would they affright me.

Patch was capering in the centre of the floor. Someone threw an orange, and he caught it deftly, speared it on his dagger, and strutted, mimicking the royal orb with his new-fashioned toy. The court howled with laughter, looking to the King for his approval, and seeing it. Patch turned a somersault, landed on a slippery square of rushes and fell on his rump. A great hound rushed snarling from under the King's table and flew at him. The fool yelled in fear and fled, round and round the Hall. Gales of laughter swept the company, and watching each face, anxious to share in their enjoyment in my unseen way, I realized that there were those who did not laugh.

The Earl of Warwick did not laugh. For the second time that day I marvelled at the icy splendour of his mien. In dark green satin crusted with rubies, the hilt of his dagger heavy with gems of price, he stood near the door, his arm about the neck of a tall, golden-haired youth, who held a brimming wine-cup. From his likeness to the King, I knew him instantly to be George, Duke of Clarence. Warwick was murmuring in his ear, gesturing the while with a glittering hand. I saw his glance fly to the little company about the King, and there again was the same disdain as when he passed the Countess's litter. George of Clarence listened, nodded, laughed a little too loud, and drank more wine.

'All artifice,' Elysande had said. I pondered on this deeply, my eyes raking the crowd. Nay, not all were happy; that was sure. One small lady, in a rose-pink drift of gown, stood alone, wistfully smiling. Middle-aged, a woman alone; but those were not the reasons for her obvious sadness. Some strange intuition told me there was more. All artifice, was it? I searched the throng deeper and saw that some were the worse for wine, lolling white and heavy-eyed back in their chairs. From my eagles' eyrie, I saw sly fingerings of naked breast and arm, hot kisses pressed on cheeks in unlit corners, quiet speech between men and men, looks of love and hate and jealousy darting like lightnings from eye to eye.

Suddenly I thought: if the case stood thus, and I could choose, there is none here I would have for my lover! If this were the court, the true splendour, for the privilege of whose enjoyment men slew each other, I was sorely disappointed. Patch had finished his joculing, and was creeping back across the hall, feigning a mortal hurt. His face a mask of pain, he crawled out of the door under my gallery and disappeared to roars of applause. Clarions sounded, and music swept into life again. The sweet wholesome sounds of viol and clavichord, shawm and lute and psaltery soared to my ears. Earl Rivers bowed to the Queen and sought her in the dance. The King urged her from her chair, kissing her hand as she descended with cool grace.

It was the music. That was all my joy. The music froze me like ice, burned me like fire. It rose to unattainable heights, wailed and sobbed and laughed. The voices of spirits were in it, songs of the laughing dead, borne on the wind of rebec and string and cromorne, and the heartbeat of the lusty living too, struck from the skin of a joyous tabor. Poetry and battle, love and death, all grew strong in that music, and my skin had lumps like those on a plucked goose, as I clasped my hands and forgot my own existence, following the courtly pattern of bright dance with misted eyes.

Footsteps were approaching along the passage and I shrank into the concealing shadow. I heard a voice muttering to itself, rude oaths, but a voice that I knew, none the less. I stepped out into the flaring torchlight.

'Patch!' I cried.

All colour fled his face.

'Jesu!' he said with quiet gladness. ''Tis a ghost, a lovesome sprite. Come to taunt poor Patch.'

''Tis truly I, Patch,' I said merrily, and kissed him on both cheeks, while he swung me off my feet.

And all he could say was 'Well met, well met' and babble about love, his favourite jest and one which I thought he always saved for me, and he swore himself a prophet, for he had vowed that I should come to court, and here I was, and he also, with all the favourable planets swimming in Heaven for him, for he had thought often of his own true love.

'Give me space for a word,' I said, laughing and struggling from him. 'Are you well? Your skill is undimmed, I see.'

'I do well enough,' he answered. 'So my lady Jacquetta brought you? The Queen Mother. Mother of the King's Grey Mare!'

Now I could laugh at an old jest. We talked of Grafton for a while, then I turned back to the embrasure, which drew me like the moon the tide.

'I have been watching the merrymaking.' I looked again to where men and women disported themselves in the Hall. Patch leaned close to me against the stone.

'A fine spectacle,' he murmured. 'Often I come up here to watch—'tis better than any May-Games, and none know we are here.'

He pointed out several celebrated people, among them a group of Bohemian knights whom the King was entertaining; the Queen's sisters and the Duke of Buckingham. He even spotted Dick and Thomas Grey, playing merels together in a corner. Tom's wife, the Duke of Exeter's daughter, was the one in the green gown. She had a furious temper. I pointed to the small lady in rose-coloured silk, the sad lady, and asked her name.

'That is Katherine, Countess of Desmond,' said the fool, and all merriment left him. 'Poor lady.'

Then he was saying other things: possibly the Countess of Desmond's history, or he may have been reciting a psalm; or making his will, for whatever he said, I heard it not. I heard no more, though his voice went on and on, as a background to the beating of my heart, which started up enough to frighten me, as if I were in mortal fever. For my idle gaze had suddenly fallen on one who had not been in the Hall when I looked before. To this, I may swear.

And had I been an old old woman with three husbands buried and twice as many children, or had I been a coal-black queen from the East with the whole of Byzantium under my hand; or had I been an idiot with no tongue, no ears, and only eyes, eyes to see whom I saw then, and a heart to feel as my heart felt; had I been any of these, I would have done as I did. And being what I was, a virgin maid, with but an armoured dream to cherish, I looked that night upon a man, and loved.

Next to the Earl of Warwick he stood, but apart from him. He was solitary, young and slender, of less than medium stature. His face had the fragile pallor of one who has fought sickness for a long time, yet in its high fine bones there was strength, and in the thin lips, resolution. His hair was dark, which made him paler still. He was alone with his thoughts. Ceaselessly he toyed with the hilt of his dagger, or twisted the ring on one finger as if he wearied of indolence and longed for action. Then he turned; I saw his eyes. Dark depths of eyes, which in one moment of changing light carried the gleam of something dangerous, and in the next, utter melancholy. And kindness too . . . compassion. They were like no other eyes in the world. Like stone I stood, and loved.

The jester was babbling in my ear, and I could not answer him. With my whole heart I hoped that he might not be one too high-born to give me a glance. I longed to know that he was an esquire, mayhap the son of some lesser noble, or a member of his retinue. Then, seeing the sumptuous fire of jewels on the restless fingers, the collar of suns and roses about his neck, I knew it all useless; my dreams but vapourings; and he on whom I looked with such love further removed than the topmost star. By rank more distant, and by riches far apart. Above all, by the way in which he stood, solitary, yet dignified by his solitude, among the noisy splendour.

In the face of this, I asked, trembling:

'Who is that young knight?'

Patch was acting craftily. 'Which one, madam? Madam, maiden, mistress, honeybee. Names, yea, names for one passing sweet, and she with many names would have a name to play with. Which name, my Venus, cozen and cuckoo-eye, which knight?'

A page was offering him wine. He waved it away.

'The one who does not drink tonight,' I said, and my voice was like a frog's croaking.

'Ho! a sober knight!' said Patch, and peered to follow my slowly pointing, wavering fingers. He dug his sharp chin into my neck.

'Certes, I had forgot you were fresh to the court,' he said with a little laugh. ' 'Tis young Dickon.'

'Dickon?'

'Yea, the sad one. The scant-worded one. The one who beds with his battle-axe. If my eye be not crossed, you point to Richard of Gloucester.'

'An Earl, a Duke?' I whispered.

'Both, and more besides. A prince. He is Richard Plantagenet, the King's brother.'

I loved. I loved, and to my surprise, the world went on its way as usual. As Elysande had foretold, there was much groaning and head-holding in the morning. Many lay abed, including the Duchess, but the King was up betimes, and after hearing Mass, rode out hunting with a large train of knights and nobles, some looking as if they would liefer have stayed quiet in their chambers, nursing the quantities of wine that churned about their bellies. But King Edward was fresh as a flower, calling his friends in a voice like a clarion, mad to spear the otter. Elizabeth was serene, smiling gently with downcast eyes as she wished her lord a successful chase. Her own chase had been wondrous profitable, I thought, as we watched the King, at the head of his entourage, gallop out between the guard and disappear beneath the toothed portcullis. Yet as soon as his back was turned, her expression suffered a brisk change. The matron of Grafton Regis returned, and soon the whole Household was flying about like souls in torment in pursuit of their various duties. Little was seen of her, but her lightest wish was keenly felt. Even so, there was space for gossip—down the corridors it crept, the arras shivering with whispers: who had quarrelled with whom last evening; whose bed had remained bare till dawning; and once again, I came on Patch, whose face served as a beacon in a bewildering world of stares that were curious, and sometimes hostile.

He looked unwell, and was wearing a hermit's robe, all rags and tatters. 'To mock the Church,' he explained, and shook with laughter at my shocked face. 'Tarry a moment,' he said, catching my fingers in the passage.

I could scarcely bother to listen; my mind was floating high, my eyes burned with a memory.

'I've been speaking to my cousin,' he said. 'Men say there will be mischief shortly.'

'Oh, do they, Patch,' I murmured.

'You seem weary, maiden,' he said inconsequentially. 'Did you not sleep? I neither. My arse is sore. Did you see me fall last night? By St Denis, I thought my back was broken.' On and on, *ad infinitum*.

'Mischief,' I reminded him, after a long space, in which he had his thoughts, and I mine.

'There are signs in the heavens that England will have war again,' he said. 'At Bedford, two weeks ago, a dame laid out her bed linen to dry.'

'So?' I said. A face crossed my mind, a young, noble, dangerous face; a face dark and pale; eyes of light and darkness, heat and cold, day and night. A face like the beginning and the ending of the world.

'And lo! it came on to rain, but the rain was not rain at all, but gouts of blood which stained the sheets and bolsters beyond repair, and all about shrieked and knelt in prayer, for this is a dread warning of things to come.'

I said naught. I wondered where the prince was, what he did. I had not seen him ride out hunting, but there had been so many in the train I could have missed seeing him, though this was unlikely. Patch, bursting with his fanciful tale, looked wounded at my inattention.

'By God's bones!' he cried. 'I might as well have speech with yonder arras, for the holy men broidered thereon would at least listen better than you!'

'Forgive me,' I said swiftly. 'Poor woman! Did she buy new sheets?'

'There is worse,' he said. His voice sank to a hollow groan.

'In Huntingdon County, there was a woman great with child. And at about the time that the washing was be-blooded, she heard the infant in her womb sobbing and crying with a great roaring noise, and she was sore affrighted, for this means sure sorrow in this realm and dolour for all men.'

This time I felt a prick of fear.

'Seek you to drive me witless with your tales, Sir Fool?'

'It is truth,' he begged.

'Once, you sickened me with a bloody heart,' I said, catching up my gown. 'Now you fright me with falseness. I'll hear no more.' And I ran, and the image of Richard Plantagenet ran with me in my mind, looking worried, and I wondered how he looked when he did laugh, and reckoned him passing fair, laughing; and ran into our chamber and slammed the door.

'Patch is like something possessed,' I told Elysande, who was sponging stains off the Duchess's red satin. I recounted the wild tales to her.

'War, hey?' she said, raising her plucked eyebrows, and went on sponging. Her calmness infected me and I put the whole matter aside. It was time to rouse the Duchess. I pinned on my sweetest smile as I sped to her chamber.

When night came, and all the upper apartments were deserted, and the merriment came loud from the Great Hall, I stole again to the gallery. Unseen, unheard, I gazed again at the bright scene below. Flattened against a pillar under the hissing torchlight, I stood for an hour. With my fingers I traced the carved faces in the embrasure, until the cold seemed to turn me to stone, as they were. I learned a great heaviness in that hour, for though the whole court assembled in glory beneath my eyes, all were effigies, without form or being. They swam like ghosts, devoid of colour or life. He was not there.

Patch came again midway through the evening, giving me sweet foolish words, snatching kisses on my cheek and neck. I smote at him as if he were a troublesome fly, and he called me cruel, so I gave him my hand to hold and together we watched the disguisings. Sir Gawayn and the Green Knight held sway on the floor below, the knight clothed in green branches, his horse also green, a little unsteady on its legs, but marvellously lifelike. I had begun to take pleasure in the play, when Patch brought back my dolour with a chance word.

'I see my lord of Warwick does not grace the company tonight,' he said. I do not care, I thought. They could all be missing, save one, and he alone would make for me a feast day.

'And George of Clarence, too, begs urgent business elsewhere,' went on the fool cunningly. 'Could it be, sweet mistress, that these two fair knights sup quietly somewhere together and talk of a lady?'

'What lady?' I said dully.

Cautiously yet pleased, Patch murmured: 'Men speak much before a fool. They think me truly *witless*, I trow when they should but substitute an "n" for an "l", and be nearer the truth.'

'Go on,' I sighed, my eyes on the court.

'George of Clarence would wed Warwick's eldest maiden,' he whispered. 'It would be a right wealthy match for him, and the great Warwick knows his mind. Isabel is the lure to draw this falcon from his royal brother's side. And across the sea, waiting, sits an old spider, a French spider. King Louis . . .'

'I know naught of these intrigues,' I answered. 'And in any case, are they not cousins, George and Warwick's daughter?'

'Dispensations have been arranged,' muttered the fool. 'The Curia is greedy. And 'twould be a weapon in the hand of Warwick, to have George as close ally. Warwick has never, will never, forgive Edward for his lowly marriage.'

I looked sharply at Patch. 'What's this?'

'Did I not love you, maiden, I would not tell you all these secrets, for you and I could be thrown in the Tower for such whisperings,' he replied, with a frightening grimace.

I pressed his hand. 'Pray, don't leave a tale in mid-air.'

'Warwick had planned a great marriage for his Grace,' Patch murmured in my ear. 'He had arranged for him to wed the Princess Bona of Savoy, sister-in-law of Louis of France. Imagine his fury when your fair widow of Grafton Regis filched the prize from under Europe's eyes! I trow the Earl writhed in his skin with rage. Think you, while we were at the May-Games that day, England was being set on its head!'

Yet I am glad, I thought, in my then arrant folly. Had all this not come about, I should not be here. I should not have seen what I have seen; should never have known this love, this love that tears my heart. I said: 'So now he seeks to wean Clarence from his Grace? Treason?'

'Of a kind,' replied the fool. 'Jesu! How the Earl must have fumed when he found his King was also a man, a frail man with a will of his own! No longer his mammet to raise to a height, to counsel and dangle . . .'

70

Suddenly, he stopped speaking, pointed down below. 'Here enters Lord Hastings. A great fighter, loves the King well.'

Lord Hastings was tall and fair, and I saw him not. For another came with him through the door, and again my heart was rent like the temple veil at Our Lord's Passing. There entered Richard, my soul's liking, Richard Plantagenet, my beloved.

This night he wore an air less lonely and distracted, and for the first time I saw him smile. He smiled when the King beckoned him over to the dais, and throwing an arm about him, placed in his brother's hands a little satin pouch or some such thing for holding jewellery. Richard opened it and drew out something small and shining, doubtless a Christmas gift from the King. A look of pleasure crossed his face. It was then I realized he was younger than I had thought; it was but his sombre expression that gave him years. He thanked the King, swiftly bent and kissed his hand, and Edward, cuffing him on the shoulder, roared with jovial laughter.

But the glad moment passed. I saw a pout forming on the Queen's lips, and with one of her white hands she touched Edward's sleeve. He turned from Richard in mid-sentence to gaze into Elizabeth's face. He looked at her as one bewitched, summoned an esquire with impatient fingers. A rosewood coffer was laid before the Queen. I craned to see what she drew from it; the white fire of diamonds leaped into life. It was a reliquary worked in beaten gold with three pearls of price dropping like tears from the lower edge. Elizabeth held it up for all to see, and whispers of admiration came from those who stepped forward to praise this kingly gift. In its lace of black enamel, diamonds big as hazel nuts vied with the pale blood of rubies dividing them.

Elizabeth also kissed the King's hand, but he kissed her mouth. Pages brought on the Christmas gifts, and Edward all but disappeared behind a veil of Woodvilles, bending the knee, kissing his fingers and the hem of his robe, smiling their thanks. Four of Elizabeth's five sisters came trailing yards of silk and sarcenet; the Lady Katherine in green, Anne in crimson, Elinor in palest blue and Mary in deep saffron. Miniver and marten banded their sleeves and veiling fell from the peak of their hennins in gem-scattered mists. Behind them, like meek lambs, came their new noble husbands: the young Duke of Buckingham; William Bourchier, son of the Earl of Essex; the young man who was the heir of the Earl of Kent; and Lord Dunster. John Woodville led his aged spouse, my lady of Norfolk, to the dais. She whispered her Yuletide greeting and looked weary, as if she lusted for her bed.

I had a sudden vision of a pack of hounds descending on a royal stag, their yelling mouths agape with greed and joy—which was strange, for all about the royal pair bore themselves demurely, with gentle looks, and courteous, loving gestures.

And Richard? Utterly isolated now from his brother the King, he turned slowly and walked across the Hall. Katherine, Countess of Desmond, came to meet him. She was smiling at him; my heart grew sore with envy. He was showing her the King's gift; she was admiring it, clipping it to the centre of the collar he wore about his neck. He looked down, fingered it, made some jest to her, and they laughed together. Then the minstrels began a French tune, the old *basse-danse* with its slow and gliding steps. The Countess was giving Richard her hand. I turned away. No more could I have watched them dance together than plunge my fingers into the torch-flame overhead. The tears filled my eyes. I knew myself possessed by some demon. Only a demon could have conjured the thoughts and wild feelings in me at that moment. I was lonely too, for Patch had returned below some time ago. I had only my cold stones for company, with the blind carved faces.

I glanced back again, anguished. The Countess looked at Richard as if she found him pleasing indeed. But the dance was over soon, and she left him, to drink wine with a group of ladies, and he was alone again. He cast an eye over to the King, but Edward was occupied, laughing, his head a spot of gold between the greying skull of Earl Rivers and the sleek locks of Anthony Woodville, who once more leaned close, talking, talking, with smiles and frowns and wise, nodding looks, while Richard toyed with his rings again, pulling off the jewel on his last finger and replacing it, over and over, a maddening gesture of disquiet and heaviness. His eyes swept the hall as one who looks for an ambush. Over the music the Woodvilles' laughter rose, as the dancing swirled about.

And he was solitary.

He was looking directly at me. I knew this could not be, as I was quite concealed in the lofty shadows, but it was as if our glances met through an arras of darkness, a tapestry woven of my dreams and desire. I made believe that he could really see me, and looked deep into his eyes, melting their

72

coldness with the ardour of my gaze, playing a foolish game with him for my own comfort, before he suddenly turned and, to my sorrow, quit the Hall.

And it was then I knew why women stooped to mix potions and simples, to wreak strange works in moonlight, for there is naught one will not do to attain the object of such craving, and this gave me remembrance of the Duchess of Bedford and that night four years ago. In my childish way I thought I understood the actions of the Queen and her mother. For if Elizabeth felt for his Grace as did I for Richard of Gloucester, we were as one.

Fresh entertainment came forward, as a pair of singers, a youth and a maid, knelt before the King. Then a soft air, a simple melody, rose to the ears of the suddenly hushed court; and for me, it was May Day again, and I was no longer cold, for the sun burned bright and the grass smelled of its soursweet bruisings and an old man fashioned a ballad for the Nut-Brown Maid, who would ever be true to her lover. I leaned towards the brightness and, in an abandonment of joy and because there was none to see, tore off my hennin and let my nut-brown hair fall to my knees. For I would be a child again, for five minutes, and remember the time when men stopped to gaze at me, with my chaplet of flowers crowning that at which they all marvelled, and longed to touch and stroke and possess. The maiden sang:

> 'Mine own heart dear, with you what cheer?
> I pray you, tell anone,
> For in my mind, of all mankind
> I love but you alone.'

I heard Patch's light step behind me in the passage, and without taking my joyful gaze from the scene below, stretched out my hand, crying:

'Ah, my friend, remember you this day! When all men called me fair, and the old ballad-maker said I would be a true maid, and fashioned this song for me ere he died! Take my hand, and say you have not forgotten!'

And I felt his hand in mine, and we stood together, listening to the music until it ended, and I turned with shining face to give him one kiss out of my true pleasure, for after all he was my friend and had shared this moment with me. And the hand which held mine did not belong to a fool, but to the King's youngest brother, who stood looking down at me with,

73

God be praised, the same look I had seen in the eyes of men that May Day long ago.

He was there, he was real. His hand, slender and warm, held mine firmly. And I was bereft of speech, as completely as if my tongue were torn out. So, of necessity, I waited, and it seemed an hour before he spoke, which when he did was in a voice passing quiet; a deep, a gentle voice.

'Is it a custom, damoiselle, to stand alone in this cold place?' he asked. 'I know the court can be wearisome, but health can suffer from these chill vigils. You should be below, enjoying the festivities.'

There was irony in his last sentence.

The torch above his head blurred and came clear again. His face was in shadow, for he had moved closer, but I could see the gleam of his eyes in the flame. Belatedly I remembered who addressed me; a royal Duke, a Knight of the Garter. I sank to the ground in curtsey, and his hands raised me swiftly.

'You do not answer,' he said. 'And I know you have a voice, for it gave me fair words just now when you bade me listen to the song.'

'Most princely grace,' I whispered, 'I am not cold. And I've no place in the Great Hall, for—I am naught!' I bit my tongue at the witlessness of my words. He was silent for a moment, then he laughed. A right lovesome laugh he had. Was there uaght of him that did not please me?

'Naught,' he said thoughtfully. 'Tell me, who shall say who is naught and who is otherwise? And, by St Paul, you do not look naught to me! Had I known you stood above I would have come before and spoken with you.'

His eyes travelled over me, as mine had over him many times, and that same awed gaze fell on my hair. I heard him breathing deeply, as if he were aroused by his thoughts; the last of my wits deserted me.

'My lord, I must go,' I said desperately. I longed to run away, to fall on my couch and weep for the tongue-tied fool I had shown myself, when the chance to be so near him might never come again. I tried to pull my hand away, but his clasp had become a grip of steel. I could not budge.

'Does my company prove so distasteful to you, then?' asked the quiet voice. 'I had hoped you would remain for a while. I tell you, I am dolorous tonight, and already you have cheered me more than a little.'

74

'I'm glad of it, my lord,' I murmured, and let my hand lie still. He asked my name and I told him, thinking even that sounded foolish. Yet he repeated it to himself, as if he took pleasure in it.

'Do you not dance then, mistress?'

'Yea, my lord, I like it well,' I replied. And I thought: Richard, Richard, only would I love to dance with you, but how shall one, who has no quality, who is shadow and not substance, think in this wise? I glanced down at the minstrels, saw the smooth movement of the viol players bowing their instruments, the swift fingers plucking the wires, and the sharp cold strains turned my heart to ice, an ice that burned as it froze. The coloured court spun in a glittering skein. I trembled all over. My skirts quivered on my legs.

'But you are cold,' he said, and chafed my fingers between his hands. I shook my head, looking wildly over his shoulder, anywhere but at his face. He had the advantage of me, for the light fell on my countenance and he could see how my colour came and went.

'To dance would warm you,' he said; and from the subtle change in his voice it came to my mind that he was not so composed as he would seem, that mayhap *he* wished to dance with me, and a little of my courage returned. And as he bowed to me, just as he had done to the Countess of Desmond, there was naught in him save chivalry and kind graciousness. So I sank before him in accession as I had seen the Countess do, and we began to dance, slowly, with only the cold stones to watch us. Moving into the torchlight, I saw his face again, and the dark eyes were fixed on mine with an intensity that took my strength.

As the music reached its height and I the peak of my intoxication, he led me easily in a circle, passing me behind him so that our backs brushed lightly. As the last note sobbed to death, we came face to face, closer than was natural, our steps meshed in the confined space. My body touched his. Even in that instant I was conscious of the strength, full marvellous in one who looked so slight, dormant in him, like a coiled whip. I felt the catlike velvet of his doublet, the sharp pain of a cold object biting into my breast. I looked down: it was the King's gift that had touched me; a silver emblem shaped like a tusked boar rampant with ruby eyes. It seemed a ferocious, snarling creature for him to wear. Already I felt a bruise forming; wild thoughts of evil omens filled my mind. I gave a trembling laugh.

'I fear he mislikes our dancing, my lord,' I said, stupid and

gay. 'For he drove his tusks into my skin as if to bid me be-
gone from his master.'

Timidly I fingered the beast, bending my head over the
pearl tusks, the fiery eyes. I felt the lightest touch, like a leaf
falling, brush the crown of my hair, and stood motionless,
staring at the boar's unwinking red orbs.

'Why did you choose this device, my lord?' I whispered.

His voice low and a trifle sad, he answered: 'The White
Boar is my special cognizance. From the Roman name for our
royal house. Ebor* . . . Eboracum; his Grace and I thought
it fitting. My late father's Duchy, too. So I took it for my
blazon.'

Then I thought of York, Salisbury and Rutland. Their
heads on Micklegate. I was lack-wit to ask, I thought. I have
excelled myself in folly this night.

Restlessly, he walked away, turned like a sentinel in the
passage and came back to me, while I leaned on the pillar
and watched him. The torch flamed up in a sudden draught
as a door at the stairfoot opened and loud voices, complaining, laughing, sounded disquietingly near. My time with
him was over.

'Farewell, my lord.' A better curtsey this time, more controlled.

'My lord of Gloucester, are you there?' bawled a voice.

'Dickon, where are you?'

Richard looked in the direction of the sounds. 'It is Lovell,'
he murmured. 'Stay, lady, I pray you.'

Frantic, I caught his sleeve. 'Sir, there will be trouble if my
lady of Bedford finds I have left my post!' I whispered. 'Sir, I
beg you, do not speak of it, or I shall be disgraced.'

He turned swiftly. 'I shall tell no one, least of all the Dowager Duchess,' he said, with a biting edge. Then he took my
hand again, and I burned in the flame of him. 'For were you
discovered I doubt you could return tomorrow evening and
that would grieve me. For it seems a lonesome nook for one,
a happy place for two.'

I listened without belief. I clung to his hand to steady my
trembling.

'You'll come?' he said.

The sounds were coming closer, shouts and laughter. A
commotion as someone fell downstairs.

'God keep my lord,' I said, and tore myself from the hand

* In mediaeval times, boar was spelled 'bore' and it is thought that
Richard's device was an anagram for EBOR (York).

that would detain me, feeling as a trapped fox which, to achieve freedom, bites through and leaves a part behind.

I dreamed no longer of my faceless knight. I dreamed that I stood on the gallery with Richard Plantagenet, that we danced together, and he told me. of the White Boar and his lips brushed my hair. And on awakening I was sad that such a fair dream must fade, until the frosty sun brought remembrance, and I roused Elysande with a hearty kiss which set her grumbling mightily, for she swore I had tossed and groaned night-long and had now broken the best of her slumber. She pushed me out of our bed and I sat on the floor and sang about the Nut-Brown Maid, while all the other women in our chamber looked affrighted, thinking I had had my brains addled by an incubus in sleep. They reckoned me a wanton little thing in any event, coming unheralded from the country under the mantle of my smile, and plying my wheedling craft upon my lady of Bedford until (they vowed) it sickened them.

Yea, and I willingly served her, disagreeable though she was that day, for 'twas through her I had attained my bliss. I massaged and perfumed her aged body, poured praises over her with the rose-water and, as if she were young and beautiful, spent hours tiring her meagre locks. I fetched her her potions and physics, held the mirror up and flattered its reflection with honey breath. She preened herself. And all the while that morning, after the dreaming night, I served her thus with great distaste in my heart, thinking about Sir Thomas Cook and the arras, and of the way the Woodvilles used Richard, with their cold glittering looks, their sharp elbows thrusting him from the King.

Of him I did not need to think. He was part of me already; wrapped close within my heart, warm and safe, with his dark eyes, fire and ice, his quiet voice, his hands that were hard and gentle. When I heard the sixty voices of the choristers in the Royal Chapel sweetly raised in the *Gloria*, I smiled for joy, for his kneeling image came so sharp and clear I knew myself in spirit at his side.

But all this made the Duchess no less capricious and tiresome. She complained of her liver, saying that the banquet last evening had not been to her taste, though Elysande whispered that she had eaten overmuch of green figs, and this was doubtless the truth. She moaned and muttered; I flew about frantically, soothing her with possets and sacred amulets upon her stomach. The Queen sent Master Dominic to tend her; he who had made such a jest out of himself at the birth of the Princess Elizabeth by so firmly prophesying a male heir; but my lady would have none of him. He in turn would have sought the skill of Doctor Serigo, the chief royal physician, but she ranted against this with such passion that he finally spread his hands despairingly and slid away to juggle with his almanac, in the chamber hung with cabalistic signs and thick with the reek of herbs. It was all most wearying, and catching a glimpse of my face I saw that I was pale, with bruises under my eyes. This cast me down, for I wished to look fresh and fair for my tryst that evening.

That he would not come I did not for a moment think. There was that in him better than honour; a lack of light-mindedness, and the cognizance of one who keeps a promise no matter to whom it is made. This trait shone from him, wordless, yet lacking no expression. My hands shook. I must be doubly careful not to spill anything, to fall prey to clumsiness and enrage the Duchess. I felt like the tumbling-women at the May-Games, balanced on sword-points, each nerve stretched in a dangerous skill. For I knew it would take but a little annoyance to drive the Duchess back to Grafton, and then I would need to work my wiles upon the Queen, a very different matter, for Elizabeth was of iron, and had plenty greater than I to flatter her. Also I had bound the Duchess to me with my sweet considerations, and I doubted she would let me leave her. So the other women shook their heads in wonder at my ceaseless toil and, murmuring that I did the work of four, shrugged their shoulders and snatched a little more leisure themselves, thanking me for a fool.

In the afternoon, Anthony Woodville came to visit the Duchess in her apartments, bringing some translations of the verses of Christine de Pisan that he had made. The gentlewomen fluttered like birds, for he was handsome. Attired like the most royal of princes, he strode through the gold-hung chamber in a journade of white velvet edged with ermine. Stylishly, he carried a tall hat on the end of his cane with an affected air. The pikes of his shoes, a quarter ell in length, were caught up at the toe and buckled about the knee with gold chains. He walked with caution. He had two new rings: a sapphire the size of a small walnut, and a pearl-and-enamel thumb-ring shaped like the royal rose. Very recently had the King bestowed on him the Order of the Garter. He knelt to kiss his mother's hand. All the women withdrew to a modest distance. Elysande pulled me down beside her on to cushions.

78

She gave me a little shadowy smile, with a teasing cock of her head in Sir Anthony's direction.

'You see his shoes? Jesu, I wonder he does not braid his legs and tumble on his face!'

I smothered a laugh.

'The Pope has sent a Bull into England,' whispered one of the other women. 'He's sorely vexed at the worldliness of this new style, and says he'll excommunicate any cordwainer who fashions such long pikes.'

'My cordwainer says his Holiness's curse won't kill a fly,' said someone.

'Are you well, Madame?' enquired Anthony Woodville tenderly of the Duchess.

She gave a loud groan, 'Nay, sir, I fear I am sick in my stomach. I'll remain in my chamber this day.'

'Shall we not see you at the feasting tonight, my lady?' he asked. 'I vow you'll enjoy the sport. The Lord of Misrule holds sway this evening.'

I held my breath. Holy Mother of God, let her decide to go! I prayed. This was a turn of events I had not foreseen. The Duchess paused for a long space, while I bit my lips as if by pain I could will the right words from her.

'I cannot say yea or nay at this time,' she answered finally, and I lusted to leap across the room and shake her till her teeth chattered.

She peered at her son.

'How goes the sport?'

'I have been in the tiltyard at Eltham, and have unhorsed eight knights without a break,' he said with satisfaction.

'So you are champion again,' she said delightedly, and he smirked with pleasure.

'Yea, Madame, as on every day,' he answered, and went on to tell her of the ingenious new harness he had designed himself, cunningly fashioned to overthrow any opponent, or so he said.

He kissed her hand again before departing, and turned at the door to bid her finally farewell.

'I trust we shall have your company this evening, madam my mother,' he said, but still she would not decide, and I began to shiver and grow chill at the thought of not being able to slip away. As he made to leave, his cold grey eyes flicked idly round the mute circle of gentlewomen and came last to me. No recognition crossed his face and I was glad of it, for as I looked at him I remembered the dark chamber at Grafton Regis, and my fear. 'Flogged, at the cart's tail.'

I went swiftly to the Duchess. 'Are you too warm, my lady?' I murmured. 'Though for sure, the fire has brought a pretty colour to your face, dare I say it.'

She looked at me, and I thought she was about to grumble, but she said:

'You are a good child—thoughtful and kindly—would that all were the same,' and she shot an evil glance at Elysande who, truth to tell, often shirked a duty, if she thought she could do so undiscovered.

'Bring me some gowns,' she commanded. 'I will choose one to wear this evening.' And my heart sprang up with gladness, for tonight I could go to the gallery, and see again the face of my love.

The Duchess sifted through damask and velvet, and sighed heavily that none pleased her.

'This one becomes you well, Madame,' and I drew out an orange satin lined with marten's fur. She threw it to the floor.

'I'll not wear that gown,' she said angrily. 'The last time I appeared in it, there were those that mocked me.'

The gentlewomen gasped in chorus. 'Never, my lady,' said Lady Scrope. 'What churl would dare?'

'I saw my lord of Warwick smile,' she said grimly, and the whole chamber seemed to darken with the venom of her look. She cast the dress away with the point of her shoe. 'Take it,' she told me. 'It needs but a little threadwork to fit you.'

Stroking the slippery richness, I murmured my thanks. Elysande was beside me, caressing the fur, eyes lowered in admiration. 'You'll look like Venus,' she whispered. My heart turned one of Patch's somersaults; now I could appear before him fittingly clad, worthy and fine. Meanwhile the Duchess tried on dress after dress. And still she would not decide.

At four o'clock, pages brought up a light meal for the Duchess, who picked at it with little heart, and if her stomach was sick, mine was sicker, with my dread that she would abstain from the feasting. At seven she vowed she would take a short rest on her couch, and at nine she still slumbered, her mouth open, the jewels at her breast catching the light as they rose and fell. Elysande and I stood and watched her.

'Could you not pour a sleeping draught between her jaws to quiet her for all night?' I whispered desperately. Elysande choked on merriment.

'Would you have us both end our days in the Fleet?' she sighed, weeping with laughter. She looked at me sideways. More than ever her eyes minded me of cursed Gyb, though they were green, not yellow.

'You are passing anxious to rid us of my lady by some means,' she murmured. 'I saw how you ran around like a frenzied stoat in your desire to robe her, and now you would have her drugged—by the Rood, that gallery must be an enchanted place! I myself have always found it too cold to stay long—but you spend half the night there and come to bed an icicle.'

'It's a diversion,' I said. 'No more.' And I turned from her, suddenly weary, all my bright dreams cold as tomorrow's fire, knowing that I had made much of naught. A few words, a dance, a kiss on the crown of the head—or had I imagined even that? A maid with long vixen-coloured hair—a moment's politeness—and all forgotten in the chase, in the tilt-yard, or checking supplies in the armoury?

At ten, one of the Queen's henchmen tapped on the door of the outer chamber, and I spoke to him. He asked whether my lady would be descending to the Hall, as all were concerned for her health. I found great difficulty in answering, and held wide the door so that he could see through into the Duchess's apartment, where the gentlewomen drowsed, Elysande kept vigil, and my lady snored.

'What a thing it is to be cursed with years,' he observed. 'My Lord of Misrule holds court below, and I warrant there will be much lusty sport, with men and women doing what they will! Do you not wish you were one of his subjects, mistress?' and he winked lewdly.

Wild imaginings burned my mind—Richard—the cool Duke of Gloucester, inflamed mayhap by some wanton, noble lady . . . I put my hand flat on the liveried chest, right over the royal badge, and gave it a shove.

'Not all have their minds crammed with bedsport, false mischiefs . . .' I gasped. 'Go! My lady sleeps and so shall we, soon.'

He twisted his body about in horrible gestures.

'Alone, mistress?' he mocked. ' 'Tis passing sad.'

From the Great Hall a roar ascended. Female shrieks and loud laughter followed. I glanced hopefully to where the Duchess lay, praying that the clamour might have awakened her, but I was disappointed.

'King Misrule will have them all kissing by now,' went on the page. 'So why should we two not kiss—fair mistress, give me your lips, I pray you.'

He lunged at me. He had been drinking ale, in some quiet corner. I thought sadly of *my* quiet corner, as I slammed the door in his face. The cold stones would be colder tonight, without me to warm them with my frail burning, and the torch flame would mutter to itself, unless others spoke and danced and touched lightly in its leaping glare. For he would not have come. I was now convinced of it.

And if by chance he had come and found me missing, a shrug of the shoulders would end that which had scarcely begun.

I could picture him, walking away, slender and agile, his jewels and his eyes of ice and fire the only points of light in the darkness of him. With his swift controlled step he would be descending the stairs, entering the Great Hall to link arms with his friend, the unseen Lovell of last evening, the fortunate one who called him Dickon.

Then they would exchange the old glances of young men. 'Did she come? Was she there? What happened?'

A shake of the head, a dagger of disdain sheathed in laughter—a draught of wine and eyes bright, seeking fresh faces to charm.

I had never seen an execution but had heard plenty of tales; how the bowels are dragged from the belly and burnt while the victim lives. I thought my pain akin to that pain. I turned and walked to where Elysande sat at her tapestry frame.

'Sweet holy Mother of God!' she cried softly. 'I vow I've never seen such a sad countenance in all my days! Grafton Regis must be the dullest place in the realm!'

'It's quiet enough. Why?' I said. The pain was growing more brutal, more real every minute.

'Well,' she said, laughing, 'it seems that having tasted the joys of spying on the great ones, you can't live without such nightly diversion! But I remember, when I came to court, I felt the same. It soon palls. Why, by St Catherine, maiden, you're weeping!'

And she sat without moving to comfort me, but looking at me with a quizzical gaze, mocking and pitying at the same time, while her face rippled and moved before my tear-filled eyes like stones on a river bed.

'Do not snivel like a slubberdegullion,' she said, sharply kind, and this was the best physic for me, for I collected myself, and managed to smile at her, weakly.

'There's more to this,' she spoke firmly. 'Will you tell me— we are friends, are we not?'

She was ever anxious to be my friend, and I was glad of it. But I could not trust myself to answer.

'You have a lover!' she said suddenly, in a pleased voice.

'No lover,' I answered. And I minded the times I had said this to others who had asked me, and my reply had mattered no more to me than the death of a falling leaf. But now the case was changed anew; I had no lover, and I was in love. I thought of my love as a perfect pearl, gleaming and warm to the touch, richly sweet as honey, fragrant as the Rose, fierce as the Boar. It had been held out to me for a little space. Unfulfilled, it must be hidden in my heart. I wondered if a heart could contain all that rich and painful sweetness, without splitting clear in two.

'No lover, Elysande,' I said again.

'But you had an assignation,' she went on, guessing, eager, kind. I shook my head, and then the Duchess stirred. She was awakening, too late. The glance I gave her was sorrowful but it held no anger. She was only the tool used by unkindly Providence, to break me up.

'I have slept well,' she announced, and Elysande and I looked at each other, lost for words.

'Do you desire aught, Madame?' I asked her, though I knew there was little method in seizing the chance to go below on an errand. My gallery would be empty, empty. It was habit that made me solicitous for her needs.

'I'll have my hair brushed,' said the Duchess. 'I feel quite renewed after my slumber. We will have a game of cards shortly,' and she clapped her hands with a fiend's delight, throwing all the nodding women into a frenzy of awakening.

So, for an hour, I brushed the Duchess's hair, and through a thin veil of unnoticed tears, I played a game that these were other locks I stroked; dark hair shining with life about a pale, noble, dangerous young face. It was difficult though; every time I made the feeling come alive, and closed my eyes the better to imagine, my lady railed at me for sleeping.

On my way to the launderer's in the morning, I passed the gallery, and stood a moment to bid it farewell. It was no longer an enchanted place. In daylight it seemed smaller and not the chamber of delight where once, long ago, he and I had been handfasted. The torch was black where it had burned through. An evil omen. There were a few people about; divers ladies of the court, white and wan with kiss-marks on their neck, and satiety hung on the air like over-heavy perfume in a hot room. I swept low as George of Clarence passed, gilt-haired, aloof, his fair brows drawn together in a headache knot.

I shifted the weight of clothes from one arm to the other and sighed. A heavier sigh from the lungs of a clever mimic, whistled past my ear. Only Patch, I thought, could have come so inopportunely; if he jests with me now, I will strike him in the face. But I had misjudged him. He seemed to sense my misery.

'Be not so doleful,' he counselled. 'I'll carry the gowns for you—Jesu! they are heavy!' He staggered under the weight of damask and fine linen.

'Give them back to me, Patch,' I said, mistrusting him. 'My lady's still wroth that one of her shifts went astray last week. God knows, you might steal one of these to wear for sport, and get me into trouble.'

Hurt, he whined: 'Cruel maid. You should know I wish you naught but good.'

So I pleaded pardon, and squeezed his arm. 'I'm in a foul humour this day, Patch,' I said.

'Then, like cat and dog, this spikes my own affection,' he answered. 'For I am joyful in truth . . . maiden, last night I had a great triumph. I was Lord of Misrule to the court, and set them all by the ears! God's bones, you never did see such sport!' and he laughed aloud with glee.

'That I can well believe,' I said, hiding my sorrow.

'I looked for you on the gallery,' he continued. 'I wished to share the laughter with you, sweeting. We could have watched them below, all in turmoil, and got great joy from it. But you never came, or at least I did not see you.'

'My lady was sick, and needed me,' I said, and turned to go, unable to bear more.

'Some folk keep strange custom,' he mused, picking up one of the Duchess's stockings which had escaped the bundle. 'For sure, I came up here to seek you, long past midnight. Yet I did but meet with Dickon of Gloucester, and I know not who was the more startled, he or I.'

Elysande had seen me talking to Patch, and noting my swift change from despair to gladness, reckoned it was he who was my paramour; and now that I had seen his wrinkled face and curving mouth again, all was well with me. So, to please her, I laughed, and thought on Piers, or Patch, for a brief space. He was clever, and scholarly, and his star was rising higher in the service of King Edward, so skilled and jocund was he. He was not ungently born and he was, I suspected, wealthy; neither was he freakish nor dwarfed, like some entertainers—he was fairly enough of proportions and far from unpleasing to look at. There would be few raised brows should I choose to

be betrothed to him. Truly it seemed that marriage for me
had faded into non-existence, these days. My mistress had
gained her heart's desire—Lady Grey was Queen of England;
and she had her relatives to look to in matters of suitable
betrothal. She had many wards—I was useful no doubt in a
minor way but of no consequence. As for my thoughts on
marriage?

There was but one to whom I would belong. And had he
been poor as the humblest cottar's son, ragged, lame, blind,
ignorant, and yet capable of offering me the wedding ring, I
would have taken him on the moment, with not one look behind, so long as he had Richard's face, and Richard's voice,
and Richard's spirit, to burn me with a steady fire, to warm
me with its young heat and make each day May Day for me.

'But you do not marry them,' I said in a whisper. By rank
far distant, and by riches further apart than the topmost star.
Elysande swam back into my vision.

'Fools, I mean.'

'Well, sweet, he is a man,' she said, laughing, and I saw
suddenly the use of this silly delusion, and caught at it
gladly.

'Yes, he is. He is, indeed,' I said, feigning coyness, and she
looked hard at me, as if unsure of her own mind.

She was hard to fathom, Elysande. French in descent, she
gave away little in confidence, never lost her temper through
weariness as did the others, and she seemed to know many at
court, some of noble birth. I had seen her only lately having
fair speech with a woman, the strangest little person I had
ever seen. She was even lower in stature than I, not a deal
higher than the comic dwarfs King Edward kept for his
pleasure, to juggle and ride the great hounds around the hall.
Far from well-favoured was this tiny lady, with a face all
bones and sharply defined as an axe, small flashing eyes and
hollow cheeks. Yet she had had two husbands, Elysande told
me, for this was Lady Margaret Beaufort. Daughter of the
Lancastrian Duke of Somerset, she had first wedded Edmund
Tudor, Earl of Richmond, when she was thirteen, bearing a
son, Henry, two months after the death of her knight.

Patch plagued me with tales of these Tudors; he seemed to
know all their history. They were some kind of distant cousin
to the King. He had witnessed a rare scene, had Patch, in
Hereford, the town where he was born.

'I can see it now,' he said, more than once. 'Old Owen
Tudor, kneeling in the market square—one blow, and he
lacked a head . . . then came this madwoman . . .'

'And combed his hair and stroked his face and wept and lighted candles all around him,' I said wearily.

'I was but a little knave,' he said, uncaring. 'Jesu, that woman must have loved him sore. Then, if a Queen loved him, why not a witless wench?'

Surprised, I murmured: 'Did a Queen love him?'

'Yeah, Queen Katherine, widow of Harry the Fifth—Harry of Agincourt. That is why they smote off his head, I vow. Slain for love,' he said romantically and sighed, rolling his eyes at me and conveniently contriving to forget all about old Owen's Lancastrian loyalties.

'Edmund Tudor was their bastard issue,' he maundered. 'Jasper and Owen and Edmund, Margaret Beaufort's first husband. Maiden, think you she has heard my tale of high romance and sorrow? Mayhap one day I will seek to interest her with it,' he said happily.

'I doubt not she is well familiar with it, Patch, as are we all.' I sighed and turned up my eyes to make him cease. And then I realized it was nearing dusk, and Tudors and Lady Beaufort fled from my mind. For they were all but as the pastry figures fashioned by cooks for the subtleties at the King's table, and my thoughts all drew together and ran to meet Richard, as I prayed for night to come swiftly.

I vowed I would wait for him until dawn. I donned the Duchess's gift as soon as she was safely below. Elysande brushed out my hair, as if I were a noble lady. The other women played at dice, casting resigned looks in our direction as we murmured and shook with mirth, though there were some who smiled to themselves, having faint remembrance of their own youth; they were all past thirty.

'They think you *lack-wit* to *love* a *fool*.' Elysande whispered, and we clutched each other and wept with our laughter. And I laughed more merrily than she at the secret jest which I enjoyed, until a sudden thought shattered my joy. In truth, I had likened Patch to a troublesome fly before, but this night, if my lord came and spoke with me, and bewitched me with his steady gaze and the clasp of his hand, the fool might prove more dangerous; a fly? nay, a hornet, with sharp jealous sting. I fell to gnawing my nails, and when Elysande asked me, sighing *what ailed me now*, I could not answer her.

She snuffed a few candles, and the chamber grew large and dark with this new riddle peering at me from the shadows. Two of the women already slept, and their quiet breathing mingled with the rattling dice and the faint music coming from below. I sat motionless.

'Your sweetheart will be looking for you,' Elysande whispered. 'Take your cloak, it is colder tonight.'

I drew the hood up over my hair.

'Why do you dally?' she hissed, holding the door open. A chill breath from the passage crept in. 'If you don't go soon, you'll not be back when my lady returns.'

'Ah, Jesu, Elysande,' I whispered. 'Will she return soon, think you?'

She smiled. 'Nay, child, she's in fine fettle tonight. From the way she spoke, she rued slumbering through the gaiety last evening.'

The door closed softly behind me. Shaken by a trembling that had naught to do with the cold, I moved vixen-silent through the familiar darkness. Around the corner, the flickering torch burned high, beckoning me with its elf-light. I heard the music and the raised voices, which by now I could almost tell apart. The King's laugh was a mighty sound, rich and golden as he, and I recognized Clarence's bibulous chuckle. Tenderly, I bent my body against the pillar, greeting the carved faces with my fingers, and looked down. I was safe from Patch for a time in any event, for a figure, all blazing yellow and red, jingling bells, leaped witlessly about before the royal dais. He had possessed himself of the gold carcanet from the neck of some knight, and was skipping with it in the manner of a young child. He will need to be careful, I thought. His glory of last night makes him wax stout and proud. For his sake, I hoped that the lord he had robbed was cup-shotten and careless.

The Woodvilles dominated the Hall. They were all gathered, and tonight also there was Lionel Woodville, lately made Bishop of Salisbury. In fine robes, he nodded and smiled at the wholesome folly before him. There was Lord Hastings, looking sour. Lord Stanley and his brother William. Katherine of Desmond, Dick and Thomas Grey, George of Clarence, and my lord of Warwick. My eyes found Warwick, found his companion, and searched no further.

He was the very reason for my birth. He was my lord, and he stood next to the Earl of Warwick, slender and elegant, dangerous and sad, and I felt my heart give one clapping rush out to him like the wings of a dying bird; and my eyes set upon him in longing love, and I heard myself, like someone far away, come forth with a little rush of loving words,

87

and his name, said over and over in the darkness. It was a moment or two before I realized that all was not well with him. He was talking to Warwick, very fast. He was pale as death. He held one hand hard down upon the hilt of his dagger as if he feared it would suddenly take on life, and kill. He was angry.

Warwick, much taller than Richard, bent his handsome head languidly to listen. A little smile fidgeted his mouth. I mistrusted that smile. And George of Clarence came strolling into the tableau, also smiling, with full pouting lips, with condescension and unmistakable mockery. And Richard talked on and on, as I watched him, his hands; the clenched fist, the spread fingers, the clasped hands like a prayer; and his brows drawing together, and his eyes bright with this unknown anger and sadness. He glanced towards the King, then back to Warwick, talking, talking. And all the time Warwick smiled that arrogant, cruel smile, and Clarence chuckled in his wine-cup.

Then Warwick laid his hand upon his own heart and spoke. One short phrase, and Clarence laughed out loud, and the colour touched Richard's face, as if each cheek had been held before the fire. Then in the next instant he was pale again, pale as one long dead.

Warwick placed an arm about George of Clarence's shoulders, and together they walked away.

Richard was looking at the King. Edward, with a moody good-humour, filled a goblet with wine and pushed it across the table, beckoning his brother to come and drink. Richard walked over to the dais. He made to lift the jewelled cup, when the Queen forestalled him. With a masterly coquetry and a cat's swiftness, she took the cup herself, pledging the King over it with large eyes. She touched it to her lips. Then she handed it over her shoulder to Anthony Woodville, who raised it high.

'The King, my lords!' he cried. 'The Sun in Splendour! Perdition to his enemies!'

With a roar, the court rose, goblets aflame. I saw them all, as if frozen in a pose, the gay court acclaiming its King, the royal pair smiling their pleasure, and the King's brother, young, solitary, fierce, his foot upon the step of the dais, glaring about as at those who sought his death. The only one to lack a cup for the loyal toast.

'Holy Jesu! Cruel, cruel!' I said out loud, and clung to the pillar, shaking.

I had been against the Countess of Desmond because she

danced with him, but I loved her the next second, for it was she who brought salvation. Snatching up a half-empty hanap from one of the side tables, she tendered it discreetly towards Richard. And Patch, the troublesome fly, the witless fool, I loved him too. For he nipped it swiftly from her hand and gave it to my lord, with a courtly bow and a wink that held no mockery. So the wheels began to turn again, and the throats of men moved in their swallow, and the thud of goblets being set down merged with the minstrels' gay tune, and the moment passed.

My heart pounded, and my palms were wet. I fixed a killing glance upon the Queen but it did not touch her, for she fluttered her lashes and her hands, and the King ogled her with looks that spoke of bed. It was only when I surveyed the company again that I saw my lord of Warwick had not drained his cup, but held it brimming still. The smile on his countenance was bland and fierce. And now the gay colours, the glory, meant little. I smelled the storm, the hidden hate. It rose up and beat about me.

Warwick bent the knee before his King. He was departing, the carved smile still on his lips, and as I marked his progress through the door, I realized that another, the other, the only one, had left before him. And I had not even watched him go; it was like a betrayal, for I had sworn I would not let him from my sight, would protect him with my gaze as his own patron saint.

I sighed. He would not come now—that was certain, for he was too distressed by whatever had befallen him down there in that hell of hot laughter. And I would not even have the chance to offer him solace. It was as I thought thus, I wondered how best I might comfort him, and lacked conclusion, for how shall one, who has no quality, who is shadow and not substance, know aught of succouring a prince of the blood

Cold and alone, I stood for a long time. My heart ached. I was full of longing and sorrow and shame, shame at myself. Last night, while the Duchess slumbered, I had tormented myself with thoughts of my love, deeming him a lightsome courtier, wayward in look and desire. Now I knew he was not even a part of the seething court; I saw him old beyond his years, constantly tortured; pricked by intrigue and spite, baited by circumstance as a bear by feast-day mastiffs. And the worst of it was I did not know all. I could not reckon what it was that branded his face with that look of angry sorrow.

And, thinking how gladly I would have shared his trouble, no matter what, I drew my cloak about me and began to make my way, sadly, back towards the Duchess's apartments.

I felt a tugging at my skirts, and turned, frightened. A pale face stared up at me, level with my waist. A child's face, a faery face, disembodied above a suit of dark livery, and green-white with fatigue. A tiny page, come by night on an errand of which he was too young and too weary to know overmuch. Very hesitantly he asked my name and looked satisfied when I nodded. Then he fumbled for my cloaked hand and gripped its coldness. He began to tug me back towards the gallery. 'Mistress, come wth me,' he muttered.

'Where?' I stood firm, while he heaved at my hand and breathed gustily as if to draw me after him by sheer strength.

'It is a command,' he insisted, and my blood turned to dreadful ice. Only the King commands. My first thought was that I had been espied on the gallery by night and that the Comptroller of the Household had been ordered to reprimand me. Or some doing of the Queen! My guilt summoned wild images of Elizabeth's displeasure. I remembered too that I wore my lady of Bedford's gown. It came to my mind that she might not recall giving it to me. I sought to hide its rich folds from the torchlight and the child's weary eyes.

'Who so commands?' I whispered. The page shook his head, mute with sleep-lust.

'Madame, 'tis this way,' he breathed, his foot pawing the ground like a pony anchored by too great a weight. And so in pity and resignation I steeled myself and went with him, along the dark ways, past the drowsy guard, who winked at me as at any fair female face, answering my uneasy smile. We ascended narrow spiralling steps to another broader passage, descended a staircase, crossed a deserted hallway and entered a part of the Palace where I had not ventured. My captor halted before an oaken door, and bruised his knuckles hammering upon it. We waited. The page looked at me, and I at him, and he twitched his pale lips in a comic grimace.

'I suppose we had better enter,' he muttered, and threw his weight against the handle. I followed him into the empty chamber, and, in the light of many candles and a great fire, saw that upon his livery was blazoned the Boar, the White Boar, and my blood turned from ice to flame.

My hand was still imprisoned. He had a duty to fulfil, and none would chide him for shirking it. I managed to smile at him.

'I shall not flee, child,' I said gently. 'How cold your hand is! Come to the warmth.'

He came, willingly, and sat in the hearth, his knees under their proud livery drawn up to his chin, while I looked around the chamber, drinking in the things that were Richard, and which gave me joy.

'Where is my lord of Gloucester?' I asked, walking about on the rich carpet.

'He was here when I left, but he must have gone about some affairs,' said the child anxiously.

'Don't fret,' I said. Now I could hardly speak. 'He will come soon.'

His chessboard lay open upon a small table, the pieces frozen in an intricate move. My fingers hovered over a bishop, then dropped to my side, for I knew little of the game. I wondered with whom he had been playing, and guessed again at Lovell, his friend of the dark staircase. A fluttering sigh came from the corner. On a rod crouched a peregrine falcon, his round eye fixing me like an angry jewel. A lute lay on a chair near by and I touched it softly. The little discord rippled and hung sobbing on the air.

I walked to his writing table. Sheets of parchment lay strewn, and some had fallen to the floor. Pens and ink—a broken quill, and a pattern of fierce words leaping to my eye. I bent to read and saw with love, his signature . . . R. Gloucester; and three words, repeated over and over, the writing a fine Italic script growing wilder and ending with an ink-smear and paper torn by a savage pen. Very recent, that writing, the last line still wet. Three words only, time and again . . .

Loyaulte me lie.

The fire spurted and hissed as it licked damp wood.

I went through into the adjoining chamber, for the door was open, and gazed at Richard's narrow bed. It looked hard, though the sheets were damask, the covers edged with ermine. The White Boar, worked in silver thread, savaged the coverlet with its tusks. Above the couch shone a tiny light, steadfast and comfortable, illuminating the statue of St George. In silence I stared at the saint, and asked his blessing on Richard Plantagenet.

'I wish he would come,' said a small voice from the antechamber. I went back to the fire and was about to try to cheer the page, when the door opened, and he did come: all my joy, all my safety and all my bliss.

He entered smiling and he too had felt the cold, for he had thrown a long cloak of dark velvet about him. He gave me no time for any curtsey; he strode across the chamber and took my hands.

'Mistress, I am happy to see you again,' he said. His voice was as I remembered it. The joy became a pain, striking my depths.

'Sir, you commanded my presence; I am happy to obey,' I said softly. He must have felt the heartbeat in my wrist; beating, beating, like a song, like a tabor. But his glance swept to the page, and his smile faded a little.

'What's this?' he demanded. 'Harry, you are becoming hard of hearing now you are old and have fully eight years! I mentioned no word of command—I did but say you were to *ask* the lady . . .'

The page's mouth opened convulsively as if to set up a bawling. Richard bent hastily and took him in his arms, setting him on the table, so that his legs dangled.

'My lord, forgive my folly,' whimpered the child. 'I have a passing bad memory—I pray you, don't beat me.' And he shot a sly glance from under his lashes, cringing and fawning like a cur who begs morsels beneath the table.

'Folly indeed,' muttered Richard. 'When have I beaten you, you knave?'

'Never, my lord,' said the page primly.

Then Richard laughed. 'Well, sir, thanks for your faithful service this night. You look over-ripe for your bed. Be gone!' and he tossed a coin up in the air which the page caught deftly, tucked into a pouch that a faery might own, and, grinning, twinkled his legs across the chamber and heaved the door shut behind him.

And we were alone; and the fire blazed and chattered on the hearth, and we stood looking at each other across a chasm of unspoken words and my thoughts that leaped and swooned and grew bright.

He was the first to move. He crossed to me and my heart raced swifter for I thought . . . I know not what I thought, but he took my cloak from about me and his glance fell on my hair and he paled slightly.

'I pray you, be seated, mistress; be comfortable.' He drew a chair for me with as much courtesy as I had been the Queen. He laid our cloaks together across the table. 'I looked for you last evening,' he said, but his voice did not reproach me. His tone was rather that of one who expects to be disappointed.

'My lord, I would gladly have talked with you on the gallery again,' I said. 'But my lady of Bedford had need of my services.'

The look of kind politeness vanished from his face as if cloven off by a sword, and he gave a bitter laugh.

'Ah, holy God!' he said, and his quiet voice was even quieter. 'It is wondrous mirthful, for even in *this*, as in all my affairs, that company conspires to thwart me.'

He turned, with his restless, trained walk moving over to where stood a flagon of wine and cups.

'Will you drink, damoiselle?' he said, holding up the crested flagon, and I sprang from my chair, for it was unseemly for him to serve me.

'I will attend you, my lord,' I said hastily, seeking to take the wine from him. He covered my hand with his own, and his dark eyes held mine as he smiled a half-smile.

'You are my guest, mistress,' he said. 'Be seated, I pray; let us have no more folly. No posturing, no sham.'

Through my wild joy, he handed me the cup. He sat opposite me, the fire burning bright between us, and stretched his legs in the hearth, the time-honoured male gesture.

'This is better than that chill nook where first we met,' he said, and smiled at me over the top of his hanap. He drank, slowly, without taking his eyes from me. Then he whispered:

'Jesu! You are fair!'

I sat and tried to be calm, feeling myself becoming fairer under his look.

'Can you play chess?' he said suddenly.

Surprised, I shook my head. 'But I will learn, my lord, if that is your desire,' I murmured.

He waved his hand dismissively. 'It matters not,' he said. 'It is a good game, however, and one that all should know. It teaches a man strategy and tactics, and, by God, I vow that in this place one should be born cognizant of such matters!'

I longed to ask him more, help him unburden himself, but I knew I must wait until he chose to speak of that which troubled and angered him so much

'How do you find the court?' he asked me, and I was sorely vexed for an answer.

'The jewels and the dresses are wondrous fine,' I ventured, and he hid a smile in his wine-cup, shaking his head, no doubt, at the light-mindedness of women.

'But I see little of the court itself, my lord, for I am neither one thing nor the other . . .' I babbled on. 'I am greater than some and lesser than some, and to speak the truth, I have not yet found my rightful place. I am pulled this way and that by standards of society, for though I came from the Queen's house at Grafton Regis, I am not of noble birth.'

He gazed at me, and there was that in his eye which reminded me of the falcon's stare, looking right through and out the other side.

'Noble birth,' he said slowly. 'Jesu, mistress, I have seen the humblest vassal conduct himself with more grace than some of noble birth! And I have seen those who, hiding their policies behind a lovesome smile, feign nobility as they were born to it. While their hands clutch power as greedily as any cutpurse in the street!'

I knew of whom he spoke, and I kept silence, though my mind shrieked agreement.

'But we are talking of you, mistress,' he said gently. 'It intrigues me much to hear you describe yourself thus—neither one thing nor the other, for I too have known this feeling, and it is strong in me tonight.'

I spread my hands, assaying to make a jest of it.

' 'Tis the best I can do,' I smiled. 'Like Patch, in his motley; half red, half yellow! That is I.'

He set down his wine, and sighed. 'And I,' he said.

Let us merge the red and the yellow then, I thought in my heart. Looking at him, dark and gleaming like a raven in the firelight, I wondered if I could contrive to touch his hand; and instantly, he must have read my thought, for his fingers reached out and closed about mine. We sat motionless, while a loving ache from his touch crept up my arm and settled in my breast.

He was quiet for so long a space, I felt bound to amuse him with conversation.

'We saw a passing marvellous sight, when we came by London Bridge,' I said. 'All the people were shouting and clamouring and everything halted for my lord of Warwick, as he rode . . .'

I bit my words off on a gasp of pain, as his hand tightened on mine like the steel of a trap. I sat enduring the agony, questioning the pallor of his face.

'Certes, the people love Warwick,' he said, through his teeth. 'It was always so, for he won their hearts with his kindliness and courtesy—none was too lowly for his notice . . . all love him, as I did.'

It was the firelight, there could be no tears in his eyes; that was impossible, I thought, for he was hard and shining like steel; a royal Duke, a King's brother, and such do not weep easily. Before I could decide, he had leaped from the chair, to lean against the polished sweep of the brass chimney-piece. He rested his forehead on his arm for a brief second. When he looked at me again, his face was so composed I thought I had imagined it. It was the firelight.

'I loved Warwick,' he said, and it was as if he spoke to an empty room. 'He was like my father, and he trained me in the arts of war as bravely as I were truly his son. I cannot bear to think of those happy times at Middleham, but when I breathe the corruption down there—' and he gestured fiercely in the direction of the Great Hall—'then I mind how sweet were the cold moors of Wensleydale with their sharp cleansing gales and haunted mists. There a man could come close to God and know himself at last. Here . . . there is naught but greed and spite and lechery . . .'

He smote the chimney-piece with his fist, and it gave off a dull booming sound. I sat quiet, and trembled.

'I wonder often, of a night when I lie sleepless,' he whispered, 'why I was blessed, or cursed, with a heart that knows one way only, and cleaves to that way as a priest to his breviary. It is easy for George—he was ever feckless and light-minded, and lets himself be swayed by the breeze of fortune whither it will. But I have cast my loves into the dust to honour my allegiance to his Grace . . . to my brother Edward. The Sun in Splendour, hidden now behind a foul cloud of locusts!'

His emotion rent me to the bone. His pain was mine.

'Do not distress yourself so, my lord,' I whispered. He did not hear me.

'When I was fourteen, I attended a great banquet,' he continued. 'My lord of Warwick made much of me, and I wore the Garter. Warwick seated me with his ladies, the Countess, Isabel, and little Anne . . . I was so honoured and happy, until I realized what he was about. He would have me turn traitor to the King. I would not take his bait, so he washed his hands of me. Did you see what befell tonight?' he demanded, turning his fiery gaze upon me.

'Yes, my lord, I knew much sadness,' I murmured.

'Jesu!' he muttered. 'He called me . . . a Woodville-lover! I, of all people, who would rather have died than see my beloved . . . his Grace, netted by that loathsome brood. And then the Queen caused me to lose face, deliberately, before all!'

His colour came and went, frighteningly, with his fierce breath. I rose and stood beside him.

95

'My lady of Desmond aided you,' I reminded him gently, and his frenzy ebbed a little.

'Yea, the dear Countess. She's a good friend to me . . . and one who has suffered much at . . . at the hands of Edward's Queen.'

As if he thought he had said too much, he glanced at me sharply. 'I may not speak of it,' he murmured. Then, in almost the same breath he said softly: 'She is widowed.' He looked at the fire. The leaping flames were red in the dark eyes. 'And worse,' he whispered. 'The shedding of infants' blood . . . Slaying women is bad enough, and no Plantagenet has ever done so, but the monstrous crime of taking children's lives deserves eternal torment.'

We were silent again, a long silence, broken only by the chirping of burning logs; and the falcon's wings softly stirring in sleep. I knew that he spoke of some secret foulness of the Queen, and wondered if he remembered that I slept by Jacquetta of Bedford. In that instant he turned to me with a faint smile.

'I will say no more,' he said. 'It is not that I do not trust your gentle face, for there is that in it which moves me to confidence. And the King knows I am loyal and would not let the Woodvilles harm me. But you are in the service of Elizabeth's mother, and open to attack. So it is better now that I should teach you chess, if that would pleasure you.'

But we remained looking at each other, and he took my hands in that same tender clasp.

'I would not betray you, my lord,' I said steadily.

'Suffice it to say this is why the Countess of Desmond and I talk together and sometimes dance in the Great Hall,' he answered. 'We find some little comfort in each other's company. And I have need of such.'

I could scarcely catch his last sentence. With my heart I watched him, for I longed to keep his image with me for ever: his dark slenderness, his pale face. I marked every aspect of him; seeing that he looked worn now from his outburst of the past few moments; that his black brows were straight as if drawn by a steady pen; that his right shoulder was slightly uneven as against the left; that he was very unhappy. For all his polished manners and his knightly grace, he was young, and woefully unhappy, and I loved him, with a love sharp as death.

He still held my hands, and my gaze, with his own.

'Have you known loneliness?' he said without emotion. And

I thought of Grafton Regis, after the old nurse died, and Agnes went away, and I nodded. All the time my limbs quivered, like branches under lightning—I was the tree, and he the storm.

'I would tell you something now, that I have not said in this past hour of high passion which I fear has wearied you,' he said. 'I am glad indeed that I wandered up to the gallery the other night . . . it gave me much pleasure when I saw you there, so fair, so kind, and welcoming me with a sweet smile and outstretched hand. Indeed, I would thank you for that, damoiselle, and for the dance we had together, and for this night, when you have listened, and soothed me with your gentle words. I feel you are a good maid. I would you were my friend.'

'I have done little, my lord,' I murmured.

'I was wroth with Harry this night,' he said, above my head. 'I did not command you to visit my apartments—that word tastes of the old *droit de seigneur* . . . I doubt not you thought I wished you here . . . to possess you, as if you were a peasant wench to tumble for an hour, when it was naught like that.'

And for all these bold and soldierly words, which could have come from the lips of Warwick himself, his voice shook slightly.

Slowly I looked at him, and, as I heard his breath quicken, knew that he would not dismiss me thus, without a kiss, and with only cool words of friendship. I shook my hair, so that it came free of my gown's collar and streamed about me, a gleaming fall, the colour of the fire.

'Call me by my name,' he whispered.

But I held it so dear my tongue could not shape the word, even to its owner.

And he reached for me with open arms, and we came together trembling, and I know not which of us shook the more, he or I, as if we lay in coldest snow, although we held each other standing in the hearth, and after a while I felt the flames warm upon the side of my gown.

'We shall be in the fire, my lord,' I said, trying to laugh, and the laugh got caught up in my throat.

'We are in the fire already,' he muttered, his face in my hair. 'We are in the fire, and burning.' And he tightened his arms about me so that I could scarcely breathe, and I felt his hard young body against mine, all steel and strength and honour, and behind my closed eyes I had a vision of him rid-

97

ing in Wensleydale, through the smoke of the mists, his hair tossed by the wind, and part of the wildness.

He kissed my eyes, and my throat, and my cheeks, and wound his hands in my hair, and I became as the soft wax of the candles and leaned back in his arms, wondering if this was how it felt to die, and attain Paradise.

The fire burned low as we stood thus in the press of love, and when he spoke his words slipped into my dream and became part of it.

'Lady, I have known no woman,' he murmured. I clasped my arms around his slender back.

'Then we are both 'prentices in love, my lord,' I said, softly smiling. 'For how can I teach you a craft of which I know naught?'

And we laughed together, all sorrow fled, and he lifted me in his arms, and I was as light as a twig. He took me to his bed and lay down with me, and we were very still for a long space, except for his hands stroking the hair which lay strewn across my cheek. He lifted his head and looked in my eyes.

'Call me by my name,' he whispered. 'Sweet heart, say it to me.'

'Richard,' I said, trembling. 'Richard, my dear love.'

He took me in his arms. He laid his lips on mine. And a flame sprang up and caught us, and we sighed in it, and were consumed by it, and there was naught in the world save its fierce glory. And he was no longer Duke of Gloucester, Earl of Cambridge, a prince of the blood, or the King's brother.

He was but Richard, and for a little space he was mine, and I was his true maid, his Nut-Brown Maid, who loved but him alone.

O Lord, what is this worldis bliss
That changeth as the moon!
My summer's day in lusty May
Is darked before the noon.
I hear you say, farewell: Nay, nay,
We depart not so soon.
Why say ye so? whither will ye go?
Alas! what have ye done?
All my welfare to sorrow and care
Should change, if ye were gone:
For in my mind, of all mankind
I love but you alone.
                    (The Nut-Brown Maid)

Now, I was part of the spring. Benevolent Saints, how I loved him! and how happy were those months! Even now, when I am old, and my body is sickly and weak so that I need the aid of others sprightlier than I that I may kneel for Lauds, I still mind that time. When the young green leaves sprouted tender as kisses, and the birds sang a merrier tune than any minstrel could pipe. When the pleasaunce at Greenwich and Shene boasted a crush of blossom nudging the velvet lawns, with brave iris and gillyflower, lilac and narcissus jousting with one another for acclaim. When the evening was haunted by lilies which, shaking in the breeze like censers, gave off a headier scent that the holy things they sought to ape, and the Rose, the White Rose, shed its splendour over all.

Yea, I have full remembrance of that time; but as my heart lies under tangling weeds and a rough stone slab, it is all as that read long ago in an old romance, and there is no movement in me, not even of sadness. Because—and for this I thank the Father in all His mercy—without a heart, there can be no sorrow, nor can there be joy. Thus, a heartless state is best during the days of waiting, which I pray will soon be over.

Yet from the time of Epiphany, when the revels ended, and order was restored to the jocund court, it became sorely difficult for Richard and me to meet. I dared not go too often to the gallery for two reasons: first because my lady of Bedford was ever demanding, lusting for this or that whim to be fulfilled, and secondly because there was no pleasure in watching him below at a distance, when I could not be in his arms. Though I did see him at the board, seated a thousand miles away at the other end of the Hall, seated below the Woodvilles, sometimes between Dick and Thomas Grey, toying with his knife, eating little, saying less, drawing his brows together as he gazed at the King, who was ever engrossed by Elizabeth's lively kinsfolk. He was all dignity and grace, sombre in the dark clothes he liked to wear, as ever courteous to all since that one burst of passion when Warwick had wounded him with words, the same night he and I first held each other—in pain, in bliss, in scorching, tender consummation.

We had been together less than a dozen times, yet I was happy beyond words. I remembered each meeting so perfectly, for I had to feed on it until the next; and once I saw him for ten minutes only, behind the tall yew hedge in the pleasaunce, while from very near the sound of the mallets in the forbidden game of 'closh' mingled with guilty laughter. There, we had stood and kissed each other softly for a few moments. I felt the sun warm on my closed eyes, my lifted face. He had said: 'Sweet heart, I had sore need of you last evening, for my heart was heavy.' And I had answered: 'My lord, my love, my heart was sad *because* I needed you.' There, in a nutshell, was the difference between us.

And that ten minutes served me for the next two weeks, for Richard was never idle, was ever conferring with older men who listened to his words with a smile, none the less impressed by his wisdom. He was meticulous over matters of policy, his commissions of oyer and terminer, and as I knew how much it pleased him when the King gave him tasks to do, I did assay to be happy on his behalf, but as he was not with me, I found it nigh impossible. Happy I was, yea, but I felt always as if the spring were gliding by too swiftly and that I was alone in the sunshine, with my own shadow darkening the gleam.

Then one evening all was well again, for Harry sought me on the spiralling stair, under the arras of gold, and I took his little hand as if we were children together and we went along light of heart in the gloom, to where the gentlemen ushers and grooms of the bedchamber turned their heads away and bent to their dice in the passages and whispered, though not of me, for they were wise men and sympathetic to the wants of lords, although they knew not what great love and joy passed between us. And Richard's chambers were deserted save for him; and if they called King Edward the Rose of Rouen, the Sun in Splendour, his youngest brother surpassed him in my eyes. Three hours I spent with him that evening, and we talked quietly of one another, of our hopes and our troubles, and our kisses grew stronger, and we were unable to withstand the whirlwind, the torrent, that burst within us. And we clung together, and forgot all but the longing to be enwrapped and enfolded within each other. And he was mine again, for three hours; and he tried to teach me to play chess, but as I sat upon his knee for the lesson and my hair swept the pieces off the board each time I turned to kiss him, it was not a success.

I wished in my heart that he had been born a cottar's son, and I betrothed to him at the village porch with a wreath of roses on my head, and the family standing ale-flushed and merry about us, and that we had been bedded together with rude mirth and left to live out our simple lives: rearing babes, toiling with smiles and frowns and days of gloom and hunger even, with our small pleasures, our bereavements, our feast days and our May Days . . . though each day would be May Day if Richard had been born thus.

Noblemen took lemen for lust, and the women went gladly through ambition, using their bodies as snares for gold and power. But he was not one of these, neither was I; for he turned to me out of the mazes of his loneliness, and I to him from the web of my love.

We were no longer 'prentices in love.

Warwick was seen no more at court. Patch, who seemed to have an ear at every door, was worse than any woman for whispering tales to me. He told me that the Earl, after a brief and unexpected Christmas appearance, had gone to his manor at Cambridge. Further, it was rumoured that George of Clarence communicated with him, and that there was more talk of Isabel, the frail fair lady with her vast estates.

'A right comely wench,' he said. 'But sickly, like her sister Anne. Though I doubt not that were she as hideous as I, the prospect of ridding London of the Woodvilles would aid Duke George to love her.'

He was waiting for me to say he was not hideous. All I said was: 'How would marrying Isabel harm the Woodvilles?'

'I fancy Lord Warwick has promised George that he will engineer this,' grinned Patch. 'But I fear 'tis delusion. You mind that Warwick was one of the Calais Earls?'

I did not, but let him continue.

'King Louis of France is a craftsman at flattery,' said the fool. 'Not long after he took the throne he made a ploy for Warwick—sought his advice on hunting dogs, wrote him fair letters at Calais, and Warwick bloomed like a peach.'

'Yet Warwick fought for Edward, and set him on the throne,' I said, confused.

'True,' he answered. 'And Warwick had the notion that once peace was made with Louis, there would be no more attacks from Margaret of Anjou. But this would mean crushing Burgundy. Edward would never agree to that. And in any event, as Elizabeth snatched the King from Bona of Savoy, Louis's sister by marriage, all Warwick's plans were halted in mid-gallop. Thus my lord loathes the Woodvilles.'

My mind flew back to an old conversation. I saw John Skelton's handsome face, heard the tale of Richard's flight to the Low Countries, and the saving of his life.

'Nay,' I said very softly. 'They would never break with Burgundy, for the Bungundians are passing kind.'

Patch laughed. 'Hardly could they, with the King's sister married to Charles, Burgundy's own Duke!'

He knew much more of politics than I. I said: 'Warwick still plots with George, then, think you?'

'Yes, and he would have done with Dickon, too,' said the fool, and my witless heart started its old dance, floundering and prancing at the name.

'I wonder if he will ever weaken,' Patch mused. 'I doubt not Warwick would give him Anne as a reward . . . 'Twould be easier if my lord had both brothers ranged against the King.'

Elysande had spoken of Richard; she had thought I was not listening. To Anne Haute she had said: 'The pull of Warwick is very strong.' Then, I did not understand. Now, I could say seriously to Patch: 'He will never yield his cause,' and the fool cocked his head to look into my face, which I kept passionless.

'As you say, mistress,' he said, and kissed my hand lightly, and bit it, and of a sudden his last speech echoed in my mind, disquieting.

'Little Anne Neville—how old is she?'

'Oh, she is not so little,' said he careless. 'About thirteen years now—slight, golden-haired. Had Earl Warwick brought his ladies here for Yule you would have seen her.'

I thought of myself at thirteen, at twelve, on my joy-day, my May Day, which I would cherish for ever together with the song, which had brought my love to me. Then, as Patch was in a confiding mood, I asked him about Katherine of Desmond, and of the matter at which Richard had only hinted. He wrenched his face about in grimaces meant to distract me, but finally told me that which all knew, but never mentioned.

'The Earl of Desmond was beheaded on a flimsy charge,' he said, in a voice even quieter than Richard's had been. 'He jested about the Queen soon after Edward married her. Last year, when the King was away, the Great Seal was purloined, and Desmond's execution ordered. They say his Grace was wroth when he returned and discovered this. Also, the Earl's two little knaves were murdered soon after their father's death, though none can swear who wrought this . . . nay, none can swear,' he said grimly, 'but all can guess.'

Then he sought to cheer me by capering about.

'How white you are,' he said cheerily. 'Come, sit a while. I have a new story, cunningly rhymed. Let me assay to cheer your dreary life a whit!'

102

I was about to tell him that my life was not so dreary, was indeed a perfect poem of bliss, on which his words had cast a fleeting shadow, when suddenly I saw, leaning on the terrace wall not far from us, the reason for my gladness.

He turned to look at me. The brightness of his look mocked the sun.

So later, when I sat with my distaff in the Duchess's apartments, assaulted by the monotonous twang of harp and lute, my thoughts could weave their own skein while my fingers idled. For though the day outside was still fair, and I must remain at my lady's side, I had seen him again. We had walked together in the quiet ways, through the Italian gardens, where none came, and for a brief time he had held my hand. His hand was not soft like that of most courtiers, but the palm was a little calloused from leather and steel, the fingers were fine-boned and delicate, the heavy rings a sweet small pain in his unconsciously hard grip. He did not link my last finger in his, custom of lovers, but walked slowly with his whole hand closed about mine. He was serious, aloof, until my frail jests brought about the swift, sweet smile peculiar to him alone.

Yet he did not smile when I mentioned the name now on everyone's lips, the name which hummed through the Palace, subject for conjecture. I had thought it romantic and said so, and he told me it was not for jesting: this Robin of Redesdale was a plaguey agitator who was stirring the whole of the north parts into a boil.

'You mark how he started the first rising in Yorkshire,' I heard his tone grow mellow on the beloved word. 'Then up springs another Robin . . .'

'Robin of Holderness,' I murmured. 'I like not that name so well.'

'As Northumberland cut him down,' he said with a little irony, 'you need not trouble about his name. But Robin of Redesdale has raised a strong following in Lancashire now. It should be quelled, and soon.'

He was frowning.

'I pray he is not becoming unwary, complacent,' he said under his breath. He often spoke of his Grace the King as if I were not with him; I did not know whether to be sad that his thoughts went from me so often, or flattered that he trusted me. In any event it was Richard's way, and therefore a joy.

'Will there be real trouble?' I asked him, remembering the

103

omens with which Patch had tried to frighten me. 'People spoke some time past of bloody rain and a child that cried out in the womb. . .'

He dropped my hand to cross himself.

'Who is Robin of Redesdale, Richard?' I asked suddenly. 'Some say he is a man of the people, others that he is the agent of some alien power sent to stir mischief. Who is he?'

He looked at me; a swift, shrewd look. I lifted my face; the sun, or his glance, danced on my eyelashes. His expression melted, became charmed, and over serious words he smiled as if he could not help it.

'My love, would that I knew,' he said. 'But I can vow this is all more than just an agitation set up by the northern citizens. Though they yelled for the return of Percy as Earl of Northumberland, saying they misliked Warwick's jurisdiction, this trouble stems from deeper things. I am convinced of it.'

Then we had reached a favourite arbour, which to my joy was unoccupied by amorous couples gowned in indolence. And we stepped softly within the shell of roses and green leaves, and like lightning I doffed my headdress for he had no need to tell me how my hair pleased him. And again he held me in his arms, and kissed my mouth, with a trembling fierceness, while I clung, breathing my love into him on a sigh. Others came soon, heralding their approach with brittle mirth.

That was the pattern of my days; to meet, to kiss and part, for privacy was more precious than the finest gems, rare as true love in this place, this time. A fleeting figure, I wondered what they thought, who came to see my lord of Gloucester sitting alone in a lovers' bower?

King Edward nearly discovered us that day. I had need to run swiftly, though I do not doubt he would have been glad to know his brother had a mistress. He came along the pleasaunce path, singing about lemen and Maying, and he had on many occasions been heard to remark that all men were frail. So he might have been pleased. Ah, I wonder.

Daily we sat with our distaffs or broidery frames in the Duchess's apartments, and the weeks slid by. Each night I lay wakeful, burned with a fever for which there was but one cure, and that denied me.

A yelp from one of the women roused me from my thoughts. A wasp had flown in through the open window. The Duchess of Bedford, who had been nodding, woke and flapped her hands angrily, and watching her, I thought how she had aged these last months. Her hair was snow white and the lines on her face deeply scored.

Elysande whispered: 'Sleep is good for the aged: but you are like a woman dead. Wake up! Answer me!'

'Forgive me,' I said. Vaguely I knew she had been asking me something, an urgent question on a breath.

'Who is Robin of Redesdale?' she murmured. 'Really, I mean. Any fool knows that name cloaks some angry lord. Who is he, say?'

The woman who had been stung rubbed her neck, listening. 'Yes, who is he?' she echoed.

''Tis the French Queen's captain' said another. 'The whore of Anjou's liegeman, Beaufort of Somerset.'

'For God's sake, soft,' said Lady Scrope. Margaret Beaufort had but lately come and gone, visiting the Duchess. Bemused on all sides, I sought diplomacy, said naught, wishing I were out, roaming the grassy fields of Bloomsbury with my lord, my love.

'Beaufort!' said another.

'Why do you not ask the fool, Patch?' Elysande said slyly. 'He seems to know all of policy; you two are hand in glove.'

'Beaufort is not in England, surely,' said Anne Haute.

The others had lost interest. They were playing with the lapdogs, yawning, picking at comfit-dishes. Elysande pulled her chair close to mine.

'By the Rood!' she whispered. 'Fools make fair paramours!'

My eyes on my work, I said: 'Why think you thus?'

She laughed softly. I was minded of Gyb's lilting purr.

'Why, maiden, you come to bed some nights with your flesh afire, blazing like the sun—I cannot bear to touch you, that I vow.' She shuddered, she watched me for some little space, her hands busy at her spindle, smiling her kind, cat's smile.

'Well, for sure,' declared Anne Haute, though none listened, 'England is safe from the Lancastrians, for my lord of Warwick's fleet lies in the Channel warding off invaders.'

The Duchess roused herself, spoke roughly. The harshness in her voice shocked me from my fading dream.

'By Christ's Blood, I would know mine enemy,' she said. 'I would know who labours against me and mine.'

Elysande whispered: 'Is Patch a fine lover? Lusty and lickerish, and hot to bed a maid?'

Removed by a thin veil from her friendly, bawdy talk, my spirit soared. I thought of Richard, and his tender, ardent lovemaking, and thought that young as he was, the fiery blood of his brother the King surely ran in his veins, for Edward had bastards which were openly acknowledged and all the maids he had bedded had long queues of knights clamouring for their hand, for that which had pleased so fair a prince was a prize in truth.

I thought thus and my heart grew heavy. For I would not now even be able to meet him of an evening, to find some chamber or terrace where we could clasp each other, kiss lingeringly, talk quietly. For tonight I must sleep at the foot of my lady's couch, and another six weeks would pass before I found my stealthy freedom, as we all served a tour of two moons tending her during the night, and this gave rise to a great sigh. And Elysande read my thought. She breathed in my ear:

'Far be it for me to stand between a lover and his maid,' she whispered. 'Would it please you, sweeting, if I cosseted my lady tonight and left you to seek your heart's lust?'

'But she clings to me,' I whispered back. 'Only I can comfort her at night.'

The Duchess had awful dreams, waking screaming and roaring.

'Men do say she is a witch,' breathed Elysande even lower, and looked at me.

There was the night at Grafton Regis, mewed up in my mind, now loosened by my friend's words. I thrust it away, took refuge in Elysande's own light laughing speech.

'You will have us thrown in the Fleet!' I said, as she had done, once.

'I jest,' said Elysande. 'But I thought you might have heard tales,' and her lips curved, and she looked down.

'I know naught,' I said. 'I have heard naught.'

'But—to our little strategy—it would please you?'

'It would delight me,' I answered.

'So be it, then,' said Elysande, and went straightway to Jacquetta of Bedford, wringing out cold cloths for her wrists against the heat, whispering sweetness in her wrinkled ear.

Seeking delight and sweetness both, I sought Richard that night, straying with trembling near to his apartments. I noticed much activity all about, even apart from the comings and goings of the esquires and yeomen of the bedchamber and the great unruly hounds. There was one face that I knew: Harry, the little page, who lingered to comfort me with saddening news, because while I would gladly have entered Richard's chamber with arms that craved him, he was not even there. For Harry told me that the King had finally listened to his advisers, and there was a council of war that night, and Richard sat on it, together with Lord Hastings and the Woodvilles; and that the King was arraying an army against Robin of Redesdale at last.

Now it was I thought I should never set eyes on him again, for although Elysande out of her charity kept the Duchess well satisfied and swore she never noticed the difference between us of a night, Richard was ever closeted with the King and his councillors. And if I knew him at all he must have been so joyful at being included in the discussions that he bore equably the presence of the Woodvilles. For, as was to be expected, King Edward's chief advisers were the Queen's father, Earl Rivers, Sir John Woodville, and Lord Anthony, laying his verses and his jousts aside to turn his talent to war.

I hung about the passages, shameless, all my conceit blown from me by the blast of my longing to be near Richard, if only for an instant, to hold his hand, to look into his unfathomable eyes. I even sought out Harry for news of him.

'How does my lord?' I asked him one evening, when thunder muffled the air and my head ached to match my heart.

He shrugged. The White Boar rose and fell on his doublet.

'There is that which gnaws at him,' he said, and my hopes leaped high for a moment, because I fancied he spoke of our separation.

'Harry . . .' I said, and ceased while he cocked an attentive brow. 'You know how dearly I love his Grace . . .'

'Mistress, I see naught, and hear less,' he said, folding his pink lips together like a night-flower, and I was moved to think how soon children grew old in this place; babes were youths, and youths, men.

'Tell him, Harry, if you see him . . . that I long to know he is in good health and spirits, I pray you,' I said miserably.

'This I'd do gladly,' he answered. 'But I scarcely have time to snatch a word with him myself—it's as if he sees me not—or any of us, for that matter. He is ever flying to the King's chambers, begging for audience, and he is in there half the night when the King has space to see him.'

'Of what do they talk?'

'Mistress,' said the little page patiently, 'how should I know what is discussed between great princes?'

'Of course,' I said, bending to kiss the small face swiftly, for the sole fact that he served Richard and had led me to his arms by night. He flinched from my sad lips and ran away.

Then one day I saw him, but he was completely surrounded by henchmen and esquires, young men who laughed with strong teeth and looked about them as if they looked at life itself and loved it. He did not laugh; his countenance was full of thoughts and he withdrew into them. He did not look around but strode on relentlessly, with full purpose and I would fain have known his mission. I stepped aside as they passed, and there were one or two who looked at me with the expression I longed to see in my lord's eyes. I willed him to see me with all my power.

But he strode on, so full of strength and grace and seriousness that my heart rose up to bursting at the sight and knowledge of him, and my lips grew cold for the touch of his. I would have thought he heard my mind crying of my long desire; for having tasted the apple no other food could sate me now, so deep in love was I.

I burned him with my gaze, and he walked on by. He was on his way to the King's chamber, on business of which I knew naught. He walked on by and did not look at me.

He had forgotten my existence.

News came to us that Robin of Redesdale rioted merrily in Lancashire. There were lootings, slayings, burning of property, but I was still curious to see this man. I was sure that he wore green and carried the long-bow, and that mayhap Maid Marian, with her false breasts, trailed wearily behind him.

The court was bored with his name by now, and new dances and sports would have taken the place of speculation, but the King wished for none of it. There was a change in him. The gallant courtier had disappeared and in his place was a stern and martial campaigner, the veteran of fearful Towton Field and Mortimer's Cross, with its holy sign of the Three Suns. Yet, paradoxically, he lingered at London, though he had ordered his tents and artillery and hundreds of jackets of murrey to be carried to Fotheringhay, whence he planned to direct his attack upon the rebels. With him he planned to take two favourite captains, Sir John Howard and Louis de Bretaylle; and Edward Brampton, a great, beetle-browed Portuguese warrior, added excitement by his arrival at court. Now the armourers polished the harness to blue-black fire, and the blacksmiths honed the swords and axes to a deadly tooth, and the banner of England with the leopards and lilies and the supporting standards of suns and roses sprouted like great dangerous blossoms wherever the eye turned. And in my heart I was glad, that though Richard could listen to those older than he laying their plans in the council chamber, all knew that the King thought him too young to join the affray. George of Clarence showed no interest in this time of preparation, for he was on one of his manors, attended by two hundred servants, basking in the sun and doubtless thinking of Isabel Neville. So men said.

The Duchess of Bedford said, waking and sleeping: I would know mine enemy.' I heard her without comprehension, through my shell of sick-heartedness. For Richard was daily cloistered with the King, and no man knew what passed between them, until I met with him again, on the last day of May.

The Duchess had been bathed and bedded, and there were few abroad save for the anonymous, hurrying servants in the passages, and I spoke with Elysande before she seated herself with her tapestry at the foot of my lady's couch.

'Think you she'll sleep?' I whispered. Come to think of it, most of our conversation took place in whispers. 'I must go out.'

Elysande's pointed teeth winked in her smile.

'Certes, what a lusty lover he must be!' she teased. 'And constant too! All these weeks you have languished for his arms!'

That I have, I thought, then gathered my wits as again she alluded to his motley dress and I was hard put to find a jocund answer. With little hope I strayed aimlessly up towards the gallery and, as it happened, I did see Patch, wandering, lack-wit as a sprite.

'I never see you now,' he said ill-humouredly.

'Well, we are on the edge of an array,' I answered. 'Shall you too put on harness?'

'I was trained for mirth not slaughter,' said he.

'Have you seen my lord of Gloucester of late?' I asked, throwing caution away.

'Certes, yesterday,' he said instantly. 'And he too was doleful as a drunkard in a dry tavern. I know not what ails folk these days . . . And as for you, mistress, become much more slender and I shall be able to nip your waist with one hand, so . . .'

I would have turned on him out of sheer misery as he stretched out what was only the hand of comfort, when my eyes fell on a small figure, patient, motionless under the torchlight a few feet away.

'Patch, good night!' I said, and left him, trying not to run, feeling his stare probing my back.

Harry took my hand.

'My lord commands . . .' he said. He had not learned his lesson. Light as air we flew, running together round and round the ascending stair, across the hall, the breeze of our passing disturbing the skirts of some tiny noble lady. 'By Saint Denis!' she cried. 'God's curse on these churlish manners!' Lady Margaret Beaufort, I thought; and she was already left far behind, to damn the sound of Harry's laughter as we ran, we flew, air-light, dove-light, down the hall, and I remembered just in time to pull my hood across my face before we knocked on the oaken door, the fairest oaken door in Christendom. A squire of the bedchamber opened to us, passed with downcast eyes, and departed as we entered.

Had it not been for Harry's lingering I would have rushed wantonly into the arms of my lord, but I waited standing before him till I heard the door close behind the page and I lifted my face and felt Richard's lips, hard and soft, cool and burning, on my brow, my eyelids, and my mouth, and I wound my arms tight about his neck, and he tasted my tears.

The chamber was the same, though it might have been a year since I was last within its loving walls. There was one addition, though. His sword, and a pair of steel gauntlets lay across the table. For all my joy, a little cold spot began to form in my mind at the sight of these accoutrements.

'Don't weep,' he said softly.

At this I had to smile, a poor watery smile, for men never know a loving woman's heart. Poor fools we are, ruled by the moon, and variable, prone to her waxing and waning, all our tides sorrow and gladness. Men never know a woman's love.

He led me to the couch where we sat hand in hand and I gazed at him. Gently I smoothed the hair from his brow. He seemed excited, and I knew that in a moment he would be up again and pacing the chamber, for I fancied I knew him as I knew myself. Still he smiled.

'My lord, my love,' I whispered. 'I am joyful we are met together again.'

And he laid his hands about my face and looked at me with that look that turned a blade in my heart, and he smiled.

'You are happy,' I murmured.

'Sweet heart,' he said, in a cramped, glad voice, 'wait till you hear my news.' I could only say: 'Whatever pleases my lord, lightens my heart.' And he held me at arm's length, and already he seemed far from me. I had a precognition of what he was going to say.

'His Highness,' he whispered. 'His most noble Grace King Edward . . .' and he swallowed his excitement and continued, calmer. '. . . After many days I have at last persuaded the King that I shall ride with him against Robin of Redesdale. We leave the day after tomorrow . . . God grant we are in time, for we should have been north long ago to crush this rising . . . Is it not fair news? Now, by St Paul, I shall have chance to prove myself, utterly fearless, utterly loyal . . . But I am ranting on like a woman,' he finished with an anxious laugh, and took me to him roughly and laughed again.

With difficulty I said: 'Your first campaign, Richard.' My voice sounded distant. 'I wish you joy, my dearest lord.'

He jumped up and walked about. And it was in that moment, all the sweetness mixed with the sour, that I knew I loved one born under the planet Mars. I fought my dismay, saying: 'I will make a novena for you, beloved.' And, because I had visions of mighty battles, thousands slain, I continued: 'I will pray that you shall smite this Robin a dolorous blow, and return in glory.'

He laughed gently. 'It will be but a little skirmish. But it is enough for my purpose. My esquires stand ready, my good friends Robert Percy, John Parr, and I shall wage more men to ride with me. His Grace will not find me lacking in resourcefulness . . .'

Then he looked at me. His eyes were tender as I ever remember them.

'Sweet heart,' he said, and he spoke my name, and sought my lips, and war battled with love in the mind and was unhorsed for a little while. I shelved my dolour while he held me in his arms, and tried to forget that the day after tomorrow he would ride north, and I knew not when I should see him again. For I ranked myself as the loving woman of a soldier, and I vowed I would train myself to be as others of that ilk, and not weep.

So when, too soon, I parted from him, and we kissed and blessed one another, I smiled a tinsel smile and carried a mask as gay as any of the nice disguisy things the mummers wore at Yuletide. And he could have known no difference in me, for again, when Elysande opened the door to me and brushed her hand against my breast in the darkness, she

111

shrank as if scalded and whispered, laughing, of the ardour of fools. Though that jest was rubbing a little thin.

It was very lonely when they had gone. Few remained at court, for most of the lords had left with the King's army, leading their own small levies, intending to wage men *en route* to the camp at Fotheringhay. The King's mother lived there, and, thinking of her for the firs time, I remembered that she was Richard's mother too, and wondered about her. She had not visited the court since I was there, for it was said that she too had little love for the Woodvilles; and besides, was pious and devout more so than many widows; she still wore mourning for the Duke of York. Men called her the Rose of Raby—she had been wondrous fair.

I did not see my lord ride away. I had been in pursuit of a duty, and when at length I had managed to reach a window the last of the baggage trains was grinding and clattering through the gate, and the stiff new banner of Gloucester, with its grim boar's head, no longer splashed its pride against the sky.

I had not even Patch to talk to, as the King had given him leave to visit his mother, who kept a cookshop in Chepe; and for this reason I was able to resume my nightly duties at Jacquetta's side. For if my lover had gone, why should there be need for Elysande to play proxy for me? I found the Duchess something altered; harder to please mayhap, I could not tell, but Elysande had little ways to which she had grown accustomed, and she grumbled more fiercely when I could not anticipate her whim.

So I withdrew into my own mind, and dreamed of my beloved; of his lips and his eyes, and of the words he had murmured to me in his quiet voice; how he had talked again, sadly, of his loves. For Clarence and Warwick had rejected him for what they mistook as the cowardice of youth, and Clarence was his tall and golden brother, lightsome and frivolous, as Richard could never be. He had told me, with a frowning smile, how the Lord Mayor of London had fallen asleep during a hearing of oyer and terminer: 'Speak softly, sirs, for the Mayor is asleep'—Clarence had provoked mirth by his wit on this occasion. It struck me that Richard, while counterfeiting disapproval, envied in secret his splendid, feckless brother. 'I know I am too serious,' he had said, and so I had assayed to make him laugh, with my foolish, loving ways, and often succeeded.

112

And Warwick! there the hurt lay deeper still, for Warwick had been his lord during the years when the will was formed, the pattern followed closely until it becomes the fabric of the soul. Warwick! who now, for the first time, disdained to ride with the King, no doubt eschewing the little skirmish as small meat for his blade to bite upon.

Richard had turned his back on Warwick, for of all his loves, there was but one. Would that it had been me.

I had alluded to the writing I had seen on that first night in his apartments, the French words of power.

'That is the code I live by,' he had said, his eyes like steel. 'Loyalty binds me. So will it always, to the Crown of England, to his Grace King Edward, and to all his kin.'

He had spoken these last five words as if they were dragged from him, for he had seen King Edward, as had all men, grow sleek and careless under the touch of a bewitching woman; one who stole the Great Seal to avenge her vanity.

'A hard road to ride,' I murmured.

'Yea, hard, foul and devious,' he said violently, and I knew that when he was violent he was sad, so I kissed his hand and held it to my cheek, for all his sorrow was my sorrow.

And now I guessed he would be glad as I was doleful, for he rode under the banner of England, and his golden brother's smile.

The flowers waved in the fair green gardens, but only in mockery. The sun had ceased to shine; the sky was blue no longer. The Duchess had a little slavering dog which jumped on my lap, shrieking shrilly. Sharp pains fleeted through my head. My lady was full of rancour and small malices. The Queen's bread was new-baked; mine was four days old, like the trenchers. I had no taste. Though the Palace still scampered with life, all who ran and walked and diced were creatures unearthly. Their voices reached me through a mist. Their faces were unreal.

I tried to conjure up his countenance, crushing my eyes closed, but I could not see him. At times a vague figure, armed and mounted, rushed through my mind, flanked by a fog of faces that mouthed silently, drowning his voice. I had no notion of how long it would take them to ride to where the rebellion flamed, but already my ears rang with the slithering crash of steel, loud formless noises, spewed out by my ignorance. My knees I wore red in prayer.

Queen Elizabeth remained calm, playing at merels and

chess with her ladies; cool, with a carved coolness, retiring early to a great bed to which no tall young form strode to visit her, and she betrayed no longings, no lusting for his arms.

It was I who quivered and shed secret tears. It was she who smiled, prayed gently, drew on again the veil of the widow of Grafton Regis, patient and resigned. Then I remembered she was more than twice my age, and thought that with the years, passions burn fainter, lips lose their clinging strength, pulses grow weaker; and I thought of Richard, and knew in my mind I lied.

Had I thought to appease my hunger by that last encounter with him, I misled myself cruelly. It soothed me for a day, two days, and then began again the pain. Once I slipped like a spy into his chambers and lay for a moment on his couch, breathing the lost scent of him, to be chased from the room by an outraged butler.

I thought of him, upon his first campaign, and grew sick with fear. I minded John Skelton's words: 'He was seventeen. And they took his head and . . . speared on pikes at the Mickle Gate.' Edmund, young Edmund Plantagenet, and sharp points in my mind for Richard his brother.

On the ninth day of this torment, I paid no heed to Elysande flinging clothes into a chest, or her anguished cries for help, until she came to shake me.

'Am I to toil alone, then?' she cried. 'I vow you are as useless as yonder popinjay!' and she gave the bird's cage a vicious clout, making it scream.

Listlessly I turned to her.

'Will they have crushed Robin of Redesdale yet, Elysande?' She dropped the lid of the chest in a burst of exasperated laughter.

'Holy Mother of God, you are the most witless . . . the most . . .' She stopped suddenly as the Duchess entered, glowering, muttering *I would know my enemy*, the old incantation.

'Do you never listen?' Elysande said softly. 'Her Grace has declared the Palace needs sweetening, and for sure, the stink is enough to make you swoon. And it was arranged before they left that . . .'

I looked out of the window again. I did not care if the Palace stank like a midden. I could not even smell the vast bed of white roses below me.

'Help me,' she pleaded.

'How long will it take them to journey north?'

'Oh, the King will not hurry,' she said easily. 'They ride first to Norwich, then to pray at Our Lady of Walsingham, then Lynn, I think, and thereafter up the Nene to meet with us at Fotheringhay.'

'What say you?' I whispered.

'Fotheringhay, half-wit!' she said patiently. 'And if you don't help me with the packing, we shall not be there until Christmas next coming.'

Right in front of her I fell to my knees, crossing my breast, my mindless thanks soaring like smoke. Hastily she lifted me, glancing round.

'They will be bringing a priest to exorcize you,' she muttered. 'Now fold these gowns, while I assay to cram my lady's vanities into this box, which is far too small.'

So we went to Fotheringhay, and I had to control myself, for I feared they would think me truly mad and have me hidden away somewhere with the gibbering and the dying, when I wanted to laugh and live. So I curbed the smile on my face and travelled cool, sparing of words, with the Duchess's new pet upon my lap; a monkey that bit me often, and whose teeth I did not feel. Fotheringhay sprawled on the north bank of the river, bounded on one side by a double moat, gazing lonely and proud over the marshes from whence came the hoarse roar of bittern and the beat of herons' wings, mingled with the seagull's lament as it winged back and forth from the distant sea. A massive place, with mighty battlements, it was built in the fetterlock shape of the old Yorkist badge. As we trundled over the drawbridge I remembered that this was Richard's birthplace, where he had grown, sickly and brave and single-hearted. And once more thought of John Skelton, and the first time I heard the name of my beloved.

We were installed in a rather bleak apartment, but one which I loved, for I could hear the wind mocking over the fens, and smell the salt sea faintly in the darkness, and I could lie listening for the sound of the King's army, for none knew quite when they would arrive. And I could not contain my longing to meet with Richard again, to feel the soft hardness of his lips and hear his whispered voice, and I planned the things I would do to make him glad, the things I would say to make him merry, when he came to me at last. At a distance, I saw the Rose of Raby. I marked her coolness when she greeted the Queen, the same courteous ice I had seen in her youngest son. She wore the widow's barbe and wimple, and on her breast hung a great reliquary like a fetter, and there was something of Richard in her face. I thought her handsome, though Elysande murmured that she was also known as 'Proud Cis' and in these parts was much envied and feared.

Vast wagon-loads of armaments rolled in, and then came soldiery, all ages, some coarse, all dusty from the dry roads with their gaping pitfalls; a few laughing, some looking up in wonder at the great castle as they assembled tents for their officers and supplies within and without the bailey. And July was almost out when a barge came up the Nene, and in it were King Edward, Earl Rivers and his sons, the Lord Chamberlain Lord Hastings, and the King's youngest brother, together with a fistful of retainers.

They came in over the drawbridge and I watched them, unseen, while the Queen stood on the castle steps with the Duchess of York. Queen Elizabeth lowered her blue eyes and smiled as the King halted below her on the stair, but the King's mother remained gazing at him, with the same steady unfathomable look I had seen in Richard's eyes. I saw these things for only the briefest moment, for I looked for Richard and found him, lithe and swift in his dark travelling cloak, ascending the steps to kiss the hands of the Queen and his mother. The Duchess of York set her lips on his cheek. The blood in my body boiled to do the same.

On the next day I saw him again. I saw him at the other end of the dining hall. I saw that he was glad, and smiled twice, and laughed once, and ate his meat, and when the royal party walked through the bowing throng to leave, he passed quite close to me. I could almost have touched him, but for two women who sat between me and the door. He wore his gold carcanet with the ruby-eyed boar, which had grazed my flesh and burnt me like a brand. His hair was sleek as the plumes of a raven; I had smoothed it from his brow. The bones of his face were as delicate as ever; I had soothed them with my fingers. His eyes were like no other eyes in this world. Strive as I might to catch them, I had no success.

For the next seven days I earned a week from my allotted span of Purgatory. Though he was in Fotheringhay, he might have been in France, for all I saw of him. I endeavoured to keep track of him, and knew that he spent most of the day below on the camp, attending to various duties, or laced into a tent together with the other officers, though I could only guess vaguely at that which they spoke of and what they planned. And each night I must tend the Duchess of Bedford, whom I had learned to hate.

The King had soft speech with his Queen daily, and lay

116

with her nightly, and I grew wondrous pale and my girdle slid about my waist, and I knew a terrible ache in my heart, and not only my heart.

So when Elysande said: 'They ride tomorrow, then,' as a matter of casual conversation, I could contain myself no more. All my sorrow broke its bounds, refreshing as a waterspout, draining as the bodily blood, reminder of Eve's fall, that purges us monthly.

'Come aloft,' she said suddenly, and taking my arm, led me up to the breezy battlements of the keep, where I saw, through the silk of my tears, the serpent Nene cleaving its coil through the marshes. And there was Richard, far below, seen as in a dream. From his horse he was talking with his mother, and he had a hawk balanced on his wrist. Slowly he stroked its feathers, as the King rode up beside them, his steed backing and tossing with its urgency, like my spirit. As they rode through the gate to their sport, I turned to Elysande. She patted the stone beside her, and we sat dangerously on top of the battlements, the wind tossing our veils.

'What's amiss?' Her voice was quiet.

My laugh was stillborn.

'You must think me blind,' she said. 'I will help you, if I can. I am your friend, am I not?'

She was, as I have said, ever anxious to be my friend. I watched the tiny figures against the blue-green marsh. The hawks were flying at heron, the snow of Edward's white gerfalcon catching the sun on its wings as it sped faster and faster through blue haze.

'You are deep in love,' she murmured. 'And yet he loves you not, for he remains in London, while you pine and wax slender, here with the Queen's household.'

So completely had I forgotten Patch's existence that I turned with a frown, and that frown told her all.

'Hey, hey!' she said. 'After all this, 'tis not the fool.'

'Of course it is not the fool.'

'Do not tell me you have been smitten by one of these,' she said, pointing with her slim hand down to the infantry's tents. 'Half of them are wedded, and will tell any tale to win a fresh maidenhead.'

I thought of my heart's lust. 'Prentice in love. I had to smile. Then I felt Elysande's hands loosening my headdress, unpinning my hair.

'Tell me his name,' she said. 'Tell me his name, and I will lie by my lady tonight, and you can seek him in the dark, and none shall know of it, save you and I.'

She began to stroke my hair gently. It waved about my face, blinding me, and her hands were like Richard's. The King's falcon was at the height of its stoop, powerful and clear against the azure mist. Silent, I watched as it dropped, beak and talons opening in a savage joy.

'Tell me his name,' she whispered. I shook my head.

Her hands clung to me. 'What does he call you?'

'Sweet heart, at times,' I whispered. I bent my head, closing my eyes under her strong, soft hands. She caressed the back of my neck, and truly it could have been Richard.

"Sweet heart,' she said very softly. 'Sweet heart, tell me his name! It will give you joy to speak it. I am your friend. I share your every woe.'

Edward's hawk had taken the heron. Like lovers, they dropped through the air, in the tender embrace of death.

'I am he,' Elysande whispered. 'Call me by my name.'

Without another thought, I told her. The gentle, stroking hands ceased for an instant.

'Certes, they fly high,' she murmured, with a little laugh.

'Who do?' I asked, in a dream.

'Why, the hawks, dear heart!' Her fingers caressed. The moments passed, grains slipping silent into eternity. I could not call them back.

'I never really thought of him in that wise,' she said. 'He looks so quiet, so serious. And yet, you have been paramours for some little time?'

'Ah, Richard,' I said, only half hearing her.

She lifted my hair from the nape of my neck, rubbing its mass between her fingers, tangling it into a skein.

'Is he a . . .'

I grew rigid. 'Ask me no more. I will not speak of it.' I closed my eyes. It was Richard who played with my hair, absently, his mind on something else.

'Tell me this, at any rate,' she said, over a tender laugh. 'I cannot ask the gentlemen of the bedchamber; they would think me wanton indeed, but you and I are dear friends and love each other. I'm curious. Sweeting, is it true, one shoulder is hideously malformed and he pads out his doublet to feign equality?'

I sprang to face her. 'Jesu, Elysande!' I cried. 'How do such tales begin?'

She shrugged; her hands stroked mine; she was my falconer, and I a trembling goshawk. 'You know how whispers wax fat from tongue to tongue,' she murmured. 'Let us therefore know the truth.'

Whatever the truth was, I would not speak of it to Elysande, and she abandoned the chase, and picked up my headdress from the stones, smoothing its windblown veil.

'I will serve the Duchess tonight, sweeting,' she said, and as I looked at her I marked how the sunlight turned her green eyes yellow, but thought her wondrous kind. We stood on the battlements and kissed each other tenderly; and a breeze sprang up and caught us. We swayed in it, and there was naught in the world save its fierce glory . . .

'I would know mine enemy,' muttered the Duchess of Bedford. The monkey chattered and wound its thin little arms about her neck.

All that long day Elysande cosseted me, staying close, smiling her gentle smile, whispering cheer as the hours wore on. She asked me no more questions about him, but made herself exceedingly useful to me, for she filtered about the castle as I would never dare, in soft enquiry as to his plans. I watched her with love and admiration, for she was clever in the way she spoke with the unfamiliar servants, the strange guards of Fotheringhay: gleaning knowledge by a half-sentence, a casual eyebrow, a disinterested nod. Certes, she was clever, Elysande.

At evening she returned triumphant.

'Proud Cis is giving a banquet in her stateroom,' she murmured. 'Let us get my lady dressed swiftly; for the sooner they have finished the feasting the earlier they will retire . . . that is, *some* will retire.' And she gave me a clip round the waist and I kissed her cheek, though an anxiousness fell upon me as I said:

'Dearest, I know not even where he lies, and there is none here who will guide me to him.'

She laughed. 'I was speaking of the King's Grace,' she said softly. 'Is it not natural that he should take his pleasure with the Queen this night, for they may not meet again in weeks. As for the other, if he keeps his usual custom, he will be down in camp, counting his men!' She covered a smile, as if she was loath to wound my feelings by jesting about him. 'They say he is so joyful at the following he has collected to ride under his blazon, he must visit them nightly, for all they were a handful of gems!'

And we laughed merrily, and cast ourselves about, until the Duchess came out from her bedchamber, and we both sped to attend her.

Much, much later, when the bed-curtains were fast on steady breathing, Elysande came to the door to bid me God-speed.

'One thing, dear heart,' she whispered.

'Anything, Elysande.'

'Ask him who is Robin of Redesdale,' she said, and I fancied her voice was a little higher than normal. But I was mad to go to him and I gave her my word. For although she did not know it, I had already asked Richard, and he had been as baffled as were we all, so I could tell her this after, and it would be truth.

It was a close evening, and the marsh mists swirled dank and warm about the castle, and I was a part of them. I clove like a ghost near to the walls until I had crossed the ward and could mingle easily with the hastening servants, grooms, carriers and soldiers who, in lantern-light, prepared for morning departure. Few lights were burning in the great fortress behind me as I threw it one last glance before halting near the drawbridge. A cart containing the chalices and trappings for the Mass was rolling towards it, and the sentinel, laughing with a fellow, casually waved it on. Covered from head to foot in my dark cloak, I ran unnoticed in the wagon's shadow across the moat, and felt the silken suck of the meadow under my soles. There were men everywhere. Never had I seen so many men. And there were horses, the great destriers of war, with hooves big as serving dishes, shifting restively at their tethers, or, forked by strong shadows, surging across my path like moving boulders of power. There was the smell of steel and sweat; and distantly, the marsh-fires burned green, brighter that night, for the demons that tended them were curious, aroused by all the activity. I crossed myself for I was more afraid than I had dreamed, and I thought of the Nut-Brown Maid, who would follow her lord into the wilds and the desolate places.

The waged men, the mercenaries, formed a vast circle. I saw their laughing faces in the light of camp fires. They were playing cards and dicing, using their leathern shields for a board, and, as I approached the dimlit shapes of the officers' tents, I saw for the first time there were women too, among the common soldiery. In one way I was glad, for I could mix with the bawds and the wenches from the nearby hamlet and none would question my presence; then, I was sorry, for as I scuttled past a little knot of men, two dark shapes rose on my either side, and I felt the touch of rough hands.

One of them kissed me, the other pulled off my hood. I felt

a beard sharp on my skin. They both laughed, and they would have wrought further, for I felt fingers at my cloak's fastenings, and I screamed. A third figure appeared carrying a light, outlined against the glimmering marsh.

'Christ's Mercy!' said a voice wearily. 'Do we ravish children? See how small she is, you great ox!'

The one who had kissed me dropped his arms and muttered something unintelligible.

'Fat Mab awaits you. On the edge of camp,' pursued the man with the lantern. I crept closer to him.

'Sir,' I whispered, 'sir, I'm no camp-follower. Bid them let me pass, I pray you.'

'Are you from the Castle?' he said.

Wildly, I stretched my mind, babbling, 'I have a message . . .'

'I'll take it then, and you can go back before this pack molest you any more,' he said slowly. I guessed then he must be one of the newly-waged men, or he would have asked why they had not sent one of the castle guard or a manservant, and not a young maid.

'It is a private message and urgent,' I whispered. 'I don't know you, sir.'

'Calthorp, mistress,' he said shortly. 'Bound in arms under my lord Duke of Gloucester.'

In all these hundreds of soldiers I had fallen on one of Richard's men. I had a message, but not one I could transmit by Master Calthorp.

'For his ears only,' I muttered, and in the lantern light, saw his mouth curve, and knew him as quite young, despite his serious way; the kind of man my lord would pick, I thought, and answered his smile.

'So be it,' he answered, and we took our way through the lines of men. Some of them were polishing their weapons, talking quietly; one was writing a letter by firelight, chewing his nails to ease the labour of it. But, dangerously near the tents, a soldier possessed one of the village trulls, unhurriedly, half-burying her in the coarse grass, and in the gloom I felt my face scarlet and closed my ears to their sighing moans. Master Calthorp whisked me past, catching my elbow as I tripped over tussocks and the edge of my cloak.

'This is my first campaign,' he said, to cover my shame. Then, inconsequentially: 'I like the Duke of Gloucester well.' Jesu, take me to him then, I thought. For I too like the Duke of Gloucester.

Suddenly, I saw him. He was standing by an open

121

tent-flap, talking with three young men. I faltered and shrank, and Master Calthorp looked round to see why I hung back.

'There he is, mistress,' he said cheerfully.

I stood and watched Richard. With the exact gesture of his brother the King, he threw his arm about the shoulder of one young man; friendly, assured, disquietingly royal. They laughed together. He seemed very joyful, and I felt lonely and lost. Calthorp storde up to him while I trailed behind, huddled in my cloak. An esquire, whom I recognized as Lord Percy's son, stepped forward protectively, hiding Richard for a moment.

'Here is one with a message for his Grace,' said Calthorp, and I drew my hood far across my face and felt the stuff quiver under my lips.

Richard turned his head as he caught the words, and waited. The three young men waited. Robert Percy waited, and so long did they all wait that Richard came forward and Calthorp held the lantern up so that it shone in my eyes. I saw Richard's hand stray to his dagger and knew that I must present a strange, shapeless figure, half human, neither young nor old, and I feared they might think me Robin of Redesdale himself, mayhap, come south to murder them. So I turned my back on the others, and for Richard's eyes alone, dropped the veil from my face, and saw his expression change. I had never seen him angry, but he was passing wroth, then, and his fingers left his knife and he started turning his finger-rings round and round, as a cat lashes its tail. 'My thanks, Master Calthorp,' he said. His voice was like the cold stones in my gallery.

Calthorp bowed swiftly and faded away. The three young men shuffled their feet.

'Good night to you, Bernard, Barney, Broom,' said Richard, and he ran their names together so that it sounded like one of Patch's conundrums, and I wanted to laugh, and cry.

'Is all well?' Robert Percy said.

'This person is my acquaintance, and doubtless brings word from the Castle,' said Richard. 'I will speak alone with her.'

'As your good lordship desires,' said Percy. 'I will remain and escort you to your apartments.'

'Nay, Robert,' Richard said. 'Get you to bed. We must be up betimes.' He held the tent-flap open for me as Percy vanished in the murk, and he followed me in, and there we were, among all the turmoil of preparation. Pieces of harness stood

122

everywhere. Richard's sword, his banner with the Boar emblem, leather jackets on a couch, a silver basin and ewer in the corner. Brigandines, and fierce, eyeless casquetals. He came and stood before me.

'Why did you come down here?' he asked quietly.

I could not answer.

'You should not have come,' he repeated, and turned away, and stood looking out of the tent-flap into the misty darkness.

'I crave your Grace's pardon,' I said, and I think there was a little hauteur in my tone, for he had welcomed my presence when he was lonely and sad, and now he was glad and occupied in the King's service, it seemed he had no further need of me.

'I will leave you, my lord, straightway, and beg your indulgence for this misconduct,' I said formally, and I heard my voice quaver. Still he did not answer, standing straight and slender of waist, with his uneven shoulders and his smooth hair falling to his neck, a dark shadow against the tent wall. So I made to walk past him and would have dived out into the unfriendly night, but his hand caught my wrist and gripped it, with a hard tenderness.

'You are angry with me,' I whispered.

He looked down, and my eyes drooped, for his glance was the same as it ever was, deeply cool and burning and loving.

'Not with you, damoiselle, but with your folly,' he said. Then, anxiously: 'Have any harmed you, sweet heart?'

Gladness nudged at my bones. I shook my head.

'Sweet mistress, this is a world of men.' It was as though my dead father spoke to me. 'No place for you, among the rude soldiery and the harlots. Women, children, things of weakness in this time of strife.'

And I marvelled at the way he spoke, calm and controlled, full of wisdom and concern as if he were old beyond his years. And while he began softly to stroke my hair, I remarked on it, aloud.

'Yes, I may seem thus,' he said, then stopped, and I said gently: 'Yea, my lord, my love?'

'My childhood ended when I was seven years old,' he said, and a heavy silence hung between us. He lowered his hand from my hair, and we both thought of the heads on Micklegate Bar.

'You know what the King did?' he murmured. I shook my head.

'A ceremony of remembrance,' he said slowly. 'Five years ago, here in this very place. We rode behind a great death

123

carriage, to the memory of my father and my brother. Under the banner of Christ in Majesty, Christ on a rainbow, flanked by the suns and roses. Gilded angels were fashioned, to cherish their souls. They lived again, that day. Then, through God's grace, and his own kingly might, Edward avenged their death. He brought peace to the realm.'

His voice shook. He turned to face me again.

'Thus, through my gratitude, have I striven to grow wise and strong, that I may be his right hand always. Great Jesu! I love him.'

A pain in my heart. Kings come and go. If only he could have said: 'Great Jesu! I love thee.' But in face of this strong and bitter love, I was no more than one of the village trulls, moaning in the long grass. I think it was then I decided my love must do for the two of us.

He went on: 'So, I will be true to him, and to his heirs, so long as I shall live.'

In the distance a woman's chuckling shriek, lewd and profane, sullied the grave quietness. For no reason at all, I thought of little Lady Beaufort.

Richard glanced round, anxiously.. He put his hands over my ears, my hair, so that I should not hear the coarse sounds. 'Sweet heart, you should not be here,' he said, his voice coming faintly through a dim, rushing noise.

Then he said: 'Why did you come?'

I put my hands on his, and he held me, on either side of my head. I had never told him how I loved him, for it would not be seemly, but this night, I felt, with a strange sadness, might be the only time I should have the chance. So I told him, all of it, and when I had ceased, his hands were trembling under mine, and the rushing in my ears had become a roar.

His voice sounded quite loud when he took his hands away.

'I wonder,' he said thoughtfully, 'if I am worthy of such love.'

I could not speak, for I was weeping, and I was angry with myself, for this was not what I had planned; I had wanted to make him glad, not bring him dolour.

I therefore took his hand and kissed it, and his rings were cold to my mouth. And he put his arm tenderly about my neck, and my hair came loose and streamed over his wrist down to the ground, as I leaned back and felt his lips on my throat, my heart.

And before I left him, because it was such a warm, damp night and he looked weary, I took a cloth with water from the ewer and washed his face as he lay on the couch. He closed his eyes for an instant and he could have been dead, with his high-boned countenance and his pallor. So hastily, to chase a demon, I signed his brow with the Cross and kissed him, and he clasped his arms tight about me, saying I was a true maid and had brought him much joy and comfort.

He summoned a sleepy young man to escort me back to the castle, one who had but lately come on duty, so that none should know, for the greenish dawn was rising over the fens and the camp would soon be stirring. He raised his hand to me as he stood between the tent-flaps, and there was a light about him that was not earthly; or it may have been the marsh fiends dimming their night-lamps behind him; I did not know.

Neither did I know that I should not see Richard Plantagenet again for many years, and then he would be greatly changed.

I never had such a friend as Elysande; and Elysande had a new dress. It was green as a willow and suited her golden skin and tilted eyes. She was kind and lovesome and I loved her. It seemed I had more need of her than ever, particularly the day they left to meet with Robin, riding to Newark in their martial blue, for to save my soul I could not watch them go. I wanted to remember him as he stood in the lambent dawn, dark figure of my fate, holding all my happiness in one lifted hand.

Elysande sat beside me, stroking my cold fingers, for no flame burned in me. Only a block of ice, and I knew not why, for he had said: 'God keep you, sweet lady, be comfortable. When we have put down this pesky rising I shall come back and all will be well with us again.'

Yet all was not well with me, for, overlaying my great sadness, another shadow had fallen upon me, out of the past, and I was full of fear.

When I was returning from Richard, walking as in a deep sleep and still with him in spirit, I had not seen the tall figure advancing noiselessly along the twilit passage until we collided fiercely. Candlelight flared above me and a drop of hot wax fell on my neck. Like a blare of trumpets, I heard the warning that tore through my mind. I raised my face and saw

125

Anthony Woodville gazing down at me from his slender height. He had just come from saying a Night Office, and his rosary beads were twisted round his fingers. Instead of frowning and passing by, he stopped and his eyes roved over me: my tumbling hair, my exposed throat and breast; my guilt.

'Well, madam?' he said. 'You are late abroad, or should I say early?'

And I was a child again, another oath broken, for I had sworn he would never again bring me fear.

'I know you, mistress, do I not?' His voice was kind, as a sword is kind until you feel the edge. I pulled my careless cloak together, confused. He had seen me more than once, sitting quietly in his mother's apartments.

'I had not recognized you before now,' he said, just as if he had read my thoughts. 'I vow—'tis those incredible headpieces you ladies wear, but now 'tis all plain . . . were you not with us at Grafton Regis?'

It was undoubtedly true. With my hair fashionably hidden, the forehead shaved for height, I owned a different countenance. Without my wealth of hair, I was but another little pale face.

His eyes, cold depths of a winter lake, held mine. My gaze showed unease, I know, but strangely so did his, as if I were some little wild animal of uncertain temper. For a moment we looked at one another, and my heart, lately lulled to bliss by Richard's touch, began to leap and bound as do the birds cruel boys fasten to stakes and stone to death.

'Yes . . .' he said, very slowly, and that one word held more meaning than the longest speech. Then suddenly he turned on his heel and strode in the direction of the Duchess's apartments, while I stayed, paralysed with dismay, for there Elysande waited to let me in. I saw him halt outside my lady's door, musing deeply, and he must have thought the hour too late or too early, for he moved away without knocking, and vanished down the staircase, his tall shadow following him.

Now fear such as I had never known held me fast. He had remembered me, and with that remembrance, had come a reprise of that night at Grafton Regis, when he had bullied me into forgetting what I had seen. And what had I seen? Something not clearly understood, something evil and dangerous. He was plainly haunted. And I feared the outcome of his malaise.

'Holy Jesu!' I whispered outside the Duchess's door. 'He will send me back to Grafton!'

He would send me back to Grafton, and I would never see Richard again. Elysande slid back the bolt and I fell into her arms, weeping as loudly as I dared.

Now she was pressing my hand gently. She had been looking out of the window.

'He rides with Edward Brampton, the Portuguese,' she murmured. 'They make a goodly show—all of them . . .' stealing a sideways glance. 'He loved you right well last night?' she whispered, and I nodded, because she was a dear friend to me and full of understanding that love was not always carnal sin, as the priests said.

'You were courageous,' she whispered. 'To venture among all the military. I warrant you saw sights to bring the colour to your face.'

Even as she spoke, I knew for certainty that she herself must have made like journeys in her time, and wondered if she had loved a soldier ever, and knew the feeling. All the while she smiled; it was as if she applied the smile with her face-paint.

'Did you ask him?' she said.

I had to tell my little lie, truth as it was, that Richard did not know the real face of Robin of Redesdale. Her smile grew broader as if it were stretched and the paint on her lips cracked a little with the sweetness of her smile.

And then, that day, Lord Anthony entered, giving us all a fair good-day, and passed through to the Duchess's chamber. And strong terror gripped me, more than I could bear, and I turned trembling to Elysande, who put her arm about me as if she had only been waiting for me to tell her the old secret that had plagued me for years.

So while my lord was closeted with his mother, I sought comfort and reassurance from sweet Elysande, and I told her all about it; the moonlight, and the manikins, and the black cat, and the herb garden, and Elizabeth Woodville's uncertainty as to the wisdom of their actions, and her mother's fierce words. I told her all, and waxed fat in the telling, for she was a kind and tender audience, and hung on every word and her eyes grew wide and she asked me many questions and showed horror and sympathy.

Then she told me to set it all from my mind, as if it were one of my bad dreams, to forget it all and be glad and think only of my dear love. How could Sir Anthony send me back to Grafton for that which was not my fault? Sure enough she was right, for naught dreadful happened, as when my lord

127

and his mother came out of the chamber they did not even look at me.

So I ceased to be disquieted, and was only full of love-longing instead, and I know which was the heavier burden.

He had told me he had written a letter to a friend while he was at Rising, for he had had no money with which to pay his men, and he had even jested about it, as we lay in each other's arms.

I wished he would write *me* a letter, but I knew he would be far too busy for that.

There came August, and a day so full of sorrow that only one other summer day can best it for its anguish and that I cannot speak of yet.

Elysande's dress was red this day, like a fair red rose, like blood, but we were not sitting quietly together on this occasion. We were at Westminster, running here and there, throwing things into chests, packing urgently, while the Household flew about as feverishly as did the panicking crowds in the street below.

For the King was taken. The King was a prisoner, and his captor was the man who had been his friend, the one who had set him on the throne, the knight Richard had loved.

Robin of Redesdale was not Robin Hood after all: he was Sir John Conyers, cousin to the Earl of Warwick; and Warwick had taken the King. Edward had left matters too late, with his hawking and his bedsport and his dalliance at Fotheringhay. While he pleasured himself thus, and his wise young brother chafed to be off, the man who made and unmade kings had been wondrous busy.

Horsemen on steaming beasts cried frenzy through London. Elysande cursed under her breath and I sought to calm my churning stomach, while we piled clothing and jewellery into coffers, bed-linen and arras into cases, helped by pallid manservants with the smell of fear about them. Hoarse shouting came in gusts over the screams of the mob. I rushed to a window; whenever I made out the word 'slain' or 'beheaded', a ghastly grinning spectre rose up to wave at me through the panes. Of a sudden I dropped the end of a Turkish rug and rushed out into the teeming passages, frantic for the news I dreaded. In a niche in the stones sat a small figure, weeping. I had never seen Harry cry before. In the midst of my demented progress I stopped and knelt to him.

He pressed his face against me, his tears fell on my bosom. He would not be comforted.

'The King's Grace is taken,' he sobbed. 'I am so afraid.'

'Don't weep, Harry,' I said, as bravely as I could. 'All will be well.'

'My sweet lord,' he whispered through snuffling tears. All my heart's blood massed in a red, icy knot.

'What say you?' I cried.

'He was wondrous kind to me,' he choked. 'Men say he has been slain . . .'

I rose and staggered on my feet, bruising my back against the carved pillar. Then I started, witlessly, to run, seeking the street, to seize the stirrup of the nearest courier and demand he give this terrible news the lie. I stumbled, and arms caught me; arms that I fought, screaming into a lined face no longer merry.

'God's Passion,' said Patch. 'Must all fly about like slaughtered fowls?' He held me fast. 'Sweeting, calm yourself.'

'Patch,' I cried. 'Patch!'

He grinned. His face looked strained and meagre; a skull-like face.

'Mary have mercy!' he said. 'I thought you had more courage than to cry havoc with the rest. So the King is taken! Was he not warned, time and again? Why all this wonder, that the great Warwick seeks vengeance on the Woodvilles?

"Pembroke and Devon are headless now.
More necks will bleed ere long, I trow."

He made a little jingle out of it. Then for a brief moment his face crumpled with grief, he crossed himself, said: 'Christ preserve the King,' and pulled me down beside him on a window-ledge.

'Ah, I love you, maiden,' he said, and I could have struck him for jesting at such a time, but felt too weak to raise my hand.

'Give me the news,' I said, trembling. 'Who is beheaded, who slain?'

'The King's favourites,' said Patch calmly. 'Sir Richard Woodville, John Woodville . . . Warwick will have the whole family's blood. Clarence stands at his right hand, now that Isabel is his bride.'

'George of Clarence—has wedded Warwick's daughter?' I cried. Patch nodded, and winked and said: 'In Calais, lately.'

'They will destroy the Woodvilles?' I gasped.

129

'In all ways possible,' said the fool. 'Tend well your mistress, maiden, for she'll need your prayers.'

I knew not what he meant, but when he started babbling again about love, and he still could not tell me where was Richard in all this, I sprang up and flew to Elysande, but she was nowhere to be seen. The Duchess's chamber was bolted from the inside, while two men stood without and spoke her name, sternly. They had a small retinue of henchmen, who wore the Bear and Ragged Staff, Warwick's livery. They stayed a few moments, then quit the chamber purposefully, while the gentlewomen huddled like terrified pigeons. Snatches of their speech crept to my ears.

'Redesdale's Proclamation likened his Grace to Richard the Second, Harry the Sixth,' said a shaking voice. 'All deposed monarchs . . .'

'Yea, and Edward the Second,' said Anne Haute, in horrified tones. She was deathly white and I remembered that she too was a Woodville. Then I thought of the King, and Richard, and of poor, unnatural Edward the Second, with his bowels burned out at Berkeley, and my stomach came up into my throat. When the blackness faded into light, Elysande was with me. She was not smiling when I opened my eyes, but as soon as I was sensible she kissed me, a loving sister. Her red gown hurt my gaze. The voices whispered on.

'The Archbishop of York . . . is in the Palace . . .'

'A Neville!' hissed another.

'Yea, and Clarence sits on the Council . . .'

'Warwick has summoned a Parliament . . .'

'The Duchess!' someone murmured anxiously.

'Who were those men . . . What have they done to her?'

Their whispers flew like arrows, rebounding on to bafflement.

Suddenly the Duchess came out from her chamber. She was yellowish, and her grim jaws were clamped together. Angrily she waved her hand at the gibbering group of women. She leaned firmly on her ivory cane, white-knuckled.

'Leave me—all of you!' she snapped.

Yet Elysande and I flew to her side, for we feared she might collapse, as the others rustled out hastily, with many a glance behind.

Ignoring me, the Duchess glared at Elysande.

'You failed me in your duty,' she said icily, and Elysande was out of countenance for a moment, and her eyes gave off sparks.

'Sweet madam, I wrought all I could, but the source ran dry,' she said, and I was bemused by her strange words.

'Where is Hastings?' asked the Duchess, and she uttered the Lord Chamberlain's name as if it were a poison on her tongue.

Elysande shrugged, as the French do.

'And young Gloucester?' My heart leaped in my throat. Before Elysande could reply, a stout knocking came on the outer door. The same two men returned who had waited to speak with the Duchess. They had waited vainly and now they would not be gainsaid. One said his name was Thomas Wake.

A panic fire had started somewhere down the street. I could hear the cracking of timber and the surging shouts from the crowd. Smoke drifted under the window.

The two men were courteous. They bowed to the Duchess, then one of them placed a parchment between her fingers.

'Madame, we will attend your presence in answer to this charge,' Thomas Wake said formally. Swiftly they left, walking clean and upright. One of them was dark and pale, like Richard.

The Duchess's fingers were stiff and curled, and the parchment dropped from her hand, so I bent to pick it up. There were many long words, and one of them was 'necromancy'.

'Holy God,' whispered Elysande.

'Ask her Grace to come,' said the Duchess firmly. I marvelled at her composure.

Elysande left and returned shortly with the Queen. For the first time ever, she came without her retinue of gentlewomen, servants, chaplains. On my knees, I glanced up at her. She was ivory-faced, but it became her, against her black dress with the jewelled girdle and the priceless reliquary Edward had given her. I wondered if she wept and feared for him as I did for my love.

'Madame, they have taken Master Daunger,' said the Duchess. And at the name I saw again, clear as crystal, the whey-faced clerk sitting at table on May Eve with the unquiet Elizabeth Woodville; galloping on May Day to Grafton Regis.

'So I am informed,' said the Queen. She also was serene, though less so. She frowned at the old woman and swept into the inner chamber, beckoning her mother to follow. Elysande and I waited. Low murmurings came from behind the closed door. I looked at my friend, and her eyes were yellow, like a wolf's eyes.

'They have Daunger,' she said, and looked at me. I said naught. I was trying to collect my thoughts, straining my ears for the cries of men bringing news of the rebellion; news of Richard.

'How fortunate that he is their only witness,' she said musingly. And then I felt afraid. The voices within were louder, raised in anger . . . that was the Queen . . .

'Even if they have his feet in the fire?'

'He will not say aught, my daughter . . .' And it was Grafton Regis all over again when she said: 'It is written, it is written . . . he is a stubborn man, and clever.'

'So there is naught to fear,' said Elizabeth, the door now ajar.

As they came out, I sought to exchange comforting glances with Elysande. She gave me a right lovesome smile. Then she stepped forward with a deep curtsey before the Queen.

'Your most noble Grace,' she said softly, and despite this formal address there was a certain familiarity in her tone as if she had known the Queen years ago, in France, mayhap, when Elizabeth served Margaret of Anjou. The Queen looked at her expressionlessly.

'Madame, there is one here,' said Elysande slowly, 'who speaks of necromancy, and sorcery . . . I know naught of it myself, for I am loyal and love your Grace. But one has told me tales of moonlight on the last day of April . . . things seen and heard. I am your servant and would safeguard you.'

She took the Queen's hand and kissed it gracefully, and Elizabeth laid her own white hand on the shoulder of my dear friend, Elysande.

They all turned and looked closely at me, while I stood shaking, and it was as if their three faces were one, with the same cold hard glance, ruthless, appraising, as if I were a pear to be plucked, a stone to be priced, a sheep to be butchered. The Duchess spoke first.

'And what folly does this one say, mistress?'

Elysande smiled. 'All, Madame. Something about evil rites and words, and ravings about fickle men and "*the o*ther".' She finished with the casual air of one who imparts the insignificant. The Queen's ivory face turned to chalk.

'Jesu, mercy,' she said quietly. Then, in the next breath and as if I were not there: 'She was but a child . . .'

'She would never withstand an inquisition,' said one of them, but by now I was falling into a black tomb and did not know who spoke.

'She is of little importance . . . she will not speak.'

132

I opened my mouth, to swear eternal silence.

'She may already have spoken,' said a voice, and I knew it by its sweetness to be that of Elysande. She came and stood beside me. I caught a glint of her red gown through a fog of fear. And Elysande said, in a voice like running water:

'Know you not, your Grace, that this one—' she indicated me with a slender sleeve-swish—'this one lies o'night with my lord of Gloucester, and doubtless bears many a pretty tale?'

It was what Richard would have called a flank attack. While I was engaged with the dangerous enemy before me, she had come down out of a mist of smiles and lovesomeness to destroy me. It was now that I knew she was truly a Woodville-lover, and always had been, despite her provoking words in my presence, her soft mocking of the sleeping Duchess. She had betrayed me.

I fell at the Queen's feet.

'You should thank me,' Elysande said. She was at the window, watching the reflections of the mob fire. Dark was falling. The glow lit up the great chamber like blood. They had been waiting for the night, for they were going to dispose of me. My mind ran rings of terror; the Tower yawned; nay, I thought, Warwick would examine all prisoners now that he was in power, and I would be of use to him.

The Queen was in Sanctuary; Elysande was on the point of joining her and the Duchess.

Ah, holy Jesu! I thought. They will kill me. They will murder me, as they did Desmond's boys. A small cry broke from me.

'I have saved your life,' said Elysande, and mayhap she did not want my blood on her slender hands, for she continued: 'The King loves Gloucester, and you are his harlot.'

I felt tears spring to my eyes at the word, for such were they who lay in long grass with soldiers, and did not give their whole heart and love to one alone.

'Young Gloucester has no power; yet if you died, and he complained to the King, Edward would be angry . . . the risk is too great. Thus you will live, cursed and forgotten.'

'He may seek me,' I said through frozen lips.

Elysande laughed, throwing back her head. 'He will not wish to seek you,' she said gaily. 'You will have vanished from the sight of men; and you have betrayed his confidence.'

'I have never betrayed him,' I whispered, shaking.

'You have spoken of him to me,' Elysande said. 'Doubtless

he will believe you have carried tales of his policies to Jacquetta of Bedford. All know there is no love lost between Richard and the Queen's kin. Has he not spoken to you of things other than love?'

I thought how I had asked him about Robin of Redesdale—in his eyes I would be a Woodville spy. I thought of his swift disdainful anger and the way he had toyed with his knife at my cloaked anonymity. My tears began to fall. Elysande went on, softly:

'He will think you to be a witch; that you had part in the rites and this is why you are no longer at court . . . a dangerous witness . . . a necromancer. One who helped secure the King for Elizabeth Woodville.'

I asked her: 'And who shall speak such foul lies?'

'Whispers wax fat,' she said, her favourite expression.

'He will seek me,' I said, and I knew I lied for comfort's sake, for there was none to succour me.

'Others will soon replace you,' she said, and watched me carefully, enjoying my anguish. 'And anyway that witless loyalty of his will destroy him . . . all the Woodvilles are scattered but Warwick's men are everywhere. I doubt not they have cut him down already on the road, together with his followers.'

'Warwick would never slay him!' I cried. 'They were as father and son!'

'Jesu! what a fool you are!' she said contemptuously. 'In war, men slay their own kin.'

And I thought with sorrow of Richard who, if he still lived, would need to ride against George of Clarence and the great Neville, and my tears turned inward, and shrouded him.

Then I heard the tramp of boots, the voices of men.

'Now all the dresses and the praises will be mine,' said Elysande, softly smiling. Outside the steps halted, and a key turned.

'You have sold me for a gown?' I cried, and she shook her head, the smile gone. 'I bore you no real malice, for I thought you wantwit, harmless, until one day,' she murmured. 'Yet you have flown exceedingly high, and striven to ape your betters, and may God have mercy . . .' and I knew she spoke of Elizabeth Woodville and the King, and Richard and me.

So they came and took me. They were silent men and we passed quickly out through the teeming streets, with the citizens with brows clubbed bloody, and here and there the glow of a fire gilding the leaning house gables. We left behind the heaps of filth and ordure which steamed and stank

134

on the cobbles, while far above them an hundred spires pointed to Paradise. And the great Tower faded, all faded, behind the veil of my tears, light as a spider's dwelling on a May dawn; and I heard them speak of the north parties of the realm, which phrase I clung to, Yorkshire being part of my lord, and therefore of me.

I wished that I had learned to play chess as he had tried to teach me, for as he said, one should be born cognizant of strategy and cunning in this world. Therefore I kept my own counsel ever afterwards, and the only words I spoke during that long rough journey northward through danger were but to ask them not to ride so fast. For I had something to protect. Under my cloak I kept my arms crossed tight, safeguarding one last small and secret joy.

The royal child, the Plantagenet. The child of my beloved.

HERE THE MAIDEN'S TALE IS BROKEN

PART TWO

THE FOOL

NOW-A-DAYS Also I have a wife; her name is Rachell.
Betwixt her and me was a great battle;
And fain of you would I here tell
Who was the most master.

NOUGHT Thy wife, Rachell, I dare 20 lies.

NOW-A-DAYS Who spake to thee, fool? Thou art not wise!

Mankind (*ca.* 1470)

I fear something's amiss with my eyes. A pale shadow dims them at moments. Should it continue, I shall go back to the wise woman, over the river at Southwark, among the stews and taverns which flourish as briskly as in the old days. She will sell me the toadstone and whisper her charms, placing her hand on my brow, and I shall almost believe it is my sweet lady. Although her hands are sisters to the lilies, and I lose no chance of kissing them; this I do needlessly, often. We are good friends, if such a thing is possible between a Queen and a mocker, a diverter of courtiers, one who hides his wit behind idiocy and keeps a well-tuned ear. I am content; I serve the one I love; men treat me with respect, and *he* likes me, for he pays me, and that is great bounty from such as his Divine Majesty. I see him now, wandering in the pleasaunce, a tatterdemalion, wine-stains down his sparse robe, scratching in his little account-book. His long face is drawn in despair over some outrageous extravagance, such as a tun of malmsey for the Spanish Ambassador last month, or one dozen candles for my lord Stanley's apartments. Poor fellow! Henry, 'tis a passing heavy business, this being a King.

This evening I will play cards with my lady. I will sit on the floor for there are few chairs since the last inventory, and the ladies will have their cushions strewn around us. There are a few pleasures left in this life, if one knows how to look at them, as one might watch a disguising, absorbing its message until one is drawn in thread by thread to become part of the picture.

We do not speak of King Richard now. Years past, she would lean the barest inch closer to me, give that small anxious cough and say:

'Tell me, Sir Fool, do you remember that revel when . . .'

And I would say, very low: 'A dreadful night, madam; when the mummers' wildman costumes caught fire and poor Geffrey was burned . . .'

Of necessity, I am a diverter. Laughing, she'd fall a little woeful at the remembrance of a real tragedy, but be amused

138

by my evasiveness and continue the game, and I would know she thought of the last Christmas before the turning of the tide . . . I have these troublesome eyes, and she laughs less than once she did; she looks weary, anxious about Arthur, for all his beauty frail enough to be blown off by a sneeze. Once, her mind was full of torment and courage and resignation, and wore mourning—truly. The darkness of it shone in her glance.

I do not know how old I am exactly, but I must be past my half a century. My Queen has great understanding, and should I repeat the rhyme I pleased her with yesterday she merely smiles like the sun. Should she desire more riotous sport, dancing, tumbling, she will call one of the younger men, Scot, or Jakes, more agile than I. It is not that my mind is wanting; more that I seem to live in two dimensions, past and present, and sometimes the two merge and the former cuts sharply through the soft outlines of reality. There I am back again, in the merry days of my lady's father, whom God assoil. The Maiden dances, dances, alone on the gallery. Was it only six moons she stayed at court? It seemed a lifetime; would to all the Saints it had been so!

King Henry has a stable full of fools. If my sight worsens, I may be blessed with a small pension and end my days in a monkery. Yet I cannot brook the thought of parting from my sweet lady. I have loved two women in my life, and they could not have been less alike, save for one trait. Pure goodness, of which many prate but few observe, for all the Masses that they hear. The court is still full of the small triumphs and betrayals which echo the bigger ones that cost the lives of men, and kings. Under the glitter, the ritual splendours, lie serpents, dormant now, but once they writhed and clung and their fangs bit deep.

Two women. One whom I have loved since she was old enough to run and tug my flaunting sleeve, beg a conundrum or a game. Elizabeth, growing into a tall flower, a beauty, destined to be Queen-Consort of England soon after the battle-blood was sunk into the ground and the dark star of Richard Plantagenet fallen for ever. The Maiden was not a deal older when I gave her my heart, and she laughed at me. She was a one for laughing. Her portrait is a second skin over my mind: her huge eyes of dark velvet, and her tiny swift body, flashing through the forbidden ways, diving with a lilt under the arms of startled guards; dodging the Dowager Duchess of Bedford . . . in all places at once, so that even I with my trained young agility could not match her.

We have had little ado here since the business of Master Perkin Warbeck. I stood in the courtyard the day they brought him in chains to confront the King. He had masqueraded as the Duke of York, my royal lady's brother, vanished long since in the bloody mist that wreathes the Tower, along with the Prince of Wales, and their uncle's reputation. Golden-haired Warbeck was a Plantagenet; one glance was enough to show, and the thought that came to me was King Edward's fondness for a pretty face, and that not always of Elizabeth Woodville. Our sovereign faced the tall rebel. Changing emotions frolicked on his sallow countenance like squirrels on a lawn. He reddened and bit his lips, and under all the just anger and coldness I saw something else, gone in an eyelid's bat—a glance like a hairshirt, a demon-haunted look.

I lingered near my lady, for I reckoned she might feel sad at the sight of such an obvious relative and a bastard. For a short space she too had known the shame of bastardy, until King Henry, in his goodness, legitimized her for their holy union. I always thought him born under a lucky planet, for had his lovely consort's brothers still been alive, he would have had to choose between her and the throne of England. Some men truly attain bliss.

I had a little monkey on my shoulder that day, and it clung close, binding its hard scaly tail about my throat. How long since they hanged Perkin? I forget. Kings are no longer addressed 'Your Grace'—their new title befits better the truly divine, the sons of Cadwallader; His Majesty is negotiating with Spain for the hand of the Infanta Caterina for Prince Arthur. That boy looks more fitted for rest and cosseting than the marriage mart.

I have been married; she died, of the new plague, the sweating sickness brought over by our King's French mercenaries when they came in 1485. I scarcely remember her; I have loved but two women.

There are particular days which seem good, when the sun
shines brighter and the cobbles are not so hard under the
soles of new shoes with the upturned points; on such a day I
strolled down Jewry and up Chepe to visit my mother, like a
dutiful son. I had no notion why I felt so gay, unless it was
that I had just seen a wench who reminded me of the
Maiden; something in her gait and the shape of her eyes
stirred me, but when I smiled at her she only swished her
gown haughtily past my legs and was gone, into the press of
people. Nor did I dwell on her, or on the one she resembled,
but went, high-spirited, abroad the bright street. Though we
had been out of Sanctuary for nearly a month, the sonorous
plainsong of the monks still trod my mind, reminding me of
my frailties. I had chosen to bide with the Queen this last
time, not only for safety, but so that I could be near the Princess Elizabeth. For her I would play the dragon or the
griffon, cavorting fearsomely, while she, leaning on her
nurse's lap, bubbled like my mother's smallest stew-pot coming to the boil. There was naught could frighten her; in her
there was more of her father, less of her mother, that gilded
icicle.

Her Grace had first flown into Westminster Sanctuary after
the collapse of that ill-starred campaign against Robin of
Redesdale, when London hovered on the lip of mob rule and
blow after blow rained on the Woodvilles. Warwick had
shown no quarter. Hard to say who had been smitten the
most: mayhap the Dowager Duchess of Bedford. No sooner
had the sorcery indictment been dropped than she had to
mourn a husband and a son. Sir John Woodville and Earl
Rivers were beheaded outside Coventry. This last had sent
her half witless for a while. Men had murmured she wrought
witchcraft for many years, but there had been no witnesses to
prove a thing. Now she crept about, a murmuring dark
mound, widowed, thought-entombed.

Anthony Woodville had embraced the religious life. I do
not mean he had taken to cloister, or to going barefoot in

monkish garb, for he rode to battle with the rest. Yet the gossiping esquires whispered he wore a hairshirt under his peer's velvet. Though he still penned verses, he was given to God, he declared. Thus can the breeze of fear blow men heavenward.

After King Edward's capture by Warwick, he had been taken by George Neville, Archbishop of York, to Coventry to meet his princely adversaries. Warwick and George of Clarence were both well-flown with triumph. His Grace displayed great cunning: he spoke his captors fair, bowed to their every wish, and went with them to Warwick Castle, then north to desolate Middleham, by night. While, in London, chaos blazed. I remained with my mother, barricading the cookshop door, while the cressets of threatening and threatened flickered past the window, and the cookboys tucked themselves under the counter, crying.

Bereft of its King, England went wild. Old enemies seized the chance to settle ancient scores—disturbances flared all over the realm. Ironically, it was such a one that proved Warwick's first undoing: while slackening his hold on the royal captive to quell a Lancastrian rising initiated by one of his own cousins, he found himself pulled up sharp. Not a soul would answer to his call until they knew the King was safe. Thus, after less than a month, King Edward revealed himself to the people of York. Lord Hastings and Richard of Gloucester rode hot to where the King lay. Neither Warwick nor his brother the Archbishop could do aught but allow these lords to escort the King whither he wished. So Edward came triumphant again to London, with his Lord Chamberlain and his youngest brother, with Suffolk, Henry, Duke of Buckingham, Essex and Arundel, Dacre and Mountjoy, and the one Neville who had remained loyal to him, John, Earl of Northumberland.

With a thousand horse they were received into London's bosom. All rejoiced, poor fools. I marvel now there was not another torrent of bloody rain to spoil the washing of good housewives, for all the mischief that lay ahead.

Misliking the Woodvilles as I did, it gave me some amusement to see young Gloucester appointed Constable of England for life in place of Lord Rivers. Although this nullified the patent for this office that was implicit in Earl Rivers's death, the King made no bones about his pride in his brother. Doubtless his Grace compared Richard's loyalty to the treachery of George of Clarence. As for Gloucester—he actually smiled, on more than one occasion. In his new capacity as

142

chief steward of Wales and the Marches, he quelled risings swiftly, was made Chief Justice and Chamberlain of South Wales, and Viceroy of those entire parts. Irony again, for these powers had lately belonged to the Earl of Warwick, with whom the King then sought to be reconciled. He had gone so far as to betroth my sweet Elizabeth to John Neville's young son, and had sought in other ways to woo Warwick, to settle the disputes without strife. To little avail though, for there came another upheaval in Lincolnshire, started by Lords Welles and Dymmock, and it was like Robin of Redesdale all over again: another ghostly, rumour-ridden attempt to shake the throne, and again, Warwick and Clarence behind it.

Welles and Dymmock went to the block after a scuffle at Empingham, and at the end of March, in the year of Our Lord 1470, the King proclaimed his brother George and the Earl of Warwick traitors. Some there were who joined forces with the two noble rebels, among them Lord Stanley; I used to see him often at court, and he was another who smiled scantily; he had a long, shrewd face, with gloomy, nervous lips, and a manner all hiver-hover. I had watched him at the board, and he was exceeding hard to please, forever waving away one dish and calling for another, as if unable to make up his mind.

Did I say the King rewarded loyalty well? Unfathomable monarch—in the midst of all the ado, he robbed the faithful John Neville of his earldom of Northumberland, restoring it to Henry Percy, that most arrogant knight. The Marquisate of Montagu seemed a poor substitute, given thus to one who had deserted his own brothers to uphold his King.

One skirmish followed another; Warwick and Clarence rode westward to join Lord Stanley; Richard of Gloucester rode after them and scattered Stanley's men. Stanely was indignant, and complained to the King! And almost as soon as Edward had proclaimed that peace was to be kept between Stanley and Gloucester, we heard, in London, how the bigger quarry had evaded him.

Warwick, Clarence, and their ladies had fled to France, to be welcomed in princely style by King Louis—'King Spider' —and to bow over the chill hand of Margaret of Anjou. And the bond to seal the bargain with Lancaster? The fair, frail Anne Neville, for the French Queen's son, Edward, Prince of Wales.

Then fortunes turned, in the bat of an eye. It was folly that King Edward wrought, robbing the Marquis of Montagu of his earldom, for that one swore he had been 'given a paltry title, and a pie's nest to maintain it with'. In September he showed his displeasure, turning on the King when he lay at Doncaster, and the next we knew was that Edward, Hastings, Rivers and Gloucester were fugitives, exiled in the Low Countries. Back to town came Warwick, wrenching half-witted Harry the Sixth from his prayers in the Tower to lead the poor wight through London, as a kind of sad harbinger of his French wife's due invasion. By this time the Queen, great with child, her ladies and her three daughters were crammed into Sanctuary, with Mother Cobb the midwife, and there was a chill corner for the King's jesters and mountebanks, all among the holy men. I could thank God for my safety—I could play with the Princess Elizabeth, and duly marvel at the new royal heir—and think of the Maiden through the sober quietness. It was not a bad time, yet we ached for news. When we heard that the King and Richard of Glouces-ter had landed at Ravenspur and gained York through some cunning policy, we were heartened. When we knew that the King offered Warwick and Clarence pardon or the hazard of battle, we were hopeful; and when we learned that Clarence at least was reconciled with his brothers, we rejoiced.

Yet again, the Nevilles paraded Harry Six through London in a ploy to rally Lancaster. Pitiful dolt! with his emblem of two foxtails on a staff drooping in the mizzling rain—men said it shamed the stomach. Then, suddenly, his Grace strode into Sanctuary, taking the Queen in his arms, kissing all the ladies, offering prayers in thanks for the fair babe. He even gripped me by the shoulder for an instant, and shed one tear of gladness. That was the sign for general weeping from all the women. I thought I should be driven mad by their noise. So I stole over to the Princess Elizabeth and saw that she was laughing, as she ever did, and that her uncle of Gloucester laughed with her.

Then the fierce struggles at Barnet, at Tewkesbury, and the thousands slain, among which were the French Queen's son, and the man who made and unmade kings, Richard Neville, Earl of Warwick.

Noble, hot-humoured Warwick, the flamboyant baron for whom the people once shouted so gladly, was dead. For War-wick had schooled his cousin well in the diversities of war and policy, and the princely pupil had overmatched him. I could not deny a vague regret—though I was right heartily the King's lover, it was as if Warwick had donned the crown and sword of Gabriel, to drive corruption from Paradise. Although there were now fewer Woodvilles, they still fed on the realm, and its bounty.

And the Sanctuary of Westminster was free of us once more; of the women and children, the servants and the nervous dogs, of the sweet Princesses, and the new heir to England, whose entry into the sinful world had brought the omens of complete victory to Edward, his father. So I walked up Chepe with the ground sunny under my soles and the taste of freedom in my belly, with only one little bit of sour.

For beside all the great personages, there was one truly insignificant but exceeding dear, of whom I had no news, for she had vanished as if she had never been.

I carried a staff along Eastchepe, to guard me from the 'prentices, who would as soon pick a quarrel as sell you an oyster-pie. Loud and impertinent, they sought to emulate the quality, dressing beyond their means, wearing tall hats, piked shoes. Their finery was the spoils of gambling; today they would lose on the dice and pawn their doublet, tomorrow be peacocking in a friend's attire, won at cards. Thus, thought I, the way of the world, the fortunes of York and Lancaster, and I smiled.

The door of the cookshop felt greasy to my palm. I went inside the brisk heat and bustle. Trade was good. Shortly before my father's death, my mother had started this enterprise, moving from Hereford to London, while I played noble houses, itinerant with a group of minstrels, and learning my craft daily. My father was a fool, his father before him, and, in the days of Coeur de Lion, my ancestor was a jongleur, and rich rewarded.

A knot of cookboys toiled at the fire, and my mother came welcoming. Short-statured like myself, she was plump as a pigeon, with grey eyes and small firm mouth. I bussed her on the cheek; it was months since we last met. We talked of small family matters, and then of the King and Queen—she was glad of a diversion from labour and heat, though all the while there seemed to be some trouble peering round her shoulder.

'So England has an heir at last.'

'Yea, the prettiest prince,' I answered.

She leaped from thought to thought.

'Did you see them bring the French Queen through the City?' She laughed. 'A right draggletail, and her eyes were

145

mindless. Some hurled filth at her but—' she lowered her voice—'I felt pity—ask me not why.'

'She's lost everything,' I said. 'Her pride and her solace, her Silver Swan.' (So they called him, this dead prince, this Anjou witch's son.)

'What of his widow?' she asked. 'Anne of Warwick?'

I told her the little I knew, from the time when Warwick had gathered up his ladies and sped them overseas. Anne and the Countess, George of Clarence's wife Isabel, great with child. The hand of the youngest daughter for the French Queen's son, and King Louis rubbing his palms over the prospect of Burgundy under his belt, and a fruitful harvest for Lancaster.

'Is it the truth?' asked my mother. 'That proud Margaret kept the Earl on his knees a full hour before she'd consent to the match?'

'Some say a half-hour, some ten minutes,' I chuckled. 'Their children were wedded at Angers, at any rate; thus is Anne Neville widowed at sixteen and lies at her sister's house. They must be right doleful together. Isabel mourns her dead child—the one born aboard ship, off the French coast.'

I gave her shreds of gossip; how Isabel's babe had been buried at sea; how it was Richard of Gloucester who persuaded Clarence to leave the ranks of his father-in-law and rejoin his brothers, before Barnet; how the swirling mists of that battle were said by some to be the product of sorcery, by others the benison of God. She drank it all, yawning at my description of the battle blows, but keen to hear everything concerning those of the blood royal and their rebellious kin.

'I did hear,' said she, 'that the Duke of Gloucester hankered to marry Anne of Warwick, time past.'

'He still does.'

She turned to clout a cookboy, who had let a pan of eels in gravy singe. When she came back her face was full of wonder.

'Why, she's under attainder, disgraced,' she murmured.

'Love makes fools of all,' I chaffed. 'And were they not children together at Middleham?'

'So has she vast estates, through her mother the Countess,' she reminded me, sharp at my sentimental drift. A woman of affairs, my mother.

'He might feel kinship, sympathy. You pitied Margaret of Anjou,' I mocked, and she coloured and dealt me a buffet in the chest, laughing.

'We shall see what manner of man he is,' she said. 'I saw him last month, heading the procession, with the banners waving and his Grace smiling behind him. How they differ, Richard and the King! Such a pale, set countenance. So sombre.'

'He's a brave fighter,' I said ungrudgingly. I admired his prowess, but otherwise I preferred Edward. There was a man, full of laughter and love, colour and light. I stole a hot sausage from the cookshop counter and blew on it. 'And a bold leader,' I added.

'And now, you say, he seeks to prove the lover,' said my mother, smiling.

I ate my sausage, good and spicy as it was, thought on Gloucester briefly, tipped him from my thoughts.

'And what of your own affairs of the heart?' I said suddenly, remembering something. 'What of Master Fray?'

'Do not speak of Daniel Fray,' she said, and angry little scars of temper bloomed on her forehead.

'Has he offended you?'

'Certes, he offends me constantly,' she said. 'I'll not speak of it before the knaves.'

She took me to the upper chamber and yielded an intelligence that made my blood simmer like the cookpots. Scarcely had she ceased when one of the kitchen maids intruded a head, saying that there was one without who would speak with her mistress. She admitted someone more like a ferret than any I have seen popping into a badger's hide. A face the colour of curds and eyes like watery rubies, he was no more than nineteen. Hesitant too. He had not even the manners to doff his greasy cap—I lifted it gently from his head with my cane. He cast a glance at me as if unsure of my humour; my mother, too, looked strangely as if she wished I were gone. I asked his business.

'My uncle and master, of the Eagle, sends words for this dame's ears,' he said, scarcely civil, and I laughed, saying: 'Prate of devils and they appear,' for I knew him now as nephew to Fray, the tavern-keeper. An unsavoury house was that, in a mean court off Butchers Lane. They watered the wine there, and harboured thieves. It had offended me at first to hear that Dan Fray dared woo my mother, then I had been amused, to hear how he came creaking lean-shanked into her shop with his declarations, vowing he sought to protect the comely widow. I was confident she could look to herself.

'Well?' I demanded.

He swivelled his red eye at my mother. 'My master your

kinsman desires a final answer,' he said, wriggling his feet about in their worn-out boots.

'You speak of kinship!' I cried, before she could reply. 'What nonsense is this? Daniel Fray is naught to me or mine, and well you know it.'

My mother looked weary.

'He vows he has proof of such, distant as it is, on your father's side,' she said. 'He has shown me letters—deeds of title; Master Priest has read them to me. He cannot make much of them, but there is something of validity.'

Forgeries, I thought. I said sharply: 'Deeds of title?'

'To half this property,' said Fray's nephew, and cast a glance around the parlour where a nice arras hung, gift from some long-deceased lord whom my father had contrived to amuse. Costly it was, woven all over with hawking knights and ladies, and bordered with hounds and grapes. His eyes took inventory; there was a fine glass window on to the street, a small coffer of Spanish chestnut, several carved oaken chairs. My mother was silent. I looked from one face to the other, starting a sweat of incredulous anger.

'My master's a fair man, sir and mistress,' said the youth. 'He bids me acquaint you again of his devotion and seeks your agreement to his proposal.'

To my relief she shook her head.

'I will have none of him.' Her voice was faint but steady. 'As to this claim to half my livelode, it is all fog and mist.'

'He will secure it without you, then,' said the ferret-face, while I gaped at him. 'Choose, dame, and I will bear your message back to my uncle. He would get these affairs settled once and for all.'

I have a temper. Looking at this young oaf, knock-kneed, his doublet foul with ale, then at my mother in her clean trim apron and neat kerchief, I came to the boil and overflowed.

'Get you gone,' I said, my words hot in my throat.

'I will go when I wish,' answered the ferret in a squeaking voice. 'Master Dan has not yet his answer.'

I stepped up close. 'Nor will he get one,' said I in a fury. 'For he sends a puling whelp to do man's work. All you see here is rightly my mother's, by her own labour, and no poxy falsified deed can say otherwise. This shop was hers while your uncle was busy stealing the rings off slain soldiers in France, and you were still at pap.'

He put up his fist to me, and I laughed out loud. I took my staff to his head, and the blood flowed on to my mother's clean boards, while he howled like a dog, folding his arms over his skull.

'Take this message to your master,' I said, and he flew downstairs, through the seething shop and out into the street. I spun his oily cap after him through the window.

I turned back to my mother, triumphant.

'It was well that I came by this day,' I said.

Her hands were trembling. 'I am not so sure,' she said anxiously. 'You should not have struck him—his uncle will be wroth indeed. Oh! and to think that villain spoke me so fair these past months!'

'There'll be no more business from that soapy pack,' I said; but I realized her feelings were wounded—that she had taken some pleasure in thinking she was still a woman to evoke tenderness.

'He will send others,' she said, distressed. 'Men stronger than that boy—he will set this place by the ears; others whispered that he wrought them ill but I didn't believe it.'

'Others?' I said.

'Mistress Petson.' Her lips were tight. 'Some tale of how he claimed she owed him money. She stood fast, and had her windows smashed by night—ruffians that ran too swiftly for the Watch to take them.'

'Extortion! In Chepe!' I cried. 'Certes, I would have thought folk were too well dined here for such ill-humoured tricks.'

'He has not been to dine with me lately—oh, let's have no more ado with it,' she said suddenly, descending again into the sweaty shop. 'I have a marriage party to look to in an hour.'

She squeezed my arm. 'Come back again to see me,' she whispered, and I promised to return soon, advising her to bar her doors by night—though I was secretly well pleased that I had sent Fray's lout off with such a straight answer, and thought we would hear no more of it.

There had been one last assault from the Lancastrians, when the Bastard of Fauconberg, with his force of Kentish men, made an attack on the south gate of London. Lords Essex and Rivers drove him back and held his army in abeyance until the King's advance guard arrived, whereupon Fauconberg took fright and fled to where his ships lay in Sandwich harbour.

Then King Edward sent his brother Gloucester to quell the

Bastard. It seemed no time at all before he returned, with the penitent Fauconberg suing for peace. This was the final campaign. I remember feeling a mixture of gratitude to God and a vague treasonable pity for those who had suffered most; the pawns on a great battle-board, a fierce game that, with real knights toppling, queens and would-be queens befouled with mud and curses.

Old, mad Harry the Sixth lay on a catafalque in St Paul's. I went with the rest to look at the waxen white face of saint or idiot, none would ever know. Still and exposed he was, between the straight figures of a guard of honour. A strangely eerie sight. The church seemed full of ghosts that shrieked silently in fury or torment. I was glad to leave the vaulted quietness and rejoin the sun-drenched crowds outside, now gaping at a new spectacle.

It was the Duke of Gloucester returning from Kent, with Fauconberg riding meekly behind him under the White Boar standard. Gloucester marked the crush of people outside Paul's, turned to his esquire with a question. 'Old Harry's dead,' they were saying. 'He pined and dwined of sheer melancholy.' For an instant I saw Gloucester's face. It whitened, he bit his lip. Some said he loved the saintly, traitorous old fool.

So peace came to England, and though his Grace laboured long of days to restore his shaken government, the merry nights returned; oh yes, we capered. And thus it befell that though I was far from forgetting my mother's anxiety and the threats of Master Dan, I had no chance to visit her for many weeks, because of my duty to the King. To amuse the Princesses was a joy, not a labour; but their mother! Marry, there was scant humour in her. More regal than any born of a long line of monarchs, she seldom thawed to a smile. Great diamonds she wore, and pigeon-blood rubies, Italian collars of silver weeping pearls large as a finger's nail, and more rings even than the French bitch was wont to wear. Mostly her gown was black—she spent hours in the Royal Chapel, and her pale confessors were seen to wander wearily after her wherever she would go.

That summer we rode down to Eltham while Baynard's Castle was being cleansed and I was glad, for I had feared we might move to Greenwich, and I had memories both sweet and sour . . . there it was I used to steal up on to the gallery to talk with the Maiden. Little did she know or care that I could have lost my post through it—each time I skipped away my heart was in my mouth that the King

150

would look for diversion among his fools and find one missing. The Maiden beggared protocol. Once, I brought her up a red apple, I who would have given her rubies, and she tossed the core over the balustrade at Thomas Grey, who turned in anger on his brother Dick, while the Maiden laughed among the shadows like a witless woman. The tears rolled down her face; I marvelled how she wept for a space long after the end of laughter. She would not tell me why.

I tried to guard that little damsel when I had the chance. I know that folk try to make out there's no such thing as love, only barter and bargain, and that women lead us all to Hell, but I loved her. I think she was fond of me, and others must have thought the same. Often I came up against that French-born witch of a friend of hers, that Elysande, who looked sly and mocking at me and spoke of paramours. I would like to have turned her skirts over her head. She was a mischief-weaver, and more than that, for the last I heard of her was in France, where she had flown to the kin of her dead husband, changing her allegiance like a running hare.

We had the jousting and the games at Eltham. Despite his hair shirt, Anthony Rivers excelled once more at all things; and when they had packed up the tents and banners and loaded the carts with all the groaning knights who had been maimed in the fierce sport, we returned to Westminster. I rode by the serjeant of the minstrels, Master Alexander Carlile. King Edward was very agreeable to him; it was the serjeant who had roused him in the middle of the night when John Neville's men were breaking down the gates at Doncaster. Doubtless this swift action saved the lives of his Grace and Lords Hastings, Rivers and Gloucester. He told me of that wild crossing to the Low Countries, and the five months' maddening exile in Bruges and Flushing.

Also we spoke of the jousting lately ended, and of old tourneys, reliving with a little mirth the most famous occasion of all: that contest between Rivers and Antoine of Burgundy, a day nearly ending in disaster.

'His Grace the Bastard of Burgundy vowed my lord used illegal harness, and weapons of trickery,' said Master Carlile.

'When he did but fight with a nag's head,' I gibed. For a time we conjured again the whole spectacle: the loges at Smithfield blazing with tapestries and the satin and silk of the nobility; King Edward in purple with the Garter; foreign diplomats dotting the stands like a pox—the ambassador of Charolais, come to finalize plans for the marriage of Edward's sister Margaret with Duke Charles; Olivier de la Marche, the

Burgundian chronicler, anxious to trap every moment; Butcher Tiptoft of Worcester, Arbiter of Chivalry for the day, smiling in complacent gladness. Then the preliminary skirmishing with swords, dismay and scandal. For when the two knights tilted fiercely at each other, the Burgundian's horse rammed its head into Lord Rivers's saddle and fell dead. The noble rider lay still, pinned beneath the destrier's weight, while the crowd rose with a thundering roar of disbelief.

'Do you recall how exceedingly displeased he seemed?'

'Yea, for when his Grace asked if he wished another mount, he replied it was "no season" and retired.'

' 'Twas well he was unharmed,' I said. I had at that moment remembered that even then Warwick was conniving in France with King Louis.

Riding through fields of harvest, the hay-apple smell sweet and bitter, we spoke of Warwick, and as night follows day, we spoke of his widow, immured in Beaulieu Sanctuary, and of his youngest daughter Anne, whom Richard Gloucester hankered to marry.

'I think his Grace will have Anne Neville,' said Master Carlile, with an unshakable air.

'I heard the King forbade the match,' I said cautiously.

'Yes, while her father lived and the Duke·would not go against him; but now he seeks his reward, and he's earned it, certes. Though George of Clarence is wroth—he is her self-appointed guardian. Vast estates she has. But the King loves Gloucester.'

Something in this tickled my spleen. I remembered the little Neville well; thin and fair and flaxen, with a gentle smile and small, anxious hands. 'Now he seeks his reward,' Master Carlile had said. Her mother's lands were forfeit to the Crown. With a sudden distaste I thought of Dan Fray, who had talked of love to my mother, and to what purpose, and then envisaged Gloucester, distant and frowning these past weeks. I had seen him wandering about the Palace at evening, preoccupied with what thoughts one could only guess at. George had married Isabel Neville—Richard's almost perverse loyalty had curbed his own ambition. As we rode I wondered whether there was a spark of tenderness in him for poor, beleaguered Anne, and saw the red eyes of greed in the face of Fray's nephew, sweeping up the contents of my mother's parlour with a glance.

'He has not seen her of late,' I said. The serjeant looked oddly at me.

'So? He saw her, and so did I, after Tewkesbury. I had

blown my last attack and the enemy were cut to pieces or drowning in the stream; my lord Stanley came to take the French Queen. She had just learned that her son was slain. By my loyalty! her screams rang in my head for days.'

'And Warwick's daughter?'

'Still, she sat, and the colour of a tallow dip. Eyes open, seeing naught. Then up rode Gloucester—harness shining with blood—even his horse's coat black with it—and he doffed his helm and looked at her. Hair wild, eyes rimmed with blood and mire on his face. And the maid, corpse-mute, staring as if he were the foul fiend.'

'Did he speak?' I asked.

'Nay, not a word. Yet he looked at her, for a long space, with a strange look. Then he turned and rode off to join the King, while Anne was taken under the protection of Duke George, to her sister's house. The Neville affairs are entirely in his hands, so he says. Thus her inheritance lies safe within his walls, until the maiden shall be married.'

I had noted the dark glances between Clarence and Gloucester. The picture was emerging.

'And yet,' he continued, 'I think my lord of Gloucester will have his way. For the King's Grace is inclined to dismiss Clarence's right of wardship as nebulous.'

I saw life as a spread chessboard neatly partitioned, though some of the black ran into the white at times. It shifted and wavered in my vision. The smallest pawn was Anne of Warwick, a little ivory figure. The Maiden and I were not on the board—we were of no importance, and I was glad of it.

Then suddenly we had reached the top of Shooters Hill, and there was London, again lying like a wanton along the breast of the swift river, while in the distance all the green turned blue as it merged with the hills of Hampstead and Highgate. Down the slope we came with a throng of people all hurrying to be within the walls by sunset. Their frantic haste put me in mind of a rhyme. I took out my tablets to snare it, and the fortunes of the nobility faded and were gone.

The Master of the Revels had his eye on me. I knew it, and he knew that I knew it. He was minded that my jests were too bold, and would have had me booted from the court had not the King unwittingly shielded me with his ready smile. None could gainsay his Grace in matters of pleasure, and I was a very small matter for dissent. Though there were a few, deeply devout, who would fain have called the Church

153

down about our ears, with their rumblings that we trouveres —to wit, 'jesters, jugglers, histrios, dancing women and harlots'—were lewd leaders to damnation and the Devil. Strong words these, for the belly of one who worked hard for his money. I would have found solace in giving the Revels Master my task for a day. He would have taken his bed a wearier man, and stiff of limb.

One late summer evening he was watching me, and he was robed and regal and ready to frown. We, the joculatores, skilled in singing, in recounting of fable spiced with mime and posture, had been summoned to the King's chamber. It was an island of informality betwixt the outer hall of reception and the inner mysteries of Edward's bedroom. Within this middle haunt the King would snatch his pleasure after hours of wrangling in the chair of Council. He sat fair-humouredly, his astute brain free to wander, like his well-shaped hands to the dish of grapes and walnuts near his couch. A few of his intimates stood about him. There was a lady there, Elizabeth Lucey, whose husband had met his death fighting for the Royal House . . . the King made much of her. Did I not say he rewarded loyalty well? In her butterfly headgear and gown of sapphire silk, she looked queenly. There is treason. Lord Hastings had his gaze on her, as she sat on her little velvet cushion, and his smooth jaw quivered with the fullness of his thoughts.

And the Master of the Revels had his eye on me.

I fancied I excelled myself at reciting one of the *Gesta Romanorum*, one of those tales fashioned by the monk Pierre Bercheur at the convent of Saint Eloi. Latin lends well to a double meaning. The King beckoned me nearer. I shot a sly complacent glance at my mentor as I drew a new pack of cards from my sleeve. I threw them high in a rainbow skein from one hand to the other. Some charlatans use a silk thread through the pack: I first mastered the trick when I was eight years old and was beaten if I dared to let them drop thereafter.

'If you, most dread Sire, would . . .'

'Take a card,' laughed Edward. He reached out his fingers. He liked cards. Dame Elizabeth Lucey stretched her fair neck like a flower. I palmed the Death Card quickly ere he should take it. Kings must only see and hear what is good. The royal astrologer stood near, fingering his pearl reliquary. Edward's hand hovered over the blind, spread fan of cards. A distant sound, growing louder, came to our ears. Heads turned at the noise of two sharp voices outside. A henchman

154

tapped, entered, knelt. He announced that the Dukes of Clarence and Gloucester sought audience. Edward raised his eyebrows.

'Bid them come.'

I stayed, one foot lightly on the dais, my eyes on my cards. Under my lids I could study George and Dickon as they entered. Clarence came first, laughing a little ill-temperedly. He flew the pink flag of temper on his cheek, but he was full of grace as he kissed the King's hand.

'Talk! talk! by my faith, it's thirsty work,' he remarked. Crossing to a side table, he lifted and drained a cup of hypocras. Edward's keen eyes smiled.

'Come, my lord, here's something to intrigue—a new piece of magic from our friend. He seeks to blind us with swift skill.'

Clarence leaned over me. The smell of wine was a heavy song on his breath. His bright hair fell about his rosy cheeks. A young pagan god was he, tall and gilded, but alas! the hand that touched the cards was over-plump, and trembled.

'Good fellow, what is it?'

Edward said softly: 'A game of chance, fair prince,' and for a brief instant the plump hand was rigid, and I knew that even my little diversion had its use, the reminder of old sins.

George laughed too loud. He straightened his back. 'I'm done with such,' he said with a candour that made me squirm. 'Besides, I am lucky in love—' he turned to include the silent Gloucester in his charming smile. 'Therefore I should not meddle with these nice tricky pastimes, neither will I.'

Gloucester moved forward into my sight. White as a ghost, more slender than ever, he looked as if he could be broken in two. His hair shone dark, and his eyes smouldered. Quietly he said: 'Your Grace, I would speak with you on a matter of gravest importance.'

'Concerning?' said Edward gently.

Richard glanced at my intruding figure almost with hatred. He fiddled with his finger-rings. In the privacy of our stable, we fools often mimicked him; but then we aped everyone, from the Dowager Duchess downwards; it was sport. Discreetly I huddled from the step, and watched him. I would have thought he might have looked happier, for lately he had again earned the King's praise. There had been trouble on the Scottish border. The North was a seat of unrest, and the King was cautious in his attitude to Lord Percy, Earl of Northumberland. Thus he had accorded his youngest brother the Wardenship of the North, all dead Warwick's commands. Richard had resigned his offices of Chief Justice and Chamberlain of Wales to the new Earl of Pembroke and now, with his northern holdings went Warwick's estates: Sheriff Hutton, Penrith and, above all, his beloved Middleham. He should have looked happier, but by his demeanour, these things were not enough. Something vexed him, and judging by Clarence's uncomfortable high spirits, I knew what it was. Earl Warwick's lands were Richard's, but not the Countess's, and the marriage ring was not yet on her daughter's finger. I heard Anne Neville's name, and knew that Gloucester still hankered. Little Anne, buffeted and tossed from the arms of the fierce, arrogant Silver Swan to those of the strange, unsmiling Silver Boar. Anne, who had looked with terror on the bloody Richard at Tewkesbury and who trailed the fetters of vast wealth. I glared at Gloucester, and catching his long dark eye, hastily turned my baleful look into a fool's grimace.

I was thinking that I must go back and see my mother, and that all men were acquisitive save for myself, who would have wedded the Maiden in the shift she stood up in, when a sudden explosion from the dais came.

'O Jesu! Cannot you, my lords, be at peace one with another?' The King's jovial mood was gone. He sat bolt upright on the couch, glowering at his brothers. Elizabeth Lucey scuttled off her cushion and fled. Lord Hastings studied his nails, while Thomas Grey smirked openly from behind the dais.

'Sire,' said Richard, 'how shall I live happily with one who will not give me answer?'

The King turned his fierce look upon Clarence.

'How say you, my lord?' he demanded. 'It seems the lady Anne is no longer in your household. Where shall my brother find her?'

Clarence turned up his eyes. 'Fair Sire,' he said eventually, 'it grieves me, by my loyalty, that I cannot ease our noble brother. Though I know he desires the lady my sister-in-law, how can I help? For, since your Grace would have it that I own no wardship over her—her whereabouts are surely no concern of mine.'

George's tongue was gold. This statement was a mingling of airy simplicity and innocent amazement. Richard kept silence under the King's troubled gaze.

'Well, sir?' said Edward.

'I'm of the opinion,' said Richard with difficulty, 'that she is concealed somewhere.'

Clarence laughed gently. 'Likely, good brother,' he murmured. 'But 'tis naught to me. London is a great place, likewise York, or Canterbury or any other fair town. She is but a little maid,' he mused.

He came over to me, where I still held the cards fanned out.

'Let us play one game of hazard, Dickon,' he said kindly, and under cover of his sleeve flicked up the cards for a lightning look. Richard stood mute, his hands behind his back. I could almost hear his thoughts, as the Countess of Warwick's lands, so nearly gained, were slipping from his grasp.

'Come!' George said. 'Won't you tempt Dame Fortune? Draw a card, and see if the omens are good!'

Gloucester was silent.

'Then I must play alone,' sighed George, and with thumb and finger tweaked out a card. I knew what it was for I had placed them; so did he, for he had cheated. Richard's face, when confronted by the Queen of Diamonds, betrayed little, and the jest went sour. He made an obeisance to the frowning King, and quit the room. The minstrels quietly gathered up their instruments.

'Certes, I found a lady,' murmured Clarence. 'A grey-eyed lady for my noble brother, but he misliked her.' I followed the tall prince in the wake of a soft French air that drifted from his lips and on the terrace waylaid him. There I showed him a little game—played with three walnut shells and a pea, and he achieved much skill with it, laughed for full five minutes, and gave me a mark.

Richard had gone, tight-lipped, down to the armoury, or I would have sought to please him with it too. Would I though? There was no humour in him, and I knew I would only be wasting my time.

Robert Hawkins played the shawm, John Green the lute, and exceptionally tuneful were they, in sounds both sacred and secular. Also they had another love, that being gambling. So, through my lord of Gloucester's whim, I had a wager of two marks with John, and the price of a good pair of hose with Robert, and I would have had the stakes doubled had it not been for their cautiousness, so sure of victory was I.

'My lord went down into Southwark two days ago,' Robert said uneasily. 'He took with him a train of henchmen, two knights and some fellows in jacks and sallets—while yesterday he was combing the ward of Bishopsgate and had an hour's talk with the Prioress of St Mary Spital.'

157

I laughed merrily and measured my leg against his, for the new hose.

'I will have them in green,' I said. 'And sure enough 'tis a fool that will place them on my feet. For does his Grace seek to find the lady all among the Bishop of Winchester's geese?'

This was a time-honoured jest amongst us. Once, the bagnios that housed the whores over the river paid rent to the Bishop's bailiffs, and brought him in a tidy sum.

'Today he went alone, and on foot,' said John. 'With but two squires to guard him.' He sighed. 'Jesu! he loves her.'

'There's no such thing as love,' I said. And I tried to believe it, for my own heart's peace.

John took up his lute. His voice was pure, castrato, silver, to set the hair on your head tingling.

> *Belle, qui tiens ma vie*
> *Captive de tes yeux,*
> *Qui ma l'âme ravie*
> *Ton souris gracieux.*
> *Vientôt me secourir*
> *Ou me faudra mourir.'*

'Pretty,' said I. 'But he will never find her. He may have slain her husband at Tewkesbury, but she'll stay widowed if my lord of Clarence has half the wit . . .'

John rested his lute on his knee. 'I never knew it was Gloucester that killed the French Queen's son,' he said, interested.

'My cousin was in the battle's thick,' I boasted. 'Were not the young princes rivals for Anne of Warwick?'

I embroidered, as Alexander Carlile had done, and my colours were even brighter than his. So is history made. Detail and truth both done to death for drama's sake, with hard bright fact concealed under the pretty swirl of histrionics. I am no worse, no better. Others have done it. But so is truth butchered, for the sake of a song.

They hung on my words, and they composed a sad little tune.

'His horse's bardings—black with the gore of the fallen.'

This I liked well, and should it be the lady's husband's blood, splashed up from Gloucester's blade, an even more thrilling ballad could be fashioned. Unluckily for me, a few words of this lay (which smacked of unchivalry) crept to my cousin's ears. He sent a boy to fetch me to where he was practising at the butts. I watched him admiringly as he drew his bow. Muscle the size of an orange blossomed under the fine hide of each sleeve. The thrum and swish of his dart caused the heads of the watching esquires to turn; against the cloudless sky it cleaved an arc, striking the target just south of the bull. My cousin swore softly, but I clapped hands and cried bravo. Anthony Rivers took up his turn, standing a good yard back from my cousin's mark, and loosed a clean quill. Under the cries of acclaim, my cousin said softly: 'So you deem yourself a chronicler, kinsman,' and flashed his steel-grey eyes at me. I was a little put out and busied myself applauding Lord Stanley's shot.

'I've heard your account of Tewkesbury,' he continued drily. 'I knew naught of my little cousin's war-lust. Mayhap I can arrange a battle for you to see all first-hand.'

The thought of fighting made me quake. 'Sir, what have I said?'

'Lies, tales of murder in the field,' he growled.

So I stood on one leg and sang:

> 'I saw a codfish corn sow,
> And a worm a whistle blow,
> And a pie treading a crow,
> I will have the whetstone, and I may.'

'Fool,' he muttered.

'Yea, 'tis my calling,' said I.

'You may yet have the whetstone,' he said. 'Hung about your neck for perjuring my account of a bloody battle nobly fought.'

'I'll do penance,' I whined. Only last week I'd seen a convicted liar in the market-place, with folk sharpening their knives on the great stone around his throat.

'Sit, then,' he commanded. 'I'll tell you of Tewkesbury.'

So I sat, and the sun was hot, and I closed my eyes the better to hear his tale; and woke with a jump to a cool breeze and his voice, quieter now, saying: 'Thus ended the House of Lancaster. Not, good friend, with silly tales of stabbings over a maid's hand, but in dust, and heat, and honour.'

'It's a fine story,' I said, blinking. He looked so sternly at me I wondered if he knew I'd been asleep. All he said was: 'More credible than yours,' and I answered meekly:

'I will have the whetstone, kinsman,' and left him. I had thought to mention Dan Fray and my mother, but I thought he might wax wroth at my clouting the nephew and risking a brawl, so I thought better of it and went to visit her myself.

The cookshop was hotter than ever. The smell of dead dinners clung to the buckram hangings of the kitchen-chamber and the rushes were greasy with fat-splashes. I leaned on one side of the fireplace until the cook, with a heavy politeness, told me I was in his way. So I retreated to watch all the diversities of cunning employed by the cook-knaves. One was preparing a venison frumenty; he had leched the meat into strips and had his wheaten soup made ready, to which he was adding egg yolks, salt and sugar. Another, more ambitious, struggled uneasily with a *fylettes en galantyne*, stirring chopped roast pork and onions into beef broth boiled with pepper, cinnamon, cloves and mace. Old Mary was grinding fresh brawn in a mortar. I watched her temper it with almond meats and strain the mess into an earthenware dish, boiling the mixture with sugar and cloves, thickening it with cinnamon and ginger. The near-solid mass took shape—a hare, was it? a hog? I was about to ask her, when my mother appeared, beckoning me from half-way up the stairs. In the upper room, I knew there had been trouble. Her face said it.

'He's been back,' I murmured.

'Yea, and none of your persuasions have swayed the uncle, for he came himself, and snared me in my own parlour, chasing me round the table. I was distressed enough to go say an Ave and a Pater at your father's tomb, I who had his Month's Mind kept all these past years.'

Rageful and sorely anxious, I said: 'You should have married Butcher Gould. You know as well as I how widows are fair game. Even now 'tis not too late to get you to the Minories.'

'Never!' she cried. 'I am not shaped for the cloister, and I'll marry none. This—' she gestured around—'is my all. 'Twill take more than Master Fray to drive me out.'

I gave her a moment to cool and she ran downstairs; she said she smelled burning and was anxious for a special order —a dozen eel-and-grape pies, coming to their peak. When she returned I asked: 'Has his nephew's pate healed yet? Tell me, that I may break it again.'

'I feared for that, too. He talked of summonsing you for assault on the lad. He held this over me if I did not submit.'

'I'm in his Grace's service,' I said wildly. Even so, I thought of John Davy, late favourite of the King, who had had his hand cut off for striking a man in front of King's Bench at Westminster Hall. I saw myself fleeing again into Sanctuary, wading into the sea after my forty days' grace crying: 'Passage, for the love of God and King Edward!' like any common felon. And the King would take unkindly to my fleeing the judgment of his Mayor—hiding beneath the clergy's mantle. Then, with relief, I remembered that Fray, with a tavern full of whores in their striped rays and Lancastrian spies thick as roaches, would be ill-advised to seek a lawsuit. All ale-sellers were reckoned guilty, whatever the matter.

'He would find no sympathy at the sessions, I'd dare my next feastday wage,' I said. 'We'll have him for trespass— we'll appeal to the Gild. He has been uttering threats against your person.'

An unwilling smile curved her mouth.

'The Gild is not much concerned with personal matters,' she murmured. 'Anyway, he said that all he offered was an honourable proposal of marriage—no threat has passed his lips—he did but offer me protection.'

'By God!' I said sourly. 'He is as cunning as Clarence! Naught to lay hold of, and in his ways as stubborn as a mule.'

She was instantly distracted.

'Ah, poor young Gloucester!' she said. 'All the City watch for him daily. My boys were in Smithfield yesterday and saw him questioning the horse-copers. Billingsgate likewise, among the fish merchants. He has paid his respects to every Abbess in town. The lady Anne has vanished from human sight, and Gloucester's like one of Arthur's knights in search of the Grail.'

'Cast in solid gold and weighty with gems,' I remarked.

'So!' she said keenly. 'Is there love?'

'Barter,' said I.

'What of Clarence?'

I told her about the playing cards and she grimaced. 'A bad jest,' and then: 'But I would not speak against Clarence outside these walls.' She gestured, east.

'Three doors down,' she said. 'Although they are under Duke George's patronage, I mislike that woman. She whispered that I gave short weight in my mutton pasties and since Corpus Christi last our dealings have been few.'

She laughed at my indignation.

'Put up your staff, before you break more heads. It will be a long while before they hang my pies about my neck on Cornhill. Words can't hurt me when I know my merchandise is good.'

'We have strayed,' I said. 'What had Fray to say finally?'

'He gave me till Michaelmas for the banns to be cried. I told him the same answer, so he waved his plaguey deeds of title before my face. I said he would have to bring this before the justices of this ward and the courts are jammed with suits. We shall have a few months' breathing space.'

'But you can't go on like this!' I cried. 'Tell him to go to the Devil!'

She squared her shoulders. 'That was my last injunction. I'll take what he brings, and I'll best him.' I leaped from the table and embraced her.

'If there's trouble . . .'

'Can I call on you?' she said timidly.

'Yes, ask Butcher Gould to send a boy to the Palace—the King thinks much of him since he succoured Elizabeth in Sanctuary. They'll give a message.'

'Only if there's real mischief.'

'I shall come straightway.' To end a disquieting hour with jesting, I told her of my wager, and bade her commend me to her silkmaid at Michaelmas to make me a costly new hose; that is, if the Duke of Gloucester had not found his lady by then.

I walked down East Chepe into the widening strip of Candlewick Street with its lines of mercers' and drapers' shops displaying rich cloth; then, because I had time to spare, strolled up Tower Street. I stopped for a swift mazer of ale in the Boar's Head. Sir John Howard was there, entertaining strangers; I made way with full courtesy, and the commonalty in turn fell back for me. The crenellated turrets of the Tower stood stark against the haze of the September afternoon. Within that building I had often entertained the King. My mind turned idly to the woman who doubtless now paced up and down behind one of those faraway slits in the great white fortress. Margaret of Anjou: I'd heard that her hair had turned grey from the loss of her son. I wondered if she wept, too, for old Harry. And Somerset—Beaufort had been her last link with a dead love; men said his father, the old Earl, had bedded with the French Queen. Like Owen Tudor and Queen Katherine.

Thinking of the slain Prince, I thought again of Anne Neville, Richard Gloucester, and the wager. I had given John and Robert until Michaelmas, and knew my money safe. He would never find her. Idly I wondered where she was, and decided she had got herself out of England—but to whom? In my mind I saw her little, childish face, blonde-framed. I had seen it often at court before the rift with Warwick; to deem her friendless made me rather sad.

That evening I brought a goat into the Hall and made a parody of John Lydgate's 'Little Short Ditty against Horns'. I dressed the beast in a hennin filched from a Flemish dancing maid, and there was much mirth and not a few red faces under the extravagant headgear of the court ladies. I plied my craft with gusto and genuine feeling—I have thought it a shame to conceal a woman's hair, her fairest possession—and when I plucked out a few hairs from the goat's brow, aping a tiring wench, and caused it to bleat and butt me in the nether end—the company laughed like demons. Therefore one did not heed the few glum and abstracted persons who sat, toying with their trenchers and staring into air. Richard Gloucester was one of these. He had come in late, a little footsore I swear and glad to be seated, his face worn and weary and unsmiling. My own magical powers took hold of me and I half-killed myself trying to make him laugh, but to no avail. By the end of the entertainment I had the strangest feeling of kinship with him. For I, too, had wandered many weeks in search of my love, and I remembered how people had chaffed me. This feeling grew stronger until I reminded myself of Gloucester's motives; I drew a callous skin over my soul and thought of how Anne Neville, if she remained hidden, would make of me a fashionable man.

Neither did the Queen smile. When the Maiden was at court, we would talk of Elizabeth—I got some sly kind of sport from the days of Grafton Regis, when food was sparse and the rod heavy on my poor sweeting's back. King Edward's wooing—ah, God! that sweet, innocent conversation:

'Lady Grey went for a walk in Whittlebury Forest and was nearly run down by the King's horse.'

Marry, what would Lady Grey expect? Everyone knew that Whittlebury was a royal chase. If that were an accident that she were there on that day, holding a fatherless boy by each hand under the Queen's Oak, then I had six toes on either foot. All sorrowful beauty would she be, suing piteously for the restoration of Bradgate, her children's inheritance. They had been dispossessed following the defeat of Lancaster at St Alban's. Sir John Grey had been knighted by Mad Harry at Colney in the spring of 1461, but had died of his wounds shortly afterwards. No wonder food was short at Grafton; Elizabeth Woodville had been near destitution. Fortune smiles on the fair. And the not so fair. As early as 1461 the King had affectionately considered the benefit of Jacquetta Duchess of Bedford, his cozen's mother. He paid her an annual stipend of 300 marks—and 100 livres in advance. Lust makes fools of all. Even Kings.

I bowed low before the royal pair, and the goat got loose and bolted round the hall, sweeping a tablecloth off with its horns. The Master of the Revels made a note in his book and looked at me, and I gave him obeisance.

In the space between the end of dinner, and supper at four, John, Robert and I, and others employed in the sweet pursuit of do-naught, would gather near the entry to Westminster Hall. There we would watch the world and his wife, and some exceeding pretty wives there were, in truth. We stood under the Clock House, and as the last deep note throbbed and burgeoned and died (and we waited for our hearing to return) Lady Elizabeth Lucey rode out from the Palace on a splendid bay. Green velvet she wore, and her headgear was almost as high as the Clochard spire with its three giant bells which, men said, soured all the drink in the town. John affected a swoon at sight of the lady. Robert said, soft and knowing:

'His Grace had me make music for that sweet face in his inner chamber.'

We trusted one another. I said: 'Love songs, I doubt not.'

He nodded. 'Well, the Queen had the costliest new device. Italianate silverwork collar and baubles for her ears—a fair bargain.'

'Riches or love, which would you?' asked Robert. I thought of Gloucester and shrugged, saying: ' 'Tis all the same, it seems.'

None could resist the King; I reckoned no surprise at it, so beautiful a person was he, and for the sheer pleasure of the words on my tongue, I quoted gently:

'Now is the Rose of Rouen grown to great honour
Therefore sing we every one blessed be that flower
I warn ye every one that he shall understand
There sprang a Rose in Rouen that spread to England
Had not the Rose of Rouen been, all England had been dour,
Y-blessed be the time God ever spread that flower.'

So we sang Edward's Coronation song, and continued to watch: the serjeants of the Crown in their silken hoods and the lawyers in long gowns of striped ray hurrying in and out the door of the great Hall of Westminster; jammed with suits, as my mother had said, like any other City Court. That splendid building was erected by King William the Red, and rebuilt in magnificence by Richard of Bordeaux; whose wife was Anne. The fellow Gloucester was on my mind again, and I shook him off like a flea. There were comings and goings from the Hall; above was the Court of Chancery, and the busy Exchequer and Star Chamber, womb of many stern laws. The Court of Common Pleas too lay within, and King's Bench, where Edward had sat for three days together at the start of his reign. All about milled the plaintiffs and defendants, the suitors and witnesses, the red robes of aldermen mingling with the commonalty's poor worsted. Flemings, in their sad-coloured smocks and hanging liripipes hawked pins and spectacles and fine felt hats, while nearby an amateur fiddler scraped a hideous noise for groats. Fierce-eyed cook-knaves, their manners more thrusting even than in Eastchepe, blustered of fine fare at the gate, clutching at hastening lawyers with their cries. Wretches hang that jurymen may dine.

Barefoot, travel-seamed, in a dust-grey habit, a Franciscan touched my sleeve. He gave me a blessing. 'Sir, I seek the London lodging of my house.'

'You'll hear the Jesus bells of St Paul's, Father,' I told him. 'North of Paul on Newgate you'll find your church and cloister.'

'And the library?' His weary eyes lit up. 'That which the Sun of Marchandy, Sir Richard Whittington, so generously endowed?'

I nodded. 'You've travelled far?'

'From Norwich.' He fingered his wooden crucifix. 'God's mercy on all there.'

I heard the inrush of breath behind me.

'Plague,' I said softly . . . He smiled wanly as John and Robert shrank from him.

'Fear naught,' he murmured. 'Weeks I lay, my bones dissolving to water, but the Lord spared me. I am whole again.'

I felt for a coin—he was not importunate, and it was luck to fill his wooden bowl. 'God be good to your house,' I said.

A slender dark shadow fell across us. I looked into the face of the Duke of Gloucester and saw it to be weary and grim with a look of restless days and nights. The Franciscan's bowl was still extended and Richard dropped a gold piece and bowed his head briefly, passing on. The friar looked after him wistfully.

'*Benedicite*,' he whispered.

'His Grace of Gloucester,' I told him.

'I have seen him before, my son,' he said gently. 'Two years ago, before all the troubles in this realm, he came to Our Lady of Walsingham with the King. I spoke with him then, though he could not have remembered me.'

But he had remembered him, I thought. As the Friar blessed us and moved away, I wondered deeply. What manner of man was Richard? There was no doubt in my mind: after two years, he had given recognition to an impoverished and anonymous friar. For some reason I began to feel much incensed. I heard the others whispering.

'He should not have come to London,' Robert said grimly. 'Death can be carried—by God, I didn't know they had plague in Norwich.'

'Nor I,' whispered John, all jelly-trembling.

'You should wear the bezoar stone,' I said, laughing again, and I fingered my talisman, smooth and round within my pouch. While I jested and saw their courage returning, I felt cold, thinking of the sudden crippling dizziness that assailed a man even in the ale-house; the orange-sized hard swelling in the armpit, the black vomit, the fires of Hell . . .

So I comforted them.

'*Carpe diem,*' Robert said: 'When his Grace sent us to play at Bungay six weeks gone, I heard no talk of plague at Norwich, for I and the King's bearward were only speaking of sickness.'

'They had no plague in Norwich,' said John, 'since August five years past, when hundreds died. Mistress Paston's household left town for fear of it.'

'One case,' Robert argued. 'The Lady Eleanor Butler. She died in the house of the Carmelites three years ago.'

'That was not the plague,' John insisted. 'At first they thought it lung fever—but she died bewitched—no prayers or simples could aid her. They said she courted death, and went willingly.'

'What a talk for a fine day!' I cried. 'Pestilence, and tombs, and white faces, and my lord of Gloucester wandering the streets like a walking curse. All be merry, as I!' and I snatched a spectacles from a Flemish pedlar, donned them and, blinded instantly, walked smack into a wall.

'Patch, I mislike this wager of ours,' said Robert.

'So you'd withdraw,' I said. 'You have not the wherewithal to pay me when I win.'

'Nay,' said Robert. He thought it too sorry a matter for gambling on. The Lady Anne was the Lord knew where, and her mother, Countess of Warwick, was in durance in the Sanctuary of Beaulieu, and it was, in effect, her money we were gaming on.

'She has petitioned the Commons that she has never done aught to offend the King; she has sought safe-conduct in vain, all her estates being forfeit. She has written most piteously to the Queen's Grace, the Duchess of York, the King's daughters, and the Dowager Duchess of Bedford, all in her own hand in the absence of clerks. She tells of great affection between herself and her daughter Anne, and craves her whereabouts. What we are about seems knavish,' he said lamely.

'God's Passion!' I cried. 'What harm can it do?' John looked down, and shuffled his feet.

'I too,' he said. 'Last night I sang a song, and incurred my lord of Gloucester's displeasure, for he looked at me with a most terrible look.'

He raised his pure boy's voice and sang a dolorous French song so beautiful it made me want to howl like a wolf. People passing smiled with joy.

'Sing it in English,' I said. 'I thought you attended the *scholae minstrallorum* in Paris—yet your accent mazes me utterly.'

He reddened. 'I had ado with many Southerners,' he said.

'Alas, of you I should indeed complain
If it please you not that I see you again
My love, who has my soul enchained.

For without I see you wherever I be
All I behold displeases me
Nor, until then, shall I sated be.'

He spoke the words.

'It loses pith in the translation.'

I thought of the Maiden, and the sun went behind a cloud.

Butcher Gould's 'prentice rode a sweating palfrey, and the beast was nearly done. He had ridden hard to Westminster Palace, nearly a league's distance, and was short of breath himself, while the horse, its sides pumping in and out, stood making water on the cobbles outside the Palace gate, a thing forbidden in the meanest streets. I had thrown my cloak on inside out in my frenzy, and was clad in my worst suiting, for I had that evening been in rehearsal—trying out the dramatization of Ovid's *Art of Love*, with many effects *ad libitum*, and I had no mind for ruining good clothes by rolling on the floor with Flemish Jeane, so ill-prepared for a night's foray was I. I had not yet dared ask the boy what kind of trouble was afoot—the one gasped word was enough.

I had been bedwards and on my way to the panterer's to get my bread and ale and candle-ends when the message came. The King was sitting late in Council; there had been no entertainment. The gateman grumbled as he let me out, but he had that very day taken two shillings from me at dice so I clattered unrebuked on my mare into the September night to where Gould's boy waited. Together we rode in the direction of the Strand. There was a last gleam in the sky as we reached the Temple Bar, but the sergeant closed the gate behind us and I was fast in the City for the night. So be it, I thought. If she needs me, I will risk reprimand. Our horses' hooves crashed on the cobbles in a dangerous, slippery ride. Few people were abroad; only the cressets of the Watch flickering on the edge of Candlewick Street, and the occasional ragged bundle in the gutter, groaning under a hunger-dream. Few people; that is, until we came into Eastchepe and saw a fair crowd. Then I knew, with sinking belly, what kind of mischief this was. The most dread enemy, after plague. Outside my mother's shop I threw my reins to one of the gawping crowd and ran into the fierce light of flames that feasted on dry timber, chuckled over greasy rushes, and roared approval as they fed.

My mother was wondrous calm. She was marshalling affairs, standing at the head of the line, swinging each bucket of water as it came to her hand through the blazing cookshop window. It looked as if the fire had been started just within, under the sill, and the frame was already destroyed. Now and then loose slivers of glass crashed to the ground. The lintel of the doorpost had caught. I seized a bucket, just as the cart drawn by two unquiet horses ground to a halt on iron wheels. 'Good man!' I cried to the driver, and filled my bucket from the slopping barrels aboard the wain. Others, silent and grimed, bent alongside me. Mistress Petson, shameless in her bedwrap, her long grey hair flying, stood wringing her hands, and I yelled to her to come fill a pail, but she seemed to have lost her reason. The frightened horses backed and plunged, so that the water barrels overflowed. Great wet patches flowed on to the cobbles, blood-red from the fire's reflection. The neighbours worked tirelessly—a swing, a splash, a deafening hiss as water fought flame. Yet the fire grew. I looked up to see the latten sign above the doorway bending in the heat, the whole square of metal drooping like a defeated banner, the gay colours blackening. A great terrible rage took hold of me. I fought my way to my mother's side.

'This is devil's work!'

'Not the devil, but his henchman.' She swung her bucket—the fire spat mockingly. I looked hard into a leaping flame and wished I saw Fray's tortured face in its midst. 'He warned me,' she gasped. 'God's curse on him.'

The barrels were empty again. With painful sloth, the wagon turned in the narrow street and made for the conduit in lumbering haste. But all the while the fire raged madly. All around were anxious faces.

'The whole street will go,' I heard.

'Yeah, by cock!'

'Mother of God, how slow it is!' And two or three ran up the street to meet the approaching cart, filling their pails before the terrified horses had halted, racing back to cast the pitifully small streams of water through the roaring doorway. Someone had foreseen to save divers belongings: I saw the arras hastily rolled and leaning against the wall. The knights still hawked upon it, the grapes still bloomed. My mother's little chestnut coffer sat impassively on the cobbles.

The cookboys were doing their best, and I joined them in beating at the flames with strips of buckram torn from the walls. One of them, Walter Cleeve, whom I had ever thought half-wit, was worse than useless. In fact, when the rats, disturbed by the heat, started to run out of the doorway in dark, firelit streaks, he set his terrier on to them, crying: "Sa, sa, cy, avaunt, sohow!' like a lord in King Edward's otter-chase. I turned and dealt him a great buffet, and shoved a pail in his hand, just as the night Watch arrived, sternly demanding that firehooks be used. My mother pleaded with them.

'Sirs, don't pull it down—the roof remains untouched! Sirs, we'll save it!' She choked on a hot gust of smoke. I looked up to see billowing black blotting out the narrow gap of sky between the houses. They could not pull down the shop. The smarting in my eyes had naught to do with smoke. Again the water-cart trundled up—willing hands dipped and threw and dipped and wiped their brows, and cursing mingled with the pluming black haze.

My mother grasped my arm. 'The well!' she screamed.

I shook my head, dull, uncomprehending. 'We have no well,' I muttered, but she pointed to where, three doors down, the woman who said my mother gave short weight, who enjoyed the Duke of Clarence's patronage, was calmly soaking her own doorframe with water.

'She has a well in her courtyard—hurry,' and I ran off, halting grimy and dishevelled before the lady, who looked at me aloofly.

'Dame, we need water.'

'You have buckets?' she said, strangely cool and pointed through to the dark recesses of her shop and I yelled to the others to follow me, while the lady went on damping her door-frame as if she were alone in the world, and in no danger. It was a good deep well and the winch well oiled. Butcher Gould and I pulled on the rope like madmen, taking the skin off our hands, running back to cast water on the laughing flames until my chest felt it would burst asunder. On my sixth journey I had to stop for an instant, and then it was I saw another leather pail, half-way up the stairs; a welcome sight for there were scarcely enough to go round. So I ran up to seize it, not caring what the unfriendly owner might say—there was a maiden coming down as I went up and we met abruptly. She carried a candle; she was frightened, for the flame quivered and shook for all that she came so steadily. I sought to pass her, and she stepped the same way. The candle almost seared my eyebrow. I dodged round the other side of her, and she had the same idea. It was a mad dance, this tripping from side to side on the stairs. We darted and feinted at one another like fighting cocks in a Southwark pit. I had to take her by the elbow, and her bones were as small as a lark's.

'Mistress, for God's love, let me by!' I cried. I took the candle from her for she was all a-quiver and dangerous. Her eyes looked into mine, and in that frantic instant I marked them as pretty eyes, nay, eyes of great beauty, the colour of woodsmoke, and filled with tears.

She said: 'Are we in danger?' She wore a serving maid's white coif and I spoke her free, for I had many happy hours of kissing and clipping, years gone, with such as she. That is, before I rose in the ranks and attained the court.

'No danger, sweet, but you would be better outside.'

She shrank from me, tears brimming.

'I cannot,' she whispered, and the next moment took the candle back from me with a thin, work-red hand; a hand so delicate that the light shone through it. And gallant as ever, in all my distress, I snatched her other hand and gave it a kiss, closing my nose to the stench of garlic and onions that perfumed it; for she was a lovesome creature, if undoubtedly somewhat loony. I could not tarry when she tore her fingers from mine and whirled away back into the upper part of the house. Seizing the pail from the stair, I hastened to fill it and ran back, just as the door-frame of my mother's shop collapsed, one beam leaning like the endpost of a gallows. I wished Fray on the gallows, and I started to pray.

I felt for my Christopher, who shielded me on summer forays when I rode forth to entertain the nobles—but it was scarcely a fit occasion for that sweet saint. I thought wildly of Barbara, to whom men call in thunder and in cannon-fire; and then remembered St Florian. Though he had been dead for twelve hundred years, I fancied him the very man for this work, and so I cried aloud to Florian of Lorch, to make the water flow faster, and the helpers run swifter, and for a miracle to save my mother's shop.

Blessed St Florian, you have ever a special place in my heart. It had been overcast all day, yet, when the first drops of rain, large as pennies, spattered on my brow, coming swift and blessedly cool, straight from Heaven's own well, I could not believe it true and thought the moisture but my own mingling tears and sweat. Then, as I heard the downpour hissing on the smouldering broken gable and the red-hot beams, and saw the cobbles awash and the disappointed flames beaten from their supper, I gave thanks from a full heart and held my mother close, in an arm so stiff from bucket-carrying I thought I would never raise it again to quaff my ale.

We had a little reprimand from the Watch of course, but my mother drew the serjeant aside and spoke to him, and he glanced across at Mistress Petson's house and nodded. The man responsible for storing the ladders and firehooks packed up his gear and we were glad to see him go. Then we inspected the damage. The counter had been destroyed, and most of the shop frontage, but it could have been a thousand times worse. A neighbour offered to make a new sign for the door, and my mother thanked him prettily. I saw then why cursed Dan Fray wanted to wed her, quite apart from her flourishing business. They carried the arras and goods back upstairs for her; and men with axes knocked away parts of the house still reckoned dangerously warm. My mother bade stupid Walter Cleeve bring up beer for all who had helped so valorously. When all were seated on those oak chairs of which she was so proud, and the boys were sweeping out the water into the street, she beckoned me and together with Agnes Petson—now conscious of her wanton appearance and full of shame—we went into that dame's house and stopped in front of her spice cupboard. A bag of pepper had burst inside it, and the sneezes of Fray's nephew mingled with his cries and thumps.

'I am sorry, mistress, to burden you with such a guest,' my mother told Agnes politely, though her lips twitched. If I have any humour in me, and men say I make them laugh, I swear I owe it to my mother. If I have any courage, that, too, is from her blood. On her own she had caught the devil's henchman, though not before he had tossed his pitch-soaked brand in through the shop window. His nose was red with pepper when the Watch came for him, and he seemed almost glad to be out of that cupboard.

'I could not lock him in my own place, in case he burned to death,' she said. I told her she was too merciful, and she quoted to me: 'Vengeance is mine, saith the Lord,' then fashioned a paradox by saying she hoped they would hang the uncle first and make an example of him.

Later we rehearsed the case against Fray, and the boys were brought in to prepare their evidence, and they told how they had been roused by the flash of flame as they slept under the counter, going to my mother's aid as she felled the nephew. And I was impressed by their wits, with the exception of Walter Cleeve, sitting stroking the dog, who had slain four rats. I compared them favourably with the servants of my mother's neighbours.

'What witless wenches she keeps,' I said, pointing towards the uncivil one's shop. My mother looked surprised.

'I always thought Jane Thomson and Dyonisia to be rather sharp young maids,' she said.

'I met one on the stairs who seemed half out of her mind,' I said, but I was yawning by now, and I looked out of the window and saw, in the square of reflected light from our chamber, my poor horse hanging her head. So I shoved her in the stall behind the shop with my mother's black pony and a sumpter horse left in pledge by some fellow who had dined and could not pay, and I bedded on the floor with the cookboys, and it was right chill there, the shop front being open to the wind. What with the smell of charred timbers and the cold, I slept exceeding ill. My body was one ache from running and throwing, my hands throbbed from their skinning on the well-rope. I lived through the whole night again, and when I rose before dawn, anxious to regain Westminster in time for Mass, I was still half-dreaming. I had been dodging the strange wild maiden on the stairs. Her mist-grey eyes looked into mine, her eyes of smoke with all their trouble and

172

anguish; and in my dreaming I saw other things that my haste had marked without the realization. The little, drooping mouth, the small round chin. As I hastened with the Household to the Royal Chapel, her face floated ahead of me—I could not move it from my mind. Behind my eyes as I prayed her hands—the hands too fine of bone for a cook-wench—clutched at me, and her face came closer. As the sweet boyish voices rose to the arch above me, I pictured that face smiling. Then all fell into place, though I would fain have dismissed it as foolishness. I would gladly have cast such thoughts aside, for she was but a cook-maid, toiling long hours, lacking privileges, abject of a bullying mistress. Yet had she smiled . . .

Those heavy eyes could easily have smiled, and I would have marked that smile journeying to the small mouth and the chin round as a child's. And, at the holy season of Christmas, four years gone, that childish face had watched my antics, and had smiled most delightfully. But then she had been seated with the Earl of Warwick, her noble father.

Up in the nave, together with others of the blood royal, Gloucester knelt. I saw his hard, pale profile; the set lips, the rigid chin.

The truth beat at me and I shrank from it.

I had found Anne Neville.

'Lo, now comes in a Fiend,' intoned the herald.

The mermaid sat wrapped in long silvery hair, with a tinsel tail made of oyster-shells. Anxious eyes peeped from under the counterfeit locks. The rosebud mouth pouted. With one hand, the mermaid held up the nether wall of a painted cave as if he feared, with good reason, it might collapse. An unpleasant youth, that mermaid, and an amateur, brought in that evening under the auspices of George of Clarence, who had been impressed by his talent at the manor. We had had words already, the mermaid and I.

'Now comes in a Fiend!' bawled the herald. I felt a thrust behind, and turned to see Alexander Carlile. Cold with horror, I realized I had missed my entrance. Robert Hawkins watched—and he ran out of spit—it's not easy to play the shawm and laugh at the same time. Some kindly soul struck fling and tinder and lit my firecrackers, and, hideously late on cue, I leaped across the Hall in a burst of flame. It's a dangerous game, the Profession.

'Sir, mind the tent,' hissed the mermaid, then broke into his

173

wailing song, his voice like a cold douche of water. I capered about, menacing him—I swear his fear was unfeigned. Closer I danced, answering his piteous song with gleeful growling—I do not pretend to have a voice; my magical powers are compensation enough. Out of mischief I brushed the cave wall on my progress, and it shook alarmingly. 'Charlatan,' whispered the mermaid, and I roared like a lion. I was almost enjoying myself. The Princess Elizabeth had been brought down for the entertainment: I heard her laughter, free and joyful as a lark's high blue song. Glancing up to see the pleasure of her, little and round as a peach beside the formidable Lady Scrope, I filled my eyes with the rest of the royal family, and my fleeting joy vanished. For the King was not even watching the play. His countenance was grim. Yet it had been he who had commissioned tonight's show—'to divert him from affairs'—so the Steward of the Household sent word to us. And I had a good notion what it was that troubled my royal and most beloved master. Gloucester: he and his fruitless quest. Gloucester's anxiety was mirrored in the King's fair face. The King loved Gloucester; and I wondered whether he himself, who had chosen the woman he craved in the face of Warwick's anger, found his sympathy enhanced by old desires. But then, the King had been in love, lustful love; and of love, Gloucester knew naught. So I thought . . . I like men that laugh, warm men of lusty heart.

All the time, near me, was a devil, a conscience devil, slowly taking shape. For why should God have chosen me as the key to this baleful mystery? It was my duty to tell Gloucester all I knew. I should have gone straightway from the cookshop to the Duke, roused him from bed, mayhap, as Alexander Carlile had roused the King at Doncaster. It was as much of a duty as that. In failing Gloucester, I had failed the King. For I could not betray Anne Neville, although my devil told me nightly that the maid was weary and soiled and very afraid. God help me, I sighed, and forgot my words.

St George stood behind the screen, his plumes wavering in a draught. He looked distraught, waiting for his cue. I was extemporizing wildly—he should have entered minutes ago, to slay me.

'And hurl us into Hell, ho, ho!' I cried, and saw St George consulting with a prompter. Under his lifted visor his face was a troubled mask. I gave up and struck my final attitude, leaning satanically upon an unsteady rock draped with buckram at the cave mouth. A brief struggle with the Saint followed, and I writhed in a death-agony. I heard him muttering 'Be still' as he prodded me with his lead-tipped sword. 'Fool I may be, but you ask much of folly,' I replied, under cover of some rather faint-hearted applause. I rolled aside as he stabbed his point into the rushes an inch from my nose. A friend of mine was butchered thus, once, and all in play. As I made myself invisible and ran from the Hall I saw that Gloucester's place was empty and remembered he had ridden north in search of Anne. I hoped he might remain there. I stood behind the screen and endured the reproofs of the Master of the Revels for a poor performance, craved his pardon, and crept away to wrestle alone with my devil.

In the passage, I heard George Clarence congratulating his protege. He was full of smiles and wine. I wondered if he knew what I knew, and what my knowledge was worth to him. In that unworthy moment I wished I had my own private confessor to run to like the King and Queen. I asked myself: how much of a sin was it? I had it in my power to ease the King, and did not do so. The King's brother was being denied the right to augment his estates, and this troubled the King. I had done nothing to alter the situation. Therefore my sin was that of non-action. My sin was silence.

I told myself for the tenth time that I had been mistaken. It was a maiden very like Warwick's daughter; a spookish trick of light, the hallucination of my frenzy. Or mayhap—and here my skin began to creep—it was a phantom. Anne Neville was dead, and because I had thought about her often lately, her spirit had wandered in my direction, appearing when I was weary and fraught and distressed for my loved ones. That night, when I slept, I shouted in slumber and woke the others. When I had made a light and sat among the straw all asweat, I saw fear on the faces of my friends.

'Jesu, he affrighted me,' said John.

'Such wild words,' whispered the man who played the rebec.

'What was I saying?' I muttered.

'Of Death, and a maiden, and the mandrake root,' he said softly, and to a man, they crossed their breasts and turned from me; and in the dark, I heard them whispering, and knew they thought me possessed. As indeed I was. I closed my fingers on the crucifix my mother had given me when I was a child. Yet the devil still sat near my head, and nibbled at me with questions. Why had I appointed myself the warden of her peace? She was a gentlewoman of lineage so rich and ancient it was almost lost in time, a Plantagenet, cousin to the King. I cringed as I remembered how I'd called her 'sweet'. She was a noble lady, such as those for whom knights maim each other in the lists. She was a pawn in the game of acquisition. The devil nudged me, and then the answer came flooding clear. She was little, and lost. She was a maiden, slender and fragile, like my own Maiden, and such pluck at my heart. Thus stands the case.

Then I slept, and the Maiden came to me in a vision. I stretched out my arms to her, and she stood in a dress the colour of water and her ardent eyes big and brown and her hair streamed about her, full of flame.

'Be happy,' she whispered. 'Dear one, be merry and glad. Be no more sad . . .' the words from that very song she loved so much, that paltry song.

I cried and ran to her, and then I saw that her loving gaze looked past me into grouped dark shadows, and the shine in her eyes grew and grew until it consumed her and she wavered into fire; and someone said: 'They are burning a witch.'

I sobbed, 'Nay! 'tis but the glory of her soul ablaze!' and woke, glad to wake, to find the year was dying, and cold to my bones.

Two days I lay sick. Word went about and his Grace sent one of Master Dominic's assistants—there was never such a King as Edward. The young physician told me that the sovereign had heard of my illness and was sorry. I asked how the King did, and he looked sober, saying that his Grace was troubled still for his brother's sake, and that other things too disquieted him. I drank a foul potion to mend me and probed further.

'The astrologer,' he said furtively. 'He had finished the charts, and men say he has told his Grace . . .' He stopped abruptly.

'Well?'

'No more.' He plucked the swollen leeches from my flesh, laid a toad-cold hand on my brow, made the Holy Sign over me and rose to go. I frowned imploringly.

'Can you not tell me?'

'I should never have begun,' he said. Then, on reaching the door, he halted, itching to share his secret, full of wavering indiscretion.

He said: 'It concerned the royal succession,' and departed.

I recovered swiftly after that, for it seemed that events were busying themselves and I was gossip-hungry. Upon rising from my bed I found that the astrologer's prophecy was not so much a secret as the doctor had made out. John had it from one of the Chapel boys, who got it from a clerk belonging to Bishop Morton of Ely, who learned it from the under-falconer, and he was enamoured of one of the Queen's tire-women, who were part of the furnishings and knew everything.

'Her Grace became sorely agitated,' John told me. 'She sent for the Dowager Duchess of Bedford and they had high words together. Her mother said she was becoming too old to do aught and went to her prayers ill-pleased. Construe it how you will.'

'And the astrologer said?'

His warm breath tickled my ear. 'That the next King's name will begin with G.'

'Surely,' I said softly, 'George Clarence would never dare aspire again to the throne, as when Warwick was alive. Pardoned, enriched, he holds all the cards.'

'Clarence was ever reckless,' said John, and we were so near talking treason, with its old familiar fearful excitement, that I had to check him swiftly.

'The Duchess Isabel is ailing,' John said.

'As ever,' I replied. 'She and her sister were always frail in body . . .' and I ceased suddenly, for with the thought of Anne there was my devil, full and venomous and real, as real as the man standing next to me. He was peering round the ribbed stone arches of the Great Hall high above, ready to spring.

There was less than a week to Michaelmas, when I could claim my wager, but the thought gave me no joy. I went down into the City one day when the river was mantled with haze, and took a penny-boat from just below Westminster Hall. I tried to enjoy the voyage; at any other time I would have risked the ebb tide and the treacherous currents under the Bridge, for with a clever boatman this could be fierce sport, but not that day. The gilt and azure and crimson of barges floated magnificently among a throng of lesser vessels. We rocked on the swell of the Earl of Essex's carved boat, sailed near the gold-hung splendour of Lord Hastings's craft. The misty river echoed the strains of pipe and viol from the barges' depths. Under the flaming banners liveried oarsmen rowed lustily, with great dipping strokes. All the way from Blackfriars to the Tower great cranes bristled bowed-headed among the myriad quays and warehouses. We passed the massive pile of Baynard's Castle and the stone fortress of the Steelyard, home of the strange, martial Hanse traders. On the southern end of the Bridge sat three heads, staring with great malancholy over the city through which their legs had walked the week before. Two galleys stocked with tuns of good Bardeaux were anchored at the Vintners' Wharf. Next moment we were beneath the Bridge, and the roar of hooves and wheels above competed with the rushing water that lapped us for a few dark moments. I saw the wooden starlings over my head, slime-green and crusted. On the other side, Brown's Wharf was boiling with trade. A Spanish merchantman was tied up low in the water from a cargo of iron and madder and oil. At the next quay a vessel Calais-bound and laden with sarplers of wool was hoisting sail. Towards St Catherine's a Flemish carvel, carrying fine Holland cloth, came slowly, like a great indolent bird.

The eel-ships were tied up at Marlowe's, and the voices of housewives fighting to board them rose shrill and impatient. The water-bailiff's men held them back while their master searched for red or undersized eels, and the women railed at his sloth. The rush-boats were in. I saw Palace servants, bent like cripples, running with their great green loads. As we pulled towards Billingsgate, the salt-cod smell wafted to my nose from an Icelandic trawler.

There was a high-masted Venetian galley wharved below the Tower, weighted with damask, velvet, and rare spices for sure, judging by the perfume. The crew were like monkeys, little and dark with gesticulating hands. My pilot spat over the side of the boat at them, and their outlandish tongue. On either bank the peter-nets lay like floating spiderwebs, dripping water as the fishers hauled in a load of salmon and barbel and flounder. The autumn sun turned the drops to jewels. A swan took flight astern of us, flying strongly east, the thin light gilding its wings. I pushed my devil to one side and tried to be happy.

I disembarked and fought the seething crush in Petty Wales, dodging the carriers and wains, asssaulted by the dreadful language of the carters, vaguely comforted by the presence of that violent life. Down Thames Street I went, turned up from the river, came into Mincing Lane and walked westward into Eastchepe. There I met Beatrice the wimple-washer with her maids all loaded with laundry, and she had linen cloths for my mother in her bundle. I took these and went on down to the cookshop. The men were chipping away plaster to fit the new door-frame in and the master carpenter told me, with shaking head, that it would be a long work, and costly. Yet we laughed together at the news

178

of Dan Fray and his nephew, lying hungry in the Fleet. To be in jail is an expensive business too.

'One meal a day, if he can pay,' said the carpenter smoothing the fractured gable.

'Or eat the rats!' said I merrily, and went into the shop to find the borrowed fire-bucket. I then made my way to the house three doors down.

I contrived to look into the back room. She was still there: Anne of Warwick, late Princess of Wales. There was no doubt in me as I watched her, slender and wearied, plunging her arms deep in greasy washing-up water. Her little chin sank on her chest. She did not look up. I marked her sorrow, felt her loneliness. The other wenches gave her sharp words, pushed past her, wearing the livery of resentment. She was an upstart, an unskilled stranger in their domain. Sick-hearted, I sought the owner, to return her bucket. I had no lust to stay. The mistress of the house raised sparse brows at me as if I were some rare beast. I stared her out. I spoke her soft. I thanked her for the loan of the fire-bucket.

''Twas naught,' she said. There was truly a nip in the air as I passed out on to the street, wishing I could leave my devil within to sour her salmon morteux.

Walter Cleeve was killing a sucking-pig when I returned. It shrieked as he smote it in the middle—I could hardly hear my mother's voice. She was full of smiles. She had appealed to the Gild; they would loan her money; not enough, mind, but better than naught. We went aloft.

'You've been sick,' she said. 'What ails you?'

I longed to tell her. I told her half of it.

'I know where Anne Neville is,' I said softly.

She said instantly: 'You have acquainted the Duke of Gloucester of this?' and when I confessed I had not, her face grew livid and her eyes like stones. Never had I seen her so angry.

''Tis your duty.' I strode maddened about the parlour, trying to explain that which made nonsense. Shortly she cooled and tried reasoning with me.

'Every maiden has a dowry—wedlock is a business . . . you have not the right.'

I knew all that, I said. I repeated Clarence's mocking words: 'She's but a little maid,' then my own thoughts: 'Alone, unloved.'

'Mary have mercy!' cried my mother. 'I have reared an idiot!' An hour we wrangled, and I grew stubborn and would tell her no more. I sought comfort and advice; she advised me and left me comfortless, only enhancing my guilt. 'The King loves Gloucester,' she said.

The King loves Gloucester, and is troubled by his trouble. God help me.

'Do not fail in your duty,' she repeated.

Thus I left her. I was shaking, and thought of going to the Boar's Head for drink and idle talk. But instead I went past the tavern and found myself at the London Stone; and on a whim went into St Swithin's, where it was dark and the wings of God beat through the mutterings of the Mass. There I knelt for an hour. The devil came into church with me and tried to look devout, sitting with folded hands on the stall-carvings above my head.

When I came out into the thin air and falling leaves of the churchyard, my mind was clear. The things about me were no longer misted as on the river trip, but sharp and solid. An old beggar lying dead against the iron bars of London Stone. A grey cat, disembowelled on the cobbles. Two disreputable players of the *scurrae vagi*, prancing to the noise of fife and tabor. A merchant, wife and daughter, dismounting outside the church. He rode a fine bay. The women shared a big white mare. I looked at the daughter, and she at me. Pale, big-breasted, with black eyes, she stared at me as her father helped her from the horse. She toyed with her beads and her gaze was unflickering. Even in my anguish of spirit I marked the wanton sparkle of that look. I fancied I saw ardour in it; a promise of forgetfulness, came the chance. Then, that warmth dazzled me—for how could I know that this was but the kindling embers of a foul humour—and that she would use me very unkindly throughout our wedded life.

I spoke of my devil to none, but there were those who, I fancied, gave me strange looks, and I had need to be doubly foolish and gay to belie my dread. Actually, my devil was not an ill-favoured fellow by any means. He had horns, for sure, and a neat little beard, and I think his feet were cloven, but as he usually had them tucked under him I could not swear to it. His face was mild and gentle, with large eyes and a protruding mouth; it was only the expression on it that chilled me, and the reproving way he wagged his head. When I was busily occupied he let me alone, but when I stopped and thought of Lady Anne Neville, abandoned among the slubberdegullions, he came nimbly down from his little niche or dropped from a flying buttress and spoke me soft. He would say: 'Go to him,' and I would shake my head, for my mind—which at one time I had thought made up—had once more turned traitor.

Gloucester was back from Sheriff Hutton, more grim-visaged than ever. Still he searched. He sent letters, he questioned folk, he took barge upriver and back again; he walked leagues, attended by his household knights. He went from the great sprawling wards of Cripplegate and Farringdon Without, to the Priory of St Bart's and the Inns of Chancery, the shops of Fleet Street, the Temple. Along the Street he walked, the Poultry, the Vintry, Jewry, up Bread Street and Milk Street; north he rode to the Grand Priory of Holy Trinity. He wandered through Moorfields, and in all these forays he spoke with an hundred holy men and women, abbots, prioresses and clerks. He dispatched emissaries to the sanctuaries with sealed writings. He was unsparing and unwearying. He grew thin and hard and eager, and the King glowered at him with an impatient, loving look. Clarence departed to tend his sick wife, the Neville inheritance still secure within his hand. I thought of Anne, and the devil swung from the vaultings and tweaked my hair.

'Tell him,' he said.

'Avaunt, Lucifer!' said I, and he looked injured. 'Give one good reason why not,' he asked. 'She is afraid,' I said. 'She is wretched,' answered the devil. 'You bear a bond for Clarence? While the maid lies low *he* is rich. You are his man in this matter?'

Nay, I was not for George Clarence, fair and jocund though he was, for he was a silly fellow to betray the King with Warwick and lucky, yea lucky, to escape retribution. The devil listened, his head on one side.

'Certes, Barnet,' he said. ' 'Twas Richard who was the peacemaker there. Blessed are they . . .' and it seemed so strange to hear a devil quoting the Scriptures that I tried to look him in the eye but it was impossible. He would just fade and become part of the stonework or curl himself up into one of the bosses on the ceiling. He was at my other ear now. 'Of what is she afraid?'

'Of being wed to Gloucester,' I said.

'All must marry,' said the devil sensibly.

'She has been married,' I said. 'A wretched, treacherous marriage—to the Lancastrian. She has been bludgeoned with bad tidings. Alone, bereft of husband, father, mother, attainted, disgraced. A pawn,' I said, and nearly choked. 'A movable.'

181

'Why a pawn?' he asked with interest. 'Pawns are not flesh and blood—they are ivory. Inanimate. Devoid of feeling.'

And I said, 'But she has feeling; I saw her tears, looked in her eyes. She should be cosseted, not hunted down for her fortune. If she must marry, let it be to a loving husband who cares not a jot for her livelode!'

The devil squinted at me and his horns moved a trifle. 'You speak as if you have designs,' he murmured. 'Were she not the Lady Anne—but I forget, you love another . . .'

At this I was so incensed that I struck at him with the cane I carried, and he flew up to the roof in fury, shrieking: 'Tell him! Tell him! Tell him!'

I saw one of the pages turn green and cross himself and walk right speedily past me down the corridor, and I realized I had better put my affairs in order before they brought in a priest.

The weather snapped into coldness. Every morning mist lingered on the Thames until dinner, and drew down sharply at dusk. We were nearly in October and the birds were taking their leave for the other edge of the world. And as the birds departed, men and women began to thread back into the city. We had watched them go in late spring, with staff and pouch, heavy with sin. Under the hot suns of Galicia they had offered a waxen leg to St James for their deliverance, and now they came from *La-Dame-sous-Terre* and from Rome, dusty yet cleansed, and lighter of purse. Trailing the severed links of their fetters they came, bearing back all that had been healed by the sight of those sacred relics: their sick hawks, their limbs, their souls. They came with a wool-thread from the chasuble of a saint; a spoonful of dust lifted from the grounds of a shrine. The shell of Compostella adorned their hat brims. They came from abroad, and from Canterbury, where a thousand candles reflected the glory of Henry Plantagenet's penitence. I had made that journey once, to see, in its canopy of beaten gold, the Regal of France, finest ruby in the realm. So they came: they had journeyed leagues and returned satisfied. Yet the Duke of Gloucester tramped London town, and came back empty.

I withdrew from the water with John and Robert. They were surprised yet pleased with my new-found sense of propriety. Did I do it to safeguard my own interests? I was not even sure myself; I knew only that the whole matter had become too odious a jest. On the day prior to the Feast of St Michael, because I could not hear the conversation of my friends for my devil's whispering, I went down to the stables to seek a mule that I might train for the coming Christmas festival. We would soon be in rehearsal and I reckoned to get all my properties in good array. I wondered whom the King would choose for Revels Master over the twelve days. Gloom ruled my every thought, I who was so merry. Along the terrace I went in my day's pale grey. In the courtyard, the pigeons searched amid sodden red leaves; the pavement was silken with damp. I went under the arches into the smell of hay and horses. I looked at the mules. Two were too docile for my purpose but the third had mischief in its gait. I set up a tub for its forelegs to stand on, in practice for when it would reach the King's dais, with me aboard. Two household stewards were grooming Lyard Duras and Lyard Lewes. Sir John Howard had chosen well in his gift to the royal couple—the fair coursers were everything that a horse should be. They struck at each other in play, with swift squealing blows. Lyard Duras kicked out, jarring a hoof on the stones.

'They can smell the mares,' said a steward. 'Even the mule won't quiet them today.'

Lyard Lewes rose on end and cried of his own beauty with quivering nostrils. His coat was silver, his haunches whorled and dappled like soaring smoke.

'He's as brave as he is fair,' called the groom, grinning. 'Today he killed a hound—cleft his skull like a nut.'

My mule was snuffing at something small behind us, something that moved and chuckled. 'Holy Mary,' whispered the groom. He lunged for the Princess Elizabeth as she ran laughing away. I never saw a five-year-old maid move so swiftly. She wanted to fondle the fair horses. She sped on across the courtyard—once, my fingers grazed her gown, but she was a hare, a light pink and golden bird, a faery. She was enjoying herself. Horsemen were approaching from the outer gate, their hooves resounding under the archway. She changed course and flew to meet them. They came strongly, their surcotes shimmering in the mist—I saw only the strong legs of the horses pounding air. She would be trampled to pulp. I foresaw her end—my sweet Elizabeth—and every man present jigging at Tyburn.

One of the front line of horsemen leaped from his mount. With a stride he was upon the Princess, grasping her by her flying hair. He wore the livery of the White Boar, and there mounted behind him was the Duke himself. The horsemen milled in a circle, exclaiming harshly, looking to see if the child had been harmed. The young knight who had caught her had been rough in his handling, and Elizabeth was on the point of tears. At that moment her nurse, the accursed, wit-less old fool, came panting flatfootedly across the yard. Gloucester dismounted, and the Princess ran to him. She threw herself against his legs—he lifted her up. He was chid-ing her gently, calling her 'sweet Bess.' She would her arms around him, burying her face in his fur collar.

Gloucester spoke to the nurse. He did not raise his voice, but its tone sent frissons down my spine.

'Well, dame?' he said, while the Princess peeped out at us with one eye.

The nurse fell to her knees, weeping and wailing.

'Is this how you guard the blood royal?' he asked. His voice was soft; soft and dangerous.

'Your Grace, I did but turn my back an instant . . .' she whimpered.

'An instant,' he repeated. 'I doubt not it would have been likewise with the Prince Edward! An instant's heinous idling —a hound at the cradle—a spark from the fire . . .' He bit his words back in fury. 'It seems that princes are cheaply be-gotten.' He turned to two of the pallid guard. 'Put this woman under arrest.'

'They'll flog her,' whispered the groom.

'They'll hang her, if he's a mind to it,' said the steward who was trying to gentle Lyard Duras. 'If he takes a leaf from the Butcher's book.'

So I thought on our last Constable of England, Tiptoft Earl of Worcester, who had devised new wondrous methods of im-palement for felons . . . a brave man, who requested his own head shorn off in three strokes to honour the Trinity. As they led the weeping woman away Gloucester took the Princess up higher in his arms. She clasped and prattled. 'Bess, my love,' I heard him say.

My devil took shape beside me, romping in the day's dour colours, pleased at the aura of recent fear.

'He is capable of tenderness,' he murmured, and I in-structed him to depart to his master, whoever that might be; while I heard Gloucester telling the Princess it was wrong to wander off, she all the time putting up great arguments—her nurse bored her and she would sooner be out of doors.

'We must all do things we mislike,' he said seriously, but she took it upon her to start kissing him, all over his face. She was more generous with kisses than protocol allowed; she had once kissed me before I could stop her. I have been kissed by a Queen.

'What great wrath lies in him too,' whispered the devil. He

was beginning to talk more subtly to me these days. 'Your Grace,' I said, in a strangled voice, but by now the Duke was disappearing through the archway. Elizabeth's hair caught the wind of their passing and lifted, cloth of gold but richer.

I feared his anger which was rare as his smile, but I also marked his gentleness with the child and sought portents in all this. But then my portents came so thick and fast I did not know what to believe, and the next thing I knew I was on my way, drearily, to his apartments. One of the young pages opened and asked my business, so I told him it was none of his. When I said it was an urgent and secret matter he seemed impressed. A pinelog fire burned in the hearth and one of Gloucester's huge hounds lay before it. It was a room of paradoxes: there was a lute, a set of tables, and Caxton's new printed book on chess, loaned from Flanders, but the Duke had a suit of harness piled against the wall, and I wondered if he contemplated joining forces with the Easterling traders, it being their custom to keep armour in every room. Then I remembered the purpose of my visit, and my heart started knocking at my ribs.

'His Grace is taking a bath,' announced the henchman.

The hound eyed me and growled. Murmuring voices came from behind the closed door of the bedchamber. I turned tail. I would shirk this odious duty. I had just convinced the page that what was important to me was of no consequence to the Duke, and was talking my way across the room when the bedchamber door opened. I heard Richard's voice as one of the Yeomen of the Body came through.

'If you will bring the book, Jervais, I'll prove both you and Lord Anthony wrong,' he called out. There was laughter.

Jervais picked up Caxton's book lovingly.

'They're arguing a point,' he told the page. 'Last night Lord Anthony vowed . . .' He saw me and raised his brows. 'You wish to see the Duke?'

'Who is it?' said the Duke from his bath.

I knew then that matters were out of my hands. The henchmen whispered together and Jervais went through to the inner room. Miserably I heard him repeat my own words 'urgent and secret' and let them escort me to where Richard sat up to his armpits in warm water. He and I faced each other through curtains and steam. The aroma of coriander and rose-water tickled my nose. He looked at me apparently without recognition and the man Jervais bent over the bathing tent and murmured: 'One of the histrios, sir,' an unkind designation which at other times would have made me burst

185

with rancour, but now I did not care. Richard nodded, then he said:

'What is this matter concerning me?'

I tried to speak and found myself dumb.

'This good man seems ailing,' Richard said mildly. 'Give him a drink.'

I gulped down a cup of Rhenish, which went straight to my head. I saw them all, grouped expectantly, save for the body servants who went on calmly pouring hot herbals over the Duke's neck and back. Francis Lovell glanced up from the *Game and Play of the Chess* and smiled. I always liked him—he had a lucky face. Richard gazed quizzically at me over the high tub. I whispered my secret.

'Come nearer,' he said with impatience, and as I did not wish him to take me for a fool, I marched up to the parted curtains of the bathing tent and told him what I knew, louder than I had intended. Something strange befell his face. He waxed white and then rosy red and the skin seemed to be stretched tight over his cheeks as his normal pallor returned.

'Help me out,' he said and extended a hand on either side. Jervais caught one, and I the other. I took the Duke's wet hand, all slippery with fine Bristol soap, and nearly had my fingers mangled by his inhuman grip. He was as thin as a whip, straight though not overtall, and well made, particularly about the shoulders. After my curiosity was sated I looked at his eyes, and ever afterwards he held my gaze with his, while they dressed him and I stood plaiting my fingers behind my back.

They dressed him with care. While one knight tied the points of his hose, the other put over his head an applebloom shirt of the finest Rennes cloth. They clothed him in the purple, the narrow-waisted doublet edged with gris, and with the new-fangled sleeves like bladders, arranging the tucks of the tunic to achieve the desired triangular effect. Two esquires knelt to introduce his legs into the soft leather thigh-boots with the grey silk lining. Jervias fastened the gold collar of York about his chest, and gave him his velvet bonnet with the pendant bauble of rubies and he said, without taking his eyes from mine:

'Now I am ready, Fran, to go a-wooing.' And under young Lovell's soft mirth, I felt murder in my soul at so sickly a jest.

He slung his cloak about him, and it too mocked my sad thoughts of Anne Neville, for it was velvet on velvet, precedent of the highest nobility. Yes, you are very grand, Dickon, I thought. I hope that the stench of onions and greasy water

186

will not taint you. Soon you will be even wealthier. May she spit on you.

London is dirtier now, under Henry Tudor. Ugly little houses clog the streets, though this is not, of course, the fault of his Divine Majesty. He has put much hard-earned money into the building of his Chapel to the Virgin at Westminster, where they sing Masses night and day for the souls of the dead. Speaking of death, he has given directions for his own funeral, commanding royal and proper magnificence but no outrageous superfluities. Such a King he is.

As I say, now it's dirtier, but on the day I walked through town with Richard of Gloucester, going a-courting, I thought I had seldom seen it so foul and knew a peculiar shame for the filthy alleys and the stench which rose about me and my sumptuous companion. I was horrified that he had decided to walk anyway—I thought we would go by boat at least, and when he marched out of the Palace gate into the howling thoroughfare, I stopped in amazement.

'I'll get horses for your Grace,' I murmured. He said grimly: 'Friend, I have walked miles on this errand which ends today. I'll see it through in like fashion,' and added, as if to himself: 'They marched further to Tewkesbury.' I reckoned he was just rambling, being so full of triumph. We went together along the Strand, with the bishops' palaces lining the south side, past Temple Bar and through Ludgate where the press thickened. I had need to run to keep up with him—all the while I was fearful that he might be assaulted or robbed, and I leaped from side to side of the street endeavouring to guard him. My disquiet must have been apparent, for at one point he stopped while I panted at his elbow.

'My lord, why have we no esquires to ease your passage?' I gasped. A smile crept over his face and he murmured:

'Good fellow, there are times when one goes where no other should penetrate,' and with that smile there was something in the back of his eyes that perplexed me utterly; that, coupled with the really mischievous look, man to man, which he gave me. I had never seen him with a woman; his habits were not those of the King and Clarence, both of whom had bastards all over England; then I remembered talk of Richard and a woman of Bruges, whom he had got with child.

Eastchepe was crammed, redolent of food and filth. I whacked the cook-knaves aside as they clutched with foul hands at us both. The Gild had prohibited the practice of soliciting, but they still did it. 'Hot sheep's feet!' they yelled. 'Ribs o' beef!' I saw a grease-smear on the Duke's velvet cloak, and, surreptitiously sponging at it with my glove, wished I had never been born. A ragged band playing harp, pipe and psaltery impeded us—they sang of 'Jenkin and Julian.' The fishmongers shouted their melwell and mackerel earsplittingly. Even the oaths sounded worse in a prince's presence. The window overhead flew open and a wife, with careless cry of 'Gardy loo!' hurled the contents of her pot almost on top of us. A dead dog, maggot-white, stank in the gutter. This was my Eastchepe, and, for the first time, I felt shame for it. 'Good lord, excuse this foulness,' I said, and was angry with myself as soon as the words were out.

'Is it all of your making, then?' he said, with a cool dark look. 'Southwark is also somewhat unsavoury, but it has a fine inn.'

'The Tabard,' I said eagerly.

'Yea, Geoffrey Chaucer's tavern. All one hears is Chaucer. He has still an ardent following, and rightly so.'

'His works would fit Master Caxton's skill,' said I, fawning. Kiss-your-arse Patch, I was. Am.

'Of course you're more familiar with such gestes than I,' he said, and I caught the hint that he thought I could be more honourably employed than amusing the court with my fellow joculatores. But his wit was only slightly barbed and we talked culture. Of course he knew more than I, yet we enjoyed the same things, and as we walked, he recited 'The Love Unfeigned,' and very well too; and when he came to the line *This world, that passeth soon as flowers fair,* I wanted to weep, as ever, and came near liking him. But then we neared the cookshop and, remembering who lay within, I thought the title of 'Dan' Chaucer's poem, coming from him, in poor taste.

My mother's shop, as we approached, looked a rather pitiful sight, and I would fain have hurried him past, but he slowed and looked up at it. 'Whose place is this?' he said, and squirming, I told him. I knew he would now think I was serving him for a reward and I felt like Judas Iscariot already without the thirty pieces being added.

'She should have compensation,' he announced, and I said that the Gild had matters in hand. He said 'Hmmm,' and was loath to drop the affair, but the next minute we were at our destination.

I went first, and the haughty mistress stepped from behind her counter unsmiling, but when Richard of Gloucester dar-

188

kened the doorway in his velvet and jewels and with his eyes like arrowheads, she swept to the ground, all her hauteur gone. As Gloucester only stood and looked about, I enquired of the mistress where the young lady might be found. Speechless, she pointed aloft, and I hung back as Richard strode through the shop. To my great dismay, for I had thought my task was done, he beckoned me from the foot of the stairs.

'Give me a watch while I talk with the Lady Anne,' he said, and turning, I saw the popping eyes of the cook-knaves. They were creeping imperceptibly towards the stairs, leaving their pies to catch at this latest entertainment. The owner was gone, I assume, to fashion an explanation for George of Clarence.

I followed Gloucester upstairs. 'Dismiss her servants,' he said, then sharply asked me why I laughed and I told him; the lady's status was not now what might be expected of Warwick's daughter, and he would find her much altered. He swore a most fearful oath, and struck the door a rap with the hilt of his knife. My heart went into my boots as Anne opened the door. Now I have witnessed many executions, and taken my due lesson from them, as is intended. I have seen the faces of those about to be hanged, disembowelled and cut up, burned in barrels, and beheaded. They have a mingling of abject terror and resignation, patched over with a fierce bravado. This vanishes into mist at the first touch of the knife. Anne Neville carried that look. I knew better than ever how Judas felt.

Richard said, 'Wait here'; then: 'Let none come up,' and I saw Anne's little white face, with the blonde hair dull from grease and her white coif smudged with dirt, blotted out by the Duke's dark shadow, as he closed the door behind him. The servants were grouped at the stairfoot. They were straining to hear like a pack of hounds at a treed quarry, but in vain. I, on the other hand, had no wish to know what went on behind that door. But it had great cracks where the oak had shrunk, and I could hear every word.

At first I thought on Daniel Fray and his lust for my mother's livelode, and wondered if that old play would be performed within, before realizing that lords do not, as a rule, chase women round tables, although the Maiden once told me a fantastic tale about King Edward threatening Elizabeth with his dagger at Grafton Regis. Well, the King was one on his own.

There was such a long silence that I was full of anguish. If he harms her, I said to myself, trembling fiercely, I will knock and enter, asking if they wish for wine. I will risk his wrath. Lord Jesu, keep my tongue still.

His first words were shockingly clear.

'This is an unseemly place to find you, my lady.'

He got no answer to this, so he said: 'Are you well, Madame?'

Had he no eyes? He could surely see she was far from well. Again she did not reply.

'I have come to fetch you away.'

'I thought you would come,' she said.

'You heard that I was seeking you,' he continued. 'Why did you not send word of your whereabouts?'

She coughed. She said, very fast: 'I was warned of you, my lord.' Then, more softly: 'I was afraid.'

'Warned? By whom? By Clarence?'

No answer.

'Yea, by my brother,' he said. He laughed harshly. 'Lord, how flown are some with ambition, how unbelievably cunning and devious . . .' Then, less bitterly: "And you? What of your feelings in this . . . this conspiracy?'

'I was not consulted, your Grace,' she said, her voice battling with tears.

'He brought you here by force,' said Richard.

'Nay, not by force. He said it would be better . . .' her words started to run away, tripping over each other. '. . . that you were so full of spleen, so hot in your desire for my mother's estates . . . so full of fury because of my treasonous marriage . . . you wished me ill. I was afraid,' she said again, and changed it. 'I am afraid.'

Do not weep, I thought. Support your soul before him, for the love of God.

'The day I called at his manor he would not let me see you,' Richard said. 'He told me you were sick—was this the truth?'

She was silent.

'Three days I waited, close by,' he said inexorably. 'Then I returned, to learn you were so ailing you could not be disturbed. And then you were vanished, utterly. I've journeyed miles to find you.'

'And now you have,' she said wearily. 'What do you wish of me, my lord?'

190

'Why, to have you with me, of course!' he cried. His voice dropped as he said: 'We have been apart too long.'

'There has been too much blood shed,' she said sadly.

The boards creaked as he started to walk about the room. ' 'Tis true, that in his Grace's service I rode against your father. Of your husband I will not speak, but you know well my one-time affection for Richard Neville. That foolish, gallant knight,' he said softly.

Her voice trembling, she said: 'Did you see him die?'

'Oxford had fled, Montagu was cut down. The Earl of Warwick made for Wrotham Wood and the Barnet Road. He was pursued and slain. Once, through the fog, I saw his standard, then I was unhorsed. My esquires were dead—I was still embroiled in the fray. Then I saw his standard flew no more, but I heard only of his death when I was in the surgeon's tent.'

' 'Tis hard for me to brook these thoughts,' she said, in great sorrow.

'And for me. I too remember Yorkshire, and happier days. But you, my lady, have been constantly in my mind.'

'The last time we met was after Tewkesbury,' she replied. 'You had a terrible aspect. You did not speak to me.'

'I was too overmatched, Madame. And, unlike my brothers, I am unlettered in fair speeches. I could but look at you . . . and love you. Be sure of this, I shall not let you go again.'

'When we were children,' she said slowly, 'I thought you loved me . . . but that was long ago.'

'At Middleham,' he said. 'My feelings have not changed. Anne, come to me.'

'I will not wed you, my lord,' she said. 'And I'm too good to be your leman.'

Her voice was that of proud Warwick's daughter. I was seized by a fit of horrid mirth, for these last words were the very same used by Elizabeth Woodville, when the King's desire ran high, as told to me by the Maiden.

'As you wish,' he said coldly, and exhaled his breath in a long sigh. The floor squeaked under his pacing, then suddenly he gave a great cry. I broke into a sweat.

'Blessed Mother of God!'

'Oh, what is it?' she said terrified.

'Anne, your hands! Your little hands! O Lord, to think that things should have come to this!'

Her steps neared the door as she evaded him. The latch lifted, the door opened a crack and slammed shut beneath the weight of his arm.

191

'Let me kiss them,' he said, and there was a taut silence, broken by a curious little noise like the last choking sob a child makes after bawling—full up with tears, struggling to scream again.

'Don't weep,' he said fiercely. 'Don't weep, Anne. Ah, Anne, I love you.'

'Your Grace,' she cried. 'I pray you, do not kneel to me. Do not kneel. Richard, get up.'

'Your little hands, Anne, red and broken as a scullion's,' he repeated, like a madman. 'I will restore them—before God, I'll restore *you*. To Middleham . . .'

'That was once my home,' she said sadly.

'Our home, Anne! Where I'll give you every joy, I swear it.'

Another silence followed, then she said: 'I am aweary of it all. Take me, Richard, do what you will. My mother's possessions are forfeit. I feel but a chattel, a necessary part of the movables, past caring. The estates are yours, and so am I.'

'To the Devil with the estates!' he cried, and my skin tingled as I realized he could shout as loud as the King when he chose. 'Anne, Anne, I love you. Love me.'

And then the silence grew longer and longer and was heavy-hung with dreaming, and I curled my toes and rolled about against the wall, feeling exceeding guilty for being there. The touch of her must have aroused old memories, for he said quite roughly: 'I have had paramours, you should know this. I have also a son, whom I shall acknowledge. Will you be wounded if he lives with us in Yorkshire?'

She did not answer for a moment.

'He is called John,' Richard said. 'He's a fine babe.'

'I love children,' Anne Neville said in a small voice.

'I will give you children, Anne. God will bless us with many children. Brave sons. Sweet Anne.'

'The Prince Edward of Lancaster . . .' she began, and he said, his voice rigid again: 'I would rather not know of that.'

She laughed gently through her tears.

'Queen Margaret would not allow him alone with me. She swore the union should not be consummated until Lancaster was strong in England. Ah, Richard, he was an arrogant, fearsome creature—he spoke only of war and beheadings.'

'I, too, know of war,' he said. 'Enough to long for peace and tranquillity with you for wife, and my friends about me . . .'

She was weeping now in earnest, and he said: 'Come, my lady, my love. Let's leave this dismal place. Lean on me.'

He opened the door so suddenly I was transfixed. However, he scarcely looked at me, only saying: 'Bring round a horse, I pray you,' and disappeared again into the chamber. My mother was out. I took her black palfrey without leave and brushed its coat. I hoped it would be a fitting mount for the Lady Anne. I tethered it outside the shop and ran up the stairs once more, into the upper room, with but a swift knocking and out again right hastily, red-eared. The Duke of Gloucester had Anne Neville close in his arms, and his mouth on hers, and in the moment of my intrusion I saw her lift her arms slowly and clasp him tightly to her, like a weary child who waits to be carried into sleep.

It was chill when we came out and moisture clung to our hair and slid down the carved beams and pentices of the houses either side of Eastchepe. Richard of Gloucester cupped his hands for Anne's foot and tossed her up lightly into the saddle and laughed, a laugh which I had seldom heard and did not recognize. She smiled down at him and her face was rose pink; and already the lady of Christmas revels, merry and safe beside a strong man, was returning. I thought he would take her back to Westminster, but he did not. On the other side of the street I walked. I walked with them and yet away from them. Their eyes never wavered from the road ahead. Once he halted, took off his fair velvet cloak and wrapped it about her, where it draped her from neck to ankles as she sat the pony. Once she touched his hand and he bore her fingers to his lips. Yet all the while they looked ahead, as if they had no wish to glance behind as long as they lived.

We went slowly along Budge Row and Watling Street as far as St Paul's churchyard and passed under the sombre shadow of the church through into Chepeside and towards Aldersgate until we saw the crenellations of the Wall. There, he halted the pony at the Sanctuary of St-Martin-le-Grand, and together they went in. He emerged alone after a little space; on his face joy and sadness gathered, overlaid with the look of one who anticipates a wearisome campaign.

My devil took flight and sped over the housetops, webbed black wings beating lustily: I never realized he had wings. Gone, no doubt, to plague some other wretch.

In a February-grey dawn I watched London, and Westminster, and all dear and familiar to me, vanish to the south-east. Coming up through Sheen, with the fingers of winter catching at my mouth, I watched it go. The Palace, and the river with its dipping cranes doing obeisance to trade, sank out of sight as we hit Watling Street, which was frost-foul. This was no May Day sally to entertain ducal households. Those were occasions spiced with good humour, singing through summer days with the minstrels and the bear loping behind on his chain, and, following, the children from every village dancing after for a league. Then I would be at the height of my power, jesting with a ceaseless cascade of fable and rhyme, and often, if time decreed, halting at a hamlet to entrap the burghers with my wit and skill. Thus had I once been myself enchanted, on the green at Stoney Stratford, by a child with hair the colour of ripe hazel nuts. I do not need to speak her name—to me, she was always but the Maiden, and save for a Queen, there was never her equal.

This was no blossomy pilgrimage of mirth, to divert Lord Hastings at Ashby, or Sir John Howard, or Sir John Fastolfe. Nor were we bound to tell sacred gestes and holy lays for mitred abbots like those at Glastonbury and St Alban's. Jolly times were those, riding forth between cowslip fields shouting with colour, and not only because the lords we pleasured were generous, but for another reason. We knew that, after our task was done, we the emissaries of the King's gaiety would be returning to London. And London was life itself to me. All those I loved were there, save she whom I had lost. All the things I knew best were there—the taverns, the reek, the jostle, the sparkling court. The sweet Princess Elizabeth. The King, who had betrayed me.

King Edward had dismissed me from his service, I that loved him so well. From the best and most innocent of intentions, he had bidden my departure on a day still edged with winter. When the Comptroller sent word to me I thought at first it was only a bad jest.

'You, sir, are to ride to Middleham, in the north parts,' said the messenger, cringing a little at my aspect, which must have shown many things.

'Alone?' I could only fashion the one word.

'You, sir, Masters Green and Hawkins—it is the royal wish,' he said, and, as there was naught to add, departed.

The King had made a gift of me to Dickon of Gloucester. A marriage gift, for Richard was wedded at last, and in a fine hurry after the final Council meeting at Sheen. Anne Neville had come forth out of Sanctuary to be his bride. After four months of Council-chatter they were man and wife, and gone from London in haste, vanishing into the wilds of the north, which I knew for a fact to be haunted by evil demons, and cheerless indeed. John had made music at the consecration of their union, and he now rode a little behind me through the foggy morning, with the Chilterns rising gloomily to the west and the rime cracking underfoot like an ill-smitten tabor. We were seven, riding north. Ahead I could see the broad backs of Sir James Tyrell and his two esquires. Directly in front of me a young tonsured clerk sat a dejected mule. I could hear John touching his lute as he rode at my rear, and Robert, lagging behind, seemed to be half asleep. We were for the cold castle of Middleham and a master still an unknown quantity. Behind me lay the royal court and all its fond memories. It seemed my days of joy and play were over, and ill fortune surely mine: I had felt this since December lately gone.

It had been a doleful Christmas. Yet we had feasted enough and been rewarded for our revel-labours, and I had ruled over Misrule once more and had got my twenty shillings from the King. Anthony Woodville fashioned a most holy play which took all our wit to justify, and I saw the Princess Elizabeth every day. Yet, as I looked to my royal master for his pleasure, and saw him fuming and sad under a dangerous golden smile, my joy was much confined. Though I rode my mule around the hall, right up to the cloth of estate and with ringing cries summoned the lords to gamble dice, which they did right heartily. Fifty joculatores crammed the Hall, wearing their tunics of blue and gold, and the guises of wildmen and angels to mask the sweating faces beneath. The pageant wagons churned through the rushes, and King Neptune sat high on the foremost ship, dressed in green cloth of gold. We played Samson, too, pulling down a temple that almost grazed the roof. One of the master-cooks invented a Nativity for the royal table so glorious that it became his swansong, for after fashioning the last gold star set in a spun-sugar sky above the Holy Child, he felt a fainting in his leg and sat down, and soon died.

The Queen's sisters danced lustily. They twirled and swooned in the bransle and saltarello, while their noble husbands, Essex, Bourchier, Kent, Lord Dunster, postured and bowed with wonderful elegance, their satin thighs stealing the torch glow from the ladies' jewels. There was a covey of holy men: Bishops Morton, Russell, Rotherham, Lionel Woodville of Salisbury. They pledged his Grace in spiced malmsey and hypocras, and if they thought the dancing wild, they did not say so.

The Queen, great with child again, was gay. The pastry cook had moulded the Virgin's face in likeness to her Grace.

195

This pleased her, likewise the collar of rubies and the sapphire girdle presented by the King's herald on gift-night. Anthony Woodville was lordly and high-hearted with prowess in the lists and at the rhyming. Young Thomas Dorset and Richard Grey were thrustingly merry, looking about with eyes that asked who dared drink deeper, dance more gracefully—and the candle of those eyes burned hot, seeking the thrown gauntlet.

And my sovereign lord? Well, truly he feasted twice, once after the vomit—in the high Roman manner, and passing bad for the belly, I have always reckoned; but I loved him no less for it. He cut a fair caper, and had he not been King I would fain have recruited him for my troupe of actors, so well did he disguise his thunderous heart. The reason for this hidden trouble was still Richard of Gloucester, whom, after the service I had done him, I had thought to see no more at court. He danced but once, and that with the Countess of Desmond, and he kissed her cheek in a filial way when all were flown with wine and goodwill. He drank but one cup to toast the King, and he stood out like a ramping tooth—Death at the feast. Ever he toyed with those accursed rings and his eyes were changing—from soft determination to hard melancholy.

George Clarence evaded the King's glance, and drank cup after cup with Lord Hastings who, like himself, shunned the Queen's kin as much as diplomacy would allow. Clarence feigned gaiety over wrath, and times looked like a naughty infant who stamps its feet for a plaything and dares a beating. His wife Isabel was there, waxing faint after a short dance, with a wonderful red colour in her thin cheeks. Clarence cherished her well, for the bright blood in that face was Neville blood. All this I saw, and because I would have had my King merry in soul and body at Yule I became furious. I therefore found satisfaction in persecuting Clarence's poxy mermaid, who was with us again, angel-voiced and simpering. For Clarence it was who had caused my King's well-disguised disquietude. He had suffered a change of humour.

I had not been wandering when I marked Gloucester's expression as he came from St-Martin-le-Grand. I said he looked as one who sees the need to do battle, and I was in sympathy with him. As soon as I had overheard his oath: 'To the Devil with the estates!' I longed to see him settled, and King Edward too. Richard had spoken to me during the Twelve Days. Half-demented from my exertions, I had gone aloft to the gallery. Now this was not like the gallery at

Greenwich, with its souvenirs of the Maiden; that was just a little stone recess where one could stand very close, and mayhap trip a measure for the sheer, silly childish joy of it. This was a broad passage with the moon coming through the openings between the corbels, and great chambers leading off on one side. Into one of these I skipped to quiet my pounding heart, and there, without candles, was Gloucester, his elbows on the window-ledge. I muttered apology, but he turned, friendly, from the night sky and I made a light for him. His face was all hollows and bones in the solitary flame. He knew me then. I would have assayed a jest and gone, but he said:

'I didn't acknowledge the service you did me in September,' whereupon I replied: 'To serve your Grace warrants pride on the servant's part, naught else,' thinking all the time how little he knew he was nearly *not* so served.

'You will not find me ungrateful,' he said, still short and brusque, and I wondered what made him so: just the absence of Anne, or was it ever his way? So I dared ask him how the Lady Anne was, and he answered she was weary of Sanctuary. He sounded sad, then.

So he must have anticipated trouble, and he was not disappointed. The court hummed with George's latest sleight-of-hand.

'A chop-house!' he had cried, feigning great wonder. 'Certes, the doings at Tewkesbury must have addled the maiden! Fortunate indeed that you found her, good brother.'

In the King's pleasure-chamber, John had twanged a false note in his excitement.

'I made a loathsome din,' he told me afterwards. 'But so amazed was I by Clarence's duplicity I forgot all Master Buckeron's teaching. One should keep the thumb fixed so, behind the neck of my lady Lute and—'

'A plague on that,' I said. 'What did the King say?'

'He looked very hard at Clarence, as if deciding this play-acting unworthy of comment. Then he turned to my lord of Gloucester, saying, "Let us now arrange your marriage with Lady Anne, and name your first-born after me." "With my whole heart, your Grace," said Gloucester, and was bending to kiss the King's hand, when Clarence gave a mighty shout. "Nay!" he cried. "He shall not have her! She is still my ward, and the Neville affairs are in my hands. Her sister is still my wife. He'll not marry her, and there's an end to it."

'The King rose and swept all his chessmen to the floor, and the blood came into his face. "By God's Blessed Lady," he said, "George, would you deny our brother the solace of marriage?" "Let him marry someone else," said Clarence, right sullen. Wherefore my lord of Gloucester murmured that this was not his desire, and I went on playing as best I could with my ears not on the tune, and got some strange looks from Master Carlile.'

Yet now they were married, after months of wrangling, and because it had so affected me, what with my devil and my anxieties, and now with my own future in the balance, I lusted to know the details. So I halted my mount until John and I rode knee to knee and spoke him soft, smothering my foul humour.

'They say it's a cheerless place, Middleham,' I murmured.

'Who says?' he asked scornfully. 'My Lady Anne seemed well disposed to ride there with her lord.'

'Tell me about the wedding.'

'It was as any other,' said he. 'The bells rang, the incense burned, the Sacrament was taken, the vows plighted. They were married.' I vowed he was an exceeding dull chronicler.

'Yet it was a quiet ado,' he mused. 'With scant ceremony. Unlike the Princess Margaret's union with Duke Charles le Temeraire.'

I scowled at him. He had been there too, in Burgundy, at the right place and time as usual. He chattered on.

'Only the direct members of the blood royal—all the Queen's kin and my lady's sister, ridden with Clarence from Warwick Castle.'

'So Clarence is at Warwick!'

'How wan of countenance she was,' he said tenderly, lost in his own drift.

'Lady Isabel is sick,' I reminded him.

'Nay, the Lady Anne. Her Grace the Queen looked proud,' he remarked, and with these few words drew a clear picture of Elizabeth, great with another royal child, all firm lips and high brow, condescending to bless the marriage of her brother-in-law with little Anne. Neville and Beauchamp Anne, before her noble father launched himself against the Woodvilles and the realm. Neville and Beauchamp still, but I could well imagine the disdainful looks from those whom the Earl once tried to overthrow.

I asked: 'What took place at the Council meeting? Clarence was so adamant.'

John said: 'Well, the brothers parted with affection, after the ceremony. Of the settlement I know little—there are more words than music in King's Chamber of Council.' He pointed ahead. 'He can sate your curiosity, if he has a mind.'

The clerk rode bowed-headed. His plainsong blew back through the brightening morning. The cold air pricked pimples on his tonsured scalp. I urged forward beside him. He was midway through a soft *Magnificat*, so I waited until he got to '*et in saecula saeculorum*' and joined him in the long '*Amen*'. He was bound for Dunstable Priory, with letters from his master, the Abbot of Croyland.

'We ride to Yorkshire,' I said, and he murmured, 'Ah, a wild part, with great abbeys and rolling heathlands,' and my heart became heavier for all this sounded somewhat gloomy. But there could be no casting back, now, and I was keen to hear his knowledge of the blood royal. I probed his mind, gently, like tickling a trout.

'I have yet to visit Croyland.' No sooner had the words left me than he was off, all a-shimmer with the Abbey's history.

'Holy St Guthlac founded it in the six hundred and ninety-ninth year of our Lord, when Croyland was bound by water,' said he. 'The house has withstood fire and earthquake. Our carved rood screen is the finest. The footbridge in the market place spans three holy streams—my master is making a new chronicle which will compass all England and its times—my hands ache with the writing of it.'

He spoke of blessed streams, and his words ran on like one of them. He talked of St Benedict of Nursia, his patron. It seemed I would never draw him on to the subject of the War-wick estates. When he paused for air, I said with cautious haste: 'Sir Clerk, I would gladly know what your master wrote of the King's Council meetings at Sheen lately,' and he replied:

'Never have I heard so many arguments put forth on either side in respect of the Lady Anne. Nor have I heard before such eloquence as that possessed by my lord of Clarence. Even the lawyers were amazed by his ingenuity. Again and again he swore that the right of wardship was his and that Gloucester should have none of her.'

'How spoke King Edward?'

'When at first my lord of Gloucester offered to relinquish all . . . the King showed anger, as if he thought him over-generous.'

'He said this?'

'During a lapse in the sessions I heard him with raised voice. "Nay, sir," he told the lord Richard. "You are my loyal and beloved brother and I will not see you cheated. But Clarence must be handled with velvet or he will wax more stubborn." Gloucester answered: "All I want, Sire, is my wife

—and Middleham." "It is not enough, by God's Blessed Lady!" said King Edward. He strode back into Council, and weeks longer they argued, Clarence full of orations, my lord of Gloucester standing quiet, and full only of thoughts.'

In my mind I could see him, pensive, unsmiling, rigid.

'Finally he grew passionate,' said the clerk. 'He marched towards the Bench and faced them, turning this way and that so that his royal brothers should know his mind. "My lords and honest citizens," he said. "I pray his Grace's indulgence, but my wish is only for marriage with the Lady Anne, and for the Castle of Middleham. My brother of Clarence can have the remainder of the Warwick lands given me by the King after Barnet Field. So can he also have my Great Chamberlainship of England. And the earldoms of Warwick and Salisbury. All I desire is my wife—and Middleham".'

Warwick Castle alone was a prize. I could scarcely believe it.

'"And Sheriff Hutton, and Penrith," said the King sternly. "So be it," said my lord of Clarence, and a long sigh rushed round the chamber. There was then only the sound of parchment being rolled, and coughing and yawning, and a great black cloud, lifting.'

'You are a poet, Sir Clerk,' I said admiringly.

'And a Parliamentary roll ordaining that no grant of lands made to Clarence ever be revoked,' he added, reproving my frivolity.

We parted near Dunstable and he gave me his blessing, and I was glad of it, for London and all I loved were slipping further and further behind down Watling Street. The first night we lodged six leagues south of Northampton and I slept well, also the following night, outside Lincoln walls. But on the morning of the fourth day, with the towns getting fewer and the great flocks of sheep rolling across our path, I waxed doleful indeed. I wondered what the Princess Elizabeth was doing, and whether the King were pleased with his new fool. I thought on my mother and the last time we met. She had been wondrous merry, pert with some hidden humour like a young maid, and when I gave her the news of my impending departure, and into whose service, she clapped her hands, saying I was a fortunate man. She then made me admire the new shop front, which gleamed black and gilded, and the brave new sign clanking in the breeze, and all I could get from her was what a noble prince was my lord of Gloucester.

'Serve him well,' she said, and when I raised my brows, she did but repeat herself and went on stroking the new timbers, like a daft woman, lovelorn. I hate secrets.

Also she asked me when I was to be married. For, over that miserable winter of '71, I had in my great folly, become betrothed to the maiden seen for the first time outside St Swithin's Church. Maiden I say, but Mistress Grace was in fact a widow of two-and-twenty, and all aflame to marry again. Mourning had not suited her heart—she was a fickle, jealous, wayward creature and for a space she fascinated me. From the moment I accepted her invitation to dine at her parents' house, things were out of my hands. Her father was a grocer and apothecary with a shop in Bucklersbury Lane, where he sold treacle of Genoa, and honey and sugar-loaves and copperas and cubebs and liquorice, as well as coarse goods in bulk. He had a house in St Laurence's Lane, next to Blossom's Inn with its sign of St Laurence the Deacon in a border of flowers. He was wealthy, but I was not without the wherewithal by any account, and both my mother and Grace's family seemed delighted by the match. So we were troth-plight-bound as if by marriage, in God's sight. I had had a strange feeling on hearing my baptismal name, used so rarely: Piers, the man, or Patch, the fool: which would you? One afternoon she well nigh tempted me to sin, in her parents' parlour. She had black eyes. We were betrothed, and I knew not if I loved her. She had not wept when I left for the north. She had only looked at me as if she couldn't wait for my return; or as if she couldn't wait.

'I will send for you,' I had told her, and she had wrapped her arms about my neck, shuddering delicately.

'Dear heart, I couldn't brook those solitary parts,' she had said. 'Mayhap I will go to the Minories for a space,' but I knew she would not. She had too much of a roving eye to cloister herself among the droning nuns. None the less, I am what I am, weak and cautious, and would not commit myself to instant matrimony, so I said: 'I will come soon again to London,' and gave her a tawny gown furred with squirrel, and a coral beads, which she wrapped round her wrist in the fashionable manner. I suppose it must have been in the back of my mind that she was my surety for a return to London, for if I asked my lord of Gloucester for leave to visit my *betrothed*, after all that had passed between him and me, and his lady, he could surely not refuse me. In any event, it was done; and as I rode north I still knew not if I loved her.

By four of the clock we were in right wild country, with

our mounts flagging from the undulations of the Fosse Way. Treacherous ice patches covered the small bogs in our path. We forded streams, plunged through thickets where the only life was the frightened duck and grouse and wild boar which started and squealed. It was as the Croyland monk had said, wild and awesome; we passed the sprawling grey shape of many an abbey and priory. Then, suddenly, a great mysterious hand threw a cloak upon us. Utterly bewildered, our company came to a stop.

'We're lost,' said John.

Ahead, I heard Sir James Tyrell in conversation with his esquires. Their voices and the chink of their horses' gear sounded dull and far in the still, enveloping greyness.

'What was that last holy dwelling?'

'Kirklees, or Hampole, my lord. I'm not sure.'

'We are off course,' said Sir James.

He murmured something else. One of the esquires rode back to us, his face a pale splash in the swirling cloud.

'We will seek shelter at the next abbey,' he told us. 'My lord says it's madness to go on.' He turned his horse, and vanished within an armsbreadth. John clutched my sleeve, fear in his face.

'It's only fog,' I said kindly. 'Bear up.'

'I thought I saw . . .' He was muttering about demons, then asked with fresh terror if we were to spend the night at Kirklees, where the wicked nun bled Robin Hood to death, and Jesu preserve us all!

We approached neither Kirklees nor Hampole. I never knew the name of that holy house, but it was a grim, solitary place and the nun at the lodge gate loath to receive us.

'We've enough to feed already,' she said, then saw Sir James looming behind us on his great black horse, and became all aflutter. 'Enter, sirs.'

We dismounted, aching from damp and the ride, and tramped through cloisters into the parlour, where the Prioress, no more than five-and-twenty, received us in rich robes. She sat motionless, a small dog on her lap. Jewels sparkled on her white hands. The *Romaunt de la Rose* lay open on the table. At the farther end of the room a fine peregrine sat on its rod. I looked keenly at the lady and decided that this was a very worldly nun. John also stared, under his lashes. I wondered if he were thinking of Master Hood, and looking for blood-irons.

'Sirs, please to be fed,' she said in a high, douce tone. 'There are two chambers you may use—we have parlour-boarders here or I would house you better.' She rang a bell and a maiden entered. She was about thirteen; no nun's habit for her, nor jewelled rings. She wore a plain grey gown and limped.

'Mistress Edyth will guide you to the guesthouse,' said Madame. 'But soft, sirs, it is long past Compline.'

We followed the shadowy Edyth along the cloister out into the fog and the cloister-garth and through to the long low building which served the corrodians and there we ate mutton in an uneasy silence. Edyth hovered; she was pale, with sad dull eyes. There was a heavy atmosphere about the place. I felt it, as I stood with John and Robert in the passage waiting while Edyth brought candles. It was so still, yet fraught with past dooms. Unconsciously I felt for my knife as a jay-bird screamed. A dog howled, a woman laughed. I lingered for a moment while the others went towards bed. I know not why. As I stood I heard a quick, light tread, and saw a flickering light bloom in the dark distance. A woman was approaching—not a nun—she wore a neat headdress with a short veil. She was as small as a faery woman, with a hand-span waist. She was the Maiden, and just as in my dreams, only better.

She stopped and peeped up at me, and it was as of old with the flame leaping round our heads and the chill darkness. The last time I had seen her she was distraught and weeping, while the King was captive and heads rolling all over the realm. Now she was calm, and older. Like a still portrait she stood with one hand on the crucifix at her breast, the other raised so that the light she held flooded us both and flickered in the draught. She had filled my thoughts for a long, long time, and I had thought to see her no more. And all my wit and power were stilled under the force of my love, and I knew not what to say to her. So I spoke her name, saying it over and over, and then I took and kissed her hand, the one that lay on the Cross. When she greeted me it was as if she were the jester, and I the maiden.

'Well, sir!' she said smiling. 'Is the King's fool to become a monk? If so, he has strayed into the wrong cloister, for we have no habit to fit him here. Or is it plans for some new disguising?'

I heard my own voice boom back from the vaulted passage. 'Sweetest of mistresses! Oh, sweet! How and what do you here, in God's name?'

She set the candle on the ledge and spread her hands, just as she used to do.

'I live here,' she said simply. 'This place is my husband in truth, for my dower feeds me, and clothes me . . .'

'I never guessed you were to buy a corrody,' I said, and she answered right swiftly: 'It was bought *for* me, my friend, and thus I eat heartily and pray long—that is, when I can, for the jargoning birds in church and dorter drive one senseless with their noise.'

So she was unhappy. To gain time I said: 'We were lost. We came here for succour. At first they were loath to open but Sir James . . .'

She cut into my speech and her lips curled scornfully.

'Pay no heed to their tales,' she said. 'It costs less to feed wayfarers than to flaunt in twenty shillings of fur on her mantle, as does the Prioress!'

When she was young, and I her only friend at court, I would hold her hand; at Christmas I had kissed her. I again took her hand and held on to it, and she curled her fingers around mine. Truly I had forgotten how deep I loved her. A sighing wind blew down the corridor and the little veil fluttered on either side of her face. I thought of her nut-brown hair, hidden this night, and I, too, sighed like the wind. Now I could rue my hasty betrothal. In the sight of God, Grace and I were one, and here was I, enchanted. The Maiden and I stared at each other, and the scent of my sorrow must have released hers, for she cried:

'Oh, Patch! this is a terrible place—there's no discipline, no peace. One of the nuns threw herself into the well, a month past.'

'Why, in heaven's name?'

'She was guilty of apostasy.'

'In what way?'

The Maiden smiled, a wonderful tight smile. 'She was in love.'

To change the subject I said: 'We are for Middleham,' and in the guttering candlelight I could have sworn her colour faded and came back.

'We can't talk here,' she said, after a pause. 'Come to the scriptorium.'

As we walked together, one of the shadows detached itself from a pillar and became the little Edyth. She took the Maiden's gown by its edge and went along with her like a dog. It was then I knew her witless, and wondered even on that, for I am far from such, yet would fain have been my sweet mistress's cur, fawning on her daily. The Maiden spoke her soft, saying: 'Go along, dear child; wait in my room,' then turned to me and murmured: 'She is not as marvellously dull as she appears; she is my beadswoman in heart and thought —indispensable.'

Yet Edyth tarried, looking at my lady with all the love I would fain have shown, until the Maiden said: 'Go! tend the jewel, she was coughing a half-hour back. I shall not be long.' And Edyth became a shadow again, merging with the darkness.

'A sick nun?' I asked.

She smiled and laughed and looked sad, all at once.

'As you wish. Aye, a young, sick nun.'

'Who is Edyth?'

'One such as I,' said my lady. 'One who rides the tide anchorless. She is gently born. A bastard. Now, what of the court?'

I drew my wits together and told her of London. Being cloistered she knew little of past events. She knew of Warwick, though.

'I cannot believe that he is dead,' she said slowly. 'Never will I forget my first sight of him—he was like one descended from Olympus.' Then she asked: 'How does the Queen's Grace, and all her many cousins?'

'Thriving,' said I. 'Waxing fat.'

'The Dowager Duchess of Bedford?'

'Dead and chested.' Remembering that the Maiden had served that lady intimately, I added, 'God assoil her.' I waited for her 'Amen' but her thoughts must have wandered for a space, for I did not hear it. She asked after Katherine and Elinor and Mary and Anne Haute and Elysande, and I was able to give her news of all these fair ones. She hounded me with questions.

'And the Princesses, and the new, blessed heir to England?'

I told her of my sweet Elizabeth, raking through last autumn's leaves for titbits to enchant her. I told of the day when Elizabeth escaped her nurse, and the Duke of Gloucester's wrath. She became very still suddenly, with the stillness of a rose before its petals drop.

'You say—Richard was angry with the dame,' she said, as if it mattered.

'Aye, white with fury and concern.'

'He was rare in his wrath, as I remember.'

'Ah, you would not know Gloucester now,' I said. 'When you were at court he was but a youth, shy, ill-fitting among the gaiety. Now he is a man, with battle scars and a will of his own. Constable and Admiral of England, and Lord of the

North. He rules these parts—from Wensleydale.' I pointed northward. 'From that gloomy fortress of his, where I am bound tomorrow.'

I hoped she would commiserate with me for she knew how I loved London. But she said, right soft: 'Wensleydale, with its sharp cleansing gales and haunted mists. There a man can come close to God and know himself at last,' and it sounded like a poem she had by rote, a song of someone else's making. 'Tell me of all the royal princes,' she said.

I knew not where to begin, but told of George of Clarence, recounting my part in the love-tale of Anne Neville. I spared no detail, for it was better than any ballad lately fashioned, being so packed with surprise and romance, and as I had been a protagonist in the strange events I recounted with gusto. And she was very quiet—the quietest audience I had had for many a geste-night.

When I paused for want of fresh embroidery she said: 'Tell on—so George thwarted the match,' and I said, with satisfaction, 'Yea, and with such cunning one could almost admire him.' Suddenly she cried: 'Friend, will you bear a letter for me?' She called for pen and paper, which the pale Edyth brought, with fresh candles. Thus she wrote, standing fine and slender like the carved scribe-stand against which she leaned, while I waited, drinking up her beauty. She rolled the paper and then she took from her pouch her seal which she held up, dark and heavy-gleaming, saying: 'My seal—at least they left me that.' She took the tallow to the flame and sealed the letter and addressed it: 'In secret, to his Grace the Duke of Gloucester,' and then as an afterthought, all his titles. She was about to give it to me when I said: 'But I didn't finish my story—do you not like it?' and added the parts I had missed, about my devil and his flying away, and she crossed herself to think of such a horrid demon plaguing me. She murmured: 'So they were wedded, eventually?' Her eyes were big and lustrous and I longed to kiss her, but on seeing her seal realized how little I had known of her, and of her family. She had always vowed herself humble, at court, with her dead father a landless knight, but in truth she had as much right there as any of the upstarts brought in over the years by the Woodvilles. It was then I felt bound to tell her a little of my thoughts, and plunged in, clumsy-footed.

'I had a dream of you last autumn.' She smiled softly. 'A fair dream, I hope?' So I told her how strange it was, and affrighting, and as I spoke I thought I saw something cousin to fear growing in her eyes. Then when I came to the end, where I fancied I saw her burning and heard the whisperings of necromancy, she cried: 'Ah, God! Do not! Say no more!' and turning from me fell upon her knees. I caught her shoulders and drew her up, full of remorse.

And all she could say, with sobs pouring, was: 'I am innocent—I had no part of it. All were lies,' and she raised her face, just the shape of a little shield, perfect and pointed. And looking at that face which was incapable of sin, I said: 'Sweet lady—it was but a foolish dream, and you never wrought witchcraft in your life, that I know.'

Yet she talked on wildly. 'You have told me, this night, that the Duchess of Bedford is dead and chested—I could have been served likewise. Ah, God help her!'

'Yes, she's dead,' I said, wondering.

She whispered: 'Was it—the block—the stake?'

'The Duchess died in her bed,' I said slowly. 'Peaceful, and shriven, with all her daughters round her, and the window wide for her spirit's passage. What talk is this of judgments?'

'But she bewitched the King!' said the Maiden, shuddering.

This I had not heard, and was full of horror for my lady's indiscretion. 'There was a charge of sorcery, indeed,' I said, very quiet. 'But it was my Lord of Warwick whom she was said to have enthralled. They said she made images of him with an iron band round his waist, to sap his strength. Not of his Grace, certès. There was a clerk named Daunger, whom Thomas Wake said had practised witchcraft years ago and knew the Duchess. But naught was proven. The arraignment was dropped, and all was fog and mist for there was none to testify.'

'Did they not speak of me?'

'At no time,' I said truthfully. I had only wished they had spoken of her, for she had vanished, and it seemed that none knew, or cared.

'Or—of love-sorcery?'

'Dear lady,' I said, patient, 'it was all a pitiful attempt to shake the Queen's kin during the rebellion—gone like summer haze. Be calm, for your soul's sake!'

She laughed, with no humour in it, more like weeping. I was nigh frantic, perplexed by her. I was almost glad when Edyth stole back into the chamber. To my lady she whispered: 'She is fretting for you.'

'Coming!' said the Maiden in a stronger voice. 'Farewell, Sir Fool.'

'Give me the letter,' I said, holding out my hand.

But she only smiled, and held the roll in the flame, and it

burnt up bright and lit all our faces with a glow like Hell Mouth at the Gild plays, and was destroyed.

'God send you good fortune,' she laid her lips most sweetly on my cheek. She was leaving, and I could not bear it.

'St Catherine have you in her keeping,' I said with difficulty.

'We shall not meet again,' she said, and was gone the next instant.

Fool that I am, I wept.

His Majesty keeps mastiffs. They lie outside his chamber of a night. Soon after his coronation we had a big baiting at Smithfield: in its way an innovation because instead of a bull, he commanded that a lion should be tried against three of his dogs. When the great tawny beast lay dead, and the curs, all gaping gory wounds, stood panting froth, King Henry ordered a strange conclusion to the sport.

'Hang them,' he said in his high Welsh voice. 'Traitorous dogs shall not rise against a king.' It took long moments for the big animals to choke on the end of a felon's halter. Some of the ladies shuddered at the unnatural sight; my sweet Elizabeth merely smiled a curious little smile. But then she knows his Majesty's mind, being wedded to him, and sees reason where most ignorant folk cannot . . .

There were many dogs at Middleham. When I rode up from the market-place, a half-dozen of Richard's hounds ran to greet me. I waved my staff with its merry moonface jester's banner, crying: 'Call off your dogs, my lord! Here enters the king of mirth and none other. My sword is wit—yet, marry, though there be no bone in the tongue it has often broken a man's head!' All this was wasted—there were only the open-mouthed stable knaves and the smith to hear me. They shook their heads, muttering that I must be a Turk or a Frenchie, so odd were my ways. Nor could I reckon much of their northern speech. I dismounted and fondled Richard's dogs: great deerhounds with a brush of wolf in them, slender running-whelps and harriers. Strong dogs.

That first evening, during supper, when I bounded into the Great Hall full of quips and favoured heraldic allusions, I looked to my new master's dais and was quite put at a loss. Though he sat under his cloth of estate with his wife and his friends about him, I had ado to recognize him. This was not the sombre, watchful young knight of the royal court. Those once guarded eyes had a light in them—like the renewed flame in those of one recovered from a dolorous sickness, or the gleam of those returning from blessed Compostella. Now and again his face broke up into smiles, as if he had no control over a deep gladness and comfort deep within. I looked along the table for the reason for his joy. In great Warwick's powerful day, my lady Anne was ever a lovesome little creature. Now it was not the rich jewels or the blue velvet that made her fair, though lovely indeed she was. She, too, had that same inner light.

He held her hand, shamelessly. Their joined hands lay on the damask; this made eating difficult, but quite often they disdained to eat, and looked at each other. My jests that night were a little diffident, as I was anxious to try the humour of this strange place, but my lord and lady laughed at everything I said, or did. I closed one eye at John and Robert. After a time the minstrels struck up *'Filles a marier'* which warns maidens against marriage because of its domestic hazards, and Anne Neville smiled, casting down her eyes, shaking her head.

Item, I had seen a friend when we passed through York. Coming up Stonegate, where they had brought the masonry to finish the fair Cathedral Church, I chanced to raise my eyes to the new houses and the gildsmen's high halls, and there, perched on a stone buttress, was my devil. I stared him out, saying under my breath: 'All this is your fault, fiend,' but to my surprise he only looked straight ahead, as if we had never been familiar, or argued about the fate of Lady Anne. I was quite wounded by his unmannerly ways.

Gloucester's friends sat about him at the high table: Francis Lovell, Robert Percy, James Harrington, William Parr, Richard Nele and Miles Metcalfe, lawyers both; and two of the Warwick kinsmen, Lord Scrope of Bolton and Baron Greystoke, Richard's loyal friends. James Tyrell was there, too. When the pale purple evening deepened to violet through the high windows, they brought torches and Gloucester beckoned me to the dais. It was for a moment reminiscent of King Edward's easy custom. He was not bent on mirth, Richard, however, for he leaned across and asked softly: 'Now, my friend, what of London?'

It seemed as if this was another pressing me for news, as if I knew more than the lords about him. I was curious, for Richard was not cloistered in a nunnery, like my sweet lady. Accordingly I gazed with innocent and lackwit eyes, saying:

'Marry, sir, the forests of Eltham mourn now that the noblest of Boars is departed,' and although his lips flickered upwards he said: 'Don't flatter me, Sir Fool,' and I thought how George of Clarence would have preened at my choice folly. I told him that the King was well, and his Queen, for diplomacy throwing in 'more beautiful than ever,' at which my lord turned to the Lady Anne. He murmured: 'Sir Fool prates of beauty. How should he know, when all beauty is at Middleham?' and this threw me adrift for a moment, to hear such words from one who had just condemned flattery—until, looking at their faces, I realized that he was in earnest.

'How does my brother of Clarence?' he said, turning to me again.

So I was to be his eyes and ears. I had warned the King, times past, about Warwick's rebellion, yet he had dallied. Richard knew of this. Men speak much before a fool—the name misguides them. In a low tone, I gave my master what I knew. George was again dabbling in conspiracy with the slippery Archbishop of York, George Neville—I cast many an anxious glance at the Lady Anne; it was a passing difficult situation for me. Richard listened and I saw his face begin to lose its lightness.

'The Archbishop is in touch with my lord of Oxford, in France,' I said. 'King Louis has tried attacking Calais, once . . .'

He gestured impatiently. 'Yea, I know of that. It's my brother who troubles me . . . surely even he would not be so . . .'

He was about to say 'so rash, so witless' but checked himself. To try and find an excuse for witless Clarence I murmured, 'Mayhap my lord Astrologer was led by a false star.'

For the prophecy, I reckoned, had given George remembrance that he was in fact, King of England, having been declared heir by the Lancastrian Parliament in '70. Now with Prince Edward of Lancaster and Harry VI entombed, who else? Then I grew cold from the look on Richard's face.

'What prophecy?' he whispered.

Holy Jesu! I thought. He had not heard of it. Impossible but true—he had been too busy looking for Anne. I told him as lightly as I could, and with growing courage, for astrology cannot be treason, that 'the next King's name would begin with "G".' I saw him whiten and cross himself, and it was like a window opening in my mind, flooding me with cold light. I thought of my lord as 'Richard'—often, to myself, I called him 'Dickon'. The name George began with G, indeed—but so did Gloucester. We stared into each other's eyes: I, the fool, he, the Lord of the North. The Great Hall with its gently laughing throng, the clatter of silver, the scurrying servants, quivered into the distance around us. Anne's laughter, rich and soft, answered some gallantry of Francis Lovell.

Gloucester took a primrose from the bowl in front of him. Young and fresh and fair, like in Chaucer's poem. He twirled the little yellow bloom between his fingers. Then he spoke and sometimes, in these clouded days, I hear his words again. 'God forbid,' he said softly. 'This—' and he embraced the whole company with one slight gesture—'this is *my* kingdom.'

His kingdom was a right wild one. Behind his court, the moors rolled upward to the sky. Middleham had stood on the slope of that dale for more than three centuries, and even before that the Conqueror's men had raised a pile of stone, the remnants of which burgeoned against the waving grasses, the shape of motte and bailey still existing. Earlier still, the ancient Celts had built a palace there—it was old as time, this place, and mysterious.

After that first evening I took care to guard my tongue—I am paid to make men merry, not distress them. We never spoke again of the prophecy, though he talked often of Clarence, and once about sending his brother an invitation to stay a while at Middleham. He was all anxiousness; I thought of how he had drawn the flickering Duke over to the King's standard again, before Barnet Field.

In his kingdom he was absorbed. He knew every inch. The flying winds, the bold sunlight that slipped across the moors with dark cloud-banners following were in his blood, as was the swift-rushing Ure, foaming on its journey down to the Mill Gill force at Aysgarth. Secretly I would watch him—for I am curious about my masters—when he rode out hawking, strong and frail, a creature of paradoxes, with his great white gerfalcon on the gauntlet. Its silver bells would catch in the breeze and jingle. Spaniels ran beside, black silk and scent-eager. Spring was coming, and Lent around the corner, the day I challenged him, for a jape, to single combat. Unsmiling, he took me to the tiltyard and with one lance-thrust . . . well, I consider myself nimble, but I fancied he had broken my wrist. Thereupon he hoisted me up with a merry laugh and bound my arm, as a brother might do, roughly gentle. 'Try hawking,' he counselled me and thereafter I accompanied him over the long slopes which opened like the scroll of a manuscript, with the great abbeys, Fountains, Jervaulx,

Rievaulx, for initial letters and the dotted thickets the lesser text. Often it was just he and I and the Lady Anne.

The blessed time of Passion and Resurrection was behind us soon. I remember how heavenly sweet the choristers lifted their voices. At one moment it seemed that their praises would burst right through the roof of the nave and up into the clear moorland air among the larks who carolled of our deliverance. There was a great freedom about that place, a sanctity. I rode down the dale with my lord and lady. Anne's mare, Cryseyde, stopped to nibble a hazel sapling. The new buds were tempting as almond milk—no matter how she tugged the rein, the beast wouldn't budge, so I disengaged horse from branch, and Lady Anne smiled her thanks, singing to herself all the while. The ballad she sang hurled my heart down into my parti-coloured boots.

> 'For if ye, as ye said,
> Be so unkind to leave behind
> Your love, the Nut-Brown Maid . . .

Why do you weep, Sir Fool?'

I shut my eyes hard, and laughed so loud that Gloucester turned back to see what we were about.

'That poor song ill-befits so fair a voice,' I said, and in a great burst of rodomontade, 'Marry, I have a song that I fancy may outshine it; if it does not please you, madame, then I will eat it, together with salt and pepper and a wing of the next duck your lord puts up.'

She clapped her hands together, joyful as a child. I had meant to hoard this poem for some special occasion, but I would fain change the tune on her lips, for at this moment, all the day's sweet was mixed with sour. So I cleared my sandy throat and gave forth with my poor effort, all in praise of the little Duchess. Her pale face flamed with pleasure. Gloucester watched her with a serious love. 'Brave, Patch,' he said. 'For that, you shall put up the first bird.'

I rode off, balancing my sparrowhawk, sending in the dogs, gently showing my hawk the light, then throwing her up into the winds. And when I looked back from the fluttering, diving birds, I saw Richard lifting his lady from her horse on to his. So gently he set his lips on her brow, on each eyelid, on her small, pale mouth. The spaniels started many birds that day, and all for me, for my master had lost interest. There are a lot of songs written about the toils of wedlock, and most of them by fools. As for the poem, the manuscript was lost long ago, but some of the lines bide with me:

> 'Now let a muse but murmur of her Grace
> Her Grace's matchless grace is well nigh matched
> For by the blessed beauty of her face
> Poor souls made radiant are, and woes dispatched.
> Hearts that behold her gentleness wax light,
> With humble joy the winds her form caress,
> Heaven's tears dry up at sight of her liesse,[1]
> And Winter yieldeth to a Rose so White.'

There was more, but only the last two lines remain:

> 'She has, and is, in Virtue every part,
> Queen of the North, and noble Gloucester's heart.'

Let no man draw from my chronicle that noble Gloucester was all for dalliance. He was too full of affairs for that, but the day on the hill stays with me, for it was spring and the world the same green world as today, where such matters are concerned. He was twenty, and she sixteen. This world that passes soon, as flowers fair.

John was in love with the Duchess. I think he saw himself as one of the old-style trouveres, who would single out a married lady in secret and, still in secret, give her his heart. He was jealous of my poem, and endeavoured to better it, but in vain. But then, neither could I sing, so the coat was as long as large. And as my lady saw the face of no man but Gloucester, however handsome or devoted, the whole business was not worth a quarrel. Neither, strangest of all, did I feel inclined to quarrelling. I had thought to be restive at Middleham, full of London-longing, but I was not. I had looked for boredom and lonesomeness in the solitary north. I was happy. The summer wore on, and the heather bloomed on the moors, and the flying song of the bees caught my troubles drowsing more than once. I dare not dwell on all this, because when joy is flown the remembrance of that joy's making brings only pain. Then, though, there were no more mists to affright me, no devils to rend my feeble, faltering soul.

The *minstralli ducis gloucestriae* gained some little esteem, as we travelled the north country at intervals. We were two bands—John belonged to the Lady Anne, so he was satisfied

1. Old French—'joy'

at any rate. I can see him still and hear his beautiful singing voice in that upper chapel at Middleham, his eyes steady on the carved roof that was as delicate as a spider-web. So can I hear the rushing river pounding the moorland slope with its message of haste—a beckoning haste that then I did not understand. I can smell the flowers in Lady Anne's garden. I can remember the names of Richard's dogs, most of whom died of old age. I say I do not dwell on that time: I lie. There are things that remain: the flight of a falcon over the dale; the sound of music in the waters of Hell Gill Beck.

I remember—and I have forgotten. Fear and spleen have made me forget all this, yet it comes again and again to taunt and reproach me. For his Divine Majesty likes music too, but the tunes are loud to my old ears, and more devious. He also likes hunting, and is exceeding skilled. He flushes out his quarry from the most secret hides, and his hawks kill with such marvellous speed that a poor fool knows not whether yesterday is today, or today tomorrow.

My Grace wrote an ill-formed hand, with characters small and straggling, and I had ado to make much of her writings. I was impatient with this, for they were full of London news, interspersed with her new gown of muster-develers, her sarcenet bonnets and additions to her father's stable. Out of this formless jumble I learned that King Edward had nipped in the bud those fresh stirrings of rebellion in George of Clarence and the Nevilles.

'My Lord Archbishop lies prisoned in Hammes Castle, off great Calais,' she wrote. 'Yet there be many flying tales in London still and men buy harness daily. It may be that Oxford will attack the realm. The King, whom Jesu preserve, keeps watch, moving from town to town. This day I saw the Princess Elizabeth go by barge to the Tower. She will grow into the fairest lady.'

Those were the lines to give me little pangs. The King, bright head grazing the clouds, sword in hand against Lancastrian foes. His eldest daughter, growing womanly.

'My mother has a green popinjay now that talks like a Christian. It pleases me you are happy at Middleham.' A great blot smeared the paper. I wondered if she had been enraged at the time of writing. I had seen her temper; she had sharp nails, and could shout as adeptly as she could wheedle and coax. We would be a right merry pair together, I thought, reading on.

'You speak much of my lord of Gloucester and his fair dealings with the northern citizens. There is like talk here, for some men of York were at my cousin's to dine and full of your good lordship. One said he offers good and indifferent justice to all, gentle or simple,—would then that the sheriff of this ward had his ear, for Master Fray came before sessions two weeks gone and—'

I threw the letter away and leaped up, smote the stone wall a violent blow with my fist, then strode about nursing the pain. Dan Fray had been acquitted. Lack of evidence, wrote Grace, but her careful, blotched characters hid the truth. Secretly I had feared this outcome, but had bargained on my mother's testimony together with that of the cook-boys to secure Fray's conviction. But Fray had done men service in his time; lords who dabbled in this and that, and whose night-walking heralds were taciturn and cloaked. Wretches hang that jurymen may dine, indeed, yet should the wretch know the right words, the jury . . . I wept with rage.

'Why so wrathful, Sir Fool?' asked Gloucester, quietly behind me. His swift eyes caught the discarded roll of writing. 'Has mischief befallen you, or yours?' His tone was the same soft emotionless one I had heard him use on the occasions when, from a quiet niche, I watched him preside at the Council of the North. Wherever the Council met, whether at Sheriff Hutton, Pontefract, or Middleham, the scene would be the same—with Master John Kendall standing, pen poised, behind, Richard would sit in the chair of estate, his red robes a bright flood against the oak. His hands would be gently folded on the table, his eye keen and intent. When he heard news that pleased him, such as the repairing of Holy Trinity Priory at York, a lightning smile would cross his mouth. When he learned at Pontefract of a poor wife dispossessed by the land-hungry overlord, he drew off his ring on his last finger and replaced it, over and over. His face betrayed little; his hands were the heralds of his distress. Once, I had thought it anger that moved them. Long hours I studied him at these council meetings, sessions that left me with a strange feeling of ignorance. In plain words, he educated me in morals and philosophy, and to judge by the startled faces of his fellows, I was not alone. Often I smiled at the dropping jaws of Lords Scrope and Greystoke and the northern justices of the Peace, when Richard, confronted by a wrangling knot of citizens, pronounced a judgment so wonderful in its simplicity that the problem, whatever it was, seemed never to have existed.

While I thought on this, he still stood by me waiting for my answer. But mine was too small a matter, I thought.

'My lady writes of bright green popinjays, your Grace, and I am jealous,' I carolled, thrusting out one red leg.

'How does your mother, at the cook-shop?' he asked, without a smile, and I was afraid he was in league with the devil and could read my thoughts. I dropped all folly on the instant.

'The villain who fired her shop walks free as air, and that displeases me.'

'A corrupt jury,' he said instantly.

'Yea, bought and sold,' I answered.

'Ah, holy God!' he cried. 'It displeases you, friend, but, by Our Lady, it *angers* me. 'Tis like a cursed, creeping plague that weakens the whole structure of our justice. Would that this matter had come before *my* Council!'

Then he asked what else, and I read on, the part not digested, and had ado to conceal a sour grin.

'Fray's nephew died in gaol,' I said. Then the satisfaction vanished, for I had no quarrel with the three yeomen and a knight, likewise chested through the same prison-fever.

'The charge was but flimsy,' wrote my betrothed. 'But they had lain in Fleet for three parts of a year so God took them, they being frail from poor diet. They will come before a higher court.' She had a keen and sarcastic wit, my lady. Richard was looking at me, pensively. He said: 'Sir Fool, what think you of this notion? If money can be exploited to sway justice, why should it not also serve to lighten the lot of those awaiting trial?'

'Pay for their victuals in gaol, my lord?'

He shook his head impatiently. 'Nay—take them from prison—rather have them stand surety in a friend's bond. Thus relieve the dreadful press within the gaols.' He looked sharp. 'Have you seen inside Ludgate, or the Fleet?'

'Never imprisoned, save by a lady's smile,' said I.

'Once I went out of curiosity,' he said softly. 'The sights stayed with me for days. It is a bitter education.'

I gaped. His reasoning had lost me long ago. Prisons were for felons; if you lay within, that was your bad fortune. An esquire came in to say the horses were ready.

'You are for London, my lord?' I asked, in a panic. They seemed to be on the point of departure, and I had not composed my reply to Grace.

'We ride to Nottingham, and the King,' he said, and gave

a peculiar smile. 'A little private business,' and left me wondering.

He also left me to amuse his lady and her companions. We sat on the warm green slope with the Castle behind us and a flourishing oak for shade. Idle days, in the sun, with the fantail doves strutting like tiny peacocks at our feet. 'My lady,' I would say, 'it is your turn to play.'

I would stare at my hand for the best part of a quarter-hour, until I knew each card by heart. I also knew what Lady Anne held; she had poor cards but I was determined she should win. She was dolorous, far away in a dream. She was ever like this—worse perhaps when he went to Scotland to investigate the regular outbreaks of fighting there. She gave a long sigh.

'Dick . . . my lord has been gone five days,' she announced, as if I were a wayfarer newly come to the estate.

'I doubt not he has many pressing affairs for King Edward's ear,' I said lamely. There was no point in jesting with her. When he was gone, she was like a flower out of water, dying by inches. It was as well he never remained absent long.

'He said it was something that would please me,' she said woefully. 'A surprise. A secret, one I would have shared.'

'Oh, my life's sovereign pleasaunce! your good lord had his reasons!' I said, remembering he had hinted about folks in durance and wondering what it was all about. Then she asked me did I know aught of love? I knew not if she spoke of love of God, home and family, country, or of man to woman, so I diced on the latter.

'Yea, "Dan" Chaucer's "dreadful joy",' I said softly. Now that the sharing of our livelode was settled and Grace's dower decided, it was time I set the marriage date. The Maiden had dismissed me. 'We shall not meet again.' My turn to sigh now. How could she be so sure?

'I do crave oranges!' said Lady Anne.

A gasping cry of delight rushed round the circle of gentlewomen. The Duchess's face was sweetly comical in its innocence. I conjured a bright fruit from my sleeve to please her. Next week it would be lemons, no doubt, or pomegranates. My mother had been the same while carrying my youngest brother—

'Little Blaise
Lived but eight days.'

I thought of Isabel Neville's stillborn babe, and resolved an extra fervent prayer for the Duchess's safe travail when her time came. Like a child herself, she sat dabbing at the orange-drops that had splashed on her gown. Lady Harrington knelt beside her.

'Now *you* have a secret for your lord, dear mouse.'

'Marry, she has her lord in a cleft stick,' said I boldly. I was glad they would leave Anne to tell the Duke herself. I anticipated his joy. There was already a child at Middleham; John, Richard's little bastard son. Lady Anne had asked for him, complete with wetnurse. She cuddled him often—he was a lovesome boy, though not pretty; the Plantagenet features were overstrong in the small face and he seemed to have inherited his father's seriousness. Watching her with this product of a gay or careless hour, I had longed to see her with a child of her own. So my day was lightened by an orange-feast.

John was called John of Gloucester, later. Years ago, I watched him go to the block, still serious, still strong of face. He died at twenty, brave Plantagenet. Traitorous dogs shall not rise against a King.

The Lady Anne's secret was very evident before my lord of Gloucester revealed his private business to any of us. He chose to surprise his wife at a great banquet one evening. The Great Hall was bulging with guests. Wreaths of poppies and roses trailed along the damask tablecloths. Pipes of hypocras and malmsey were borne in from the buttery, with baked swan and pheasant, roast capon and sucking-pig, doucettes and subtleties, and a great White Rose fashioned of frosting and honey. A barrowload of fragrant gillyflowers had been mingled with the rushes underfoot. Outside, against a greenish sky, bats dived and swooped past the window arches, and a drowsy thrush chortled. Anne Neville concealed her proud secret behind the high table; it was strange to see her so round, elsewhere she was exceeding slender. I teased her gently, saying I knew it would be the fairest babe ever, and in all virtues like her Grace, save in the 'very, very thing' for I knew Richard longed for an heir. He had given us all an increase in wages.

We had an honoured guest that evening: one whose shadow cast itself over my lord's affairs constantly: Lord Percy, Earl of Northumberland. Grim and arrogant, he had sworn before King's Council to respect Richard's superiority in the northern marches. Richard had likewise taken oath to be his good and gracious lord and give him due considerations in all matters of policy. My lord often entertained this awkward nobleman, made him joint arbiter in the disputes arising amongst the barons, and spoke him fair. Yet the vice Envy gnawed, and my master never touched Northumberland's heart. I capered and mocked and declaimed great double-witted praises on the noble earl and his ancestry which I fancied he might be too slow to grasp, while John and Robert twanged and bugled in the gallery. Lord Percy fed on roast heron and sugared violets, while Richard discoursed with him upon the Scots wars and Middle March jurors, listening cordially to his opinions, firm and cool. Lord Percy could be offensive in a careful, veiled way, but Richard never showed a flicker. There they sat, these two great men: the young, royal Lord of the North, and Henry Percy, whose family had ruled that same North for generations with a heavy hand, and in whose belly this new arrangement lay right sour. Richard, however, had got him laughing when I looked up once from the floor of the Hall. I felt jealous; this was my job. Then I heard Gloucester say: 'They are late.' One of his henchmen leaned down from behind the cloth of estate and whispered. Richard smiled and turned to Lady Anne, pointing to the door, through which strode Sir James Tyrell, dusty from riding, and beside him a frail, ageing lady.

Richard rose and came down the steps to embrace the Countess of Warwick. Sciatica made her hobble at every step, her face was drawn. He kissed her on each cheek and led her to the vacant seat beside her daughter. I had mused about that empty place all evening. Anne was weeping. All she could say was: 'Ah, sweet mother!'

'Tis all thanks to your good lordship,' said the Countess of Warwick wearily. Richard leaned to wipe up tears with a napkin, signalled to me to start a jape, while the servers came forward with food for the fragile old dame.

This then was his well-kept secret. I found out afterwards that King Edward had taken some persuading. None knew why he was so reluctant to release the Countess from Beaulieu Sanctuary, but Richard's pleas at Nottingham had finally succeeded. And he had his reward in the one burning, loving look from his little wife. I would like a woman to look at me like that, if only once. But then, I am not Richard Plantagenet. I am of no importance, and alive.

'It is four winters since we plighted our troth,' wrote my lady. 'I find you a false wretch, as false a knave as ever my eyes
219

beheld, for you say you cannot come to London and I could not support the cold of the north, without that I had a gown furred with the red fox and a dozen pairs of warm shoes, and such an unfeeling creature as yourself would seem ill-disposed to furnish me therewith. I trow you are without a heart.'

Lord! how she did rail! But to good cause, I admit, for over the sweet, fleeting years at Middleham I had become a crafts-man in procrastination. None could hiver-hover like I. Yet I looked forward to her letters, for she still spoke of the King and the weather of policy in and around the capital, furnish-ing me with precious news.

'Since my lord Oxford found himself adrift on St Michael's Mount, he showed good sense in throwing himself upon the King's mercy. My lord Clarence is full proud and lusts for this and that supplementation, and maybe more than just added livelode. The lady Isabel's boy, now Earl of Warwick, thrives and will be the same age as your Duchess Anne's child, bearing the same name, that of his Grace. Katherine my sister is with child again and bound for Calais to succour her lord who received grievous wounds. His wool-ship was plundered by the heathen Scots three days out of Dover. I have a new brachet, bought me by an old friend, you do not know him, he is a gentleman. My lord Clarence left the King's Parliament lately right joyous now that he has Claver-ing in Essex and the manor of Le Herber, that which Earl Warwick used to own. It seems that the King has one thought and that only for his brothers to be at peace together.'

At one juncture it had seemed that Gloucester might lose Middleham. Anxious days those, while Clarence agitated again for the redistribution of the Warwick estates. Lady Anne had wept in the arms of her gentlewomen.

'Why must he have these cravings?' she sobbed. 'Can he not live in harmony?'

'There, dear heart,' said Lady Lovell uneasily.

'My lord thinks as I do. Today he said, "Why can he not be content as I?"'

Thereon I had burst into the room with mad grimace and silly song, and dried their tears within five minutes. Yea, the Church may frown on craftsmen like myself, but I vow there is virtue in folly at times. Then, Dame Jane Collins brought in her precious charge, Edward of Middleham, with his play-fellow, and their sport together put mine to shame. For when Edward bumped his head, little John it was that bawled.

I will speak now of Edward, for he is as clear in my mind as the red rose I wear in my cap today. He was, as I had forecast, the fairest babe I ever saw: light and delicate as a rainbow, with the gentle features of his mother, and Gloucester's dark blue eyes. He wore a white velvet doublet and a tiny dagger, blunt as an old man's wits, and he played the soldier, challenging little John and besting him, for all that he lacked a year of his age.

'Item,' wrote Grace. 'I hear that by the means of the Duke of Gloucester my Lord Archbishop Neville has come home. It passes my understanding that your lord should so concern himself with one who has laboured so treacherously and should have other deserts. I saw the Archbishop leaving ship at St Catherine's. His time in prison has made an old man of him—he could scarce mount the steps. As for you, right worshipful and well beloved, I am likewise waxed frail in your absence, and would wear your ring soon for naught lasts ever, neither beauty, nor money, nor kindness, and my humours change daily, as the moon wanes and waxes. Let no earthly creature see this bill.'

I was about to tear it into shreds accordingly, when her scratched postscript caught my eye. 'Item, your mother is sick.'

Just that. If Grace had wanted to get me to London, she had chosen the right halter to lead me. The letter was a sennight old and the packman who brought it north must have been riding a snail. Not so the courier who arrived at Middleham an hour after I had finished reading my lady's hard words.

His horse was dying. It staggered on its feet, keeled over and lay with blown belly. The rider, a young harnessed knight, strode clear of the kicking hooves and made for the castle steps. He came swiftly, clutching his dispatches hard against his side and doffing his helm with its dark blue mantling. He was not one of the Middleham knights, but was gently born with the right to bear arms of the bend sinister, like Gloucester's John. I did not recognize the other charges on his tabard. Besides I was taken with his eyes. Cold eyes, the colour of ice, and a black ring round the pale candle, like the eyes in a mad horse. There was excitement in him—folk could smell it—they came hastily: the horse-leech and the slaughter-man, the grooms and two of the guard. Then more sedately, a chantry priest and my friends Robert and John, fresh from the delightful toils of music. 'What news?'

221

The young man's eyes, when he smiled, were not cold at all.

'History in the making!' he said. 'I have gained the north in four days from London. Five spent horses and one squire weeping by the road without York! As for the news, you will hear it from his Grace. Where's my lord of Gloucester?'

The guard pointed across the drawbridge. In the long distance, two horsemen were approaching, tiny figures.

'The Duke rode to Rievaulx this day. Is that he returning?'

The strange knight stepped forward a pace. He looked for a long moment into the far blue and green of the spring day. 'Nay, that's Lord Percy's man,' he said finally. 'He bears the silver crescent on his shield.' He stared longer. 'And the Earl's son, Sir Robert, rides with him. He's smiling.'

No man had sight like that, I thought. I made up my mind that he was a braggart and began to chaff him delicately with riddles, while all the time the riders grew closer and closer and came up over the drawbridge and dismounted, hastily, with the same elated air as this keen-sighted gentleman at arms. And they were Robert Percy and his esquire, of the silver crescent and the smiling face.

'We are for France, and war!' they cried.

So it came that I did not ride London-ward alone. At first we were an hundred, then double that number, and by the time of reaching York walls, our band had burgeoned to five hundred northern men; armed knights, archers and swordsmen, on foot and mounted. They wore brigandines, spiked pauldrons at the shoulder, heavy greaves on the leg; they sported jacks and sallets, carried bright swords and bills and leaden mauls; and if the mail sat on some better than others, or there were weapons that had lain idle overlong, it was nevertheless a heartening sight. From Northallerton and Boroughbridge and Knaresborough and Pontefract they came, and at York the column swelled to a thousand and then five hundred more. I could not fight, but I could sing, and so we did, with lewd jests against King Spider, to be wound in his own web, and praises sung for Charles of Burgundy, awaiting at St Omer the flower of England's invading host. Their fathers had taught them the Agincourt song, and now was the time for its airing. So they rode to war, these men of the north—hard and swift of ire and slow to laughter, and they raised their steel-framed eyes often to the standard that flew above the long, glittering file: the snarling Boar of Gloucester.

I contented myself with riding up and down the line with

quip and sally, dodging many a blow from men who could not wait to strike at something. One of these looked at me with scorn and muttered of coxcombs; whereon I rode knee to knee with him and strangled him with a paradox as we came to York, heart-high. On Lendal Bridge, the Friars of St Augustine raised blessing hands—Gloucester bowed; they were his friends. We clattered down Micklegate and either side was hemmed with women whose lords and husbands moved out to mingle with our throng. Under ghost-hung Mickle Bar we rode, and an old man wavered from the walls: 'Jesu preserve his Grace! God for England!' for he had fought beside King Harry, and come back limbless. This then was the army of the North; men bred in the cold moors' solitude, who knew little of the court and its silken coils. Their loves were those of Gloucester, and they were Gloucester's men.

My lord of Northumberland smiled a wonderful sour smile and set his shining back, for it was plain how these northern men loved Gloucester, who took the time to listen to their grievances in all the blaze of his great affairs, and once these had been Percy's people. To quote one small incident: there was that matter of the fishgarths. These traps, said the men of York, littered the Ouse and Humber to such a degree that poor folk could scarcely make a catch; but the Bishop of Durham and those like him needed this meat for their holy houses—an outrageous monopoly, vowed the northern magistrates. Such sacred souls are fat and powerful—it took a King's brother to find the solution. The plaintiffs came to the Council of the North with their pleas, and went away satisfied. So thereafter was fish on the table of clergy and laity alike, and one day fish on the Duke of Gloucester's board—perch and tench and demain bread and pipes of wine—gifts from the grateful aldermen of York. Oh, how that fish stuck in Lord Percy's craw!

When we emerged from Galtres Forest a party of knights awaited us at Bootham Bar. At that time I rode near the man of keen sight. I could only distinguish a vague shape of colour drifting from the standard-bearer's pole, but the young knight said calmly: 'The Company of Taylors and Drapers—a goodly sight.' And again I would not give him credence until he murmured: 'Or, a pavilion purpure lined ermine on a chief azure, a lion's head cabooshed affronte or over all, two Robes of Estate ermine lined purpure. Is your name Thomas, by chance, Sir Fool?'

Throughout London they were arming. In Eastchepe the merchants were leaving their houses on richly caparisoned mounts. I went first to my mother's place, and stood aside for the band of archers who strode down the street, singing grimly.

'Godspeed, lads!' I called.

One stopped, mischievous-faced. 'Don't you wish you were coming, Sir Fool?' he cried. 'Frenchwomen are fair, I'm told, and fairer when they struggle!'

'Bring me a souvenir!'

'A French purse?'

'A French pox, more like!' I cried, then stepped into the cook-shop, my heart sinking, for there was the sickness smell, and no customers. My mother lay abed, small in a mountain of pillows. I pushed between the curtains and embraced her. My sister had come from Kent and stood at the fireplace with her back to me, stoking the flames as if for a lying-in.

'Open the window,' my mother said. 'I would hear the men riding by.' This I did, and the sound of tramping feet rose clear from the cobbles, a never-ending clatter. 'I shall soon be well,' she said, and would not talk about her ailments, but gossiped with me as before, of the Royal household, London life, and trade, which had not been so good lately.

'Folk have not the wherewithal,' she said. 'And there has been too much costly strife in London—quarrels breed heavy fines, and besides, the King, God cherish him, asks much of his people.'

'How?'

'The *benevolences*, he calls them. Even here I've heard grumblings. You cannot milk a dry cow.'

'Why, I thought the King could pluck his jaybirds with such skill that they never cry out.'

'No more. And this war is expensive. God send him victorious.'

'Amen to that,' said I.

She smiled weakly. 'As for this French affair—it is his intent to cool their humours with a real battle."

I felt a wish to see the King. She said, 'You may find him changed,' but would say no more, so I asked about his royal offspring.

'The Prince of Wales is at Ludlow,' she said. 'With his noble governor,' and pulled a little face, saying that some servants of Anthony Woodville, Earl Rivers, had been in the shop lately and brawled with Lord Hastings's men. There had been bloody noses and a table broken. 'Let us hope he is teaching the Prince Edward better manners.'

'The Earl is schooling him in all ways of urbanity and nurture,' said my sister from the fireplace, and I winked at her.

'Let us hope they will not make a milksop of him,' I said boldly, thinking of the Woodvilles' creeping elegance.

'Speaking of heirs,' my mother said, 'you must wed Mistress Grace.' This was the moment I had wished to avoid. I acted right shiftily, causing my mother to plead and my sister to frown.

'Do not deny me grandchildren,' said my mother. I told her I had affairs to see to, and left her with a kiss, trying not to notice her sad face. My sister followed me down; she was weeping.

' 'Tis canker,' she whispered. 'She has a growth on her belly the size of an orange. The doctor would have cut her, but it goes too deep. I mislike your lady Grace, but it would please our mother to see you settled and the line continued.'

'Then *you* have a son,' I said, bitter with grief.

'My son died,' she said, going pale. 'I have been to Canterbury, but I am still barren.'

So I went out into the street, and made my way, heavy-hearted, to Grace's house. I had forgotten how foul London was. The streets were littered with filth that once I had hardly noticed. Had anyone, times past, told me I would crave the moors of Wensleydale, I would have struck him for a traitor.

On the corner of Fish Street I jostled a real popinjay of a fellow who cursed me. My mother had said that folk were tightening their belts against the press of Edward's benevolences, but this man was exceedingly well-endowed. He was no nobleman yet he wore violet satin and carried a gold-headed cane. His hat was a green velvet carrot, with silver tassels. He had a fair, rosy, maiden's face, and his voice, even when raised in oaths, was like a warbling thrush. It was Clarence's mermaid, his protege who sang so sweet. A member of the Profession, so I spoke him soft.

'Life treats you well, friend.' He smiled a double-edged smile at this.

'Certes, I have a good master,' he answered, and flickered past me into Candlewick Street. I watched him disappear into The Parys, a tavern frequented by the wealthiest lords, and I pondered on him all the way to the house of my betrothed.

Well, the banns were cried, and Grace and I were married, and my mother came to church in a litter borne by two of her oldest servants, who had burned to ride on the second Agincourt but were too full of years. The candles gleamed, and we plighted our eternal troth in God's holy house, and took the wedding breakfast at my mother's. There were smiles all round, even on my face, because not for naught was I trained as an actor. Then I took my lady and got her with child; and in the dark, she had very long, soft hair.

Grace was rounding to the grandchild which my mother would never see, the day I sat in the Boar's Head and watched the men returning from war, and saw the faces no longer smiling and heard the voices that no longer sang. Some of them passed through the tavern without words and quaffed ale as if to sate a thirst for blood. Their faces were such I thought it more prudent to sit silent until a figure I knew entered. It was my cousin, who halted at my bench, standing splay-legged, tall and fearsome with eyes like iron bolts.

'You should have come with us,' he said, sickly with scorn. 'For that was a fool's errand, yea, a fool's errand, by Jesu!'

'How went the battle?' I said, frightened. He lobbed his spit over the table edge and down by my feet.

'You should have been there,' he repeated. 'For there was much hearty jesting, and dancing, and sport, sweet talk, fair words. By Our Lord, I need drink! Tapster, wine here!'

'And the fighting? How many casualties—how many men did Charles of Burgundy send?'

'Not a blow was struck,' he said, on a great swallow. 'Not one blow. And as for Burgundy . . .'

There was a clamour at the inn door and a company of young archers came in shouting. They were spoiling for a fight. There had been no booty, no plunder for them in France. Outside, a minor riot was developing among lewd soldiery who had ravished no women, plundered no dwellings. One of the archers was a little flown with drink.

'You liar!' he cried to a fellow. 'My father paid taxes to make war, not sign treaties!'

Blows followed, and the landlord seized a truncheon from the wall and ran among them. It looked a good fight—I fingered my staff, then felt my cousin's fingers gripping my arm. He was gazing through the window where could be seen the livery of the King's Peace officers. 'Be still,' he muttered, and I obeyed, watching while they entered and arrested four, five, six of these young hotbloods, clapping them in manacles and dragging them away, still foamy-mouthed with ale and passion. Then my kinsman told me all.

King Edward had signed a peace treaty with France on the bridge at Picquigny. Charles of Burgundy had never arrived at all; he had gone wandering off to besiege Neuss at the crucial moment. It had been a bloodless truce.

'Disgrace,' I whispered, feeling torn to pieces. 'Oh God, dishonour!'

'I warn you never to speak thus,' my cousin said grimly. 'His Grace has said farewell to mercy.'

He told me that times were a-changing; that the King now intended to punish—with the swiftness of the Almighty—all miscreants in word or deed: thieves, murderers, and those of seditious tongue. 'He may have signed for gold with Louis, but he is still our King, by God's grace, fearful and omnipotent. You'll see.'

'And all the lords stand with him,' I said miserably.

'Yea, they were well pleased with the fine presents King Louis showered . . . save for one, that is.'

'My lord of Gloucester?' I murmured, and he said, somewhat shortly, why did I ask him of the doings in France, if I knew them already?

'He was as angry as any out there.' He pointed to the grumble-haunted street.

'Don't ask me to believe he quarrelled with the King,' I said.

'The Devil have my soul, when I see that day,' said my cousin with a laugh. 'Louis sought to woo him full lovingly, but the more he smiled the more fiercely did Gloucester scowl. He would not dine with the French King, as did my lord of Clarence and de Bretaylle. At the King's direction he accepted Louis's presents, but with as much wrath as if he thought he'd sold himself.'

'Though the Boar is rooted in the Rose,' I mused. 'It seems our King could set the realm in flames and his brother would cleave to him.'

'I know not which he loves more, England or his Grace.'

'They are one and the same,' I said. 'Whatever the end, France is conquered.'

'And Hogan keeps his head.'

'That charlatan!' I roared. On all his perambulations round England the wily old soothsayer stirred up the people. No matter which way the wind blew he could lay claim to foresight and this day no exception. He had forecast that France would be conquered—so had she been, for 50,000 crowns a year and a trade agreement.

'The Princess Elizabeth is promised in marriage to the Dauphin.'

This was the end for me. 'I would leave London,' said I. 'I would go home.'

He smiled. 'So the north is now home to you. You've caught a tincture of its speech—d'you know it?'

Gloucester had taken his anger back to Middleham, yet I was still in London when they burned John Goos for heresy. My mother was fading fast and Grace's time near, like the ebb and flow of the tide. The cook-shop would be mine by my mother's will. Grace expressed the urge to manage it, though I would liefer have put in some trusted body to see to these affairs, and have my wife and child by me in Yorkshire. We quarrelled over it. If I ever conjure her into my mind these days, which I do rarely, I see my lady with her weapons of war to hand: a kettle, a pewter platter, a ginger-jar. Once, she heaved a whole pig's head, hot from the fire, at me. That was one missile I did not catch, but on the whole she fumed in impotence at my dexterity. Though she had her way over the shop.

'I will have no Month's Mind kept,' my mother said, in a whisper.

'If that be your wish,' I answered with regret. I wanted to remember her publicly and in honour, came the anniversary of her departing. The physician approached and set leeches to her temples. Her pallor deepened and her eyes closed in pain. I could not brook remaining in that hot room heavy with sickness and my sister's sorrow. Grace's kinfolk were there too: her haughty brothers and her sister Kate, who was tender to my mother as if she were truly of her blood. I walked with long marching steps through London. Aimlessly I went Tower-ward, where Margaret of Anjou no longer lay; for the King had ransomed her as part of the peace bargain with Louis, and she had returned to France, no longer fair, an old woman.

On Tower Hill there was a vast crowd and some who recognized me. So I gave them a heel-and-toe and a bawdy rhyme, before the real revel began and they led Master Goos, self-confessed Lollard, to the stake. The sheriffs and priests stood about him with stern pleading. He had a sallow, gentle face; and even at that late hour he spoke of Wyclif with quiet conviction as if the whole matter had been decided for him years ago. They beseeched him to die a Christian man but he shook his head. So they looked at one another with thunderous cold looks, and made fast the chains about his body. The smell of the pitch rose high as they soaked the faggots and touched them with flame.

One prist persisted, stepping close in the whirling smoke. 'My son, my son, is not the Holy Sacrament Christ's Body?'

'It is but bread,' gasped the heretic.

When the blackened head drooped, there was a woman who writhed on the ground and wept, despite the tuggings and hushing glances of her friends. There is ever, I have found, one woman who mourns a death. Many may weep but there is always one who loves, and most times she is unknown. Like the dame who cried for Owen Tydder, with his poll on the highest point of Hereford Market Cross. Some unwise philosophy made me say aloud: 'He died for what he thought was right.'

'Yea, he did and is damned for it,' said a great-bellied cordwainer who stood by me, and spat towards the sinking flames.

There were many such sights that year. King Edward was better than his word. He said farewell to mercy and he spared none, not even his own domestic. There were hangings by the score, quarterings and beheadings. Ears were nailed to cartwheels and their owners given a knife and told to leave town. There was even a boiling, but I did not see it. The gaols were straining at the seams. But there were no more mutterings of England's dishonour, for the people were, in a strange way, comforted. They still had their strong fierce monarch, their Rose of Rouen, even if the Rose's petals had curled a little. I saw him a couple of times in the distance. On the first occasion I might have thought him slightly changed for there seemed an unfamiliar fullness about his person. The second time was on the day I returned from the graveyard, walking behind the empty carriage with its big black horses (many accompanied me; my mother was respected). My heart turned a little even in its sadness as the King passed. He was half hidden by his gentlemen-at-arms but what I saw seemed foggy, with no clear outline. It may have been the last of my grief confusing me, but he did not seem so strong and sharp as in my remembrance. It was to be twelve months before I knew the truth of this.

'Right worshipful husband,' wrote Grace after my return north. 'I have had occasion to dismiss Master Bates and Mistress Mary Slone, for idleness was upon them and the woman Slone was in the habit of wasting scraps on back-door vagrants. She was insolent and spoke of going to the Gild for settlement but my brothers talked with her and she will cause no trouble now.'

Mary had been with my mother for fifteen years. It had been her custom to feed beggars; my mother had turned a blind eye.

'My brothers have found a dozen fresh knaves for the work; they are stout fellows and loyal to us. We do not find business to be so thriving as you told me, I know not why. Master Fray came in the shop last week. He said he hoped all was pardoned and we shook hands on it, as I see no call to harbour dead grudges.'

I began to wish she would cease to write me. Then the next bit caught my fancy. 'Duchess Isabel has been passing sick, and was brought to bed of a boy lately. Men say she will not live, her lungs are bad. It is hard to be warm in London, so you freeze, no doubt, in the north parts.' With this joyful thought she commended me to the Almighty, bidding me burn the letter. I turned it sideways to read the postscript.

'Item, the Duchess Isabel is dead.'

That cast a shadow on Lady Anne's Christmas, the year of 1476, though she herself was well, and rosy from the sharp weather. Edward throve, and little John waxed strong. My lord of Gloucester rode against the Scots and returned victorious. I made them good cheer and we were peaceful together —until the King summoned Gloucester to the Great Council at Westminster. There had been grave tidings of a death, and that of one more important than the quiet Isabel. Charles of Burgundy was dead; not of anger over the Picquigny scandal, but from a surfeit of steel in his noble body. Rash as his nickname, the Duke had been besieging Nancy with a depleted force. Thus, in January snow, perish great princes. I stood behind Lady Anne on the castle stair and watched my lord depart. His company moved out of the gate and down the dale, and the spring day was a little dimmed for my Duchess.

'Truly, he seems never at home.'

'Duty robs Beauty, 'tis the thief of joy,' said I.

'He hates London,' she murmured.

King Louis had made a proclamation. Now that Charles was dead he declared Burgundy to be his, all its domains reverting to the Crown of France.

'This day I saw the lords ride to Westminster,' wrote my lady. 'His Grace, whom God uphold, has it in mind to stand with Burgundy, but he would liefer not upset the Frenchie. My lord of Gloucester has advised taking arms, but my lord of Clarence has the notion, men say, to wed the Princess Mary and thus rule Burgundy himself. He is wonderfully strong in his wishes, but I fancy the King does not share this ardour. Messengers take ship daily to the Duchess Margaret but none yet know her mind, that of her late lord's heir, or indeed, the mind of our King.

'Item, my sister's husband is sore afraid lest we fail to keep Flanders. Is it not enough that his ships have trouble with the false Scots and the Hanse traders? For another cargo of wool was taken three days past, and he fears that should we lose our ally, he will lose his livelode.

Item, Mistress Petson's man was fined £1 this day for scalding hogs in the street. Your son has been sick, but is well again.'

We were to know the King's mind, and that of Clarence, before the end of summer. A company came back from London, among them minstrel John, laden with new songs for my lady's delectation. I met him near the smithy, in sunlight.

'This is a fair rondeau,' he said, joyful. '*J'ai pris amours de ma devise.*'

'That's the music of Flanders,' I said. 'And how are they singing in that realm?'

'There's most wonderful mischief.' He drew close. 'Clarence's suit was rebuffed.'

'By the Princess Mary?' I smiled. 'George stuck in her gorge, then?'

'Nay, 'twas the King would not allow it,' he said urgently. 'And as for names, the lady might fare worse to consider St Anthony Woodville.'

'Earl Rivers?'

' 'Tis the Queen's wish, but they say she will not have him, either. As for Clarence . . .'

'Tell me naught,' I chuckled. 'He is enraged, and stalks about the town, vowing the Woodvilles have blighted his troth. Blighted his plight, he wanders meatless and Maryless, making his moan.'

'Far worse. There was a woman hanged by his jurors, and they all in fear of their lives and property to prove other than her guilt.'

'What woman, why?'

'Ankarette Twynhoe,' he whispered.

I remembered Ankarette from the court days. She was Duchess Isabel's chamberwoman, a nice old soul. John told a strange tale.

'My lord swore she had poisoned the Duchess. He sent

231

eighty armed men to her dwelling to drag her from her bed. She was tried speedily and hanged quicker. *Yet the one who should have dangled wears a crown.*'

'You're witless from fast London living,' I said, stupefied by this.

'Clarence vows it. He burst into the King's council chamber while his Grace was at Windsor and said all manner of terrible things. How that the King, the Queen and her kin had plotted against him, had given money to the woman Twynhoe for this murder. And that a Woodville servant had slain his infant son.'

'What else?' Could there be aught else, I wondered. The cards were surely stacked against George, now.

'He has cast a taint upon the King's lineage,' he murmured. 'He would have it that he is the rightful sovereign, his Grace of bastard stock. His men whisper that the King has dabbled in the Black Art,' he said, crossing himself.

'Say no more.' This was treason of the worst kind.

'He courts disaster,' said gentle John, strangely bold. 'I'll say what I wish—there are no spies at Middleham. Not like London, where the Queen's kin are everywhere, whisper, whisper in the alehouse, in church. How that Clarence seeks the downfall of those who lie at Windsor and at Ludlow, surely as the blood of Sir John Woodville and his father stains the Duke's hands.'

'Robin of Redesdale, do his archers shoot from the grave?' I said, wondering.

'But men also say there is some secret Clarence holds,' murmured John. All this was too much for me. I got me to London, full as a plum with curiosity.

I bent to my wife's lips, and she gave me her cheek. So be it, I thought, and kissed my son instead, who knocked off my hat in a loving fury, seized the feather and endeavoured to choke himself with it. My pleasure was only dimmed when I saw him treat my wife's brothers in the same familiar fashion. I did not stay long; I was for the court, all agog to see the King again. The closer I came to him the more I longed to see his smile, his handsome face, and I asked Grace how he did, while clothing myself for the ride to Windsor.

'Easier now that Clarence lies at the Tower,' she replied.

'In the royal apartments?' I asked, lack-wit.

'In a dungeon, dolt!' she said. 'The Queen's kin did their work well. Guard your tongue, no man is safe.' We had one

232

thing in common, my wife and I: the name Woodville bred a hearty mistrust.

'He'll soon pardon him again,' I said. 'Blood is thicker than water.'

'The King has a new leman,' she said suddenly. 'Mistress Shore.'

I burst out laughing. 'Not Will Shore's wife!'

'She is beautiful—none can resist her. She laughs excessively, and is kind besides.'

'I remember her,' I said. 'So it's farewell to lovely Lucey, and all the other queans, for the mercer's finest ware?'

'Oh, he still has others,' she replied. 'The holiest, the fairest, and Jane, the merriest harlot in the realm.' I hastened through the autumn noon to see for myself.

I met Anne Neville outside the royal apartments with her ladies and she gave me a pale smile; the journey south had wearied her. We had left Edward behind at Middleham, and I knew his little fair face haunted her. Richard was nowhere to be found. I had not yet seen the Rose of Rouen, but I had crossed swords with the King's resident fool, and he had bowed to my greater experience. So we had made a pact that he should sing and I would dance, we would both tumble, and when one grew weary the other should relieve him. I was armed with a thousand new jests, suited in purple and green with silver bells on my boots and a longing in my heart to hear the sovereign laughter. The King's laughter—he of the old royal blood. That evening Windsor Great Hall was the same, and the company therein, save for those who were dead or absent for other reasons; the hot perfumed air was as my dreaming nose recalled it. Queen Elizabeth sat lily-cool, and some witchcraft had chained the years at her door, for her beauty was untouched. Beside her, my King.

O Jesu! he was fat! he was well nigh gross, and his complexion marred by threads of scarlet running down into the pouched flesh at his jowl. Those gem-like eyes were fighting for room above full cheeks. The rings cut into his fingers. No one had told me he would look like this. I had need to turn my grief into mockery, vowing that it was joy at seeing him which made me weep.

A printed book was being passed from hand to hand. Over the high wailing music I heard the remarks, and between the velvet sleeves of the Queen's kinfolk saw the flash of gems on its binding.

'What a mind! What a man! Truly the sayings of the Philosophers could have no finer translator. I felicitate you, my lord.' This was Doctor Morton, Master of the Rolls. Barbed whiskers at his chin, he leaned at Anthony Woodville's side.

'Master Caxton has laboured well too,' said my lord of Gloucester, in that emotionless voice. He had come midway through the revel, straight from Horton Quay where his Admiralty had been hearing a case. Soberly dressed, his plumage was markedly dull beside that of his companion. Henry Stafford, Duke of Buckingham, who stood with his arm through Gloucester's, was dizened like a peacock, with his device of the flaming wheel powdered on purple satin. At one time this young man had not excited my curiosity, being only the one wed to Kate Woodville so that the Queen's sister should not die a poor spinster, and the Queen's tears be staunched. Now he glittered, and Richard liked him. There was a lot of Clarence in young Buck, the same languid voice, and fluent charm.

Earl Rivers bore his treasure to the King's dais, smirking, and Edward pored over it. I turned and set off round the hall at a run, flattering the ladies outrageously, conjuring eggs and serpents from the sleeves of bemused lords, capering on the bounds of what was seemly. I leaped on a table and down again, head over arse. I brought two monkeys and staged a wedding. The company loved me. Jane Shore's was a lovely name to juggle with. Better even than the princely stables and the King's Grey Mare.

> 'For Shore is gold a prince's treasure
> And shorely he should take his pleasure.'

Or:

> 'I trow no sailor asks for more—
> Than to come safely into Shore.'

(This last I kept for my friends.) She was fair, as Grace said, and there was much warmth in her. Rosy and round, a little thing, with elegant manners; much kindness did she for men, and her wit was almost equal to mine. Still there were those who reckoned her last name should begin with W, not S, for varying reasons. She danced with Lord Hastings, and once, brushed lightly against Gloucester as he stood with Anne and bright Buckingham. He bowed stiffly to her—his eyes were cold. He was sad that night—an Israelite in Babylon.

Some of the old faces had new husbands. Lady Margaret Beaufort was wed for the third time, now to Lord Stanley.

King Edward had approved this gladly, so said my wife. For Margaret was Lancastrian as well as learned, and Stanley was loyal enough to curb these leanings.

'She brought her son to court, a month past,' Grace told me. 'Dressed like a peasant, with scarce a word to say for himself.'

King Edward had received young Henry Tudor generously, while the court muttered a little at Lady Margaret's effrontery. Some sniggered at his gaucherie and Welsh accent.

There are times when I feel I have lived too long, and seen overmuch. It makes an old man dizzy, the way the wheel spins.

Then there was the night we went down drinking in Southwark, and came out of the inn late, a little cup-shotten but not so mad with wine that we neglected to look well for the Watch or the special constables prowling the darkness. Robert was anxious lest he be locked out. John—well, I had ado to stop him singing. He reeled about and almost pulled me down, and some of his verses would have made the King roar and my Lord Gloucester look very sharp indeed. We rolled up the street, a fine uncaring trinity, being barked at by dogs and cursed by people already abed. It was I who had suggested this foray. Once again I was dolorous: not only because of the King's looks, his loss of something beautiful and remembered that pained me still. Richard seemed full of gloom, his lady choked with anxiety about her faraway son, and Grace—I had had occasion that day to remind her that there were penances for scolds, rich and poor alike, and hang the disgrace of it. It was the hour between dog and wolf, and as the drink soured in my belly old sins kept me company. I should not have been amazed to see my devil, and I had just decided to become a monk when a dreadful, groaning yell convinced me I was too late in my good intentions.

'O Jesu, what was that?' whispered John. He dropped our light in a patch of snow. Cursing, we stood in darkness. I could not find my tinder; I was shivering so much. Robert snatched up the lantern.

'You are a brace of old women,' he said angrily, but the flint was damp. He swore and struggled while my fearful ears strained for other manifestations of Hell. Feet were approaching, their swift thudding accompanied by the sound of gasping breath. There were two people—earthly at that, but in the blackness we could only discern vague shapes. We cringed against the wall. Robert got the lantern going all of a sudden. It flamed up as the shadows passed at a jog-trot; I got a flash of half-hidden white faces, black cloaks and the dull spark of steel. Then they were gone. We breathed again, drunkenly comforted by the absence of ghosts.

'Go carefully,' said Robert. We sidled round the next corner in our little isle of light. The snow was dirty underfoot from the day's traffic. I felt pity for a poor beggar lying in the gutter. He was rolled in a houpeland of fine cloth for such as he; his breath snored whistling through the filth of his pillow. As cup-shotten fools will do, we stood and contemplated him.

'Friends,' said John, 'let us lay him against the wall or he will be trampled.'

'Let him alone,' Robert said. 'Sleep's his only comfort.'

And so, as is ever my way, I did the opposite and rolled the limp form an inch over the cobbles. I saw then that he had been stuck with a dagger; his fine wool doublet was sopped with blood all round the protruding hilt. I called Robert to bring down the light so I could see the face of this well-clad vagrant. It was Clarence's mermaid, and he was not quite dead. The snoring stopped and he gave a bubbling cough. I had found him arrogant but he was after all one of my ilk, an entertainer, so I took his head on my arm and he opened his eyes.

'Sir Fool, tell my lord,' he said, in quite a strong voice. I remembered how beautifully he sang, and I felt great sorrow.

'Peace, friend, lie quiet.'

His breath came quicker, horrible to hear.

'I have done my duty,' he gasped. Then he was babbling in a whisper, babbling and bubbling like a slaughtered beast, and my hands became sticky with his blood. He had a tale for my lord of Clarence, but Clarence was in the Tower, waiting on the abatement of the King's rage. So I tried to quiet the wanderings of this grievous wound, which were a jumble of nonsense, words plaited in a wanton skein, among them being . . . 'the house of the Carmelites' and something that sounded like either 'bastard whelps' or 'Bath and Wells'. I stroked his face with a chilling hand, trying to hush him, while he coughed and then became stark dead. We did not linger, of course. 'Did you know those two?' I asked, as we ran. Robert shook his head but John clutched my arm.

'The one I know,' he whispered. 'He writes ballads. Sometimes he sings.'

'Well, he has sung one there to death,' I said, frozen to the bone.

'He's Earl Rivers's man, I think,' John gasped, running on.

Lady Anne Neville stretched out her hand. 'My lord! Dickon, let me see the letter.' With great reluctance he gave her the precious missive lately received from Middleham, and he smiled for the first time in weeks.

'God be praised, he's well,' she sighed, reading. ' 'Twas a little fever he had. My sweet son!' She kissed the letter as if it were Edward himself. Anne had a cough. She was not so well in London, and touched her amulet constantly; she wore it against her continuing barrenness. We had been gambling in my lord's apartment; a nonsense game, for the Regal of France, the London Stone, and the Forest of Eltham, and I was winning all. While they both read and re-read the letter, their heads together like children, a rap came at the door, and quite a small company entered.

'We are honoured, my lord,' said Richard, rising.

Anthony Woodville, Earl Rivers, was cordial in scarlet satin. Thomas Grey, Marquess of Dorset, looked about him with a little contempt. With them came two boys, neither of whom I had seen for years. Prince Edward had grown fair as a maid, and pouted like one. Richard, Duke of York, was smaller, a swift bright bird. He tugged impatiently at his heavy state robes as if he would fain have put them off. His sleeves were too long—he pushed back the ermine from his wrists like one keen to deal out blows. I knelt before our future monarch, who leaned, languor-pale, on Earl Rivers's arm.

'His princely Grace expressed the wish to see you, Sir," said Rivers, and laughed rather unquietly.

'My brother wanted to hear about the fighting in Scotland,' said Prince Edward quietly. He stepped forward, but Rivers held his hand. There was no holding back the Duke of York, however. He nipped up and took the stance of a grown man, feet crossed, against the table where Gloucester sat. They gazed seriously at one another.

'Sir! Have you slain many men?' enquired the little Duke.

'As many as was needful, my lord,' said Gloucester, with a faint smile.

'How many?' asked Richard of York, and I could foresee a long conversation.

'As many as would have slain my troops, had matters gone otherwise,' replied Gloucester calmly.

'Why do you not recite your verses to his Grace?' asked Rivers, all hasty.

'How many dead?' said Richard of York. 'How many, I say? Did you use guns? Bang! Bang! I have a new pony,' he added. He darted closer to Gloucester, until he leaned on his knee.

'My lord uncle, excuse my brother. He's but an infant,' said the seven-year-old Prince. He disengaged from Rivers's clasp and came to stand by Richard. 'He's to be married soon,' he said confidentially, as if this explained the Duke's wildness.

'Is the lady fair, my lord?' asked Richard of Gloucester.

'She is the Duchess of Norfolk,' said Prince Edward.

'She's taller than me,' said the prospective bridegroom.

'So Richard shall have Anne,' said Gloucester. 'To me, that augurs well for future joy.'

'Did you go in a ship to Scotland?' said the Duke of York. 'Have you many ships? I went in a ship once . . . to a big place and there was a lady . . .'

'That was a barge,' said Prince Edward wearily. 'On the Thames. But I too would dearly love to sail the sea. My lord, when did you first take ship?'

Gloucester looked at the small boy, suddenly serious. 'When I was your age,' he replied, and his voice was quiet. Thomas Grey cleared his throat.

'My Prince, tell his Grace what you have learned of Cicero.'

Edward remained, staring at his uncle. 'Sir, shall I be a soldier and captain like you?' he asked. At this, Gloucester looked straight into Earl Rivers's eyes, saying: 'The finest, good Prince. But better than I. Like the King your father, who raised the great Sun banner and was rewarded by God, in snow, in fog, and in foul country. Skilled in war and courage, as well as in verse and music.' The way he said these last three words made me cringe, and hide my lute behind a cushion.

'What's necromancy?' asked the Duke of York, loud and sudden. Earl Rivers and Grey both moved forward at once.

'Come, my lords, it grows late.'

Obediently the Prince Edward gave his hand again to Earl Rivers, smiling up at him. But little York lingered, staring at my lord, on whose face there was a trace of the old grimness.

"Where's my uncle of Clarence?' the boy demanded suddenly. '*He* makes me laugh. Where's he gone?'

'Come, my lord,' said Thomas Grey. 'Your brother waits,' adding to Gloucester, with a charming smile, 'They are inseparable.' Dickon of York stumbled over his robes in the doorway. This seemed to unleash a tide of passion in him, and we listened to his diminishing shrieks. 'I want to see my Uncle George!'

'Here's a new rhyme,' I began, wriggling in anguish.

Neither my lord nor his lady paid any heed.

'He's Edward's age,' whispered Lady Anne. 'He cannot comprehend all.'

Richard rose slowly, white as a skull. 'Give me your prayers, my lady,' he said, and strode to the door. She stretched out her hands to him, but he was gone, marching through to the King's apartments in a fury of decision. I fidgeted, watching her. She was very thin, and sad.

'Read the letter,' I said, and soon she was lost in it again, murmuring little thoughts like beads. 'Dirick has made him new shoes. Green, silver buckles. Medcalf and Pacock took him to Aysgarth lately—they guard him well, those men.' So I left her and stole away. For that day was the Eve of St Nicholas, the first night of the revels, and I had plans for a spectacular entrance. I would leap from the minstrels' gallery on to the shoulders of the Vice Titivillius 'who snares neglected prayers, words dropped at Mass', and hoped they would pick a sturdy fellow for the part. I had some measurements to make; it would be a mighty leap. So along the passage I went and into the gloom of the small recess, bumping over lecterns and scattering sheets of music. I leaned over the rail to study the drop, and there below, within spitting distance, was proceeding a play, a tragedy by the look of it. In the deserted Hall, the King held court. He had just returned from the chase; there was snow on his boots. The dull gold of his head throbbed in the twilight as he lay wearily in his chair. Richard of Gloucester knelt before him, gripping the sovereign robe by its hem. The Queen looked on. Her hand lay on the back of the King's chair, close to his neck. Her pointed pale face was in shadow but I saw the gleam of her little teeth as she chewed her lip. Edward's voice grated on my ear.

'I have shown mercy,' he said. 'He has betrayed me. Not once but many times, and I have pardoned him. No more.'

'Your most noble Grace,' said Richard, very low, 'does not our Saviour say: forgive not once, but seventy times seven?'

'My lord,' Edward answered heavily, 'I have spoken my mind. The traitor must be punished. It is God's will.'

Elizabeth's soft voice from the shadows said: 'Yea, my lord, the King's grace speaks wisely. For my children are not safe while Clarence lives.'

The King raised his hand, touched white fingers lightly.

'Soft, Bess,' he said gently. 'I have promised. None shall harm our blessed heirs.' She slid away in a rustle of dark satin and diamonds. King Edward rose from his chair, and Richard from his knees.

'Edward my lord,' Gloucester said, 'will you not hear me? Have you forgotten all we have known together? Have you forgotten we are of one blood?'

The King was not wroth. He leaned and kissed Richard, but his tone was stern.

'He is a traitor,' he repeated. 'He has called me bastard and practiser of witchcraft. He has sown death, and shall reap it. Leave me now.'

'Your Grace, he is my brother!' Gloucester's cry chilled me.

'He's mine also, Dickon,' the King said wearily. 'Go from me.'

I watched Gloucester quit the Hall. The Lord of the North —tears poured down his face. Quiet in the gallery, I thought many things as the King sat below, his head cupped in his hand. It seemed plain that the name Woodville had brought a deal of dolour to the Court, this way and that. A jest leaped to mind. I could not shame the Queen and live, but there were others. Edward was calling for wine.

'And I am dispirited,' he told the page. 'Summon Mistress Shore.'

I crept out.

The King was drunk early that night. Lord Hastings saw to that; he plied him with wine as if he gained more pleasure from double drunkenness. They shared a void with Jane, vowing that her lips gave added sweetness to the drink. St Nicholas paraded with his crook and mitre, and the Vice Titivillius was there, a strong lad, with his long pouch full of *Glorias* and *Misercordias* and all the other bits the priests gabble over. But I had a better entrance than the one planned previously. I waited patiently until Anthony Woodville was present. Behind the screen there were gasps at my costume; it was lewd in the extreme. The coat reached only to my middle and the hose—well, they would not be delivered of me uncut, for they revealed all: in plain words, my privy parts, so close were they shaped. The points of my hoses were long enough to stretch half across the Hall. In my hand I bore a marsh pike, and so I entered, to screams.

The King was not so flown; he blinked at me as I neared the cloth of estate.

'Ha, Sir Fool!' he said. 'Why this guise?'

I took a full breath, for a loud voice.

'Upon my word, Sir King,' said I, 'I have been absent from court too long. For I trow, the Rivers are so high in your realm, I could not hope to ford them without the help of this staff.'

Thinking back, 'twas a feeble jest, but they were ripe for it. All the old nobility whose noses had been disjointed by the Queen's kin bayed like dogs. Elizabeth froze. King Edward looked a little hard at me for a moment, started to tremble, then opened his mouth with the fair white teeth and his wonderful rich laughter came pouring forth. He threw back his head. The portly chins vanished, and he was, for a brief space, the Rose of Rouen once more. All the company was mine, from that instant, and I would not let it rest there. All night I pranced in my shameless garb, tripping past Earl Rivers with my nose in the air, crying: 'High, high! By my loyalty, they are high!' It was a fair victory. As for the Queen's brother, he bore himself well; he smiled adequately though he was very tight of countenance. Once I caught him gazing at Gloucester, who had also raised a smile at my folly. I believe there were some who congratulated him on having such a clever fellow in his household. Those such as I wax fat on praise, and I listened afterwards to the comments. Lord Hastings had helped the King to bed and folk were dispersing, dizzy with wine and food, as I kept my ears wide in nook and cranny and torchlit corridor. Thus it was I heard the opinion of Earl Rivers; he seemed displeased. He stood round a bend in the passage, the wind blowing chill on his shadow and that of his companion.

'It was but a harmless jest, my lord,' said Doctor Morton soothingly.

Rivers laughed sourly. 'Harmless indeed,' he said. 'The King took pleasure in it.'

'Do not trouble about the humour of his Grace's brother, my lord,' said Morton. 'He has doubtless grown unfamiliar with our culture, living his rude, far existence.'

Instead of comforting the Earl, this seemed to enrage him further.

'Yea, by God!' he said violently. 'He may have a tame popinjay to pipe his insults, but I have a prince in my schoolroom.'

'Soft, my lord,' said Morton uncomfortably.

'One day it may be Gloucester who needs a marsh pike to ford the realm,' said Rivers, and their voices grew fainter, and went away.

If a man stood in Petty Wales, between Billingsgate and the Tower, he could watch royal retinues issuing from the fine apartments. He could laugh heartily to see them fuming in the moil of traffic that barred their way. The carters did not care: they carried on, foul-mouthed, whipping their horses through spaces too narrow, upsetting drays laden with flax and rope, thread, grain and fish. A man could also listen for news of those who lay within Tower gaol. Whenever there was an execution, I found that the quickest way to gain the truth of the matter was to enter a cook-shop in that quarter, for within the hour all would come to my ears. It was simpler to chaff the tidings out of the wife of a loose-tongued under-warder than wait to be told in formal proclamation at Paul's Cross. The Tower in those days was like a beehive, heavy with gossip. Not so now; they are not such a jolly crew, and less informative. Or less informed.

I left behind a London that was partly scandalized, partly amused by the marvellous novelty of Clarence's demise. My friends at Middleham were inclined to disbelieve me, until I elaborated.

'He was drowned in wine,' I said. 'The doorway of his cell was too small, so they took him to the butt instead, trussed like a fowl. The malmsey was of the finest, and his favourite.'

'I would rather have my head struck off,' said Dirick the shoemaker. 'For I know I would try to drink deep, and be defeated.'

'Well, it was at his own request,' I said, feeling rather sickly. For I remembered Clarence: fair, jocund, lovesome traitor. This last gesture had in it a jesting princeliness, a snapping of the fingers at death. I could not help but wonder what became of the malmsey, after they drew out the dead Duke. Then all my frivolous thoughts fled away. From the chantry came a file of monks and priests and poor men from the village, all clad in sombre mourning. The great cross at the head of the procession caught the winking sunshine, the requiem bell tolled in time with each step. Behind the smallest pair of singing-boys came the lady Anne, holding her son by the hand, and last of all, my lord of Gloucester, in black, his eyes swollen with weeping.

The King had agreed to Gloucester's wish that he should

found two colleges, one at Middleham, the other at Barnard Castle; and ceaselessly the bells were sounded at both establishments. Each day the priests named in solemn obituary those of the House of York who had gone: my lord's father Richard, his brother Rutland, his uncle Salisbury, and, latest in this company, the fair, foolish George of Clarence.

Gloucester went no more to court, but kept himself within the northern territories. He was often away from home, for King Edward kept him busy. So for the amusement of the lady Anne I wrote poems about him and his fierce punishment of the heathen Scots, and these gave her as much pleasure as her lord's martial exploits did the King. For King Louis had persuaded the Scottish James to violate his truce with England, and for want of the loving words I could not pen, I gave Grace the news in my southbound bills.

'Right well beloved wife, it may be that you will receive my fool's cap with the head yet inside of it, for we are to be besieged by those false kilted creatures north of us and I know not what will befall. I leave all in the hands of my lord of Gloucester, and through Him that sits higher than all earthly princes, we shall prevail. I read what you say about the tax which the King's government has levied upon our livelode; may the Saints attend his Grace's wisdom and may the pinch be worth the penny.'

In truth I only wrote thus to affright her, and in hopes perchance of a kind word or two, for I had no doubt whatever of Richard Gloucester's strength and strategy. His blistering assaults upon Dumfries and Berwick, and his capture of Edinburgh without the loss of a single man; well, these are still talked of today, albeit softly. King Edward was full with his brother's success. He himself did not come northward; he had not the humour, he said. He wrote to his Holiness the Pope thanking the Giver of all good gifts for his most loving brother, whose proven success was enough to chastise the whole of Scotland.

'Right worshipful husband, I have taken as a parlour boarder the kinsman of Master Fray. He is a man skilled in penmanship and will help me with the accountancy. You will know that Calais was attacked lately; it is as well that your Duke of Gloucester has subdued the Scots though never did I think to see the day when England could call on those for aid, which state you say his lordship has brought about. Hogan sings loud as ever, he did say the Bull would swim and the Boar would triumph. Item, Louis of France has broken his son's troth with our Princess Elizabeth. This day I

243

saw her, and she was more fair even than yesterday. She was merry. Yet marriage is a blissful state is it not? The price of hogs has risen.'

Elizabeth was not sad when she was young; not even when the Dauphin was withdrawn from her by his devious father. Yet my Queen looks sad today. She has that look of anxious love familiar to me from the days with Lady Anne Neville. When Edward ailed and my lord was away she had a moonbeam look troubled by trailing clouds. I think it is Arthur who grieves my lady, and he has the look of Anne Neville, too white, too rosy. Life is full of paradoxes. Each mirrors the other.

I saw his Divine Majesty eye me last evening. I thought he was going to say I was too old to earn my money but he did not. None the less, I tried to put on a younger aspect—then I thought he might say I was too wise. One must either be young and silly, or wise and feeble. I am what I am. I live in past and present, then suddenly both come together with a fierce clash like an axe on armour and I am shaken into confusion—ah, this white mist over my eyes . . .

There are particular days in life which seem good, when the sun shines and the air sings sweet down to the well of the lungs, and on such a day I walked through York for Corpus Christi. Long before dawn the Gild Masters readied the wagons for their slow journey around the City. Five hundred actors waited on Toft Green. I followed each pageant with eagerness, from Holy Trinity Priory on Micklegate, across to All Saints, Davygate, where they lighted the beacon for wayfarers in Lantern Tower. The wagons halted before the houses of great lords, who stood at their windows to watch the rise and fall of mankind, and threw gold for their lesson.

Eve was very fair, and shamed by her nakedness when the Prince of Darkness tempted her in serpent-guise. On Lendal Bridge Noah built his ark, and who better to advise him than the gildsmen of the Shipwrights, the Fishmongers and Mariners? The actors of the Vintners' Gild dealt with the Miracle at Cana, where Our Lord changed water into wine. The tyrant Herod was wonderfully fierce. He leaped from his chariot to buffet his head upon the stones, foaming at the mouth. He used lye soap and gunpowder for this; the Gild Master had fined him the year before for not having given enough pith to his part. As we moved towards the great new Cathedral Church, there came the soldiers of Herod who took and slew with daggers the Holy Innocents, wrenching them from their mothers' arms. The women's screams were like icicles.

Lady Anne filled her large grey eyes with tears at the dreadful scene. My lord of Gloucester, as he watched, laid his hand upon his small son's head.

And as was right and proper, darkness had covered the City when they nailed Christ to the Tree, so that the faces of the singing boys wavered like the candle flames they carried, and there was soft sobbing in the dusk. Very low and sweet they sang the old carol, those little boys with their innocent faces.

> Lully, lulley, lully, lulley,
> The faucon has borne my make away.
> He bare him up, he bare him down,
> He bare him into an orchard brown,
> In that orchard there was an hall
> That was hanged with purple and pall.
> And in that hall there was a bed
> It was hanged with gold so red.
> And in that bed there lieth a knight
> His wounds bleeding both day and night.
> By that bed side kneeleth a may
> And she weepeth both night and day.
> And by that bedside there standeth a stone,
> *Corpus Christi* written thereon.

I could have been a devil at Doomsday had I paid pageant-pence and volunteered, but there seemed enough cunning players to drag humanity into Hell already. The discipline was strict: I saw one of the fraternity chastising a devil who came in late on his entrance after quaffing a mazer of ale behind Hell Mouth. They fined him four pence on the spot. In his black hose embroidered with pitchforks he leaped on the platform, declaring that he had been unjustly used. God, in six skins of white leather, frowned from his pinnacled throne. And they hurled them into Hell: the men and women, the lustful and those who had shown no charity, the adulterers and the murderers, those of unkind tongue and all who had taken no pity on those who lie in prison or are otherwise persecuted. For no reason that I can name I turned and emptied my purse into the hand of a blind man who stood behind me. He dropped some of the coins, they ran tinkling away. I looked up at the other side of the stage where the silver steps led to Heaven, and saw a great progress of angels and men ascending to the bright robes of Christ, and found myself weeping.

245

The following day they made my lord and his lady members of the Corpus Christi Gild. With bishops and priests they walked, glimpsed by the people through a forest of mitres and chasubles, shaded by the cloth of silver banners and crosses of gold. In its jewelled shrine the Host went before them, and thus, from Holy Trinity they went all the way to the Cathedral Church. The air was full of singing. And, with my eternally curious ears, I listened to the men of York chanting a fauxbourdon to these solemn hymns as my lord walked through town, straight and rigid with a soldier's step. Snips of thought were blown to my hearing like birds in a storm. 'Gloucester settled the matter, and all was well.' 'Through my lord's aid, we are friendly once more.' 'Because my man's father was sick, he . . .' 'I rode beside Richard—he fought like ten!' 'Our gracious Lord . . .' 'He set their kilts afire!' Laughter. 'Our son lay in goal and he . . .' One booming voice, full of self-importance: 'You prate of small matters—when all was feared lost, he saved his City's Charter!'

At the ale in Eden Berrys on Goodramgate it was 'Dickon, God preserve him!' from one roisterer who should have known better.

All the way it was Richard, Richard, Richard. From the Merchant Adventurers to the smallest craftsman. They loaded his table with the choicest food in Gildhall, they set before him the finest wines. They arrayed the aldermen in scarlet by the score and horsed them grandly for his welcome at Bootham Bar. The banners danced above him. The trumpets blared for his entrance. He wore York like a jewel in his bonnet.

Lord Percy rode a little behind him, and was deafened by the noise.

And there are days in life which start out so fair, and end up black, like the hand of God descending to chasten men for their sins, for none knows when the Day will be. Hogan and others had prophesied the world's end in the year 1500, but I still live to speak of a day I hold in my mind clearer than many.

The sun was shining. I was a little anxious about my sparrow-hawk; she was baiting, and I took off her hood to look into her misted eye. She would not eat, not even the choicest morsels, and I did not want to spoil her for future sport with temptation, so I left her with the falconer and walked across the ward. The drawbridge was down, for a horseman had lately ridden in, flecked with spur-blood and spume. In the green meadow across the moat, I could see Edward on his pony, trotting in a circle, round and round like a leaf in the breeze. He was laughing. Little John sat on a sturdy bay in the corner of the meadow, watching Edward as a priest guards a shrine.

I walked back to the Castle. Folk were gathered at the foot of the steps and more were issuing from the great door. I raised my eyes to the battlements; they were lowering the standard that flew there in the moorland wind. At the same moment as a bell began to boom slowly, the horseman I had seen emerged and ran down the steps, unwashed, foam-spattered cloak wafting about him. He called for fresh horses. A page ran beside him, and passed close, so I caught at his sleeve. He wore Lord Hastings's livery.

'What news?' I said. He looked excited and fearfully pale.

'The King is dead,' he said, shrugging me off in his haste.

It was like a blow, a douche of icy water. The whole ward shimmered before me into something alien and fierce. I caught at the boy as he hurried past.

'You lie,' I said softly.

Then I looked again towards the Castle and saw Lady Anne, Lady Lovell and a few other women. Anne Neville was descending the steps; I fell on my knees and offered her my arm, for she almost stumbled in her haste to reach the level of the yard. She leaned on me briefly—like a willow tree she was, for she wore palest green and she trembled and shivered and swayed like a willow in the wind.

'What tidings, my lady?' I cried. 'Pray, go carefully,' for her feet caught in the hem of her gown. 'Ill tidings,' she whispered, as people came running to strain for her words. Her voice rose from a mere breath to a sorrowful cry.

'Our Sovereign Lord is dead!' Then, softer: 'O Jesu, Edward is dead! And Dick is in Scotland! He has been cold a week; our Sovereign Lord is dead!'

Over and over she cried it. We all knew it was impossible. Yet it was true.

Thus ended my time at Middleham.

The sun was brighter then.

HERE ENDS THE FOOL'S TALE

PART THREE

THE MAN OF KEEN SIGHT

It standeth so: a deed is do
Whereof great harm shall grow;
My destiny is for to die
A shameful death, I trow.
Or else to flee, the t'one must be,
None other way I know
But to withdraw as an outlaw
And take me to my bow.
Wherefore adieu, my own heart true!
None other rede I can;
For I must to the greenwood go,
Alone, a banished man.

The Nut-Brown Maid

The King of England is dead, and they have taken him away, I know not where. He will have no magnificent funeral rites, no sumptuous weeping or solemn obsequies, as did his brother, whose death I also witnessed. King Edward died with tears in his eyes, begging his ministers to embrace one another, and it is only today that I fully comprehend the reason for this. For King Edward, upon whom I have thought almost with hate, bestowed a fine legacy of sorrow and confusion upon us all, and especially upon one whom I loved better than any brother. King Edward was tall and sheen, and he died in his bed. It was his lust for a fair woman that helped bring about this day of death. There was another king, a youngling, uncrowned. Bastard slips shall take no root. He did not die; not even of shame. All the fat whispers in the world cannot render the living dead. Death is brought by the axe, the cudgel, a swordthrust. Or by an arrow in the face, as died yet another king of England defending his realm, long ago.

The King is dead, and I am well-disposed to follow him, for I loved him, and never more than this week lately gone and on the day of his fall. They have shed his blood, they have used his body more shamefully than any man's, let alone a King anointed with the Chrism. They have despoiled him of his life, his flesh, but his honour and his fame they cannot touch. This makes them angry. The wrath on their faces is like a mask hiding fear-sweat, for Death has nudged them, and the passing breeze of something greater . . .

Richard is gone from us, yet his name fascinates every tongue. A thorn bush received his crown, and on a humble beast his corpse was carried, yet a beast as lowly bore Our Saviour into Jerusalem. Did they not think on this? When they flung my liege lord over his poor mount?

There are a half dozen of us, knights and yeomen, a few from distant shires whose tongue I cannot understand. Close beside me, standing patiently in this foul cell, are Master William Brecher and his son Thomas. Brave warriors both, despite their simple stock. I fought beside them in the battle and marked the honour of young Thomas. He is afraid now, but has himself in hand. We are to be executed for our treason. Outside I can hear them erecting the gallows, with steady knocking blows, and my own heart echoes each rap. The roll has been read, the indictment signed, and in great haste, for the Dragon would be on his way to London to take up the reins of the kingdom into his long pale hands. We are traitors. And the cognizance of our treason? We fought too well in the King's service. We bore too high the standard of Blanc Sanglier. His raison was ours. *Loyaulte me lie.*

I am shriven. For the past hour I have made my devotions. I am thirty-three years old, and I have served three reigns and seen the separate and singular manner of their ending. A fourth reign I shall not see, nor would I wish it. There is no King, save the King of Heaven, other than the third Richard. Across my knuckles I have a scar. It was not got in battle, but in friendship. Dead white, it is shaped like an arrow-head, and pricks and burns at the most unlikely moments. Looking at this talisman, my mind is full of days stretching back like a long rolling road; without seeking my saddle I can ride that road again to its beginning. I will close my ears to the hammerings that build my doom and, in love, remember Richard. Then he was Duke of Gloucester, and seventeen. Now he is but 'the traitor Plantagenet' and he is dead.

I shall think of the day when, for the first time, he asked: 'Will you ride with me?'

1469

It was a fair, hot June when I rode to Hellesden to visit the Pastons, they being my guardian's distant kin by marriage. I had ridden alone from Kent, leaving my lord's chaplain muttering into his beard at the unwisdom of it, and I had turned to salute him with an edge of mockery in my farewell. I had seventeen years behind me, silver spurs, and the right to wear my sword without the belt. I was so gay as I journeyed through the cherry orchards that I returned the obeisance of the villeins with low bows, as if I were the Earl of Warwick. They gaped at me, standing like stricken fowls in their tunics of coarseweave and their wide straw hats. One of the wenches threw me a bunch of fruit. They looked like rubies and tasted of wine. The people seemed happiest when they were in the fields; it was only the confinement of the manor court which appeared to bring about an increase in choler. I had sat for hours listening to their arguments. Of course they had their rights, but some tenants were cunning in their abuse and I had seen many a slow-witted farmer protesting to our stewards against a new title he had had no notion existed. I tried to take an interest in these matters. For the past year or so there had been talk from my guardian's tongue of sending me to study law at Cambridge so as to equip myself with better understanding of such affairs; as for my own half-stifled ambitions, they seeped through all the forecastings of my mentors. For the sport of gentlemen, the serious subject of the Statute of Winchester, had become, to me, an addition. O, you pagan god or devil, I know not, O Toxophilus, you had me by the throat. My friends dreamed of maidens, and other sinful joys. I dreamed of a sweet bow easy in the hand, one that does not kick: a bow fashioned of the finest Spanish yew, with its demoniacal paradox of sapwood and heartwood, the one resistant as an unschooled colt, the other pliant and gracious as Our Lady's smile. And as I grew in length, so did my bow become tall and strong as I; and on my seventeenth birthday, my Saint's day, I became the owner of the finest, the real *taxus baccata*, whose tip exactly matched the crown of my own yellow head.

In an indiscreet moment, I had mentioned my longing to become an archer *de maison*, for was I not the champion of three shires? My guardian's lady had shrieked out loud and feigned to swoon, vowing that I should look upward, and that to labour thus would be but to demean myself. For did not common yeomen so employ themselves, and had I forgotten my lineage? Which in itself was foolishness, for having seen my father once, and marked his blazon and his heritage, I should have been want-wit to be heedless of it. I should of course see my father no more, and his terrible death did not haunt me, even when I burnt his Month's Mind candle. As for my mother, why she was something fairer than motherly —proudly glad to wear the barbe and wimple of Lady Abbess. For these reasons, and for the thongs of kindliness and fair dealing, the Kentish castle was the only home I knew. But at seventeen the blood is hot, and the long struggle for independence begins. The trumpets have sounded, but the battle is yet to be joined. I did not think to find one in Norwich, for the Pastons' quarrel with the Dukes of Norfolk and Suffolk was none of my affair. It had been going on for too long, and there was little to be done. None the less, I felt sad for young John Paston, and a little guilty besides, for not long after my arrival at Hellesden I had bested him at the butts and I took his money, three shillings and eight pence. Young John (I called him so to distinguish him from his brother John, a knight older but more frivolous) would have been deeply dishonoured otherwise. And he was full of misery. With the two Dukes biting great pieces out of the Paston estates, he said he had had no time to write to me, and with equally gloomy sympathy I replied that it mattered little, for I had no army yet to raise on his behalf, and most of my money was in trust until I came of age. The Pastons were always writing letters. Every day one or other of them would be pacing a room, feeding a yawning clerk with phrases, while trouble chased hope across their brows like a fox pursues a weasel.

And in the pleasant garden at Hellesden, with a great hole in the wall through which one of Suffolk's cannon balls had plunged, I cast Young John further into despair. Through a faultless hold and a draw that perchance Pandarus himself might have admired, I beat him at the pricks, and above his little wistful murmur heard someone say: 'What a beautiful loose he has,' and smiled to myself.

I smiled, not just through boastful pride. For none watching knew of the struggle I had waged with my own recalcitrant body, over the years, to perfect the sport I loved the best. Because I am cursed with long-sightedness, the archer's enemy.

The physicians had studied my eyes. As a tiny knave I remember how they pried with their bright round circles of polished brass. They hummed sadly together over my strange sight, for they too realized it could jeopardize my skill. How can an archer study the nock and the unwavering hold when already the fat white clout dangles close to his nose? If I looked closely at the image for a moment it would come rushing up to me. At first I had been a little afraid of how to construe this magic. I could mark the strike of a hawk far away over a plain or high above a thicket. I could see what prey dangled from its talons, down to the glazing eye. I could scan the face of friend or foe long before they knew who approached them. The charges on their shields, the powderings on their garments and the emblems on their horses' housings were known to me outside the fifth part of a league. Once my keen sight had saved a child being swept away by the millrace. Others had thought it to be a cat in the water, but my eyes saw her black hair and clothing, and I had crossed a meadow to seize her from the flood. That day, I had even mused that I might, through this trick of nature, do some great person a service.

But archery, my leman! For that only, I battled with this useful fault. To ignore the abusing nearness of the target, to fix only upon the precious nock, to feel the urgent hemp pulled low to the right pap with a hand that wags neither up nor down, as Homer instructs us: the swift glance, the straight back and out-thrust chest—best for profit and seemliness—the yell of 'Fast!' and the unspoken command to those wilful eyes—thus did I conquer. It was a struggle, and at times I almost succumbed in the Castle of Perseverance. But it was the hand, the hand and the mind, and never the butt, wooed too soon by so many, which I bent to my will.

Enough of me. I would to my friend, the future King of Care.

Young John sighed, delving in his purse.

'By troth,' he said, 'I would you lived nearer to help preserve us from our enemies.'

This made me laugh.

'You would have me stand upon the keep and pick off Norfolk's men? With Master Calle to fill my cocker with arrows plucked from the slain?'

'Aye, Norfolk, or cursed de la Pole,' muttered Young John. 'And Suffolk married to the King's sister . . .'

'With Suffolk wed to Lady Bess,' I said, 'I would have thought an appeal might bear more force. Now that John your brother is at court.'

'He wrote lately,' said Young John bitterly. 'Of tourneys at Eltham, folderols, fat horseflesh and fair ladies. I would liefer see him here, or at our poor Caister, than at the joust even against Lord Rivers. He had become betrothed to Mistress Haute,' he added. 'A Woodville kinswoman. He thinks to gain favour. Meantime we sit awaiting the place burned about our ears.'

Master Gloys came hurrying over the green towards us.

'Sir, more trouble?' asked Young John warily.

The Chaplain shook his head. 'Not in these parts. But the King rides near, waging men to quell the northern rising.'

I had no intention of riding to war that day. So when the King's train rode by it was only through curiosity that I mounted and followed them. They split into two bunches of knights and esquires, one of which passed through the orchard and down to the remains of a lodge, ruined by Suffolk's men. It was then I first set eyes on Lord Rivers, marking his blazon at a distance; Young John was anxiously talking with him. Rivers wore white velvet over harness, and a sympathetic smile. Where the Woodvilles were, I thought, there would the King be also, so I rode off down the path and under the trees towards the lodge, hoping to spy out his Grace.

The lodge was a sad sight. Suffolk's men had burst doors with battering-rams, and had planted a few accurate cannon-shots through roof and windows. They had then tried to start a fire, for the gaping doorway revealed blackened floorboards and a crumbling pit down to the cellar. Green weeds and grass sprouted from the masonry, like hairs in an old man's ears.

There was someone standing a little inside the entrance, very still. A dark youth, of about my age, in demi-armour. There was not much to him, or of him, for that matter. He stood in shadow. He was alone. And that was my first ever impression of him; his utter loneliness. His horse cropped grass outside. I dismounted and went to join him. He appeared to be talking to himself. This was a habit I, too, enjoyed, when I needed to straighten something out in my mind.

'Brutal,' he was saying.

I was in agreement. 'Yea, is it not?' I said. I kicked the door-post and a piece of it disintegrated and fell clashing through the floor with a great choke of filth. My companion stepped back a length.

'This is not the way,' he said. 'Unnecessary violence. It is wrong.'

'Violence is well, if the cause be good,' I remarked.

He said sharply: 'This cause is ill. For centuries the philosophers have argued over what constitutes a good cause, and cheating, tyranny, never were such, and never shall be.'

'It was a fine place once,' I said, looking about me.

'And now despoiled,' he said softly. 'Doesn't it sadden you? Thinking that masons and craftsmen once laboured to the glory of God for something of beauty?'

'And now the vainglory of man has plucked it down,' I murmured. He gave me a quick, peculiar smile, no sooner born than dead.

'You renew my faith,' he said. 'I shall speak to the King about this.'

I thought him to be like John Paston, assaying to make his mark in Edward's household.

'How do you pleasure yourselves at court?' I asked. His face darkened.

'Well enough,' he said shortly.

'Let us go outside,' I said. A huge bat dived out of the darkness and round our heads. My companion remained inside, picking up a piece of oak and weighing it in his hand. He had very slender hands, with fine jewels.

'Sir, what's your name?' I asked.

'Richard,' he said, musing.

'Richard . . . what?'

He turned and came into the sunlight.

'Gloucester,' he said, and his lips twitched. I saw everything at once, too late. I saw the Silver Boar on his mail, the unmistakable Plantagenet face. I saw that I had been talking to the King's brother with no more respect than I would have shown Young John Paston. I saw myself a fool, and knelt.

'Gracious lordship . . .' I began, and heard him laughing softly. He struck my shoulder with his gauntlet, mocking me with knighthood.

'Arise, sir,' he said. 'I have the advantage of you.' He touched the arms upon my mantle, laughing again. 'It is a pleasant sensation.' We were then both merry together, when Sir Thomas Wingfield, of the King's household, rode up to remind us that the King awaited his brother's witness to the breaking-down of the lodge by Suffolk's men.

'A moment,' Richard said, and faced me fully. 'There's rebellion in the north country. I need men. All who can draw a bow, wield an axe. Will you fight under my standard? Will you ride with me?'

Something, the name of which I shall never know, took possession of my soul. I had no intention of going to war, but before his last word was out I was again upon my knee, and in the presence of Sir Thomas Wingfield and others I do not remember, I became Richard of Gloucester's sworn man.

We were a diverse company, that day we went forth on our first campaign. Four friends of John Paston rode by me: Bernard and Barney, Will Calthorp and Broom; my brothers under the Blanc Sanglier. As for that, there was just enough of a fair wind to make it fly, among the host of other banners dwarfed by the great arms of England. In the fields, men set down their tools and donned jacks and sallets to march with us. The wagons with their barrels of harness grumbled along the pitted ways, and the King's falconers with the priceless gerfalcons and peregrines; the sovereign's dogs; the coffer with the royal book collection guarded by the slavering, swaying deerhound atop of it. Up ahead rode the King. I could count the petals of the fleur-de-lys and the leopard's claws on the royal standard.

Gloucester rode in the middle of the train, his squire bearing his shield and accoutrements. He talked to his henchmen in snatches—the ragged wind blew back his voice. Even in his harness he was very thin. Yet he could never have passed unnoticed. He was sober and gracious, and I spurred to ride near him, past the elegant back of Lord Rivers. The richly attired Lord Anthony, his father and young brother, were flamboyant and gay, tossing Latin quips and fragments of wit to one another, marvellously regal; hard to believe that their lineage was baser than my own.

Young John had no such doubts. The words he used about them were strong for such a gentle fellow.

'Rivers came again,' he said finally. 'He spoke me fair, and said he could do naught for us. Then he would have me ride with him—I have no stomach for it.' And Young John, looking old, had called for his clerk and started a rush of dictation, all about life's hardship, begging his brother to succour them in their accursed hour.

My sorrel laid back her ears, and nipped at Gloucester's horse. I gave her a swift stroke with the flat of my sword, and she flaunted forward jostling the line. Sir John Woodville, scarcely two years older than I, half-turned to his esquire with a little sneer. 'Green as grass, I vow, some of my lord's waged men,' and I would lief have asked him what *he* knew of fighting, or how his aged bride did. Then I saw Richard of Gloucester smiling at me, a little sadly.

'The Pastons are friends of yours,' he said, and I had the notion he knew everything about me. 'I am truly sorry I could not help there,' he continued. 'His Highness said that they should have put the case before the oyer and terminer a month after it happened. And now he has this rebellion astir in his mind.' His gaze went ahead to royal Edward, who sat tall and gleaming on his black horse. I saw that Richard's face wore the same guise as when I had observed him at Mass that morning, mingled with that of my maiden-haunted friends. I said, truthfully: 'What a glorious prince he is.' Richard turned to me, shining like the sun.

'Yes, and he has a great heart,' he murmured. He started to tell me what I already knew: that during the commencement of the war with Lancaster he himself—a little boy of seven or eight—had been lodged in London with the Pastons.

'He came every day to visit us, my brother Clarence and me,' he said. 'Every single day, mark you, full of affairs as he was; though he was striving to put this land to rights. I shall never forget how eagerly I looked for him. He would ride through the gate like . . . like Phoebus, or blessed St Michael. He brought us gifts and clasped us in his arms. Strong arms,' he said a shade wistfully; and I noticed a slight unevenness about his own body. The right pauldron of his mail was fashioned larger than the left. He caught me glancing at it.

'I have suffered much ill-health,' he said, and he seemed rather amused. 'So, to counteract my frailty, I wielded arms so lustily that it left me with more in the right, less in the left. It was a battle of my own; a battle with the battle-axe, and made me doubly puissant thus,' and he rapped his shoulder with his mailed fist, making it ring.

'And I have unnatural sight,' I said, rather softly in case I should be put off by any as a wizard. 'Long eyes—and I love archery.'

'But you conquered,' he said, looking ahead as he rode.

'I did, my lord,' I said, and saw his little satisfied nod.

He was so easy with me. He looked gratified, then vexed, then tortured, his face hiding no thought. He talked of Yorkshire, and ere long I was passing eager to see this land which, according to Richard, was Paradise on earth and, sadly, as unattainable to him as the hidden Grail which all men strive to find. So I kept an acute silence, sorry to think that Elizabeth Woodville had marred his future by marrying the King and alienating Warwick.

Our progress was slow. We passed through cornfields and apple orchards; and when we finally rode up the incline to Castle Rising and saw its hundred steep steps, the King took it in his head to go hunting, and went off accompanied by the Woodvilles. I was left with Richard, and Robert Percy, and others engaged in overseeing the provisions and armour and marshalling of the troops. In the ward, knots of men muttered together. One song was in every mouth: 'When is the paymaster coming?'

The faces of the gently born wore little sneers; the rough soldiery shuffled their feet and jangled the groats in their purses as if to turn them into marks by necromancy. In front of the treasurer's tent they formed a line; the men of Sir John Woodville and his father, and those of Lord Anthony and the King; the archers doffing their metal helmets, rubbing their sweated palms on the breast of their deerskins. The close line merged forward, swaying like wheat, and the lightness on those faces as they came away was like a ripple of sun on corn. Money chinked in their hands. But Lord Richard of Gloucester's men, his precious men whom he had asked to ride with him, stood jostling their feet in the long meadowgrass, and whispering of niggardly masters. Bernard, Barney, Broom and Calthorp murmured that there would be no dicing that night. Robert Percy and Thomas Parr conferred with Gloucester.

'This has gone beyond jesting,' said Sir Thomas.

Robert Percy had a mouth that looked as if it always smiled. Though he was a good friend to Richard, I do not like faces which smile without cease. Yet Robert smiled, saying: 'They are full of rancour surely; they foresee victuals neither for their horses nor for themselves, I vow.'

'They will be fed,' said Sir Thomas roughly.

'I spoke of other needs,' said Robert Percy. 'Ale and cards and gowns for their womenfolk.'

I heard my lord of Gloucester's voice.

'By Christ's Passion,' he said, 'they will be *deserting!*' This

260

cast the others into silence. Richard looked in my direction. I bowed slightly. Suddenly I wished I had money for him.

'Where is my clerk?' he asked suddenly, still gazing towards me. I moved forward as a young man carried pens and inkhorn into the tent.

'Would that I could aid you, my lord,' I said.

'There may yet be time for that.' He started to pace about the tent. 'Right trusty and well-beloved,' he began, and we all listened to the rasp of quill on parchment, while outside a lark sang madly. A little haltingly he dictated, and when he came to the part explaining how the King had summoned him to attend his highness in the north parties, and yet had left him so ill-purveyed of money as to need beg a loan from this old lord and trusty follower, I marvelled still more at Edward's forgetfulness. Yet verily, he was always a marvellous creature, King Edward the Fourth.

Still unfinished, Richard turned to Sir Thomas Parr.

'How much will I need?' he asked.

'Say an hundred pounds, Richard my lord,' suggested the knight.

'Until Easter next coming,' murmured Richard. 'Tell him I will repay in full—and will serve him the same if ever he needs it.'

The clerk set it down. Suddenly Richard snatched up a pen. 'Sir, I pray you that you fail me not . . .' and I saw that his hand matched his voice, and trembled.

His esquires withdrew, but I stayed. I wanted to offer him some word of good cheering counsel, out of all my seventeen winters. Half-jesting I said:

'Sir, it seems his Grace would rather chase the stag than see his brother and his brother's army satisfied. It would seem ill-considered . . .' And then I all but cut off my tongue with my teeth, for he swung round upon me like a true boar, with lowered tusks, and the first fireflash I had yet seen in his eyes.

'You speak against the King?' he said softly.

I should have knelt, but I was fixed. His face came very near. There was sweat-dew on it.

'No treason, my lord,' I said, clearing my gullet.

He gave a deep shudder, and his body lost its tension and became pliant again, like the heartwood—sapwood in a fine bow.

'Words . . .' he muttered.

'My words were fool's words,' I continued. 'For his Grace . . .'

'His Grace is supreme,' he said, without violence. 'My

261

brother his highness is omnipotent. Yea, my friend—' and all his swift powerful anger was vanished in the joy of speaking of King Edward—'he can do no wrong. I am but his humblest servant—we are all his liege men, bound till death.'

'Noblest prince, give me leave to excuse myself,' I said, affected by his own fervour. 'May Our Lord empower him with great glory and a thousand blessings. Always.'

'Amen,' he said, as the constraint between us lifted. He then made a retreat into his own mind, for the line between his smooth brows came hard and then faded—I watched him. He was saying something about it being a full day's ride, and I leaped into the breach, mad to make atonement. 'Sir, my horse is . . .'

'Strong? Fleet?' He turned, anxious and amused, guessing my desires.

I looked in his eyes. 'I am no royal herald, my lord,' I said. 'But I will have the money in your hands by day's beginning.'

He smiled. "You would go through the night, with an hundred pounds in gold across your saddle-horn?'

'I will take armed men, if it please you.'

A rich laugh he had; you could warm your hands at it.

'That you will . . . the stoutest!'

He would trust me with his money. Fleetingly, it came to me how willingly he trusted. The esquires were ready, and I marked with some dismay how weighty with harness they were. I determined not to let them impede my progress.

'My friend will house you overnight,' said Richard. 'Guard well my wages.'

'With my blood,' I answered.

'Or we shall have a rebellion of our own here,' he said, and added, a little mockingly: 'I will have prayers said for your safe passage.' Then he grasped my forearm, and I his, and I turned into the southwest wind, glad to feel it, for the morning sun looked on me with fierce eyes. And I thought, riding, of the gesture of good-fellowship from a sovereign prince, and set my spurs in sorrel hide the faster to do his bidding.

That was a good mare of mine. She lived long, and was well-tempered and puissant, and was speared under me finally by a dozen shafts. (So, also, died White Surrey . . .)

I slept ill that night, though the bed in the old lord's castle was soft enough to please the noblest lady. My host asked with great love after Richard and the King, but when in all innocence I mentioned some doing of Anthony Woodville he could scarce contain his apoplexy, and swore oaths, ill-fitting such a great knight of ancient line. Thereafter I took a secret vow of silence, and fancied as I lay to hear a voice grumbling, night-long. Again, I had touched anathema, and lashed myself with penitent prayers.

I went straight from Mass into the June morning. There was a waist-high white veil, spreading over the fields, gilded to cloth of silver by the sun, hiding the boles of trees and changing the forest into a place enchanted. The spiders had woven night-long, and their tapestries brushed dew on my cheek as we rode. Through wild country I glimpsed thick clustering bluebells, and delicate damp buds of thorn unfurling. Waywardly I pushed my mount; her feet seemed to leave the ground; my half-armour was weightless, the money-pouch across my mare's withers light as air. My tongue gave gold to a summer song, while behind me I heard the thud of the pursuing esquires.

I had to rein in and wait for them. They pounded up, their helms shiny with dew.

'You ride fast, my lord,' one said, gasping.

'I'm no sluggard,' I answered gaily.

'There are thieves about . . .'

'Stay by me, then!' I cried. 'My lord of Gloucester waits!' I felt like one who had drunk deep. 'Sweet life!' I shouted, and was off again, a creature possessed, hearing the grunts of my followers, and the rattle of their mail. I left them a bows-length behind, then the gap stretched into a quarter-league. I felt the sun hot upon my parted lips, the breeze warm in my teeth. I dreamed of the archery. I was champion of all England—I was master bowman of Burgundy. I was my lord of Gloucester's trusted fellow, and wild with delight; so full of virtue, in fact, that I omitted to watch for the foul wounded roads, downfall of better than I. The sorrel was dainty of foot for so big a mare, but I had driven her cruelly. She fell, her nose between her forelegs, and rolled, and for me it was a starless night, a sense of buffeting blows on my skull and a sun bright with pain.

I lay near a gateway, and the light flickered down through foliage on to my face. I had a great dint in my breastplate but was otherwise whole, save for the deathly fear when I thought of Richard's wages. When I saw the mare, standing shamed but still gold-laden, near to me, I knelt and gave thanks to the blessed St Anthony for saving what was deemed lost. As I prayed, I heard a faint chuckling and looked up warily to see a figure mounted on a gate, a man who laughed at me with a sound too high-pitched for beauty. He must have come from the field, likewise the black-garbed, weeping woman who sat on a mule the other side of the hedge. He had a longish beard, dung-coloured, though he was about five-and-thirty; he was dressed in a hermit's robe, and looked unclean.

'Too fast, fair sir, too fast.' He wagged his head, and his beard swung, like an old goat chewing hay.

'Why does she weep?' I asked, still dazed.

Again he chuckled. 'She weeps ever. To good cause.' I felt a pain in my nose, and tasted blood. My head seemed invaded by a hive of bees.

'A sorry fall,' said the stranger. 'Where, so hastily?'

I gathered my fuddled wits. 'My affairs are not yours, fellow,' I replied.

'Your speech is that of Kent,' he said, as if he had been on earth for hundreds of years.

'How are you called?' I asked. My hands were still shaking. He was laughing quietly. 'My name is Hogan.'

I looked at the woman. She quivered with sobs, sitting her mule under a hawthorn tree.

'Your wife?' I was curious.

'Her tears are for the doom of man, not because she is wed to me,' he answered. He slipped down from the gate and came close. He had a sideways gait, and I felt strongly chill, as if the sun were less bright.

'So,' he said. 'A Kentishman. They have fought and died, in fury and despair.'

I reckoned him struck by the moon.

'Many have died,' I said.

His laughter ceased. 'As will many more. This England will be a stew of red life. Yours also. You have few years left. Pleasure yourself, my fair young sir.'

I was not afraid, only angry. I wiped the blood from my nose and glowered, hating this Hogan, who had cooled my day. 'By the Rood, you lie!'

He laughed again, knowingly, pointing to the weeping woman, then at the tree under which her mule stood patiently.

'The Thorn of Joseph,' he said. 'In a dream, I saw it— crowns rolling, wondrous death, and the end of the House of Plantagenet.'

I crossed myself, rage bubbling.

'False harlot!' I said, trembling. 'You shall be whipped to

the stocks an the King hears of your heresy!' I cast round for my esquires, separated from me by the forest.

Hogan smiled.

'You . . .' he said. 'And your King . . . the foot that strikes the stone shall turn into a head, and the bones tossed on a dunghill, *to stink for ever.*'

He was raving mad. He should be exorcized. My guardian's chaplain would have soon drawn out his devils—he was ever rebuking me, mostly for swearing on the Wounds of Our Lord. He would say: 'Think, my son! Think on His Pain!' I searched my soul for compassion towards this poor wight.

'Are you hungered?' I asked, feeling in my pouch.

His beard wagged to and fro. 'Never, for I live on my wits,' he said. And then I heard the scudding of hooves in the distance. They were catching me up. I mounted, feeling the warm nobbly sacks of money at my saddle-bow, feeling sober and shamed, turning my back upon the madman Hogan. When I faced the gateway again, astride my horse, he was gone. And the woman. There was only the wind wavering the grasses.

The men-at-arms came up at a gallop, hot with relief.

'Come!' I cried, all my gaiety gone. 'The King's army awaits us!'

After Lynn, and our brief sojourn at Croyland, we cooled our heels for a week at Fotheringhay, where Richard conferred with the captains: which was the best place to flank the archers if we should encounter rebels on a plain, or a hillock, or in wooded country. All the strategies of war were meat for his keen mind. He asked questions, gave opinions: even the seasoned warriors Louis de Bretaylle and Edward Brampton seemed moved by his sense. It was upon reaching Newark that I first had speech with King Edward. I had been shooting with Richard. I was his master here, but only just. He had paid me. I had received his wager with thanks and a pledge that he would recover it at the dice later. We were handing our bows back to the royal stewards when I looked across the meadow and saw a party of horse approaching.

'It is his Grace, riding from the hunt,' I said, absently.

Richard was cognizant of my keen-sightedness and said, with great good-humour: 'And is he sad, sombre, gay?'

I caught the King's face within the candle of my eye. A face so fair and clean it was almost too beautiful. A short face with a mouth for kissing, as well as giving commands. His rippling golden hair hung to the level of his chin. His gold collar shone upon his breast. His blue eyes gleamed above rosy cheeks.

'He smiles,' I answered.

Walking over the green, Edward towered above his followers. He saw his brother, and his smile spread.

'Well, Dickon,' he said.

I tried not to stare at the King, but I had seldom seen him so close. Then his glance caught mine, and I saw the jewelled hand raised in a beckoning gesture. It seemed a long way across the grass to where he stood. We had had a little rain, and as I knelt I felt the dew soaking the knee of my hose.

'You are one of my brother's henchmen I do not know,' he said, and I saw a knight of his—it may have been Sir John Fogge—making a note on parchment. The King's eyes took in the quarterings on my mantle.

'Your father was a brave knight—I do not need to tell you this.'

'Sire, if I can be as true a man, I will lack no reassurance.' The answer seemed to please him. He set his arm about my neck: I am tall, but my head reached only to his shoulder.

'I have not the honour yet, Sire, to be your brother's henchman.' His arm around me was warm as sunlight. I could see the hairs curling golden on his neck. I decided instantly that Richard was right: this was a King whom all would obey, as long as life lasted. His hounds fawned about him, covering his slender satin-clad thighs with pawmarks, while he fondled them carelessly.

'By God's Blessed Lady, why not?' he asked suddenly. He turned with a smile to Sir John Woodville and the others who pressed up behind him. 'One day, my lords, I declare I will have a Book of my Houehold made, written clear, and thus exclude all unwanted followers.'

'Such as my lord of Warwick,' a voice said, but the King gave no sign of having heard this. His arm was still fast about my shoulder, and his glance returning downward to mine bade me admire him, do him homage.

'Watch his Grace my brother, then,' he said, releasing me. 'He will keep you wakeful half the night with chess.' The Woodvilles' laughter was like tinkling cymbals. I bowed, kissed the royal hand and retreated, as the party passed on.

'He is pleased with you,' Richard said softly. I thought for a moment how Sir John Paston would give his teeth for my chance. And I was not betrothed to anyone.

Thereafter being a gentleman usher to my lord of Gloucester, I shot in a bow with him each day. We played games— we liked the same things: the works of Ovid and Cicero, battle-talk and music-making. I found his mind like a rainbow, all varied colours, some coming hard and clear and bright, then waning, as do the parts of a rainbow grow brilliant and pale, when God manifests his thoughts to the eyes of man. He had a statue of St George, to which he sometimes spoke aloud. Often, he made me feel a whit frivolous, when I accompanied him and his esquires on the nightly forays around the swelling ranks of men, familiarizing myself with the supplies of armaments: the barrels of harness, the hundreds of spears, cross-bows, bills, leaden mauls; the fine horses. I looked with distrust on the few handguns which had been engaged, and more so when Richard recounted to me how even King James the Second of Scotland had blown himself heavenward while firing one of these imperfect weapons. Verily the devilish inventions seemed to me vastly inferior to the sweet surety of a longbow, or the keen and whirling tooth of the axe. Only once did my lord and I speak of maidens. I told him how my guardian was seeking an heiress for me. I had never met Margetta, but reckoned hers a pretty name. She was twelve or thirteen years old; I often mused on whether her colour was dark or fair, or if she were tall or little. My guardian knew only that she was well-purveyed of money and would bring me a good dower. Richard fell very silent and released no confidences. It was Robert Percy who told me one day, while my lord was busied with letter-writing, that the King had plans to marry his brother to a foreign princess.

'As his Grace should himself have been wedded, had Lord Warwick not been outwitted,' said that one, with a calm smile.

A storm, and something else, hung over us at Newark. I felt it as we sat at cards and the day drew in a little. The hounds were restless. One raised its muzzle and growled, like thunder.

Richard's voice made me start a little.

'We should be moving northward,' he said. 'I feel . . . as if we have tarried overlong here.'

One of the other young men shuffled his feet in assent. Robert Percy stretched out his legs under the table. I laid down my cards.

'His Grace will move off shortly,' someone said.

'Who is Robin of Redesdale?' asked another.

'Christ's Passion!' said Richard impatiently. 'A rebel. An agitator bought by the Lancastrians to cause strife. As for his *nom de guerre*, possibly he thinks it romantic!' He gave a short laugh, and the hound thundered again.

So we sat on and played, yawning; and supper faded into the past and bed drew near, or a look at the men, until that idle pattern was suddenly broken by a noise of shouting that coiled up the stairway. It was not yet dusk but as we descended the circling stairs and emerged from the root of the tower the glow of torches grew and lapped around the busy scene. A dozen men-at-arms surrounded one knave—as we came into the courtyard I saw him clubbed to the ground, rise to his knee and remain, bowed-headed.

'They have taken a rebel agent,' Richard said softly.

'*Halte, au nom du roi!*' roared a voice. Louis de Bretaylle strode across to the mute prisoner. He thrust aside the men-at-arms, with his free hand searching inside the man's garment. It was a piece of parchment which he drew out, soiled with journey sweat, too tough to tear. The rebel clung to it, tried to devour it but was knocked to the ground and lay retching in the shadow of a great form to whom all knelt.

King Edward had arrived, and at leisure was reading this, Robin of Redesdale's proclamation. My keen sight took in the smile of contempt, the indrawn brows, the look like the ring of steel in a scabbard.

A courier was riding in over the drawbridge. Behind him came two more prisoners: one limping beside his captor's mount, a rope binding his arms; another swaying on the pillion. I saw the fine trickle of blood at his brows. I saw all manner of things which others could not. These men wore a familiar emblem powdered small on their garments, over the dusty harness that still picked up a gleam from the departing sun. The courier reached King Edward first. He threw himself down before the King.

'Hush, fellow!' said one. 'His Grace reads of most wonderful treason. Hold your peace until he has finished.'

'Sire, you must get to Nottingham!' cried the courier.

'So!' said King Edward in a low, distinct voice. 'He likens me to those of the old royal blood who have been deposed, murdered! He likens me to those whose favourites led them to ruin! By God, now I will show him a true likeness . . .'

In my ear came another voice, like the wind that rushed up through the trees, bringing the first drops of rain: 'Tell me,' Richard of Gloucester said, 'of whom does he speak?'

'That I know not, sir,' I muttered, my sight still fixed on

the distant oncoming prisoners. Their powderings showed sharp and clear.

'What then of your far-sightedness?' he said mockingly, and stung, I replied:

'I am at your disposal, my lord.'

'The captured esquires—what emblem do they carry?'

And I turned to look fully at him, not knowing the great agony I should see upon his face as I answered: 'The Bear and Ragged Staff, your Grace.'

He staggered a little, but shook off this frailty quickly and stood braced against something that lashed him from within, as the wind now lashed the trees. The ward was filling with armed men, and the captains were running to their weapons and to take mount. One of these surged by me as I stood near Richard, waiting for him to speak again, which he did not do for a long time. It was Sir John Fogge, his face fearfilled.

'To Nottingham!' he cried. 'Earl Warwick approaches with a great puissance of men. By Christ, we have tarried too long! Where are my squires! My lord . . .' and he was gone, his voice trailing off in a lonesome cry.

In a jostle we harnessed Richard, and ourselves, with hands that shook from excitement and the sharp thrill of fright. So busy was I, indeed, that I did not notice the tears in Richard's eyes, though others whispered of them afterwards.

And then, for us, more waiting for extra men. He kept me wakeful at Nottingham. Within that stout pile, hewn from a sheer grey shoot of rock, I passed many an unquiet hour with Richard Plantagenet. Sir John Conyers, calling himself Robin of Redesdale, had raised a great force. The Woodville knights were no more with us; they were fled all ways, fear-shodden. We played chess. Chess, yea, and talking long into the night, and when at length I sought my weary couch beside Richard's bed, I knew no easement or rest. For he would oft-times move with sudden, fretful plungings and murmurings to make me start up, thinking he had called me.

'How can I ease you?' I took up a lute. 'A song, a story?'

He looked at me, but without seeing.

'This palace . . .' he said. 'I feel a chill . . .' He shuddered. 'Old ghosts. Or sorrows to come, mayhap.'

I stood silent, touching a soft lute-chord.

'It is a care-ridden place,' he said finally. Then a great reversal of humour took him. He cried: 'Yea, let us have entertainment. Sing the airs of Burgundy, which I loved when a puling knave. Or tell the lay of Beowulf,' which was as much for my pleasure as his own, for he knew of my affection for the old meadhalls . . . long before Kentishmen fought and died in blood and despair . . . Hogan—curse him.

With music I conquered his strange melancholy, but not so, later, when we learned of Clarence's disaffection. Richard laughed softly at this news; a joyless sound, the strained mirth summoned by an old, bad jest; and later he woke me roughly by crying of 'Three Suns'.

'The parhelion.' He shivered with sweat. 'At Mortimer's Cross. The King . . . a man called by God Himself. The Saviour of our noble House. And now betrayed *by his own* brother. God's Blessed Lady,' he said using Edward's oath. 'The folly, and the shame! Has he forgot that we are all one blood?'

'I know. My lord. Richard,' I said humbly.

'George was born in Dublin,' he said, with a sickly smile. 'The Irish runes are powerful—mayhap some wanton sprite looked on his cradle . . . What think you?'

I merely cried—sounding like my Kentish chaplain: 'Let not hatred put your soul in jeopardy, my lord.' I cursed my tongue and was relieved when he answered calmly:

'Tell me then what is hatred, for I know it not. He is my brother, and I love him. But loyalty binds me to Edward until death. And beyond.'

He slid from the bed.

'Pray with me,' he said simply. 'Pray for a settlement to this mischief.'

So we knelt together, like children, two pairs of hands joined at the point of the chin, and above us the statue of St George flickered and gleamed in the waning rushlamp hung below; and I grew sleepy and leaped with horror out of a dream of archery to hear his muttered: '. . . *donna nobis pacem.*'

'Mayhap our reinforcements will come in the morning . . . Lords Pembroke and Devon . . .' I said hopefully, thinking his orison to be over; yet he breathed again: '*Agnus Dei,*' the gleam falling on his bent head. As I watched him carefully, there came an old and puzzling remembrance of another evening when I was just as slothful.

It was at Fotheringhay, and I had gone down into the camp, late, with some message. Everything was steaming with damp summer heat and in the musky darkness I discovered him with a young maid, whom he bade me guard

270

through the ranks and deliver to the Duchess of Bedford's apartments.

Kneeling beside him, I remembered more. I had thought it prudent to offer the damsel my arm, as she struggled through the trailing briars. Her hand on mine was like a small smooth flame. She stopped suddenly when we had gone a few steps and turned to look back.

'Ah Jesu!' she whispered. 'How he shines!'

I fixed my sight upon the pale Duke, bringing him near in the lanternlight. A moth flew round his face and he lifted his hand to brush it away. The maiden smiled, in tears.

'There is a light . . . a light,' she sighed.

'What then, mistress?'

She had looked up at me from the cavern of her hood.

'A light about him not of this world,' she said.

I could see naught but the fen-fires, burning malefically.

We were at supper when I had my first sight of Lord Hastings. We were still immured at Nottingham, our leaders sorrowfully depleted. I gnawed on a leg of spiced heron and wondered with anxiety how Lord Anthony Woodville was faring; whether that handsome and cultured nobleman had reached his Lynn estates still owning a head; likewise Sir John Fogge, and the Queen's father, and her arrogant young brother. Yet we still had Louis de Bretaylle, and Sir Edward Brampton, so swarthy and blackbrowed, and torturing the English tongue with what sounded like 'Heesoo Kristo' for the Holy Name. Richard told me that he was the King's godson, had forsaken Judaism for the True Faith, was a brave warrior and a seaman of renown. Brampton was also an astute trader and useful in the concourse with Flanders, having many kinfolk there—including a Mademoiselle Warbecque, who was said to have great beauty.

The King was eating heartily, tearing at choice meats with purpose, dabbling his fingers into scented water as if to wash off treachery, when the door of the hall crashed open, to shiver the silver goblets with its din, bring the dogs roaring out from beneath the trestles, and admit the Lord Chamberlain.

I summoned Lord Hastings's face clear into the matrix of my sight: fair like the King's but narrower; the mouth somewhat overfleshed; the eyes crowned with a hard glitter. His gait along the hall bore the stiffness of fierce riding.

The King got up and the prone servers raised themselves

271

from the floor to make way for Hastings. Looking at Richard, I saw the lightening of his countenance. Another trusted one here, I thought; another beloved; and I determined to eschew all criticism of this great lord.

The King and Hastings embraced briefly.

'What news?' Edward asked.

'Good and ill,' answered Hastings, and in that moment I, too, shivered under the chill of Nottingham Castle, which had bred sleeplack in Richard and in me.

Hastings announced that we were cut off from London by Robin of Redesdale—he had skirted Nottingham to the west.

'Pembroke?' asked the King, wiping his hands on a napkin.

'He leads but a small force of Welsh pikemen, hastening northeast to aid your Grace.'

'The Earl of Devon?'

'Likewise, with his West Country archers, but Warwick himself rides hard to forestall them both,' said Hastings.

'Eat, my lord,' said Edward, thinking hard. The servers ringed Lord Hastings with laden salvers.

'Your brother Clarence is married,' said the Lord Chamberlain, biting into a roast. I caught a gasp from Richard, drowned by the angry thunder of Edward's fist on the board.

'He bribed your Grace's own agent at the Papal court so as to wed Warwick's Isabella,' remarked Hastings coolly.

'Mother of God!' said the King. His angry eye fell upon Richard, and softened. 'Jesu be thanked that I have one loyal brother remaining.'

'We are all loyal, your Grace,' said Hastings, downing a void of wine in one draught. 'Yet I fear that the Queen's kinfolk may be the butt of Lord Warwick's wrath.' He did not sound displeased at the thought, his tone being neither black nor white, but full of grey shadows.

Edward was controlling his anger. 'We will tarry three days,' he announced, and I thought, yet more waiting! I caught Richard's face in my eye, knowing that he could not see me as well, being low down the hall as I was, yet noting the sadness and the impatience which chased across his brow.

On the third day we rose from the little death of impotence and took horse in the direction of Buckingham Shire. And Richard had eyes for two now; his brother, on whom he looked with loving care, and Hastings, upon whom he cast the glances of a trustful son.

'Thank Christ there are those still loyal,' he repeated again and yet again, and, God forgive me, I sighed a little within me at times, and dreamed of Toxophilus, my leman. But at Olney, it was I who first saw the distant cloud—a little greyish-brown haze, swirling like smoke, growing into the shapes of sweat-slimed horses and weary men who gave tongue, as they rode, of fear and the sword, too close for safety. Blood on their hands, their harness, some wound-weak, they came upon us at a fair wallop, singing of danger. I recall a dying man who spoke of great peril; how he vomited blood while crying: 'The hosts of Warwick and Clarence are at our heels! The Herberts slain—Lord Pembroke—Sir John Woodville—her Grace's father . . . fly, O King!' And with the bright red life bursting from him, rolled from his horse and into a ditch, still and suddenly dead. I recall how Edward turned to his dwindling army, bidding them act as the stiffening fellow under the hedge had advised; and how swiftly they spurred their horses' sides—passing in a cloud of shouting dust—gone.

My sorrel shifted under me at the ambience of fear. I watched Richard, who sat his horse like a stone statue; Hastings too, grim and still. And coming nearer, a vast party of mounted men, their harness splattered with triumphant blood. It was the Church that came to take the King; the Archbishop of York, Earl Warwick's brother. Edward rode up to greet him.

'So you are come, my lord, from your Manor of the Moor,' he said quietly. 'I had hoped that the rumour did not run as I had heard, but it seems—by God's Blessed Lady—that even Kings can be led astray.' He looked around at us, the score or so of men who remained behind him. 'Well, my lord,' he continued, 'will you at least spare these men, who ride under my standard of their own volition?'

The Archbishop smiled nastily. 'Is it not your own prerogative, your Grace, to cry: "Kill the Lords! Disregard the commons!"? Pembroke died bravely,' he added.

King Edward's tongue was an ice-sword. 'Where is your noble brother Northumberland, my lord?' An unwilling flush ran up under the Archbishop's stout steel helm.

'Sir John is so blinded by folly he will not join us in this enterprise,' he replied.

'This treason,' said the King, still marvellously sweet. 'Or should it be considered a Holy War?'

The Archbishop swung his horse about and came up close to Edward. Foam gathered at his lips. 'Yea, your Grace. A purge of this realm, levied upon upstart knaves who lead a King into the paths of wantonness. *Succubi*,' he said, clutch-

ing at his dangling crucifix as if it were a Woodville throat—
'*succubi* that drain your Grace's strength and treasure.'

Somewhere in the royal ranks sounded the hiss of a slow-drawn sword. Instantly a knot of the Archbishop's armed men surrounded the King.

'I am ready,' said Edward pleasantly. 'Whither do we ride? To Pontefract? A fitting manor for the murder of Kings, if memory of Lancastrian treachery serves.'

The Archbishop looked ill at ease. 'I wear the cloth of Holy Church,' he said uncomfortably. 'We have no hand in such devilish work, any more, Sir King, than you have choice but to do my lord of Warwick's bidding.'

Smiling still, Edward drove spurs inward and moved up. 'I had hoped,' he said, 'that my kinsman was not so ill-disposed as it might seem. But I would meet with your Robin of Redesdale. Perchance I can best him at the pricks, for I too am a fair archer, my lord.' To Hastings he said quietly: 'Disperse your men.' Richard's horse reared up, fretted by its rider's nerve-tense hand. The King looked at him, as if for the first time.

'And my brother Gloucester?' he asked the Archbishop, maid-meek. 'I fear you will find him more difficult to seduce than fickle Clarence. Mayhap my lord of Warwick has forgot he is no longer a child—he is a fierce young man. Do you not fear him?'

The Archbishop Neville disregarded this irony. 'Come, your Grace,' he said firmly. 'It was only your royal person that was desired.' His captains formed up their spearmen in a solid line.

'I am ready,' said the King again, rosy mouth smiling. 'I trust I shall be housed and fed better than poor Dickon of Bordeaux. For you have enjoyed in plenty my hospitality at one time.' Then he was gone, close guarded, riding along the dusty June road, taller by a head than the rest; full as a ripe cherry with the juice of wit and courage. And we were left, with one accord turning to the Lord Chamberlain for succour, for the reshaping of our life's pattern, now that the King was taken. And Richard of Gloucester spurred up close to his King's best friend, and looked with trust into his face. Our worst fears realized, our first campaign brought to a startling climax, I sheered away from the forecast of a madman: 'The foot that strikes the stone shall turn into a head—and the bones cast on a dunghill for ever;' but in Richard's late nameless fears I did believe, and for a short while I too

274

thought on Nottingham as a care-ridden place. I feared for the King.

Edward Brampton spoke. 'I guess zey vill take him north,' he said.

The north. The unenvisaged north. A vast cache of secrets: wild, dangerous, adjoining the fearsome borderers' domain. The north by day, lonesomely lit by plover-cries and the grave-song of wolf; peopled with cloaked assassins and sombre, holy men. God there in the north, but fiends also. A place for swift riding, back-looking. The north by night—Jesu preserve all who travel in that direction! The north a refuge also; to glean safety from its solitude, to bite through danger with the sword of determination. The north, hiding, hole for captives, for those whose presence is an embarrassment; for those in peril from their enemies. Just as a sanctuary can be a prison, so is a northern fortress likewise a place of safekeeping. The north. A stout chalice for the old royal blood.

And they took the King north, under cover of dark, although we did not learn of this until the moon had waxed fat and thinned, and again grown heavy with the child of night, during which time we remained together. We rode quietly, a small company cleaving to the hidden pathways, every so often one of us detaching himself from the rest and riding for a night or a day to return laden with whispers. The King was at Coventry, and had been stabbed in a quarrel with his brother Clarence. Nay, the King was at Warwick, sound and hearty. The King lay at Pomfret, in chains. I began to think that Hogan was not so mad after all, only armed with a foul and peculiar intelligence. Then one day we met on the road a merchant, fleeing from London with his wife and two young daughters, and servants with fear-green faces. Lord Hastings stepped out to meet them.

'We ride to my kinsman at Sawley Abbey, my lord,' gasped the merchant. He eyed our harness, the teeth of our lances, and seemed minded to die of fright. His wife, contrarily, bestrode her great dappled horse like a soldier. Her curling red smile hid scorn.

'Fool and husband, be at peace,' she said sharply, and I wondered if my Margetta would turn out to be a scold, fine dowry or not. 'These are King's men. He is sick, my lord,' she explained. 'London is a city gone mad. Our premises among many have been despoiled. There is fighting in every ward.'

'Yet the people love Warwick,' I heard Robert Percy say.

'Certes, sir,' she answered, with a wit like crackling leaves.

275

'That's why they brawl so fiercely over the King's capture.'
The two little maids peeped from their litter. One was blackbrowed and swart as Brampton. The other owned a head like
a golden angel—the kind men trade secrets for.

'What is the talk in London?' asked Sir Thomas Parr.

'There is a Parliament of sorts,' she said, to a withering
shrug. 'A pretty gathering, with none willing to bend the
knee to any noble earl while his Grace's fate is shaped by a
scaffold. We love our King,' she said, sad-proud, and the tiny
maid, crooning to a baby-doll, leaned from the litter, Planta-
genet-fair.

Lord Hastings motioned the men aside. 'God speed you,
dame,' he said. 'May you find redress, once this mischief is at
an end.'

'Pray Jesu this is soon,' she replied, and led the husband,
headhanging, forward and through our lines, halting for a
brief instant before my lord of Gloucester, who sat his horse
close by me.

'Your Grace,' she murmured, inclining her head. 'Good
lordship, give us back our King, soon. Oft-times he spoke of
his sweet Richard,' she said with the honey reserved for royal
blood in the dark hours when all are equal.

'Madame, our pledge,' said Richard, spear-stiff. The bold
lady then passed on; a queenly quean.

'They will take him northward,' said Lord Hastings, and
Sir Edward Brampton sighed, a little, patient, alien sigh.
Then Hastings said: 'Or will they?'

Richard spoke slowly. 'If London is divided, the Nevilles
will not risk disaffection. My Lord Chamberlain, what say
you?' Hastings sat silent, full lips sucked thoughtfully in.

'Who knows my lord of Warwick best?' asked Robert
Percy. He looked at Richard, smiling, smiling. I too stared,
and thought, if Gloucester waxes any whiter he will vanish
from the sight of man; and my mind asked me: Jesu, has he
ever known any happiness? I mused on my own careless life,
and thought: it is hard to be the brother of a King.

Richard set his mailed hand upon the Lord Chamberlain's
arm.

'Lead us, my lord,' he said simply. 'Lead us to my brother
—or to death. We are ready.'

Upon the road behind there was the thundering of many
horse.

'God's Passion!' said Robert Percy with a laugh. ' 'Tis a Neville. Can you believe that the sight of such warms my heart!'

Northumberland drew up his horse so sharply that its hind

276

legs slithered on the road, and the score of men behind him merged into a wheeling coil of bright armour, pennons, flying tails and plumes. Fire leaped from the steel-smitten ground.

'Gather a force, my lord,' said John of Northumberland without ceremony. 'The King lies at Pomfret. In my brother's keeping. None will strike a blow for Earl Warwick until the King's person is revealed unharmed. My agents have laboured well. The time is now.'

Hastings turned to the whole company, but it was to Richard of Gloucester that he spoke.

'Come, good prince,' he said. 'You and I will ride together. We will shortly have his Grace again at Westminster.' And Richard smiled, his colour returning. Hastings spurred forward. 'King's men!' he cried, holding up his sword. Richard watched him. 'My lords, muster all the men you are able in the north country. We ride to free a King!'

John Neville's sweated mount brushed my leg in passing. 'How does my lord of Gloucester?' he asked Richard softly.

'Grateful, sir, for your fidelity.'

'The King has given me the favour of a great earldom,' answered Northumberland. 'I could do naught else.'

'Would that all were grateful,' said Richard.

We mustered a great company, and set Yorkshire aflame with our own holy war, our pledge to rescue an anointed King. We were not at York to see Edward standing in the market-place, whole and sound; neither did we hear the cheers, nor see the dark glances of disapproval for Earl Warwick and Clarence. For we were busy. I rode with Northumberland and watched our ranks swell with lords and commonalty alike, while to the west the standards of Hastings and Gloucester summoned both the loyal and the wavering until all were armed, shouting for the Rose, the golden Rose, who answered from Pomfret Castle with a proclamation that made Robin of Redesdale's pitiful shaft break midway, like the ill-oiled, unprepared thing it was.

I have seen King Edward's smile often. A cunning smile, or a kindly glance, or a mischievous smile full of white bodies and soft beds; never, however, a sad smile that I saw. But I remember, over the tearful, bloody years, the smile he wore at Pomfret when we rode, calm and sharp of blade, to escort him back to London. We left the Nevilles weak as a woman lately up from childbed. We rode into London accompanied by the greatest lords of England, welcomed by the Aldermen of the City, in loyalty's blue.

Richard of Gloucester was horsed between King Edward

and the Lord Chamberlain. For the White Boar had drawn men, as it had drawn me—ask me not why. He had rallied hundreds to his standard. He looked drained and proud. Verily, I thought him happy at last. And the King was not ungrateful, for he gave Richard honourable commissions in Wales.

As for my part, the King was still pleased with me. He brought me into his Household as Gentleman Usher; many were the tasks I undertook beside the guarding of his royal person. Cleanly and strong archers, gentle men—was the stipulation. But King Edward also loved love. I was quiet, I was discreet, and if I were a little surprised at times, I did not show it. Gentleman Usher—that is good! Many women did I usher in to that god-like presence.

I saw Richard once before he departed for the Welsh marches. He took my hand.

'My thanks for your loyalty in this affair.'

'I hope to meet your Grace in less turbulent times,' I answered. 'I recall, you owe me three shillings.'

'Ah,' he said. 'Leave it—as surety that we shall dice together again. Besides, I find myself sorely ill-purveyed of money.' And we laughed together in remembrance, for it was a good jest, the King having rewarded him well. He said: 'Gloucester does not go back upon his word. You shall have your debt in full—the next time we come upon each other.'

'May it be soon, Richard my lord,' I answered.

'I feel you are a good man,' he said softly. 'Give me your prayers, sometimes.'

I saw him hardly at all for some two years, during which time the King kept me occupied with all manner of pleasurable duty. Many the cloaked lady; many the whisper. Toxophilus was still my leman, but wantonness led my rein. O Jesu! I was a laggard lover of Richard those days, for if ever I spoke his name at Mass, it was only when others did so in accord, and without deep thought. Fitting, perchance, that the next time our paths crossed it was in the face of danger.

Again, the enemy Warwick. But a Warwick better prepared, and we so unready. Mad, furious flight, easterly that September; a night ride through chill mists sad with the warnings of winter. To Norfolk, with the mud of the King's horse stinging up into my face. From Doncaster, where I had been waked by the rude cries of the *rex minstrallorum*. Enemies had come to take the King; allies of Earl Warwick, with an army that far outnumbered our own. Again, the same frail company: Lord Hastings, galloping stirrup by stirrup with the King. Sir Richard of Gloucester; a few esquires. A score of men-at-arms, hastily and inadequately harnessed. An addition: Sir Anthony Woodville, now Earl Rivers. He had misplaced his helm, and his bright yellow hair streamed about his face, and once he gave me a smile, riding, saying softly: 'The pity of it! I was having a wondrous dream; saints in their golden crowns.'

An omission: no faithful John of Northumberland this time! Alas, the fickleness of princes—and the irony of circumstance! No longer Earl of Northumberland, but plain Marquess Montagu, it was from him and an army doubly outnumbering the King's that we fled.

Four or five woolships bobbed against the quay at Lynn. It was the King himself who marched over the cobbles and spoke with the harbour-master. A few incurious eyes watched. A greybeard sitting on a coil of rope spat in the sea and muttered: 'Heigh-ho! Kings sail out—Queens sail in,' and cackled, the horrid laugh of the ancient. The captain of the wool fleet was likewise unmoved.

'Your Grace wishes my ships—to take you to Flanders?' Despite the imminence of our danger, Edward pressed him but gently.

'You will be well rewarded.'

The other answered, shoulders hunched: 'King's men will steal the room for my cargo.' One of Edward's esquires dropped a pouch of gold into the captain's hand. He shifted it to his other palm, saying: 'This will not redress the lack of my livelode.'

The King was taking off his cloak, the purple cloak lined with ermine into which I had eased him what seemed years before, though it was but a matter of some hours.

'When we return,' he said gallantly, 'I will give you a far richer garment. Meanwhile, keep the King's cloak warm for him. Pray for him.' This, with a smile to charm the blood.

Behind me, Richard of Gloucester was talking.

'He has him,' he said softly. 'Would Jesu that men followed me, like they do his Grace.'

I all but turned, but checked myself, for I fain would have told him: Ah, they do, Richard, my lord! You may not have the bright glory of Edward; your countenance may be sober and overanxious, yet, there was one once that dropped his dreams and took horse at your bidding. Even the Welsh respect you—you need have no fear. And I looked at Anthony

Woodville, with his calm fairness and devotion to the King, and I thought: we may be fugitives now, but I am proud to sail into exile with such great men. So clever, charming and devout. All thoughts of Earl Rivers's base lineage and past Lancastrian loyalties had long been chased from my mind.

As I leaped over the vessel's side and dropped down on deck, an aiding hand caught mine. A familiar, tense grip.

'How does the man of keen sight?' Richard asked, before I could beg his pardon for having used him as I would a page, then: 'Exiles—equal in exile. But mark me, we shall return in glory.'

And when they raised anchor, in a wave of fish-stinking sea, I marvelled at Gloucester's confidence, for London was swamped now by the adherents of Warwick and Clarence and the fearsome Frenchwoman, the French Bitch, Queen Margaret, who men said was half-mad with ambition and love for her whelp Edward.

I walked behind Richard on the hatches, looking the last on England. The quay swung away and a high-calling flock of seabirds lifted around our vessel. And then my mind brought back Margetta, for her breast was verily the colour of those crying gulls, and her eyes . . . why, gazing at the whipping grey water, sucked back in pools by the wind . . . surely, she could see *me!* Margetta my betrothed, whom by now I had met, and loved.

I sat down upon a sarpler of wool, hatefully wet from an early squall, and cursed Northumberland, he that was, well— I cursed Montagu then, the Neville who had turned through rancour to treason. King Edward stood by the masthead, under the sail which waxed as a woman but newly with child; and I thought on Margetta and, for an instant, spitefully, upon the King. For the *culpa* was surely his; he had traded an earldom for a kingdom, and had lost. John Neville had been crazed with spleen. I had heard his very words from Earl Rivers, reading a letter borne in after the event.

'My lord vows,' he said, laughing on each word, 'that the King has robbed him unjustly. Is this how he rewards loyalty (asks my lord)? For here is a rich Earldom forfeit to Lord Percy, and for what? A paltry Marquisate—and a pie's nest to maintain it with!' He and Thomas Grey had laughed, loud and long. Rich, warm laughter. Until their gay humour was shortened by the avenging pursuit of six thousand men.

I was ocean-soaked again already, my clothes only just having dried from our earlier crossing of the Wash. I walked upon the hatches beside Richard. The sails of our little craft fattened now, like a woman well-ripened with love's fruit. Richard was saying: 'They should fly England aloft,' looking up at the mainsail; and I had need gently to remind him that we had only the garments we stood up in, let alone the Royal standard, or pennoncelles.

It had been so easy—Margetta and me. She had been like a flower in the meadow-grass, yet whiter than the daisies, her eyes changing from grey to black and back to grey; her smile clearer than sunlight. And her sweet body—once a little nook, now a door open only to me . . . when I returned. Holy God! *If* I returned! There were others who had sought her favours and been turned upon with a pouting lip which served but to madden them further. I cursed Montagu, and his pie's nest.

It began to rain great drops which, against an unnaturally red sky, looked like blood.

I curled myself into damp, miserable sleep, to be wakened hours later by a call from the look-out.

'A strange fleet astern, Captain, and your Grace,' he said, uncertain as to which he should address first: his familiar master or a fugitive King.

'I can't see what they are flying, but they come in haste,' and he craned out from half-way up the rigging until he looked like an old figurehead of Saxon time. 'Great speed!' he yelled. His voice was whipped away as the wind changed and nudged us southerly.

'I will look,' I said, and hoisted myself high, burning my hands with the fierce sheet's tooth. Margetta waited far away, and I had no wish to drown—not in that dark draught at any rate. One glance only, and that enough to make me assume mastership, crying in unashamed fear:

'The Easterlings! Cram on all sail!' and sliding down in readiness to fight by the side of my lord, and my King.

They were out for our cargo, and our lives. The dreaded Hanseatic League, spiders of the sea, coming nearer and nearer with each bounding gust. Great ships, manned by grim, pitiless men. Topsail, mainsail, each straining inch of belly, not like a woman now, more like an old man hard-swollen with the dropsy of death; and the foolish, loving wind, as like to change as a King's whim, sweeping us up in its embrace. The cross-currents buffeted us hither and thither, and we swore, and called on St Peter and Blessed Nicholas. Again my keen sight picked up the blandly fierce faces of the

Hanse traders, and their snarling blazon, and the fire of their steel, and I saw their pointing arms, and the spideriness of them, working up and down their rigging for a closer look.

'Now may God be with York!' cried Richard, for this was verily a battle-charge, against an accursed, shifting wind; then I knew us humbled by a miracle, for our look-out cried: 'Landfall!' while at the same moment a detachment of armed craft showing the pennons of the Seigneur de la Gruthuyse hove into sight, come from the nearing shore of Alkmaar to drive off the men of the Hanse towns. So we were delivered from distress.

'Blessed be Jesus!'

'Amen and amen,' said I, then: 'Soon we shall be on Flanders soil for the first time, your Grace.'

'For your first time,' Richard said, sad and sharp and gentle. 'On my part—it is like a wicked dream come round once more.' He looked instantly at Edward, fine-coloured from the sprayful wind. Be calm, my lord, thought I; the one who expunged your evil dreams before is still within a handgrasp and will not fail you—no more than he did when you were seven years old. You see how I was as the wind is? Full of pride and all a-bluster with good counsel, yet veering one side to the other, and whirling in currents of rancour, admiration, envy and love!

The horse they gave me for the ride to Bruges was not to be compared with my sorrel, and the sere terrain of Flanders far less pleasing than the flower-starred fields of Bloomsbury, where Margetta and I had lain together. The Seigneur de la Gruthuyse was a great man, tall and round-bellied. When he embraced King Edward, the Governor's gold collar, weighty with rubies, caught for a moment on the salt-soaked doublet of his Grace, and, doubtless showing his cognizance of this brotherly omen, Gruthuyse took it off, placing it lovingly about Edward's neck.

'My house is yours, cousin,' he said, in what passed for English. 'Yaa! Like bird in storm the King of England comes. One day—bird strong: he fly away—pouf! To deliver us all from those who plague us.' And I looked at the woolships nudging the quay, and thought on King Spider, Queen Margaret—and Margetta.

'A bird, yea,' said King Edward ruthlessly. ' 'Twill be a hawk that returns to England. Now, its prey flies high, and makes a great clamouring, but after—why, if men desire to know who struck the fiercest blows, ask the ones who felt them.'

The Governor laughed wonderfully at this jest, and then they fell to speaking in Flemish, most of it that I could gather concerning King Louis, the threat of invasion to precious trade. And Gruthuyse told us that his horses, men and house were ours, and he was better than his word, for we were lodged most splendidly in his mansion at Bruges.

My window frame was coiled and carved with all manner of device. Looking down, I could see the bustling street, and the women of Bruges in their high caps. Sir John Paston had once written home about these women, saying that they were fiercer than any man in lust; yet, writing thus, he had not seemed displeased by the notion. And there was I, standing watching them. The wintry wind caught at these very caps, twirling the veiling like frost about the lovesome faces, lifting the skirts higher than was seemly. John Paston had said they were easily led from virtue. I fingered the window frame and felt the shape of a marguerite. Moon daisy. In Bloomsbury, growing tall. Margetta, easily seduced, and a grey whipping sea between us. Misery breeds on idleness, and the Seigneur de la Gruthuyse had swamped the King with gentlemen and boys to work his every will; so I was no longer called to swathe him in towels, rub rose-water into his great bare body, or play the lute and sing. I was treated with respect as one of his Grace's entourage, and as one who would retrieve the bleeding bird of York, along with the thousands waiting somewhere in mist. But amid the costly fog which clouded the Governor's soul and all our days of exile, I thought on my love, and, in a chamber fraught with snoring Flemish gentlemen, nightly lay trembling upon my own mind.

I was in this unholy state when I met with Richard of Gloucester, one evening after supper. The King had gone with the Governor to Tournai, for there was a freeman of that city whom Edward desired to meet, being possessed of the fairest wife in Flanders . . . Catherine de Faro. The young pig stewed in Rhenish lay languidly in my belly as I left the chamber.

'How does my lord?' I asked mechanically.

He seemed restless. 'I am but lately returned from Lille,' he said. 'From my sister, the Duchess Margaret. The King has tried all persuasions, but my brother-in-law will not yet commit himself.'

Charles le Temeraire, your rashness must be sleeping, I said to myself; and then aloud, in a sudden uprush of woe:

'Sir, will the Duke ever bring himself to aid our cause?

Will he wait until King Louis invades Flanders? Shall we never return to England?'

He studied me. 'You are dolorous,' he remarked. 'Would that your keen sight could pierce the future!'

'I am no seer, my lord,' I answered. 'To my mind, it is a sin against Holy Church.' Cackling, greybearded Hogan. English fields. Marguerites. Margetta.

Richard was smiling, his look still intent. 'Yet how much easement we should know at this time, if you were blessed, or cursed, with such a gift.'

'The King's astrologer fills his office well,' I said nervously. 'My sight is but good for spying out devices, warships and the like.'

'And faces,' he said gently, and as I did not know how to reply to this, he went on, laughing: 'A plague on my musing. Let us leave it to Master Astrologer, and when we are both crabbed old men, we will see how sure his shaft struck the blazon!'

I sighed at this last word, for he was speaking already like the Flemish archers, of the squared board divided into differing values, and not the homely English butt and marker. Oft-times I saw these squares so close they merged into one and I had been bested that day by an arrogant young knight from St Pol.

'Come,' he said, touching my arm lightly. 'A diversion would be well—for both of us. I know a fine inn, where you shall recover from me your three shillings.'

A cluster of esquires came darting, gibbering in the alien tongue I was beginning to hate. They brought us cloak and horse and, riding down the cobbled slope across the square, where pigeons, wind-frozen, snuggled together, we shook off their company; they were but foreigners, and weakly.

I had to stoop to enter the tavern, and he did not, yet it was at him that they looked. There was an unreality about the people within. A line of brawny young men occupied the bench along one wall. They rolled their heads about against the panels, laughing lackteeth at some frolic. A brace of them confronted one another, palms clasped, elbows sliding in a puddle of spilled ale. With gruff cries they urged each other on, in this test of strength. Two merchants sat at a far table, their voices softer by a breath than the slight chink of coin passing from hand to hand, muffled by velvet pouch. Three

Flemish women nodded over hot ale, their faces plain as platters. A Spanish seaman like a monkey postured and smirked, offering (in Latin too, the holy tongue of philosophers and the Church!) to sing of his adventures. Jesu! I thought, when shall I hear English voices about me again? The landlord shuffled forward, and it was all unreal, like a tableau set up for a play. His eyes were crusted by a film of age and sickness. He made owlish looks at my lord, who stood wrapped in his plain blue cloak (a present from the Governor). The tavern-keeper did not know him; I was on the point of crying: 'Make way, master, for a prince of England,' when I heard Richard say, in courteous French:

'Your best, a flagon, friend, and a private chamber.'

'You are merchants? *Hoe veel gelt?*' said the landlord, his eyes crawling from Richard to me.

'We are thirsty men,' replied my lord. 'If you would know our names, mine is Dickon Broome, this gentleman . . . Mark —Mark Eye.' Ah! the whims of princes! Yet my counterfeit name pleased me, for it smacked of Toxophilus. Gloucester took money from his pouch—I missed its value but it drew a smile from our host's withered gums, and he shed ten winters. *'Als't u belieft,'* he said, taking a handful of flickering light from one of the tables. He urged us up steep stairs into a small firelit room. He crept about for a moment, casting on fresh peats, then poured a dark-looking wine into pewter hanaps, and left us.

'I am grateful to my lord,' I said, feeling warmed at last.

He laughed. 'It is the Governor's money.' Though he spoke cheerily, I knew that this fact irked him, and that his flashing mood was a match to mine that night. We were like two restive steeds.

'To your Grace!' I drank, and knew this wine would undo me. All the fierce foreign suns had been spawned in it. A dagger's white fire had bred mischief in it. My bold and melancholy humour rose to meet its downward thrust. I sat opposite Richard, and the carvèd wood pressed my back, so stiff was I, so martial and controlled.

'How like you your name, Mark Eye?' he said. 'I had to think of something pleasing to you.'

'I like it well, my lord,' I answered. 'And your own trips easily from the tongue.'

'Broome,' he murmured. 'The glorious *planta genista*. Plantagenet wearing a coat of yellow flowers. Geoffrey d'Anjou's blazon. Edward used to do this,' he said, pleased as a child.

'He would enter houses under a pseudonym and folk would become enamoured of his charm and graciousness. They would talk to him as if he were not the King of England.'

For a while then we cast the dice, and again he won; feigning despondency, I drank deep with a mocking smile. He did for me the service I was bound to do for him in England—he poured the drink before I could guess his intent. He was still unquiet; his hands were not as steady as his eyes. ---

'I know little of you. Only that you come from Kent.'

'Yea, that is where I was raised, my lord.'

'You love it well,' he said.

'I love it well,' (repeating the lesson). 'As you love Middleham.'

'It is the fairest land in all the world,' he said softly. 'Though I have seen but little of the world. Every hope, every dream, every desire I ever knew was there.' The steady eyes dropped to the hanap which he turned round and round.

'Be of good cheer, my lord,' I said. I sought to fill his cup, misjudged—my sight all gone to perdition—and sat down again, shaking the table.

'There is no sky like that sky,' he said softly. 'No earthly winds could shake my spirit as they did; and in the Hall at evening, although a great fire warms the body, they still cry from without the walls. They run like ghosts, whispering and roaring.'

'Strange thoughts,' I muttered. I took a gulp of my wine, swallowing air, and shivered.

'Do they affright you?' he asked with a smile. ' 'Tis needless fear. Those are not demons of whom I speak. Beings of good, not evil—spirits to ward off spirits—the protectors.'

As if I had been there, the Great Hall at Middleham emerged in my mind's sight. There were hounds, and laughing children, and noble Warwick. Cursed Warwick. Many bright candles, unlike the rushlight that smoked between us on the table. There was music, and the moorland winds within that music. Dulcimer and viol and cromorne.

'Out of the dark—into the light,' said the wine. I shook my fuddled head.

Richard of Gloucester sat waiting.

'There was an ancient, holy man.' This, foolishly, for the wine had run off with a venerable name. 'Who told his King: "Lo, while we sit in the Hall in fireglow and brightness, there enters in a sparrow from out of the storm. He flies the length of the Hall and is gone, through the window. Thus, he departs, after a brief space in the gaiety and the company, again into the darkness. And who shall say that our span of life is not like unto this sparrow's flight? For none knows from what dark bourne he came, neither do they know whither he departs".'

I tilted the flagon. He set his palm across the rim of his cup. 'No more drink,' he said softly. His eyes were far away, so I drifted out of the dark into the light, and back again.

'Are you betrothed?' he asked. It was like a sword-thrust. I just nodded, looking down at my cup and tracing the devices climbing on it. God preserve me, they were marguerites.

'Then you have the advantage of me,' he said stiffly. Ah, Margetta, Margetta, I thought. Your neck the stem; your mouth the bloom. Would Jesu that I lay upon your breast. Gloucester was talking, steadily: '. . . she would hold my hand, beneath the table, out of the sight of her father and the butlers . . . her Saint's Day, when she was eight years old . . .'

Mocker wine, you mock me!

'. . . silly children . . . her hand all sticky with comfits.' He was laughing at his own womanish talk, as if he feared his own laughter. 'So were we bound, in sweetness.'

Sweetness, sweetness. I have sinned with Margetta. Nay, we are troth-plight. When I took her from her horse in the meadow—she laughed so lustily I was angered. So I cast her down among the grass and changed that mirth to tears and tears to smiles. In that sea of flowers she was the whitest flower of all. Ah, by St Valentine, she showed me the hottest love, after the first moments when she pleaded against my terrible work. And her parting speech! Lord! the bold quean! The honey of her! With a smile to blind the keenest sight (tears in my eyes, now): 'I think—I shall not mislike marriage . . . my nurse lied!' I silenced her with each fierce kiss: 'Lady, beloved. Cease this wanton talk. You *will* like marriage, an I have aught to do with it!'

Now I have naught to do with it. I am in Flanders. With the fathomless North Sea between. My lusting, lovely lady. She has sinned with me. Is she, perchance, lying lovelocked with another at this hour? I sit a table's breadth from the Duke of Gloucester, who is murmuring of Master Caxton, lately visited . . . Richard, who neither knows, nor cares; while the King, through his own shoddy treatment of John Neville, lies merrily with Madame de Faro and lets his kingdom be rent by wolves. French wolves. White wolves. Margetta in the meadow-grass. Daisies pied. A pie's nest.

Some fellow, it may have been I, sprang up with the clatter of a wine-cup. The pie's nest struck the board with a great din, and pain entered my clenched hand.

'God's curse on his pie's nest. And on those who . . . who make such the dole of faithful followers!'

Then I seated myself, very wet and glistening around the lips, and my wine sang a merry lay inside my head.

My lord of Gloucester was looking at me.

'Does he speak of the King?' he murmured. His eyes dropped; he traced a little wine pattern on the oak.

'Sir, I spoke without thinking,' was all that I could manage.

'Nay, you spoke from the heart,' he replied evenly. 'But as you are mad with drink, I must restore you first to your senses before you answer the pledge I would put to you.'

I had cursed the King! He had but to reveal himself, summon Gruthuyse's guard, and forever, farewell, Margetta. Yet all he did was to reach out and close his left hand around mine, speaking slowly.

'Below, those *bourgeoisie*. You saw? Trying their strength and skill. Let us essay our force likewise. Will you play?' He went on as if I were not there: 'Can he really be such a bold and traitorous fellow?' He raised his eyes, and our looks swam together. He stripped his sleeve in one swift movement. Holy Mother, his arm is slender as a maid's beside mine—I shall break his bones. But I laid my forearm up against his and our fingers locked in mid-air, wavering like the little bowl of flame beneath them on the table.

'Do not fear the fire,' he said. I gripped the ringless hand. 'I am ready,' I whispered. I should have marked his look, for it was the same that he had worn at Rising, when I had spoken of the King's folly, and then through ignorance, not wine. He bent his wrist, a little, gentle pressure. He was so slender. I would go softly at first and release his hand ere it touched the flame. One does not burn a royal Duke.

'Montagu was wrong,' he said, as a strange pain was born in my wrist. 'Once, he was loyal. Now, he wreaks treason on his Grace. Warwick—likewise. Clarence—ever. Gloucester—never. How strange are the hearts of men!'

He was steel and rock. I felt gouts of sweat in my oxters, my neck. God! he was using his left hand—what must his right hand be like? I felt the pain, effort straining at my throat, deep in my belly I caught the drag of his unassailable strength, hearing sinew and muscle shrieking for release. The little flame burned nearer—he held my hand over it and my eyes within his own wise, melancholy gaze. I struggled to raise my arm, watching the vein wax full on his brow, then tasted fire with the back of my hand, and our mingling sweat hissed in the flame. He held me, and I began to burn.

'Swear your loyalty,' he said quickly.

'Under duress, my lord?' I gasped.

He released me instantly and rose, turning away, while I sucked at the forming blister. A mark like an arrow head. When he looked back his face was ravaged. 'I have used you ill,' he said. 'Grant me pardon,' and took my hand again, looking at the burgeoning mark. 'Remember me,' he said. 'Think on me by this brand. But above all, his Grace. It is men like you whom he needs. Men who will fight and die for that great prince.'

I went on my knee, wept, told him of Margetta. He listened, as a father might.

'Well, Mark Eye,' he said, and touched my hanap with his. 'What shall be our toast, now?'

'His Grace King Edward.'

'York, and Plantagenet.'

'Victory, or death, your Grace.'

'St George for England.'

He was silent, briefly. 'We are exiles—equal in exile,' he said. 'Call me Dickon.'

And it was then the chamber door opened rudely to admit two of the fairest ladies I had ever seen, and one had eyes grey as glass, like Margetta. They were in a demanding humour, saying that the room was theirs that evening for private conversation; and who, for the love of St Catherine, were we, pray?

Were these, I thought, gaping, the women of Bruges, of the same that had buffeted Sir John Paston with their strong whorish love? I had thought to find them bold-featured, with that thrusting hip-swing which fed guffaws in the stews of Southwark, but these were delicate, fair. There was not a penny's grace to choose betwixt the two, although they were unalike, and calling one another 'cousin' in the prettiest fractured English, for our benefit.

The tavern-keeper came crawling up the stairs like a sea-slug, all flurried, not knowing which party to offend: his own country-women, or two high-flying English gentlemen with gold sound to the bite.

'*Pardon, mille fois,*' he creaked, but I could not tell whom he addressed, and he was not sure.

The tall woman, with the eyes like holy Madame Eglentyne in Chaucer's Tale, loosed a pack of fast gibberish at

289

him, meant to be scolding, no doubt of it. Yet her voice itself was so douce in timbre that it robbed her speech of all harshness. And her red mouth was wide, her brows the very shape of a sweet easy bow, set close over the lids and tapering off at each outer end; while her breasts were trussed up high so that the long throat merged into an arrow of darkness at the edge of her bodice. As to her companion, her cousin, her butty (as I would have named her had they been men and we shooting in a bow—a vulgar, and an apt, comparison!) why, she was a little sugarplum creature. Pale, with cast-down eyes; grey eyes too, but not the snapping sea-black wind-sucked grey of the tall damsel (for in her real or feigned anger at the landlord I watched those eyes change and saw Margetta in them, which made me sadly happy). Nay, the little one had the colour of sunlight through rabbit's fur between her white lids, and that rabbit hopped almost unseen from Dickon to me, from me to Dickon, and vanished in a faint, downward smile.

'Mesdames, we will withdraw,' said my lord, to my momentary surprise, as I had forgotten he was still playing Prince 'Prentice.

'*Mijn Got!*' said the tall wench. 'Jehan, I cannot believe you would play us false. When you said there were English merchants aloft, I thought it a jest. *Sainte Vierge*, how the blond one stares!' I glanced away in haste, feeling hot all over.

'Go to, go to,' said the landlord unhappily. 'Sirs, I have taken your gold. The fault is mine,' and he looked as if he wished we would all vanish into mist.

Dickon drained his wine, bowed slightly.

'Beauty commands. Mesdames, the room is yours,' he said, very gallant.

'The chamber is large enough for four,' said I. The wine still owned a small voice. 'We shall be deaf to your secrets.'

Richard let his cloak, raised in readiness for departing, slide from one shoulder.

'Blind to your whispers,' he said.

'Fie! Unchaperoned!' cried the tall one, and her look mocked me. The little one spoke at last.

'Cousin, these are English gentlemen,' she said sweetly. 'See—' she stretched out an ankle tiny and round as a willow-stem—'do we not wear fine English cloth?' revealing the hem of a broidered kirtle. 'Yesterday I saw the King Edward. He is in manner and person comely enough for a god. For his sake alone I will gladly take wine with Englishmen!' With that, she sat down, opposite Dickon, and fixed her pointed chin in her hands, and Lord! if I had been accused of staring, she was my master by a league, for she commenced to devour Gloucester with her eyes, from the crown of his hair, to his mouth, and his hands, and back again, while he returned her look with calm amusement.

This has all been forecast, I thought wildly, as the tall woman seated herself. Margetta, I would that those long white hands which lie so close to mine along the table were yours. For comfort then, I went swimming in the sea-grey eyes and watched them wax full in darkness, and felt my lord of Gloucester's shoulder, nay, *Dickon's* shoulder, press lightly against me in companionship, and I tasted the cup . . . and I was happy, and sad.

'What do you trade in?' asked my lady.

'Wool,' said I.

'Weapons,' said Dickon, and we sucked in our breath on laughter that threatened to consume us both, and I began 'My lord . . .' and felt his shoulder nudge me so hard that I flew higher than ever with delight and had to take a great draught to stop it bursting forth.

'It is bad, this war in England?' asked the small woman.

'All will be well,' I said, as Gloucester did not answer.

'My sister wrote me from Angers,' said the tall one, 'how Queen Margaret's son was wedded to Lord Warwick's daughter.' She had some difficulty with the Neville's name and it emerged as 'War-weak'. I felt a slight shuddering begin in Dickon's body, as she talked on. 'King Louis had the French-woman and the Earl swear by True Cross to keep their faith.'

'It was an evil work,' I said, empty-handed for a stronger retort.

'I would not sell *my* daughter for a crown,' said the tall one artlessly. 'Tell me, sir—' this to me—'is it true that in England they do not marry for love?'

'Sometimes they do,' I murmured, being sucked deep into Margetta's eyes. 'Men say the French prince is fierce, like a wolf,' she mused.

The small one made a soft angry noise. She was acute, that little wench. Her gaze never left the face of my lord, not for one instant.

'All will be well,' I said again, like an idiot.

The little woman slid the goblet towards Dickon. 'Drink,' she said, more motherly than natural for twenty or there-abouts; she is no virgin, I thought. She is cognizant with the humours of men, gay and lusty and sorrowful within the space of moments.

'We have but the one vessel,' said he, taking the hand that held it. I felt a pressure under the table. The woman who owned Margetta's eyes was closing upon me like a huntress. Her ankle rubbed mine, as if she stroked a dog.

'Then we must have a loving-cup!' she said, with great merriment; she stretched that long white neck to the brimming draught, raised her face and smiled at me. Her eyes were whirlpools. Droplets clung redly to her lips. My vile body swam out of control. I gulped down wine, lusting to have her. Her mouth an inch away, she said calmly: 'Jehan has been watering the drink. Sir, can you sing?'

Madame, if my guess is right 'tis no lullaby you would hear. And at this time I could not raise a whistle. 'My lord sings better than I,' said I, forgetting.

'Why do you call him thus?' she murmured, and looked at Gloucester. The small face opposite his had chased away his frown. He smiled. She chattered. He held her hand still.

My lady rose, tall, high-breasted and took a viol from above the chimney piece. *'Mijn Got*, they are dull company,' she sighed mockingly. 'I am left with the entertainment!' So she undid me finally with her singing. She sang the celebrated *'J'ai pris amours'*; next a little lay so bawdy that it could not be fitly construed into English; then, her great pride accompanied her in a true song of England:

> '. . . I will you take, and lady make,
> As shortly as I can:
> Thus have you won an Earles son
> And not a banished man.'

It was *The Nut-Brown Maid*, with its many verses, and such a mocking air that I knew her undeceived by our counterfeit guise, and at this I sprang up regardless of the other two deep in their soft converse, and calling her 'Eve' and 'temptress', I held the wine to her lips and my mouth to her breast for an instant before she leaped away, calling for her 'cousin'. Margetta, Margetta, where were you then?

'Sirs, we wish you a good night,' said the witch of Bruges, near the doorway.

'I'll stay,' said the little one, her eyes on Richard.

'Tell me,' murmured my undoing, as I spun her cloak about her, longing to remove that high cap. 'Tell me, Sir, of your friend. Is he not the Duke of Gloucester?'

I nodded, casting back to where Dickon sat, calm and comfortable and light, while my lady flitted across to her 'cousin', bidding her good evening with a kiss, and a trifle of whispering, which I did not heed and cared naught for.

Margetta was not with me as I hurried after the woman of Bruges, whose tall shadow tripped ahead like a banshee, I cajoling and she laughing and headshaking all the while . . . and Margetta was not with me in the mad-breathing darkness of the passage when I caught that woman and bent her over my arm; and she struck me a great blow amidships with her slender thigh, and I knew then what Sir John meant.

It was Margetta whom I betrayed that night, yet, strangely, Margetta who lay with me; and fumbling in dawn's twilight for my clothing I heard my bedmate say, even while she stretched to detain me, like Potiphar's wife . . . 'Heart's joy, you are very forgetful.'

'Why for?' I said, mazed by the stirrings of shame.

'My name is Anneke . . . all night you called me otherwise.'

(God preserve me, I shot better than ever the following day. I had heard that bedsport improved a man's marksmanship, and had dismissed this as all fable and nonsense. Yet it is true.)

Yea. I betrayed Margetta. I have said my *culpa* for that, but the night stayed with me for years. Not for that strong supple body, and the alien delights showered upon me. Not for the wine, the laugher or the music. But for the fact that I sat shoulder by shoulder with Dickon of Gloucester, as equals in exile, and we shared the follies that plague and enchant all young men.

When I saw him some days after, he gave me one look only, sufficient to declare that which needed no speech; thus we both knew what had passed between us two, and the women of Bruges.

My tongue is a dry stick in my mouth. Here in Leicester Gaol, we, the privileged traitors, have to ourselves a cell which stinks of past fear, and pride, and piss, and death. Here, thought rides me like a nighthag. There are pauses in the hammering without, for building a scaffold is thirsty work. I have lately seen a skull cleft as an apple and the bursting brains splattered upon the outer wall not far from my face. And all that my mind told me was: 'He was one of Norfolk's men, and Norfolk is dead.' So, oddly, it was fitting that he should fall in flight. I am filled with envy; beside my destiny and doom this hasty ending was honourable. Ah, Tacitus, how could you foresee such circumstance as mine? And Tacitus wrestles, in answer, with Saul's armour-bearer, who fell upon his sword.

The chaplain has gone. I think he was one of Morton's priests. Yet, none the less, I saw him only as a man of God and loosed my sin-sorrow into his pale hands. Despite my dear lord's words to us all, I am of a mind he would not wish me to pawn my own soul. For there are other sins than those of slaying my fellows . . . acts born of impulse and folly and the unwitting devil which led me once. My tongue is a sere bough betwixt my lips. Would that it had been torn out long ago. It would have been kindness. The mischief it has bred. Yet I was one among many. Many. I lave myself with possets of this vain comfort, as William Brecher kneels beside his son who has broken at last. He lies in the straw, a boy, a child, his broad placid face like stone, yet stone which the masons have attacked with chisel ill-tempered; his flesh is cloven into a thousand little lines of despair. He has shoulders like a bull, for all his youth, and on the death-day I watched them rise and fall, to deliver great buffeting blows with club and bill and maul; and at one moment he seized the giant Brandon's bloody sword from his dead hand and struck down a Breton knight with such puissance and skill, bringing the gore bursting from his shattered hauberk in bright clustering gouts. I thought then: He should surely be knighted for this work. Soon now he will feel the hemp, and not the steel, about those mighty shoulders. I will give him such consolation as I can.

His brow is wet, and the tow-coloured hair, matted with dust and bog-mire, curls flatly. We are all bound upon the same road, but he is still a yeoman and I a knight, so he attempts to rise. Swiftly I kneel beside him, facing his father, and we are like two priests beside a corpse, for he is dumb and still. In kneeling I realize that I have taken a wound—rather that my old injury has renewed itself. It is far from mortal, a piercing of the hip where, thirteen winters ago, a sword-point fleshed betwixt the steel lappets of my brigandine. Now, a glancing cudgel-blow has broken it afresh. Master William Brecher has noticed my cumbrousness in kneeling.

'You are hurt, zur?'

They are from Devon, these men. Their harvest will be wasted this year. Unless there are other sons to garner the apples and the grain. Or bring in the hay under a thunderous blue sky . . . next year. The year after. The last scraps of

294

flesh will have rotted from our heads by then. I pray my wife will not come Leicester-ward to see the face she once possessed, caressed, speared high upon a pike.

I place my arm about the boy. The roving eyes fall to the welt of dried blood upon my side. His thick fingers reach out and touch gently.

'Do it give pain?' he asks curiously.

I shake my head. 'Nay, master. The hurt left it many years ago.'

'*I* am not wounded,' he says with pride.

'You fought valorously.'

My answer throws him into a fit of shuddering, while his father clicks his tongue and our glances meet—his begging pardon for what he reckons a craven display.

'His first battle,' he says in exoneration.

And his last. Your last, Master William; and mine. And my King's. I would tell them of past battles, though those are long-gone, fallen victim to this ecstasy of despair. There is only the Now, with its hourglass and scythe.

'It is the waiting,' I say, and Master Brecher bows his head. There is a man-at-arms from York who has cursed and sworn day-long, calling up all the demons in Hell to smite one H.T., and he stands belabouring the door, shouting for water, which comes slopping in a greenslime bucket and is passed from mouth to mouth. I hold the water to young Brecher's lips. He smiles. His teeth are like fence-posts ill set-up, and I love him. The father is speaking.

'When he was little, I talked often to him of battles.'

'You fought for King Edward?'

'I was at Barnet Field,' he answers. And from the deep reaches of desperation, lo, there comes a bad jest:

'I did not see you there,' say I.

He can still smile; and there, I have them both smiling, one from water, the other from wit.

'I saw naught but mist,' says Master Brecher.

I saw blood at Barnet. I saw thick fog, laden with groans and screams of man and horse. I saw confusion, with the Silver Star of Oxford shimmering in the thick dawn. And while swearing and blind-striking in that broth, I saw the wheeling flanks of Montagu robbed of reason, for they chopped down their own allies like men bewitched.

'They thought it to be King Edward's standard.'

'Yea, the Sun in Splendour, with its streaming rays.' They turned, they clashed with one another, crying of treason, and were slain.

I saw the end of the House of Neville on that day. And, lying in the surgeon's tent, I cursed beneath the doctor's probe, and watched them bring in Richard Plantagenet, who dropped blood from his wrist, and talked wildly of his esquires.

'John Milwater—I saw him fall. Is there news?' he asked.

'Dead, my lord,' said the surgeon, watching a fresh red seeping through clean linen.

'Thomas Parr . . . he was beside me when I took this blow. . .'

And just then they carried in that same knight, stripped of course of his rings and his purse, and with the life only lately gone from him; and those who brought him cried with joyful tongue that Earl Warwick had gone deathward, trampled underfoot, but whole enough to be displayed in St Paul's on the morrow, together with his brother Montagu of the Pie's Nest. And Richard Plantagenet, plucking his arm from the surgeon's ministry, walked with unsteady step over to the corpse of Sir Thomas Parr, and kissed its face, and wept; wept, for Warwick and all that was gone.

But is there only the Now? Could I not counterfeit a dream, a dream that will soon be ended? Master Brecher's son has closed his eyes. How old is he? Seventeen? Eighteen? And there I was calling him a child. It is because I am old to his eyes. A grandad in his mind. My dream, if I can will it back again, it still full of steel-shriek and the dog-like moans of the dying. I was nineteen, at Tewkesbury. I had a fair young wife in my bed, and the kiss of a King on my cheek, for my work at Barnet Field.

'In the Name of Father, Son and Holy Ghost, I create thee a knight.' The heavy jewelled sword descending. That great golden face against mine. The joy, the wound-forgetting; the upsurging renewal. Richard Plantagenet, standing palely by the King. And the sound of the Frenchwoman's host already sharpening our steel again. The men of the West Country behind her; the armies of Somerset, Dorset and Wiltshire rallying to her fanatical voice. We had but a month to lick our hurts, to gather our force, and to borrow our money. Now I knew the meaning of livery and maintenance, but from the other end of the scale! Jasper Tudor (yea, the Dragon's own uncle) waited in Wales for Queen Margaret to join him. I waged a stout company of friends. Some of those lives still hang heavy on my soul.

Tewkesbury was a fair little town, tranquil and flower-framed, with a sweet-running river girdling the Abbey and its green fields. I gazed at that stream with fierce longing, and craved above all to rid me of my harness and plunge into the clear flood. The past hours weighed on me burdensome as the steel lapping my body. Our march had started, long before day's beginning, from Sodbury Hill northward to Gloucester. There, a hasty recognizance that its gates were barred to the French Queen; then hot on her heels all day. Hot, God's truth, the heat of hell fire from a pitiless sun turning our mail into an oven. I stewed gently in my own sweat, my sodden shirt a penance. A choking dust, and no drink. All the streams we came upon were like cesspits from the host that fled before us. My sorrel dropped her nose and sucked up mud, and I pressed her on. At times I fancied I had died and was in Purgatory, until I shook the sweat out of my eyes and looked for our leaders, and saw that if this were truth I was in fair company. For the King, and Hastings, Sir John Howard and Richard Gloucester, struggled ahead of me, encased in full harness; thus was I shamed and counted myself lucky to be only wearing brigandines; and wondered if they envied me; then began to look jealous at my own men in their jacks and sallets, light as the deer that had once worn the skins clothing them.

Sir John Howard had given me words of comfort during that ride. 'Remember,' he said with his furrowing smile, 'our quarry has fear as well as heat to combat. Jesu! one can almost scent their fear! *Her* fear!' Watching him spur on, I pondered on loyalty; for he had sworn to have the elder John Paston's head. I had lately learned that my erstwhile friend fought for Lancaster. So where did loyalty lie? There was naught to counsel me but the chafe of my flesh and the river running beneath my armour and the racing thoughts that numbed my mind—would the Frenchwoman wear harness and wield a sword? Like the saintly witch whom they burned before my time?

Thus we came to Tewkesbury in a fine moil, and took a field, because the Queen had done so, and we were all among thickets and bogs and thorn-hedges, and there were not three suns on that day, only the great yellow device on the royal pursuivant's staff, and that blazing orb above. I swept my eyes along our array. The banners hung quiet, for there was little wind to stir them. Now and then a breeze touched at the Silver Lion of the Howards; Clarence's Bull shook shyly in my keen sight. Its owner, however, was full of grace, plump with a pardon from his royal brother. George, my lord, where do you keep your allegiance? thought I, then I cast

297

round at the thousands of men ranked behind us. I saw through the shimmering distance my sorrel, standing in the horse-park. One of the baggage-boys sat at her feet. And all this I marked over the fifth part of a league. The archers were thick on our wings, while on my either side steel mirrored steel. I glanced toward the vanguard, and was blinded.

Flame filled my eyes like a lightning stroke, and I was afraid, for I was minded of the physicians in my childhood days with their reflectors, which had caused me to cringe and them to mutter, perplexed by my unnatural sight. Is this, then, I thought in the great terror which was only battle-anxiety bloating my conscience, to be the end of my seeing? Yet as suddenly the fire left my eyes, for a cloud settled on the sun and I gave a laugh of relief which set my esquires looking at one another. My keen sight had caught and burned in Richard Gloucester's mail, that was all. A foolish, witching phrase popped from memory. 'A light about him, not of this world.' Ah, who on earth . . . if it mattered. My mind went idling—a bad moment to choose.

Sir John Howard was readying our wing. We were spread out—Hastings's men so close to the stream that the last man in his flank was braced against a willow-tree and glancing down at the ripples, then back to where all eyes looked greedily. For in the Abbey's stone shadow lay the enemy. A great puissance of men, and no Frenchwoman among them that I could see. But one little figure in the distance, opposite our King. I strained for the cognizance, and saw that his standard-bearer flaunted the Silver Swan. My eyes went to the right wing and who there but Beaufort of Somerset, closing his visor. Placed no doubt to aid the French Prince. And Lord Wenlock . . . and our clarions sounding, and the throat-tearing cries of: 'England! England!' and 'York! A Edward! A Howard! Clarence!' immediately followed by that sound of a thousand geese in flight, the air-thrashing swoop of arrow-shot, and the uncertain cannon bludgeoning the ear. Then the two stout lines ran at one another like lovers long-parted and a tall knight mantled with the lilies of France sought me out and blunted his weapon on my shield while I hammered at his weakest join, finding the rift between neck and shoulder and feeling my sword in flesh, and glad of it. All around it seemed as if banners fell like trees in a storm. Two friends kept close and we struck in harmony, with a fine rhythmic force, the parry and the feint and the clang, clang of steel on iron, on steel, on lead, and the sweet suck of metal in the body of a foe. Why, this is but a little skirmish,

I thought, and also thought how the sound of man's dying is nearly always one of surprise—not a scream of anguish but a long grunting 'aaaah' and there was another of the French traitress's henchmen gone to his just reward; then my boastful bloody humour turned to dismay as a body of men, with Beaufort at its head, smashed into our left flank from behind, and we were all swept together in a flailing mass near to the thickets where they had concealed themselves during the first moments of close confusion. Two came for me at once. A knight of John Howard appeared alongside me, and did well, for he struck off the hand of one assailant cleaner than any surgeon or headsman might. And we were still hard pressed. Back and back. I slithered on someone's bowels, spread out on the ground like a glistening white necklace. Naught separated us from the enemy save a carpet of slain. And all the time we were cumbered by the foul lanes and the hedgerows and the clumps of briar which ruined many a fair stroke and gave solace and shelter to many a French dog. One such kept harassing me. He bore the powderings of the Prince Edward, and he was like a ghost in harness, for while I fought him back against a clump of oak trees, and struck at him again and again, still he dodged aside and came at me thundering blows on my shield, striking fire from his heavy broadsword, and we feinted and thrust until in amazement I felt the ground becoming reedy and treacherous under my feet and knew then that he had tricked me down towards the river and I actually heard him laugh behind his visor, which chilled me through, for my steps had no purchase yet he seemed light as air and nimble as a court-dancer or a tumbler, while my leg which had taken a blade at Barnet was stiffer than it should be. My eyes were full of red dust—my ears crammed with a thousand sensations: the roar of the battle around me, the rasping music of my own mail, and the great dolorous boom of the Abbey's bell, sounding out as if the House of God were shocked by this slaughter so near its precincts. Then we were rolling down the bank, my adversary and I, and the cool swim I had promised to myself became reality. He flailed at me with the flat of his sword, raising waves as I rolled with him out of the shallows and dived for his legs and drew him under, and we must have resembled two great steely salmon floundering together; for while I sought to ride him underneath the ripples he clawed at my visor and got it open and his poignard came close to my face before I kicked him in the belly. But Jesu! he was full of strength and valour and he came for me again, the sun catching the edge of his blade like it winks off the monstrance uplifted in Church . . . and I would have had no face left had not fortune been with me in the shape of a dead man-at-arms, one who came plunging down the slope to hurtle head over heels on top of us both . . . and in that moment of confusion when victory was mine I did not recognize him as one of my own waged men and feel sorrow and gratitude, for I was busy serving the silver-swan-bearer with the coup he would have bestowed on me. I wrenched his helm apart like one of Sir John Howard's Colchester oysters, and stuck him to the death, my knife spitting him through his teeth, right to the back of the skull. Then, pulling myself up the bank with my hands full of rushes and mud, I saw that the tide of war had turned in our favour, that Beaufort of Somerset was besieged from the rear in his turn. 'God bless our King!' I shouted, hastening upward to see the small band of spears who roared like ten thousand, bearing down on the enemy. Edward had foreseen the contingency, stationing these upon a little knoll. Our flank no longer gave ground. I saw Gloucester, his bright mail bloody, and the Blanc Sanglier held aloft; I heard the command—'Reform your lines!' hot-followed by the trumpet-bray. I saw briefly Sir John Howard and the other captains, and then we were no longer a sinking straggling mass, but running together in orderly puissance and the fine dance-like rhythm of hack and stab and thrust, feint and weave and parry rich-flowing once more. I came close to Richard Gloucester—a few yards away, I saw the bright windmill of his swinging axe: one, two, three, they went down, he pressed on, keen-footed, swift-sighted, chivvying and maiming and killing, his esquires body-hot around him. And as I looked I realized how far forward we had moved and Jesu! the host of Lancaster was falling back. The cries around me took on a savage note of triumph; fierce laughter mingled with the oaths . . . the baggage-boy whom I had sighted beforehand was suddenly at my side. 'Up ahead!' he cried. 'Look! Ah, good sir, 'tis sport! They are butchering each other!'

So they were, Lord Wenlock and Somerset. From a vantage point the boy had picked out what seemed only a boil of confusion. . . . Beaufort splitting Wenlock's skull in a rage, calling him traitor—we learned after that he vowed he'd played him false, not giving him of his strength against Gloucester's wing. But at that moment we only wished to know they were in flight. They ran like hares towards the town, towards the Abbey, plunging into the river, fear-crazed, sinking like stones under a hail of arrows and the weight of their own harness. They raced across the meadow, whose green carpet had grown red flowers, and we were after them, yelling derision at the lumbering lords mail-burdened, and the terrified commons all spread out in flight across the field. I cried for my horse, and my esquires, singing their delight, pitched me into the saddle and I rode like a madman, for all are mad in war, close upon the heels of the waving Bull of Clarence and those who upheld it, and our quarry who was young, and royal, and his French bitch of a mother's heart's pride; and the heat went out of me as our prey turned with face bared to George Plantagenet. I saw that face, like a young wolf, as the woman of Bruges had said; yet a brave white young wolf, with lip back-curling and fear clothing the fangs, and my keen sight picked out the fierce eyes that had doubtless once smiled in friendship at turncoat Clarence. And I turned away hearing his scream of 'Mercy!' for whether or not he was begotten of the Holy Spirit, or, as men said, from the loins of an Earl of Somerset, he had been but lately hand-fasted with Prince George, and it was George's men who struck at him, ringing him round so that he went down with a soundless fountain of blood spurting from that young wolfish face, and they hacking at him in laughter. So where, ah where, does loyalty lie? But there was no time to ponder on such riddles, for all around was the beat of hooves and the triumph-cry of a victorious army and I too was swept up within it, and possessed by the grim glory that beset my captain and the three Plantagenet princes. The river grew thick with corpses, its clear stream running heavy and red.

We trod down the Beauchamp Swan, the Griffin of Montagu. The lilies of France bloomed bloody. I saw all: the sweeping, fear-crazed rout going in waves before us, my horse's ears rising before me as we plunged through a hedge and were enfolded in the shade of the Abbey.

King Edward dismounted at the North Door. He raised a sword clotted with hair and blood, and struck the oak a fierce blow. Slowly the door swung back, but not so slowly that I could not hear the force of that blow still thundering and rolling up the length of the great vaulted aisles—past the sleeping forms of long-gone knights and priests, like the harbinger of all the evil at which Hogan had hinted. And I was suddenly sore afraid as I saw the old Abbot framed small by the huge portal, sad of countenance and upholding the golden Tree of Christ, while behind him trembled an acolyte with the pyx and Eucharist in his hands. So the King and the

301

Church confronted each other, while the banners flared above us, the Sun in Splendour, the Bull, the Lion, the Boar, and my own gay emblem of the bend sinister.

'Holy Father, let us pass.' The King's voice was hoarse from the cries of war.

'Sir King,' said the Abbot steadily, 'there are men within who seek succour in God's House. Go in peace. It is the law of Holy Church.'

For a moment I thought the King's humour would soften. Then his eyes raked the darknesses behind the upraised cross and I saw that look redden like the river behind us.

'Beaufort!' The name itself a death sentence. 'Stand back, my Lord Abbot!'

The old man had no choice, as we, a mailed wave, poured powerfully over the threshold. And it was only knowing that Tewkesbury was not by law a Sanctuary[1] that nerved my arm as I ran with the others among that forest of pillars and fought, my breath a snarl of war-lust, up the nave to the High Altar where the candles, thick as a man's thigh, burned coldly. There was a knight who shrieked like a trapped rat while aiming fiercely for my head with his axe, and my sword bit a slice from one of the tall Norman columns as my unbelieving eyes saw the quarterings on the tiles all overspilled with gore. I fought this rat of Lancaster into the south transept and there, by the gilt tomb of the Despensers, I found a weakened rivet and took his life away, and came limping back through the aisle to see them dragging out Beaufort of Somerset past the stiff stone form of a Saxon Abbot, who looked as if he had sprung fresh dreadful wounds, for his effigy ran with blood.

As Beaufort panted out his spleen, mad Hogan's words rang newly in my ears . . . 'This England will be a stew of red life . . .' and I grudged him right on one count.

They straightway tried them, Beaufort and the other traitors. A few were pardoned, among them Morton, lawyer and churchman, who threw himself upon the King's mercy and pledged allegiance. King Edward seemed anxious to see the affair concluded, but Richard Gloucester came in, tardy, to sit beside Sir John Howard. He had his robe flung hastily over his mail; his eyes wore a red glaze, but he held the mace of Constable of England firm enough as he pronounced sentence

[1] *Author's Note:* Although most churches were by canon law sanctuaries, Tewkesbury had neither royal charter nor papal bull to this effect.

upon Beaufort and watched him pass, heavy guarded, through into the market-place. I stood beside Richard, waiting while a priest shrove Beaufort, and I thought briefly on our sojourn in Flanders. He was not changed, I decided, only sadder, and battle-weary, as were we all.

'You fought with marvellous strength, my lord Richard,' I said.

'A bloody business,' he said bitterly. 'The Lord Abbot says the Church must now be closed for reconsecration—the first time since its beginning,' and he shook all over. I, thinking he had taken a secret wound, gripped his arm.

'I have seen her,' he said, looking straight ahead at the waiting scaffold. 'Anne. Anne Neville. By the holy house at Gupshill. Once more . . . and by the Rood! She hates and fears me!'

I had no space to reply, for they brought Beaufort then, handsome Beaufort. When they loosened the neck of his jerkin for the axe, we saw that he carried near his heart a sweat-soaked device. A marguerite, in cloth of silver.

'So, Beaufort!' said Clarence derisively. 'For all you bore her emblem close, your Queen's cause is lost. Finished forever.'

'You forget, Plantagenet,' said Beaufort, showing his teeth. 'I have a cousin whose name also lends itself to this cognizance.'

Lady Margaret, I thought. What hazard she? What hazard any weak woman? and then I was not so sure, thinking on the Queen, wily and beautiful; Margetta, who had well-nigh driven me mad with worry while parted from her, and the woman of Bruges, who had conquered me through my own knavish lust. And Richard, who had a woman in his mind that moment and shook with dolour. 'She hates and fears me,' he said again.

Beaufort mounted the block under enough May sun to turn the axe to fire as it fell. (How was it, Beaufort, that swift death? Would Jesu that I knew.)

There was neither fear nor hate in Anne Neville when I rode to Middleham six years later with the call to arms against France. Never have I seen woman cling closer to her lord.

I killed a horse on that ride to Middleham. My blood was high with the foretaste of glorious war. I killed a horse, and that was all I killed. I could almost smile now at the remembered sight of Louis on the Bridge at Picquigny: dressed like a mountebank, all motley colours, and his aide and chronicler, Philippe de Commynes, clad in facsimile; Oh Louis, so full of mefiance that he dreaded assassination even with his hand clasped on the fragment of True Cross, and over King Edward's.

The fifty thousand crowns. The priceless plate, the betrothal between Edward's Elizabeth and the Dauphin. The sumptuous banquet—spoiled only by Richard of Gloucester's humour. For we had been so merry together, and so busy on the crossing and ride inland from Calais that I had envisioned the old fugitive time together and the brotherhood reborn between us. Not so, however. One look at his countenance, filled with a mixture of sadness and disbelief, halted my move towards him; and I stood, solitary, west of the Bridge, while all around me they rolled the fine fat casks of Gascon wine and ale and started the fires under the spitted oxen, and turned the wenches out of doors like so many Salomes writhing for England's head. And the soldiers fell to with a will, while I watched, empty-minded: the worst state in which to find oneself, for devils enter.

'Come, sir, why so dour! A fair day for England!'

Anthony Woodville spoke; horsed, sparkling and smiling and shining, with his helm streaming its silver mantling, like a winged god, packed with poesy and music and more learning than I could ever hope to attain. My friend and good lord.

'Fair, yea, Sir Anthony. The sun shines, but I doubt if Harry Five would have smiled upon this day.'

He shook his jewelled bridle. Even that sounded like a song.

'Are you ailing?' he enquired. 'Forsooth, you are gay enough at court. And this is a time for rejoicing. No more debts for England . . . by St James, you are grown dour as others I should not name.'

And with one accord our glances crossed to Richard Plantagenet, stiff as a lance on his great bay horse.

'I am a Woodville, and some of England does not care for me,' he went on. 'In fact,' he mused, 'it would seem there are those who reckon England's honour weighted in the dust by that handful of gold.' He paused. 'But what is the designation of honour?'

'What is honour?' I repeated in obedience. The back of my hand began to sting and burn and I slapped at it, but the louse or wasp or whatever it was had vanished. There was only my old white scar, talisman of Flanders. Unsightly brand, I thought, drawing on my glove.

Thereupon Sir Anthony began to talk to me, about honour in love, and in war, and how the changing values of his life render honour impossible to examine, century by century, and when he reminded me that even Antisthenes had spoken of 'how modesty and fidelity and justice and truth are fled' I got his drift plainer than ever before, and looked at the King with even greater worship, seeing in his extended hands, and in the treasurers loading their coffers with Louis's first peace payment, a new era beginning, where all men smiled, and victory no longer wore a bloody gown.

Sir Anthony sent me a dish from his own table that evening. Sturgeon, and venison frumenty. I saw him raise his flagon to me once, flashing a smile, and I watched how closely he loved King Edward, and charmed King Louis on three occasions with a tittle of verse to the honourable event, *ad libitum*. And I also watched Dickon of Gloucester, knight of the dolorous countenance, and was impatient with him in my heart. And then Thomas Grey, Marquess of Dorset, climbed over the trestle to sit by me, though I knew him but slightly; and he enquired with great kindness after my estates and fee-farms, and Margetta, inviting me to describe her beauty and worthiness. He vowed he would come one day to take a cup with me on my manor—when the King could spare us from our duties, that was; and he spoke of young Ned, and little York.

'Jewels, both,' he swore, kissing his fingers. 'Priceless jewels. Mischievous, the younger, yet a true prince.'

He took a sliver of meat delicately from my platter and ate it with strong teeth. He looked around the crowded chamber, redolent with music and crushed flowers, strong wine, rich food, and gave a happy sigh.

'This is indeed a time for joy,' he said. 'Peace with France —York and Lancaster united at last, and at Ludlow a noble infant heir, waxing beautiful. For that then, doubly a toast to my royal mother.'

We clashed hanaps. 'The Queen!' I said obediently. Then he enquired: 'Did you bring many men to his Grace's bidding?' I could laugh with wine in my belly.

'They were lusty for war,' I said. 'Yea, as many as my ships could carry,' and I told him, even boasting a little. For a moment I thought I saw a look on him like that of Sir John Fogge, noting my blazon when I first approached the King. I preened under his interest while the distant fife and tabor from the streets mingled with the sound of Louis's dulcimers.

'How they do caper!' I said.

'Even Gloucester's sad Yorkshiremen,' said he gaily. 'Many followed him, did they not?'

I told him the exact number.

'I have never seen so many stony faces,' he said lightly. 'By God's Body, the north would not be to my taste. How did you find Middleham?'

'It has a kind of peace,' I said truthfully. 'And the Lady Anne prospers—the ambience suits her health, and that of the boy.'

'Sickly, sickly, the Nevilles,' he said soberly, then went on with his swift courteous converse, dropping on first one topic, then another, with a kind of light and schoolboyish lift to his manner which was disarming.

'My lord of Gloucester seems a fair judge of men.'

'He's loved in the north country,' I answered. This I had noted during my short sojourn there. It had been like stepping into a foreign land where Richard was King. I had sat at his Council and felt the warmth emanating from behind those stony faces. I had seen his justice, and an old woman bending to kiss his shadow as it fell across Bootham Bar . . . Dorset was laughing.

'I was thinking of Lord Stanley. Stanley is blessed with infinite patience and there! Richard has him sitting without the gates of Berwick all those days and nights . . . are they well reconciled, those two great lords?'

'Jesu! that's an old quarrel,' I said. I myself could hardly remember it. 'Stanley was wavering once, and Richard cut him off ere he could ride against the King. Now he follows, says Richard, as well as the next man.'

'As well as the next man,' mused Dorset. 'That I like well. For who indeed, is this next man we hear of so often? By troth, my noble uncle could fashion a paradox on that!' He laughed again, his fresh young sound.

'In rhyme, of course,' I said.

'You shall come to Ludlow,' he said, his elbows on the board. 'You shall come and see the royal heir. A gem of price,' he said, as if he were not a fleshly little boy at all, but something hard and glittering. 'When we return to London, speak with my uncle, Lord Edward—regard my kin your friends.' Why, these Woodvilles are not half the grasping, callous persons that the barons say, I thought, clasping the arm of Queen Elizabeth's son, and half-hearing his flashing words. 'So Stanley is docile and loyal? What of his wife, though? Eh, friend? To what end think you she puts her terrible learning? For she's fuller of philosophy than becomes any dame. Their place is at the loom and in the bed, I vow. Mistress Shore . . . there's a woman! Empty as a fowl, but those little, dewy paps . . .' He stopped short, with quirking brow. 'So! Lady Margaret! Has Stanley tamed her?'

I firmed my thumb on the table-damask. He glanced down. 'He on she, or *vice versa*?' he asked, and I was about to tell him the little I knew of this turbulent match, and to ask also his knowledge of the mysterious Henry Tudor, when there was a great uprising as the King of France called a toast to the King of England, and the toast-master came riding up to the dais with a golden cup and the whole evening blurred into merriment, unmarred for me except by my damned hand, which pricked and burned like the very devil.

I recall that Dorset said again: 'You must ride to Ludlow,' for all the world as if he owned that castle, and he bade me go watch the royal prince at his schooling, for it was one of heaven's delights, said he. And he made me smile with tales of Mistress Shore; of her wit, her amorousness—ah, did she not belong to the King, said he, he would joyfully seek her bed, delicious creature. So his talk flowed all the way back to Calais and England. And Gloucester rode north again, without a word for me, and I rode London-ward to Margetta; and for the next five years it was a jewelled time, all the jewels being counterfeit, had I but known it.

In the midst of the pleasure and the glad service I hung like a fool between two factions: the charming Woodvilles, and Hastings's party, who chewed their thumbs down to the bone at sight of the Queen's kinfolk still, and I got some spice of delight from it all. I promised myself that I would journey to Ludlow and see the future king at his lessons; I promised this for full five years and was too busy and too idle to fulfil even a pledge to myself. When the time came for that ride, it was full of weeping.

'Come closer,' said King Edward. 'My Lord Chamberlain. Ah, Will, my good old friend!' He stretched out a hand and Hastings tenderly took linen and wiped the King's face, the froth from the mouth, the sweat from the purpling cheeks.

'Can you do naught to ease him?' Hastings turned on the physicians. 'For Christ's love, Master Hobbes! Have you no more tricks, no more potions? He burns like fire.'

'I will not be bled again,' said Edward querulously. Then

he chuckled. He had laughed before, during the days and nights when we had watched him, all of us grouped about the great plumed bed and empty with fatigue. I had fixed my eyes upon the Sun device behind the King's head, and it had seared my brain, each flickering point bidding me believe what I would not. For Edward could not die. He was a lion, untouched by war and pestilence, he was forty or thereabouts, but he was supreme and would live to three score years. He had been gay at Christmas, laughing lustily then at the players' antics, bawling sarcastic quips against the sombre mummings of World, Flesh and Devil in the Hall, and it was only a week since he had laughed himself silly on the fishing trip up-river—a clumsy young henchman capsized the boat containing Lord Dacre's mistress; she went in head-first, revealing plump naked privy parts; he had laughed too, in his fever-madness, rearing in the bed. He could not die, and there he was, dying, of an April damp taken spearing the salmon, or so ran the diagnosis of Master Hobbes and Brother Dominic. And when their noxious draughts failed to remedy the ill, they set blood-irons to the royal veins and vainly all but drained that vast body. They placed a little dog upon his chest to suck the evil humours out, and he cast it down, saying, 'Take the poor beast away; why should she share my sorrow?' They even sent pages to Southwark in search of old Tib, but they found her gibbering wantwit with all her simples gone useless and a green and powdery skin, like the fur of a frog, atop each jar.

The chantry priests had gone, but one young monk knelt in the corner, murmuring mechanically: 'Ave Maria, gratia plena,' fervently oblivious of his betters; of Lionel Woodville, Bishop of Salisbury, Sir Edward, Lord Richard Grey and Thomas Dorset, Hastings, and Stanley. The King's bed was an abyss. The Woodvilles stood together on one side; Hastings did not look at them, but Stanley did, sometimes, with that lip-chewing wavery glance. Sir John Fogge knelt at the foot of the couch, hands clasped on swordhilt. I hovered near Dorset. Fantasies assailed my weary mind, old soothsayings returning like bats at dusk; 'How shall we know that our life's span is not like unto that sparrow's light?'; looking down at the cicatrix upon my hand, and up again to catch the sombre smile of Dorset, or the markings on the astrologer's robe, all the Zodiac starring its black silk, or the Sun in Splendour, whereunder the King tossed and burned up.

The astrologer stirred a dark liquid in a little vial. This he handed to the taster who swilled a mouthful, said 'Drink,

Sire,' handing it to the King. Edward sucked the brew and spat it out, saying: 'By troth, friend, your potions are worse than your prophecies!' and there was a fierce clash of glances betwixt Hastings and the Queen's kinfolk as an old spectre rose. 'Your Grace's pardon for past errors; 'twas the dark of the moon,' whimpered the astrologer.

The King's eyes were a hard blue above the fleshy cheeks. 'Nay,' he said, with renewed vigour. 'There was no "G" . . . no "G" for King. No fault of yours. I forgive.' He plucked at the coverlet, while the air waxed stale with hate.

Master Hobbes was feeding him saffron-water, a harmless draught to allay the congestion in his bowels, and he said, with a weak laugh: ' 'Tis naught, sir, 'tis naught for that. But mix me a purge to drive the Treaty of Arras from my belly and I'll give you knighthood.' Then he began to weep a little, and I had to quit the room for a space, or swoon and be shamed.

So from the tremendous heat of that chamber I stepped, to find half the court without. Mingling with the awed, yawning pages there were women, one of whom clutched my sleeve.

'How is he?' she gasped.

For a space I did not recognize Mistress Shore. Her face wore a bruised look, as if she had been beaten by her grief.

'His Grace is passing sick,' I said, then added: 'Don't weep, good Jane.' This I called her by custom, as did all men, though she was far from such, being free with her body. Yet she was kind, and had given gladness to the King, so I spoke her thus. She made a muffled sound and withdrew into the shadows, as another figure, taller, more slender, rose from before a prie-dieu and came to me, attended by the ladies Scrope and Beaufort. Elizabeth of York was beautiful as ever.

She asked: 'How does my noble father?' with firm lips.

'Madame, he fights his last battle,' I answered, and I did not speak of the Treaty of Arras, for if we had lost Burgundy, Artois, and 50,000 crowns a year through Louis's treachery, she had lost the Dauphin to the German Emperor's daughter.

'Is he in there?' she asked with sorrowful scorn. I knew she spoke of the astrologer. 'Surely his presence will worsen the ill.'

'He's full of sadness, not prophecy, your Grace.'

'One day,' she said bitterly, 'I met my father walking in the pleasaunce, with tears. The charlatan had said that his blood would never rule England . . . that no Plantagenet would grace the throne through Edward's sons.' Her lips lost their set line and quivered. Then she said: 'I would my uncle of

309

Gloucester were here. He can comfort him best.' I bowed down, kissed the hem of her garment and left her; and leaving, caught the eye of Lady Margaret Beaufort. An eye like a lizard's, motionless, but very alive.

The ways were black with priests and monks. Holy men, familiar hooded faces, some strange to me, for the clergy had ridden from far to be with the King in this melancholy. There, an old bishop, heavy with winters and sorrowful of countenance, walked falteringly through the close-packed corridor; I bowing in reverence, looked up to see this face of great trouble under the golden mitre. And looking, knew him from long ago. The Bishop Stillington, of Bath and Wells. A frugal man, I had heard, who did not revel or sate himself with glories such as many other prelates.

'He is weaker?'

'Hourly, my lord.'

The deep groan startled me.

'May Our Blessed Lord preserve him,' he said, and then, shaking his head, murmured softly, 'I am an old man. Too old, too old, ah, Christ Jesu!'

I left him, uncomprehending, to his privy sorrow and returned to the King's bedchamber, where Lord Audley was speaking.

'Shall we summon the Queen, Sire?'

Edward shook his head, wearily, offering no reason. There was a little hiss of breath from Doctor Morton, Master of the Rolls.

'Your daughters then, lord?'

He sighed. 'Ah, sweet Bess,' he muttered. 'The cursed Treaty robbed her sore. Nay, let them stay without. For I fear that same poison will be my end.' His physicians looked gravely at one another, and began to pack their medicines away, for now the King confessed what had been in all our hearts. The rocking at his realm had been too much for our sovereign lord. Edward's eye roved round, settled on Lord Stanley, who knelt at the bedside.

'Your Grace?'

'My lord, keep your lady . . .'

'Sire?'

'Keep your lady in submission,' the King said faintly. 'And let not that impudent son of hers aspire to stir my realm— that Tydder—on your loyalty, let him not harass my heir with his threats once I am gone.'

'Henry Tudor is in Brittany, lord,' said Stanley stoutly. 'And my wife is loyal as I, to York.'

Edward sighed again. 'That is well. God's Blessed Lady!' he said suddenly, and it was strange to hear the fierce familiar oath on dying lips. 'There *is* one face I would kiss ere I depart. Dickon . . .'

Thomas Dorset leaned forward. 'His Grace is on the Scottish border, Sire. Too far, I fear.'

Edward smiled, paling. 'Yea, God keep him. The only man, the only strength to tame those barbarians. Ha! to think he's made them denizens of England. To fight the French—and all our foes . . . to fight . . . to die . . .' He closed his eyes and a gasping breeze rose in the chamber.

'The Eucharist! hurry!'

Yet Edward spoke again, still with lids closed.

'First summon my executors,' he said.

They came, five noble prelates and three great lords, Stanley among them. The death-smell grew stronger, and with it the fiercer stench of enmity and strife. Kneeling by the King, Sir Edward Woodville and I raised the huge, gross body, bloated like a wine-bag. We heard the fat choking from organs ill-purveyed to fight this enemy. We propped him on pillows, and saw his eyes open on a film of tears.

'My lords,' he said, and we all drew near at the urgency in his tone. 'My good friends, soon I shall be no more. Before I return to Him who made me, I would have your promise. I, who have granted many boons, ask one now in exchange. A simple, gentle thing . . .'

'Aught for your easement, O King,' said Hastings thickly. Edward looked at him, slow, then at Stanley, then at the Woodvilles, flanked like archers on the other side of the bed.

'Love one another,' said the King. 'As Christ Jesus loved the world, and in His Name. Let there be an end to quarrelling, to envy and spite. Let the past be washed away. For the sake of my son and heir I beseech you all, be as brothers henceforward. Forgive all wrongs. Live at peace.'

I was still supporting him and a great tear fell upon my hand.

'Your arm, Dorset,' he said, while the water coursed down his cheeks. Thomas stretched out an arm straight as a lance.

'And yours, sweet Will.'

Hastings extended his hand. With difficulty, King Edward joined them in a clasp. A hard, invincible grip, wrist locked on wrist, each set of fingers gripping the other's sleeve.

'Love one another,' he said again, and Dorset began to weep.

'My promise, Sire,' muttered Hastings, and I looked up to

see that he too wept, and so did Sir Edward, and Lords Audley and Howard, and the Bishop of Salisbury; and Stanley buried his face in a kerchief, and sobbed out loud.

'And mine,' Dorset cried, as the ambient air waxed full with love and sorrow. Edward gave a great shudder and rolled on his right side.

'Do my will,' he said, and those who were incapable of speech, nodded fervently.

'*Kyrie eleison*,' intoned the young monk from his corner.

Weak from the heat and heaviness of that hour, I listened to King Edward's last bequests, the slow painful words broken by great gaps while he sought breath, and the spaces filled by the scraping of quill on parchment.

'. . . and rectify any extortions of which we may be guilty . . . paying all our just debts . . . Your hand, Will, I feel cold. And to the poor people of London, we bequeath . . . and I pray you have Masses aplenty for my soul, and to this end . . .'

So he apportioned all his worldly goods, and laboured for air, while Hastings held his hand, and somewhere without I heard a woman wailing and wondered if it were the Queen. Then he was silent, and with great care the clerk under the eye of Doctor Morton began to burn the wax for the imprint of the Great Seal and Edward's signature, when the King spoke again, with a suddenness that startled us all.

'And having in mind,' he said deliberately, 'our dear son Edward, Prince of Wales, he having only tender years and being the future monarch of this realm, we hereby appoint . . .'

He was taken with a seizure and brought up blood. So it was with blood on his mouth that he said:

'. . . sole Protector and Defensor of the realm and our heir, our entirely beloved brother Richard Plantagenet, Knight of the most noble order of the Garter, Duke of Gloucester, Earl of Cambridge and Constable of England . . . Set it down.'

He raised himself to watch the clerk write. When the rustling pen ceased he signed with difficulty and said: 'So be it. Shrive me now, Father, for I have much to confess. All men are frail.'

They came with the Host and the heavy-hearted incense, and we withdrew for a space, and none looked at another, and the tumult of thought was well-concealed.

About an hour later he awoke from fretful sleep and cried: 'Ah, Dickon! It grows dark!'

Thereafter my blindness, the witching of my keen sight. There were stars I should have followed, portents I should have recognized; I, who was wont to scan men's faces hungrily for their intent. I know not if it were sloth and ignorance that lamed my perspicacity, or the ringing promise that boomed in my ears. The bells said it: 'Love one another!' cried the tolling voice of St-Dunstan-in-the-West. 'Our promise, Sire!' sighed the sweeter tongue of St John of Clerkenwell. Throughout London was the song of mourning translated in my mind as loyalty proclaimed to a dead King. An end to strife and the subtle warring waged within the court, all bound in that one note which swung out upon the funereal air: from St-Martin-in-the-Fields, from St Olave's at Southwark, St Peter in Chepe and St Mary Woolchurch. And in the great Abbey's tumultuous voice, overwhelmed by the brassy note of Paul on Ludgate Hill.

I should have known. I should have heard that the great bell of Westminister sang a warning as well as sorrow and an empty pledge. I should have even remembered mad Hogan's words on a distant June morning. I should have listened well to the splendid bidding prayer, which ran: '. . . for our dead sovereign Edward V and the lady queen Elizabeth, his mother'; and went on grandly, paying homage to 'all of the blood royal, and all the nobles and people of our new prince'. All of them, vowed the bidding prayer. All. Save one.

I might have put my keen sight to employment over the humours of Mistress Shore. Yet what did I but stand gaping at Dorset's elbow in the antechamber by where the quiet figures in their new-donned mourning robes passed in and out during the King's last sleep. I stood, and Jane wept and sighed, and Dorset bit his lip and looked at her, while the Lord Chamberlain stood at her flank, close, as if to glimpse again the memory of Edward in her, his merry harlot.

'Christ have mercy on him,' she gasped. Then she cried, unfittingly: 'What will become of me?' and even I, stupefied by this new world a-making, saw the look she urged upon Dorset. A gusty look that, through all her grief, enveloped him from head to foot: his youth, his slender thighs in their well-turned hose, his tight-pulled waist and massive shoulders, his fair Woodville face. A glance in replica of that carried by the fen-maid of Fotheringhay, who vowed that Dickon of Gloucester shone so bright. A look like flame.

'Sweet Jane,' said Thomas Dorset, and childlike, she stretched out her hand, while her face trembled. He tipped up her chin and kissed her, a kiss too short for Jane, for her

313

eyes were still closed as he addressed himself, over the tip of her spiked bonnet, to the Lord Chamberlain:

'Good my lord, will you not comfort our late sovereign's comforter?'

Hastings's tongue passed over his lips, a swift, nervous movement.

'Go to him, Jane,' said Dorset kindly. And like a child she clung until he placed her in Hastings's arm, which closed tightly about her.

'Let us love one another,' Dorset said. The great bell echoed his words.

I should have marked that Hastings was old, and Dorset young, and Shore a woman—a woman in love at that, which makes them twice as foolish, and ready to pawn their own souls. I should not have ridden to my manor that day to tell Margetta of the King's death, nor should I have tarried there until the secret Council meeting was over. I remember how I punished an alehouse ancient on one of my farms who cried: 'Woe to the realm that's ruled by a child!' My moon was in eclipse, and the promising bells deafened me.

I should have marked how Bishop Morton went straightway to the Queen, and that there were no tears in his eye. For I saw all this, and without seeing.

And had I followed a saner star, what odds?

For how shall we know that our life span is not like unto a sparrow's flight?

'Get you to Ludlow,' said Thomas Grey, Marquess of Dorset.

There was a saw of which old Sir John Paston was very fond. 'Get you lordship and friendship at any cost,' he had been told: *Quia ibi pendet tota lex et prophetae*. This advice had he been given whilst he hivered betwixt Norfolk and Suffolk and their changing moods, and thus had he bidden Calle, his bailiff, who suffered much hardship during service for the Pastons, being beaten from manors and gaoled constantly.

The King was dead. There had been a council meeting, and there were sundry rumours that the Woodvilles had overstepped themselves. The Queen and her daughters were closeted away in some part of the palace, and everywhere was black and shrouded, even the thoughts of men. Here, then, was my good lordship in these changing days.

'Get you to my uncle, Earl Rivers,' repeated Dorset. 'He

and Bishop Alcock will break the news to his Grace the King.'

King Edward is dead, I thought stupidly. Long live King Edward. The crown will sit heavy upon a twelve-year-old head. Praise be that Gloucester is skilled to advise him.

'Take men.'

'Men?' said I.

'Certes, sir, men,' he repeated, with his flashing Woodville smile. 'You raised a fine force for the French enterprise, I recall. How many can you find me now? Two—three hundred? A stout bodyguard for the infant King. Arm them well.'

I must have looked aghast. He struck me on the shoulder, bidding me not to disquiet myself, telling me I would not be alone on this precious commission; that Edward, God assoil him, had entrusted him, Dorset, with troops and armaments for the especial safety of his heirs, that he as Constable of the Tower could furnish others loyal and willing to bear the young king to London, but that I was a direct, swift-riding and capable man. And so saying, he weighed my hands with a purse of gold that nearly dropped me on the floor.

'Ride under my blazon and with my blessing,' he said, and I nodded. Pleased.

'Who will take the news to the Lord Protector?'

His face became a shop-front with the shutters down.

'I could reach Middleham in four days,' I suggested.

He waved my words away. 'Ride where I decree,' he said a little shortly. 'You have my friendship. Heard you not our King's words a-dying? How he bade us use each other kindly.' I looked away swiftly, hearing his gentle voice. 'My lord of Gloucester will know soon enough,' he said.

So they brought to me Dorset's own barrels of harness from out the Tower, and I sought men, henchmen and esquires from off my own manor, and those bound to me by livery and maintenance (ironic jest), who would do aught for gold and colours. Yet before I rode meekly out from London, I was confronted in the courtyard by the Lord Chamberlain, pallid, and at his side Richard Ratcliffe, who had ever been one to bear me cordiality, and with whom I had shot in a bow many times. And Hastings's guard slithered their pikes across my face, while the Lord Chamberlain stared, and my sad humour waxed impatient.

'Your pardon, my lords,' I said, taking up haft of one weapon to push it from me.

'You go hastily, sir,' said Ratcliffe. 'Should one ask whither?'

Through an archway I could see my men, harnessing themselves. They flew Dorset's standard. I could see one or two of the serjeants glancing in my direction. Their mail was in good order, burnished bright. I fancied such a guard of honour would please the prince, in all his sorrow.

'I ride to Ludlow, with others,' I said, more sharp than chivalrous.

Hastings looked over my shoulder. 'A strong force for such a sober task,' he remarked.

'But two hundred, or less,' I answered. ''Tis a wild ride from the marches.'

'So you aim to protect him, then,' said Ratcliffe, unsmiling. 'I fancied there was one already appointed by our late sovereign lord for that work.'

'The Lord Protector of England,' said Hastings, looking again toward the troops, then back to me.

'I ride for the Marquess of Dorset,' I said, angry.

'So I see,' said Hastings slowly, glancing at the standards, and for the second time I saw his face lose its hard determination and his eyes waver a little, and tongue on lip as when he had looked at Mistress Shore. He struck up the halberds with a gesture.

'Pass on, sir,' he said. 'Two hundred men is a fair number to escort a king.' He turned his back upon me and walked towards the palace.

And Ratcliffe? He with whom I had shot and played and laughed many times, when he was not at Middleham with Gloucester: he looked me up and down and then he spat and with his heel scraped the spittle into the stone, and left me gaping like an idiot.

I had been dreaming. I stood in the round Norman Chapel, the chapel to St Mary Magdalene at Ludlow, and heard again Earl Rivers honouring the little Prince in the St George ceremony, as he had done some hours before I took my bed. There were more bells in my dream, long after the six tongues of St Laurence had ceased and the curfew sounded for the town's closing. There were songs in my head, as if I had been given some witch's root, henbell or wolfsbane, for I saw visions: the jewelled mitre of Bishop Alcock turning to the horned headdress of an old pagan priest, the shimmering robes of Earl Rivers leaping like fire. I heard voices, whispering, and the whispers rushed around my senses, friendly, drowsy ghouls. Then I came to full consciousness and knew that the sighing sounds were real, and in the chill April dawn I slipped from my couch and opened the chamber door a fingersbreadth. The Great Hall lay lapped in shadow. Sleeping dogs and pages littered the hearthstone, where smoke from a last smoulder of fire wound upward. Three figures were closebound in conversation. There was Sir Anthony Woodville, Earl Rivers himself, his hairshirt itching him, for he ran a finger round his neck and shuddered while he talked in the same low tone that had disturbed my sleep; my eyes growing used to the twilight, I recognized Sir Thomas Vaughan, whom I had seen cosset the young King in his first grief when the news came to Ludlow; and Lord Richard Grey, the Queen's youngest son by her first marriage. Prince Edward's childhood counsellors, and Woodvilles all. They had been well pleased with the escort I had brought them.

Standing shivering in my *robe de chambre*, I admired them. Close by my hand lay a volume, richly dight with pearls, and every leaf gold-edged. Earl Rivers had loaned it to me in part payment, he said, for swift service, and the *Romance of Alexander* had lulled me to sleep and perchance had given me my mystic dreams. I remembered this book well: I had seen it first at London, when they had little York read from it. He had snapped shut the clasps and declaimed the verses by heart, adding that his lord uncle's saintly father had brought it back from pilgrimage.

'He was a great and holy man,' he had volunteered, coming close to the dais where his mother sat with her icy smile. 'And he was cruelly slain by the villain Warwick, who had the face of a serpent and lion's teeth. My good brother Dorset told me so.'

My thoughts turned to the new King. In his years at Ludlow he had grown upward, pale and slender as a lily. After the ceremony they had seated him between Earl Rivers and the Bishop, and his maiden's face he had kept low, as if the chains of kingship already hung hard upon him. And little did he say in answer to his subjects' greeting, for he looked ever and anon at the Earl like an actor with lines ill-prepared. While Rivers, kindly, bent to the pale child's head and whispered in his ear until a faint smile accompanied the ever-faithful words, 'It's as you say, dear uncle.'

I stood and admired the three clever men. Absently I listened to their voices. They whispered no longer.

'Pray God Dorset comes soon,' said Lord Richard Grey. Rivers laughed softly, moving to the dying fire.

'You were ever anxious, nephew,' he said. 'He will be here, with force the like of which those sad northern birds have never seen.'

Vaughan was chafing his hands together.

'Even if we are gone before they arrive,' he said, 'so much the better. Your captains have their orders?'

'They know what their work is,' said Rivers. 'They will have stout bands strung all along the road to London. He will not pass.'

'You are sure?' asked Grey unquietly. 'By the Passion of God, I would not meet him unprepared. He fights like Samson when provoked, men say.'

'He has great courage,' said Vaughan.

'Too much, for our safety,' murmured Grey.

'And, perhaps, for his own,' said Sir Anthony, with another musing laugh. 'Neither he nor his rusty yokels will suspect aught. Every contingency is covered. My brother Edward blockades the Channel—good Dorset has a fair armoury beneath his belt. He will not—shall not pass.'

'One would think he had forgiven us brother Clarence,' Vaughan said. 'He of the drunken, clappering tongue. For he wrote you courteously, did he not?'

'Yea,' said Rivers, with some contempt. 'But by God's Grace, Elizabeth's letter cheered my fainting heart. Did man ever have such a sister?'

'I would she had given us more time, though,' said Grey.

'God will stretch the days,' said Rivers fervently. 'The boy will be crowned on fourth of May. Fear naught. Ah, my lords!' he said, his voice rising higher, 'what a future lies before us!'

'The riches of England!' said Grey breathlessly.

'The sea, the Tower, the treasure!'

'And the consecrated King!' said Rivers. He nudged a slumbering boy with his foot. 'Good John, bring wine! Certes, we have talked long. 'Tis cock-crow, near enough.'

'I pray that all goes well,' said Grey once more. 'I would liefer not meet the Hog in battle.'

Anthony Woodville sighed deeply, taking wine from the page.

'Hear me well, nephew,' he said, in the same voice as when he showed the young Edward his lessons. 'Know you not by this time that we are so important that we can, with impunity, make and enforce the law? A fig for any deathbed decree! 'Tis no treason—the King wandered in his mind. As for Gloucester—he will fall like a flower beneath the harvest-

318

er's scythe . . . enough of this womanish talk! Gentlemen! I give you King Edward the Fifth!'

They drank meekly. Their swallow sounded loud in the stillness.

'And his noble councillors!' said Richard Grey, bold at last.

'Perdition to Protectors!' said Vaughan, laughing, then Rivers laughed, and in that moment, my restless shifting in the doorway loosed the hasp and it swung wide open so that I stood, unguarded, a target for the turning faces wild with joy.

'Come in, sir, come in!' said Earl Rivers, hand outstretched. 'Will you not share a toast to better days?'

They gave a coconut cup into my hand. Its fanciful stem was inlaid with silver. They gave me wine, and sweet Christ Jesu pardon me, Dickon, I drank to your destruction! Then, instead of dashing down the cup and feeling the steel in my throat for my championing words, what did I next? I walked with the Prince Edward's governors to the oriel and looked out to see the dawn, clear-coloured like a plover's egg, limning the Shropshire hills and the Teme valley; and I saw also that the drawbridge of Ludlow was down, and that over Dinan Bridge and Ludford too, poured an endless stream of armed men, a throng that crowded the bailey, traitors all, and I their chief.

'Two thousand at a guess,' said Grey, satisfied.

'A fair escort for an infant King,' said Rivers, smiling at me.

The scar upon my hand burned white; while the palace grew astir with preparation and the Mass bell of St Peter's chapel groaned 'Love one another' mockingly.

Then Rivers bade us get going with all speed, and Richard Grey turned to him with renewed disquiet.

'You will ride with us?'

The Earl wagged his head. 'I have another strategy,' he said. 'I shall play Gloucester like a salmon on the line. My men and I will meet him in courtesy at Northampton and hinder his progress. But you shall take the main force onward and get the King to London. Station your fellows as you ride south—in every copse from Stoney Stratford. I will blind him with fair words—the axe and spear will complete my work. Later.'

'We'll meet with you in London, then,' said Grey, to a ghastly smile. Did he muse on whether the Earl might play us false? Once, King Edward had rebuked him for going off on pilgrimage during the campaign against Margaret of Anjou . . .

'Yea!' said Rivers heartily. 'And noble Dorset too. At our fair sovereign's coronation.'

'Take care,' said Vaughan. 'Hastings may have got word to him of our contrivance. And Plantagenet is no fool.'

'I will tie him in a true-love knot,' said Rivers, then smote Grey upon the shoulder, saying: 'Get you gone.'

'Can you not make a potion of his wine?' asked Vaughan, also a little unhappy at this change of plan. 'Hemlock or mandragora?'

'Like my grandam used lusty Edward?' smiled Grey, his colour returning. 'That five-leaf grass with Jupiter strong and the moon applying . . . amorous herb. Jesu! Clever dame! To send a King so wantwit that he wedded where he merely should have . . .'

'Tongue, wanton tongue, get you gone, my lords,' said Rivers, sword-sharp, and this I knew was something so black that it was unfitted for the ears of even a paid traitor like myself. Grey bit his lip and ran calling for his henchmen, and I followed, sick and dolorous, bought and sold, and prepared to join the pack of men whose mailed feet trod down the bailey's green grass.

Through April rain and flickering sun we went. From every hedge demons leered acclaim for my weakness. Earl Rivers had given me a gold collar when I came to Ludlow; it hung about my neck like lead. The little King sighed aloud, complaining of a toothache, and Vaughan cheered him merrily. I was both sorry and amused to hear the boy's reply.

'When I am crowned, my first command . . .' he began, his voice jounced breathless by the pace.

'Sire?' smiled Vaughan, riding hard beside him.

'To have my brother York as squire,' cried Edward. 'To keep him close by me again. His wit could ever chase away these gripings in my head and I have missed him sorely.'

'It shall be as you say, O King,' said Grey, with a sidelong glance at Richard Haute, who slept beside the boy of a night. 'But God grant you will not cast us off, who love you so.'

We rode through Northampton and the townfolk came out to stare. A few doffed their caps and held them on the heart, but in God's own truth, we went so swiftly that they had scarce time to glimpse the King. And from each holy house by which we fled the requiem bell tolled out so that our ride seemed yet unseemly with Edward the Fourth lately entombed. Our hoofbeats splintered the cobbles of Stoney Stratford towards evening, and we were fourteen miles nearer London. Suddenly the surging line ahead of me wheeled to a halt. Leaving my own contingent rubbing their chafed thighs I rode up to the front of the train. The young King was near to tears, so thin and pale, the men about him grimly strong.

'My lords, I can go no more,' he said. 'My accursed jaw pains me. I must rest.'

'Your Grace, London awaits you,' said Haute coaxingly. 'Do you not long for your coronation? It will be splendid—all will bear you homage. There will be fine gifts, clarions alight with exultation . . .'

'God grant me rest a space,' cried the boy.

'His Grace is weary,' admitted Grey anxiously.

'As are we all,' I said. The first words I had spoken to them on that mad, treasonous ride. Behind, I could hear a grumble of assent. Grey pulled his horse near to mine. Two knights were helping escort the young King into a tavern; his knees buckled.

'He cannot ride through the night,' Grey said. 'He will fall sick—he must be well for crowning. Tomorrow will see us in London.'

'And the Hog will not ride by night either,' Vaughan replied. 'Even now, I doubt not your good uncle entertains him with delay.'

'Anthony is clever,' said Grey, then yawned. 'I am bone-weary. Come! Tomorrow we will press on and leave our watchdogs on the road. Tapster, ho! Are there inns enough in this town for a king's escort?'

There was a bed for me. My esquires had the floor. I was soulsick. I threw myself into sleep.

I rode a lame-legged horse through a thicket where once holy rowan trees black and twisted resembled vicious spirits; then I was in a clearing filled with tall marguerites, their stems thicker than my arm, and each pretty daisy-face was Margetta's face, all wet with tears, and my horse trampled the blooms and ground that lovesome face while every flower sobbed and screamed aloud. Then the darkness came before me again and a copse lay ahead denser than the first and I would fain have pulled my horse aside so as not to enter, but my hobbling mount walked on with iron neck and will unconquerable, into a glowering den of evil with Margetta's screams behind me and a growing noise ahead. And came a whirl of blinding light and out of it a fearsome snarling Boar, with tusks like the unicorn's spear and slavering bloody jaws; and about him the rattle of all the horsemen who had ever forged into war; and the Boar came at me and I heard my own desolate shriek as he caught me on his tusks and shook me, and a voice said: 'My lord, awake!'

'Sir, your harness, quickly.' I felt them buckling on my cuirass and greaves, handing me my helm, the mantling limp from yesterday's spring storms. Below the window there was a noise of horsemen, and dream-bewitched I said: 'The Hog is coming.'

'Nay, sir,' said one of the squires comfortably. 'We must make haste, though. Lords Grey and Vaughan are calling horse already. The day begins.'

Knights were lifting the young King into the saddle when I gained the street. Vaughan, Haute and Grey were horsed and impatient. The first detachment swung off down the road; their speartips caught the early sun. Behind them went trundling a score of loaded arms-wagons.

'Gentlemen! Your Grace!' said Grey. 'To London!'

Young Edward had bluish rings beneath his eyes. He called for his pet hawk. Grey's temper was shortening.

'Sire, there will be no time for sport this day,' he said, and while they argued my spirit shifted within me from great misery as I thought what evil this day would bring to a man I had not seen for full five years, yet with whom I had once sat in friendship, sharing wine and ladies' smiles; and I heard one of the squires say softly: 'Sir, you have hurt your hand.' I looked down at the flaming mark upon my flesh which stabbed and burned beyond belief for such an ancient wound, and a ghostly voice spoke in my mind.

'Think on me by this brand,' it said. 'Remember . . . Remember . . .'

Then there came hooves, and those not of our own departing force whose steel pricked the air, but from the rear. And I caught Grey's face in the candle of my eye as he turned, and Vaughan's likewise, and all our captains', and saw the mouths fall open clownishly as slackens the jaw of a corpse, and I twisted on my mount, and the old fear of witchcraft shook me to the bones.

Richard Plantagenet rode toward us at a steady pace. Clad entirely in black, he forked a great white horse, and he was very pale. Behind him there came riding a silent company, all unarmed, all in deep mourning, all quiet with a dangerous quietness. A black community cool and sad, and if these were the rusty yokels Rivers had jested about he was never further from the truth. Wildly I took in the quarterings, the faces. The arms of Neville and Northumberland, Scrope, Greystoke,

322

Ratcliffe—he there in person, as was Sir Francis Lovell and William Catesby. The gentlemen of the North, come London-ward to mourn a King. The Lord Protector of England, riding south in requiem and duty.

His eyes held mine for an instant and I bowed my head, for had he spoken the words would have come no clearer. 'You also,' said the dark eyes in the lean pale countenance. Then, possibly: 'How strange are the hearts of men!'

As one silent man, the gentlemen of the North dismounted to kneel in obeisance. The young King sat his horse nervously, waiting as Richard Plantagenet strode towards him between the bowed, black ranks. The Lord Protector was not alone. For one instant I thought that George of Clarence was back from the tomb; the man who walked proud at Richard's side was cast in the same mould: flushed and sheen, with arrogant head held high, and a smile of goodly triumph on his lips. And I marvelled at the likeness, seeing then no wraith of a dead duke, but Harry Stafford of Buckingham, whom all had thought whiling away his days on a manor at Brecon. Yes, those were Brecon foot-soldiers behind him . . .

The young King spoke, high and womanish and timorous, shifting on his horse.

'Is it not my uncle of Gloucester?' he said uncertainly. 'We are for London. I . . . I had not thought to see you here.'

Richard Plantagenet did not speak. He went on his knees before the young King, taking the hem of Edward's gown to his lips. Buckingham did likewise, with flamboyant grace. Vaughan and Haute and Grey were grave-quiet.

'What means this, good uncle?' asked Edward, shriller now.

Richard Plantagenet rose, his garments dusty from the ground.

'My liege lord,' he said, very low, so that only those near could catch his words, 'I share your grief in this your noble father's passing. And by his ordinance I offer you my heart and will. God grant I may show you a true and loyal protection. In every way.'

Edward turned, quivering, to Lord Grey.

'What ordinance?' he demanded. 'You are my guardians; 'tis all settled. And where's my Uncle Rivers? Speak, sirs, I pray you!'

Haute and Vaughan looked sickly at each other. Grey looked at the ground. Buckingham spoke, imperiously.

'Your Grace, these gentlemen are no friends of yours. They seek to use you as a pawn in their own sport of kingship.

323

Your uncle Rivers lies at Northampton under close arrest, guarded by my own true men. And this, my lord of Gloucester, is named Protector of your person by royal decree. Ha! they flew high, these counsellors of yours. Your Grace has been sadly deceived, make no mistake of it . . .' His voice grew louder. Richard Plantagenet gave him a swift look, reproving, oddly weary. Buckingham continued.

'We shall console your Grace,' he said. 'The Lord Protector will advise you in the ruling of this realm, and I . . .'

Edward broke in.

'My lords, my lady mother and the nobles of her court are pledged to support me,' he said in a trembling voice.

Buckingham laughed. 'Ruling is not for women,' he said gratingly. 'The Queen has no rightful authority, no more than did Joan of Kent or Katherine of France. Here is one of the old royal blood, as I am. The Lord Protector of England.' He indicated Richard as a revels-master produces his most cunning player.

'I knew of no Protectorship,' said Edward, and then, like April rain, began to weep.

Richard Plantagenet frowned deeply.

'Hush, Harry,' he said with sharpness. 'His Grace is weary and, to me, looks ailing. My lord Edward, will you not dismount?' He stretched out his arms for the boy, who shrank away.

'Jesu, what have they told you of me?' Richard said, very low. Then, to the young King: 'My lord, listen. All that my cousin Buckingham has said is true. Those who nurtured you at Ludlow have also conspired to deprive me of the Protectorship. Your father's will most treasonously overpassed. But loyalty bound me to his Grace and henceforth to you. Will you not be content with your own father's ordinance?'

Richard Grey found his tongue at last.

'My lord of Gloucester will not prevail upon our charge,' he said haughtily. Buckingham was on him in a flash.

'Hold your peace, my lord,' he cried. 'Soon you shall hold it for ever, traitor and knave. You! Dare you speak when you have laboured with others to destroy me and my cousin of Gloucester? Were it not for Lord Hastings we would be dead in our blood!' And he raved at them for a space until the Protector raised his hand in silence. I grew a deep cold within me. I was young. I did not wish to die. And it was meet that I should. I had led men for Dorset. I was guilty as he.

Remorse surged over me like a sea wave, beating at my breast, my head, the flesh of my face, catching at my tongue, my wilful wanton tongue that had been so ready to swear allegiance to a bright smile and a fat purse. I am not alone, not alone, I whispered to myself. I looked at the other captains standing motionless around me. I am no worse, no better than they. But they have no brand upon their sword-hand—they gave no little pledge in secret, over a testing flame with fingers locked in those of a good man. Yea, a good man. Through all my wavering wantonness this sang clear, knife-sharp. I looked at him once more, Richard Plantagenet. He was lifting the sobbing boy down from his horse; he kissed him lightly on the brow.

I wished with my heart that my raison had been that of Richard Plantagenet. I looked at his gentlemen of the north: the broad, honest, fierce faces, and with my keen sight picked out the smallest page, dirty with travel at the end of the line. With my whole heart I wished I were he, in Gloucester's service. Now I should do his will only upon the scaffold.

'It is best that you ride in comfort,' he was saying softly to Edward, who wiped his eyes.

'Yea, a litter for his Grace!' called Buckingham. Two esquires were already backing a moorland mare into the shafts of the barrel-shaped carriage. The young King said something in a low voice. Richard laughed.

'No disgrace, good prince,' he said. 'My own son goes often in this fashion. When he is ailing.' The laughter went out of his voice. 'But then I tell him, rest easy now, and when he is grown, he shall ride my own White Surrey, a puissant beast in truth. No weakness this, my liege.'

Edward ascended into the swaying wagon, and all awaited the Protector's next command. Many looked anxious. A stiff knot of Buckingham's foot-soldiers surrounded the Woodville trinity.

'To London, Dickon?' asked Sir Francis Lovell.

The Protector shook his head gravely.

'We shall return to Northampton. Rivers must be taken northward under close vigilance, like these three. But the people of London shall see the mischief he has wrought. Display the barrels of harness through the City gates.'

'It shall be done, my lord,' said the glowing Buckingham.

'And send to Lord Hastings that all is well,' said Richard, preparing to mount.

Now our fate, thought I. Our destiny, our well-merited doom. Behind, my men-at-arms stood like rock.

Mounted again, Richard turned and surveyed us. White Surrey lifted one great hoof and tore fiercely at the ground. I waited for the Protector to denounce us traitors. He was looking at me, once more straight into the eyes. There was no anger, only regret and a bitter kind of humour. He spoke with sudden swiftness.

'This accursed livery and maintenance!' he said—in itself an incautious remark, which brought a very faint whispering from some of his own followers, and a great jolting of the heart to me. He knew, he knew, how easy it had been.

'Disperse your men,' he said quietly. 'Go to your homes, and be good a-bearing. All of you. And come Londonward for King Edward's coronation, which shall be when Parliament decrees. Come, Harry! Your Grace, are you comfortable?'

They turned, they rode swiftly. They were disappearing in a cloud of dark plumage down the sunlit road. From out of my sight he rode, black on white. I loved him. I took Dorset's standard from the limp hand of Long Wat beside me, and cast it in the dust.

I set spurs deep and rode after Richard Plantagenet.

He offered no word of reproach and there may even have been some gladness in his look as I kenlt before him. He said little, only reminding me that we all had a duty to fulfil, and I was abysmally grateful. Deep within me I would lief have called him Dickon, but those days were gone, and I foreknew that never again would I see that lightness about him. We were no longer eighteen, and Flanders was a time and place far distant.

I overheard something that he said to Sir Francis Lovell on the ride south. Meant for Lovell's ears only, it warmed me through, and rekindled my shame.

'I must be a Protector in turth,' he said, rather sadly. 'Yea, not only of the lives and comfort of my dear brother's children, but of this war-weary England. Poor England!'

'She has bled long,' said Lovell.

'God aid me to steer this child's mind into the way of peace. And—' he turned a hard bright look upon Sir Francis —'there will be no peace if the Queen's kin take command. The barons will boil. Certes, this seems like another battle, and I thought I was done with them. A battle of a dangerous, insidious breed.'

Then I heard Lovell bid him take courage, the courage he had never lacked, and as we neared Barnet old memories waked in him, for he fell silent. Also on the journey he talked of Hastings, and at one little church hard by St Albans he dismounted to give thanks kneeling for his own deliverance from the hands of his enemies, and for the Lord Chamberlain's foresight and fidelity. I fancied Buckingham misliked this; he grew very quiet, and wore a jealous mien. When we crossed Barnet Plain, Richard Plantagenet bade the young King look from his litter and hear of the mighty battle which his uncles had fought there, together with his father, whom God assoil. And how valiantly Lord Hastings had battled; and at Tewkesbury also, and reaching further, whom God assoil. And how valiantly Lord Hastings had battled; and at Tewkesbury also, and reaching further back into the past, he recounted to the boy Hastings's marvellous wit and cunning when they rode to rescue the captured King. Buckingham laughed louder than the Protector, applauding his soft halting tale, flaunting in the sunlight. At mention of Hastings he waxed jealous as a woman.

'What of *my* prudence and fidelity, lord?' he asked. Richard, leaning, clasped his arm.

'Good cousin, I give thanks to God also for your keen wits at this time,' he said fervently. 'And for your warlike aid.'

'Then I need no reward,' said Buckingham, turning up his eyes.

'Yea, you shall be rewarded,' Richard said, with a wry smile. Buckingham grew silent again.

Upon the City walls the populace craned and cheered the King and his entourage. Before us rolled the wagons of harness with the Woodville arms blazoned thereon, and the heralds cried of treason. I thought briefly of Rivers, heavy-guarded at Sheriff Hutton, Grey at Middleham and Vaughan at Pontefract. The air was infected with excitement, Buckingham bowed and smiled, but Richard was sombre, in his gown of coarse black cloth. The little King, horsed again, and in blue velvet, looked bewildered at the array which surged to greet him. Behind the Mayor and Aldermen, scarlet-clad, five hundred burgesses blossomd in violet silk. Grandly they came, and grandly pledged the oath of fealty to Edward the Fifth.

Hastings was there. As we moved down Ludgate Hill he rode with us, and the tension dropped from Richard's face, revealing plain love and admiration. He was quiet no longer. He jested with the little King, fixing a smile on the boy's pale puzzlement.

'Jesu preserve you, William,' I heard the Protector say, more than once.

'And you, Sir Richard,' answered Hastings, his glance flaring to Buckingham. 'I am glad to see you found a worthy follower. How does your lady wife, my lord?' This brought a poppy flush to Buckingham's cheek and a laugh to my own throat, for I had forgotten that this new bright star was wedded to a Woodville.

The little King's eyes searched the throng as we reached his lodgings at the Bishop of London's Palace. So obviously cast down was he that Richard asked the nature of his distress. 'I had thought to see my brother York awaiting me,' he said plaintively.

Richard Ratcliffe, whose pardon for my actions I had begged upon the road, walked beside me into the Great Hall. He whispered in my ear: 'His Grace will remain disappointed, an the Queen has aught to do with it. She has the younger boy fast in Sanctuary, together with her daughters, Bishop Lionel, and half the Tower's treasure!' He laughed under cover of a shadowed archway. 'In the instant the plottings were uncovered, her Grace flew into Westminster, hawk-swift. Lord! she burst down the Sanctuary wall for easier passage of her goods. Chests, boxes, fardels of gold and silver, gems of price, furnishings, carpets to clothe the palaces of Europe.'

'What of Dorset?'

His smile faded. 'Fled to France, men say,' he murmured. 'With more gold, but Sir Edward Woodville had the best pickings—a fleet of stout ships and treasure enough to sink them.'

Buckingham was displeased by the Bishop's Palace; it was well the Bishop was a little deaf.

'This is not a fitting lodge for his Grace,' Buckingham said firmly. 'Did not Harry Six seek refuge here many days? To me, these chambers, smack of weak wits, frail bodies.'

'Why not the Hospital of St John?' suggested Francis Lovell.

'Or Westminster?' murmured Hastings.

An exclamation burst from Buckingham. 'What madness!' he cried. 'Too near the Sanctuary, my lords. Who knows what treachery is still a-making?'

Richard Plantagenet frowned. 'The Council shall decide,' he said sharply. 'We must do what is best for his Grace. Remember always, he is our charge, our duty.'

Buckingham was unquelled. 'I have it!' he said, with a sudden finger-snapping. "Our King must enjoy the royal custom. The Tower, my lords.'

I glanced toward the boy. He was talking courteously with the Bishop of London. The Protector spoke.

'It is a large, bewildering place for one of tender years,' he said. 'Those apartments grow hot in June. I remember my last sojourn there . . . my wife was ill . . . the mists rise from the river at evening. Nay, my lords. The Council shall decide.'

'Sir,' Buckingham said obstinately, 'is it not the privilege of Kings to occupy the Tower before their crowning?' He moved closer, taking the Protector's sleeve. 'And is it not a place of safety for the boy against his enemies? From those who labour to seize his royal person?'

Hastings, with Woodville-anger doubtless aboil in his mind, said 'Yea!' loudly.

The Protector sighed. 'There is much to be done,' he said. 'The bidding letters to be sent for those who will receive knighthood at our sovereign's hand; the coronation gowns to be made. And the settling of Edward's crowning day.'

Buckingham leaned eagerly. 'When should that be, my lord?'

'In good time,' said the Protector. 'The Nativity of St John Baptist, mayhap. It is not long to Midsummer. But we must have no dissension. I must persuade her Grace to leave Sanctuary. The Coronation cannot proceed without the Queen-Dowager.'

Hastings said 'Yeah!' again, so loudly that I looked at him. I know my eye has a strange colour, and pierces through, but that was surely no reason for him to flush and lick his lip and turn away completely out of countenance, for he had looked at me before and I at him, many times.

'The Council shall decide,' said Buckingham comfortably, sliding his arm in that of the Protector.

At Crosby's Place, Richard's town house, I was well content, for I was again in his service, like many others who were separately bound to him through old ties of the blood and through plain devotion. His men of York upheld him in the Protectorship: Francis Lovell, Richard Ratcliffe, William Catesby. And his Council! Such a core of loyal supporters: Thomas Rotherham, Archbishop of York, my lord William Stanley and his brother cursed Thomas, ever-faithful Hastings, and oh, the cleverest of them all, Morton, Bishop of Ely. I could laugh weeping, were it not for young Brecher's face watching me from the fouled straw. I could laugh at the irony of it, and at our singular blindness.

He trusted them. He trusted me. Sweet Jesu, how easily he trusted!

329

I served him at bed and board, I bore letters, waiting while the young King appended the laborious *Edwardus Quintus*, watching each bill kissed by the red wax and the Great Seal or the Privy Seal or the Signet Seal, and witnessed by the Chancellor, John Russell, at the royal apartments of the Tower, where Edward awaited his coronation. He was not ill-pleased with his sumptuous chambers, Edward. There he reached full realization that he was part of the long pattern of monarchs, sleeping and eating where previous kings had done, and submitting daily to the fussing ministry of Piers Curteys, who while measuring him for the robes of state, vowed his Grace to be overlong in the leg, yet wonderfully slender in the waist. Edward grew less pale and pouting, but there was one thing that he craved: he longed for little York, his brother.

I recall one day at the Tower. It was excessively hot for June. The reflected river lapped brightly on the stone walls, the gay arras. Lady Anne Neville was talking with the little King.

'Madam, I miss him sorely,' he said. 'Sir Robert Brackenbury puts himself out to entertain, but he is not my brother Richard.'

The Constable of the Tower pulled a long face.

'He is not as young as your brother, Sire,' he said ruefully.

We were laughing together when the Protector entered, Buckingham's flashing figure at his side. The young King moved swiftly, forestalling his uncle's obeisance.

'Have you news?' he asked hesitantly.

The Protector's eyes swept over the boy, moved to Lady Anne, grew troubled.

'Again, I shall disappoint your Grace,' he said slowly. 'The Queen your mother remains adamant. She will not leave Sanctuary, nor will she allow my lord of York to do so. All our persuasions have come to naught.' He touched his wife's cheek. 'Madame, you are wan today,' he said. 'Like a lily.'

'Then I must go to them,' said Edward decisively.

Richard Plantagenet turned, walked to the window in silence. Buckingham's tongue, however, tripped gaily as one of his Welsh mountain streams. He grasped the boy about the shoulder.

'It's better you remain,' he laughed. 'Certes, it is safest—safety above all, eh, my lord? We would not have you witched away in the black of night by certain parties . . . Be patient, good my lord.'

330

Edward, puzzled, unquiet, glanced from one to the other. 'What did my mother say?' he asked timidly.

Buckingham laughed again. 'The deputation records that she sings the same, alas!' he said merrily. 'The Queen-Dowager weeps anon. There's a vast hole in Sanctuary wall where they brought her treasures—coffers of jewels, bolts of satin, cloth of gold. She sits surrounded by richness, and she weeps.'

The Protector turned with a frowning glance.

'Be comfortable, good my liege,' he said. 'Tomorrow, we will endeavour to bend her to your will. We shall send Sir Robert here, and the Archbishop of York, Chancellor Russell too . . .'

'Can you not send Bishop Morton?' asked Edward eagerly. 'I remember when I was at London before, my mother said he was the most cunning prelate in the realm and the best friend in the world to all her kin.'

In the breath-holding silence that very prelate was ushered in, smiling. He looked richly bland, the chalky cheeks folded like a lizard's. Lady Margaret Beaufort had an eye like a lizard, well I recall . . . And a Dragon, what is he but a monstrous lizard, spewing slime . . .

Behind Morton strode Sir Edward Brampton, fresh off his ship, with salt-stained cloak. His fierce sailor's eyes fastened on the Protector.

'Sir Edward has news,' said Morton amiably, returning our bows. 'Faugh! It is stifling in here, my lords. His Grace should have more fresh air, dare I say so.'

Robert Brackenbury turned to the young King.

'Will you best me at the butts again, Sire?' he asked. 'Despoil my purse an you will. I deem it honour,' and he went out, a giant, a clown, with the willing boy. Brampton fidgeted with excitement, as the door clashed shut. Men clustered round him.

'Well?' asked Buckingham impatiently.

'Not vell, my lords,' said Brampton in his twisted English. 'I go, as you decree, to fetch back Sir Edvard Voodville. I spread the offer of pardon through his fleet as it lie off the Downs and sure! the captain's, being Italian, see the sense in obeying England's governance. First they fill up the guard with vine and bludgeon them to sleep. They are at the quay now, vaiting the King's pleasure. But Sir Edvard! Alas!'

'What of him?'

'Gone,' said Brampton bluntly. 'In two fast Genoese carracks—svift, svift, despite his decks being veighted with gold platters and jewels from this very palace!'

'So!' said Buckingham, in great dismay. 'Dorset flown—and now the other traitor gone—where? Do you know this?'

'My lords, can't you guess?' said Brampton with a wry smile.

Richard Plantagenet drew in his breath, slow yet sharp.

'Brittany,' he said.

'To Duke Francis,' said Brampton. 'And to Henry Tudor.'

'Henry—Tydder,' said Richard softly. 'With money, and ships.' He shuddered. 'How cold it is!' he said.

Morton himself leaned to close the window, and I felt the sweat flower upon my lip as the sun beat through.

Beneath the ordered preparations for the crowning, there were stirrings . . . no more than the shift and whisper heard in a field at night. The Woodvilles' presence was felt, for all that they were fast in the north country. Their long shadow stretched southward and their sullen adherents were everywhere. Despite the outward composure of Crosby's Place, of the Tower and Baynard's Castle, where Richard's mother lay, under the surface of town there heaved and fermented a boil of faction. There were sundry murmurs, rising and gone next moment like an echo; many flying tales, down Chepe and Bread Street, in Petty Wales and Poultry. Again the cry from those who well remembered witless Harry Six in infancy: 'Woe, woe to the realm that's ruled by a child!' London moved gently, a many-mouthed monster. The agents of the Privy Council went quietly abroad, and I was one of them. Yet it was my wife, in all her innocence, who should have earned my dole.

Margetta was amorous for a gown in blue cloth of silver trimmed with marten's fur. She vowed she would not be eclipsed at the coronation by Sir John Howard's wife; I chided her, for the Howards were good friends to Richard. She, at this, pouted and frowned, smote her stomacher, gold butterfly passement and all, and tried another tack, saying that if she were not given a new dress, our babe would break forth in Westminster itself, so close confined was he. With that, she kissed me. Ah, Margetta, Margetta! *Never* come to Leicester!

I was in her bower, big and awkward among the trinkets and tiring-women. Neat as doves, they came 'twixt her and me, and finally I sent them off and took the comb myself to the rippled black silk that cloaked her. I bade her close her eyes and dream I was her abigail.

'So talk, Margetta,' I said gaily. 'Gossip to me as I were Jane, or Tib.'

'What news of Mistress Shore, sweet Tib?' she said obligingly. 'Are men still lusty for the wanton wench?' I went on combing, soft easy strokes. Her shoulders beneath the black silk were wonderful whiteness. I grew hot for her.

'Will she return to poor Will, think you, Tib?' asked my lady. 'Poor luckless Will Shore, to lose a beauty, a prize. And to see her spurned—but that should make him laugh. Verily, it was judgment that Dorset left her as he did!' Her eyes opened on sharp anger. 'The bawd! No sooner our King laid low than she flies to Dorset's bed. Shameless, shameless!'

'He did not keep her long,' I said, wondering where in France Dorset was.

'Long enough,' said Margetta viciously. The game was over. 'She spoke of taking poison when he quit the realm. The wanton whore.'

'She comforted the King,' I said.

'She is a fool,' Margetta cried, glaring at her mirror. 'She will do aught for Dorset. Even her life, I vow, hangs easy on his tongue.' And I perceived how much my wife hated Mistress Shore, with the guilty wrath of one who has lain in meadow-grass with a young man hot as a rooster . . . I turned her to face me.

'Remember the marguerites,' I said, busy at her lacings.

Crying, she fought me off. 'The child, my lord!'

I set my lips to the rounded white belly. 'I shall not harm our son,' I said. 'Yet should I? Is there danger in it? Yea, perchance he will think ill of the intrusion . . . Now, Mistress Shore, she's not with child, is she?'

I ducked her swingeing blow and laid her on the bed. In Flanders, Spain and Italy, they say the English do not know of love. And the French too, are skilled liars . . .

I returned from somewhere dim and far. Margetta was babbling of the day's bread, that it would be overdone. She must go to the kitchen.

'Yea, your bread is nicely risen, lady,' I said. 'Lord's bread, by my faith. Lie quiet.'

She struggled and sighed and was still in my arms. Yet fair Jane danced again in her mind, for she said:

'This day my maid told me how she met with Mistress Shore. Disguised as a nun. Ha! A fine nun! She had speech

333

with a man in Bucklersbury. Meg knew her, and would have followed had she not been late with the spices.'

I pressed her rosy pap. 'Where did Jane go!' I asked idly.

'I know not,' she shrugged. Then the hour struck somewhere and she cried: 'What sin, what madness this! Let me up, my lord.'

'Up, wanton,' I said, with a last kiss.

She turned a loving look on me. 'She is not fairer than I?' she asked, and I shook my head, smiling at the body like a fat white candle-flame.

'I know not where she went,' said Margetta, coiling her hair. 'But I know she came from Westminster Sanctuary. She had been to see the Queen Dowager. So tell that to Richard Plantagenet, and he'll give you an earldom.'

I lay, thought-lapped. 'You have busied yourself,' I said. 'Is there more?'

She knelt, a mischief, and fuzzed my ear with whispers. I became stiff with unbelief, heavy with the evil from my wife's sweet tongue. I shall not rise, I thought. Soon they will come to lay me in the chantry, my toes and helm pointing heavenward, my little bitch Bronia curled beneath my feet. For this new knowledge verily makes me of stone.

'Woman, woman, what say you?'

'And not only does she lie with *Hastings* of a night,' said Margetta, clothed, the respectable matron once more, 'but she succours the Queen by day. Meg's brother is a servant at Westminster.'

'Holy Jesu,' I said, rising.

'What then, dear heart?' asked Margetta.

'This is evil news, my lady,' I said, and because she had done such a great service through her clappermouthed alewife, I took her again into my arms and she closed her eyes, while I stared at the bronze mirror and thought: how jealous Buckingham will rejoice! (Can Richard withstand this foulness? We must be sure. We must be sure, for this will break him up.)

There were others who had laboured to the same intent, and we were all of us only too sure when, a week later, we waited with our news at Richard's mansion.

We had marked our man: Hastings, the loved and trusted. The double-dissembler. My keen eyes had seen the flush of guilt. All his avowals—his hearty concurrence with the royal design—all feigned, treacherous and counterfeit. Even his calling me to halt on my departure for Ludlow—a masked displeasure as a token of his loyalty to the Crown. What moved him thus? I asked myself as we stood in the antechamber of Crosby's Place. And the answer: ever the same. Power. I heard Buckingham's voice, raised commandingly; fainter, the Protector's mild reply. Power. Power and jealousy. My fingers cracked round the letters in my hand. Letters to send four men to the block, Shore to the stake, and Elizabeth Woodville—I knew not how Richard would deal with her, but doubtless she would weep, whatever befell, tears being her weapon.

Two knights of Buckingham stood beside me. Their tongues were hot. They smiled. And I was not happy with the burden Ratcliffe and I bore; the sole joy I got from this sorry business was that Richard Plantagenet would live.

How they had planned it I could only conjecture, but it was writ plain, the date his life should end, by poison or the knife along some darkly shadowed way, surrounded—his escort outnumbered, fighting desperately in black hopelessness . . . there were gold-hungry assassins in every Southwark tavern, and traitors eager to shame their knighthood for a few acres of livelode. Then, Rivers freed, the young king once more his. A gem of price . . . like holding England in the palm . . . They would need to kill Buckingham too. Buckingham, the glorious. A bright sacrifice on Envy's altar.

The seneschal stood in the doorway.

'His Grace bids you enter.'

But there was one coming out who impeded our passage. An artisan, small, rat-like. He clutched to his breast a roll of parchment, the wax on it new. From his patched garments rose the reek of back-street London. His pale face gleamed up at me. As he passed, Buckingham's knights recoiled a little with crimping noses.

'Fourteen years,' he said in a small rusty voice. 'Fourteen years have I waited for this title. None would ever listen before. They said I had neither case, nor hope of such. Jesu preserve that man.' He went suddenly red. 'That—that sun of York.'

Then we were standing beneath the fine hammerbeam roof of the council chamber. The sun of York sat at the board. John Kendall, his secretary, sprinkled sand upon the last of his writings for that day. Richard was in pleasant humour, while Buckingham fairly sparkled. Again, approaching the dais, I was struck by his likeness to Clarence. Ruthless and gold and gallant; even the way he tossed the cup's contents down his throat, with one showman's gulp, was token of Clarence, who had drowned in wine.

'Will my lord join me?' smiled Buckingham.

'Later, Harry, later,' said Richard, handing a bundle of bills to Chancellor Russell. 'I shall need your advice on the distribution of these enfeaoffments. For the King's signet,' he added to John Kendall, rolling yet another parchment. 'Harry —' he rose, linking arms with Buckingham—'the Spanish have a proverb: "The man drinks the first cup, the second cup drinks the first, and the third drinks the man." Very well —' at Buckingham's laugh of protest. 'Pleasure yourself, good friend. We have laboured long today.'

Then he saw us, aligned before him. The smile left him and was reborn on Buckingham's face.

'My lord, these friends of ours have something to impart,' Buckingham said smoothly. 'I fancy they have flushed out the rats which made those rustlings lately in the realm. With your permission, sir,' and he stepped forward and twitched from my hand the letters I carried, letters to Jane Shore of blackest treason, letters from her lover, and letters from the Queen Dowager. He thrust them towards the Protector, who remained motionless.

'I do beseech you, read them, cousin,' he said. 'My eyes are sore . . .' The last words retreated into silence.

'By God's Body,' said Buckingham, with a little whistling noise. 'Rats indeed, my lord—but these are greater rats than you or I had dreamed. Treason, my lord. Treason writ large. Will you hear the rats' names, my lord?'

He was enjoying it. The Protector's lips grew thin with blank despair at the foreknowledge of those names; yet George of Clarence was cruel too, men said, and had called the childish Gloucester 'changeling'. So Buckingham smiled as he read the words:

'Rotherham, my lord.'

'Yea,' Richard said, without expression. 'He was chagrined because I took away his high office. That, for his wild and wanton action with the Queen. He gave into her hands the Great Seal. I was justified.'

Buckingham gave him a queer, swift look. 'None doubt it, sir,' he said. 'Shall I go on?' His brows shot up as he read: 'Morton, Bishop of Ely! Certes, how the cloth of Holy Church is rent this day!'

Richard was beginning to look calmer. 'A cunning prelate, as our young king said. Is there more?'

'Stanley,' Buckingham said with bitterness. 'Despite his

336

great estates bestowed by your sovereign brother, my lord. The shame. Ingrate. He should be punished duly . . .'

This time Richard laughed, a hoarse, unlovely sound.

'Stanley goes where the wind of change blows him,' he said. 'Loyalty was never one of his virtues. Yet . . .' he hesitated, and his stern face looked almost bewildered. 'I fancied that he loved me well enough.' He poured wine before the page could read his wish, his hand shaking like a tortured bird.

'So, Harry. And who was captain of this conspiracy? Which of these three foolish lords prized his head the least?'

This, then, was Buckingham, the magician, producing the bauble from the air. The serpent in lieu of a fish.

'Another that loved you well, my lord,' he said softly. 'So well that he now plans your death, the seizing of the infant king, the plunder of the royal bounty. Love so great for you that he is now handfasted with Elizabeth, the Woodville Queen, Rivers, Vaughan, Grey, and the harlot Shore! Verily was he fast with *her*, my lord. He lay with her last night, and loved you well. My lord . . .'

'Nay,' said Richard, turning his back on Buckingham. 'Not Hastings. Before God, spare me this.'

He was spilling the wine, and it dripped down his doublet like dark blood. Buckingham lowered the parchment.

'It is all here, my lord,' he said softly. 'We should thank Christ for the swift sagacity of our agents . . .' A purse, corpse-cold, weighted my palm. I let it slide, watching the Protector's stooping back. He was resting his hands upon the table, his head low. One of the marks fell and rolled, tinkling. Then there was only silence, which Buckingham broke with a tossing laugh. He stepped forward to grip the Protector's shoulder, the one which was a little malformed from axe-work.

'Cousin, my lord,' he said, 'we were to die, you and I. Our lives cut off, and England left to the mercy of the greedy Woodville tribe. As to Hastings—he loved you once, mayhap. Now, no more. Denounce him.'

'He was the loyalest of them all,' said Richard.

'Cousin, our lives are in peril!' said Buckingham urgently. 'Tomorrow night would see us in our blood!'

There was another beside Richard now, one with a gentle face.

'Your life is mine, Dickon.'

I had not even noticed Anne Neville's presence. She sat so quietly in her corner of the big window, with her tapestry,

337

her little hound. A frail, small woman, she came into this conflict of battling knights.

'Arrest him, my lord.' This, from Francis Lovell.

'The traitor!' John Howard's fierce growl.

The Protector turned. He looked sick.

'So be it,' he said, very quietly. 'Summon these four lords to a Council meeting. At ten in the morning. Friday, June thirteenth. A luckless day.'

And he drank his wine, and sat down again, heavily, and I felt Ratcliffe nip my sleeve, for he knew Richard well, and we withdrew, leaving the Protector to Buckingham's bright ministry. Later I prayed to the small blue Virgin above my bed. I prayed for the courage that I knew he never lacked. I prayed that he would have the strength to brook the severance of a good right arm. And I said all the missed Aves I should have given him, and asked his health and comfort in the long years ahead. Long years ahead! O Jesu! Even then, it was 1483, and the shadows just beginning to gather.

Were I to live unto an old man, I would remember always that morning in the White Tower. The lords entered with a stiff rustle. Richard stood to greet them, aloof and sword-straight, still but for the unquiet fingers which turned the ring upon his right hand. The Bishops took their chairs each side of the board. Morton looked very splendid that day, in his ermine cloak. He talked of strawberries; he had a fine crop in his Holborn garden—would my lords care for a mess of them?

I think they foreknew, Hastings particularly. He sat motionless, while the others coughed and shifted and, in the following hush, looked expectantly at the Protector, and Buckingham, behind his chair. So Richard began to speak, with a cold, queer controlled passion, and I shrank from his voice, for there was grief in it that rang harder on the ear than any shout of rage. And I was anxious lest the four conspirators should hear it too, and, construing this as cowardice, defy him outwardly. But then I heard him declare before the Council how the plots had been discovered, and at the one word 'Treason!' a buzzing struck up, which swept through the room and hid among the arras, and the June sun departed suddenly so that the place grew cool. And when Richard spoke of Rivers, Grey and Vaughan, I was glad to hear the virtue of his wrath.

'These Woodvilles have paralysed my arm. I can do naught

for England and its sovereign lord. Their treacherous plottings cripple my endeavour. They have despoiled the realm, they have worked most evilly to render the Protectorship null and void. And further, they have schemed against my life!'

The buzzing became a stormy silence. Then Richard Plantagenet was on his feet, leaning over the table.

'My life means little. What the treasonous knaves have not thought on is this!' Drawing his knife, he drove it hard into the board, where it sprang and quivered.

'If I should die this day, as was intended, twenty thousand men of York would rise to avenge me! Is this what they hoped? Yet another bath of blood for England? A dagger in England's heart?'

His hand pointed.

'I accuse you, William, Lord Hastings, of plotting with the harlot Shore, with the Queen Dowager and her kin. Hastings, I accuse—' and for a terrible moment I thought he was about to weep, and my hand flew to my swordhilt, for I knew they awaited weakness like kites round a raw head—'I accuse you of high treason,' he said, and turned his fierce blue eyes upon the blanching company.

'And you, Thomas Rotherham, likewise. And you, John Morton, of connivance with the Woodville brood. And you, Thomas, Lord Stanley, for conspiracy against the King and his government. Traitors all!'

'Thus are you named,' Buckingham said grimly.

I had never feared Richard more. I watched those craven faces register this confrontation in their singular ways. Rotherham felt gingerly for his weapon, got it half out of the scabbard, and saw it struck from his hand by John Howard's blade. And then suddenly Stanley fell on his knees before the Protector, mouthing pleas as if he were an actor playing the scene rehearsed for many hours. Morton turned aside, masking the quiver at his jaw with a lean, stroking hand.

But Hastings stood firm, and looked deeply at the Protector.

'Richard,' he said.

'Treason, my lord.'

'Richard, Richard, your Grace,' Hastings said again. 'For Edward's sake—for the Sun in Splendour. Have you forgotten the glory?'

The Protector wheeled to face him.

'Yeah, by Christ's Passion,' he said, through his teeth. 'The glory you destroyed! You, and the strumpet Shore! Night after night, cup after cup! Leading him in wantonness, making of him a sot, a drunkard. Speak not to me of his glory! I was made sick by the sights I saw at Sheen, at Greenwich . . .'

'Richard,' said Hastings desperately. 'For all that is gone, I beseech you . . .'

'For all that is gone!' said Richard, with hissing breath. 'Do you remember Clarence? Put to death through these your chosen allies! Christ, I still mourn . . . and you, you above all, handfasted now with *them*!' Like a dropping wind the anger left him. 'You shall be tried,' he said coldly. 'You shall receive just punishment. Take him.'

The pikemen moved forward to flank Hastings.

'Yea,' he said suddenly. 'I am indeed guilty. And I would no longer live.'

Richard made no answer, but turned once more, walking to the window near to me so that I caught the sound of his swallowed tears.

'My lord,' said Buckingham urgently to the Protector's back, 'shall these Woodvilles go unpunished in this affair? Shall Rivers, Vaughan and Grey not feel the Council's anger? And the Queen . . .'

'The Queen Dowager is my brother's royal widow,' said Richard, without looking round. 'She can but be revered as such. As to the others—yea! my patience ends this day, as they shall.'

The tramp, tramp of Hastings's guard struck a fading echo in the passage without.

'And there,' said the Protector, in a hard voice, and turning, 'goes one better than all Woodvilles ever spawned. One whose quarterings put a blush upon their meagre blazon. Judases,' he said, froth at his lips. 'Betraying him into sin, as he betrayed us all.' He spoke to Catesby. 'Yea, send to Pontefract, Sheriff Hutton, Middleham. Set up a jury. And let them taste the Council's wrath.'

He paced up and down. All watched him, and none keener than Morton, who looked as if, had he tablets, he would have written all this down.

'I have sworn to avenge my brother of Clarence,' Richard said. 'And now, another I loved dies through these Woodvilles' treachery. This, then, shall be my vengeance. Their deaths shall shroud my brother's ghost. Ride north,' he told Catesby.

As Catesby quit the room, Morton moved forward one pace, bowed low before the Protector.

'My Lord,' he said smoothly, 'Stanley has thrown himself upon your mercy. Now must I do likewise. *Mea culpa,* your Grace.'

The wraith of a smile chased across the Protector's lips.

'Your head is safe enough, my lord,' he said drily. 'Yet mayhap you need a little space to think. It is no secret to me, my lord, how, by troth, you were made giddy by your own aspirations! Cardinal Archbishop! a fair title, sir, and one day yours mayhap, but for your treason. Now, I fear, never. Your strawberries have a passing foul taste . . .'

Someone chuckled softly. A vein at the corner of Morton's mouth swelled and twitched.

'Where shall your Grace put me to think on this?' he said quietly.

It was Buckingham who had laughed.

'Brecon, my lord,' he said cheerfully. 'Stout fortress, mine. I think you might instruct me in the ways of spiritual grace.' He raised a brow at the Protector.

'Yea,' said Richard, dully.

When the heavy escort about Stanley, contrite and trembling, Rotherham, green with fear, and Morton, still, like a slumbering lizard, had quit the chamber, Richard called for John Kendall.

'Write, good John,' he said softly. 'Draw up a bill for the King's signet. That none of William, Lord Hastings's lands or livelode be forfeit. That his widow, Katherine, shall enjoy all these goods and privileges, and my protection, as long as she lives. That she shall ever be defended against those who may seek to defraud her of her rights.' His voice shook on the final sentence: 'And that William, Lord Hastings shall never be attainted, and shall be interred in St George's Chapel at Windsor, near to our late sovereign lord. As per his royal decree.'

Margetta went eagerly to see Jane Shore do penance. She came home pouting, saying that men had wept at the beauty of her naked breasts, limned in the glow of the candle that she carried all the way from Bishopsgate to Paul's Cross, and that though some jeered, many there were who spat their lust upon the cobbles.

'She was thrown into Newgate, bare as a worm,' Margetta said as we lay nestled together at night.

'So are the others gaoled,' I said. 'Stanley, Rotherham, and Morton; he is a prisoner of honour, that one, at Brecon.'

341

'Whyfor?' asked Margetta. 'I count him a flickering fellow for all he is a great, clever Bishop. Why did my lord not send all three to the block?'

Sweet Margetta, you spoke truth that night! Why, why indeed?

'I reckon Mistress Shore full fortunate,' she went on, while a bird cried dreamily outside the window and the night Watch pursued some felon down the street with oaths. 'Richard could have had her head. He hates wanton women. So men say.'

I stretched. I felt weary, and jaded beyond belief.

'He would not harm her,' I said, yawning. 'No Plantagenet has ever shed a woman's blood.'

'Earl Rivers made a song before he died,' Margetta said, punching the bolster with loud slaps. ' 'Twas fair indeed . . .

'Somewhat musing, and more mourning . . . in remembering Th'unsteadfastness, This world being,
Of such wheeling, Me contrarying,
What may I guess?'

'My lady, sleep, for God's love,' I said desperately. Through the window a chink of light came from across the courtyard. And I knew where that flame burned so late and sad. The sleeplack was once more with Richard Plantagenet.

'And were you there, zur, when they crowned him King?' asks William Brecher, kneeling by me on the foul prison straw.

They have lately brought Catesby in, flight-grimed, and still with the drought of fear upon his tongue. He does not speak, not even to answer the fierce rebukes of the man from York. That one is angered, his talk is never-ending. Powerlessly immured, he would kill with a curse. He rails of Northumberland, the shame of the North. Northumberland, who has knelt in homage to the Dragon. The stench here is noisome, and waxes more poisonous each hour. How many days and nights? I know not. The sun rose with thunder this morning, as if heaven were angry. But Brecher is speaking and this, my last duty, to comfort him and myself, by talking of . . . ah God, where have they taken him, all in his felon's halter? He, who was so fine, so fair . . .

'Yes, my friend,' I say, soft. 'I was there, in truth. I saw all.' And I saw also the withered countenance of Fortune. In

the plays and the disguisings, Fortune is a lovesome woman.
But I have seen Fortune, have seen it smile on Richard, with
a smile full of dolour and woe, sitting sadly upon the face of
an aged man. Like an old song, that smile hung heavy on the
heart.

So came this sombre-clad Fortune, within a week after little
York was taken at last from Sanctuary. I was one who went
upriver from Crosby's Place to carry out this mission for the
Council. And how Elizabeth Woodville stormed! When we
entered, she was seated low on the rushes, babbling of
injustice, raising a gossamer veil of real and imaginary tribu-
lation, blinking her blue eyes as she cried of her brother's
cruel beheading. And she sobbed piteously of how one son
was gone from her, all the while clinging closely to little York.
She contrived to loose her hair until it hung like a gilded
shroud, and Archbishop Bourchier, ill-ease at any event at
this violation of Sanctuary, looked anywhere but at her
beauty. Then all her grief ceased of a sudden; she began to
abuse the Council, the Protector, Buckingham, and all of us,
and little York writhed from her grip.

So we took him from Westminster, and the Archbishop en-
treated Elizabeth to follow likewise, with all her daughters,
and be welcome at the house of the Protector, to which plea
she all but growled, headshaking, a golden tigress with her
cubs about her, sharp claws beneath the silk. I looked deep in
her eyes from afar, and marked she was afraid. Of what?
Dare say of retribution. She did not know the Protector, for
she had never chosen to know him, and had she power, I
doubt not she would have ground him beneath her heel.
Watching her guilt, her fury, I was minded to laugh, and
must indeed have smiled, and so doing, caught the eye of tall
Princess Elizabeth, who looked as if *she* would fain be out of
Sanctuary, and with her brothers. Eighteen and beautiful,
more Plantagenet than Woodville, and a gem of price.

While Richard waited, we were mindful that the Parliament could no longer support this obloquy upon its being
and, further, that the King waxed sorrowful without my lord
of York. Thus we delivered little Dick to Edward's apartments at the Tower, and saw the young King step down
from his dais to embrace the younger boy; the joy on each
face lit smiles like lamps.

So it was that both awaited the coronation there, while the
gowns were fashioned, the bidding letters written to the gen-

tlemen whom King Edward would honour with knighthood, and the cloth of gold, the satin, velvet and sarcenet cut and slashed and broidered for the banners and the hangings and the horses' trappings. And the Nativity of St John Baptist drew near, and with it came a knocking on the Privy Council door which split our destiny down the centre, as a thunderbolt an oak. I remember well the place of revelation, and even the one who kept the door that day. For we attended the Protector in the Star Chamber, and William Colyngbourne, Gentleman Usher, stood guard.

Richard had the great Book of the Household open before him, and was dictating to Kendall, at times snatching a pen to add some postscript, smiling, knitting his brows over a wardrobe account, a jeweller's bill. He looked up at Colyngbourne of the white face and twitching hands, asking: 'Who comes? Can they not wait?'

'My lord,' said Colyngbourne, strangely unquiet, 'the Bishop of Bath and Wells seeks audience.'

'Stillington?' Richard set down his quill. 'Is he in London? I have not seen him since Clarence . . . I have not seen him for years.' Musing, he said: 'We are hard pressed—'

'He has waited long, your Grace,' answered Colyngbourne. 'He begs . . .'

'A boon, I doubt not,' laughed Buckingham. 'We have had our fill of Bishops, ha, Dickon?'

Buckingham waxed hourly more stout and proud; his body in its peacock raiment was bloated by arrogance.

'Some feud in his diocese, I'll warrant,' he went on. 'Some brawling of priests. So he comes to the Council as a last resort. He must be three score years at least.'

Richard got up instantly. 'Let him enter.'

Sir Robert Stillington came in, and he took long to approach the Council bench, for he was verily an old man, who seemed to have gathered many years in the two months since I saw him last. Then, outside King Edward's chamber of death, he had grieved to excess, and that sorrow was still with him, mingled with a kind of bitter desperation. His cheeks were grey, his hair stark white, and the hand extended for the Protector's salutation fluttered and shook. Buckingham offered wine.

'I will not drink,' said the Bishop in a voice like crackling leaves. 'Neither drink nor meat before I have spoken. For speak this day I must, or die.'

Waveringly he seated himself, and passed a hand before his eyes.

'Come, my lord,' said Buckingham. 'Do not talk thus of death.'

'Is your Grace sick?' asked Richard. 'The fault is mine; we have delayed you overlong.'

'Not you, my lord,' said the Bishop, with a faint smile. (The pallid smile of Fortune.) 'Mine the delay, mine the fault, and mine the reaping.' A cloud settled on his face, leaving it drawn. 'I hope only that God will not judge me for this same delay.' With this he ceased, clamping his mouth, while his glance roamed over Buckingham, Lovell, John Howard, Catesby, Ratcliffe, Kendall, Brackenbury; Piers Curteys, standing with a bolt of green silk in his arms, Lord Scrope of Bolton, the two men in the livery of the Goldsmith's Gild, myself, Colyngbourne and the henchmen. Then his eyes returned to Richard Plantagenet, and stayed there.

'Well, my lord Bishop?' said the Protector.

And Stillington was dumb, and I began to wonder whether age would addle my wits too, and mused if it were not better to die young, with all the senses sharp and clear, then Harry Buckingham coughed loudly, and the Bishop's eyes fastened on his face.

'I would speak with my lord Duke of Gloucester,' said Stillington gravely.

'He awaits your words,' smiled Buckingham.

'Alone,' said the Bishop.

Almost before the flame of anger rose on Buckingham's face, Richard leaned over to lay his hand upon the Bishop's sleeve.

'Your Grace knows that all here are my good friends and advisers,' he said gently.

The Bishop looked down at his velvet lap.

'Speak, my lord, for Jesu's love,' said Buckingham harshly. 'We are not here to judge your Grace. If 'tis some boon, I doubt not it will be granted. If some error, the lord Protector will no doubt be lenient. He loves loyalty—' with a flashing glance at Richard—'and you come as a loyal subject of the Crown of England, do you not, your Grace?'

'Ah, certes,' said the Bishop heavily. 'In truth, I do.'

'Gentlemen, good day,' said Richard to the goldsmiths, at the same time nodding dismissal to his henchmen. They withdrew, looking wonderingly at one another.

'Now, sir,' said Buckingham.

'I have sinned,' said the Bishop softly.

Buckingham's lips made a hard line. 'Why are you come before us, my lord? Would you bring wisdom to the government? Or have you some request? For you make us your confessors—how can we offer penance to a Bishop?' Then in a voice wily with friendship: 'Was your Grace not once immured by King Edward? If my memory serves me, I knew not why.'

The Bishop began to shake, and not only his hands. His voice was a breath as he answered: 'For speaking words defamatory to the King's Grace.'

Buckingham became an inquisitor. 'Words, my lord? But were you not the tutor of Bishop Alcock?'

The Bishop said quietly: 'He was indeed pupil to me, sir; he rose to great estate. He kept me close to him.'

By now the chamber was full of muttering; I heard the hiss of 'Woodville-lover' from one corner.

'He kept *you* close, my lord?' cried Buckingham, incredulously. 'What a world is ours, when pupil can bid master come and go? Or was there—' his tone became harsh again—'was there some bond betwixt the two of you . . . some privy tithe he owed you, or *you owed him?*'

The Bishop's eye roved wildly again to the Protector.

'My lord of Gloucester,' he said faintly, 'I bear news which may set our world upon its head. God has moved me to come here this day. But all this is for one only. He of the old royal blood.'

Richard spoke quietly. 'My cousin here is Plantagenet, your Grace, and without these my councillors I am as naught,' he said.

I saw the gleam of a tear in the Bishop's eye.

'Sir, you are true brother to our late sovereign lord,' he said. 'I am an old man. Full heavy with this burden that I bear.'

Even Richard's patience was waning. 'Your Grace forgets that we are busy men,' he said shortly. 'Each hour is precious. The time is short until my nephew's coronation.'

Stillington drew a great breath.

'There can be no coronation,' he said. 'I have toiled long with this secret. While King Edward lived, I could only hold my peace. But now . . .' and the tear in his eye started its journey down. 'I cannot see a bastard receive sacred Chrism. I cannot see a bastard on the throne of England.'

Piers Curteys dropped his bale of silk and it spread out, richly green over the lozenged tiles. The sound of its fall was like a corpse upon hard ground. And there was an end to quiet. Amid the gasps, the stifled oaths, I heard the word 'Blayborgne' and an old image leaped to my mind: the leer-

346

ing face of a French ambassador's henchman, with whom I had once passed an hour, an hour that had ended in blows when he, drunken and tongue-loose, had whispered of our King's own parentage, as it was sung in France.

'*Le fils d'un archier*,' he had sniggered, swaying on his bench. 'So tall, so blonde, that Blayborgne . . . so low, so dark, the Duke of York, God him pardon. Proud Cis was not too proud . . .' Then it was that I struck him, to rob him of three teeth and send him asprawl and bloody . . . Buckingham had heard of it too. For Buckingham, drunk with a kind of madness, was daring to voice it. Through the confusion of my own stunned dream I heard Richard's answer, and trembled for fear of him.

'May God forgive you, cousin,' he said, on his feet and stumbling with rage. He turned savagely to the Bishop.

'And you, my lord? Would you impugn our royal line? Do you prate of old, vile rumour in this Chamber? Do you question my late brother's ancestry? Mine too? For you but lately called me true brother to his Grace. We, who are descended by pure blood from Edward Third? Would you cast filth upon the name of Plantagenet?' The blood left his face and with a gasp he caught at the throat of his own doublet.

'I lie at Baynard's Castle,' he said, in a choking voice. 'Think you that I can brook such evil and kiss my mother's hand this night?'

For the first time, Buckingham looked uneasy, and glanced towards the door, perchance wishing he were hunting, or drinking. And the Bishop stayed calm, old, and far beyond passion.

'My lords, you misconstrue my words,' he said with a ghostly smile.

Next instant, Buckingham was babbling to the Protector. 'Your Grace, forgive my folly! Am I not your true friend and lover? It is but that you, my lord, resemble in face and body both, your father Richard, whom God assoil. Aye, you, sir, more than any other man.'

The Protector's breathing shuddered and slowed. His eyes were still fixed on the Bishop.

'Have done with this,' he said in a tight voice. 'Speak now. And, by the Blood of Christ, speak plain.'

Stillington bowed his head. 'I do not, dare not, question the royal lineage of King Edward the Fourth,' he said. 'The bastardy is rooted in his heirs. The young Princes, and the maidens. Bastards all, and unfit to reign in the sight of God and man.'

347

'Unfit to reign?' whispered the Protector.

The Bishop's eyes were closed. 'How should they reign, my lord?' he asked. 'They are all issue of an unholy union, contracted in a profane place, between Elizabeth Woodville and a man already trothplight to another. The King, my lord, was wedded when he took Elizabeth to wife.'

'Say on,' said Richard in a frozen voice.

'Her Grace the Duchess of York wrought all she could to prevent it,' said Stillington gently. 'I have myself seen letters where she implores the King not to commit this sin. For the sake of his immortal soul and for his heirs.'

'And for England,' said Richard dully. 'Yet he would have his way. Always . . .' He looked sharply at the Bishop. 'What proof have you of this union? There are ever strumpets ready to court perjury for gain. Who was the woman? Was it Elizabeth Lucey? She bore him children . . . O, Jesu!' He laughed harshly. 'Not the creature Shore! Nay, she would be but a little maid . . . who was this wife of Edward? And who the priest that joined them?'

Smiling faintly, Stillington opened his eyes.

'No strumpet, your Grace,' he said. 'None but Great Talbot's daughter, the Lady Eleanor Butler.' Under the burden of gasps ringing round the chamber he said: 'And I it was who, in the first year of Edward's reign, bound them until death.'

Sir John Howard spoke, harshly. 'The mighty Talbot's wench,' he said. 'Where is she now?'

'Dead, these fifteen years,' answered the Bishop. 'In the house of the Carmelites at Norwich, of a strange melancholy.'

'Was he mad?' said Richard softly, as if to himself. 'Some battle-blow at Towton might have loosened his senses for a while . . . How could he do this thing? Tell us, my lord Bishop. Tell us all.'

'He was bewitched,' answered Stillington. 'By Jacquetta, Duchess of Bedford, mistress of the Black Art, and her daughter. They fed him potions to drive reason out and lechery in.'

'Who knows of this?' said Richard, crossing himself.

'There are half an hundred witnesses whose lips were sealed,' said the Bishop steadily. 'Persons of no account, clerks and nuns—but men have died by this knowledge . . . Elizabeth was sore afraid.'

Richard looked straight at the Bishop's eyes.

'My brother . . .' he said haltingly.

'Yea, my lord,' Stillington nodded. 'Your brother of Clarence knew all. I was more fortunate, being cast in gaôl.'

The ruby upon Richard's finger struck spears of light as he twirled it round. 'By God, this is an evil day,' he said.

> Upon this hill I found a tree,
> Under a tree a man sitting;
> From head to foot wounded was he;
> His hearte blood I saw bleeding.
> A seemly man to be a king,
> A gracious face to look unto.
> I askèd why he had paining:
> *Quia amore langueo.*
>
> XIVth century: Anon.

Now, strangely, only swift bright thoughts like birds. For the days thereafter moved too fast, though I lived through them as knowingly as he did, and heard the same voices; above all, the brassy note of glowing Buckingham, come into his own at last. Buckingham, now no longer dead Clarence, but dead Warwick, the maker of kings. Buckingham's marvellous address to the mayor and burgesses of London, eloquent, and florid as a pierced vein's yield.

'Know you not, good citizens, that this noble Prince is true son and heir of Richard, Duke of York? That he, England-born, is by blood and birthright truly English!' Lightly he leaped on Edward's evil diet, then as the wine of oratory touched his soul, he gave them Stillington's sad secret, like one who throws a whole fresh beast to starving dogs.

The witchcraft moved them. Powerful fear lashed the stout merchant men; they muttered.

'Know you not that there is none other to defend this realm against such evil than Richard, Duke of Gloucester, most mighty Prince, skilled in wise counsel, and in battle Hector's kin?'

There were men in Gildhall who had fought by him, at Barnet, at Tewkesbury. The murmurings swelled; there came bench-rappings, shouts of 'Yea, yea!' and *'Bene!'* from the lettered, as if they attended a tutorial in dialectics. My sight grew keener. The conserve of rue I habitually ate strengthened not only my eyes, but gave me an inner seeing. Thus, watching Buckingham, I saw not only his bright mouth and blazon of the flaming wheel, but also the grants which Richard had already heaped upon his loyalty. Constable of Shropshire, Hereford, Somerset, Dorset and Wiltshire was he; Chief Justice and Chamberlain in the north and south parties of Wales; Constable and Steward of all the Welsh manors of Lancaster and March. I saw his eyes on the Protector, saw his greedy love.

'The great wit of this Prince, the prudence, justice and noble courage!' On and on. And Richard, unsmiling. I saw his brows draw up once, when Buckingham alluded to Edward's past lecheries and unwisdom, and to Clarence's attainder for high treason . . .

'There is none other living who is fit to rule! The issue of George, Duke of Clarence; attainted in the sight of God and man . . .'

Young Warwick at Baynard's Castle. Frail Isabel's child, clinging to his aunt, the spittle dripping off his chin. His vague, empty laughter. Anne Neville's soothing hand upon the overlarge skull. And little Edward, Richard's son, a faery child, looking up amazed from the lessons that Warwick could not grasp. Young Warwick, screaming in fright before the motleyed fool who sought to cheer him.

Richard had not his Middleham fool with him; the one whom I had ever reckoned so wanton and dangerous a fellow, and marvelled that he kept his head—that one had gone, all fury, to sit at the feet of Princess Elizabeth in Sanctuary. He vowed he loved her more now she was bastard; he caused much mirth among the other players by his departure.

A hot July the first, licked by the smouldering heat of June's last day, and bursting into flame. Anne Neville paler, with a dangerous bright spot on each fair cheek. Her cough, dry as the roads. Her swoon one evening at the feasting board; the white neck snapped forward, a broken flower. And Richard himself lifting her in his arms, leaving the Spanish and Portuguese ambassadors and his stern old mother. He carried her weightlessly away, pursued by anxious, twittering gentlewomen. Her pale returning; and his kiss upon her hand, that left a mark . . .

Bishop Shaw's sermon from the erection on Paul's Cross: 'Bastard slips shall take no root.' The people. Scrivener, cordwainer, fletcher, cooper, lodging-house keeper, tapster, silversmith, mercer and cook. Whore and beggar and cutpouch. Gaping, gaping upward. Alderman and priest and friar. Black gown, red and grey. The turnings and noddings as they, good London folk, sucked in the sense of their country's new design.

The men of York, four thousand strong, who came at Richard's bidding—the Londoners jeered at their ramshackle harness, their outlandish speech. Yet the tongues were hushed when Richard rode out to greet them. They were all drawn up in a great circle in Moorfields. He passed among them on foot, with bowed head. Some towered over him. I saw their looks of love. 'Dickon, God bless him!' they said.

And the long bright hill down which we all rushed, into the unknown enclosure of a new reign. Margetta and I went out in it, to catch its humour. Into seething London.

'King Edward kissed me once—he said I was fair, a hinny.' Stout bosom heaved with old conceits.

'And took twenty marks from your pouch straightway, for his archers' folderols.' Blue buskins beneath a worsted gown. Squinting eyes, one looking east, the other west.

'This one's a sober man. There'd be no kissing . . .'

'Well, mayhap no benevolences!' said the squint-eyed witch gaily.

'Bastard slips shall take no root,' said her husband, and spat.

'What of Clarence's son—he's no bastard, is he?' demanded the fat one.

'He is an idiot—and attainted—by your King Edward,' said the witch-woman with triumph.

'Did we but know Gloucester . . . he was ever up in the north country.'

'Dust'a speak of my lord?' enquired a grim voice. 'I'm from Knaresborough. I know him. The best good lordship York ever had . . .'

At court, an emissary from King Louis, sent obviously to spy. And the French chronicler, Commynes, scratching away like a clerk, watching everything and everybody, and suiting it doubtless to fit the designs of his spiderly master.

And sorrow in the Garden Tower. The sorrow and the hate. Prince Edward, the once and never King, receiving his uncle with white dignity. They stood to face each other, and there was little they could say, in truth. Richard spoke of the Law of God, the Law of Nature; that their position as royal bastards would rank them high within the court, but Edward stiffened and looked on him with his mother's eyes, cold, outraged . . . 'Is there aught you require, my lord?' asked Gloucester.

'Naught, sir, for what was mine you have already . . . the Crown of England.' The gracious turning from him to hide tears. Little York, the merriest of men, resorting to rude faces at Buckingham's back.

And in Chepe, where Buckingham's lieutenants bawled of Richard's birthright, I saw Hogan again, together with his woman, who had wept beneath the hawthorn tree. She was not veiled that day; I saw her face and the great purple wen that disfigured it, a fleshly curse from mouth to eyebrow. A press of people blocked me, and over the shoulder of a mighty fletcher, I saw Hogan look me-ward. And he nodded, once, twice, with an expression on his face that chilled me, while the scarfaced woman followed his gaze so sadly that I would fain have crossed myself had I had room in the crush. I leaped through the crowd. A swirl of people withstood my buffeting, and when I finally gained the place where he had stood, with his malevolent half-smile, he had vanished as if he had been there only in my own mind.

A dozen Woodville agents were brought before the Protectorship. The many-mouthed monster still moved under cover of night. Scant news of Sir Edward, or Dorset, but their names augured the looming of a longer shadow. That barren twig of Lancaster, that impudent son of Margaret Beaufort, that Henry . . . Tydder. Duke Francis kept him snug in Brittany—'Till he is strong enough to fight?' Richard asked the weary messenger, with an ironic smile.

Then all these sundry sparks together kindled a great flame in the Parliament. The lords spiritual and temporal assembled with most of the barons of the realm; the Lords and Commons, bent on the one and only course left to them, swimming desperately in that uncertain sea towards the last harbour: man, not child true-born, not bastard . . .

The great roll of supplication drawn up for him, stating his claim in plain words . . . 'that the said King Edward was . . . married and trothplight to one Dame Eleanor Butler, daughter of the old Earl of Shrewsbury . . . his said pretended marriage with Elizabeth Grey . . . they lived together sinfully and damnably in adultery . . . that all their issue have been bastards, and unable to inherit or to claim any thing by inheritance, by the law and custom of England . . .'

They wrote of the great noblesse of his birth and blood. 'You are descended of the three most royal Houses in Christendom, England, France and Spain . . . By this our writing choose you, high and mighty Prince, unto our King and Sovereign Lord . . . according to this election of us the three Estates of this land, as by your true inheritance . . . accept and take upon you the said Crown and royal dignity . . . We promise to serve and to assist your highness, as true and

352

faithful subjects and liegemen, and to live and die with you . . .'

So ran the Act of Titulus Regius, a great unwieldy parchment sealed in state, with haste, and with many a backward glance to France and Brittany, and secret thoughts, no doubt, of the creeping Woodville net, in every town, on either shore.

His countenance at Baynard's Castle, so stern and white that the amorous stout one, who cherished foolish memory of Edward's lips, would surely have retreated in disgust. He stood on the great stairhead, while Titulus Regius was read by a hoarse herald who took full half an hour in the reading, and outside the walls came the buzz of the commonalty, stirred at last; and my own mounting joy and longing for his acceptance.

Three times they offered him the Crown. He said:

'Yet for the entire love and reverend respect I owe to my brother deceased and to his children, you must give me leave more to regard mine honour and fame in other realms. For where the truth and certain proceedings here are not known, it may be thought ambition in me to seek what you voluntarily proffer, which would charge so deep a reproach and stain upon my honour and sincerity as I would not bear for the world's diadem . . .'

I saw him glance downward at his son. Then, as he listened to the solemn talk of the ancient laws and customs of the realm, and I stood, hand clenched upon my dagger and ready to live and die—the pallor faded from his face and it waxed rosy, as he bowed his head. And Buckingham hastened to his loudest henchman, who slipped outside . . . came the cry, after a moment's silence of 'Richard!' The buzzing hive turned loose, as though in full flight.

He knew, despite the varied motives of the Parliament, that there was none other.

He rode to Westminster. He seated himself in the marble chair on King's Bench. The royal oath—faintly heard upon his quiet lips.

His lecture to the Justices of Common Pleas and the Serjeants of the Law—unprecedented and, I think, not altogether welcome . . .

'I charge you, one and all, to dispense justice without fear or favour. I say unto you' (hands knotted and poised upon the Bench) 'that all men, whatever their estate, shall be equal, in the sight of God and the Law. I charge you straitly to follow my will in this.'

353

Then he rose, and took the hand of Sir John Fogge, one of the staunchest Woodville adherents. He took his hand; he welcomed him in love and trust—he made him Justice of the Peace, God help me, for my own Kent! Fogge smirked a little under his obeisance.

The surprised looks.

Richard reinstating Bishop Rotherham to the Privy Council.

Richard, begging justice for all men.

Richard, summoning Lord Stanley, a little pallid, from out the Tower dungeon. His speech of forgiveness. Lady Margaret Beaufort was there, to rejoice with her lord.

I took to bathing my eyes with hawkweed, that plant shaped like the human eye and miraculously endowed. Even then, I knew I would need my keen sight.

The sun emerged as we made our way to Westminster, and the crowd, one great jostling gawk, showed its upturned chin in wonder. That augurs well, they said, with ohhhh and ahhh, then writhed to crush one another in their frenzy to see the King walking barefooted to his Coronation, on a broad crimson ribbon two ells in width. He walked far ahead of me, preceded by clarions and heralds, the leopards and lilies of England blazoned on each stiff tabard, the fringed pennons asway in the sunlit air. Before him, the great Cross flamed its high splendour. Far ahead of me he went, but through the long train of monks and priests, abbots and bishops, I could glimpse the rich purple of his robe, his dark head, carried on a steady, measured walk. Then the light faded, as we were gone from the sun, and into the dark arching vastness of the Abbey. At the end of the train I came, in my red and white, the colours of Plantagenet. And tall Northumberland sealed off my view of him, so that I looked upon the pointless sword of mercy, and a great diapason of singing rang against the stone, a high ethereal swell like one might hear upon the time of dying . . .

And the dark was changed again to light, a softer light bestowed by a thousand candles, and the slowly dropping banners grew transparent, unearthly with an unearthly jewelled glory, and the colours of the nobles took on a mysteriousness, sad flames, the reds like blood, the azures darkening as a storm-rocked sea. And the splendour faded a little when I saw who carried the Mace of Lord High Constable: Stanley himself, restored, and meek of step beside the King he swore to love for ever. The soft rustling beat of our steps was translated—in my mind alone—into Viscount Lovell's voice, as he walked ahead, carrying one of the pointed swords of justice: 'My lord, forget not he betrayed you once—why do him such honour?' And Richard (the throng swayed apart momentarily and I had him again within my sight): 'I shall show him justice and mercy, Francis, he will repay me in kind.'

The state robes hung heavy on Anne Neville. The long train dragged at her small shoulders, and I had a sudden longing to take all that rich strain over my own arms, but there was one already destined for that dignity. Stanley's wife smiled as she went, behind the progress of frail Anne. She had grown in stature, Lady Margaret, what with the chopines boosting her soles and the rich hennin floating above her head, and her well-concealed pride. She held the cloth loosely between her hands, unlike Buckingham, who gripped Richard's train until his knuckles blanched white.

The Earl of Lincoln bore the orb, Suffolk the sceptre. And above Richard's head, the golden canopy, carried by the Wardens of the Cinque Ports, gave back prisms of coloured light from one great window, filtering rainbowlike over the slow procession and resting lovingly upon the Crown of England. Bold John Howard bore the Crown; Howard, friend and servant of Richard for many years; Howard, newmade Duke of Norfolk. Up the nave I went, feeling the slight red wrinkling of the carpet beneath my feet, beside Richard Ratcliffe, behind Sir John Fogge, while the singing in the misericords rose and rose; the high cold voices, the organ like a bell!

Richard and Anne stepped forward, and merged with a sea of grey amices, gold mitres and croziers. Caught up in destiny, while the Latin and prick-song resounded from the old stones of the Abbey; they *were* England. I wanted to shout, to weep. They rose from their seats of estate and walked, small figures in the candled distance, up to the High Table of God. Four priests divested them of their upper clothing. The thick wavering light shone upon their flesh. The dark head bowed. The fair head drooped. The choir was silent.

He was anointed with the sacred oil, on brow and breast and hands, and there came a little gushing sigh from the walls of the Abbey, where hundreds on hundreds of citizens and holy men, earls and barons and dukes, formed one great eye; and somewhere in the cold upper darkness of the church a power stirred that was not of this world, and the Chrism gleamed upon the flesh of Richard, and of Anne.

Yea, I was there, Master Brecher, when they crowned him King. I watched him anointed, King Richard the Third, and saw, through the haze and the pungent shrouding incense, a young man, distressed by the bloodshed in Tewkesbury Abbey. I saw him with bare head slowly circling the rusted ranks of the men of York in Moorfields, thanking them for their presence. I saw him laughing across the table in a Bruges inn. I saw also a little artificer, clutching his deed of title, while the stink of London rose about him. And the face of a young maid, mouthing a long-forgotten echo . . . 'Holy Jesu! how he shines!' All this I saw, and without seeing.

They were arrayed in cloth of gold. In the last moment of silence, Cardinal Bourchier set crowns upon their heads, and the organ burst into a swelling paean of song, while the monks of Westminster lifted their hearts in the *Te Deum Laudamus*, and King Richard took in his hands the crown of St Edward and the holy relics, offering them at the Confessor's Shrine.

Outside, the jubilation had already begun. It was an awful sound; although I knew it to be the thunder of welcome, it had the puissance of a great fire, wantonly directed.

So he came out into this inferno of acclaim, crowned, with darkness and the trace of tears beneath his eyes; with Anne, his Queen, white and rosy and smiling; and they stood a moment listening to the cries. In the courtyard of the almonry outside the West Door hung the Red Pale, Caxton's emblem, and unwittingly my thoughts fleeted to his achievements. Books to laud the martyrdom of saints, the past honours of English fighting men—and the greatness of kings. And who would be written of more gloriously than King Richard the Third?

Little stays with me, of the banquet that followed. Except that Buckingham was Master of Ceremonies, that Stanley and his lady were prominent, and that I served the King with wine. Lord Audley carved his meat, Lovell and Robert Percy tendered him dishes of gold and silver. The servers lay prone at his feet; each time he, or the Queen, touched food, four henchmen raised the cloth of estate high above their heads. At opposite boards bishops and knights surveyed one another across Westminster Hall, and the whole peerage of England observed their King. There were contented looks, and when Sir Robert Dymmock, the King's Challenger, rode in through the great door in pure white armour, forking a steed barded with the colours of Plantagenet, there was a growing murmur that swelled even as he brandished his sword and called on any who would fight him for the King's honour. Thrice he challenged the company, and before his last cry was out, the answering roar came from a thousand throats . . .

'King Richard! King Richard!'

And Dymmock took from the golden cup a great draught, then, casting the wine upon the ground, rode swiftly from the Hall, while the spilled redness soaked the rushes, like the blood of a dying man.

He yearned for the North, at once.

After the long exhausting revel we made him ready for bed. It was late, and the fire was down; so I lit new candles, coaxed the logs into brightness, and divested him of his Queen's coronation gift, a habit of purple cloth of gold, starred with white roses and the Garter emblem. He stood at the window, I behind him, holding out his bedrobe and looking over his shoulder on to the Thames to where the lamps hung like fireflies in the rigging of visiting craft, and at St Edward's diadem gleaming round the great dark curve of the river. Far below, the unseen black tide flowed, muttering a strange nocturne.

I do not attempt conceit, that I could always read his mind, yet I knew then how he was full of self-doubt. Twice that evening he had bidden a henchman see that the Lords Bastard were comfortable in Garden Tower. Brackenbury had told Ratcliffe and me that the Lord Edward would speak to none, but that the Lord Richard had regained spirits and was playing soldiers with a page, avoiding the set, white face of his brother.

He stood so long before the open window that the cold air blistered his naked flesh. He said without turning:

'They gave me a fair ovation this night.'

'In truth, Sire, they did.'

'How does my Queen?'

'Well, if a little weary, lord,' answered Lovell.

'My son?'

'Asleep, your Grace.'

He turned swiftly for me to gown him. He took up a candle. Its light made his shadow tall. We followed him along the wavering corridor, to the apartments of the little Prince. We entered so soft the tutor did not wake, and only one page stirred at the bed's foot, groaning in a dream.

'Gentlemen, your future King,' said Richard quietly.

I have seen many looks of love. The love of a good priest for Holy Church, or a wanton for a fair young knight, or a miser for his purse. Never before, or hereafter, have I witnessed such as the sublime look King Richard dropped upon his sleeping son. The child lay with his hands thrown upward above his head. A briar-scratch creased one palm. His mouth bloomed moist. A small blue vein in his temple fluttered softly, like the wings of a nesting bird.

'Francis.'

'Your Grace?'

'I would not set my bastard John on England's throne.'

'No more you would, Sire,' said Lovell, in swift comprehension.

'By true blood and birthright,' said the King.

Lovell was moved. He sank upon his knee.

'By true birth and blood, my lord, you are our sovereign. This day, and for ever.'

The King looked down at his bent head.

'You give me great comfort,' he said. Then, taking up the candle again: 'Tomorrow, I will plan a great progress through my realm. Worcester, Gloucester, Coventry. And York, of course. We will ride north.'

None of us had an inkling of how unwise and how ill-chosen his moment to reap all that sweet glory, that swell of growing homage, like the organ and the high splendour of the voices at his coronation. A praise waxing more frantic the farther north we went. At Oxford, the students, thronging the streets, banded and unruly as only students are, and joyful at the holiday. Their lecturers and tutors, gowned in sombre magnificence; the chief dignitaries of church and town and the founder of Magdalen, welcomed him at the college gates.

The disputation held for his entertainment, between Dr Taylor and Master Grocin. Theology, philosophy. Their premises darted like hares around the hall. I was swamped in a great lake of logic. King Richard sat entranced, thanked them heartily after, with a new-killed buck, and money.

At broad-tongued Gloucester, the King's own duchy, Harry Buckingham joined us. I saw a hardening change in him that amazed me, though I knew he had come close to quarrelling before we left London. Ratcliffe had told me.

'The King said that my lord of Buck must surely be the hardest fellow to satisfy ever, being ill-content with the Great Chamberlainship and Constableship of England . . . and Harry took the rebuke badly. "Sire, you get great store by loyalty," said he. "The de Bohun lands are surely less than my due." And the King looked at him right steadily, while Buckingham grew like a peevish, greedy wife, and touched the King's heart right sore. For he spoke of Earl Warwick, and of how he, Harry, had set Dickon on King's Bench as truly as the Neville once aided Edward Fourth. And (mad, or drunk, or over-certain of the King's favour) he spoke of how those that make kings warrant especial privilege, and he used Warwick's name again, in the shadow of a threat.

'And the King sat very still, then he ordained the de Bohun lands, all fifty, to Buckingham, but there was a look on him that soured this gift, certes. As if a favourite hound had turned to maul him. That Harry Buckingham flies high since Richard said to Bishop Stillington: "My cousin is also Plantagenet".'

The Mayor and aldermen of Gloucester had a welcome for the King, and a brass coffer of more money than I had ever seen at once, about a thousand pounds, and he refused it. He took the uncertain hands in his, and spoke of their Englishness, and of his affection. He enquired after their grievances, and a long line of petitioners came forth and were contented by him. He spoke an hour with one man, whose property had been unlawfully annexed by a neighbour. 'A clerk it was, Sire, from Cambridge, and lettered in Latin; I was uncertain of the law,' and a thoughtfulness came on Richard at this.

His generous new charter of liberties laid Gloucester prone with gratitude. As to Buckingham, that word was not in his lexicon, though we did not know it. He parted from us at Gloucester. I can see him now, tall on a jewelled mount.

'Farewell, your Grace.' There was unfeigned mockery in his obeisance.

'So you leave us, Harry,' said the King carefully.

'With regret, Sire. Business is pressing.'

I stood by Richard, as the Duke rode close to us.

'Your Grace's answer remains the same?' he asked softly.

There was a look like flint that Richard could employ at times.

'You know me well enough, my lord,' he said. 'I never retract my word. About your pressing business then, I pray you. We shall, I think, miss your company.'

'Farewell, Sire,' Buckingham said again. He clipped spurs, two diamonds, into sleek hide and took off along the Hereford road, Brecon bound. There were two children clinging to the walls.

'Look! The King!' cried one. He clambered down swiftly, almost beneath the heels of Buckingham's train.

'Silly Billy, that's not King Richard!' But the other, child-like, ran waving, and Buckingham, pleased, dropped gold with a laugh, and rode from the town. That was the last I ever saw of him.

Passing through Sudbury Gate into Worcester, where the Welsh lilt grew stronger and the faces narrower with slanted eyes, we were greeted by Bishop and Mayor. They had a strongbox containing more than a thousand pounds for Richard, and again he refused it. 'Rather your heart than your money,' he said, with a smile.

'He's not like Edward,' said a butcher from the Shambles.

'But he has a good face,' his daughter said, jumping on tip-toe to see.

'He's gone into the church. To see King John's tomb.'

'He's up at Castle Gaol,' said one blackbrowed adventurer, caressing his bawd and laughing.

'He's letting out all the prisoners!' cried the landlord of the Talbot.

'Peace, peace,' called a friar. 'He is but hearing their grievances. He observes their diet, sniffs the air they breathe, listens to their double-tongued, knavish tales. He's not like Edward . . .'

'I like well his countenance,' said the butcher's daughter. 'And when he smiles 'tis fair.'

At Tewkesbury, a change clothed him. The gaiety was forsworn. He walked slowly up the flags to the North Door. There was no blood, no harness gutted with blows, as on the last occasion. In the royal purple, with his crown, he knelt in penance before the aged Abbot. Then we followed him past the sleeping Saxons, the Despenser tombs and beneath the soaring massed stones of Norman craft, into a long-gone age. Queen Anne's young husband lay beneath the misericords; behind the altar George of Clarence and Isabel; all free of this transient life.

The King lay prone for some minutes, then, rising, took the Abbot's hand.

'Three hundred pounds for this church,' he ordained. 'Three hundred pounds for that day.'

At Warwick Castle the Queen awaited us, with a simpering Spanish envoy. She was bright, and uplifted by the tales of our progress; she was downcast from the news that Edward, at Middleham, was ailing again—his sojourn in London and the journey back had wearied him, but they would see him

360

again soon, at York. 'Oh, my lord, let us not delay too long!' pleaded Anne.

The Spaniard, by name Gaufidius de Sasiola, was a clown. Even his Latin sounded foreign. He was like a small black monkey, and his message, though welcome, held much irony. His royal mistress, Isabella, sought peace with England. King Louis had played them false. The envoy would have been sent years ago, only . . .

'My Queen was full of fury. Her royal hand in the offing for King Edward and yet he chose another . . . the Woodville lady! My Queen had the wrath . . . *del infierno!*'

He also told us that King Louis was very sick, and this, together with the news from James of Scotland that his country wished for permanent peace, sent us gladdened on our way. But there was still Brittany to shade the brightness of those days. At Richard's command, Dr Thomas Hutton came and went to Duke Francis and returned empty. Sir Edward Woodville still lay in safe harbour. Of the Tydder no one spoke.

So we came at last to York, on the last day of August. The city sprang, like a jewel in a circlet of water, from out the rolling dale. Its walls winked white, and the northern breeze fluttered Margetta's veil as she rode beside me. Behind the high sheriffs went the King and Queen, splendidly mounted, and at their side rolled the little painted chariot containing Prince Edward. He leaned from his litter, waving, his pinched face clothed in smiles. Queen Anne had well-nigh thrown herself from her horse on meeting with him again at Pontefract; I had caught her weightless fall upon my arm. She had not thought to see him until York. He had been caught up in her arms, while, regardless of the crowd, she rained kisses on his face. The King had received his son's obeisance gravely, with a proud, burning look. Coming into York, Margetta's grey brushed against my mount as she said softly:

'Mark you the King's countenance! He sheds ten years!' The winds of York tugged at his purple robe; whipped youth into his face. Near him jogged a plague of bishops: Worcester, Coventry, Lichfield, Durham, St Asaph's, St David's; and clotted all around him were his powerful noblemen—Surrey, Huntingdon, and Lincoln, Lovell, Dudley, Morley and Scrope, Northumberland and Stanley. Yet in the midst of all this might, he seemed, most strangely, to be alone. When we approached the high barbican of Micklegate, two skulls, neatly cleaned by kites, stared out across the dale. As Richard reined in his horse, the sheriffs frowned at one another. There should have been banners only to trap the city wall. Richard paused fleetingly, and then spurred through, to shroud his father's ghost with joy.

For they extolled him above the skies. At each bridge and gate there was a pageant lovingly enacted for his diversion—speeches of honour—cheering, with solid faces split with grins—unashamed welcome under the banners of Christ in Majesty and behind the scenes at the Creed Play. Leaping, they ran alongside us, seeking to touch his robes, and reeling back under the whacks of the perspiring henchmen—light whacks those, for there was no mischief in the clamorous throngs, only a great torrent of affection . . . he was in truth *Ricardus Tertius, Rex Angliae,* yet he was still Dickon, their especial good lord.

In the great new Cathedral Church of St Peter, Edward received his investiture as Prince of Wales. For this, barrels of raiment had come hustling up from London; yards of Holland cloth for all the Household: doublets, gowns, gilt spurs, coats of arms beaten with pure gold, a thousand pennons, and thirteen thousand rampant White Boars for our livery.

Prince Edward took the golden wreath about his brows, the gold wand in his hand. His face was a windflower, pointed and pale. He bore himself nobly, walking hand-in-hand with his parents through the city. And so glorious was this day, men said elsewhere that Richard had celebrated a second coronation . . .

The Ouse lapped against the walls of Gildhall as the King spoke lovingly to York.

'As Englishmen, I cherish you dearly. And I charge you, in all wisdom, to let justice and mercy be your watchwords. Let them illumine your path. Succour those that are oppressed, relieve the poor, and guard your juries against corruption. Every man, be he rich or poor, gentle or simple, warants fair trial. Let not hearsay and malice sway your hearts. *Ita fiat, amen.*'

Then he came down from his dais into the hushed press of people, and took the hands of as many as was possible, and thanked them for their loyalty over the years that had gone. He summoned Kendall and ordained a statute of relief, exempting them from half the tax which York had hitherto paid the Crown.

He left York in joy and glory. The Queen and Prince Edward went north to Middleham, while we rode down to Lincoln, a city of bad and shameful tidings.

Summer was over. The messenger was plastered with mire and dead September leaves.

'Speak,' said Richard tight-voiced. 'Hold naught from your King.'

The messenger—a page named Harry, who had served Richard for many years—rose from his knee and staggered against the King's chair of estate.

'Your Grace's pardon,' he said, choking. 'I have ridden hard from Brecon.'

'Brecon,' said Richard, the surprise fading from his voice. 'I pray you, go on.'

'Yea, Sire, I thought it prudent . . . there is great mischief a-making; I have heard and seen much during my sojourn there. Pray God I am in time to warn your Grace—your friend the Duke of Buckingham . . .'

Here he crimsoned and clutched his left side, speechless.

'My chief minister and trusted ally,' said Richard, expressionlessly.

'. . . has risen in revolt against you, Sire.'

'Did he give reason?' asked Richard.

'Yea, your Grace, but I cannot speak of it . . .'

'Then you are foolish, Harry—you that have served me so well.'

Harry's words came as a cataract, tumbling over one another.

'He vowed that he would have as many Stafford knots as Warwick had ragged staves. Night and day he and Bishop Morton kept company. They grew close, like lovers, and walked together in the quiet ways and spoke together long o' nights. There were messengers . . .'

'Messengers?' Norfolk came close to the young man's side.

'Yea, my lord, from Westminster Sanctuary. That's a hive of treason—Lionel Woodville is arming—the Queen Dow—that is, the Lady Grey, sends thousands of their followers. At first there was talk of storming the Tower to seize the Lords Bastard once again . . . but then Morton—O Sire, I heard William Colyngbourne say . . .'

The King breached the flood with a sharp laugh.

'Colyngbourne! William the Silent—my own Usher!'

'He said that Morton swore vengeance on your Grace for such base treatment that had fallen to his lot.' He turned red again. 'More he said—vile words and imprecations . . . that Morton would show my lord of Buckingham a method of making rulers that would not go unrewarded . . .'

'Unrewarded! Sweet Jesu!' muttered Norfolk.

'Dorset, too, joins the rising.'

'Dorset is in France!' said Richard.

'Nay, lord, he is *not*!' cried Harry, breathless. 'He has been seen in the north parties—none knows who is in the north and who is not!'

'Certes! said Richard, and his eyes looked inward for a moment. 'A wild place—a place of safety. Go on.'

'It is worse, your Grace,' said Harry. He glanced uneasily towards Lord Stanley, who stood near, thin and devout. 'There is one even more powerful in ambition . . .'

'His name?' rapped the King.

'A lady, Sire,' said Harry. 'The Countess of Richmond, Lady Margaret Beaufort.' And with this he cast down his eyes, while Stanley came forward, harried, crablike, with outstretched hands.

'Sweet lord, the shame!' he cried. 'My own wife! It is a madness that comes upon her . . . She thinks overmuch of Henry, her son . . .'

'Of her son upon the throne of England,' said Harry, with a lordly glance at Stanley, who looked furious.

'Hearken to this knave, this popinjay!'

'No knave, Thomas,' said the King. 'He serves me well. Are *you* as loyal, my lord?'

He looked down as Stanley fell to the ground, kissing his robe. Harry had ceased his gasping for breath.

'Tell me what moved my lord of Buckingham,' said Richard.

Harry looked steadily into the King's face.

'Sire, it was but that you would not grant his wish before you quit London, to wed his daughter to your infant son. He would lief be the father of a Queen.'

'As I thought,' said Richard, with a queer smile. 'So now he would be King? How many Pretenders are there, I ask you? He often spoke of his mottled lineage—boasting of Thomas of Woodstock . . . sweet Christ!'

'Yea, your Grace, he lusted to rule,' answered the page. 'But Morton prevailed upon him. 'Tis Henry Tydder whom Morton would have as King,' and he sank his angry young eye again on to Lord Stanley, to whom Richard also turned, with that look of flint.

'How bold my henchman is!' he remarked. 'Should I have him whipped, my lord?'

'Nay, Sire,' said Stanley, cringing. 'He serves you well, that I vow.'

'As you shall,' answered the King. 'To arms! All of you.

Summon up the levies. Now, my friend, what is their number? Which road do they take? Have they guns? Who are their captains? Oxford, I warrant, fruit of Lancaster . . .'

There was a sudden activity in the Hall as the listening company thawed from their strait positions and began hurriedly to disperse, calling for their esquires, sending to rouse the blacksmiths from supper. But Harry lingered, tears in his eyes.

'Henry Tydder makes ready to invade this isle,' he said quietly. 'He and Sir Edward Woodville have a fine fleet.'

'Henry Tydder,' said the King, equally soft. 'That bloody, bastard dog . . . You weep, Harry.'

'Great King, I love thee,' said Harry in a whisper. 'There is more I have not said. Concerning the Lords Bastard in the Tower . . .'

A most peculiar, shuttered look came over Richard's face. 'They shall not have them,' he said. 'No rebellion will begin over the heads of those children . . . Harry, be comfortable.'

'Sire, I shall continue to love thee,' sobbed Harry.

'You have done great service this night,' said Richard. 'Get you gone.'

Harry slid from the tall step, turning quickly. His eyes were sad, like an animal's eyes. Richard beckoned him back. 'What ails you?' he asked.

Harry came closer. 'While they were arming . . .' he said.

'Well?'

'Bishop Morton spoke his mind . . . things of great evil . . . he spoke of the Lords Bastard, Richard and Ned. He said that he will destroy your Grace—if not by the sword, then by the spoken word. By calumny in this isle and abroad.' Terror crossed his face. 'All these things they said . . . and yet I knew not the meaning. Nor do I know it now.'

God sent kind weather to us, that fall. Not sunshine and late flowers, but a fierce, whipping storm that buffeted the ships of Henry Tydder back to Paimpol no less than two days after Duke Francis had sent them out, so gloriously equipped. Men told how they had seen a brace of lonely battered craft still lurking off the Dorset coast, but the shore of Poole was lined with Norfolk's men, and soon the Tydder turned upon the heaving sea with the kick of the wind behind him and English jeers to speed his journey west.

Nor was there mercy for Buckingham, in the eyes of God.

Before our main body launched itself southward, King's men under the command of Humphry Stafford were up ahead of Buckingham, and with a stout and filthy band were wrecking bridges, sealing off passes and making the whole of Hereford Shire an ambush for the Duke. My faithful newsbearer, Richard Ratcliffe, was one of these.

Lying in his bathing-tent, he grinned up at me.

'More hot water!' he cried. 'Pour it on my head, good fellow.' Spluttering, he emerged from the scented cascade. 'Holy Mother, that is good! All the dirt of England clings to me still. Forsooth, a short but muddy little skirmish!'

All over the Palace men were cleansing themselves of that march. And at Salisbury, six feet of the same autumn mire clothed Buckingham.

'How did he die?' I asked.

Ratcliffe grimaced. 'Hotly, and without grace,' he answered. 'He would have felt better, I trow, had one blow been struck. Ah, Richard! What a strategist!' And he launched into a eulogy of the King, of his tactics in driving the wedge between Buckingham and the rebels in the west and south, bubbling soap and enthusiasm while the *valetti* washed him and listened wide-eyed.

'But I ever deemed the Duke was mad,' he said bluntly. 'To set himself against a warrior like the King, and all ill-armed and ill-prepared, with such a scanty following and the cautious Tydder hovering mid-sea . . .' He soaped his hands, lost in his thought. 'I went to call him from his cell to face the jury. He knelt to me, and wept, begging to see the King. "One word only," he repeated, ever and anon. "Take me to him—he will not refuse my plea." And when we told him that Richard utterly abjured his request he smiled strangely and said: "Richard loved me well—he saw dead George in me".'

'Richard would not see him?'

'Nay—he turned his face from those who bore the message and said, hot and cold: "He is the most untrue creature living," and went away. This I told to the Duke, who took his finger from his eye and grew red once more, like a turkey-cock. Then it was I reckoned him mad, in truth, for he babbled of the Lords Bastard, of all things, and said the King would rue the day.'

'What day?'

Ratcliffe shrugged water from his back. 'That day, I trow,' he said vaguely. 'The day they sliced Buckingham's head from his shoulders and the hand off his wrist to brand him a traitor. Mad he was, then and always. Power turns men.'

'So he died bereft of all.'

'Bereft of Morton, his chief adviser,' said Ratcliffe suddenly. 'And there is one who is *not* mad. As wise and cunning as ever Elizabeth Woodville deemed him. We ran him to the monastery of Croyland, in his own diocese of Ely, and there we lost him. He has the Devil's luck.'

'And where lies he now?'

Ratcliffe laughed, shortly. 'Who knows? Men vow he is in Brittany, licking the hurt pride of his Welsh Pretender.' He shuddered. 'Jesu! I would see that prelate's head upon a pike. More hot water, sirs! I am not yet cleansed!'

All this I recounted to Margetta, whom I had not seen for far too long. I swear her wenches lit candles against my lechery. It was not seemly, they whispered, withdrawing from her bower under my gaze. Yet she was not for bedsport that day. She put me off with little words, and as on another occasion, Mistress Shore filled her head.

'By St Catherine, you know what now?' This, with eyes that dulled her diamond reliquary.

'What now, sweeting?'

'The King's Solicitor-General, Sir Thomas Lynom . . .' she whispered.

I stretched upon her bed—coarse fellow, with my boots on.

'A good man, and well-purveyed of livelode,' I said, nodding and smirking.

'He went to see her in Newgate, and now he wants to marry her!'

'Perchance he likes well her body,' I said gently.

'He petitioned the King. Tib told me.'

'Yea, he petitioned his Grace,' I answered.

'What a fool! What hope!' she snapped. 'She is destined to rot and die in Newgate. She wrought great treason against the King.'

'Certes, that she did.'

'Well?' she said angrily. 'What think you of that?'

I summoned my strength. Tall, strong Margetta, I pulled her down beneath me, and bared her twin roses.

'What breasts! What paps!' I murmured. 'There were never such in the whole realm . . . Jenny Shore is an empty gourd compared with this . . . and this . . .' the robe slipped farther . . . 'and there was never such a Mount of Venus in the world . . . not even in Bruges' (Satan on my tongue) 'where the women are wondrous fair.'

'At least I am not a traitor.' She gave a little whine.

'Nay, lady,' said I. 'Yet even an you were, the King would pardon you. For—' holding her tight, arms pinioned—'King Richard has written kindly to the Bishop of London regarding Jane. He would see his Solicitor-General content, and thinks that Jane has suffered over-long in gaol . . . He has had her removed from Newgate, to the care of her father, and says that if good Sir Thomas is still so inclined . . . he . . . shall . . . have her.'

Therewith, feeling and not feeling her little rageful hands beating my back, I did such that made her cry shame, and made me exceedingly well content.

'You live in the old times, sweeting. For it is surely no longer sin to love one's own wife!'

'I am a wicked, envious woman,' she said, beginning to weep.

'Come, be merry,' I said. 'What of my children?'

'The one you gave me that kept me long in York . . . well, you can hear him, bawling for his sire.' And sure enough, little Richard, for so I had named him in the King's honour, was cutting the near-by air with lusty cries.

'Josina is well. She can read better than I. But Edmund—' here she sighed.

'Tall, strong, handy with a bow already,' I said happily.

'My lord, he is past eight years,' she said, frowning. ' 'Tis full time that he left our home. I spoke with my lady of Norfolk lately, wondering where best to place him.'

'Does he still cough?' for Edmund had a grinding in his breast that I had heard before, during the sad hot-weather days of Queen Anne. A thought grew in me, how that Anne waxed pale in London, strong in the north. The King had manors away from all dirt and disease, where henchmen were ever welcome. I began to count off Richard's strongholds in my mind. Sheriff Hutton—his bastard John lived there, young Warwick too, and John, Earl of Lincoln, son of Richard's sister, Elizabeth of Suffolk. Then there was Middleham, wild and beautiful; Pontefract, and Barnard Castle, where, men said, the singing-boys excelled. Edmund had a fair pure voice —he could do well.

I called Edmund and the nurse brought him. His hair was Italian black; he looked foreign. His eyes were grey and looked through me.

I told him he was going away.

'Where, sir?' he asked equably.

'Barnard Castle, an the King sees fit.'

'Yea, good Father,' he answered, and glanced up, with the straight square look of a bowman.

'Shall you speak to King Richard?' Margetta asked.

I deliberated.

'Brackenbury has lately been made Constable of Barnard Castle as well as of the Tower,' I said. 'He shall speak for me.' I looked sharply at Margetta, who was, by her countenance, ill-pleased again.

'Does it not content you?' I asked.

'I was thinking about Jane Shore,' she said. 'Husband, is the King altogether wise? To pardon that strumpet who has wrought him such ill—to approve her marriage with such a great knight. And Stanley! See how he cherishes him, making him Constable of England in lieu of Buckingham, while it was that wife of his who worked this latest mischief. By God, he should hang them all.'

'You would have made a passing fierce monarch,' I said.

'He has not even punished Lady Beaufort,' she said. 'Only bound her to be good a-bearing in surety of her husband. Tib told me.'

'Tib should be an agent of the Crown,' I said a little bitterly, for some days I seemed fogged by ignorance of what was afoot.

'Tib thinks the King is over-gentle,' Margetta said, with a curious look.

'Tib thinks overmuch. Tib will have her tongue in a brace,' I said, angry.

'He's not like Edward,' Margetta said meekly.

'Does Tib know the King?' I shouted. 'Do you know him, my lady? Because he does not milch the City with benevolences—because he does not punish and slay willy-nilly—because he does not lie with every mercer's wife in Bishopsgate —does he displease you? God's Bones, lady, do you know the King?'

Margetta raised eyes, diamond-bright.

'Do *you*, my lord?' she asked.

'My horse!' I shouted, and a page leaped from the hearth-stone. It was because she, my wife, had touched off voiceless doubts lying ever in my mind that I shouted. She might as well have called Richard weak, and I had seen him fighting on the field, a superhuman strength within that frail body— so I was powerfully angered at her *insouciance*.

'I will sup with Sir Robert Brackenbury,' I said, and while she bent again, smiling, to some pretty tapestry of hawks and saints, the echo of my own anger beat at me, for who *does* know a King? As I rode through London, its pavements slimed with dead leaves, I thought to myself: Do I know him? Truly?

There was a mist rising from the river, full of November rot. The Tower, all four hundred years of it, hung ghostly and tall, its feet in fog, its crenellated heights almost gathered into the dark. There was a knot of common people standing beneath the walls of Garden Tower, craning upward as for a visitation. I rode on past them and dismounted at the postern gate, through which a dim red light shone. My second rap brought the sentinel peering through the bars. I asked for Sir Robert.

'He is not here,' said the guard unceremoniously.

I knew these knaves, suspicious, well-flown with pride from sitting in their little brazier-lit cavern, jangling their keys, and kings in their own right.

'Open,' I commanded, raising my shield so that my quarterings were visible.

He disappeared in a cacophony of creaking wards as the great lock yielded. The door groaned upon, revealing familiar sights: scurrying henchmen, great hounds tearing at a bone, a fool with a popinjay, a boy sitting cross-legged, mending a shattered hauberk. A couple of pages wrestled in one corner, oblivious of the fury of two Augustin friars poring over a sacred chronicle. The Constable of the Tower was absent, in truth.

I thought of Sir James Tyrell. He would bear my message, to Sir Robert, if not to the King himself.

'Not here, sir,' said the guard.

'Well, where, then?' I asked hotly. 'And where is Sir Robert?'

'Ridden out,' he said, and looking down, began to whittle a piece of wood.

'Take a message,' I said, my impatience rising.

'Mayhap,' he said, not looking up.

'It is *important*,' I said, between my teeth.

'Great knight,' he answered, 'I know not when Sir Robert will return. He had pressing business in the . . . realm.'

The fellow was concealing something. On whose behalf I knew not, but it made me angrier. I jerked him close to me, and he stared me out, unfeared.

'Do you know me?' I asked.

'Nay, sir,' he said, still staring.

'Why did you open?'

'You are King Richard's man,' he said simply.

I let him go. He was broad as a bull, and seemed twice as dumb. Yet his eyes were crystal clear.

'Can you give this message to Sir Robert on his return?'

'Yea, if he returns,' he said.

'It concerns my son. Tell him I would place him as a henchman. He is eight years, full strong in body and wit. Sir Robert has the wardship of Baynard Castle.'

'None shall enter Baynard Castle,' he said, swaying a little on his feet. If ever I saw one repeating a lesson, here was he. 'There is no room for pages there. It bursts at the seams with boys, Sir Knight.'

Fate was against me, then. This man knew more than I, it seemed. He and Tib would have made a fine pair.

When I rode out the sky towards Westminster was flushed with red as the sun went down, and the little gathering of people still stood with their quiet talk, beneath Tower wall, pointing upward. I reined in by them, following their gaze up to the empty battlements almost completely shrouded by dusk. They talked in low tones: a carter, an old hag, and a young wench who lacked only the gown of ray to play a harlot. Standing a little apart from them was a cowled monk. I caught the tail of their talk.

'Up there they were,' said the carter. 'Each day of last Mayor's term I watched them, shooting at the butts. And a beautiful loose had the little one; he always won.'

'It's not true, certes,' said the young woman, and I heard her start weeping. 'An it is, poor, poor little knaves!'

'Yea, a-playing and laughing they were, lovesome and young,' grindled the old crone. 'Like his father, was Neddie —tall and straight. A-playing and a-growing, unto St Michael near enough.'

The carter spat. 'Aye, 'twas Michaelmas I saw them last—then I saw them not, and thought it naught, till this night when the brother here . . .'

I saw the monk's face, a thin arrow of white beneath his black hood. Then suddenly he spun on his heel, drew fast his robe and went with a steady measured lope across the strip of green, over the cobbles and down to the watergate, whence came presently the plash of oars, fading.

'And never gave us his blessing!' said the carter indignantly.

They saw me, and were a little taken aback. The carter hung his head. The young wench ogled me nervously, but the old crone cried for alms, spreading her ragged skirts. I spun a groat into the darkling air.

'It grows late for sight-seeing,' I said.

'Sir . . . we were looking for a glimpse of . . . King Edward's sons.'

'And did you see them?' I asked pleasantly enough.

'Not for a full moon,' said the carter stoutly.

The old woman came and took my stirrup in her filthy claw. She looked at me with the horrible knavish confidence of the ancient. I felt her spittle-spray.

'The good brother knows,' she whispered, fondling the coin I had thrown her.

'He that was here lately?'

She glanced down toward the dark river. 'Yea,' she muttered. 'Terrible things he told—ah, tales bloody and black. He knows all manner of privy things. About the King . . .'

The carter, tugging, was at her elbow. 'Come home, Meg,' he said, with curses. 'Good my lord, she's old, ale-fuddled. Now she'll drink more, through your lordship's aid. Dame, come away,' he said angrily, prodding her like a sheep.

'What of his Grace?' I said. It was no longer damp, misty, chill November. It was dead winter, and I was in its grip.

'Naught, sir, naught,' said the carter, hauling Meg away. She struck at him, tripping on her kirtle and turning with a swift aimless rage to bawl the last of her precious message.

'The shedding of infants' blood!' she cried, and went flapping across the green.

So was I left, with a piece of ice in my chest and trembling so much that my horse trembled, and the young strumpet stared at me, saying: 'Heed her not, sir,' and looking uneasy: ' 'Twas the holy man who turned her with his talk.'

I looked upon the river and the closing blackness.

'I would speak with yonder holy man,' I said.

She laughed, twisting her hands together. 'He is from afar off. Some land surrounded by water, so he said, where run the blessed streams of righteousness.' She looked down at her feet. 'I have never been out of London, sir.'

My mind took up her words as a man takes up a rotting apple, and spat them out. I thought on Richard Plantagenet. My King. My wife's voice beat at me from the shadows: 'Husband, do you know him? Truly?' How, in God's Name, shall one know a King . . . there have been many Kings, men who lived and squandered and laughed, Kings who wept and prayed and went mad, little Kings deposed by Fortune. King Richard, in glory. All that splendour, at Westminster, in York. All counterfeit? The rarity of his smile. Did that sombre quietness mask a heavy soul? His lenience, his rich bequests

—could they all be made null and void by one dark aching voice? The look upon his face when young Harry spoke of the boys . . . his stillness, his slow but powerful anger, his swift deeds of retribution; no less, and no more, certes, than King Edward's . . . his mercilessness to the traitor Buckingham, who would in truth have shown him none . . . mercilessness even so; his mercy to the Stanleys, Rotherham, Jane Shore . . . ah, Jesu! who should know a King!

As to Edward, the once and never King and his brother . . . the meek Lords Bastard . . . For deposed Kings had been slain before my time. Dickon of Bordeaux had met his end at the hands of his uncles—yet Dickon had defied them, had struck Arundel bloodily upon the mouth in Westminister Abbey, struck him in insult over the corpse of dead Queen Anne. Dickon had died. Men said it. And now men said the Princes were no more. So groaned the treadmill of my thought.

The wench was staring at me. I could not answer her, or myself.

That was the evening of the first whisper. I rode home, wounded most grievously, in the chill dark.

'Do you know the King, Margetta?'

'My lord?'

'Would you know him?'

She little guessed how lustily I owned that longing. For I now watched Richard with a great unbelieving fear, a hope and then a sadness, seeing his quiet, quiet countenance, remembering him when he had caught at my heart in his black mourning on White Surrey—when he had known my fault, had pardoned me. I scanned his face as closely as I were his leman, anxious for any sign that might give me the knowledge I feared, the release I longed for.

And I would with all my heart that we were again brothers in exile, that he were Dickon and I were Mark Eye, and I could lean over the table and ask him, with my branded hand on his: 'Are the Lords Bastard safe, my friend?'

I took my daily walk around the Tower, and there were at most times little idling crowds, upward-looking. Two days before Epiphany I heard another whisper. My ears were strained for such murmurs, as for an ambush. Two friars it was this time. One was counting the day's gettings, and his words were punctuated by the sharp rattle of coin.

'I had it on good authority,' he said. Clink.

The other crossed himself, his lips moved in a novena, while he looked envious at the other's purse. He was stout, like Hood's henchman in the ballads. His voice was like a draught of oil.

'Tell me, tell me. What method did they use?'

'Oh, that I know not,' said the counting friar. 'But he is wise, my friend, and vows they are no more.'

'Crushed to death?' said the stout one quizzically. 'Strangled? Sancta Maria, what wickedness rules us now!'

'Man was ever cursed,' said the other. 'Pray for their souls.' Clink.

'Ah God, yea,' babbled the fat one lugubriously. 'For they went violently, and all unassoiled!' Then, thinking so hard that a crease threaded his plump brow: 'I would have staked all that . . . hm, hmm, that he was a devout man. I would not have deemed him one to leave any without *Dirige* and *Placebo*—whatever the deed . . . say, tell me again, who spoke you of all this?'

'A monk of Calais,' said the other, counting still. 'A Cluniac, well schooled and born in Paris . . .'

'A Frenchman,' said the fat one doubtfully.

The other dropped a mark, retrieved it with creaking joints.

'Men say,' he murmured calmly, 'men say the princes are no more. In France they sing of it. And in the fen country where English live and die . . .' Clink. 'They write of it. It is the truth.'

'Shall we wager on it?' said the fat friar wickedly. The other snapped his shoulders, cast a glance up at the Tower ramparts.

'An you will,' he said. 'Five marks they are not seen again —' he pointed—'where once they played so merrily.'

It was January when I asked Margetta would she know the King, and I took her to the special Court in the White Hall, which Richard had initiated to hear solely the pleas and grievances of the commonalty. Me, I had no mind any more. I watched my wife as she listened to the requests and to the answers they received at the King's signet.

'. . . that Robert Bolman, under-clerk in the Privy Seal office, has been overpassed in the promotion list by one Richard Bele—who by gift of money and by corruption of the other clerks has unlawfully attained such promotion; that this stranger, never brought up in the said office, should be ordered to stand down, and Robert Bolman succeed to the post, for his good and diligent service. Richard Bele, however, to be granted a clerkship at the first vacancy.'

'. . . that the Prior of Carlisle being hard pressed to meet the £8 fee to Chancery for his royal licence . . . let the Clerk of the Hanaper return these monies gratis.'

'. . . that the Vicar-General of Paynton, Master John Combe, shall promote Master Rauf Scrope to the Vicarage, which Master John Combe has presented himself by crafty dealing and to the undoing of Master Rauf . . .'

'An annuity to our faithful minstrels, John Green and Robert Hawkins, who have served us well.'

'The sum of forty-six pounds thirteen shillings and four pence to the repairing of the Church of Creyke, County Norfolk, lately destroyed by fire.'

'. . . that Edmund Filpot of Twickenham, a bricklayer, who by misfortune had all his thirteen tenements, his dwelling and his goods suddenly burnt to his utter undoing, and who kept in his household a great degree of poor creatures much refreshed by his generosity—a Royal protection requiring of alms for the rebuilding of same.'

'To one Master John Bently, clerk of poor estate, four pounds to defray his expenses at Oxford University . . .'

'Know you the King?' I asked Margetta harshly, as we left the White Hall.

She shook her head. She looked a little dazed.

'He seems a fair man,' was all that she could say. And ever, the roll read to the juries who tried cases in the Court of Common Pleas:

'We charge you straitly to defend all our commons against oppressors and extortioners, to dispense justice without fear or favour, in merc and fairness to all men, guarding against bribery and corruption. Justice for each man, be he humble or great. We charge you directly to follow our will in this.'

And all the time my treacherous heart beat out the rhythm of my pain. Where are the sons of Edward? Where? Where?

A cloud born of the news of the Tydder crept across the sun, word of a fresh invasion, of which King Richard disdained to speak in his correspondence with Brittany, as if deeming the Pretender of scant importance. Yet he was wary. Soon after the final sitting of his Parliament we took horse for Nottingham. That gloomy rock, that impenetrable fortress. At its feet, the town sprawled, straggling; all around for many leagues the flat counties, bristling black forest, lay under our surveillance. Here, the King's hand rested upon the heart of the Midlands; a dozen couriers stood ready. Here, he could watch and wait, as he and I had once done together, young knaves, coaxing the nervous hours with chess. I was closer to him then. I asked him many questions and got fair answer, that other time at Nottingham. You shall ask a Duke but not a King. Had kingship changed him so utterly, or was it my own dread mefiance?

March yielded to April on our ride. A soft April of beauty, of stark branches suddenly clothed in tender green, and, new-washed by the drifting rain, each tight bud at last abandoned to flutter and show against the sun's gleam; then a fast-flying oyster sky, then sun again. The calling throstle and robin dropped beads of song like jewels; in every tree there was a cuckoo, bold and full-throated and mocking. Gentle tips of green encroached upon the road. It grew hotter. On one side there was beauty, a field palled with gold and white, buttercup and dog's-eye; on the other, merriment, as a rabbit washed behind its ears, saluting our splendour from a moss-green dais.

The Queen was sad, none the less. Gently, springshowerly sad. Her escort hung back and I took his place, on my sorrel, old now but still prancing the merry season out under her hoofs. Anne smiled at me.

'It will be beautiful, northward, now, your Grace.'

'The beck will be in spate,' she said, bowing her head. I cursed my tongue. We were not riding that far north. Not to Middleham, and Edward of Middleham, who made all things green.

'How does the Prince of Wales?'

Before she could answer, there was a scudding of hoofs and black regal looks from the Earl of Northumberland, come with tidings of the rebels still free, who had espoused Buckingham's cause and roamed the country. The Crown Lieutenant read of the latest captures: Turbyrville, and Colyngbourne had been sighted. Twitching, sparse-spoken William had a price on his head. Last Tuesday forenoon he had been pursued and lost in London.

'What news of France?' asked the King.

'Divided, and squabbling, since Louis's passing.'

'A minority rule moves people thus,' said Francis Lovell. He rode close to Richard, making him laugh, touching his sleeve, pointing to a soaring lark and sending up his peregrine halfway to heaven in swift victory.

'So perish your Grace's enemies,' he remarked, as the two birds clashed mid-sky. Sir William Catesby and Richard Ratcliffe jogged at the King's side. They talked of the Parliament.

'Justice for all,' said Ratcliffe soberly. 'How they extolled your Grace! And the statute of bail—why, they cried for Richard an 'twere Cœur de Lion returned!'

'It was but their due,' said Richard, and his face beneath the black velvet bonnet with its pearl brooch became a little more set. So Lovell cut in with a quip, peering forward to see his sovereign's thoughtful smile. He loved him deeply, that was plain, as did Ratcliffe—and there was near-worship on John Kendall's face. Had they heard the whispers? I mused; could they feel and do thus, if they had? They were none of them dissemblers—they were heartily pleased with the new Parliament and clung close to their King. Northumberland thought differently. With all his unhampered governance of the North, the Parliament gave him no joy. I had learned this through my need for a flagon of ale on a fierce March day, a fortnight earlier.

In the Mermaid, the booths are built like prayer-stalls, dark, high-backed. So it was only Northumberland's voice, buzzing to my ear through four-inch oak, that told me of his presence. Neither had he seen me enter, from Friday Street. He had companions with him, two familiar voices and one to which I could not fit a face. They spoke of the King's new statutes, with the incautiousness born of anger. Disgust rode high in Northumberland's voice.

'And at Oxford, because there was a man, a common peasant, who tattled of some poxy deed, said he'd been misused. . . .'

'Dog should have been whipped,' said Sir William Stanley.

'Misused, because he could not read the law!' pursued Northumberland. 'Thus, old Dick—' this contemptuously— 'turns the world about—commands the statutes *writ in Eng-*

377

lish! Jesu, now every snivelling dunghill whelp shall know himself a lettered man—like you, or I.'

'The swine love him for't.'

'Yea. Perchance he would compose his Council of poor clerks and alewives!'

' 'Tis what he deserves, certes,' said the voice unknown.

'Push not so hot.' (Thomas Stanley's voice.) 'Kneel to the King. Always.'

'I had no other thoughts,' said Northumberland mildly.

Someone laughed. There was brief silence.

Then: 'For how would you raise your levies now?' A fist boomed on the table.

'The evils of livery and maintenance!' came Northumberland's voice, cold with anger. 'When he spoke out thus against it—Sweet Christ, I had ado to hold my tongue!'

Yea, Richard had forbidden this practice of binding oneself to a lesser lord and, fleetingly, I saw myself riding beneath Dorset's standard. Yea, my lords, thought I, how will you raise your murderers now? Then, that righteous glow died in me, for to murder a murderer is surely just. God, where are the sons of Edward?

'Yea, but how would you?' persisted that quiet, unidentifiable voice.

'By loyalty, the King says,' and there was a general burst of mirth.

'You look princely yourself, today,' said the younger Stanley.

'God be praised, I am well-purveyed,' answered Northumberland. Then, fiercer: 'Long may I continue . . . know you he has halved the Crown dues on no less than eighteen cities?'

'Soft, sir,' said Lord Stanley unexpectedly. 'I . . . I fear him.'

Caxton had entered then, bearing the *Order of Chivalry*, its words still moist. He had promised it for Sir Robert Brackenbury, but could not resist showing it to a few friends. I glimpsed the dedication: 'Long life to King Richard, prosperous welfare and victory over all his foes.' Caxton smiled, bearded, gentle and with that pungent whiff of ink that clung to all his gowns, more sumptuous now than in days past.

'His Grace came to see me at work yesterday,' he said proudly. 'We talked of the old time in Flanders. I had forgot most, but not he; how I showed him the Jason tapestry and the Palace of Wonder at Hesdin. A little, stern knave he was.

378

"York will triumph," he would say, staring me in the eye. "My brother will give us the victory." 'Tis years ago. Then, I did trade in clothing . . .' he tapped the book tenderly, blew invisible dust from its cover, 'not this.'

Then I heard Northumberland's party leaving. With spur-song and hush of velvet they were gone, out into Bread Street, but the faint rustle behind me told that one of them remained. I heard him swallow and set his cup down. The Flemish Friedeswide, the tapwench, came to me smoothing her kirtle. I asked her: 'Who sups there, alone?'

She peeped round the corner of the booth.

' 'Tis but a poor old monk,' she said, shrugging. 'Brother Jasper, they call him.'

A customer shouted for her, pressed a mark into her hand put his fist into her bosom. I heard steps behind me, as one unseen joined Brother Jasper. There was a trifle of whis-pering, like rats in the woodwork.

'So, how goes it?'

'Well enough,' said the new voice.

'From shore to shore?'

'Hardly, my friend. Scarcely. *Yet.*'

A deep sigh. 'Time hangs.'

'Rather time than ourselves . . .' Murmurings. '. . . he sends greeting to all his followers . . . something embittered by delay . . . he is a passionate young man.'

'Yet my lady's commands must be obeyed.'

'Yea, forsooth, slowly and with great care. A pinprick here, another there, until the time be full . . .'

'Holy God, I cannot wait!' Sudden emotion charged the monk's voice.

'But wait you must,' said the other sharply. 'Dame, bring double-beer!' and of a sudden he began talking of fee-farms and the price of corn. Such a curious conversation would not have stuck in my mind had I been happy and sound, as once I was, but now I listened to everything, in mortal dread.

As I moved towards the door, my thigh struck a table at which sat an ancient man, his crusted beard dribbling in spilled drink. He cursed me wantonly. Angerless, I clapped down a coin in recompense and made to pass on. To my sur-prise he swept the money from the table and glared at me drunkenly.

'This will na' buy me wine.'

'Wine is rich for an old belly.' I saw red gold clutched tightly in his hand. Too feeble for a cut-pouch, too silly for an extortionist. Drinking Rhenish in the Mermaid. His eyes fixed on my livery and the Boar emblem at my breast. Then, leaning, he let fall a gob of spittle near to where I stood.

'King's man!' he said softly, and it could have been the worst oath, the cruellest miscalling in the world. So I waited, not angry, no longer wondering. He rose a little from his bench, wavered and sat again.

'He will be judged.' His eyes were closed. Sweat crowned their lids. 'He will be judged for't. God in His Heaven will punish him. Mark me well.'

I could have called him out for blasphemy, heresy, treason. Yet I feared his words so much that I called only Friedeswide, said, a puny potentate: 'Serve him no more drink,' and passed out into the wind that whipped my eyes to tears, so that I of the keen sight could not even see across Friday Street. Therefore . . . even had I looked back into the dark tavern at those who had murmured behind me, I would not have recognized the marguerite of Reynold Bray, Lady Beaufort's clerk, or the face of Jasper Tydder, blood-kin to the Dragon.

I could have spoken to Lovell, Norfolk, Ratcliffe; to any of the King's lawyers and chaplains. I could have described those who spoke against his Grace and they would have been discovered in their hovels, for all were lowly and mean and stupid, the sort King Richard loved best, going by his statutes. They were so dreadful to me. Their faces hung mouthing above my sleep. The Mermaid whisper was, I think, the worst. In all its drunken utterance it was passive, logical. One night I awoke howling like a dog. For I had seen Richard, black-clad, his feet upon the Boar, and the Boar was devouring something . . .

I spoke only to Margetta, for I feared the truth.

Tib had heard naught. I made my lady question her and she, in turn, questioned me, touching my face with her velvet fingers, saying I grew lined and old and surly, and that she loved me. So I closed all the doors and windows and told her a very little, as much as I dared. She went and picked up the infant, Richard, and called Josina, whom she held at her knee, close-clipped.

'Well, what then?' she said, her voice hard and steady. 'He is King, is he not?'

'Yea, anointed in the sight of God. And in the sight of God, I love him still. Am I, in my own heart, a traitor?'

'So!' she said. 'Enthroned, he rules England. You prate of whisperings: can they uncrown a King?'

She was holding Josina so tight that the child squirmed away. She looked down at the babe's head.

'Do the whispers speak sooth, my lord?'

But my thoughts were running, leaping like a third voice under the weight of our conversation. My thoughts were nonsense, sliding into a vision inopportune. Myself, a young knave in Kent. My guardian had had cut for me two dozen arrows, tipped with the grey goose wing. I, churlishly lingering on a hold, had spoiled the shoot, seeing my fine new dart thrust out across a stream. In a wheatfield I sought it, hearing already my tutor's scolding, dreading the lash across my buttocks. In every furrow I had parted wet green blades, running, bending, groping. Even so did I chase my own elusive thoughts, seeking the shape of that third voice which uttered words heard somewhere once before, all in a hurry . . .

A young, tearful voice: '. . . to destroy your Grace, not by the sword . . .'

Young Harry the page, regal in his mud.

Margetta was talking. 'He is secure—only the Tydder threatens, and he's a coward, by all reckoning . . . Richard cannot be slain by a whisper.'

('Not by the sword, your Grace—not by the sword . . .')

'You do not answer me,' said Margetta, and suddenly a tear dropped upon the babe's head. 'O God, did any labour to harm my children, I would haunt him with a curse, unto my last breath. I would find blackest poison to sweat the bowels from him who touched my babes . . . I would give my body to be burned . . .'

I had them all against my heart. My gold collar rasped Josina's cheek and she began to cry, which set the infant bawling. At other times we would have laughed, been gay.

'Hush,' I said, 'hush,' and rocked them, like a cumbersome wetnurse.

Even now, and now especially, I shrink from the remembrance of one evening in Nottingham. He had ever disliked the place, and it brought to me the echo of our sleeplack and his nightlong prayer, in the time when we rode together against Clarence and Warwick. Devout he was! I tried to look upon him without love. Devout he was still, but had kingship changed him?

While climbing the hundred steps of the sheer face of Nottingham's grey fortress, I caught the thread of his heart and knew him determined to lift the gloom of that castle with gaiety. In truth, he had food for rejoicing; for the Scots were clamouring for peace.

It was the day the envoy came, monstrous tall with great grey eyes and the tartan of Lyle, to stand before the king who had given his country so many hard buffets. I had heard that such as he were wont to give terrible skirling cries in battle, like the fiends of Hell, yet there he stood, calm enough, and wondering 'was there no better way to end the matter?' Queen Anne, under her state canopy, smiled a little at the Scot and pressed her hands together, as if also hoping the business mended, and then, mayhap, a release from Nottingham, which was not far north enough for Anne. And a bird came rap-tapping at the high rock-hewn window over her head, dancing on a sprig of wild roses and tapping as if the window were a snail. The halting negotiations continued; the Scot was difficult to comprehend—at times the King spoke French and things went better, while in idleness I watched that bird, who tapped and tapped discourteously above the royal dais, and then seemed to court madness, for it ceased suddenly and began to dash itself at the oriel's pane ever and anon, its soft body thudding against the cruel glass. After a while the King remarked the interruption, motioned a page to drive the bird away. He glanced swiftly at his Queen, leaned to her, whispered, then asked the Scot:

'Will my lord continue the discussion over supper?'

The gathering in the hall dispersed, and outside I heard men talking.

'His Grace has ordered a banquet this evening, and entertainment.'

'What, for the kilted one, of the red beard and knees?'

'Nay, for the Queen's pleasure; he thought she seemed cast down.'

What kind of a man, thought I. What manner of man? Ruthless and secretive, the purveyor of black and bloody things, and yet, so kindly? Then I thought, in my great cleverness, of the Archer's Paradox: the loosed arrow strikes a course not followed by the string—it is bent a little away on one side. It regains its straight trajectory on following the bow. Was Richard Plantagenet then, a paradox, cast in flesh? I summoned all my loathing and looked on him, and his quiet face bemused me.

The Scot seemed impressed by the revel. Me, I moved among the thronging dancers, courting the fairest; I pleasured myself; I watched the King. I listened, idly though. There were no whispers at Nottingham.

'Heard you the news? Francis of Brittany has gone mad.'

'Then there's an end to the King's hopes of a treaty.'

'Nay, the reverse. Landois is weak, and hated by the nobles. He'll be glad to treat with Richard. Mark me.'

'And where will the Pretender be then?' Loud, joyful laughter.

'Restored back to his native soil, given a beating, sent supperless . . .'

'And we could leave this thorny spot.'

'The waiting galls me too . . . *will* he invade, think you?'

'Certes, I fear his lady mother more than he! 'Tis against nature for woman to be so learned!'

Verily, they were gay.

What of Richard, and Anne? He danced with none other, and for a soldier he was graceful, while she was like apple-bloom, drifting on the wind. Slowly, as the coming of spring after an iron-fierce winter, her sombre mien faded; she yielded to joy. He took her in the fair old basse-danse: *'Belle, qui tiens ma vie'*. As she hopped and twirled her saffron silks flew out and her Florentine collar of pearl-and-silver, the King's gift, wept beauty in the dancing light. The candles wore down. He kissed her, and she broke a rose from the table-trimmings and placed it in his cap.

I watched them, in their last moment of happiness.

It was not late when they left the Hall, hand in hand. The minstrels were packing their instruments away. There had been a woman from the town, who sang with a fiddle, a sweet, mystic song of love and death. The air was warm with crushed flowers and the breath of wine. A trailing spray of white violets clung to my shoe as I climbed the stair. It was not quite dusk, so I went up on to the battlements. The air curled about my face, soft; it would be a fine day on the morrow. At each corner the lookout stood like granite. I leaned under the greenish sky, sniffing the breeze, scanning the darkening plain. Below, the town covered its fires; each little point of light wavered, burnt up bright, and was stilled to blackness. My sight was good that night, keen and far to where the winding road, outlined by pale thorn trees, clove through the meadow; the road north, for which Anne yearned. One star was out, and half the moon pricked my sight. A boy I once knew had seen God among the stars, in a great trailing grey robe, and thought his day of judgment to be at hand, and swooned, never the same after. I looked swiftly downward, over the sweep of rock, past the jagged stones girdling the foot of the castle, and saw a horseman riding through the bailey. A lone horseman, who rode so slowl[y] that it was easy for my eye to catch at his dusky colours, an[d] know him for a royal herald; but his face bowed low upon hi[s] breast as if he were loath to enter Nottingham. As loath t[o] look upward as was that boy, after seeing the Judgment o[f] God.

There were too many of us, outside the royal chamber. Wit[h] scarcely room to breathe in the corridor, it was like a beehive[,] the priests muttering all together in the confined space. [I] thought then: there should be only one, or two, to knock and enter. I would not be that one, but I am here, who woul[d] fain be elsewhere. When the Squire of the Body drew bac[k] the latch he looked frightened, unsure. He murmured; 'Th[e] King and Queen have retired,' and pointed at the inner cham[-] ber, then Norfolk bent to whisper in his ear and we went in[,] without a sound, the priests no longer murmuring of comfort[,] the boards beneath too dolorous to creak.

Richard and Anne sat by the dying fire, robed for th[e] night. Her hair hung down, pale against the flames, and hi[s] hands, nurse-tender, caressed its wealth. He rose upon seeing us, while Anne's women moved nervously to her side. H[e] asked, with less annoyance than I would have shown: 'Wha[t] means this?'

He glanced from one to the other, at the white, crowding faces, and none spoke.

'Ill news?' he asked.

Norfolk cleared his throat, a dreadful, grating noise.

'Ill news, Sire.'

The King came to us, brows drawn together.

'Well?' he said quietly. 'Is there ever aught else? Tell m[e] . . . the rebels have invaded? Come, tell me the worst.'

His eyes still moved, calm, questing. The silence grew in- supportable. I looked sharply at Francis Lovell who stood clenching and unclenching his hands, waxing red and white, bright-eyed.

'Sirs,' said the King uneasily, 'your news, I pray you.'

Lovell stepped forward, and stumbled.

'Sire,' he whispered, 'I would give every drop of blood in my heart to spare you this . . .' Then, reason forsook him and he said: 'Ah, Dickon, Dickon . . .'

'Speak,' said Richard. The word dropped like an icy pelle[t] of rain.

'Your son is dead,' said Lovell.

384

The Queen's first scream brought sweat gushing on my brow. She ran forward, her hair streaming like a shroud, ghostly in the tortured air, and she clawed at it, tearing out great hanks; she screamed and screamed and ran, from table to chair, from door to arras, beating and tearing at her own head while her women sought in vain to grasp her.

Norfolk and I caught the King as he fell.

At first I thought that he too would die, but he was strong and, as he said, ever inured to ill-fortune. Yet from that day I never heard him laugh, and for many weeks, when he had learned to sleep o'nights without weeping, he did not smile. With others, I nursed him, as well as I could. He lay on the borders of madness. And I was rent by his whispering voice, crying in the depths of his anguish: 'My son, my son, my sweet son!'

I fed him the root of mandragora that brought him an evil, drugged rest. I sang to him on the harp, like David . . . I talked ceaselessly until he bade me silence, and what I talked of, or what he answered, I know not. I remember only one thing he said during those terrible days at Nottingham.

'Truly,' he said, looking about him with vacant gaze, 'truly, this is the Castle of my Care.'

'My entirely beloved son, whom God pardon.'

Thus spoke Richard, leaving Middleham for the last time. The castle's great shadow stretched forward and touched us darkly. Edward lay at Sheriff Hutton; they had embalmed him, from his pale windflower face to his small straight feet. He slept beneath a heavy load of finest marble, bright with the quarterings of Neville and Plantagenet, and he played somewhere beyond the stars. He had not been sick, said Dame Jane Collins, when she could still her sobs—he was hale in the forenoon, then later complained of pain in his head and his bowels and burned up, despite all, all, most dread Sire. He sank into fever sleep and sleeping, died.

Ratcliffe called me to the King's presence.

'He is pleased by your watching with him in his sorrow.'

Irony. My bearing with him, of God's judgment.

'He commands you to remain north.'

Irony. Ratcliffe said sharply: 'He does you honour.'

From the chantry came the thin high sound of Edward's first requiem. Ratcliffe glanced towards the singing.

'May blessed St Anthony guard him ever.'

At Middleham, the figure of Anthony, richly carved, gazed down from the priest's stall. Anthony, patron saint of youth. And of swineherds, having the boar at his feet.

'He would ask me often the story of the boar,' Richard said, looking somewhere over our heads. Deep lines graved his face, as if newly carved by some mischievous mason. His cheeks were gaunt as a hollowed hand. I missed a feature hitherto taken for granted; the brightness of his eyes. I saw them dull, like riverstones, eyes at the bottom of a stream, and thought, without satisfaction and in great sadness: thus has his judgment maimed him.

'Yea, Sire, the Boar, the White Boar,' muttered Lovell, so put about still by grief that he would have talked nonsense, had the King wished it.

'Lady Croft spoke me often of boars when I was five, puling and sickly,' said Richard dementedly. 'She called me the Tantony Pig . . . a boar guards her tomb, she loved me. Ah God! the world is full of tombs. They weigh it down.'

A robin (that same harbinger of death?) alighted in the window and, jouncing on an ivy twig, began its exquisite song.

'How does my Queen?' he asked, and even here there was no comfort, for Anne it was now who had to be conveyed in a chariot; Anne, who had wept every league to Middleham and, if she attempted to rise, swooned. She broke her sleep with little sobbing cries which turned to coughing, coughing. No balm could ease that cough.

'Should she stay here?' he said doubtfully to old Dr Hobbes. 'I must to Scarborough; our fleet is ready and Norfolk needs my eye, my signet; but the Queen cannot ride . . .'

'Your Grace will not leave without her,' said Master Hobbes, with a little smile. 'Not one mile shall you be apart now. She vows it.'

It was then that Richard quit the room, to sit beside the Queen, clasping her hand for many hours.

Thus, that summer of 1484—why, 'twas last summer!—I spent at York, and participated in the Council of the North, which was a machine of such wonderful ordinance that it was famed abroad. And I made journeys to the ridge of Scotland and back, a royal letter-bearer, one of many who kicked up England's turves in King Richard's courier system. By means of relay, so could a man in London get his bills within two days and a transaction be complete in less than a week. So the saying 'news travels fast' gave birth to rememberings in me, and, o'nights, lonely without Margetta, I thought of the two poor sons of Edward, sticked with a dagger so men said, and cast into the ocean. Yet, strangely, there was half the despair in those thoughts while I lived in the north country. Among those barren crags and wild rapids, with the sudden natural shocks abounding—a bleak moor crowned with a noble abbey, the majesty of bright water falling through pure rocks, and trees to shame the emerald—there was the flavour of peace, of continuity. Stern country it was, in truth, but when it smiled . . . !

I came again to London, in November, where the King lay sick of a fever. And there, I was sorry. It burns me with sorrow, Master Brecher, to think on this.

By river I went, straightway to Westminster, shunning the public ways. For although, north, I had been free of whispers, the knowledge of their being sucked at my soul like a tapeworm in the belly of a child. My waterman, hunched raven-like against the fog, cried of the latest news over his shoulder. Tidings good and bad—trade with abroad was flourishing—piracy was less. His uncle, or cousin (Lord, how he prattled!) got reparation for a ship taken by French privateers last month. London was thronged with Germans and Scots devils. The King's Grace had not been seen for days— did I think he was laying plans to withstand the invasion— for the Earl of Richmond would surely assay, come spring, to rape the realm?

So the Tydder called himself Richmond, now. Impudent. King Edward, dying, had termed him so, to Stanley, bidding him watch his wife . . . 'Let not her impudent son aspire to harass my heir . . .' Dear Jesu, I would not think on that heir, or his brother. I would fold my mind as the boatman folded the wool about his ears against the creeping fog. For I was bound to the service of King Richard, and I would fain forget a little, seeing that he was sick.

We whirled on a full-flowing cross current, passing beneath the bridge. The Tower, far behind, was a white blur in the greyness. Becalmed again, the oarsman sang to me, gaily, of Henry Tydder.

'Does his mother live yet?' he asked me.

I would not think on Edward's sons, for should I be called to nurse the King, I might harm him with a thought. Yet . . . were they stabbed in the throat, and with whose blade? Not

Brackenbury's, by all the saints, or Tyrell's . . . there would have been assassins, paid silent men. King Richard's men, snuffing those lives with gold-gloved hand.

'Aye, fellow, the Countess is hearty.'

'Then he is not Earl of Richmond,' bawled the boatman, shipping his oars, his riddle solved. At Westminster pier I paid him his penny, while the Devil himself hung cackling at my elbow: 'See you aught of the Lords Bastard?' I watched his brow wrinkling, saw him counting the months, and dared not wait on his answer.

So I went on up the slimy stair, and without the Palace gate there was a herb-seller, standing with her pannier full of sweetness, wondrous fresh and fair, a maid that looked up at me with her virgin's eyes, child-eyes clear and sheen.

'Look, Sir Knight!' she said, pushing the little bunches towards me. 'Good spice! Brought all the way from Eden—down the river that flows from Paradise!'

I looked, at her shining face, and the nepenthe she offered me, and I stooped to kiss her soft mouth, and then I bought from her a root of the Black Hellebore, perchance to ease my melancholy, and a sprig of Valerian, Our Lady's blessed herb, that drives all ills away. She looked up at where the royal standard hung in mist, and said simply: 'God send the King good fortunes,' and so fair was she, she minded me of another clean young face I had once seen, and forgotten. And I ran up the steps through the stony guard, and entered Westminster.

'On your life, let none know he is sick.' This was Lovell, gliding like a wraith beside me in the passage.

'What ails his Grace?'

'I am not a physician,' he said, frowning. 'I know only that he has pushed himself to the edge of disaster this summer. Since the Prince of Wales died, he was wont to ride ten leagues a day and work half the night. He came from revictualling the fleet at Scarborough worn to the bone.'

We reached the King's chamber.

'Only yesterday could he bring himself to name his heir,' said Lovell softly. 'He wanted Warwick, but the child's near-idiot, and under attainder . . .'

'Who, then?'

'John, Earl of Lincoln,' said Lovell. 'Also a true Plantagenet.'

I entered the King's chamber, afraid. Flames ate steadily at a great log the length of the hearth, while the doctors clucked and chaffered around the King, who sat uneasily in a chair near the warmth, with the shadow of the flames licking his cheek. Papers lay strewn before him, and Kendall leaned to catch words and write them down, words wellnigh buried beneath the fussing voice of Masters Hobbes itching to use his blood-irons.

Kneeling, I presented the dispatches from York. I fastened my gaze upon the hands lowered to me, and their heavy rings. On his thumb the King wore a skull wrought from a ruby, wondrous small. A *memento mori*, of God's Death, and the ultimate destiny of man; I heard my voice expressing my sorrow in his sickness.

'It is little,' he said. ' 'Twill soon be mended.'

'If your Grace would only rest!' cried Hobbes despairingly.

I looked up at last, to see the King's profile flickering against the flames.

'You make much of naught,' said Richard.

I could hear one of the other physicians muttering crossly: 'Fits, faints, swoons! May I go hang if these are naught!'

'Is York still fair?' Richard asked me.

'Yea, lord, the fairest city in your realm . . . in great St Peter's the choir excels . . .

He was scanning the rolls I had brought, eagerly murmuring to himself each signature as it unrolled beneath his eye; the Mayor and burgesses; the Council of the North; the writings from the Gaol delivery. Once, he said: 'Good!' then he knit his brows, held the paper closer, sighed, let it fall, and passed a hand over his eyes. The physicians stopped whispering and waited.

' 'Tis more an agony of spirit, this,' he said, so softly that only a few caught it. 'I shall retire now.'

They pulled out the trestles from under the King's bed. I knew that four or five would watch him this night, as he was so unwell. I picked up the parchment he had dropped, a bill for the Masses at Sheriff Hutton, for Edward's soulkeeping. Then, amid a rising babble of protest, he said: 'I would be alone tonight. One only shall guard me,' and his eyes, with the red firelight still in them, fell and rested on my wretched face.

'You shall give me the news of York,' he said softly. 'That will bring sleep, better than any potion.'

They withdrew swiftly, too swiftly, all of them, while I, seeking to calm a strange new trembling, put the great dog which seldom left him outside to the grooms' hands, and drew the bolt stoutly across, and went with my drawn sword behind the arras and in the gardrobe; I smoothed back the damask sheets and the purple coverlet, and set the Night Livery, the bread, the wine, on a side table ready for his need. I received his jewelled collar, and turned a key upon it. I unrobed him of the silk shirt, the fine hose, and felt them burning damp, like a marsh-fire. And I gowned him for bed to which he climbed, to lie looking at me. So was I left alone, with the King who, men said, had had his nephews put to bed for ever.

I had not been alone with him before, not even at Nottingham, and there, in any case, he hardly knew me, for he was in Hell.

How should I sleep? Close to his feet I lay, houndlike, staring at the ceiling. The fiery shadows played games there, dark demons among running blood, open-mouthed faces screaming without noise. There were no sounds, but once, faintly, I thought I heard the clank of a halberd outside the door; again, lying wide-eyed, I seemed to hear quiet coughing . . . Lovell said that the Queen coughed all night. A sick Queen, a sick King. A dead Prince. God's indignation at its mightiest. All quiet again.

He had been kindly to me in Flanders, when I had worried and wept over Margetta, and for this reason I sat up and looked, over the mounded quilts, to whence the King's soft breathing came. I saw the dark of his head against the rich carvings, thrown into sharp relief by the flickering fire. I looked at him, and at the panels depicting the Holy Sepulchre on this bed, the only bed that he could sleep in, and which, said Lovell, he took everywhere. It could be broken down and amassed again within the hour. He was breathing almost noiselessly, and I lay low again, thinking great treason —the same thoughts of course, and I was thankful that thoughts are soul-sealed, to be given tongue only by the old, the drunk, the mad.

I know not how long I mused thus, feeling my trembling that grew and grew until the trestle quaked beneath me, nay, shook the great bed of the King, until I was afeared I would awaken him, and, trying to still my limbs, knew with a start that it was not my trembling, but his, Richard's. It shook the bed, my trestle, as if a giant's hand rocked it. Then I heard him moan once, through his teeth, and like an arrow I was at his side.

I touched his hand, to find it cold as glass, like an empty hearth in a ravaged castle. Chill moisture stood on his brow, and yet the room was warm still, warmer than comfortable—and Richard cold.

I ran and poked the fire, clattering the irons about. I chafed his frigid hands in mine, piled furs upon the bed. Even in the half-light I could see his pallor, and how his eyes roved about. And I thought: Is there no end to this judgment? He is still my King.

'Sire, you are frozen—a posset—I will fetch Master Hobbes—' I said wildly.

He caught my hand. A grip as hard, as cold as stone.

'Nay,' he said, and his teeth chattered. 'They are . . . too many . . . good doctors all, but they stifle me with their ardour . . . there's no cure for this sickness. I am not sick.'

I stepped away from him, to lap his feet in blankets, poured wine, which he spilled on the sheet through his trembling, and said again:

'I will send for our Grace's physician straightway.'

He said, strongly: 'I forbid. Lord! I am cold!' and he touched his heart, saying: 'In every vein here—I feel it . . . like snow on the moors, deep, and hard.'

I could not warm him. I rose from the bed, thinking to get a brand from the fire to hold near his hands, but those same hands detained me.

'Stay!' he said. His head sank on the pillows, beneath the Holy Sepulchre. So I looked at him for a space, with the two poor sons of Edward howling in my mind, and Richard being my King and I his body-knight, I did assay to do the best I could. I lay beside him. I took him in my arms, his face against my breast, and held him closely, and warmed him. Presently, his shuddering ended, he slept, and I, warning myself to stay awake, slept also.

His first anguished cry tore my slumber apart. Seeking wildly his presence by my side, I found him gone. The fire was almost out, but in the corner of the room a small blue flame, lit by him, illumined the statue of St George; a youthful relic, gleaming tranquilly for all that a King lay prone beneath it. With spinning head I left the couch, hearing again that dreadful sound. One word, muffled, yet stark with meaning.

'Peccavi!'

I went on tiptoe, miserable, unsure, and knelt, close to one of his outflung hands. He clutched a heavy silver crucifix; I tried to pray, but when I heard once more: 'Peccavi!' I thought only: Aye, lord, you have sinned, in truth; then next: he will be chilled again and the fault mine—so I lightly laid my hand on his, and all but drew back from its heat.

If he had been cold before, an inferno now raged in his blood and I was sore afraid, for so had King Edward seethed before the dying. Thus it was that I knew I loved Richard, despite all, and it was passing hard to witness his privy sorrow, for a crime that had robbed him of all hope of Heaven. So I kept my hand on his and in a quivering silence said: 'Peace, my dear lord.' And he rose up from his face and, kneeling, looked at me, and when he said, 'You are a good man,' I felt an aching in my heart and was glad my thoughts were hid from him. He gazed again at the little flame and the George, who guards pure knighthood, and said, deeply:

'May God forgive me! For sending *him* to the block!'

In that moment I did not understand. He began to talk swiftly, in the way he had, half to himself, but with the tincture of anguish in each syllable.

'I! who once talked of forgiveness—of Our Lord forgiving seventy-fold . . . I! who could not forgive!'

He swung round and caught my arm; he was mindless and fever-hot. All rapid grief, his voice hammered my ears.

'Perchance . . . well . . . aye, 'twas because I loved him so dear—I could not have borne him near me afterward, knowing of his treachery . . . Morton and Stanley . . . sometimes I wonder about Stanley . . . they did not cut so deep! Yea, his was the bitterest betrayal of all. Sweet Christ, how I regret that day! Ah, Hastings, who led us northward once to find a King! Ah, William, William!"

He beat his breast, weeping. Sweat ran down his face.

'Verily, I was loath to lose him,' he said.

I spoke not one word. I had seen the King's guilt, like a bare, bleeding wound. And it was Hastings that he repined— Hastings, grown man and traitor, who had courted death and deserved it. I saw Richard Plantagenet, sick with penitence in the dark hours. For Hastings, justly slain, like the traitor Beaufort, the traitor Buckingham. And with never a thought to his true victims . . . two little knaves, lying somewhere deep, all unassoiled . . .

Men said the Princes were no more. They told it in the taverns, and holy men, washed by the blessed streams of righteousness, saddened folk with the story. Even the shadows shrieked it.

Yet Richard, wanton-tongued with grief and fever, repented Hastings only.

I milled the hellebore fresh root, milled it extra fine, while he sat limp and sweating like a blood horse that has been pushed too hard. I bent eye and ear upon the handmill so as not to look at him, or to hear the murmured words that poured from him still. He was bound on self-castigation; the evil humours boiling in his body had touched his brain, undamming a stream of guilt. My thoughts were dreadful thoughts. I milled faster. The smell of the root, mouldy and sharp at the same time, rose up. Hellebore, for mania, melancholia. I laid the powder on a crust and took it to him, looking down at his feet, at his calves rubbed raw from saddle-hours, anywhere but at his face. I tried to be deaf, while he raved, quietly, of Hastings, of past sins, little sins of the flesh, of impatience and passion . . . he would make me his confessor and I longed to fly the room, for soon I thought he would speak of the worst thing of all . . . I offered him the medicine, with lowered head.

'What is it?' he asked sadly.

'A simple to cure your grief, Sire. A plant of easement.' Then, shaking, I told him what the herb-maid had said.

'Ah God, yea,' he said, taking the crust from me. 'The river that flows from Paradise! Give me of it, then, my friend. Give me aught of Paradise. It seems I have lost mine.'

He would make me his confessor, and I could not bear it. He would speak of the Princes, crying of how, in a moment of temptation, the Devil got him by the soul—the details of how they died, and why. Why? Why, deposed Kings had been killed before my time. Men said it.

He would make me share his burden, and I was not strong enough.

'Eat, Sire.'

He looked at the bread, then at my face. My eyes flew away quickly.

'You think only of my comfort,' he said softly. 'Am I worthy?' I felt my hot blood rising. 'Your Grace!' But feeble words could not hold back his thought.

'There was none other,' he said desperately. 'A bastard cannot rule. Ah, holy God! Did I do right to wear the Crown?'

'Sire. Hush and hush, I implore you,' I muttered. For he opened his heart, as no King should do before one such as I; opened all, like the besieged gates of a famished city. And my thoughts were dreadful beyond knowing. For he did not speak of the Princes, the Lords Bastard, and a growing fear stole over me, clouding my eyes—a dread I dared not name but one which rose up and shaped itself from whispers,

393

screaming skulls, bogles in the dark night; whispers, bloated and fat and obscene, pursuing Truth down a long hill into the valley where dead men lay . . . a dread of my own thoughts, my own past beliefs. I did not see him rise from his chair. Suddenly he was by the hearth, nudging the cold grey ashes with one foot. The log he touched crumbled apart, fell to powder, cold and dead.

'So burns away a dynasty,' he said softly. 'So lies my only son. Next year, I would have buckled the Garter about his knee . . . now . . . all finished. Saw you the Queen today? My Anne—' his face contorted—'will bear me no more children.'

Now, my mind craved his confession. I would fain have him talk of the Lords Bastard . . . how they were done to death, a matter of privy policy. He had been judged. It was enough. Let him unburden himself to me and have it marked down after as mere sick ravings . . . let him take away the dreadful doubt, the doubt I could not own.

The knowledge that my sight had failed me, that I had listened where I should have looked—that I had given credence to foul lies . . . I felt faint suddenly. He had his hand upon my shoulder, and he was talking yet.

'All my hopes,' he said. 'Gone, like a dream. England would have smiled under my son's hand . . . would to God he had been strong and hearty, like my dear bastard John! Shall the name Plantagenet be thus swept away for ever? Our rich, royal line . . . how shall we be remembered?'

The pressure of his hand grew, bowing me at his feet.

'I have endeavoured to show favour and mercy. I have tried to do what is right. For England. Yet . . .'

He ceased. The tabor of my heart went drumming. I kept my eyes upon the King's bare feet. There was wood-ash on the toes.

'Yet there are those who speak great treason against me,' he said, very quietly.

Three pains had I. One behind each eye, a deep burning soreness where a swelling river ran, and another, across the knuckles of my hand, at which I looked to see an old scar, talisman of faith, upsurging as if newly branded.

His voice came to me through a cloud.

'Always, you brought me comfort,' he was saying. 'This night, you gave me your good warmth. You cooled my blood with herbs. Now, I pray you, ease my spirit.'

It came with difficulty. 'How, your Grace?'

His hand crossed my vision, pointing. 'Take up the Book of Hours, and read.'

I lit candles. I took the *Horae* from a chest, undid its clasps. I opened at the first page, a Collect of St Ninian, scrolled at the beginning of each line.

'Turn to the end,' he said almost inaudibly. It was a prayer, plain, black and unembellished. Someone had borne very heavily on the page when writing.

' "Most merciful Lord Jesu Christ, very God, who wast sent into the world by the Almighty Father to loose our bonds, to lead Thy flock back to the fold, to minister to contrite hearts, to comfort the sad, the mourning and the bereaved, deliver us from affliction, temptation, sorrow, sickness and distress of mind or estate, and from all perils in which we stand".'

No penance I could do would ever be great enough. If the whispers, lying, had snared me in their filthy web . . . ten thousand candles would not burn my shame away.

' "Stretch out Thine arm, show Thy grace to us, and free us from the sorrows which we endure. Even as Thou didst free Abraham from the Chaldees, and Isaac from the sacrifice; Jacob from the hands of his brother Esau, Joseph from the hands of his brethren, Noah in the ark from the waters of the Deluge, Lot from the City of Sodom, and Thy servants Moses and Aaron, with the children of Israel, from the hand of Pharaoh and the bondage of Egypt . . ." '

He knew this prayer by heart; I could hear him echoing my voice in a breath. I read as never before, giving each fair round phrase its proper emphasis, breathing comfort into every word.

' "Saul on the Mount of Gilboa; David the King from the power of Saul and Goliath the giant. Even as . . ." '

The script merged, blurred. Had I been prepared, I might have managed it, but even that I doubt.

' "Even as . . . even as . . ." '

A cry was choking in my throat. My power of sight was gone. There was only silence, mine and his.

' "Even as Thou didst save Susannah from false accusation", he said, in his beautiful voice.

Knave and fool, I stood, while the leaves of the *Horae* trembled and fell together. Just before the trumpet sounds, and the graves are opened, the silence will be as that silence.

'Read on,' he said, gently.

I could not read, neither could I see. I, of the keen sight.

'Why do you not look at your King?' he asked.

My blood answered him, by rushing in redness over my neck and face. Then, I heard him laugh, a truly awful sound.

'You too?' he said, passing soft. 'You too have searched your heart in prayer and found me guilty?'

The floor was hard under my knees.

'Yea,' said Richard. 'Men speak treason against me. Need I repeat you what they say?'

He began to pace about, talking the while, a quiet, hard tirade that swelled and faded as he turned.

'They say that I have destroyed Ned and Dickon—to what end God only knows. Once, you spoke to me of hatred and I answered that I knew it not. Ah God! now I feel that my soul is indeed endangered by that passion . . .' He stopped, both talking and walking, and I prayed that he had done, but he went on, his voice like a leaden maul on steel.

'They also murmur,' he said raspingly, 'that Our Blessed Lord sent retribution when He took my son, laid low my wife . . . do I, then, know your heart?'

I looked up. The gathering shadows seemed to suck him into their midst. He was King Richard once more, not the sick young man I had held in my arms. A distant clock struck, thrice, and on the third note's death I said, whispering:

'I can brook no evil thoughts against your Grace.'

He laughed, a bitter sound. 'Because I am your liege lord? How short, then, is the memory of mankind. Certes, I feel sometimes I have the longest memory of all.'

He beckoned me from my knees, and came near. The candle of his eye was very large, perchance from the medicine. He was all eyes, dark, shining.

'Cast back your mind,' he said. 'We were brothers in exile, at Bruges.'

I managed to speak, steadily enough.

'I remember well,' I said. 'When you held my hand in fire and asked my allegiance.'

'Which you betrayed,' he said, sword-swift.

'All unwittingly and to my own sorrow since, Sire,' I answered. 'I have said my *culpa* many times, since Stoney Stratford. I would thrust my head, not my hand, in fire now, to your service. It was my folly that I trusted Sir Anthony . . . he spoke so fair and King Edward had an oath, while dying . . .'

He cut me short, placing his fingers on my lips.

'You are right,' he said. ''Tis past. O Lord! the mistrust that treachery has bred in me! Tell me, is there any loyalty? Any love? Any kindness left? Any gratitude?'

'You are exceedingly well beloved, your Grace,' I whispered, my keen sight gone swimming in a mill-stream of tears. His fingers rested on my arm, with a kind heaviness.

'You have known all my loves,' he said. 'My people, my wretched, oppressed poor. My Englishmen, proud and warlike and true. Even John's mother . . .' he pinched my arm with a little forced jocularity, Dickon Broome again! 'Ah, she was fair.'

And we were quiet, remembering.

'Recount the rest,' he said suddenly, and, glad to spare him their tender names, I muttered: 'The most noble Queen Anne Neville, God strengthen her . . . Edward, Prince of Wales, whom Our Lady keep ever . . .'

'Also George Duke of Clarence, and our late Sovereign, King Edward Fourth,' he said very strongly.

'Yea, Sir,' I murmured. 'You loved him well.'

He did not reply. He moved to a small ivory coffer with the Yorkist Rose studding the lid with pearls. This he unlocked. From this, searching, he lifted out parchments, rolled and bound, a few coins, the seal of his dead son, even a flower, withered and brown. Then, from the root of the coffer's jackdaw-hoard of years he took a paper, tawny with age, but with writing plain and black. He held it, down-curling for my eyes, across the room.

'How reads my man of keen sight?' he asked.

It was his raison, in a boyish hand. *Loyaulte me lie.*

'When I was sixteen years, and ill at ease as any man could be,' he said, closing the coffer. 'When I was pushed from place to place and severed from all that I loved, I made a choice. It was not Warwick, God assoil him, neither was it my sweet Anne. That choice was our late sovereign, my brother. The Rose of Rouen. The Sun in Splendour. One night I wrote it down, set down my heart on paper, in the midst of all my loneliness. I have never swerved, despite his marriage, despite the vicissitudes to which he laid open my life by his unwisdom.

'Of all my loves, he was the greatest.'

He came to me, and he was smiling, a half-smile that had all of the past in it, sweetness and bitterness and despair; a smile also of resignation, and even a little ironic amusement.

'Do you think,' he asked quietly, 'that I would harm the fruit of his loins?'

There were apartments at the Tower which I had never seen. There were a myriad passages and secret rooms where they could be. All the battlements in my mind crumbled before the truth in that smile, the smile of Richard.

'The Lords Bastard are quite safe,' he said, still smiling, 'though I can trust none with the secret of their safety. Yet, for the friendship we once knew, and for your comfort of me this night I will say this. Seek them not in the Tower of London.'

The night was nearly spent when he said: 'We did not finish the prayer.' The fever had left him, though he looked weary.

Loving him utterly, I took up the *Horae* once more and read:

' "By the blessings which Thou hast brought me, since Thou hast made me of nought and hast redeemed me, bringing me from everlasting Hell to eternal life, I beseech Thee, sweetest Lord Jesu, that Thou wilt deliver me from evil".'

He spoke the last line with closed eyes:

' "And after this transient life wilt lead me to Thee, O God of Life and Truth".'

Strange, Master Brecher, that I should step from that chamber a different man, bound to the King for ever, and in my first breath, betray him.

This is the sin for which I should be hanged.

For I met a man, loitering, whom I knew as Humphrey Brereton, Lord Stanley's esquire, and he greeted me pleasantly, saying I looked worn out.

'Is the King sick?' he asked, and I, cautious on Lovell's instructions, answered, nay, he was in good fettle, and Brereton, looking closer, said:

'He has kept you wakeful—can he not sleep?'

'He passed a bad night,' I said, swaying on my feet.

'His Grace is devout, is he not? Did he pray? Leap from the bed and pray, I mean?'

Yea, I answered, King Richard left his bed most of the night, and he prayed too.

Brereton said: 'So!' smiling like the sun, and told me where to get velvet at a third the price, and went off with peculiar haste . . .

Now I can guess what was made of it. The King could not sleep, leaped from his couch as if haunted, wept and prayed . . . but it seemed little to me then.

'Twas a great disservice that I wrought, that day.

398

So little time is left to my remembrance. A prison cell, deeper than this, down through the teeming spirals of the Tower, thronged night and day with servants (where Richard, unseen by human eye, had had the Lords Bastard buried privy, that being one version of the treasonous tune sung out. That it would have necessitated the Tower being peopled only with blind men had not curbed the sting, the rot. Men will think what they will think.)

I stood and heard all from the twitching white lips of William Colyngbourne, captured at last, calm with desperation, mocking like Hogan, prophesying almost, under the shadow of the Council's wrath. Colyngbourne, of the filthy rhyme:

'The Cat, the Rat, and Lovell our Dog
Do rule all England under an Hog.'

Half London had seen it before they wrenched the crude writings from St Paul's door. Catesby—you, who fled the bloody field—I see you now, I saw you then, so angry . . . you said: 'The Speaker of the Commons to be named thus! By God's Body, 'twill be a Cat, to hunt this vermin down.' And Ratcliffe, sweet Ratcliffe, whom I shall see no more upon this earth . . . you cried aloud not at your own rude designation, but at the insult to our King. Lovell, brave dog, you did but finger the silver hound dancing at your collar, distaste writ plain, and with the greater treason worrying your mind. While Colyngbourne gobbled gruel and seemed detached from all. He had grown thinner during the fugitive months, more slithersome, with a tic that closed one eye at times.

'The King has prisoned Turbyrville,' he said, slopping food. 'He will soon be free. The King mislikes to see folk long in gaol.'

He had a raw head, souvenir of someone's anger.

'He'll not hang me,' he said. 'Not for a rhyme.'

'Not for a rhyme on a church door,' answered Norfolk. 'But for your treason with our worst enemies.'

Colyngbourne dropped spoon and platter in the straw.

'He is so *merciful*,' he said again. 'What proof, my lords?'

'Eight pounds' worth,' said Norfolk. Holding a soiled parchment he read: ' "To my good friend, Thomas Yate, in secret. I hereby urge you to bear our future sovereign these tidings . . . that the miserable usurper (whose tusks be sharp) bears no good will to France, that no French envoy is safe under his roof, that he intends war on our noble cousins

399

of that realm . . . and especially to our liege to be, Henry of Richmond, that he shall make all haste to invade this autumn, when the Hog shall be from London, and my lord of Buck shall give to England a new King . . ."'

Colyngbourne stopped twitching, as if already dead.

'Tom Yate,' he said cravenly. 'A traitor, skilled in forgery.'

'Your seal, your hand.'

'Lies,' muttered Colyngbourne. Then madness took him for he tittered and smiled with long sharp teeth. He raised his cup of ale.

'I hate Richard,' he said. 'Health to my master, across the sea. God save Prince Henry!' He started to sing; he liked a rhyme, it seemed.

> 'Jasper will breed for us a Dragon—
> Of the fortunate blood of Brutus is he,
> A Bull of Anglesey to achieve,
> He is the hope of our race . . .'

Someone whispered: 'Kill him,' and behind my head there was a scuffle of restraint. They tried him when the snow lay pretty on the roof of Gildhall. Norfolk sat on King's Bench, with Suffolk, Nottingham and Surrey, Lovell and Lisle, a commission of great dignity. They sentenced him, and no word came from Richard. Thus we knew how much he loathed the Tydder, and all he stood for. After, I saw Colyngbourne in his cell waiting on execution, and he was as one wakened roughly from sleep; he wept and pleaded before a handful of guards.

'Let me have speech with his Grace,' he cried. And when they turned, disgusted, from his shame, he babbled of lost rebellion, and scratched in his rat-mind for the key to lock out death.

'I would help his Grace,' he whined. 'His Grace would not listen to my lord of Buckingham, yet he could have served Richard, better than any dreamed . . .'

'Hold your row,' said one of the guard.

Colyngbourne beat with the flat of his hand against damp stone.

'He will pardon me!' he cried. 'My secrets are his . . . all that Bishop Morton planned against him . . .'

The guard looked at one another. Contempt rode high.

'How they turn their coats! 'Tis the smell of the hemp.'

'Morton was your ally, sir,' said one.

'Curse Morton!' said Colyngbourne wildly. 'He left us all,

stricken, mid-march. Listen, lords! I trade you Morton's secret for my life . . . I pray you, tell the King . . .'

'He will not hear you,' I said, looking at the white face, eyes like holes in snow. He clasped his manacled hands before me.

'Hear me out,' he whispered. 'Bishop Morton plots against the King's honour, and through his fame, his life . . . he has spread the word like plague, that Richard did murder the Lords Bastard . . . from shore to shore he vows that all shall know it. To turn the people's heart against the King. To speak treason but in whispers only . . . he gave gold, to many, to destroy his Grace . . . not by the sword, but . . .'

Myself, a young knave in Kent, and the third voice, leaping, running alongside all my doubts. The green wheatfield, in which I had found my arrow, clean and bright, still waving in the corn. Even so did I remember young Harry, muddy, regal in his mud.

'. . . to destroy your Grace, not by the sword, but by the spoken word. He talked of the Lords Bastard, but I knew not his meaning.'

So it was Morton who had put the poison in their mouths. That cunning, cunning prelate! Father of the whispers that had made my life, my King's, a purgatory. The monk! From afar off, where run the blessed streams of righteousness—where else but Croyland, and whose diocese but that of Morton? The meaty tale with which a Cluniac had seduced two friars . . . a Frenchman, and Morton doubtless now lying his way through France. Red gold in the tavern. Red loathing in my eyes, misty.

'. . . so that the King's favour should be weakened, and the people learn to hate him . . . stories in legion, that they were smothered and cast into a pit, digged deep.'

Even the guard listened, open-mouthed.

'Where is this pit?' I asked stonily. Even Morton, a devil from Hell if ever one breathed, could not conjure two corpses from air.

'It is all falseness,' said Colyngbourne desperately. 'Morton knew the King would take them from the Tower, once he himself was crowned. It is a place only for Kings . . . or traitors like me. Pray Richard to spare me.'

I marvelled at him. 'Spare you? God have mercy on your soul.'

'He pardoned Lady Beaufort's man!' he cried as I reached the door. 'Reynold Bray goes free, treason still on his tongue! Long live the King! Beg him watch his noble person well

. . . Spare me and I will praise him. I will say he sleeps easy, not . . .'

'What? How?' I turned.

'Not as others instruct. That his chamberers tell in secret how he never passes a quiet night, goes about privily fenced, starting up in the dark, ghost-ridden, crying sorrow for the slaying of Ned, of Dickon . . .'

Humphrey Brereton, asking me with a smile, how the King slept. Here, I heard the King's fever-grief translated into treason. The fault, mine. I knew great bitterness, and, more urgent, the voice of warning. For was not Brereton Stanley's squire? And was not the Tydder Stanley's stepson? Ah, Richard! You must watch Lord Stanley well.

Snow on Tower Hill, and a fierce joy in me. For the good people of London were there to see Colyngbourne drawn on a hurdle to the new gallows; folk stood muffled against the cold. The pedlars were busy.

'Ripe apples!'

'Is your knife sharp, butcher?'

'Death, death, death!' they chanted.

A woman jostled, her face wild with glee. 'Saw you the rhyme he penned? O God! against our King! Death! Slow death!'

'You love the King?' I said, cold hands, cold feet, and a great warmth spreading over my heart. She grasped my arm with hurting fingers.

'Love him!' she cried against the tumult as Colyngbourne, bound, climbed to the scaffold. 'Never did any do more good for me and mine! Fie! I can't see!' She leaped in the air, turned to an ox-fellow standing by. 'Lift me, Jack!' With a coarse jest, he set her on his shoulder, while an unnameable thrill, like lust, or battle-glory, started on the fringe of the crowd and ran, wind on the wheat, for they swayed and shivered and moaned softly, as the noose clipped Colyngbourne's neck and the trestle was jerked away, so that he danced and plunged.

He began to twitch in earnest, as he had never twitched in his life. They screamed, 'Don't kill him!' A terrible mercy, for there were fresh pleasures—a keen knife and a bright fire of straw burning. The butcher loosened the strangling rope, nursing the life in him like a skilful doctor, and I saw his eyes, just the whites showing. I could not pity him, for half my own soul suffered there, the worst half, that had believed the evil he had fostered. Would it had been Morton's belly gleaming for the knife, whiter than the snow. One downward

402

slash and his hose fell away, revealing privy parts, shameless and spouting fear. A great hush, broken by Colyngbourne's shriek as he was castrated; the golden fire hissed when the butcher tossed the bloody members in, and shriek and hiss and crowd-roar merged for an instant. A further silence, broken by the wretch's screams as the blade, blood-mottled, slashed down again. Colyngbourne's belly opened like a rose and entrails, purpling white and red, came bulging out. Still he lived, even under the second stroke that gashed the other way this time to make a gay crosswork of his body, for he screamed, and the crowd shook with fearful quiet mirth, afraid of the demons within them that feasted on the sight. The butcher rolled his sleeve, plunged a great fist into the mass of spewing bowels, ripped and tore. A shuddering groan escaped Colyngbourne's lips. All around the gallows the snow was sodden red.

'O Lord Jesus, yet more trouble,' he groaned, and his head fell back.

How they laughed! as the living bowels died in the flame. He was a prophet, Colyngbourne.

I wanted to cry aloud to those who whispered. I longed to take a woman by the hand, a woman, blonde, slender and haughty of mien, and drag her through the cheapnesses of London. I lusted to stand with her upon Paul's Cross, roaring: 'Here then, behold! Look well upon her! Here is Richard's advocate!'

Of course, I did no such thing. I only watched her, Elizabeth Woodville, mother of the Lords Bastard, still lovesome, still bejewelled, sitting at dinner with the King, and I flew to Margetta demanding, with a kind of wondering fury, why was I not told that the woman was out of Sanctuary?

'Husband,' she said meekly, 'you were full of other things, quiet and dolorous, since your return from York.'

I could not deny it. I had shunned even my Margetta's presence, and naught to do with York. It was since the night in Richard's chamber. I had bought candles for my shame . . . His soul burned bright on many an altar.

'Tell me, quickly, of the Queen.'

'Anne is woefully sick,' she said sadly.

Impatience. 'Nay, the false Queen. Elizabeth.'

Her frown gave way to mischief. 'Dame Grey. Thus is she known, an honest name befitting her rank, which is no more than that of . . . of Katherine Bassingbourne.'

'Who's that?'

'A goodwife whom Richard helped of late; he took her case of hardship before the Common Pleas. Ragged, scarce able to state her grievance—some neighbour had defrauded her. The King made a great pother and ordered restitution. I was there. Some thought it an ado over naught, but folk cheered after the hearing . . .'

'Tell of Elizabeth.'

The week of our departure for Nottingham, said Margetta, Dame Elizabeth Grey had come from Sanctuary, of her own free will, and bringing all her daughters. Unsolicited, she had placed them in King Richard's hands.

'Winter strikes cold in Sanctuary,' said Margetta with a smile.

'*All* her daughters?'

'All five, to the King's safekeeping. She wished it. He has promised them protection, good marriages for them all, that none ever mistreat them, and, on their betrothal, two hundred marks a year in perpetuity.'

'Say on.'

'Dorset, her son.'

'Yea, traitor Dorset.' I saw again bright eyes, strong teeth, whispered voice seducing me with gaiety. 'What of him?'

'She has written to Dorset, begging him to return. She has asked that he pledge loyalty to Richard, who will pardon him freely. My lord . . .' and a line scarred her brow again, and she looked at me in a kind of sorrowful, hurting way.

'What ails you?' I asked gently.

'Once, you spoke to me of things that pained you, made me weep . . . Dame Grey is, like me, a mother. Surely, you were wrong?'

I strode to the window, watching the whirling snow settling pure and white upon the gable opposite.

'Never more so,' I said, so quietly that she came to me to repeat it and we stood hugged against the tooth and sight of winter.

'Seven hundred marks a year,' said my lady. 'To Elizabeth. She's well content.'

Seven hundred marks is not a fortune. I stroked the smooth tail of Margetta, as I shall do no more.

'And I, my love,' I said. 'And I.'

Epiphany. Richard restive and sad, and the fiddles wailing their sweet, threadbare joy. A mockery of a feast; death made

404

all counterfeit, sitting so close by Anne of the broken heart. For all the rich gowns the King bought her, and the gems with which he girdled her throat, she was his no longer, nor was she shapely and fair, but a pitiful, cough-racked shell; she was claimed already, yet he kept his hand on hers, as if to stay her going. She wore bright April-leaf velvet slashed with scarlet like the raging blood in her lungs, a dress one would have thought past copying. Yet a blowing breeze, an usher's lusty voice:

'Dame Grey, and her daughters.'

Quiet, speculative mirth. Dame Grey was clad in black, befittingly demure in her reverence to the dais. But Bess! Elizabeth of York—she drew all eyes, her bared swelling breasts thrusting above a gown of April green with scarlet slashings. Thus came the two Elizabeths, leading a train of sisters richly dressed at the King's expense, and young Bess's face was transparent as a glass window. At her glowing approach, Queen Anne seemed to diminish. A ripe, swooning look lay on the bastard daughter of King Edward. Her eyes sought Richard's: it was no way for a niece to look upon her uncle, not that pleading, hungry glance of love.

I danced with her, a thing I should have hesitated over once, when she was a Princess. She was bold and charming, with her blue eyes ever over my shoulder.

'Can you read the cards, Sir Knight?'

'Nay, madame, I cannot read the cards, and your dress mocks at my King's dear love.'

'You like my gown? Her Grace had some stuff left over . . . Richard is fond of green.'

How long, I wondered, had this rich wound been festering? Dancing, I spun her in a reel, felt her hard paps press me, right through my doublet's cloth . . . the viols shrieked louder and Patch, her self-appointed fool, mimicked and smirked like the madman he was, feigning jealousy . . . Bess seized a cup of wine and drained it even while Anne's coughing rose above the music. In almost a gay tone she said, with a French prince's jilting behind her (for I must excuse the maid, she did but love):

'Ah, God! Will the Queen never die?'

I could not answer, and what I wold have said is now past thought, for there was a tumult at the door that moment and two couriers ran in, flushed and rain-soaked. As I watched Richard rising slowly with the candlelight gleaming on his crown, with the music dying and the hot dance stilled, I knew with the foreknowledge that makes words null, that this was the tide turning. And I saw him extraordinarily changed. A sudden lightness and youthfulness fell upon him. His strong voice carried down the Hall.

'News, my lords,' he said. 'Of Henry Tydder, calling himself Richmond, the adversary of our might. Through our spies across the sea, it is known beyond question. He gathers a force even now and plans to invade our realm.'

A rushing tumult of cries.

'When, Sire?'

Richard leaned forward. The gleam had reached his eyes. 'This coming summer,' he said. 'And to his cost.'

My gaze swept them all. On one side of the room, Catesby, Ratcliffe, Norfolk, Lovell, Metcalfe, Brackenbury. One the other, Sir William Stanley, Lord Thomas Stanley; Lord Strange, his son, Lady Margaret, his wife. And Dame Grey, veiling herself for the solemn occasion. She looked at Richard too, but not, like her daughter, at his mouth, his hands, or his hair. Only, unmistakably, at the Crown of England on his head.

I am afraid. So, to sheathe my craven fear, I plunge into a chaos of thought. Memory. Disjointed. I call it back like a faithful hound. The good and the bad mingling.

They tolled the bells one day . . . March it was, a month of treacherous, whispering winds, and Richard ordering the commissions of array to guard the coast towns, spending days in the Tower Armoury among the ranks of burnished steel. Richard keeping Lord Stanley waiting on audience one day while he spoke with, and rewarded, King Edward's aged nurse, whom, he said, mankind seemed to have forgotten . . . they tolled the bells, and there was wailing in the Queen's apartment, and he said, looking up: 'What means this?' with a fearful, fragile countenance, and Anne crying: 'They say that I am dead!' with her hair hanging loose and wringing her hands in the cold corridor . . .

They tore him from her bodily, the physicians, protocol forgotten for an instant. 'Her sickness is mortal, mortal, your Grace, you must not enter her chamber!'

And he, seeking comfort, turned to Bishop Rotherham with a sad and piteous look: 'So I have lost everything. Everything.' Rotherham's velvet arm through his. His turncoat smile. Would he had come to me for comfort! It would have assuaged a little of my present grief.

John of Gloucester, kneeling for his father's kiss. John, a

fine boy, God preserve him, Plantagenet nose and chin, and the grey eyes, rabbit-fur in sunlight, of Anne's Flemish substitute. 'We appoint our dear bastard son, John, who is both quick in wits and agile of body, Captain of Calais from this day forward . . .'

Anne dying, quietly as she had lived. And no sooner was she chested and the King's tears sealed with her under stone in Westminster, than a poisonous wave, another riot of rumour, sprang up. It came from the lips of Rotherham, he who had clave closest to the King in his sorrow. The face of Bess was made hideous to me in all its beauty, for her cruel young words came back. 'Will the Queen never die?' We could hear only the whispers and watch the guileless faces on the stair; we could do naught. Until there was one day a crying on Paul's Cross, of Richard's patience ended. And in the pleasaunce, when the daffodils had blown their trumpets ragged, I met with Bess again, smelling of gillyflowers and honey, but half-mad. I had never seen her so distraught. I could have embraced her, but I did not wish it. She wept and tore her hair.

'Why do they treat him thus?' she cried. 'The evil that men say outweighs the good.'

'What do men say, lady?'

'Evil, evil,' she sobbed. 'To say he gave her poison! Why, I hated her because he loved her so!'

She wound both hands in the neck of her gown till the fine silk split and tore.

'He is my joy and maker in this world,' she said. 'I am his in heart and thought. I would have him. I would bed with him and bear him the sons he never got on the sickly Neville Queen. I would give him joy, gladness . . .'

Brutally, to quell her storm, I said:

'What of your brothers? You know how the rumour runs? That Richard . . .'

'Lies!' she screamed. 'Two bastard boys! What harm they? What harm any of us? O God, that I had knives to carve the tongues from those who speak against him! Know you not, Sir Knight—' she put her face up close to mine, and her breath was no longer sweet, but rank with hatred—'that they are the cause of my sorrow?'

'Lady, you are raving,' I said sadly.

'Nay, sir,' she said, clutching my arm. 'For to wed poor Bess the King would need to legitimize me—no bastard Queen for Richard Plantagenet! And my brothers then by custom made the same. The stain wiped out. Christ, sir,' she said, weeping again, 'I wrote in love to my uncle of Norfolk, giving my whole self to the King. And what did Richard, for England's sake? He sent a herald on Paul's Cross, crying me bastard, vowing he would not marry me!'

'He cannot marry you,' I said. ' 'Twould be vile, incestuous . . .'

Her eyes slitted, mere threads of blue. 'The Pope would grant a dispensation,' she murmured, trembling. 'In ancient Egypt, brother and sister married . . . why not uncle and niece . . . my lady mother says it; once, a woman, an Egyptian, told me I should be Queen of England; I was but a babe, but my mother tells me . . .'

'Speak not to me of your mother,' I said bitterly. 'For I know she would see a crown upon your head and herself Queen-Dowager again. Not through you, but through Ned or Dickon. Then, again, the old warry dance. Speak not of your mother.'

'She would have me wed,' she said tightly.

'I doubt not,' I said furiously, seeing again Richard's face at Anne's burying. 'I doubt not she has for you a second choice. Another pretty bridegroom . . . across the sea, lady? Do I speak truth?'

She blanched. In all my hurt, there was satisfaction. My sight was still keen. I left her and went to tell Richard, who knew already. During my absence in York, Dame Grey had offered her daughter to Henry Tydder.

Margetta loved Richard too, and reverenced him. I never knew how much until we said farewell in June. It was raining, and she, looking from the solar window, said quietly:

'It rains. They even blame him for the rain. They say that God is angry with the Plantagenets. There are factions set against him, like some devil that would do him harm. Yet Bishop Langley . . . head you how he wrote to the Prior of Christ Church?'

I touched her hand. Still looking at the rain, she said:

' "He contents the people where he goes best that ever did prince; for many a poor man that has suffered wrong many days has been relieved and helped by him and his commands. On my truth I liked never the conditions of any prince so well as his; God hath sent him to us for the weal of us all".'

'You have it by heart,' I said.

I thought, I do think, of the gaols and the prisoners who through his kindliness had parted company; of the newly endowed College of Arms; of the jurymen who nevermore would fall prey to corruption; of the poor men who knew their rights through the Statutes writ in English, of the cheating and sharp practice to which he had put an end . . . and the steadily rising poem to God in King's College Chapel, Cambridge . . . and the little Priory of Holy Trinity, York, rebuilt when he was Lord of the North. And his words, at Worcester, Gloucester, Coventry: 'Nay, my friends: rather your hearts than your money'—with that rare smile. The one phrase the epitome of his desire—love in lieu of ambition. And I grew suddenly affrighted, for in a world as sinful as ours, I thought, what man could prosper by such philosophy?

What man could fail by such courage, I thought, as Richard, looking from Nottingham keep at the thunderous sky, said: 'Pray Jesu this foe of mine comes soon! Oh, sweet chance! the time is full to crush him.'

His prayer answered. Fair winds, that swept the enemy fleet round the western tip of England, while to north and south sped the commissions of array—the call to arms, for England, and Plantagenet.

Then came Thomas, Lord Stanley, in August, this August, month of death and sorrow, with his thin shrewd face drawn in a mask of regret. A thunderstorm grumbling outside the castle walls. I recall how Stanley remained on his knees throughout the whole of his talk with Richard, a gesture, in all its servitude, oddly contemptuous: I wondered at my own strange thought. Cordially Richard informed him of the royal force's disposition, the flow of armed men streaming in great puissance to his side, and then expressed his hope in Stanley's support.

'You are, no doubt, defensibly arrayed to do me service.' He meant, of course, the marshalling of Stanley's great levies, from Denbigh and the Welsh Marches, of his force in Cheshire and Lancaster. And Stanley, wagging his eyes up and down, his lean face leaner, his body still obedient, saying:

'Your Grace is assured of my devotion,' and in the next breath, begging leave to retire to his estates for a time.

'I am unwell; I would rest and refresh myself,' he said.

The long moment of thunder-broken quiet, and the infinitesimal change of Richard's mien, as if he greeted a familiar acquaintance, a guest unwelcome yet inevitable, and his smile like a chilling wind.

'I trust you will ride with us on this campaign,' said the King.

'As soon as invasion takes place, I shall be close at hand.'

Richard said, as he had said to me, his fickle lover, 'You serve me well,' and the next instant Stanley was gone from the chamber, while Lovell, Kendall, Norfolk, Metcalfe, converged about the King, in a full spate of protest.

'Your Grace, for the love of God! Call him back!'

'Sire, with his command of *Wales!*'

'Dickon, he wavered ever! I pray you . . .'

'Pray *for* me, Francis,' said Richard, still frozen in a smile. 'Nay, good friend. I do not trust him, have no fear. Any more than I trust Dame Grey. But I would trust him, and have his love.'

'Sire, command Lord Stanley,' said Norfolk fiercely.

'Command him naught,' replied the King. 'Yet . . .' he turned to me, asking: 'Is his son still in the castle?'

From the window, I could see Lord Strange and his father, preparing to mount up. They smiled at some jest.

'Delay Lord Strange at my pleasure,' said Richard. 'He shall be surety for his father, and may Jesu pardon my mistrust.'

'Madness!' some voice said quietly.

'Yea, perchance I am a little mad,' Richard said, turning away. 'The evil noised against me is food for madness.' Following his own thought, he said: 'I have sent Bess to Sheriff Hutton . . . they would not find her there.' A hiss like a drawn sword, of breath intaken at the first hint that matters could go awry. Then Richard spoke of the Tydder's advance round the cheek of Pembrokeshire.

'He hates the Plantagenets,' he said, without emotion. 'The enmity of envy. In my soul I know that he would give no quarter. Because he is of bastard, mongrel stock.'

Sherwood Forest, lonely and green in the waiting. His new Icelandic gerfalcon, winging, winging. A sure strike over the treetops, and the bells on its legs a sweet thin music on the heavy air. He looked at me and smiled, saying it was a fair omen. One night he dreamed, in the Castle of Care. Rolled in the bed and cried of Anne. A white owl drifting near the battlements mocked at his cry.

Brackenbury's coming south with a force of knights and gentry, gorgeously equipped, and tall fellows in jacks and sallets; a goodly, half-forgotten sight, the brave long-bows, the sparkling brigandines. And Brackenbury saying:

'Dickon thrives, but the Lord Edward is ailing. 'Tis an obstruction in his jaw that gives him much pain,' and I realized that he spoke of King Edward's sons. I saw the subtle, warning look pass 'twixt Brackenbury and the King, who could trust none with the secret of their safety. Richard asking: 'Liked he the new clothes?'

In March I had seen that bill made out, two doublets of silk, one jacket of silk, one gown, two shirts and two bonnets, for my Lords Bastard: I had thought them to be for John.[1]

At Beskwood Lodge, where the trees brushed the roof, two men arrived. John Sponer, Macebearer of York, and his messenger Nicholson, dusty, troubled. Richard asking: 'Where are my troops from York?'

'Delayed, Sire, but they come, as many as they can muster.'

Richard giving thanks, but asking, warily, why the delay? Sponer shuffling, down-looking.

'My Lord of Northumberland, Sire. Because of the plague, he said it was improvident to summon the levies.'

'York has plague? How bad is it?'

More fidgets, a look of suffering allegiance.

'I've seen it worse, your Grace.'

The deep sigh from Richard and his: 'So! Northumberland!'

Northumberland, the shame of the North.

Lord Strange, handsome, frightened, calling for Norfolk in the middle of the night.

'Tell the King my father and uncle mean to forsake him; they are pledged to Henry Tudor.'

And Richard, unwilling to believe what was writ plain, saying: 'Send your father a letter—remind him of all that is gone.'

Lord Strange, with juddering pen, touched not upon the past honours granted by the King to Stanley, but only of his own terrible danger.

'He will not betray you now,' he said, looking at Richard with tearful, haggard face.

An end to waiting.

A courier, sweating excitement. Young Harry again, under the grime, witness to an invasion. A dead mare outside.

'When the Tydder landed, he knelt and kissed the shore of Milford Haven, tongued a psalm . . . *"Judica me, Deus, et*

1. *Author's Note*: This bill is extant.

discerne causam meam . . ." He lay last night without Lichfield town . . . Shrewsbury opened to them. He marches under the Dragon of Cadwallader . . .'

'Already, they have penetrated my kingdom to the heart,' Richard said slowly. 'Who are his allies?'

'Rhys ap Thomas, Sir John Savage . . .'

'The Welsh chieftains!' Richard's stark cry, clipped short. He had known them well, ruling them when he was nineteen and Lord of the Marches. Only lately, Rhys ap Thomas had vowed the rebels would need pass over his belly to enter . . .

'The Earl of Oxford . . .'

Naught surprising there, nor with the others, Sir Edward Woodville, Piers of Exeter, Jasper Tydder, now calling himself Earl of Pembroke.

'Reynold Bray, servant of Lady Margaret Beaufort.'

'Yea.' Richard's faint smile again.

'John Cheney, William Brandon. Arundel, Guildford and Berkeley.'

The rebel force numbered some two thousand, said Harry. And they were the sweepings of all the gaols in Normandy. Poxy, scrofulous, Breton-Welsh, born in the gutter, ragged, lousy, some armed only with rough baulks of timber, at each scrabbling step cursing the King they had never seen.

'My Lord Stanley and his brother—ride they in this distinguished company?' Harry's headshake, and a lightening of the King's stern face.

'They are encamped between Lichfield and Leicester—a little apart. I fancy they await your Grace's coming.'

Richard's glance, pert, mischievous almost, sweeping all of us. Mark well, said his eyes. Stanley will not betray me. I looked for the loyalty in him and I shall find it.

The sun shone greenly through and touched Harry's steel, lifted in salute. Tenderly the King looked at him.

'Will you ride with me?' he asked. 'You, and men like you?'

'Yea, your Grace,' I said, speaking out of turn. 'To the world's end.' And my throat felt tight, as if there were a rope round it.

Southward, to meet with the enemy. A cramped, busy night at the White Boar Inn in Leicester. My weapons in good order—how bright my bow, how sharp my sword! In square battle order we marched from the town, the good and the bad mingling. On the King's left side rode Howard of Norfolk, the Silver Lion glaring savagely from his shield, his hawk eyes blazing through his visor slits; on Richard's right,

Northumberland, come lately in a feigned lather of speed, full of charming apology for his tardiness, sweeping, magnificent, with an ostentatious kiss on the King's hand. Forming the vanguard, the men at arms and archers were screened by the cavalry and backed by the trundling baggage-wagons. Behind Richard rode Lord Zouche, Lord Scrope of Bolton, Scrope of Upsale and Dacre, Greystoke and Ferrers of Chartley. Lord Strange, under guard. Far behind the van, Northumberland's men.

The people of Leicester were out to see their King. Mailed and bareheaded save for the golden crown, he was worth the seeing. White Surrey's coat shone like cloth of silver. Our train blazed with light. The colours of England flamed on tabard and drum and banner. Flailed by the sun, the air was alive with spanking hoof and jingling bridle, and the tramp, tramp, rat-atat-tat of drummers on the march, their lilies and leopards like jewels, beating out Death! Death! Woe to the foe! sang the drums, in a low, sonorous voice of warning, and the clarions caught it, with a wild bray, shrill to split the ear, to fire the brain under a brassy sky, through a warm wind, while the people, the treacherous, fickle people, came running into Swine Market to see their King.

It happened as we came over Bow Bridge. I was thinking: pray Jesu the wooden joists will stand our weight! when there was a commotion up ahead and I saw White Surrey's ears and head rise up in a wild terrified plunge across the bridge, halting the whole train, prancing sideways until I feared he might leap the parapet into the River Soar. Richard held him with firm ease—then I saw what had made the destrier shy. Quietly sitting on the bridge was a woman, a harpy, ragged, ageing, with a great purple wen disfiguring her face. I could scarcely credit it, but in truth, it was she, Hogan's woman, still wearing that dreadful, dolorous look.

White Surrey hated her. Rearing and sidling, he leaped close against the opposite side of the bridge; Richard's mailed foot struck fire and harsh music from the stone. The woman left her perch and ran alongside, shouting.

'Turn back, Plantagenet!' she cried. ' 'Tis the sign!' and she pointed at the long gash made by Richard's spur in the stonework of the bridge.

'Your head, Plantagenet, when you return!' she screamed. They called her witless, poured on over the bridge. But Hogan returned to me, clear as day, mouthing his old riddle. 'The foot that strikes the stone shall turn into a head . . .'

I too, deemed her witless, for I would fain believe her so.

So we came from Leicester, through the lonely, smiling fields of Kirkby Mallory, towards Sutton Cheney and Market Bosworth. And to the old Saxon hill, called Una Beame. Ambien Hill. The hill of one tree.

We halted first at Sutton Cheney, for there, among a sprinkling of cottars' dwellings and lean, rootling hogs, stood a church whose porch had seen mayhap a thousand weddings. Squarely built by Normans, with no pretence at grandeur, it had a welcoming look. Raising his hand, the King halted the detachment. His swift, turning gesture encompassed his Household Knights and esquires. He sought to dismount; I took his weight upon my hand. Then, with those who lived closest to him, he entered the porch; he stopped, removed the crown, and I took it at his command. The first time I had held it—it glowed red in the climbing sun, a perfect ellipse with the points delicately chased and wrought. Cool and burning, this was the thing over which his father Richard of York had striven in vain, that had sent Margaret of Anjou mad with ambition, had weighed heavy on the skull of Harry Six, had been won in blood, worn like a bauble by Edward Fourth. It lay surprisingly light in my hands as I followed into the dim-lit nave.

He knelt before the altar, with its patched vestments. The vicar was stout, ruddy, incurious. Without haste, he consecrated the Bread and Wine, and ministered slowly to the strange young knight.

'In Nomine Patris, Filii, et Spiritus Sancti . . .'

There was no choir, no candles. But a single bird spoke questingly outside and a wistful finger of sun pried through to light the King's bent head, and vanish in a cloud. The church darkened again with promise of more thunder.

As night fell, I stood with my arms in good order outside the King's tent, from which he appeared briefly at times to receive news . . .

'The rebels now number some five thousand. They waged more men at Shrewsbury and Lichfield; they have left Watling Street and advance towards us; they'll make camp upon the plain called Redmore . . .'

. . . and to deliver messages:

'Go to Northumberland—ask him to draw up his line close to Norfolk.'

I could see their fires, spreading in a long straight glimmer north and south, parallel to our own wing.

'Send to Lord Stanley—bid him to attend me here.'

The messenger, panting back through our lines.

'Sire, Lord Stanley would lie between you and the enemy —when the time comes he can serve you better thus. So he says.'

'And his brother?'

'Sir William speaks likewise, your Grace.'

Due south, the lights of Stanley's camp flowered duskily. Beyond the ridge, an answering glow marked his brother's army, to the north.

In a near-by tent, Lord Strange lay, whistling a mournful tune.

The supper of bread and meat was sour in my mouth. The King refused victuals, stood for an hour gazing at the crouched animal of Ambien Hillock. Once he murmured: 'A Godsent point of strategy, that mound; it must be ours before the dawn.'

Lovell, Norfolk and Kendall sat with the King, while I fingered the gold-fringed tent flap and wished the morrow here. The darkness disgorged Brackenbury, with a boy. John of Gloucester, saddle-weary, bright with excitement.

Richard raised him quickly from his knees.

'Sire? Am I to fight at last?'

The disappointment writ quickly on his face as Richard said:

'I sent for you to hear my counsel. Get you to Sheriff Hutton and stay quiet. If, tomorrow, things should go amiss . . .'

'God will give your Grace the victory,' muttered John, then, burstingly: 'Father, sweet Father!'

'I wished to see your face again. Remember, you are Plantagenet. Guard yourself.' He kissed him, blessed him. 'But have no fear, our parting will be short.' And John went, weeping.

North-west, a further cluster of lights, like marsh demons, marked the Tydder's camp. I stared, summoning old curses, swallowing tomorrow's glory down, fighting the hours with joyful trembling. Then, a horse's pale shape stirring the drowsy line. A tall, dark figure that tripped on a spread tent-fold and cursed loudly in a heavy, un-English tongue.

'By Heesoo Christo!' it said. 'Where lies my King tonight?'

I stiffened and challenged him with sword and lantern, and knew him before he spoke again. Knew his black brows, his sensual mouth, his sailor's gait. It was the Portuguese man of war and none other.

'Sir Edward Brampton.' He bowed, flashed strong teeth; Kendall came from the tent and urged him in to where Richard sat; I glimpsed him through the flaps for one instant, his shirt opened against the sultry night.

'Please you, let none enter,' said Kendall, right serious, and they were gone from my sight. I stood, with naked sword, thinking clearly for the first time in my life of Richard, about how much I loved him. More than brother, friend or father, wife or child; my every sense was sharpened through this knowledge. I picked out a man's face at the end of our wing, felt his yawn crack my own jaw, saw him raise a twig and toss it at the campfire. I counted Stanley's lights again. A night-jar shrieked, steel hissed on stone, a horse blew wetly down its nose, stamped and jingled. Closer, the King's voice, mellow, distinct.

'I feared you would not get here soon enough.'

Brampton's deep tones, answering: 'We had to dodge that pack at Atherstone. Heesoo! Saw you such a clique! Your Grace should wear great confidence . . .'

'Before God, I *am* confident,' said Richard, ice-cold. 'But I will take no hazard. Not with the lives of certain persons. You know why you are come?'

'Would that it was to fight,' said Brampton gruffly.

'You have a commission none other can fulfil.'

The flap swung open an inch and I saw the King, still seated, looking up at Brampton's tough harnessed shape. After a short silence Brampton said, sighingly:

'You had my word on this many months ago.'

'Is your ship ready?'

Brampton chuckled. 'I have a vessel like a bird, trimmed to a hair. I have a crew to fright even the Easterlings. And I can whistle up the wind to your Grace's bidding.'

'Then hear me,' Richard said. 'Lie without Leicester until the battle is ended. If all goes well, and the Boar brings down this . . . this Dragon . . .'

'As he will, by God!' said Norfolk fiercely, somewhere within the tent.

'. . . then shall you fetch back the Lords Bastard to Westminster.'

'And if things go otherwise?'

'Take them with all speed from England. To Tournai.'

'To my kinswoman, Frau Warbecque? She's a good woman.'

'Yea, Catherine de Faro; she bore a son to my royal brother . . . take them to Tournai; then seek my sister's aid. The Duchess Margaret . . .'

'The Lord Edward is somewhat sick,' Brackenbury interposed. 'He has a festering jaw. I pray no need for all this; he might not withstand a sea crossing.'

'Your Grace, think you this Tydder would . . .' It was murmured low. I could not hear.

'I have no doubt on it,' said Richard. 'He has hankered for Bess and the crown longer than any know.' His voice, softening: 'Poor little knaves! Pawns, they, in this deathly game. Get you gone, Brampton.'

'We'll meet again, in glory.'

'At Westminster.' A pause. 'God speed you, Brampton.'

Another rich chuckle, rising to a laugh. 'Your Grace forgets how close this secret has been kept. I'll go straightway, when I know which road to ride. Sire, where are the Princes?'

Someone laughed reluctantly, for Brampton, a sailor, was ignorant of the sickness wound about this jest. Sir Robert Brackenbury, stern and courteous, took keys from his pouch, a ring from his finger, and gave them to Bramtpon, who ceased smiling.

'They are at Baynard Castle, in the Kingdom of the North,' said Sir Robert. 'None may enter without these tokens. Cherish well the young Princes. As his Grace has done.'

He came and stood beside me towards dawn; he could not sleep. Together we listened to the night-croaking of the frogs from the distant marsh, the snores of the men stretched in a line beside their weapons. He laid his arm across my shoulder. As on our first meeting, he was the loneliest creature I had ever seen.

'Your Grace,' I said haltingly. 'Remember you that day at Hellesden and the breaking of the lodge?'

'Your friends the Pastons. I mind it well. They do not ride in battle today.'

I was more glad than sad. I might have had to kill Young John and I would have done it, for Richard, without a pang.

'They never forgave my brother. He had not time to deal with their grievance. I was always sorry.'

I thought, but did not say, that Edward had much to answer for. A little word, some sixteen years ago, a little gold, and Young John would even now ride with the King . . .

'All my life,' Richard was saying, 'has waited on this moment. A final settlement of scores. Peace eternal.'

The dew was cold. I shivered.

'Edward Third had many sons,' he said. 'Brave knights, whom I would give respect. But today I fight one who has no claim; feigned offshoot of a bastard line. Christ's Passion! small wonder that he would marry Bess! Only through her could he consolidate his vile, usurping lust.'

I felt his anger in the dawnstruck night.

'The times are changing,' he said. 'Once he lies dead, the shadows on me will be lifted. My nephews brought back, safe from mine enemies. It has been a hard lesson, these last two years. I fear I have grown less merciful . . .'

He was staring at the hill's dim shape, when Norfolk's night guard came running through the dark. A piece of paper fluttered in his hand; he gasped, thrusting it forward and I made a light.

'Pinned to my lord's tent, Sire.'

> Jockey of Norfolk, be not so bold,
> For Dickon, thy master, is bought and sold.

Richard crushed the writings in a ball.

'Send again to Lord Stanley,' he said. And to me, while my heart filled up: 'Stay by me this day. I may have need of you.'

The first, faint cock-crow, and the damp stirring like a huge stealthy beast. And to north, south, and north-west, the fires going out. So it was time to make ready. By lantern-light and the dawn's first paleness, I was one who helped to arm him. We girded on him the harness he had worn at Tewkesbury, worked in fine Nuremberg steel, and with the one pauldron fashioned large to house the battle-axe shoulder we had once jested about. There were still scratches on his cuirass that would never yield to polishing with salt and hide-cloth . . . he wore an assortment of tokens and talismens hidden near his heart, as I did, the sprig of yellow broom, the white rose cut from silk. He left off his helm for the moment, as he wished the men to see his face when he addressed them. When I had buckled the greaves on his legs, and ensured the sword hung free at his waist, there was almost a father's pride in me, for standing there, he seemed very young, a slim boy. His dark hair hung on the bright and powerful shoulders; the great fans of steel were like wings. He shone.

He said to me: 'I have a thirst,' so I brought him wine in a cup from which I drank for safety and he shook his head, smiling a little at my over-anxiety. I would have liked to talk to him then, but all our conversation had been done last night, and it was full time for us to escort him to where his army waited on his words.

Mailed man upon mailed horse, he pitched his voice high over the dim ranks, the row on row of quiet, attentive heads, the winking spear-tips. He told them the number of the rebel host, then that of his own—some three and a half thousand men.

'And today there rides Sir William Stanley, with two and a half thousand, Thomas, Lord Stanley, three and a half thousand,' he said, with a tight emphasis that drove eyes left and right to where the Stanley's lay, then back to the King in acceptance, awareness. The standard-bearers were motionless. White Boar, Royal Arms, and Silver Crescent (for Northumberland sat a black horse near by) drooped from their staves. York men around Northumberland were hanging on the King's words, yet obedient to their commander.

'My Lord of Northumberland leads three thousand men,' said Richard. 'Norfolk, how numbers your force?'

'Two thousand, five hundred, Sire.'

About four score Knights of the Household, richly armed, supported the King, and it was at them he looked when he spoke next.

'This day will see a change in England,' he said. 'Should the rebel who offends our might be by some means victorious, he will spare none of the scions of York. You know as well as I that he will rule by fear; because fear attends a man who has no right. Fear will be his sword. So, if you would see justice, fight this day as you have never fought.'

He paused. White Surrey tossed and snorted.

'And,' he went on, his voice dropping, 'if I, by God's grace, prove the conqueror, there will still be change. I tell you this. Always, I have sought loyalty, have pardoned freely those who turn against me . . .' Hawkwise, he looked at Northumberland, who fussed with a rivet in his harness.

'But from today, I give my word. Justice will remain, but mercy will be dead hereafter. You will find me ruthless with those who would betray me, and deaf to pleading. If there are any that would leave me, let them now depart. Choose well, and if you would still fight for me, God and St George be with you, and send us this day.'

A muted roaring, like surf on rock: his name, lashing the dry throats of men who cared naught for tomorrow. 'Richard! Richard!' muttered lovingly in the dawning.

'Sire,' said Kendall. He had a vambrace dressed back to front; never before had he put on harness. 'Sire, there are no chaplains in the camp.'

'John, our cause is God's,' said Richard. 'Let no man repent slaying another in the name of England.'

'Your Grace, answer from Lord Stanley,' broke in a messenger at the King's side. 'He is not of a mind to join you!'

'What?'

'He says,' the man faltered, 'that though you hold Lord Strange, he has other sons.'

'By the Blood of Christ,' said Richard, blanching white. He turned, cried to the guard: 'Then execute Lord Strange for his father's treachery!'

They pressed round him, remonstrating. Norfolk begged him not to jeopardize his soul before the battle—to wait, dear lord, and let the wager of war decide. The fire left him, and he said, 'So be it,' dropping the sword raised in anger, and lifting instead his gauntleted hand to the eminence growing in the lightening dawn. 'Sound the advance!' he said.

Lovell came forward with his helm, the golden crown circling its rim.

'This is folly,' I heard him say. 'The enemy will mark you clearly.'

Richard set it upon his head.

'I beg you, Sire, don't wear the crown,' said Lovell unhappily.

Richard smiled. 'I will live and die King of England.'

White Surrey moved forward; the head of the column was already ascending the ridge. Northumberland's men lay far behind.

Cries, groans. Steel on steel, steel on wood, steel on bone. The dissonant blare of warring trumpets. 'Attack! Retreat!' Under the sun, rebel army and royal force lashed back and forward like the sea, or some great hydra-headed beast bristling with bloody points of light. I stood by the King, on the hill; in my ear rattled the stream of his commands. Watching, each mortal shock beat at me, I yearned to be in the melee; small detachments thundered minute by minute down the slope, were engulfed in the running tide of combat below. I turned once to him, praying, 'One bow-shot, for Jesu's love,' and he nodded, still staring outward. I marked my man, his face, it seemed, a yard in front of me, loosed a good arrow from the trembling hemp—saw his dying hand clutch at the shaft that pierced his eye and watched his fall. From further

420

down below the ridge came the boom of serpentines, a knot of men shattered to fragments, red blood, white bone.

I marked Oxford's streaming Star and sent a sweet death-song into the flailing line with which the Silver Lion fought so valiantly; the Lion which even at that instant broke and wavered into a crescent, dangerously thin at the centre. Richard's order rapped out: some threescore men raced from our vantage to mend that hateful gap; the horns of Norfolk's phalanx started to weave inward, crushing the enemy into a block where they struggled and swarmed like maggots . . . Oxford's trumpet shrilled: 'Retire to the standards!' They fell back; I saw Norfolk looking along his line, heard the wisp of cheering rise, the clarions scream, the renewed cried of 'Howard! Howard!' and beheld the moving wave pour once more forward . . .

It was then I first saw you, Brecher, fighting so valorously. You dealt with six of Oxford's men; and your son—no son of mine could better that sweet bull-thrust . . . Then from my eye's tail I caught the standard of Ferrers dipping, surrounded by a boil of striking men, and no sooner had I marked the danger, where but a moment ago that flank had been pressing hard on Oxford's van—it was but a short moment—then chaos overtook the Silver Lion. Norfolk himself, scummed by a yelling, pounding sea, Surrey his son, his harness gashed, staggering under the fall of his own dead squire. The lines wavered and plunged, were lines no longer, but wedges, circles, scatterings of men tried to the death yet fighting, fighting, for England, for Plantagenet. It was not until then I realized the whole implication of the cursed Stanleys' whim. We were too few.

Crying aloud, I rode along the ridge, frenzied, I wheeled and rode back to the King. I could not get near him, he was surrounded by his Household Knights, jerking their steeds about. White Surrey, inflamed by the battle-smell, was rearing, the blood in his wide nostrils. Richard was shouting: 'A Norfolk! A Surrey!' and a farther body of the reserve swept down towards the surging death, while a man-at-arms, black-faced with bloody dust, came scrambling up the bank. He fell against Lovell's stirrup, gasping of Norfolk.

'Ah, God!' I looked down. The Silver Lion had fallen.

'Norfolk—slain?'

'Ah, sweet Jesu, Norfolk dead!'

One cry, wrenched from the King, lived but a moment as with mailed arm he swept a bunch of men down to bolster Surrey's standard. In the distance, a tiny flaunting figure, horse and man, detached itself from Oxford's wing and rode north across the plain towards the blurred mass of Sir William Stanley's waiting vanguard. Silent, as we watched, our thoughts linking, I felt my bowels draw up. That man bore tidings of how matters went against us.

'My lord, my lord!' Ratcliffe's desperate voice. 'Where is Northumberland?'

Pale, tight-lipped beneath his helm, Richard spun his nervous horse. He leaned to clutch the shoulder of a pursuivant, crying above a blast of cannon-fire:

'Summon the Earl—bid him advance at once to my standard,' then, looking at the butchery below, said: 'Ah, God, how they perish!' in the most dreadful, dolorous tone. Beneath the colours of Scrope and Dacre men of York swayed and groaned and hacked, part of the tangled monster on Redmore Plain, whose sunspecked green was pooled by now with strewn dead. I lifted my eyes and searched the horizon. Tiny moving shapes and the swing of a banner were token that Henry Tydder also watched, unseen.

The pursuivant returned, limping badly. He had caught a foot in a caltrap and half his steel shoe was torn away; he crested Ambien Hill gratefully, leaving bloody prints.

'Northumberland will not join your Grace; he feels it prudent to remain rearward, he says; in order to guard against Lord Stanley.'

Catesby came forward, pallid with fear. Fresh horses milled behind him.

'O Jesu, Sire, let us withdraw, all is lost . . . these traitors aim to cut us down . . . what's one battle more or less?'

Richard sat quiet, straining his glance over the seething plain, while I saw Catesby stealthily mounting a fast bay, edging through the still ranks, his back to the King, his head bobbing lower and lower as he descended the slope: the hot spit of scorn rose in me. I watched Richard, all dappled by the shading solitary tree, followed his far gaze across the field to where, somewhere, stood Henry Tydder. Then he spoke the words for which my life was shaped.

'Where is my man of keen sight?' he said.

I was at his side, he did not look at me; I was no longer a face, a name, but the instrument of his fate, the angel of his justice. He pointed north-west, to the mist of men.

'Mark my enemy!' he said.

There was a little hummock, higher than the tree. I stood in my stirrups upon it, willing the clear day to part for me. I called to my service the God-given, recalcitrant eyes, the eyes that had saved a child from drowning, that could know the strike of a hawk, the powderings on a garment, the charges on a shield, outside the fifth part of a league. Through those eyes, that had bewildered the physicians with their terrible magic, I poured my strength. The green earth, the bloody tumps, the hawthorn bushes, came rushing up, mine. Mine the horizon, mine the clustering mass upon it, dividing into groups, into standards, horses, men. And so it was that I saw him.

Beneath the gory Dragon of Cadwallader, he stood housed in a surcote of slavering beasts, his mail a little ill-fitting, one hand gauntleted, one bare, his visor open full so I could see his countenance, pointed, sallow, young and not young, sunken dark eyes, a long mouth neither weak nor strong but so thin that its character was nameless. A face that could be hungry, or calculating, or mean, a grey, starveling face from which all emotions save one had fled. This, then, was the Dragon of Cadwallader, Henry Tudor. And he was mortally afraid.

Returning, I heard that Lord Ferrers was slain, clubbed down by a dozen French mercenaries. But the King's swift tears vanished at my message.

'You see him?'

'Yea, Dickon, I had him in my sight—and he's half dead with fear!'

The name was out before I knew—there was no time for shame, neither did he wish it, for he smiled, following my hand with his eyes to where the red Dragon bloomed, mighty brave and blustering like a coward's spleen. He turned to the Household. Lovell, Brackenbury, Ratcliffe, Kendall, Humphrey Stafford, Thomas Montgomery, Ralph Assheton, Robert Percy, Marmaduke Constable, Harrington, Metcalfe, Sapcote and Burgh, Blanc Sanglier Pursuivant, Gloucester Herald, and the Royal Standard, France and England quarterly, rich azure and gules and gold, rippling in a soft breeze. He looked at the faces of stern love. They numbered less than one hundred, and it may be they foreknew the hazard he would have them dare. I remember only their quietness, and how they gave no answer to his words, but only nodded. Raising himself high in the stirrups, he said:

'We ride to seek Henry Tydder. Once he is slain, their cause is lost. Let us make an end to this slaughter. Sirs, will you ride with me?'

They came forward, a swift mounted line, closing visors, tightening harness. I felt young Harry's colt bump against my sorrel; he whispered:

'Sweet Christ! would I can cut the Dragon's claws!'

Richard heard him and, grimly chaffing, said:

'Nay, touch him not! He is mine! My booty, my prize!'

They gave him his axe. He weighed its balance, marked approvingly its cruel, wafer edge and, on White Surrey, led us down the slope. To our left, the battle tossed, a troubled sea, broken by cliffs of slain. Harry's steel-muffled voice tapped at my ear again.

''Tis wondrous strategy: once he sees us victorious, Stanley will follow!'

I rode after the rider on the white horse. The sun was growing high.

'He wavered ever, my lord Stanley,' said Harry, faint and far.

We descended unnoticed to the plain. At the hill foot, the ground sucked at hooves where a spring, rainswollen, bubbled over lichen into a mossy cup. Richard dismounted and, wondering, I did likewise. He knelt beside the water. He set helm and crown upon a little rock.

'I have a terrible thirst,' he said.

I filled my own casquetal from the stream, watching while he drank deep, bathed his face, poured the clear drops over his head.

'A penance,' he said, into the pool's dark eye. 'For those I am about to slay.'

The water ran down his face as he looked up. 'What did we once decide? That the span of a life is like a sparrow's flight?' He smiled, suddenly gay, rose, donned his helm. 'Let us see how fast this sparrow can fly!'

He glanced back at the little gushing stream.

'May this for ever be known as Dickon's Well,' he said mockingly. He climbed from my cupped hands into the saddle and rode to where his Household waited, taut as hemp.

One glance at their tight battle order and he raised his hand. The trumpeter spat, clamped his lips around gold and loosed a fierce, valiant call, and White Surrey sprang forward, the air beneath fluttering his housings, the flaying breeze above filling the standards so that they lifted at last and streamed above the King like the sail of a fighting ship, and the Boar ramped and snarled upon his azure field; a bloodfleck from Richard's spur dappled my sorrel's coat, and the torrent of battle to our left was past and gone already.

For we rode the wind, that day, across the plain; we rode the turbulent ocean, coming on in the wake of a white horse, to the screaming triumph of clarions and the mail-rattling roar of 'Richard! Richard! Richard!' and England's own voice, the snap and flame of the great standard, the leopards and lilies quarterly, the tug and stream of the bloody Cross of George held high, and the sun itself, bright-hot, reeling in heaven to see this madness, yea, madness it was, glorious insanity, a handful of men thundering to guard England, to the song of 'Richard!' and 'Loyaulte me lie!' Shapes ran towards us from where the Dragon stood, and the banner of Cadwallader came wavering down borne by a horseman, without the Tydder, though, by Jesu, for him I still had between my steel-slits and he cringed and seized the arm of another who stood beside him with gaping mouth. Beside me, John Kendall sang over the thunder of our ride: 'King's men! King's men!' and I too cried out with a giant's voice, and my eyes filled with the puny creatures that ran and rode into our ranks, fools they, to meet with Richard Plantagenet. His axe was whirling in a terrible arc. Two of them, with broadswords, broad faces, came at him and fell shrieking as he sliced the head from one, the arm clean from another—a mounted man clashed with him— was borne back by White Surrey's deathly striking hoof, took Richard's axe between neck and shoulder while I made a roaring chicken of one fellow, spitting him through harness on my lance and breaking it, feeling for my sword and smiting one who would have stabbed Ratcliffe, busy with another —and there was young Harry, idiot-bold, helm open the better to cry his challenge, but thrusting like a wise old warrior . . . and the drone of fury from behind Brackenbury's visor as the rabble came upon him and he buffeted them, one, two, three, till their brains burst white on his sword, and there, of all men, were you, Brecher, and your son, come to the King's service on stolen horses across the field . . . maiming and killing with the strength of ten. And we were sweeping on, on towards the man who cowered by some thorn bushes, wringing his hands, one gauntleted, one bare, I would strike at that bare hand, nay, I would not strike, for he was Richard's prize, to lighten his darkness, he was for Richard, cutting a swathe through rebel flesh with his terrible axe, while the crown clave to his helm and Harry Five would surely have smiled upon this day . . .

Frantic, the Tydder's guard were trying to form a line, from which came one horsed and snarling to meet our advance, with bull's horns blazoned on his surcote, Sir John

Cheney, twenty stone of him; and he marked the golden circlet and the man on the white horse, flinging himself forward, an oak to crush a sapling, but the crowned sapling raised his steel, shattered Cheney's weapon with a blow, shattered the arm that held it, milled his justice in a fierce fall of light, and Cheney's dying weight dragged down his own horse so that both lay pooled in death.

Here was the Dragon's standard, and charging down upon us, its bearer, William Brandon, with the red teeth and claws flying above, and Richard there to meet him, killing him stark dead with one sweep, and White Surrey's hooves pounding the painted Dragon into the marshy ground, as Richard rushed on to slay his fleshly counterpart whom I saw again, so near. I saw his craven pleading and laughed joyfully, for but a few parted him from Richard Plantagenet, whose might none could withstand. But even as we rushed up the little slope towards him there was a crying at my left hand, not of joy but of despair, and staggering through the ranks came Gloucester Herald—leading fresh horses and screaming above the tumult: 'Your Grace! Fly! for the love of God!' and I looked to where his hand pointed and saw through a haze of fear, the red-coated army of Sir William Stanley, mailed and mounted, hundred on hundred of them, bearing down upon us at a gallop.

The golden crown marked him clearly. They made straight for him, a silent, gleaming host, while Lovell and Ratcliffe and I tried desperately to shield him. I took a heavy blow on the side, felt my horse go down, speared through the heart, saw Ratcliffe clubbed backwards amid a fountain of blood. I was pinned underneath my mount among the trampling death. Then someone cried: 'Richard!' despairingly and I saw him, unhorsed, straddling the neck of dead White Surrey, laying about him with his axe, killing and maiming still . . . a club struck the helm from his brow and the crown flew in a golden arc, tumbling into a clump of bushes; I saw his face, one cheek gashed open, saw his axe smitten at last from his hand by a score of Stanley's men, who surrounded him, beating him to his knees, cutting his harness to pieces with their sharp hate. I saw his bleeding face, his broken sword raised once—heard his last, anguished cry:

'Treason! Treason!'

Then he was gone, lost beneath a stabbing, striking wave, a foam of anger that hacked at him as if he were all the evil in this world, to be utterly exterminated . . . Thus he died, fighting manfully in the thickest press of his enemies, to the great heaviness of us all.

I lay wounded, trapped, weeping. Near me Brackenbury was down, two Breton oafs kneeling on his hapless body. They wrenched his visor open and shore his face with hatchets, again and again. Not far from my mount's corpse lay John Kendall, his head half severed, arms outstretched, in an oddly suppliant gesture . . . and young Harry. The bright sun stung my face. The marsh seeped cold through a rift in my harness. The sun should snuff out, the marsh dry up.

The sun was scarcely at noon, and Richard was dead.

Through mist I saw them; they struck my face and made me look. They were all there, Reynold Bray, even Morton, for where else would he be in this great moment? There was now a fine colour in the Dragon's cheeks, the thin mouth smiled. Nuncle Jasper stood close, with satisfied hands. And, O God, Northumberland, come at last from his rearward post.

Through tears I saw them: Lord Stanley, plucking the crown from a tangle of hawthorn. The Crown of England, a little bent and misshapen . . . He placed it on the Dragon's head.

'Thus ends Plantagenet! The Devil's Brood!'

You are wrong, my base-born lords, I thought. There are still Plantagenets. The rich blood of Edward surges in their veins. They still could rule . . .

They were shouting, around Richard, as if the cry had been bottled in their throats for years.

'Drag him through Leicester! Let them see their King! He who shed the blood of infants!'

They were stripping him of his harness. He was clothed only in blood. They looped a felon's halter about his neck, and they threw him crosswise, over a trembling mule. I turned, vomiting grief. Their cries beat in every vein of my heart.

'Display the accursed!' they chanted. 'God was with us this day!'

And God was silent.

The long waiting is ended, and we are glad of it. The saints reward you, Brecher, for your comfort of me, these past days. For now I admit, it was *you* that cheered *me*, Brecher, t'other was self-delusion. For Tacitus wrote that it was sin for a man to quit the field alive, once the leader was fallen. Yet we are to be hanged for our loyalty, and that's a warming thing. Tacitus wrote much. Caxton used to talk of him; Caxton will go on, inky and mild, printing great works, the lives of saints and martyrs, and kings. What will they write of Richard?

I shall not read those books, but they cannot lie. His honour and his fame they cannot touch. They would need to invent a devil in human shape, so great was his glory. I shall never know.

Pray Jesu Brampton had a fair crossing . . .

They are coming for us. They laugh; and outside, I hear the growl of people, ready to enjoy our torment.

I am afraid. Jesu, Jesu receive my soul.

O Richard! Is there a place for me beside you, above the stars?

HERE THE MAN'S TALE IS ENDED

PART FOUR

THE NUN

Whatever befall, I never shall
Of this thing be upbraid:
But if ye go, and leave me so,
Then have ye me betrayed.
Remember you wele, how that ye dele;
For if ye, as ye said,
Be so unkind to leave behind
Your love, the Nut-Brown Maid,
Trust me truly that I shall die
Soon after ye be gone:
For in my mind, of all mankind
I love but you alone.

The Nut-Brown Maid

There is a malady peculiar to such as we. I have known this mingling of boredom and melancholia; Dame Johanna, who was scornful and cruel, called it *l'accidie*. She misused me but once and thereafter deemed I had power and became afraid. Power! pitiful that, pitiful me, who nêver realized the strength in a word, a name. A name of riches. A rich name, unspoken.

I broke my vow of self-counsel, though, in Yorkshire, shocked out of vigilance by Patch, come dripping rain and folly, off the moor and out of the past, and I, loving and hating him for that reason, saw his loonish eye flicker, felt his wide lips upon my hand and longed to scream: 'What of my lord, Sir Fool? What, what of my love?'

I did not ask straightway. Instead, we talked of apostasy; it was meet that I could do so, not being professed myself . . .

They came and took me, and they were silent men but kindly for all that they wore the livery of Jacquetta of Bedford, and they rode hard with me through the night, day, night, and I kept my own arms clipped tight beneath my cloak to guard that which I held most dear . . .

Apostasy we talked of, the apostasy of love, while Patch mocked with his eye and feigned a tear.

. . . North they brought me, and so I vanished as though I had never been. And I think Dame Johanna was passing glad of me for she took the hand-to-hand gold purse from the man who had ridden at the head of our company and looked me over, saying right loving: 'I would not have priced her so high,' and one of those who stood with us peered just as hard at that douce and sinful face under the rich wimple and fingered his hose, breathing little ugly words. She was a knight's daughter and I remember her but vaguely. For as life has taken me, shaken and slain me and restored me to a half-life which in itself is peace, the middle years are less

430

clear than youth and childhood; mercifully even these are something veiled. I say mercifully, for if all that were to come again so sharp and clear I could not support the remembrance of what followed after.

I have descended into the depths of Hell. I have tasted the grave's earth. I have died, yet I live: a witless old nun with words half-listened to, and always, always forgotten. Truly, I have known death, and am risen, not to glory but to a plain of calm shadows. Folk are passing kind to me, I have my daily bread and ale; I have my herbs and my garden and the everliving consolation of Him who died on Tree, whose agony I am well-purveyed to share. I know the tormenting ache of His Side, the fierce pain of His Wounds; I know the colours of death, the flavour of grief, as surely as if I had sat beneath that long sundown shadow, with Mary and the Harlot.

Merry Patch, do you live yet? I spared him the full tale of the one who cast herself into the well, for he would not have got my drift. I did but touch on it and he cocked his head, interested, for I spoke of love which was ever his prerogative (in a silly mocking way to speak, making fair foul and what was bright, unclean).

. . . They took me, those strong men who lusted for a comely nun, to a wild place, a cold cloistered realm of bells and secrets. There were never such vigorous bells as in that house in Yorkshire; they frightened me. It was as though their clangour would shroud all that took place within, unseemly for the sight of God. Their wildness struck at the flourishing elms, sent the pigeons clapping high around the taut vibrating tower, shivered the reeds crowding the stream that ran northerly through the cloister-garth. Constant were those bells, like the heart of a true maid, and the only loyal entity in that corrupt house; sweet Edyth tolled them, doubtless that was why. Prime, Terce, Sext, Nones, Vespers, Compline. My heart hung heavy on each stroke.

I was not put to sleep in the dorter. An abject of the Queen's will, I had a cell in the guest house, with a low pallet, a deep window at which I stood that first summer evening, staring at the dark trees and the night-greying sprawl of the frater and chapel buildings. There were no stars, nor were there tears left in me. I had three gowns: a journey-splashed blue silk, a black dress of muster-develers and God! O God! Jacquetta's orange satin, which the flames had scorched.

I remember casting wildly about me, to divert my mind. A

small figure of Our Lady hung over the bed and I flung myself before her; I caught up my beads and began, feverishly, to tell them, but with the first touch of the coral I became heretic for I cried not on the Virgin's name but on another, one of such richness that the cell seemed to throb and glow from its sound and the walls to weep in concert with my cry, for there was water trickling somewhere near, the spring which fed the troutstream and the lake, though this I did not know. Right outside my window it ran and, low down in one corner of the room, where a stone had been plucked out by storm, moisture lapped sadly through, like a little, flickering tongue. A patina of damp lay on the floor, and mould grew up the feet of the bed. How long since I shared a silken bed? How long since I nestled in sleep by Elysande? Hot and secret and trusting, sharing with her the most precious of my heart's estate; a slack and loving fool, dreaming while she schemed.

I thought on Elysande with sadness, marvelling at her treachery, and heard once more her soft voice, while she was still my friend . . . 'But, sweet, you do but kiss, and where's the harm?' and my own silly trembling answer, and the hawks flying high over Fotheringhay. She, in our small privacy, clipping me close and murmuring that she too had lost her maidenhead when twelve years old and none the worse . . . gripping the bedstead with its sheen of tomb-rouge, I prayed that she had not watched me too closely through those final days, that she knew naught of the pledge he had left within me; so thinking, I rose quickly from the stone to honour a silent voice that said guard yourself.

My whole heart enveloped the child full lovingly.

The child. Am I to finish the tale, then? It will give me a plenteousness of woe. Ah, now it comes, clearer than I would wish. Child. Pray for me.

My eyes, when I touched them, were swollen and burning, and my mass of hair seemed to drag at me, sapping my strength; I thought—now I suppose they will cut it off. My hair, my only beauty! for I knew not the limits of their power, nor indeed, in whose power I was. I knew only that here was the end to dreaming and to glory, that this severance from my own heart's liking, my own true knightly love, was sharp as the knife they would need to shear away my hair (for that, in all its nut-brown show, could have no place in cloister). And I thought to save them the labour, turning and turning

432

again in the cell, spying for any glint that might betoken a
blade, or a mirror. There again: no mirrors in cloister! though
to reflect the past, ghosts aplenty. Each thought conjured
them from the shadows. Images, and words . . .

> As, cut your hair up by your ear,
> Your kirtle by the knee;
> With bow in hand for to withstand
> Your enemies, if need be . . .

I had not withstood *my* enemies. The Duchess of Bedford's
great burnished glass shone in my mind. Her face, too, set in
it like a toad, unwinking, raddled beauty, while behind it,
mine, white and attenuated, with plum-blue bruising round
the eyes from the worry, worry, that she might rob me of a
minute, a second in *his* arms. Even in my own mind I would
not name him. He was he, and I was utterly his, and I would
never again give his name a voice, I held it too dear. I would
not dishonour it.

Great black bats began their sweeping dance between
earth and heaven. Framed by the pointed grey arch of my
window, they flew, silent as treachery. A bell tolled, heavy,
urgent, the metal of the soul. I sat on the bed, and felt its
dew soak through my gown. Motionless, I thought: my love
has entombed me. Old thoughts and new flittered like the
bats. The Duchess would have rushed into Sanctuary with
her mirror and the Jerusalem Tapestry—that cloth of Arras
for which Sir Thomas Cook had paid so dear. And Elizabeth,
Elizabeth! who had flown so high and to good purpose—was
her glory, too, crumbling like mine? Did she weep, and did
she love? For the King was taken. The King was taken, and
his brother, and the dampness of the chamber made me
shake as I saw my love, fighting that moment to the death,
against proud Warwick.

He would fight bravely, on his first campaign, striving to
shield the worshipped King. Were he taken hostage, he
would not cringe or seek the sanctuary of defeat, would give
no fair words to sneering Warwick. Even his voice, crying his
challenge against terrible odds, for St George and Plantagenet, would wear an edge. And if they took his sword, it
would be in their own flesh. Would to God I were fighting for
him, my hair cut off, the child asleep within me. Would the
tears stand in his eyes, I wondered, when he saw his foe, the
friend turned enemy? 'Yea, the people love Warwick. All love
him, as I did.' Would his colour come and go, like the fire-

light, when he saw the cruel Bear and Ragged Staff? And I decided yea, and yea again, hearing through my fear's torment the hammer of his steel. This, then, would be his mien. For I knew him as I knew myself.

Warwick, maddened by a usurping woman, would show him no quarter. Warwick, forgetting past love, would sanction his death.

Night fell, and I laid a curse upon Elizabeth. Laid it, and lifted it. For if Elizabeth loved, as I, and would have her love, to lie beside him all night and wake warm with him at day's beginning, we were truly sisters, and cursing her, I cursed myself. Yet Elizabeth had done many things which I could not. There were Desmond's boys, and Desmond himself, who still plagued me. Patch had told me: 'Foully murdered, for their father's affront to the vanity of her Grace.' That is, if Patch could be believed, with his loose and dangerous wit.

Long after, hearing how matters really went, and how Warwick was outwitted, I could have mocked at my own thoughts, but perchance that evening saw the beginnings of my madness. For in those first few hours, I deemed myself truly mad. Made mad by love, and a cruel parting. Others in that house shared my longing, knew well the colour of my thought, but I had yet to learn of this.

There came a scratching at the door, and I kept silence trembling, for I still thought that there were those who sought my death, and I marvelled that none unlocked the chamber door and entered. I sat watching that broad piece of oak, like a cat—God save us! like Gyb spying on a mouse!— and wondering what lay without. Thus, with my growing dread, all the monsters I had even seen, in books and dreams, scratched on the door; I reckoned the Duchess in her mercy could have sent a headsman, a handman, to slay me for my crimes—what crimes? And the scratching grew more insistent, past bearing, so that I cried, in what was almost a scream: 'Enter! in Our Lady's Name!' then called thrice upon the Trinity, and well that I did, for the door, that was not locked, crept open and there entered a spirit, a creature unearthly, from which I shrank in terror. Dear Edyth, how you affrighted me! You, who would not harm the smallest thing alive, whom I have seen shed your cloak rather than jolt a slumbering butterfly, you little know how close I was to death that instant!

For the being that came silently in was green, green as a waternixie, possessing a drowned, dead look, the flesh of its face made a more ghastly green by the quavering light it carried, and the arms, twig-thin, loaded with sour greenness, a great slithering mass that rustled and shook—a green pillow to smother me.

I beat out my hands to ward it off. But it came on, this apparition, steadily, flashing me one glance from great hollow eyes in a twilight face. And dropped its bundle on the ground, so that its true form in a gown greenish-grey was revealed to be thinner even than mine. The light it held up to my face, and the dropping gleam lit up its own, so that I shuddered this time with relief to see the countenance of a child. A child, spare to gauntness, a pale sad mouth, a body clothed in shrunken grey, wisps of hair lying like river-reeds upon its neck. A maid, with naught but duty in her face. Sweat ran down my sides in a sudden gush of warmth. I started to laugh, and the laughter shook me with its wanton witlessness. You looked puzzled, Edyth, then my laughter pleased you, for you too peered closely for the jest, saw it not and joined me, none the less, with a high tittering sound like the cry of some sad bird. When I had done, you also ceased, composed your little face into its old apathy and bent to your bundle, untying the bonds from its lush greenness, and spreading it with your feet all round the chamber.

'Rushes,' she said. 'Rushes fair and green.'

Kick, kick. Then, the ridged, bending spine, the hands flying like pale fish in a dark-green river, patting, smoothing, a meticulous procedure. I saw that one of the trampling feet was twice the other's size; all but one thong of the sandal shoe had been severed to accommodate a clumped, malformed mass. Now and then she stopped, peeped back over her bowed shoulder to give me the quarter of a smile. When she came to the corner where the wet seeped through, she thrust two fingers into her mouth and stood, considering deeply. She looked back at me.

'Wet,' she said. 'By my faith, 'tis wet.'

She turned again to survey the rippling damp, and, dumb, I watched for a long moment the workings of her intelligence. Sudden energy seized her. She pulled the thickest sheaf of rushes into the corner, packed them tightly, and bending, so spare, so under-cherished, dammed the flow. Then she rose and hesitatingly came to me and laid a hand upon my arm, the first soft touch I had felt for many days. She began to stroke the silk of my sleeve. Now, I felt anger at myself for having feared her; she was no more than eleven years old, stroking, stroking, face bent, the pallid, bumpy brow close to my chin.

' 'Tis fair, this,' she murmured, rubbing the stuff between two fingers. Together we stood, our foolish silence broken only by the bird's claw hand chafing on silk. Our conversation, as it ran its course, was like the sighing of two branches in the wind, separate, alien one to the other.

'A fine gown had I, once,' she said.

'What is this place? Your name?'

'Madame sold it. Madame sold my gown. She said 'twas not fitting for such as I.'

Is Madame the Prioress? I thought, but did not ask. I would that the shocks came stealthily, on tiptoe one by one, for I felt as a bowstring must feel, drawn to the last aching limit.

'Are you from York, lady?' She looked up, frail-faced.

'Nay, London,' I said.

'Sister Adelysia is of York.' Her eyes studied mine. 'She wept again today, and would not have my comfort.'

Jesu, what place is this, I thought. This crippled child, midway 'twixt death and life, herself assuaging sorrow. Yet more sorrow?

'Where's London?'

'Child, what ails your foot?'

Raising the hem of her gown, she looked at the misshapen member as if for the first time, and blew a little puffing breath.

' 'Tis larger than its fellow,' she said, then looked full at me, the dull eyes suddenly lit with remembrance. 'For when my mother bore me in her womb, she was wont to sleep o' nights with legs crossed, left over right. So were the evil humours bred, and I lamed.' She smiled. 'They cry me idiot to the same purpose. But I am wise, really.'

I twitched my sleeve from her clinging fingers and went to the window. For until this night, I had forgot much, all the wise women's tales, the ladies' solar-gossip, the vital knowledge of what one should and should not do. I had not yet thought of myself in this connection. Toads, spiders, serpents. How many had crossed my unseeing path? Even a hare! ah God! to ruin, running, my baby's mouth with sidelong stare! And the journey north, so rough, so rude, despite my entreaties. Enough to drive the life from this royal child, this cherished thing.

'I must have medicines,' I whispered.

I swung round to ask in desperation, if there was a leech, a good infirmaress, who might aid me to avert disaster, and stopped myself. Another moment and I would have betrayed my secret. I had seen the steel of my enemies, and trusted none. I had become a pawn in the privy policy of the court. Friendless and in great peril, mayhap, I was held in unknown hands. Let the child wax weak or strong in silence. For if they knew, might they not, for reasons of their own, do it harm? I felt the cold sweat on my brow, imagining the child being drawn from me by some alchemy before its time. Better to treat myself. I would be my own leech, my own counsellor.

'Where is the knot-garden?' I peered anxiously out at the reddening dusk. She understood. She came and pointed towards the far corner of the cloister-garth. I could see only a straggling mass of thistle and dandelion choking a tangle of herbs weakened by their own overgrowth. I spied a fennel, a celandine, a trail of white stitchwort, the bell-flowers of Venus's navel. There were others, in a desolate moil of crowded life, like an army in confusion. There was the herb of grace, of sorrow, of repentance.

'I see there's rue aplenty,' I murmured. Tall yellow tansy battled with a savage cluster of nettles. The Sun in Splendour, cut down by Warwick's Ragged Staff? I turned away. I would think no more on that, or die, and the royal child with me. I must guard myself.

'I'll bind both my legs to the bedstead of a night,' I whispered. Edyth did not hear me. She was looking again at her own bewitched foot.

'But then, Dame Bridget says,' she murmured, 'that it was a judgment, for my mother was but leman to her lord.'

Ah God, she was, after all, a creature of Hell, some demon come to torment me! I clutched and shook her with all my strength. I had not known that I could be so cruel. She stood, unresisting, head lolling. She, whose last words were like hot iron in a wound. She, who smiled even as I punished her.

'Yea, shake me, dear lady!' she cried, with jolting speech. 'Shake sense into me, as the others do! For I would fain be sensible!'

My hands fell away to a great uprising of shame. With face averted, I asked her pardon. The next moment I felt her hand, her cold, rough claw, moving on my cheek, which she stroked as she had my sleeve.

She was still ill-pleased with the room, for she glanced round and said again: ' 'Tis wet.' Then I asked her where the Prioress lay and she clapped a hand over her mouth, having forgotten the main purpose of her visit, which was to summon me to Dame Johanna's supper table; a privilege, I learned after, enjoyed by all corrodians on their first evening. I was a little surprised. I had thought all would eat in the refectory, as they had done at Leicester. Leicester, still recalled by me with the love of a child grown up.

'Come, lady,' said Edyth.

She went ahead, out into the chill, vaulted passage, carrying the light. Without looking back, she put out her hand and gripped mine, to anchor me through the dark ways.

And the last remaining tears stung my throat, for that instant she was Harry, little Harry, leading me again to the chamber of love.

It was a court, and Dame Johanna Queen. She sat at her own high table, beautifully caparisoned with damask and gold thread, a flower-strewn board upon which, up and down, a sleek little dog ramped freely. It was the dog I noticed first, and her hands caressing it. She would sweep it up at times to kiss its slavering face, pinch it in her lap and lose interest, so that its black nose soon peeped again over the table top, its white paws appeared on the board, and its body gambolled once more under her lustrous, uncaring eyes.

A short nun, robin-round, opening the door to reveal this sight, wished me good evening and resumed a low gabble which I thought at first to be prayer; then, listening harder, knew as grumbling, an eternal flow of little words, French and Latin and English mixed up together. She swept me with her glance, dismissed me from it to encompass Edyth with a mingling of pity and scorn.

'You're late, child,' she said in a heavy accent.

A brisk, hard trembling shook Edyth. She seemed literally to melt backward into the arching shadows. 'Yes, Dame Joan,' she murmured.

Joan smiled at her; I was caught by the tail of that gat-toothed smile. She had one tooth east and west, and none between.

'Be chary, *enfant*,' she told Edyth. 'Madame is proud tonight. Serve not the sturgeon too hot.'

With that, she gathered a mouthful of phlegm, and shot it into the dark, where it dripped down a stone column, like a snail-trail. A little of it fouled my sleeve.

'Pardon, pardon,' she said blandly. Seeing my distaste, she laughed. 'What ails you? Don't they spit at court?'

So she knew my origin, already.

438

'Yea, they do. But their aim is better,' I said, stiff with misery.

'I should not spit,' she said mockingly. 'I have defied a rule,' gave a yelp of laughter and took my arm in a hard, clumsy grip.

'Enter, enter,' she said. 'And *bon appetit!*' She stared up towards the Prioress, with an uncompromising look of hate. 'Good victuals, I trow! Better, *pardieu,* than any that touches our throats!'

The heat of an hundred candles washed me like a warm wind. I walked, foolish, alone, towards the dais, on the steps at either side of which stood a habited form. The nun on the right was reading aloud; I recognized the work instantly—Thomas a Kempis, *Imitatio Christi,* in the Latin. And as I went hesitantly in I felt my heart move suddenly, with an older longing and sorrow than that of the past months. All faded for an instant and I saw only my mother's face, and the face of my spiritual mother, the gentle dame of Leicester. For, in the old days we three were wont to read that same book together, and I would oft-times fall asleep, to be jounced awake by some sonorous phrase and catch the mild eye upon me not without tenderness, under the proud grey wimple so recently assumed. Thereafter would come my mother's shame. 'Forgive her, Mother,' she would say. And the douce answer . . . 'She's but a little maid, let her slumber. There's time aplenty . . .'

'She's but a child. She would not withstand an inquisition . . .' Queen Elizabeth's cold eyes, with death, and death's fear, shifting in their depths.

I knelt before the Queen, the Prioress. Rays of fire smoked off a great ruby and emerald cluster on the lifted white hand, and the dog leaped from her lap to sniff around my skirts. I had to crane upward to observe Dame Johanna properly, and for the second time was amazed, for between this Prioress and the ladies of court there was but a hair's-breadth of difference; indeed, her habit was of stuff far richer than worn by, say, Anne Haute, a frugal soul. Brows had she none, they had been plucked out fine and fashionable, and the breadth of forehead above was like a wide white river. Certes, she was beautiful, with glass-green eyes sharply halved by lids of cream, and a full, small mouth. No princess would have scorned her jewels. She was mayhap ten years older than I, no more. Bemusedly I stared at her. Was there some little pleading in my gaze, for what I know not; for charity, or understanding, perchance? In any event, my glance disaffected hers and she looked away, snapping her white fingers to the dog, while the drone of Thomas a Kempis's writings went on above my head.

'*Soyez la bienvenue,*' said Dame Johanna, still looking away. I moved nearer, kissed the icy jewel extended to me, whispered 'Gramercy,' and took my seat at a side table two steps down from the Prioress's dais, ill-ease and wild of mind, wondering to hear the courtly tongue in a House of God, looking at the fair table appointments, the heavy silver salt inlaid with beryl, the fat gold goblet at Dame Johanna's elbow, and glancing up covertly to study the two nuns on the dais steps.

The one reading had a visage saffron yellow and long as a ram's. She clipped each word with close, rat teeth. Black hairs prickled coarsely on her upper lip. She followed each line in the book with a tall curved nail, so that now and again her eyes could safely stray from the text and rest on Dame Johanna's face in a curious glance both servile and truculent. It was, I decided, an envious, cunning face and heavy with secrets, and I turned quickly from it to have my own gaze caught up in that of the other, silent nun, who stared, and continued to stare, at me.

Although the eyes, half-closed, looked as if they had wept for years, a thread of dark intelligence struck at me from between the slits. A strange, wavering light that glowed and flattened and was extinguished even as I gazed. The rest of the face was common-place. Pale, puffed cheeks and fleshy, dough-coloured chin surrounded a soft mouth oddly childish, hanging a little open to reveal blackened teeth, while deep lines stretched upward to the nostrils. An ordinary enough face, as faces go, save for the look about the eyes. That woman looked at me as if she knew my very soul and all its secrets, as perchance she did. There was madness in those eyes; two demons straining at a chafed thread, and sorrow, and murder, and yet, despite these evil things, a cry for help, a desperate yearning for succour which those eyes knew would be ever late in coming. And all manner of dolorousness: the courier ambushed on the road, the poison drunk before the bride-groom's arrival, the last standard falling beneath a field of spears . . . Within a few breaths' space, I knew that those eyes could infect me with whatever sickness had their owner in thrall. So I looked down, smoothing the cloth with trembling fingers, picked up my trencherknife and replaced it, while the heat of the candles and Dame Bridget's stare shrivelled my senses.

The Prioress said grace, liltingly, stumbling on one phrase, winding up in a rush with a slurred 'Amen'. She laughed merrily, clapped her hands, and the dog shrilled a yap. I sat, feeling Dame Bridget still watching me.

"Bring meat!" cried the Prioress. 'By my hand, I've an appetite! Juliana, close that book! Those dull writings turn my stomach. Read something other. Read Geoffrey of Monmouth, the tale of Merlin and Arthur. Bridget, the wine!'

Bridget went smoothly to the flagon, poured a red stream into the shining goblet upheld. Juliana laid down her book, shook back her wimple, long face set.

'Madame, *we* have not yet eaten,' she said peevishly.

The Prioress laughed again. 'Fie!' she cried. 'Leave reading, then! Sit down, and sup with me! Let us be entertained this night; we have a guest from court!'

All three looked at me. There was a small lightening of Juliana's horse-face. At Bridget I did not look.

'Shall we continue to speak French?' asked the Prioress, sweetly enough.

I sat dumb. This was not how I recalled the life in cloister. At Leicester, meals were taken in silence. There were the signs, of course; the hands wagged sideways, rippling (for one who desired fish)—the pinching of thumb and forefinger (for salt)—the nose-rubbing (for mustard), all overlaid by the companionable Lives of the Saints, the click of knife on platter. There was no question of what language we should use; our hands said all that was necessary.

'English then, mistress,' said the Prioress, a trifle sharper. Then, suddenly alert: 'Ah, here comes our supper!'

Although the room was not large, it seemed to take Edyth an hour to traverse it, laden and limping. Spiced steam rose from the great trencher she carried. She carved well as I watched her, as well as any of the King's henchmen. Dame Johanna spied every morsel on to the plate, choosing a slice of baked venison, the breast of a partridge dripping with Burgundy juice, carrots like tiny golden daggers, lord's bread white as snow. She served her dog at table; it slobbered from silver, paws on the cloth. And so stealthily did Edyth go with her ladle and platter that I failed to notice how high she piled my plate also. Chunks of meat, its rich rankness disguised by basil and cinnamon. I felt my bowels twist within me, and, hands clenched under the cloth, prayed that I would not vomit, as I was wont to do of late.

When she was partially assuaged, Dame Johanna leaned forward.

'What of the court, then, mistress?' she asked, showing little teeth.

' 'Twas in confusion, when I saw it last,' I murmured. 'And many, many—in dire peril.' Grief, steam, candlelight mingled to choke me.

The Prioress looked at Juliana, who was eating as if it were her last meal.

'So 'tis true, then,' she said. 'Her Grace's henchman told me that Warwick was arming, but he's a great liar, that man.'

'While our sister here speaks only gospel,' said the Sub-Prioress spitefully. Juliana did not like me, that was plain from her glance, yet I did not fear her. It was Bridget, or rather, something in her, that I feared. The Prioress looked hard at me.

'Yea, I think she does,' she said slowly. 'What of Neville of York?'

'The Archbishop is at London.'

She smiled. 'That is well,' she mused. 'With his mind full of war, he will scarcely have time for us, I think.'

I could not follow her drift. I watched her downward smirk, her toying with a piece of bread; and the rainbow-changes on Juliana's face, primness, sourness, unwilling gratification, all writ plain. But the next probing question chilled my blood.

'How does her Grace of Bedford? I heard talk of witchcraft—some vile and slanderous charge? How say you to this?'

'There was an arraignment,' I whispered, bone-cold.

'Foulness,' said the Prioress. 'Is my lady safe?'

I stared at my load of cooling partridge. 'She is in Sanctuary,' I said dully. But Johanna was not listening. Johanna, the Woodville-lover; her greedy eyes were fixed on the pantry door.

'The sturgeon!' she cried, as the odorous darkness yielded Edyth. Serve it not too hot, Edyth. Go carefully, with your cumbrous foot.

She had almost reached the dais when an ankle turned beneath her. Truth to tell, it looked well-nigh deliberate, but there was naught planned in the hurting way she fell, clutching at the hanging damask to save herself, letting go of the vast silver salver so that the succulent fish shot on to the rushes, spewing gravy and lemon-slices, all broken and steaming on the ground. The dog leaped yapping from its

442

chair and rushed upon the wreckage, burnt its mouth, screamed and flew back under the table.

Johanna rose and came unhurriedly down the steps, and in one lightning moment I knew that she willingly sacrificed her meal to sate another lust. I looked once only as her open hand descended across Edyth's face with the sound of a whiplash. I sat head in hands, fighting the rising demon in my belly, while the noise cracked out again and again. After what seemed a lapse in time, there was silence, and, looking up with one eye to see if she had killed Edyth, I saw the Prioress, refreshed, back in her chair, drinking wine. There was no sign of her victim.

'Now, mistress,' she said to me. And of a sudden, I was wondrous calm. I was alive. In a world of strife and violence, I was alive. I sat erect. Dame Bridget was no longer there and I was calm.

'You will be professed, of course,' Johanna said, not looking at me.

'I will not,' I said out of my calmness.

This startled her and her eyes shot round. She drank more wine. I watched the movement of her thoughts.

'I understood that you would be professed,' she said again, and her fractional hesitancy gave me courage.

'Her Grace of Bedford laid no injunction on that score,' I said, gambling as hard as I had ever done.

She looked away swiftly. 'Nay, neither did she.'

'I brought a good corrody,' I said boldly. All the money, in fact, that my father had entrusted to Sir Richard Woodville for my marriage or for my profession. I was not married. I would not be professed. Witless little fool that I was, I was learning. By sheer will I dragged her eyes back to mine and hung upon them, while she pondered, flickered, and shrugged suddenly.

''Tis naught to me,' she finally said, and drank. And I drank, holding her over the cup with my eyes, and before I drank I pledged my sweet heart in sweet wine, for a safe passage of arms, a fair meal and a soft bed, and I was truly a little mad, that night.

They were waiting for me, at the foot of the curving frater stair. Dame Joan, weighed by a flagon of strong ale, gibbering with combined wrath and excitement, was anxious to know my thoughts on her skill as cellaress, her training of the cook. She strutted in the meagre warmth of a tallow dip; the others

443

were only shadows, but their breathing rose hissing from the dark cloister.

'Do not punish Edyth,' I heard myself say. 'She was cruelly beaten.'

Joan sucked in her cheeks. '*Pardieu, parbleu!*' she exploded, then began to quiver, round and bird-like in mirth. 'So Madame was cheated of her favourite dish! I trow our lady's face was worth a mark, and she marked Edyth's face, so I'll reward the child.' She jutted upon me in laughter.

'*You* did not eat,' she said accusingly.

' 'Twas all too splendid for my stomach,' I replied.

'Courtly manners!' she said with approval.

'The court!' came whispered from the darkness. Yea, the court, the court. All around rose a hushed sea of pleading. 'Tell us of the court.'

'*I* was at court,' quavered an old voice. 'When Harry reigned, crazed as an owl. The Frenchwoman turned him, men said, with her bedsport . . . marry, he was holy.'

'By St Loy!' Joan cried suddenly. 'We'll pleasure ourselves, now. Will you take ale, lady, in the misericord?'

Sweeping with mockery, she led me, while the following shadows loomed behind, down a low passage with a dim, fanned roof and gilded bosses.

'A shapely building, this,' I murmured, looking about.

'Bawl bawl!' answered Joan. 'The place is falling about our heads. For all the wool she sells from one hundred sheep, not a groat does Madame spend on its upkeep. Wait you.' She gripped my arm, riotously. "Wait till the next visitation by my lord Bishop's bailiffs. Then will I settle old scores . . .'

Around the wall-angle a light guttered suddenly and burned up bright, to the most dreadful sobbing sound, and I thought: Edyth! Yet it was Dame Bridget who came slowly towards us, with tears falling like rain; great round drops dripping over the barbe at her chin, splashing darkly on the darker stuff of her habit. Blind she walked on, blind to us all, and when she had turned the corner, the noise of her sobs lingered on the dark air.

'Jesu! what ails her?' I cried.

Joan, turning, made a knowledgeable moue and winked at someone in the dark.

'Again, so soon,' she remarked, over my head. 'They took her but a fortnight past, these fits. I fancy . . .'

'Dame, what ails her?' It was of great importance; I feared the weeping nun so much. Joan threw open the door to the misericord. Light streaked about her mischievous face.

444

' 'Tis a sickness,' she said lightly. 'Madame has a fanciful name for it; she calls it *l'accidie.*'

So we sat, fairly companionably in the misericord, while Joan sucked at bread-soppets in her beer. The ale, warring with the Prioress's strong wines, set my head to spinning, and the line of black-garbed faces opposite to swinging in my view. The nuns observed me, incurious, wistful, weary, uninterested. In one corner slept an old woman in secular dress. Tethered to a perch, a jaybird sat quietly, its head beneath its wing.

'Good bread, eh?' demanded Joan, waving a great black crust. 'Dame Gertrude does our baking.'

A wizened little nun, her face crossed and ribboned with lines, half-rose, bowed to me doubtfully. In a voice like a breathy harp, she said, pointing to the bread and ale: 'Wafers and hypocras.' A jest at which only she smiled.

'The King's Grace takes such, before retiring.' So spoke the nun who had known the court when Harry Six kept it.

'Yea,' I said.

Joan turned sharply on the aged nun. 'Baw! How can you remember! And you were there only a month, if at all.'

'Agatha was ever puffed up,' said Dame Gertrude. Her spiteful little eye crept sideways amid the forest of wrinkles.

'It was so!' cried Agatha querulously. ' 'Twas so, is now, ever shall be.' With surprising vigour, she picked up a roll of bread and threw it, smiting Joan in the chest. 'And your bread chokes my gullet!' she added to Dame Gertrude, whose face reddened with fury. The jay awoke, emitting a piercing shriek. A nun with skin pitted and pocked like an orange seized the bird off its perch and began stroking its feathers, calling it her hinny, her dear, in loud raucous tones. The old corrodian slept on, snoring through the din. I got up, sat down again. From above, faintly, then loud, came the plink of lute and the hollow note of tabor. A gay dance tune. As we listened, the door opened and a nun rushed in, harassed, angry, pointing at the ceiling with one hand, snatching up a pitcher with the other.

'Give me ale, for mercy's sake!' she cried. 'So! Madame sports aloft, while I sit in the gatehouse, starving!' (Her looks belied this, she was stout as a cask.) 'Dance, does she? They who dance have the Devil's bell about their neck! And when he hears them jangle, he says. "Ho, hoo, my cow is with yet!"'

'Our Sub-Prioress makes merry, too,' said D̶̶̶̶̶̶ ̶̶̶ ̶̶ ̶marked

'Yea, Juliana's in favour this night.'

nun, rolling up her eyes. 'For how long, though?'

'There'll soon be strife again,' muttered Gertrude, emerging from her sulk.

'More for the reckoning, come my Lord's visitation,' said Dame Joan, with a suck and a gloat. 'Her ways, her airs, her tongue.'

For some reason unknown, the stout nun became incensed.

'Speaking of tongues,' she said, glowering. 'I know others ripe for chastisement. Even from the hostillaria I could hear. Blasphemer!'

'Who, me?' cried Joan. 'In faith, you lie. Or you're bewitched, or I'm besotted. I'll feign deafness.'

'*I'm* deaf, from your foul oaths,' pursued the porteress. 'Day in, day out. By St Jude, by St Anne, by the Holy Book, and Holy Church and by Our Blessed Lord Himself. As for poor St Loy, you've worn his name to a thread. Come the visitation, they'll cut you a piece of red cloth, shaped like a tongue, to wear beneath your godless chin.'

Joan drummed on the board.

'By St Loy, you vex me, Dame,' she cried. 'Yet I'll not answer, for I know you lust to fight.'

'Certes, ask me out,' said the fat nun grimly. They were like demons. I had never heard women quarrel so before, for such scant cause. Dame Agatha roused herself to observe that the cellaress should have been whipped more as a young maid; in her corner, the snoring parlour-boarder remained the sole element of peace. While Joan, to my surprise, bore insults with equanimity, gums folded round a sucket of bread. It seemed she was not averse to goad, but herself would not be drawn.

'In faith, I mislike your countenance,' persisted the stout one. She feinted at Dame Joan with the end of a custy loaf. Frightened by the sudden movement, the jaybird lunged at the porteress with beak and claws, got tangled in her wimple, broke free screaming and circled the room like a clatter-winged fiend. I rose, unable to bear it, forgetful of my youth, my newness, my grief.

'My ladies, for the love of God!'

They fell silent and looked at me wonderingly. I think they had forgotten my presence, all in their anger's joy.

'Yea, tell of the court,' said Dame Gertrude, and they arranged themselves like children at lessons, bunched together with eagerness, waiting, and I was anxious again, not knowing to begin, what to say, for the court, in truth, had place through which I walked unseeing, deaf

446

and blind to its richness and its music, eyes fixed or searching a face, a name, a smile, senses tuned only to a voice, hands, a look, did he look sad today, or glad today, and did he take his meat with good appetite; was he walking in the pleasaunce—yea, he must be there among the swans and flowers, for the sun shone as it would ever shine, on him, fortunate sun.

Was he alive tonight, in peril this night, was his horse steady under him, was he backed up against a thicket with his men, was there blood upon his sword, blood on his mouth, blood on the Boar, the snowy Boar upon its azure field, and would he, would he think of me, if only fleetingly in a slack moment (if such moments there be)—a maid, there was a maid once—yea, perchance he'd think like that—a maid, who loved him more than life and sharp as death, who carried within her the child of his body—of which he knew naught.

'. . . he is truly fair?' came a voice, leagues distant.

'Yea, fairer than truth,' said my own voice, equally far.

'They say he stands four handbreadths higher than other men—gold-headed; is't so?'

'Nay. He's dark. Blue eyes, almost black, and of low stature.'

They digested this. They must have formed a passing false notion of King Edward. But I went on, no doubt a little foolishly, and as I talked, all my fears renewed themselves. Thus, after weaving a fine saga, like cloth of Arras, of jousts and revelry, I bit off its splendid thread and asked that which I could no longer withhold. I asked them: 'What of the rebellion?' Their barbed, dreaming eyes were suddenly keen.

Dame Gertrude said, waspishly: 'How say you, Dame? What should *we* know of it?' And the stout and warlike porteress cried out marry, *she* had never been in London, never in fact further than Middleham, and looked askance as if now she doubted all my words, thought me counterfeit. My own voice, uncaring in hope and dread, asked was Middleham far? She answered it was half a day's journey years ago, the roads being foul and likely so remained, but as for Middleham Castle being far, why, as the crow flies, nay.

Each time she said the name it speared me like a toothache, pain and pleasure in the pain. I had not thought to be so near his joy.

A bell clamoured, wild and dark, erratic in its vigour, arousing the aged dame in a fit of coughing. The nuns got up hurriedly, brushing off crumbs, swilling the dregs of ale.

'I'll hear Compline,' Dame Joan announced. 'For I could die this night.'

Was there a choice, I wondered? Or had mischief, this child of indiscipline, bred complete heresy in the women? Yet they went dutifully, folding their wimples tight about bowed heads, fingers clothed by their beads, and, admittedly, Joan did turn to me as we walked, saying with grinning gums: 'Fear not! I *always* hear Compline!'

The chapel, like my room, needed repair. Fearful light-chinks gleamed through the tower masonry. It was cold, like all such places, with a smell of stale incense and onions. The nuns filed into their stalls on either side the nave. I knelt alone, heart-heavy, a little way behind the old corrodian. I saw Juliana come in, redly flurried, wiping her mouth; I looked nervously for Dame Bridget and saw her not. Madame's dog, unwearied by close of day, rollicked up and down the aisle, hunting a mouse behind the roodscreen. The pock-faced nun brought in her pet bird, unholy jay; it shrieked and chattered, drowning the voice of a fat little priest. And never had I heard an office taken with such scant regard of form or meaning—he rampaged through as if reciting for a wager against all the other scattered clerks in Christendom who might be saying the same words at a steadier pace.

Did *he*, perchance, hear Compline at this hour? Or was he, unthinkably, past hearing?

The chaplain's assistant was a fair young man, too well-favoured ever to have taken orders. A rufus, his tonsure like an auburn crown. It was better when he began to sing, after his master had tripped and staggered through the versicle, throwing whole pieces to the four winds, starting a line, forgetting it, and leaping gaily on to something halfway down the page; riding the versicle out like a night-hag, while I tried vainly to follow his whim in my missal. But when the red-haired young man took up the reading, his voice was rich as well-brewed mead.

'I will lay me down in peace and sleep; for thou, O Lord, only makest me to dwell in safety,' sang the nuns in response.

O Lord! Make him, dear Lord, to dwell in safety. If it means my own life's taking.

In the choir, someone belched, said audibly: 'My belly's afire, that I vow.' My growing godly vision curled and died like a scythed flower.

'Into thy hands, O Lord,' sang the chaplain's assistant, pure and high.

448

'For thou hast redeemed me, O Lord, thou God of truth,' replied the nuns, half-voiced.

'Gloria!' screamed the jaybird—was it the jaybird?—hopping fiendlike along the back of my stall.

Into thy hands, O Lord, I commend my spirit. I stayed, kneeling low, while the chaplain threw his outer vestment over one of the candles and scuttled away as if he had instant business at the other end of England. His fellow priest followed more leisurely, and the nuns, a chaos of mirth and black plumage, tramped down the nave and were gone, presumably to their beds in the dorter. So in quietness I took the breviary and murmured my own Compline, missing out naught, and added the *nobis quoque peccatoribus*, the Great Intercession, for the living—and the dead.

Then I saw the Cross, a stain stretched out before the altar, dark in the waning light. A feigned vision, for it moved, dissolved before my eyes, reared to a kneeling posture, sobbing, fell down again, spreading human arms against the stone. I heard the murmured words of penitence, while the light faded more, bats beat against the clerestory and I grew sad to be witness. After a time, the nun arose, gathered her habit around her and came lightly down the nave to where I sat in silence. Her wimple had slipped back from her face, and a little of her cropped hair was visible, tiny curls like you would see on the head of a young page, or the back of a yearling lamb. Tear-tracks lined her thin cheek. She was about twenty. Rising, I asked her pardon.

'''Tis naught,' she said, twining her rosary. She had a mouth flower-soft, gentle eyes.

'The others know, so why not you?' She looked closer. 'You are the London lady,' she said. 'Young. Young,' she repeated thoughtfully, 'fair, and kindly by your countenance. God grant, child, you never bear such as I.'

She bent and gave me a light kiss, a courtly salute with true warmth in it, then said: 'My name is Adelysia,' and, shockingly: 'And my soul is for ever damned.'

Moments passed, then I said: 'Jesu have mercy on it,' trembling for her. She stood, steadfast, sadly smiling, and I whispered: 'Is there no penance . . . to absolve you?'

'Daily,' she answered, and took a little scourge from her girdle, flicking it around her neck where a rich welt glowed, instantly.

'If . . . you are penitent . . .'

'God's mercy?'

'Surely, His infinite mercy.'

'You do not know my sin,' she said almost gaily.

''Tis not my affair,' I said, leaving the chapel. She came with me, like a quiet wind.

'The Queen's Grace sent you, did she not? Will you be happy here?'

How could I be happy, I asked her, when I would fain be elsewhere? And it seemed this was a peaceless place, with one and the other. Little Edyth . . . the nuns who bickered like alewives, comported themselves like madwomen.

'Come,' Adelysia said, taking my arm. 'Walk in the cloister-garth until bedtime. The air will soothe you.'

I was moved to her. In all her own distress, she cared for my comfort.

'The nuns act so,' she said, as we trod the succulent green-sward, 'because they have lived and slept, eaten and prayed together for so long that when they quarrel, it is as if they rage against their own selves. Their chatter is like that of birds, the birds they bring into church, wanton and senseless and over quickly. If, with a knife, they could change each other's countenance, they would be passing glad. But it is all like little dogs barking, little children fighting. Truly, they are good women.'

'The Prioress . . .'

She tucked her arm close in mine. 'Dangerous,' she said softly. 'High born and wilful, and sailing close to the wind. As for Juliana, she loves and hates. She plans to be on the winning side, come the reckoning. There are men like that, too,' she said in a changed tone.

'And Dame Bridget,' I said. She stopped walking, became still as the carved gravestones by which we paced.

'She . . . has *l'accidie*,' she whispered.

Dame Joan had spoken of this, and I was curious.

'*Accidia*, in the Roman tongue,' Adelysia said, looking across at a grove of yews. '*Accidia*. The most deadly thing upon God's earth. Born of sadness and boredom, and melan-cholia. Men go mad because of it. They lose their faith in thrall to it. And, because of it, eventually they perish, and die, and are everlastingly consumed.' Her eyes grew enormous and dark.

'There was a monk, not far from here,' she continued. 'A holy man, who for no reason save that he had been in cloister fifty years, contracted the sinful malady of *accidia*. He dreamed o'nights that he drowned in the waters of Hell (for there is water in Hell, along with the lake of fire) and daily he was cast down into a pit where God could not reach him.

450

Shut off from God and the Saints, he came no more in church. They found him in the fishpond, where the weeds shrouded him.'

I could not answer. My brow felt very cold.

'After thirty-eight years, Bridget comes no more to Church,' said Adelysia. We paced on. I looked uneasily at the troutstream, saw, horrified, a giant toad leap clumsily across the green. The child! O God, should I perchance do penance?

'What is your sin, Sister?' An unpardonable question, born of frenzy.

'Later, later,' she said, not offended. 'Guard against *accidia*, lady. It is allied to Tristitia, and Sloth. And . . .'

'Yea, Sister?'

'And there is also Wanhope,' she said, her voice dull. 'That comes of too much outrageous sorrow.'

Wanhope. Ah, a good word. Too much outrageous sorrow. My lord, my lord. There was a maid once . . . with nut-brown hair. She loved me, Frank—and I, enamoured for a space, dishonoured her. Mind you those revels, the twelve days of Christmas? An easy light o' love, she even chased me to Fotheringhay . . .

Wanhope. A good word. A word to bring madness, replace fond memory with a lie. Call back, then, the obedient horses of the mind . . .

'Jesu! You are fair!'

'I wonder, am I worthy of such love?'

'Sweet heart, my true maid, you brought me much joy and comfort.'

Ah, Wanhope, can you bring me Richard back?

'I loved, and lusted.' It was Adelysia speaking, not my thoughts. 'Saw you the young chaplain . . . with the sun girdling his head? Sunset-red, his hair. I lust, and love.'

'And he?'

'He pursues me. Even when he offers me the Host, his eyes lick mine. I am in mortal sin.'

In the dusk, she saw my questioning look.

'Nay,' she said bitterly. 'But in my soul I've lain with him, I'm guilty. Thank God my father is no more. He gave much gold for my profession when I was six years old. It was his pious wish. Pray Jesu he does not see me now. Apostate, and at heart, a whore!'

We had reached the end of the cloister, and the arched portal of the guest-house. A dark figure filled it, at whose sight Adelysia sought her crucifix. Dame Bridget stepped out of the shade. She had done with weeping.

'You're penitent?'

Adelysia's voice, a breath, answered: 'Yes, Dame, as ever.'

'There is no salvation,' the other said. 'There is none to save us. I have sought one, listened for his voice, and heard silence. This day, clearer than ever. Black, eternal depths.'

'And that, I cannot believe,' I said. Adelysia turned and looked at me, miserably clutching at my hope.

'You, Dame, have also sinned, no doubt,' Bridget said, ice and stillness. 'But this one, guilty of apostasy, heresy, foul lusts . . . know you, Sister, what the Fiend has in store?'

'Black waters, that do not purify, for all that they burn as they freeze. Living weeds, which wrap around the soul and drag it down. The demons of the undersea, slimed, crawling monsters. Sharp beaks to rend and tear . . . No warmth, no pity . . . Sister, hear me out!'

'*Ab omnibus malis. Libera nos, Domine,*' said Adelysia fervently. Once, long ago, Anthony Woodville had returned to Grafton Regis full of miracles, having been at St James's tomb in Compostella. Among other things he spoke long of a painting he had seen in Spain. He crossed himself while talking of it. For this portrayed the fleshly lusts, the just reward to follow, and obscene tortures of the damned so dreadful . . . the act of love itself a torture, made so by fire and sharp instruments. There were men stripped of the wayward flesh, white ribcages with witches feasting within, flames kindled in their bowels . . . women pierced by flowers like swords . . . men strung on viols, impaled by harpstrings . . . the devil-dance in full flood . . .

Yet all great men had lemen. Even Kings, anointed by the Chrism.

I came out of my stark dream. Adelysia wept, and I guided her to the dorter, while she clung upon my neck. To comfort her and quiet my own fear I said softly:

'I too have loved.'

'But you are not a nun,' she said sorrowfully, and touched my lips as she melted into the dark.

I stumbled towards bed. I would ask the Prioress for a penance, for my sake and the child's, and above all, as surety for the life and deliverance of my lord. Somehow I knew that he lived. Had he been dead, I would have known that, too. I would do penance, whatever Dame Johanna gave me.

My cell was transformed. Edyth had been, was still there in fact, and she had brought every conceivable form of bed covering for my pleasure, three or four blankets, a moth-chewed fur, her own meagre cloak. And, in the corner neatly arranged upon a hempen bag, were sweet herbs for my well-being. Agrimony for the eyes, aloes for the heart (full dangerous), the sloe's fruit for the bowels. Saffron for the eyes, flowers of the valley lily, also for the heart, rose petals, rue, the King's Evil root for kidney pains, dried elderberries for a fever. She had an infusion of ginger hot for me, and she herself was in my bed, to make it warm. Having heard my whispered need for medicines, she had acted upon it. If Edyth was witless, may all my friends be simple in the head.

In the night she cherished me, slipping away twice to ring Matins and Lauds, and did her utmost to shield me from the damp; yet I know it was in that place began the rheumatism which plagues me now.

The snow was drifted halfway up the window. Sacrificed on its summit lay a sparrow, stiffly dead. Snow scurried like powder under a sharp wind, heaping the corpse with white. Across the moor that same wind raged and cracked branches made brittle by the ice of weeks. A few of the sheep had ventured near to the house and stood mournfully nestled together, their thick wool hanging matted almost to the ground. They stood out dark against the snow. Even the trees seemed to be crowding closer, too. Behind me, the Prioress chafed hands by the fire. I could still feel her eyes upon my body.

'Now I know why you asked for a penance,' she said softly, and blew on her fingers.

She had been loath enough to give it to me, four months earlier. First, she could not find her book, in which were set out the statutory penances for this and that; then, she vowed it was passing awkward, the rules for a nun not being applicable for a corrodian, and further . . . which was where I broke in, heartrent, and babbled something about asking his Grace the Bishop when he next descended on us. Whatever my words, she flew straightway into great agitation and gave me answer in the next breath. I was to fast for three days, come last into church for a month, during which time I was to say seven psalters. And, as my sin was *de lapsu carnis* (all I would tell her) I could go barefoot the length of the cloister for seven days, upon the hour of None. All this I did, and the nuns came peeping, open-mouthed, as if at a miracle. And as I walked I prayed for his deliverance, and the stone was not even chill beneath my soles. Edyth walked with me. I could not stop her. She had taken the notion to grip my garment by its side, one fold pinched between her fingers.

'In truth, you're my shadow,' I told her in amazement, on the sixth day. She shook her head vigorously.

'Say not so, lady,' and looked afraid. 'Dame Bridget speaks of a shadow. 'Tis evil. 'Tis within us,' she said, hissing-breathed, and as I was growing sick from Bridget's dreadful talk, I said hastily: 'Then you're no shadow, little one.'

'I pray for you,' she answered.

'Then you're my beadswoman.'

Now the Prioress studied what was no longer secret.

'They did not tell me, lady, that your dower was meant to feed two mouths.'

During this interview, I said very little. Yet here, I felt bound to remind her that there was no more money from that source. This I did with equanimity, knowing that my dower was ample for myself and for my babe.

'And the gentleman?' Arrogantly sounded, this—she is of no account, likewise he is of no account, but marry, let us have his name, and see how my poor house may benefit thereby.

I thought of Elysande. I had learned my lesson well. I shook my head, I even smiled a little. Knight of the most noble Order of the Garter, Knight of the Bath, Earl of Cambridge, Duke of Gloucester. Hidden from me behind the edge of war. Mine. Mine for a little space. Within my heart for ever.

I said naught, but looked pleasant, and Dame Johanna's eyes began to slide away, as they ever did.

'Daughter or son, I wonder?' she said, surprisingly. I could not know what went on in her mind, and even when she mused, 'You may bear a wench—when is your time?' I saw naught of significance. I answered: 'In the spring,' and we parted from each other, both wondering and neither wise.

I went down to the scriptorium, passing by where some of the lay sisters were spinning, under the eyes of Dame Bridget. She walked among them, face vacant save for a glower, while the younger ones tittered behind her back. Madame Brygge, the old corrodian, worked industriously on a shift for herself. Deaf as a stone, she was unconscious of the maddening chirr-r that rose and fell like the wings of a giant imprisoned moth, or of Bridget's voice. Adelysia sat numbly by the window, her fingers limp about the distaff. Misery ringed her like a nimbus. I passed on to see Dame Joan. In my departing ears I could hear Dame Bridget, strangely vigorous that day. 'Spin! curse you all! Spin!'

So they span.

Joan was sighing over some bills.

'Baw! I can't read what last I writ,' she declared mourningly.

'What's that?' I asked, pointing.

'Red herrings,' she gloomed. 'Four kemps of oil and salt fish. Three pound, six pence.'

'In beef and eggs,' I read out. 'From St Michael, to St Simon and Jude. Ten shillings and three ha'pence. That's a lot of victuals, Joan.'

'There speaks the Prioress!' said she, in a rage. 'Dame, Dame, you run me into debt! How shall my pocket feed such hearty wenches? Fat, fat you all are! Am I fat?' she demanded. 'Is Gertrude fat? You might play tabor on her ribs. You could stop a door-draught with Edyth. Are *you* fat, mistress?'

'Yea, Joan,' I said, with a little smile. 'Behold me.'

Her temper died at once.

'Do you prosper, child?' she asked. 'No fevers, sweatings, dreams?' She hoisted my skirt to see my ankles, pursed her mouth and nodded judiciously. Then she prodded my belly. 'Leaps he lively, the lusty lord?'

'Nay,' I said, puzzled.

'Then, mayhap he's a lazy lord,' she said, passing kindly. 'What? Weeping anon? Faugh!' she said, dabbing at the blot I had made on her household book. 'What a running river I have about me! That Adelysia . . . and you, who I thought might cheer us with tales o' London, you're dolorous as a bereft ewelamb. I'll need to rewrite this page.'

'I'm not always sad,' I said, choking. 'We've laughed together. When I showed you the old basse-danse, and Bridget caught us . . .'

'Nay! Nay!' said she, with a clumsy twirl. 'I'm a cross creature.'

'Let me repair the writing,' I said. You are not cross, Joan, I thought. No more than is Gertrude, or Agatha. All, as Adelysia said, like little dogs barking at one another, little children quarrelling. And God has preserved you from the sin of accidia. I don't have *l'accidie*, she had told me, grinning. *Pardieu!* I live too much in this world to be deranged by such unearthly pangs. For good Dame Joan was a businesswoman. All the convent hinds were afraid of her. She bullied one James Mustarde, supposed to be solely employed in tending the hogs. Each slaughter-day merciless Joan had him boiling up vats of lard for the tallow dips which she sold to the monks at Fountains, herself riding over the fell on an old dun mare to barter with the cellarer. It was a charitable act, she said, in expiation. It saved the good brothers much trouble, and gave them more time for prayer. None the less, she drove a sharp bargain. I often wondered what the Bishop would say about it, likewise her manner of accosting travellers on the moorland road, crying: 'Has your belly canker, good sirs? Take a root of King's Clover. Madame, your face is yellowish. Try my Corn Campion, blessed by the Baptist. Lemon Thyme for lung-rot! And a farthing-worth of fennel seed for fasting days!'

She was totting her own secret hoard, managing all the time to keep an eye on me as I wrote, to see I did it properly.

'A clerkly hand, yours,' she said musingly. 'There is a prayer that Brother Tom wants copying. Think you . . .'

'Certes, Joan, I'll do it,' I said, smiling again.

'I shall but take a quarter fee,' she said, all hasty. 'By St Loy! I was forgetting.' She fumbled among a dozen great rusted keys for her waist pouch. I felt the press of cold coin in my hand.

'For your threadwork,' she said, almost apologetically. 'The Abbot was well pleased. He had never seen Our Lady's monogram wrought so fine. Had it not been for the one slipped stitch he would have hung it in his own Chapel.'

I was warmed, more than I could say. Proud, too, to think of my work at Fountains, acknowledged by those grim, quiet men. I thought of all the good linen swaddlings I might buy for the babe. Loyalty's blue, a princely hue . . .

'Mayhap your lord will come soon to see you,' she said slyly. 'For I fancy he *is* a lord, and you a lady, once, at court.'

Did she taunt me? Nay, not Joan. Did she expect an answer? Did she think me mad, never to speak of him? to have no pittance from him, the father of my child? Did she deem him dead? And with that thought, the snow started again, silently swirling, each flake a ghost, a white flame in the greyness. Did she deem him dead, in truth?

'God's nails!' cried Joan, and clapped a hand over her mouth, slipped gabbling down her beads in swift penitence. 'I pray you, Madame, cease that crying!'

'It's Christmas,' I said.

'Holy and joyous season!' she cried. She marched me to the window. 'Here! Watch for the minstrels!'

I stood against the glass. Cold wind eddied about my face. And in the embrasure, with carven grin, was a little stone monk, his features rugged under my hand. The chill, carved faces, and music in the wind, a cold song ringing, rising high, an ice that burned as it froze. He was dancing, dancing with Katherine of Desmond. So agile and gracious, so light in the dance. The velvet of his doublet was a dark fire. His sombre eyes gleamed. Once, I saw him laugh—it pleased her, she looked at him as if she thought him pleasing indeed, and I was not jealous, for she was his good friend, and widowed, and used cruelly—a husband headed, and two little knaves, ah, what, what had he said, all white and red? The shedding of infants' blood? Those who do such . . . what then? For my life, I could not remember, though all his words lurked ever on the lip of my mind. I could only watch him, hearing the plangent lute, feeling again the gallery's icy cold which turned to such heat, such flowering warmth, such madness, at one touch of my lord's hand. I saw the sway and shimmer of gay Edward's poisonous court, far below me on the rose-painted floor. And eyes looked on me from the darkness, eyes like no other eyes in the world, and there was the feel of velvet cloth, the bruise of a heavy jewel crushed on my breast. And Richard's arms, and the Blessed Mass of Christ, holy and joyous season. And despair, to ring me round. The music fell faster, and the snow sang full strongly, I could distinguish each instrument now, rebec and reed, tambourin and harsh cromorne, but he was gone, and so was Countess Katherine, and the rose-decked floor laid waste, a white wilderness, and he was gone, I knew him gone, and felt Joan's arm, black-smith-brawny, about my shoulder, red drink roaring down my gullet.

'Don't spill it,' she said. ' 'Tis of my best. Good Clary wine.'

'They gave his mother that,' I heard myself say. 'Each night before sleep. A cure for childbed vapours.'

'Whose mother?' said Joan crossly. 'Drink.'

'He's dead,' I cried. 'Hear you the music?'

They were playing, strong and sprightly.

> Beauty, who keeps my heart,
> Captive within thine eyes.

I rolled my head in my hands. The music was within.

'You hear it, Dame?'

'Yea, the music,' she said, releasing her grip, moving away. 'They must have crept through the snow. Now Madame has them at their craft, wet clothes and all. Good fellows, too,' she said, tapping her foot. '*Belle, qui tiens ma vie!*' She sang, out of tune. 'How I love Christmas!' she said.

457

I was reeling. 'I must lie down,' I said. The words drifted away, unheard.

'Two moons ago, you promised me the receipt for hypocras.' She had her roll ready, pen poised, saying we might as well pleasure ourselves at Christmas, if ever. It would do Gertrude good, Gertrude who was frail and old, and I must lie down, and weep, fully, without the fear of chiding.

'Later, later, Dame.'

'Hypocras, child,' she said firmly. 'Haven't I given you of my best Clary?' A bargain was a bargain to Joan.

'*Aqua vitae*, 5 ounces.' How slow she wrote, while he lay dead by sword or bludgeon! 'Pepper, two ounces.' There was poison in the knot garden, swift and sure.

'Two ounces ginger.' The dreadful unknowing, not daring to know.

'Cloves, of the same.' He was dead. Dead, yet dancing?

'Grains of Paradise.' The quill broke, she fumbled and clicked her tongue.

'Ambergris, five grains.' Costly, costly. Was the King dead too?

'Musk, two grains.' To perdition with the King.

'Infuse for a night and a day.'

Joan sighed. 'How much sugar? How well they play! London lads were ever best, yet these were trained in France, that I warrant. By St Loy! I can't afford this drink. Not unless I teach young Mustarde threadwork too. How say you, mistress, if we . . .'

'You say they're from London?' Trembling breath, and hands gone witless, flying to my throat, my heart.

'Fresh from London, gossip-choked,' she said, and may have laughed at me a little, I did not stay to see.

There was one tall curly-haired boy, and the only one who did not snigger behind hands at the sight of me, young, unwed, swelling with child in a nunnery. I knew that they made songs about such as I. He was however kind, polite, and winked only once towards the ribald cheer that rose from his fellows as I, unthinkingly shameless, pulled him into an alcove, pleading, begging.

'Worth a kiss, is it?' he asked agreeably.

'I would hear of his Grace the King,' I said, trembling hard, and, so that there should be no confusion: 'His Grace King Edward Fourth, and his family.'

He gazed at me frankly. 'Stands the case so?' he said, with a little more respect, and I knew that he thought me one of Edward's lemen, and I wanted to laugh at the incredible thought, but checked myself, for the words from this young lutanist's tongue were more pricelsss than all the jewels round Elizabeth Woodville's throat, more precious than any of Joan's costly hypocras, and yet, my wits knew not how to mine for them. I looked up at him, saw his blond curls dabbled with melted snow, his merry, shining eyes, saw him not. His mouth took mine then, cool, ale-fresh, hearty. The kiss marked me, emboldened me, like the opening phrase of a song. Softly I asked him: 'How should Earl Warwick loose so royal a captive?'

He laughed, his contempt veiled in kind sadness.

'Dame, I would not for the Kingdom of Heaven,' he said, and stopped, and laughed anew. 'Nay, that's too high a price. For Heaven's estate, and that only, would I trade my condition for yours. 'Tis passing sad. To dwell here at the world's end. To have September's news for Christmas!'

O God! We were interrupted then by the nuns. They came into the frater with a great commotion, Dame Bridget harrying them. The minstrels watched, grinning covertly.

'Accursed, accursed. To leave off spinning thus!'

'I've spun enough,' said Agatha rudely. ''Tis Christmas. I'll hear Vespers, then I'll enjoy myself.'

Fiercely gay, she tripped on by, touched the lute in passing as one might stroke a baby's face. Its owner stood splay-legged and watched Bridget, reflectively chewing his top lip.

'She's poison, that one,' he remarked. He plucked a chord.

> 'Like marsh grass is my lady's countenance,
> Both wild and sour . . .'

'I kissed you,' I said desperately. 'The news now. The London news, for Jesu's love.'

He was looking this time at Adelysia, who came tapping, beads swinging to that light, quick tread.

'A special tune for you, holy fair,' he cried.

She smiled wanly. The chaplain had gone to York for Christmas, to the house of his benefactor, a wealthy merchant taylor, leaving the fat gabbler to say all the offices alone, much to his displeasure. Adelysia therefore could have flung herself into devotion; should have been merry, heart-free. She was not, however. Tortured, heretic, solitary, Adelysia loved. I could have spared her a thought. I, who had once comforted the lonely, the tormented—yea, dear Lord! could have halved her burden. I have often been sorry.

'The King does well, then? *And* all his henchmen?' Mad, I

was willing to buy news with another kiss, but his eyes were straying again, this time over my shoulder. I felt a grasping at my gown and had no need to turn, but saw the minstrel's face, a little taken aback. Edyth, so thin and green, could shake one's soul at times, with her unearthliness. And she wanted something.

'Yea, what is it?'

' 'Tis hard,' she said, her usual fashion. Hard it is, I thought, to bend to your prattling while news of my love is so near. But the well was solid ice, she said. She was strong but not that strong. Dame Joan was roaring for water. Edyth had been prodding for an hour.

'I'll do it,' the minstrel said. We went out into the snow. Black ice lay on the lake. The stream was patched over with the same. Here and there a trout, dark and sullen, rose thrustingly to the brittle surface. White and silver the reeds, and stiff as swords. Was he safe? happy? alive? I stood mute while the minstrel drove his staff at the well's hard depths. Edyth held his legs as he leaned dangerously over the side.

'Certes, it's good and deep,' he said, peering, as water began to suck and trickle through. He turned the winch, tore his hands, cursed, and said: 'An easy drowning death, I think.'

'Not for me,' one of us answered.

'But for some,' he said, grinning. 'Yon sour-faced nun, perchance?'

Yea, he's right, thought I. Here were the grasping depths, the darkness, the slime. The goal of accidia. Bridget could well drown herself, in one of her melancholy spasms. But he was walking back towards the house, and I was running, all thoughts of Bridget, and Adelysia, and Edyth flown from my mind, straining to hear. What did he say? That the King was taken to Pomfret by Warwick, and from there, rescued. And how cleverly they turned the trick! One shot an arrow into the bailey while His Grace walked the lawn, signifying their presence. Another climbed the wall and asked would the King go hunting. Edward liked the audacity, the jest. (What a man, what a King!) Made brash by their endeavour, he sent word that he would gladly hunt, an the quarry be fair. Send all my lords to Pomfret, he said, and I'll go there to meet them.

'But he was already at Pomfret!'

'Nay, Middleham,' he said, cross and careless. 'Did I say Pomfret? Are you faint, mistress?'

'I thought . . . the King were dead,' I whispered.

460

(He was at Middleham. So near.)

''Twas but one of those flying tales.'

'Who . . . who were the lords that rescued him?' I could scarcely shape the words.

'Hastings, they say,' he replied. 'Young Buckingham, that I do know. Suffolk, I think. A few good archers. Archbishop Neville is disgraced. The See of York will soon be vacant. Earl Warwick fumes, but can do naught. Daft Harry's in the Tower again, Clarence in France, and Edward on the throne. Jesu, mistress! Aren't you glad I came your way?'

Never was there a more garbled tale, like a skein on a loom all twisted, with the colours showing the wrong way round, yet with a semblance of truth. But if the colours shone bright, I cared not a jot.

'And all were safe.'

'Not a head broken,' he said gaily. 'A good young man, the King's brother. Scarcely rest nor food did he take, till Ned was safe.'

'Gloucester.' Oh, the pain and bliss of saying it. A wound within the mouth.

'Yea, Dickon. He's in Wales now, Governor of the Marches. Didn't I say Earl Warwick fumed? All his old commissions gone to the stripling Duke . . .'

A wound, born of a kiss.

We were at the door of the frater. Be good to him, Wales, fortunate Welsh. The players struck up again, each note a sweet, cold icicle.

Vientôt me secourir
Ou me faudra mourir . . .

Aid me or I die. He was beyond my call. He was conferring with his Welsh chieftains, hearing the oyer and terminer in wild valleys. Bards hymned him on the harp. He rode a black mare over the mountains. He did not think of me. He was alive.

He was alive.

Within me I felt the joy. It leaped and sang in my breast, in my belly. Startlingly potent, it turned and fluttered within my bowels, at the burning core of all my loyalty and my hope. Joy leaped lustily, with such vehemence that I swayed, clutched the cold, stone, searing wall, a wall of flame. Richard lived. My joy bounded through me like a bird.

His child reeled within me. Richard lived.

'The Welsh seem greatly attached to him,' said the lute-player, departing.

The room was full of people and shadows and pain.

'This is surely the true penance,' said an awed voice. Soft though they were whispered, the words lashed me like a running sea. My mind seemed split in two. One half was dead, the other knew everything sharp and clear. I did not know my name. I knew that the sun had shone all day, fierce for April. I did not know that they had built a great blaze in the hearth. I knew that night had come, but the sun's heat still poured over me, they had brought the sun into the chamber. I knew that Edyth was in church, praying for me to St Bernard, yet Edyth knelt beside the bed—so Edyth could be in two places at once, sweet Edyth with her green marsh-face, and therefore she was a witch and I screamed for they were going to burn her. Nay, it was Jacquetta of Bedford they were going to burn. I took their pains upon me, double pains, too much to bear, and screamed in the flame. Yet it was meet they should burn Jacquetta, she of the mischievous potion and the little lead lovers twining beneath the moon. Vervain and cinquefoil, aconite and amanita, she had given them to the King. Nay, I had given them, had mixed them in his wine, and they were burning me. They burned me slowly, in a fierce foreign garden. Even white-muzzled Gyb had come to watch the burning. He sat on my belly and sharpened his claws, a cat painted from out of the air by a man with raw Spanish colour on his brush. He stroked the colours on me one by one. Each was a molten pain as it ran down, he moaned as he worked, he did not want to hurt me, but it was written, my daughter, men are fickle, fiickle, forget not the other!

'Jesu, mercy,' said Elizabeth Woodville, and crossed herself. I fell at the Queen's feet. I was in darkness for a space, while the fires died down. Above my head came a muttering.

'The fever abates,' I heard. ' 'Twas the yarrow-flower water she took. It never fails.'

'Nay, the Saint answered. I looked just now. The candles are right down, and burning.'

Burning. I saw horsemen, their harness rent and bloody, arching dark vaults peopled by demons, the devils of the green fens with their malefic lights held high to shine in my eyes. They were tearing my sinful flesh with pincers. A shrieking voice curled around the ceiling. 'O blessed Lady, help me! Sweet Bernard, succour me!' I wondered, through my agony, what poor soul cried in such anguish.

'The creature is right small; I fear she's not mighty enough in body.' Hands stroked my hair, a rough stale touch unused to caressing. With difficulty I looked to see a stout red face, the sweat-soaked wimple clinging to either cheek. The lips moved.

'Help me, child,' they said. 'Give life. Come, give life to your lazy lord.'

Monstrous, Gyb fell on me again, a swollen-furred tiger.

I did not know that Joan was such a skilled accoucheuse. She told me later she had learned her craft in Citeaux, before entering the Founder House. They held a crucifix before my eyes; on that I hung, while my strength ebbed and waned and became as a mere dot of life, suspended for a spell, utterly contained in its stark shape. And the cross spoke to me, in a woman's voice, saying:

'She has a maid—right fair and lovesome it is, too.' Another wiped the sweat from out of my eyes and I saw the stern and kindly faces about my bed, then looked down, and for the first time beheld my Katherine, who had the nut-brown hair, to say naught of the blood royal.

A royal bastard maid. Born to glory, death and sorrow, like her father. Like all the ill-starred Plantagenets.

I had her named Katherine. All the nuns lost their wits over her. Even Juliana, the most unlikely person, kissed her often when she thought no one was looking, and gave her a blue beads to keep her from harm. Bridget kept away from her, and the Prioress said naught, which should have warned me. And the nuns exalted my choice of a name for her, as Catherine is the patron saint of maidens, and reflected well on all of us. Yet they did not know my own reasons for calling her thus.

I did it in remembrance of my Lady of Desmond, who had been kind to him.

I recall when I began, vainly, to care about Adelysia. It was the Feast of St Hilary of Poitiers, a sharp black January in the eleventh year of Edward's reign, and I was teaching Katherine the opening passage of the Credo, and to say *Jube, Domine, benedicere*, though that will not go down in the chronicles. She was almost two, full of wit and fair beyond belief. Venus was strong on her natal day. I should not, cannot, speak much more in this wise. There are things past

463

bearing, made harder because they are unforgettable. She impressed Dame Joan, ever vigilant for a show of sharp wits. She had her on her lap, giving her French endearments. This vexed me, I grant it. I went from the scriptorium, leaving them together. I was always jealous. I know not who petted her the most: Edyth, with her timid amorousness, Joan, who made her laugh, or long-faced Juliana. It was only when I learned that Juliana, before being professed, had miscarried of a child, that I understood. In those days I was so single-minded, clinging desperately to my heart's one token, I was blind to the hardship of others. Kate was a fleshly covenant, and all beauty. And I wished with my soul that he could see her. I myself never wearied of looking at her. And what was it I sought? Of course, of course. In morning and evening light, I turned her about, smoothed back her rich hazel hair. I gazed in her eyes, and prayed for one glimmer, one shadow, striking in the same way. On the Feast of St Hilary, it was there. She looked at me obliquely, and my breath caught up in my throat. She sat in kind, cursed Joan's lap, with her hands joined like a wreath of flowers. The winter sunshine made her eyes long and oddly tilted at the outer edge. She had in no way a childish face, there was scant roundness about it. The fine high bones showed clear. I saw that spiritual, fatal arrogance, that delicacy. I kissed her so hard that she was frightened, and Joan gave me a slap.

'Cool off, Madame,' she said sternly. 'Don't cry, doucette. Go, you. Pull me a bagful of roots for drying. Spring's coming. There'll be some travellers on the Scotland road. They'll need my draughts to ward off all the heathen ills. Ah, she smiles, anon!'

Her mouth was not like mine, not red and full. It was not in the least like mine, nor were her eyes. Trembling, happy and sad, I tore myself away then and went into the knot-garden. A year of my planting and nurture had wrought a difference. Each bed was enclosed by a thick, neat row of box. Some of the herbs were sleeping, but under the stiff brown earth I felt them with my mind, their life pulsed through my fingers as I scratched at the ground. It was all there, life abundant, not dead but slumbering, awaiting its own Resurrection; a silent token of faith beneath the soil. There were rabbit droppings, too. Though the winter had not been so severe, it seemed that lately these pests had braved the half-wild cats who roamed our estate and had come to scavenge my precious patch. I felt a strange, sharp anger. Little things seemed to annoy me more each day; I found myself snapping at Joan, at Edyth, closing my mind to the dreadful fear which accompanied these tempers. For it was unthinkable that I should fall prey to accidia. I was armed against it, yet often enough I caught myself thinking, in horror: Is this the beginning? They said it was allied to Tristitia and Sloth; therefore I kept well occupied and, to flaunt in the face of sadness, I had Kate, I believed in God's infinite mercy. But I had heard strong, shattering words, I lived in a shaken world, and two things were uppermost in my mind. How long should I be here? and, unheralded by any forethought: Could I not write to him? But there was also Wanhope, which comes of too much outrageous sorrow, and the Duchess of Bedford had made me a gift of that. While she lived, I dare not write to him. I had been more than fortunate. I had my Katherine, and my life.

So I thought of Jacquetta and was minded of how it all began. With a herb border at Grafton, from which I peeped to see a King embracing his heart's lust. I shuddered at the reality of my vision, for there were a man and woman standing in each other's arms, right before my eyes, against the cloister wall. And it was as of old; I could not move, or look away. He had her close, pressed back against the sunwarmed stone, and he was kissing her neck under the barbe and wimple pulled aside, while his hands strayed over her body. His tonsured aureole flamed. Adelysia's face was white, her head hung back, with eyes tight shut, as if to blot out sin.

Only an instant did I look before I fled, my hands full of earth and foliage, my heart pounding so that it hurt me. I ran desperately, dodging and weaving along the paths, through the untended grass. I think I moaned as I ran, under the burden of the great bell tolling for Sext. Full of shame and sympathy for Adelysia, I fled towards the church, more to pray for my own soul than to intercede against my sister's damnation. For that sight, which had bruised my very eyes, had brought again, sharp as death, the remembrance of him and me, together. I, who had thought I had contrived to forget. Forget! My flesh had not forgotten his lips nor my spirit his nearness . . . And the night when the marsh lights flickered about us in silent menace as we lay in the darkness of the tent, and it was not like that first time when we loved each other so swiftly and hastened partly because we were 'prentices in love and partly because we could have been disturbed at any moment. I said: 'Shall I loosen my gown, my lord?' and he said: 'Yea, take it off,' and tried to help me with the laces, his hands that were so sure in handling a bow, or a

465

horse, or a pen, strangely, dearly awkward, and of a sudden he burst out laughing and said: 'I would make an exceeding poor abigail!' Then he laughed no more, but tore fiercely at the fastenings of my garment, I too casting all away until I lay in his arms just as I had come into the world, and knew no sense of sin, all was too fair . . . wicked, wicked me! Happy me! Ah, Richard, Richard.

I ran, and Bridget blocked my path. She leaned against the well, her face livid with sullen grief. There was a ferosity about her that I had not seen. She caught my wrist, thrust her other hand amid my fallen hair just as if she knew the throughts that wept and sang within me. She forced me against the well—its hard lip cut into my breast. Knowing her mad, I suffered the pressure of her hand upon the nape of my neck, and wondered if I too were mad, and Adelysia, likewise the whole world, and bent my eyes where she would have me look.

'The black deeps,' she said, in a love's voice. 'See! See the just doom that awaits us all!'

A pretty little frog was climbing the side of the well. Transparent, slimy and green, its frail heart beat fast as it inched upward with splayed, lucent feet through the moss and delicate weed that lined its circular tomb. Tenderly it clawed for the heights. It wavered and fell with a splash into the rank, dark water. Scum closed over its head. I am the frog, I thought, this cursed, unhappy place my well.

'There is no mercy,' said Bridget amorously. Her grip slackened. She leaned far over the well's side.

'Forty years.' So soft she whispered. 'Forty years, yet He betrays me.'

'You account His existence, then,' I said timorously.

'Nay!' she cried. 'There is no God!'

I wrenched from her and ran on, blind, with her behind me, calling; and I went like a hare, terror-stricken, running from her, and above all, from my own thoughts of the time that would never come again, however much I wished it, full of fear. I felt a grasping hand, struck back into a soft side, a body too soft for Bridget, and Adelysia caught me in her arms, and I would have none of her. Cruel that I was, yet caring, I turned away.

'Scourge me,' she begged. 'I am afraid. Scourge me.'

She proffered the little knout, its threads sadly worn. She thrust it into my hands that were full of the good Yorkshire earth, the soil that he loved, and how should I chastise her? But she ripped the habit from shoulders all mottled by lust's purple flower, a cruel lover, the young chaplain, I thought, staring at the bright marks of his mouth. She fell forward on her knees.

'Scourge me,' she whispered. 'God has given me up!'

From the tower the bell clamoured darkly, with a new, furious insistence, and in one of the tall elms a covey of rooks was holding court. The bare twigs shook under their weight. They were very quiet, but now and then one cried menacingly and the others lifted great black wings in assent. One bird sat alone, its plumage folded like a coak. The criminal, on whom the others now passed sentence. While Adelysia knelt bowed-headed and the bell for Sext plunged and boomed about us, I watched, and the feathered Parliament broke into raucous accusation. On ugly, ponderous legs they advanced through the branches. Shrouded in its black cloak, the offender waited motionless for death. Completely alone, it did not even attempt to fly. Its eyes would be the first target for a score of beaks. It seemed a terrible thing, which was strange, for I had seen it all before, this cruel justice, this one against many. The scourge lay idle at my feet.

I turned, lifted Adelysia, dragged her dress together, wondering sadly why she came to me above all other, I that was not even professed. Seeing her poor little face all swollen and blubbered with tears, I cried over the roaring bell:

'Throw your whip away. Come to church, Adelysia.'

Like a blind woman Adelysia went with me, to that place where most of her waking hours were spent, in quiet, cruciform penitence, or kneeling alone daily in her stall while old Dame Brygge snored and the nuns chattered and played. I soothed her as we went, planning her support. We reached the porch and, turning to give her a last encouraging word before we entered, I saw her face white as milk, her eyes staring into the dark nave as if they beheld the terrors of Purgatory. I started to pull her gently in through the door.

In a strangled voice she said: 'I cannot. His House is closed to me, from this day on. Ah, Jesu! did I not tell you I was damned for ever?'

I had no time to reason with her, though I called her name desperately, but she was gone too quickly, running faster this time, disappearing through the grove of rowan trees behind the church. I saw her head bobbing between the gravestones, saw her stumble, rise, run on, till she was lost to my sight amid the fringe of the forest. I would have gone after her but Joan came to meet me, bursting like an egg with mischief. The church was full. For once the whole community was

467

gathered, and for no holy purpose either. Joan pointed down the aisle. A delighted smirk carved itself on her face. Beneath a gilt canopy knelt the Prioress, so seldom seen in church. Face covered discreetly in her hands, with taut, straight back, she gave no heed to the hubbub that boiled and hissed behind her under the vaulted roof. There was a stranger in the church. A tall, lean, sickle-nosed man, who genuflected briskly in the nave, then marched back to kneel straightly against a pillar not far from us. On his garment shone the quarterings of the episcopal see of York. The Archbishop's emissary, I thought, whoever the Archbishop may be in this precarious time, and gaped. Behind me came a shuffling commotion and I was rudely thrust against Dame Joan. The fast priest entered, cherry red. His hands trembled beneath the holy plate he carried so that the soiled linen which covered the chalice quivered and blew. Behind him strode the chaplain, hair like a new coin, seemingly unperturbed. Had he known what I had witnessed, he might not have spoken with such sweet authority.

'Good sisters, I pray, be silent for the Mass,' he said, and somewhere from the choir came coarse female laughter, followed by the jaybird's shriek.

'Does he think to quell them at this late hour?' There was such delight in Joan's voice that I looked at her amazed. Her eyes were fixed upon the Prioress.

'*Introibo in altare Dei*,' sang the priest, at half his customary speed. His little brutish eye rolled sideways as he struggled to see if the Archbishop's man were watching him.

'He brought all manner of news,' Joan muttered as we stood side by side. 'All about the two dreadful battles we heard rumoured, and how the King was exiled abroad, came back, and killed Warwick at Barnet. And there were more doings at a place called Gups Hill, where Warwick's youngest was borne screaming from a nunnery by one of the King's brothers.'

Anne Neville. I had not thought of her in years, nor of the tender way he spoke of her once, calling her 'little Anne'. Would he, could he, tear her screaming from Sanctuary?

' 'Twas the Duke of Clarence,' breathed Joan. 'Then she disappeared from the sight of man. By St Loy, I wager Madame would gladly be in her place!'

The Prioress was still kneeling, while the Mass progressed. I could see she was not wearing her pearl and gold rosary, but a plain one of arbutus wood.

'*Quia tu es Deus fortitudo mea, dum affligit me inimicus?*'

468

chattered the priest, making nonsense of the whole phrase. Not for his life could he amend old, bad habits.

'What did the Prioress say when the emissary arrived?' I murmured.

'She came forth with the words of Job,' chuckled Dame Joan. 'Gave a shriek and fell into her chair, saying: "That which I feared most is come upon me!"'

She started to laugh again, so mockingly that there was something distasteful in it, even to me, who had no love for the Prioress.

'*Spera in Deo, quoniam adhuc confitebor illi . . .*' Wait for God's help. Was that what she did, kneeling so waxen straight? And did Adelysia, alone in the cold forest? And did I?

It must be admitted, the Prioress remained splendidly calm. Though, standing quite close to her in the porch after Mass, I saw she could not meet the eyes of the Archbishop's man. Neither could Juliana, for a different reason. She stood behind her mistress, lids cast down, stroking the beads at her waist. Once only did she look up, to reveal a glance of triumph so burning it made Dame Joan's glee seem like indifference.

'*Pax vobiscum,*' said the hook-nosed man. It sounded like a curse.

'I fear my lord's visit is ill-timed,' the Prioress said demurely. 'Our household books have yet to be reckoned for last quarter and I vow! a thousand things!'

Beneath a habit of unusually coarse, poor stuff, her spine shivered and twitched like a flea-maddened dog. Now and then her thumb and finger made an involuntary groping movement as if dying to scratch, and at times a spasm of agony fleeted across her fair pale face.

'I have no plans to stay, Holy Mother,' said the Archbishop's man coolly. He looked about, missing not a thing. His sharp curved nostrils dilated. He could see, smell, taste, count, forecast, without visible effort. I knew, watching him, that he could tell the altar lacked its full complement of silver plate; that a latten alloy had been substituted in the T-bar of the gold crucifix, that there was a large hole in the side-chapel and daws nesting in the tower. He knew our number without seeming to reckon, knew our ages, the state of our health, even what we had eaten that day. He knew that Edyth was lame and defective. With those fearsome eyes, he might even know about Adelysia, though the chaplain stood meekly, hands in prayer, earning my hate.

469

'I am for London,' he said, after a moment's disquieting scrutiny. 'My lords have arranged to visit your house at St Valentine. Prepare to house ten of them. You may then render a full account. Can that be a dog barking?' he said, with an air of absolute repugnance. 'My lord dislikes dogs. Expect the visitation in one month. God be with you.'

A shoal of grinning faces watched him cross the yard. James Mustarde, in dung-spattered smock, held his horse for him. Madame Brygge, who had not heard a word, rambled behind me of a son long dead. He too had been stern and tall. I felt for Kate's little hand, but she was yawning on a hassock, completely hidden behind the deep stall. She rose and came to stand by me, looking up artlessly at the Prioress. I watched the trembling of Dame Johanna's back, and identified the cause at last. She was wearing a hair shirt for the first time in her life, and her tender skin rebelled.

'One month,' said Juliana, vituperatively calm, and provocative. 'I, for one, will be ashamed. For surely my lords will see how our house is in disrepair!'

The Prioress answered quietly. Her eyes were fixed on a point somewhere near my knee. What was it at which she stared to such hard purpose?

'It can yet be mended,' she said.

She would use any means, I knew it. So I became instantly, mortally afraid, seeing her eyes fixed so, guessing her mind.

She was looking at Katherine.

Old Madame Brygge spoke but rarely , but when she did, her words were a falling flood, not to be dammed. Naught could quell the mumbling drone of her talk. Being deaf, she demanded no answer but was content to roam, shrunken face champing, amid the debris of lost years.

'When I was a young maid,' she maundered amiably, 'I travelled much. I was in Rouen to see them burn La Pucelle. Heretic to the last, she had impudence enough to ask for Christ's Cross at the stake. I stood near young King Harry and his uncles; he, the lily, wept, and vomited from the stench of her flesh roasting. She was a witch, I trow. For I miscarried of a child soon after I returned to England. They have that power, know it well. And they can also hinder a conception, for all the man be lusty. Yea, the Witch Woman of Orleans, they called her. She lost me a fine daughter.' She wagged her head, and chewed a fold of her wimple.

'Yea, gag yourself,' muttered Joan, entering the misericord in time to catch half of her speech. 'Some there were that called her a saint.' Madame Brygge said 'Eh?' and cupped her ear.

'*Pardieu!* What's the use?' cried Joan. But she was in a savage good-humour, bred of the Prioress's impending disgrace. She could think of little else, single-minded as I, who was aware only that the Prioress had something ill in mind that concerned Katherine, and that Katherine had a cough, had been coughing for the past two nights. That cursed, damp chamber, I thought in fury; pray God the Archbishop's deputation include my foul quarters in their search. Kate leaned on my knee, her face fever-tinged, her eyes moving curiously from Joan to Dame Brygge, while Edyth, kneeling, coaxed her with a spoonful of elderflower wine.

'A child of my first husband I lost,' continued Madame Brygge. 'He that was killed at Agincourt. One of the few, poor sweeting. Nay,' she added, her muddled wits clearing. 'That can't be. 'Twas by my second. His name was Thomas, too. True Thomas.' Her hand shot out, and jerked the spoon away from Edyth. She tasted the potion, shook her head. 'You should give the infant tincture of elecampane. 'Tis stronger for the chest than this rot. Tall, yellow, daisy-flower . . .'

'In February?' I snapped, grabbing the spoon back.

'And then I married Brygge,' she mumbled. 'A Merchant of the Staple. Niggardly Ned. Each morning he'd have me sew the lips of his purse up tight, so he shouldn't be tempted to spend. For all his airs, I had to tend my own kitchen with but two wenches. Mean as a muckworm, he, though he was looked up to in the City. Never a night's rest had I. He'd rise and run down to count his money at all hours. Ha! he died of the flux, too close to call an apothecary.'

Katherine was flushed. She would do better in bed, I thought wildly, if only the bed were warm, the floor dry. Holy Jesu, what would her father say, to see her thus? It was not as if I could not write, a fair clerkly hand at that. I toyed with the sweet thought of a letter to him.

'So all his virgin gold came to me,' cackled the old dame. 'He was saving it for his age; now it soothes mine. Ha! I can sleep all day here. And here I stay!'

She had almost the determination of fear; fear that the old

order might change, and her easy, snoring life be swept away. Then Katherine coughed again, and again.

'Joan, what other remedies have you?'

Joan was still wrapped in her world of vengeance.

'Certes, you should have heard Juliana,' she bragged. 'So cold and clean. "Nay, I can't aid you, Madame," she said. "And why should Madame need my aid?" Cat and mouse, in truth.'

Adelysia had said it: 'Juliana loves and hates; she plans to be on the winning side, come the reckoning.' I had not seen Adelysia for days. Her stall in choir was empty. Yet once I thought I glimpsed her wandering sadly, a slim dark figure, near the porteress's lodge. And Bridget was in thrall to one of her fits again, weeping and roaring.

'I was thinking,' said Dame Joan craftily, 'that with God's help, and a little word from me, my cousin from the Founder House might fill Johanna's stall. Now, there's a saint! If she were to eat roast sturgeon, then should we all; were there gems on her finger, ours would not go bare. The Queen is dead! Long live the Queen!'

Her fanaticism frightened me. Kate was coughing. I lost head and temper and slapped Dame Joan hard, thinking instantly: Is this the beginning? She stopped midspeech and looked at me, the turning worm.

'What ails *you*?' she demanded.

'My babe's sick,' I said, shaken with rage. 'Do something, for Jesu's love.'

She shook her head mazedly. 'Yes,' she said, quieter. 'Edyth, fetch the brown jar from my shelf. And a gallon of well-water. I'll make an infusion.'

Edyth kissed Katherine tenderly. 'Stay quiet, honey sweet,' she said. Only when she spoke to Kate did all the knots in her tongue come loose. Her leg dragging, she went out.

'Don't you want the Prioress shamed?' Joan asked curiously. 'She took your dower and misused it, like she did to that old fool Brygge. It's just that she should be punished.'

'If that were all . . .' I began, and Joan threw back her head, braying.

'All! By St Loy, let me list her crimes.' She hooked thumbs into her wimple, aping a lawyer. 'Madame is guilty of: using the nuns like beasts of toil; simony in its direst form; selling the holy plate and the wool to pay for her own sports; luting and dancing after Compline; letting the house and all its demesne fall into disrepair.'

I was thinking of the rooks and their parliament. Black and

ugly, waddling towards the lone infidel, a vast, vengeful crowd, the one against many. Yet Johanna was a Woodville-lover. Bless them that curse you.

Joan was still recounting the Prioress's shortcomings: 'Not setting a good example to her sisters; neglecting to go to Confession; ill-temper—'

'Ill-temper!' I cried. 'Why, you have the illest temper of all!'

She ceased, and glared at me. Her eye rolled red.

'Would you then be her advocate?' she asked with menace. At that moment the door opened and Edyth came back. Joan pointed, crying: 'You saw her strike that child! Can you love her, after that?'

And I was about to say, Nay, a thousand times, Joan, when I saw Edyth's face. She could go no paler, but her eyes were sunken as if she had sustained an hundred fresh blows.

'Where's the water?' Joan asked.

Edyth's lips trembled on a hoarse sound.

'The well . . .' Her words dragged out. 'I saw. Drowning. Deep.'

So at last, Bridget has made an end, I thought, as we hurried across the cloister-garth. And as she seemed to lust for death and was so unhappy, I was glad.

But I was not glad a moment later, when James Mustarde, who had brought hooks and a rope, leaned with his lantern over the well's black mouth, or when the swinging light picked out a shape that bobbed beneath the slime. Slime clung to the face, a trail of weed made blind the staring eyes, and one hand, lapped like a lily by the water, clung on the crucifix at its breast.

'What's that on her cross?' asked James Mustarde, fishing brutally with his hooks.

Even the depths could not darken the flaming glory of a wisp of hair twined shockingly around the dead Christ.

Ah, Adelysia, Adelysia. Was it *l'accidie* that ruined you, or was it love?

'Sweet mistress,' said Patch rapturously. 'Sweet mistress. I never knew you were to buy a corrody.'

Because for several moments I could not own him anything but a ghost, I held the guttering dip high over my head so that its light filled the upper air and ringed him round. Demons love only the darkness.

He did not vanish; he was real. Fog filmed his cloak and

473

dew shone in the creases of his cheeks. A rude diamond sat on the end of his nose. He looked hearty and roguish and robust as ever, and he was glad to see me. Round a waist grown mayhap a trifle stouter he wore a broad leather belt in which was tucked his knife and his jester's bauble, the one with the full-moon face, the same, I vow, with which he had tormented the lords at court. He took my hand and held it tight in broad calloused palm. I had held my hand out for his once, and he not there to take it, but another, and three years fled away . . .

Take my hand, and say you have not forgotten!

And turn your face about, sweet, silly, shivering country maid, and see what God has sent you under cover of a song. A royal Duke, no less!

I wondered instantly whether he knew. Gossip was his second trade. Worse than a woman for whispering tales, he was the sort that kings employ. Sow the seed where it can fruit the most. Out of the past he came; I loved and hated him. I let my hand lie still in his. I remembered a bad moment, a moment that could have been direst humiliation for my lord, and how Patch had averted it, merely by handing him a cup of wine. My thanks for that, Patch. I began to jest with him, my heart warming a little. He would make a fine monk, I said, or some such heathen banter, I can't recall.

We talked first of the Prioress, and I was moved by poor Adelysia's death to make some gibe about her clothes, for in a more disciplined house Adelysia might have lived happy, grown old and saintly and attained Paradise; had Johanna spent less time at board and hawk and lute, that is. They had not let Adelysia lie within the cloister. James Mustarde had buried her, and worse, had sworn he had seen her walking through the rowans one night since, when he was feeding the swine, so that none now went near that place, save I. It was sad, among the shady rowans, but I was not afraid of poor sweet Adelysia, and I made the Intercession at that shallow grave, little dreaming, as I shaped my tools of prayer, that I would use them to cut a far more bitter grief.

I told Patch none of this. He would not have got my drift. I spoke only of apostasy, and love, and my changing colour may have shown kinship with Adelysia's trial. Either that, or Patch was acute beyond my understanding. He began at once to speak fully of the court, all that I could ask no stranger, and I did not even need to probe him. I heard the story of their exile. I knew that Warwick was dead, slain outside London, at the place called Barnet, where King Edward sought the aid of a White Witch, Friar Bungay, who conjured fog to blind the enemy.

Nobly stern looked Earl Warwick, lying in stately death. Young Dickon (no need for him to tell me this) took it hard. Then he went down to Kent, and, returning, found they had executed Daft King Harry, or that Harry had pined and died from sheer melancholy. Men said he took this harder still. Why did he call him young Dickon? Sheer habit, a nickname, for he was twenty—a man in truth, Constable and Admiral of England, wounded at Barnet—Lord of the North, and dwelling at Middleham. And Patch was his servant, bound to entertain him on the morrow, with song and caper.

I could not say a word. He was again at Middleham, and I ignorant of it till now. He would have passed again along our road, coming up through the Fosse Way and on to York and into Galtres Forest, to Wensleydale, with its harsh cleansing gales and haunted mists, while I was—what? praying, eating, tending Katherine, sleeping, weeping, over Adelysia, or myself—or him.

Ah, holy God! *He* could not have been driven by fog into our cloister, nay, not he, only Patch, who stood there gibbering courtly silliness at me before launching into yet another tale.

And a fanciful one indeed, all about cookshops, and a fire, with himself playing the hero's part, and Lady Anne Neville, she that was Princess of Wales, greasy as a penny pie and nicely restored into the arms of her loving cousin, Sir Richard of Gloucester, the same. I wondered if Patch heard my heart thumping in the quiet room. If he did, it was not apparent.

Edyth came timidly to listen, and I sent her away. Now Patch brought in George of Clarence, laughing so much over some private victory that some of his words were lost. And how George forbade the match. What match? Why, Richard to Anne, of course.

Though I knew it to be, on my part, arrant foolishness, for I had always known he must marry somebody, this did not make it any less a mortal blow. I stood in front of Patch, while he shook his bauble, parading it up and down his arm to demonstrate how George addressed the Bench. 'He—shall—not—have—her!' he shouted, while I stood there alive, but dying, all the blood in my heart draining away and my spirit flickering up and down, like the rushlight. Had he tried to be cruel, he could not have laboured to greater effect, for even then he gave me a reprieve, led me to think that George had utterly, irrevocably forbidden the marriage, so that I, like one in the last moments before the axe falls, half in death, half in life, seized parchment and pen.

'Will you bear a letter?'

Patch was for Middleham, to his service. I would have changed places with Patch, envying not only his destiny but his light, unloving heart. Patch would see him tomorrow, could pass my letter into his very hands. Patch had been sent by heaven. He watched me write; I turned the roll away from his eyes.

And I knew not how to begin, for the usual greeting—Right Worshipful and well beloved—used by all, meant naught, even if I wrote it in my blood. So after thinking, I began 'Your Grace', for he was indeed gracious, and lovely beyond belief, and I wrote it somehow, telling him of Katherine. Even now, I wonder, would he have smiled had that letter ever reached him? It was a piteous, wanton, desperate bill.

'All that I told my lord when last we met is changed. Then, it was meant only with my whole heart. Since then my heart has grown ten thousand times. Today the bell struck nine: I thought of him. It struck again, nine times, my thoughts had never left him, and a day was gone. This, then, the pattern of my days.'

The saints whose blessing I invoked upon him filled half of the page. Without planning it, I ended with St Jude, the patron of lost causes. Only now do I know that this was hindsight.

Patch was a skilled executioner. He watched me roll and seal the letter, and then he let fall the axe. My voice was marvellously gay as I replied: 'So they were married after all,' while part of me rolled bloody in the dust. It was only when he went on to tell me, casual as ever, that the Duchess of Bedford was dead, and letting me think they had burned her for necromancy, that dreadful fears overcame me: I wept and cried aloud. A good torturer, Patch; again, in his next breath, she had died in her bed. I saw his shocked eyes as I raved of love-sorcery; then, before him, I burned the letter. Jude's name was the last to go.

I kissed him when we parted; he was for Middleham, and the Duke of Gloucester. There was a Duchess of Gloucester too, so I kissed Patch farewell, nevermore to meet. That was the sum of it, a little like Joan's counterfeit household book; plain and black on the face, yet rife with hidden reason. I could never go to Middleham.

Not for hours did I see the one blessing in Patch's dreadful visit. The Duchess of Bedford was dead. My chains were off.

I did not lie down all that night, but stood at the window. Just before Matins, the heavy fog that had lain on us for days lifted, and I strained my sight through the grim grey arch, trying to push back the long distance to where he lay. I saw only dark trees, their branches raised like weapons against the sullen moor. Then arose one of the sudden sharp winds peculiar to those parts. There was a verse that I had to remember, from the foolish song that kept me sane.

> Though in the wood I understood
> Ye had a paramour,
> All this may nought remove my thought,
> But that I will be your.
> And she shall find me soft and kind
> And courteous every hour;
> Glad to fulfil all that she will
> Command me, to my power:
> For had ye, lo, an hundred mo',
> Yet would I be that one:
> For in my mind, of all mankind
> I love but you alone.

I listened vainly for his voice in the wind's howling. The curlew's shriek blew back my cry, and the night-owl, bird of heresy, joined in our lament.

Dried peas, black and brittle, filled a cask to the brim. Carlings, Joan called them; before coming to Yorkshire I had never heard the name, but in Lent, on Care Sunday, each nun received a little sack of them to eat in token of remembrance. This year, I foresaw difficulty in tackling the hard food myself. I had something wrong with my gums, they wept blood and all my teeth were loose; in fact I had pulled one with ease and saw myself getting as gatfaced as Joan. I had not looked in a glass for nearly three years, and all the fishpond told me was that I was very pale. There was only one mirror in the convent, and even that had lately disappeared, for it had hung in the Prioress's room, which in itself had undergone the startling change to complete austerity. Holy symbols hung everywhere; the walls were draped in black. Her lutes and hunting whips had vanished, and she herself preserved a silent withdrawal. It was the week before Valentine.

Edyth sat beside me, sorting the carlings, while Katherine, at my right hand, rolled the peas about. I was making the little bags, a task in which my mind could wander. Most of my thoughts were of a grim thankfulness that Kate was better, for Joan's inhalations had worked a miracle of sorts, a mixed blessing, for now Edyth had the cough, just as if Joan by alchemy had transferred it. And Edyth's cough was worse even than Kate's had been. She was coughing now; the poison rattled in her chest like the carlings in their tub. In the corner, Dame Joan swilled ale, while James Mustarde, protesting mildly, filled with peas the bags I had made.

'Pack them hard, boy,' I heard her say. 'Madame shall take some with her into banishment. I warrant she'll have care aplenty!' She laughed at her own jest.

'I must feed my swine,' muttered James. Then, anxiously: 'Reverend Dame, if the Mother is sent away, shall I lose my employment?'

'Nay, never!' she cried. 'When my cousin from Citeaux is installed, you'll wear a silk smock. You'll wait on us both, and I'll share my lady's chamber!'

'I'd liefer tend the hogs,' said James wistfully.

So Joan will be another Juliana, I thought. And, should her cousin offend against Holy Church, would she, in turn, betray her as Juliana did the Prioress? For the hundredth time, I wondered what the Mother at Leicester would think. If I saw her again, if I told her that to my mind, three-quarters of the world were wholly bad, would she sigh agreement? Yet she was ever merciful. When, in my childhood, troubled by unknown fears and hate against those who had slain my father, I was suffering an infant Wanhope, she would say: 'Look around, child. See that flower, that bird, that tree. The Master wrought them all, in their beauty. Who shall fear to fall into the hands of Him that made these things? It is the pattern. And the pattern is God's mercy, reflected in man.'

Does she still live, I wondered. Holy in a true sense, I remembered also her warm worldliness. She loved to laugh. There was never spite in her laughter. She liked a tale, and if it were bawdy, she was never outraged. She did not judge. Long ago, there was a plague at Leicester, and one house that none would enter save her. She soaked her habit in asafoetida and garlic and nursed one man back to health. The other members of the household she shrove before they died. She had never had plague herself, yet she tended that man until the boil beneath his arm burst and the evil humours ran out black and stinking. He kissed her feet. And the people of

478

Leicester stoned her when she came into the street, for bringing a risk to their noses, so that her right eyebrow was scarred where a flint had left its mark. And what did she? She laughed, a whit proudly, and said: 'Poor creatures! Lack of faith has made them afraid.' There was much trouble afterwards, I remember, and many came to beg her pardon, but the rest is lost. I remember her beating me soundly, and that I deserved it. I know she loved me.

Sitting thus, with my arms about Edyth and Katherine, and the carling-bags slipping unheeded off my lap, I thought on Leicester and the Mother, wondering again if she were still alive.

The sun, good and hot for February, made patterns on the broken floor. Edyth whispered that she must ring for Terce, and coughed long and shatteringly. I bade her let another do it, so she sat on, until presently we heard the bell's swooning clamour, and Joan got up.

'Come,' she said. 'I would watch Madame praying for a miracle.'

Madame was in church, but not praying; she looked angry. Her little white dog sat happily in the stall, tongue lolling. Near by, Juliana's long face was like a block of yellow stone. Between these two women flew a snapping whisper which grew in strength and passion until it outdid the priest's gabble. Again and again I heard the Prioress mutter: 'You lie! You lie!'

'That I do not,' said Juliana with steady heat. Amazed, I saw Dame Johanna fall on her knees, arms outstretched not to the altar where the priest, open-mouthed, waited halfway through a Homily, but to Juliana, who turned away, haughty and grave.

'I beg you, Dame,' cried the Prioress. 'It's my whole life!'

Juliana shook her head. 'I will not be your compurgatress,' she said, and began her beads. The priest rang the Sanctus bell, but none heeded it. Like great black birds the nuns encroached in a circle upon the two women. The priest waited, and the chaplain, for he too was there, twined his hands, looking anxious for the first time.

'But you helped me before,' said the Prioress, very low.

'Yea, I perjured myself,' replied Juliana. 'Till my soul was nigh as dark as yours. I denied your misdoings, covered your sins. On the last visitation I did it. Yet you still treat me like —' her glance slid downward—'nay, not like a dog! Like a slave, a craven beast. I shall tell my lords—'

479

The Prioress rose, no longer a suppliant, eyes arched menacingly.

'Well, Dame,' she said, still quiet. 'What will you tell them?'

'All,' said Juliana. Unerringly her finger pointed to the chaplain. 'Including the tale of our poor sister. How she died, and why.'

The Prioress let out a shriek. As if signalled to the chase, the dog flew from her side and launched itself at Juliana, nipping and worrying the hem of her robe. Its hind-quarters writhed under a flurry of black cloth. Juliana raised her sandalled foot and gave the animal a kick, and its yelp was drowned by the Prioress's second furious scream. In a trice, she had Juliana by the neck. Tall and strong, she tore off the other's wimple with a rending crack, revealing Juliana's head, stubbled with grey hair. She had Juliana in a stranglehold. Caught round the neck in her own garment; and holding her thus, she dragged the nun up and down the nave, striking her in the face with her free hand.

'Beggar! Harlot!' she cried. The dog bawled limping at her side.

I felt Edyth press close to me in fear. I felt the crispness of Katherine's little headdress under my hand. Gently I turned her, and held her face against my thigh. I closed my eyes.

That same day she sent for me. I had known it would be soon, for she had so little time. Even so, this preparedness did not stop my bowels from turning to jelly when the summons came. Edyth held on to my gown all the way through the frater. 'Sweet mistress,' she said. She always called me that.

'Madame will not strike *me*,' I said, laughing. An awful laugh it must have been. But she will not harm me, I told myself; there is a boon, a favour she would beg, a request that may become an order. I must therefore be as steel, as adamantine; I must not lose what wits are left to me, nay, I must be cleverer than ever I was. For I knew the Prioress's mind, as surely as if the interview was already begun, and the knowledge brought fear. Dame Johanna's door looked big and black.

'I'll wait,' said Edyth.

When I went in, the Prioress was standing by the fire, shivering gently as if she were cold. This set up an even deeper dread in me, like entering a tomb. Then she faced me and smiled with pretty teeth. So like Elysande was she at that

480

moment that I felt the hair lift on my scalp. Her dog was there, growling sulkily, with a bandaged paw.

'Hush!' she told it crisply, like one anxious to set a cordial mood. Then she murmured: ' 'Tis cold for February, think you?'

So she would sharpen her blade upon the weather. Very well.

'I am always cold, Madame.'

She was solicitous. It suited her ill.

'Winter does strike hard,' she remarked.

'Summer or winter,' I pursued. I tried to catch her sliding gaze. She said calmly:

'You shall have more bedcovers. Dame Joan can give you some lengths of stuff. I hear you are passing skilled at thread-work.'

Dread from her unnatural kindliness grew in me, and, paradoxically, courage.

'Even damask wouldn't mend a rotten wall, Madame. My cell's like a marsh.'

Silent, she took two paces right, two left, the hem of her coarse, poor habit, newly donned, rasping on the stone.

'We are a penurious household,' she said suddenly, looking somewhere above my head. 'Would I could have the place repaired, fitting and seemly. To please my lords. I am embarrassed, ashamed.'

She takes me for a fool, I thought wildly. Does she think me ignorant of her simony?

'You are happy here?' she asked, eyes on the ceiling.

'Nay, Madame.'

The heavy-lidded gaze swept down. 'But you have no cares,' she said softly. 'You have food and shelter. You have your daughter, have you not?'

Like the trumpet call before a tourney, a warning sounded in me. Beasts are sensitive to such a mood-change; the little dog yapped suddenly, then began to whine. I looked at it.

'The Archbishop detests dogs,' I heard myself say. I was quoting the emissary, and she knew it. I was sounding the attack. I waited.

'But he loves children.' Her full lips closed round each word as if it were a plum. 'I've heard it said that a little holy maid touches him like naught else.'

I waited.

'Where is Mistress Katherine?' she asked gently. 'Bring her here.'

Edyth brought her, while I stood calm and chill and wish-

481

ing I were a man, a powerful man with a keen weapon in my hand, and an army behind me. Edyth must in some uncanny way have shared my thought. She had robed Katherine royally, like a gay banner, in the orange satin gown which I had cut down to fit, the neck and sleeves slashed and hemmed with fine linen bleached to cream. She wore a short hennin and veil made of the same fiery cloth. Her hair hung down, as befits a maid. No jewels, save for her eyes. She looked brave. There was no other word, and, as she came sedately, holding up her gown, I knew that here was army and sword, drawn and cast from my own heart's blood.

She walked well until she reached the Prioress, when she sat down hard and suddenly on the floor, a gold bloom sprung from the stone. Johanna stretched out the arms that had beaten Edyth so cruelly, and a restrained madness took me so that I bit my tongue and sought silence in the pain. The Prioress's hands raised Katherine; I fancied Kate was soiled by the touch, and wildly, irrelevantly, thought: Fool, fool! not to have sent that letter! But to have sent it would have been like presenting myself at the gates of Middleham, and the Lady Anne doubtless enjoying her honeymonth . . . ah, God! not to think on that! the Lady Anne, proud Warwick's daughter, would surely look askance, but would her lord? I knew not, I only conjured his spirit into the room to shield Katherine, thinking how well he would abash the Prioress with his icy chivalry, his stern will . . . I saw the Prioress's hands on Katherine, heard her chanting a blessing, as if in conspiracy with the child.

'What say we at the ending, Kate?' the soft voice asked.

Katherine turned to give me a smile. '*Te rogamus*,' she said obligingly. Then she went pell-mell through her brief repertoire, *Jube, Domine, benedicere* and all, and *Bye, Baby Bunting* crept in somewhere too, which had certainly no part in the office, but as good as any of the fat priest's gibberish.

The Prioress rose. 'She has a marvellous keen wit,' she said. 'I vow her advent was a blessing to this House.'

I had dreaded the guess, and guessed right. She was bending again, holding Kate by the shoulders.

'Shall you like to be a nun, Mistress Katherine?'

I had planned to be calm, but one cry burst from me, I could not help it. Across the floor in an instant, I snatched Katherine up into my arms.

'She will not be professed,' I said through clenched teeth. 'Not in this evil house. Nor any house. She will grow strong and fair and marry a good man. By Jesu!' I said, starting to laugh and cry. 'She's scarcely two years old!'

Dame Johanna came very close. She took a snippet of Katherine's orange gown, my gown, the Duchess of Bedford's gown, in thumb and finger. Holding it, she said quietly: 'You refused to be professed. The corrody pays only for one. This child is the property of Holy Church.'

I did not know all of the law, but I knew a lie when I heard it, and said so, screamed it into her face.

'Then there will be food only for one,' said Johanna, kindly.

I abused her, weeping. I said her day would soon be done, and that the new Prioress would look after us both. Anger bleached her face.

'You are a fool,' she said. 'Your dower was small enough, God knows. (In all my frenzy, I knew this to be another lie; I recalled her saying: 'I would not have priced her so high,' to the men who brought me.)

'Well then, Dame,' she said, hard yet cunning. 'What do you propose? There are walls and roofs to be repaired as you say. Has your knightly father more money? Or am I to please the Archbishop with a new postulant?'

'My father is dead,' I said, trembling. 'Sir Richard Woodville is dead also. There is no more money.'

In my frantic grasp, Katherine stirred fretfully. Dame Johanna's long white finger stole out to touch her cheek.

'Kate, you'll make a fine nun,' she said, and smiled like a serpent. 'I shall write to my lady of Bedford, asking her blessing—it is only courteous.'

But that's impossible! I thought stupidly. Then realization, a great bolt of it, struck me. Immured here in the north, the Prioress was far more ignorant than I. *She* had no Patch, to bring her grief and joy and news. Accursed and blessed Patch!

'The Duchess of Bedford is dead,' I said.

She did not speak for a long time. Then she whispered: 'Who told you? Sir James Tyrrel? By God—he told me naught! He said the foggy ride had wearied him and he needed sleep!'

Quietly I said: 'The jester who came with him,' and she knew I spoke the truth. Now she did not seem so tall. She was a little crouched, a preying beast.

'Once, I gave you a penance,' she said. 'I fancy it was not enough. Give me the child, I'll say no more. The man who got you with child—he's dead, the nuns whispered it at

Christmas. Dame Joan thought you would miscarry. You are alone. Resist me, and I'll have you scourged as a harlot.'

Anthony Woodville once threatened to have me whipped at the cart's tail. I looked down at Katherine. The child of my beloved. We were two. Such threats could never more affright me.

'My lord lives,' I said. Kate smiled and yawned. 'He lives, and he is Constable of England, Lord of the North. The King's brother. Richard of Gloucester.' (And mine for a little space, and I his true maid, his Nut-Brown Maid, who loved but him alone.) I did not say this, of course. I only said, as I watched the lost power, and the fear in her eyes, as I quit the room and joined Edyth, coughing outside:

'Remember his name. The first and last time I shall ever speak it in this house.'

When I saw that Edyth, in my chamber, had a bundle fashioned of my one remaining gown, threadbare as a hermit's shift, my seal, my cake of lye soap, and Katherine's few little garments, all tied with hemp and thrust on a pole, I did not ask her how she knew my mind. Nor if she was coming with me, for I could tell there was no gainsaying her. One pocket bulged bread, and in her hand a leather flask was hard with water.

'The porteress sleeps,' she said, and I answered:

'But it's a long way, Edyth. And for us, farther than any pilgrimage.' In love and pity, I looked at her misshapen foot.

'I'm strong,' she said. She put out the hand that was to lead me through the dark.

None travel by night, but we did. And none should attempt such a long journey on foot with a child and a cripple, without it be on pilgrimage, that being another matter, for my parents had once walked from Worcester to Canterbury, but during daylight and lodging in religious houses on the way. There was only one house I wished to see, and it was far. Leicester. Edyth, whose mind was already made up, never even asked where we were bound. I told her it was a place where they would take good care of us.

'Middleham,' she said instantly, and for the first few miles would not have it otherwise. I gathered from her that I cried the name in sleep, and wondered what else I had said. There were always dreams, of course. And often of Middleham. But in one dream particularly, I was at Eltham, where the men were working on the new Hall commissioned by King Edward. It was to have round windows all along the upper wall with the *rose en soleil* and the falcon of York alternating in fine coloured glass. Elysande had told me about it all. Running down to the lawns hard by the tilt-yard, there was a little stone tunnel, its mouth draped with suckling vines, wild-growing roses. Only in dreams had I seen Eltham, had I waited for him there. Though he never came, I was always certain of his coming, so the dream was neither happy nor sad.

The Priory weathervane, etched black upon the fragile sky, shivered north-west. We struck out into the wind, keeping close to the trees; we went soft as rabbits, three trembling does, one full of her own conceit. James Mustarde's dim shape, moving drearily among the sunset hogs, was the last I saw of the Priory inhabitants. For a heartstopping moment he looked up, and I darted behind an oak tree, pulling Edyth down. But he merely glanced in an aimless circle, blew his nose on his fingers, and shuffled off. For once I gave thanks that the house was in such decay; the outer wall was virtually in pieces and we slipped neatly through a gap in the stone and found the rough-trodden moorland path beneath our feet. So we began our journey: we must go south, that I knew, and in my crazed conceit trusted that the rest would follow, that once upon a good road the way would uncoil before us like an obedient map. Edyth walked well, with a peculiar, swinging sideways gait, not delaying me as I had anticipated, and she *was* strong: for Katherine, swaddled like a beehive in her warmest clothing, she carried easily. Thinking back on it, 'twas a wicked, heartless act, pardonable only if I had waited till summer, to take a child out into the unknown night. But fear, illogical and instinctive, had mastered me. Despite my proud words to Dame Johanna, I felt that, did we wait for summer, we would both be dead.

It lacked half an hour or so to sundown, and my steps were strong and light. As the moorland slope cut off our view of the Priory, a kind of dauntless rhythm came into my stride. Left foot, then right, steady and strong. The Priory was a league behind. There was freedom in my urgent, springing step. Freedom. At least five miles between the evil and ourselves, and the sun downing for Compline—who would toll the bell? Not Edyth. We went faster. Edyth should never ring Compline again. The short coarse grass pushed at my heels and spurred me on. Even the wind was a whip, whispering freedom round my face. We came to a patch of rising ground, and the summit ran to meet us. We fled gratefully down the other side, our feet going faster than our bodies; we slithered on pebbles, strode through sucking moisture in a sheltering copse, right, left, right. I became momentarily changed, uncaring if the brambles tore at my gown, talking wildly to Edyth in an effort to cheer her, who needed no cheering, intoxicated by my thoughts. We were free. Free to die. But I did not think on this.

I had not planned the date of this, our flight, but perchance my woman's body had, for there was a moon, good and big, watching us with full yellow eye through the upper branches of the wood. A good omen; I was minded that all of this was meant, was written long ago. So it was, of course. Everything is, good and ill, but I was so proud and conceited at that moment I fancied I was master of my own fate, could bend even the planets to my will. I think it was the recent speaking of his name made me feel thus. It gave me so much joy. His name armed my very feet. Left, right, left. So easy and light. I began to weave fancies. He would be riding through the next wood—alone. He would draw up his horse at sight of us. I'd call: 'God greet my lord,' and he would marvel: 'Sweet heart, what do you here?' a little shocked, but pleased and pitying, and he would lift me up. I watched the moon, and smiled. I ran. Mad was I. I said, as he wound his arms about me, as he shook his horse's reins, whose leather I could even smell . . . as I leaned my head upon his breast: 'Ah, Richard, Richard, you are my joy in all this world. I would not leave you—I was taken. Ah, Richard, my heart's blood!'

I could not read the stars, but watched the moon, chased it down the crackly, stony track, through briars and bushes and the spreading, frosty branches of oak and elm and trees unknown, brought perchance by the Romans, centuries ago. We went stoutly through deep underbrush and, when the moon wholly commanded the stiff icy night, my first doubt awoke and stretched its limbs. We seemed to have been on the same rough road for hours, and the moon, into which at one time we seemed about to walk, now hung at our right hand, as if wearied of the journey and standing to bid us farewell.

'We'll not turn back,' I said out loud. 'Edyth, are you cold?'

'She's warm,' Edyth answered, feeling one of the hands which protruded from the mass of Kate's clothing. She was at one with Kate, and I, suddenly put to shame by her selflessness, asked no more of her comfort. All about us rose a symphony of night noises, the owl's high, mounting moan and, farther off, the blundering squeal of wild boar. A fox, whip-sleek, darted across our path; at sight of the lithe creature I smiled, but Edyth, for some reason, fell into a quiet tempest of fear and came close, hugging Katherine. I looked up at the free wide sky. Dark puffs of cloud rode the moon's face. The fox snuffed and ran for cover. I watched the bushes fold thornily behind it, and I laughed. I was not afraid. Vixen-colour, my hair! Edyth pressed me, and something hard swung at my hip. I said, madly gay: 'Are you armed, fair Edyth?' She stopped, looked sadly at me through the gloom and fumbling, produced yet another leathern flask, so tightly filled with milk it felt like stone, milk for my Katherine, and again I felt ashamed that she, who always had been derided for her dearth of sense, had had the forethought which I lacked.

'Tis well we have you to look after us, Edyth,' I said, shaken.

'I knew you would want to go,' she said, shifting Katherine to her left arm so that she could hold the edge of my cloak. 'When I heard Madame so wroth. Will they make Kate a nun at this new place, sweet mistress?'

Never had she spoken so well. It was as if, free from the poisonous air of sorrow we had left behind, all her crushed intelligence bloomed at last.

'Nay, she'll be a great lady,' I said softly, but I was only half listening. Our road had narrowed to a mere trickle of flint, and my first creeping doubt grew large and was joined by another. I began to hear a voice inside my head, and words long pushed away for their very hatefulness. 'You have flown exceeding high, and may God have mercy . . .' The road was disappearing, likewise the spring in my step. There was an ache in the sole of each one-time courageous foot, starting as a prickling cramp and mounting to my calves and thighs like a fountain of hidden fire. And ahead, the road vanished among bare arched trees curving black and frostily like demanding hands, and an aperture laced and criss-crossed with twigs, like a wicked mouth, which we must enter. A road cannot go nowhere, I thought. I took Kate from Edyth's arms. She was quiet, easy breathing, warm as coal. As soon as I relieved her of Katherine's weight, Edyth began to cough. She coughed and coughed, staggering under each spasm as if it were a blow. She flung herself on the ground to cough better. When it was over, she got up, shook herself like a dog, and smiled.

487

' 'Tis done,' she said.

We must go on, I told myself. So we went into the black thorny depths, for what seemed hours and hours, and I left part of my cloak and a great clump of my hair in the eager grasp of one clawing tree, for they were like real creatures, those forest-dwellers, bare and silent. And I suddenly knew how cold I was, cold and sweating, going bent low over Katherine with her face folded into my bosom to save it from the tearing thorns, and that the soles of my shoes, patched a score of times, were there no longer. I took every thorn, every stinging pebble, every gob of mud, between my naked toes. And all this was naught, all this, the cold and the dark and the weariness, compared to the voice going on and on inside my head. It said: You will never get there. Never, never, never. And if you do, what then? You have no money, no money. They will turn you away. Katherine should have been a nun. Mayhap it was the will of God! But I replied, God's will in that house? A godless place, by my loyalty, and Kate shall be a lady, have the gladness and comfort I knew but once in my ill-starred life. The voice said: Kate will be neither nun nor lady; Kate will walk the world a beggar, and through your fault. Through your fault. Hear Edyth cough! Your fault, your fault. Ah yes, that too! *Peccavi nimis cogitatione, verbo, et opere; mea culpa, mea culpa, mea maxima culpa* . . . My doubts writhed like serpents, each feeding the other. They would turn us away. When we reached the door, they would slide the little grille to one side—and what was her name, the one who kept the gate? Would she still be there? Nay, it would be a strange, hostile face, a head-shaking face. Useless to cry 'Remember me?' They would turn us out. My sore teeth chattered together.

Then the trees parted, the path widened slightly before us to a glade into which we went, passing slow and silent and sick at heart, with the pale light on our backs. The bread was all eaten, the milk drunk. There was a little water, at which Kate sucked fiercely. I fancied she was too quiet. I kissed her fine-boned face. My arms burned from carrying her. I thought of St Christopher bearing Our Lord over the stream.

Less than a bowshot away, I saw the wolf. The size of a yearling calf, it lifted its snout to the fretful moon, haunches drooping, its long banner of a tail carried low. It sensed us, but was not sure of us; its gaunt body quivered as it searched the wind, as we stood like stone. It slowly turned to gaze in our direction, and the emerald depths of its eyes glowed. I felt my own eyes starting from my head; behind them somewhere the silent voice spoke. 'Eaten by wolves,' it said casually. I knew someone once whose son was . . . there was scarce enough to say a Mass for. Your fault, said the voice. Your fault, your fault, your fault. He gave you a precious child of the rich blood royal and you let the beasts have it. I thought: Forgive me, my lord. Forgive me, sweet my lord, closing my eyes in redness for the snarling spring, for the sharp mouth that would need to tear me first. Then I heard Edyth's slow breath, hissing out long and low, like a boiling pot.

' 'Tis gone,' she said, flat-voiced.

I looked. The moonlit glade was empty. Only the hill, against which the wolf had stood, loomed dark and high and near, a mountain, stretching to heaven. And I was so weary. No one in the world could breast that hill.

'One more step, sweet mistress,' she said, and my bleeding, burning feet obeyed her. 'And another,' she said. Lord! she was strong. She had fashioned a cradle out of her cloak, and within it, Kate clung to her back. So she bore a double weight, what with her body bent under the child and her arms straining about my waist as she cajoled and supported me. I wept a little for my own weakness which should have been strength, and promised her the earth for her courage and kindness—a furred gown every day of the week, three hot meals taken in mirth and leisure, with love in abundance, when we came to Leicester. Because, through her, the hill curved down and away behind, and I saw the road going on between what looked like dwellings. There was a light in one of them, moving slowly like a willywisp, and Edyth, I said, should be a lady, when we came to Leicester. I swear it was no idle promise. In my pain, each step a screaming, burning agony, I would have said aught to keep from crying out loud, so I said what was meant and uppermost in my heart. I think Edyth was possessed of some holy or unholy spirit that strengthened her on that hill, so, as we staggered towards the clustering dark building I was near to reverencing as well as thanking her, and was only reminded that poor Edyth was— well, as she was, by her asking:

'Is this Leicester, sweet mistress?'

It was a cottar's settlement, with one poor cabin surrounded by a number of byres and barns. Spent, half-frozen, we threw ourselves against the first door. Within there was hay-smelling darkness, redolent of warm animals. I touched a cow's lean flank. I fell, and lay in straw that smelled of dung and lost summers. O, God! It was sweeter than the fairest bed. One final pain stabbed through my legs, I called 'Katherine!' tried to reach out for her, then a whirlwind lifted me and I was gone, conscious at the last of having failed us all.

I woke to soft light, and voices. Lying there, filthy, my hair matted with thistle heads, I saw Edyth, sitting on a milking stool, giving only the shortest answers to a huge man. Although he was seated astride a block of wood, his shadow, cast by a rush lantern, sprang and wavered almost to the roof. A sheep's fleece, worn over a leather tunic, hung about his shoulders. A wild grey beard spread itself on his chest. He had Katherine comfortably in the crook of his arm, she was sound asleep, one hand curled round a half-empty mug of milk. I lay and watched the man's face, which was like a badly chiselled stone saint's, or a pagan god's, a crag, a cliff; I lay, and was aware that someone had washed my feet and bound them with strips of wool. 'Edyth?' I said weakly. The giant peered across.

'Tha' be safe,' he said, as if quietening a child, then continued talking to Edyth, a lengthy tale in a dialect so tortuous that I could catch about one word in ten. He spoke of past villainies wrought against him. Too dark to see now, this was his common land, allotted to him unto the farthest tree, and he and his Alison had had the right to pasture four beasts thereon until last month, when he, John, had found that right superseded, one of his cows maimed, and Spinney Field overrun with pigs. It was not as if his neighbour needed the pasture so sore. *He* paid no servile dues, but commuted in hard coin. And he did not lack friends; that was plain when John took the matter to law. John could not ken half of what the Bench said, nor could he read the lumberous legalities concerning it, but he had marked well the sly glances, the veiled smiles from eye to eye. The day after, Alison had driven the cows down as usual, notwithstanding. *He* had been waiting, with others. They flung her to the ground, she was a young woman—a little sport, that was all that was intended, they said. So it was mere accident that his horse had trampled her as she lay. The law had nodded and hummed. And the jury . . .

He gave us bread and ale and cheese, and packed more for us on the morrow. We ate ravenously. He talked on; Kate slumbered, his beard pillowing her head.

. . . Every man paid to do perjury. There was no appeal. They told him go home, or be pilloried for a nuisance. He took Alison's bloody body away, and buried her himself. Yea, we could bide. No harm should come nigh. There was only him, now. Alison had looked a whit like Edyth, only stouter. We slept, among the smells of fecund earth. I have not forgotten. Long John of Derbyshire.

At dawn, he saddled two horses. On a moorland pony he looked comical, his great legs nigh touching the ground, but holy too, with his wild beard blowing beneath that hewn-stone face. He would ride with us to the high road, he said, then he must take the horses back. I wore dead Alison's shoes, and no payment asked. The thanks would not come; there were not words enough, nor would he have them.

'Tha' sholl keep the river at thy left hand till Lincoln,' he said, painstaking slow and clear. 'Then comes the Fosse Way. Keep on't. Tha' sholl ask anew at Nottingham.'

Riding through a gathering of great oaks, I tried to say, in a way that he would understand: 'Tha'art good, Master John.'

A smile like the mirthless gash in a torn oak tree split his face. He was looking ahead to the wood's edge. A man hung there, his body spiralling slowly from a taut branch, hanging high with dead, violet face, bird-ravaged eye-sockets. The feet dangled heavily, in line with my head. Whoever put him there must have been a tall man. John reined in. Gazing, he said thunderously:

'Vengeance is mine, the Lord saith. So blarts Master Priest. He lies. They all lie.'

I looked in the stricken eyes.

'My vengeance,' he said. 'At this spot 'twas *he*—' pointing at the thing that gently spun and jerked in the morning wind —'took my Alison's life away.'

We rode on. When the high road came in sight and, a few fields distant, the frosty river glinted, I ventured to warn him. He would not have my counsel.

'I'll bide,' he said. 'And when they come . . .' With difficulty I learned that they would be foolish, if they valued their necks. 'For naught matters now,' he said, lifting me from my horse. 'They took my Alison.'

The river, on our left, saw us in Lincoln just before curfew. And I dared not stop within the town, not even at a religious house. For I mistrusted everybody, and we had no money, and we would not find another John. There was one place only that I would be, and I thought: surely, it's not much further now. Lincoln town frightened me. We slunk close to the houses, two dirty, unkempt women with a sad little child, being jostled by evening revellers. We were catcalled once or twice, and I thought once a watchman looked suspiciously at Edyth. I hurried us through Lincoln, ashamed. I thought: if my lord could see me now! I swallowed the salt blood from my gums and held my head high. High and haughty in the air, to avoid the stink of my own body.

Then we were on the Fosse Way, and again, it was night.

I do not like to think on this, but it must be told, all of it, because what passed was of my folly, my making. Unable to hide from it, I let my memory reproach me now. We had been on the broad way for some three hours. Last night's moon, a sliver gnawed from its pale cheek, whitened the road. Though I went stiffly on bloated legs, my feet no longer pained so much; dead Alison's shoes, too wide and wadded with fleece, protected their wounds, and some of my courage had returned, warmed by John's food and kindliness. To our distant right, I saw the murky shape of a town and thought: Nottingham already! in careless glee.

'Leicester?' Edyth asked, and if her voice was a little more dull and weary, I did not notice. For I was busy turning my joy into dismay. It was midnight; the gates would be fast against us. And now, I was mad to go on. That was my criminal folly. If we had only found a sheltered sty and lain outside those walls till morning, if we had crept into an aleyard, or rung at some house of charity—or snuggled in the shadow of a wall even—a thousand ifs!

But I was mad. And when a late-returning pedlar with his empty mule hailed us from behind, I was madder still.

'Leicester?' he said, pushing back his hood to scratch. 'Nottingham first, surely. Five leagues or so.'

He looked us over disapprovingly. Another three hours' walk, I thought, puzzled and disappointed.

'That there's Newark!' he pointed in answer to the dim town. Then he said: 'Running away?'

Doubtless it was a jest. One which lit a tremor in me.

'Lord! How yon maid does cough!' he said. Edyth hung back, writhing and rasping. I turned and took Katherine from her. Impatiently.

'A babe, too?' said the pedlar, amazed. His mule blew a wet sigh.

'See here,' he said hesitantly. 'My sister keeps a tavern without Newark town gate. I could knock them up.'

If only I had listened, been wise. But I had been badly frightened.

'We have no money,' I said, hating the worn phrase. I felt

492

for the remainder of John's food, the reassuring flask of milk, tucked inside my bodice.

'We'll go on.'

Edyth choked assent. We left the pedlar muttering, were we too haughty to draw ale, wash dishes, in payment? Muttering of my madness.

It took us nearly double the three hours to Nottingham, and while the moon slid up and over the great dome of night, impatience pushed me on, supernormally renewed at first, then dogged, counting a million steps, a million stars. The frost-bitten sky received our fiery breath, puffed out in little heralding clouds. Our feet cracked on brittle ground, the night breeze played with our ragged skirts. A deep hole yawned in the road, and I fell into it and rose with my cloak dabbled to the knee in icy mud. Katherine cried, a soft pitiful sound that tore me worse than the thorns, or the fatiguing cold or the noise, half-heard, of Edyth's anguished lungs. We crawled up a long hill and down into a wood where the road became a bog, treacherous with fallen branches. My clothes dragged like a dirty shroud, but through those trees lay Nottingham, and I thought I felt the first essence of dawn, colder than the night. By this time Edyth and I walked as if drunk, weaving a pattern in the road. My mud-brown hair, like sin, pulled me down.

> As cut your hair off by your ear,
> Your kirtle by the knee.

Thou, O God, art all my strength, why hast Thou cast me out? Why do I go, mourning, with enemies pressing me so hard?

> And this same night, before daylight,
> To woodward will I flee . . .

Kate was so heavy. Warm on my chilled breast, she weighed the whole world. Edyth tugged at me.

'Sweet mistress, let me bear the jewel.'

So, reluctantly, I gave her up, and we ploughed on, through the foul black mud and the tangling briars. Pale clouds crossed the moon, so that we struck our steps and reeled together, and I was fearful for Katherine, but Edyth, whom fools called witless, held her as if she were the Crown of England. And I thought of Richard, whose face was now scarcely more than a sad heartbeat and strangely not so clear as that of Long John, who by now they had likely taken, and killed. Then Richard came to me again, sharp and clear, the hoofbeats of his horse ringing behind me on the road. We staggered and slipped, and I began to laugh with sobs at the thought of it all and reckoned how Patch would have relished the scene. Two feckless wenches fled from cloister, and a prince's daughter in their arms!

The hoofs came closer. They were real. Men, riding hard and dangerous, like those who had slain Alison for sport. I heard the rape and murder in their swift jingling ride. Stiff with terror, we crouched behind a bush, its twigs were sparse, and the traitor moon grew bright.

Edyth began to cough, a fiendish noise, her mouth a black cavern. She roared and whooped and choked. Saying, Hush, for the love of God, I clapped a frantic hand over the cough and held her juddering body close while the horsemen galloped by. And they were, in truth, robbers, boasting to each other of their latest feat—a knight dead on the York road and his gold filling their saddle-bags. Kate whimpered, puppy-like. I took my hand from Edyth's mouth—the palm showed dark and slippery wet, I wiped it on my cloak. She seemed hardly to breathe. Then she said, quite normally:

'Is this Leicester, sweet . . . ah, Jesu!'

'A pain?' I cried.

Slowly, she stood up.

'Nay, not a pain. More like . . . a stone, breaking.' She touched her breast.

'We must go on,' I said.

Now, I bore the double burden. With Kate clinging to my neck and Edyth clipped beneath my left arm, her own about my waist, our progress slowed to well nigh naught. Left foot, then right, but each step a torment of sloth, especially for Edyth. Her great, misshapen foot, the wages of sin, trailed in the slime, her head hung down. Now it seemed that I carried her, then, I hooked my thigh behind hers, pushing her steps forward as if we were two cripples tied together. And all the time I cheered her with talk of Leicester. For the Mother would be there, I told us both.

'A furred gown for Edyth,' she said, very faint, and tried to cough and failed.

'Every day of the week!' I cried triumphantly, for we lurched round a bend in the road and there was Nottingham Castle, high on its rocky shelf, with turrets shimmering in the weird light of dawn. I looked at it, and the life drained from me. For it gazed back, as if it nodded in grim acknowledge-

ment, and I knew without question that it was a place built
by evil spirits. I saw Nottingham, in the greenish dawn, and
from it, across the sleeping meadows, came pouring a wave
of such dreadful sadness that it struck into my very soul. I
stood there weeping as I had never wept, and knew not why.
I kissed Katherine; my tears fell upon her icy face. She was
very cold; her hands were stiff. Edyth lay in the mud at my
feet. I could not raise her up. I could not stir, while Nottingham Castle stood to watch me weep.

A dream of riders surrounded me, bearing bright tabards,
burnished arms. Voices assailed me, courtly exclamations. A
standard flew over Nottingham, weeping gay colours. They
asked my name, and something broke in me . . .

It was not swooning, in truth, more like a cloud of unknowing that covered me, and I heard my own sad voice crying:
'Leicester! Leicester!' and calling on my own dear Mother in
the House of Peace . . .

Yet when one of the knights said, in all regret: 'This child
is dead!' I gave up, and fell against his arm, and knew no
more till I woke, raving, in my own childhood cell, indeed at
Leicester, and they told me. They gave me sorrow and joy in
a breath. For it was Edyth who had died, and not my Katherine.

And then I knew that everything I touched must die.

She was still there. She had not changed. Though for days I
lay unconscious, I knew, with some unslumbering part of me,
that the hands that washed and turned me skilfully, that performed the bodily services of which I was incapable, were
hers, and none other's. Without words, the vibrations of those
hands spoke comfort to me, penetrating that fog of unknowing, and, when it was time to return to the world with its
guilt and regret, I was unafraid. My eyes opened on the
Mother. She sat at my bedside, her ivory face bent over the
book in which she was writing. Ten years had ploughed new
lines, like the sun's rays on water, at the corners of her eyes.
The scar at her temple was, I fancied, faded, but the whole
structure of her face seemed more delicate. Leaf-fragile, the
skin across her bones stretched taut, probably from a surfeit
of fasting. Yet the essence of her had not changed. My gaze
roamed the arched roof, across the lacing of bosses, one a
cluster of oak leaves, the next a rose, then a fleur-de-lys, then
down to the empty fireplace and the salt cupboards, one on
either side, each packed with bottles and jars—all unremem-

bered mysteries. Through the high round window the sun caressed scoured flag-stones. I had dreamed they laid me in my old chamber when they brought me, when they told me of Edyth. Memory, which I would gladly have lost, flooded back. They had moved me—this was the Infirmary. The Mother had stopped writing. I saw her eyes, pale periwinkles. When she was angered, they could blaze blue fire, as if she looked into a fiercely lighted room. Now they were merely a troubled pool, reflecting heaven. She lowered her book.

'We shall say a prayer of thanksgiving for your deliverance,' she said, rising. 'And then I must tend your gums, or all your teeth will be gone.'

And with this double proposal, which merged comfort of the body with that of the soul and was utterly typical of her, she knelt beside my bed, shutting her gracious eyes. I was still very weak. I began silently to cry, then remembered she despised tears, and wiped my face on the coverlet before she crossed herself at the final psalm.

I crept from the bed and stood infirmly before her, in a shift which must have been worn by a lady passing tall. I could not have walked in it without tripping. I fancied a smile glimmered on the Mother's face. I opened my mouth wide at her command, while she dabbed my swollen gums with a piece of wool soaked in a pleasant-tasting amber fluid. Then she bade me sit on the bed while she unwrapped my feet from their bandages. Both great toe nails were gone, but my feet seemed to have no part of me any more. A young nun, not one I remembered from the old days, brought water and smiled cheerfully at me before departing. Then the Mother washed my feet. The pain was terrible, but the shame was worse. She, of all people, should not serve me thus, I thought, cringing with humility. She applied a yellowish balm to my toes, and bandaged them again, telling me it was Tansy juice, a wondrous wound herb, and, for my mouth, the Greater Celandine, ruled by the Sun. The Sun draws out the pain, she said. But Tansy! that could nigh bring back a man from death. She had treated one of the few who escaped Tewkesbury's Bloody Meadow. His fearsome wounds! One of the Prince Edward's men.

'A Lancastrian?'

'Lancaster or York,' she replied. 'The soul needs a house. I treated his body and asked his policies after.'

An awful, self-pitying wave washed over me. I had suffered, dear Mother, I said, excuse me. I had suffered, and I had sinned. She looked me levelly in the eye. 'But you are alive,' she said, and that broke me completely and I babbled of Edyth—of my sorrow, and my hideous culpability.

'Peace,' she said. She took me in her arms. I could never remember her doing such a thing before. I hid my face against her steady heartbeat.

'You did well to come to us,' she said. 'You and your little maid. Your Katherine Plantagenet.'

So she knew. I guessed rightly that in my fevered state I had said much, and was glad to be spared the recounting of a sad tale. But I itched to tell her of all the other trials—I had not seen her since I went to live at Grafton Regis, and I had my mind made up to tell her all, right from the beginning, and above all, to get her opinion on how such things could be, as took place in the Yorkshire house. She sat by me on the bed's edge and listened, gravely, to the story of May Eve and the Duchess of Bedford's strange work, a brief hint of my happiness at court, and the doings subsequent to War-wick's rebellion. I stinted naught in the telling; it was such a relief to be free of Dame Johanna, Bridget with her accidia, the skimped offices and the dreadful, damp dilapidation. It was so wonderful to talk of these things in the tense of Then and not Now, that at times I was afraid I was dreaming, one of my better dreams. When I described the fat priest's parody of the Mass, she surprised me by smiling.

'Titivillius,' she said. 'Don't you remember the *Mirror of Our Lady?*'

In truth, I had forgotten.

'When a holy Cistercian Abbot was in choir at Matins, he saw a fiend with a long bag about his neck, gathering up all dropped letters, words, and failings made by the priest and the nuns in their office. The Abbot asked his name; he was called Titivillius, and he had to bring to his master, the Lord of Evil, a thousand such bags daily—full of dropped phrases and misread psalms. Or else he was sore beaten. I like to hear you laugh,' she said unexpectedly. 'Your laughter was always full sweet. Go on.'

I told her that Dame Joan counterfeited the household accounts, but that she was passing kind to me. I told of the dreadful scene in Chapel. The Prioress's dog, and hair shirt, came in for dry comment, but when, reluctantly, I told her about Adelysia, her face grew like a thundercloud and she paced the room.

'They mock the frailty of women,' she said fiercely. 'But, on my soul, 'tis the men that make them so! I trust your fire-haired chaplain will be excommunicated.'

I began now to see that I was wrong; she had changed, most subtly, in some way that I could not quite fathom. Though I was not very wise, I knew without telling that this kind of philosophy would not make her popular with the bishops. And I loved her for it. I was able to talk of Long John, and she agreed he had been cruelly misused. But he was wrong to take the vengeance upon himself, though she did not judge him for it. I spoke again, trembling, of poor Edyth, and she said naught. I touched on accidia. She had read of its existence. Accidia, I said. Was it not a dreadful, inevitable thing?

'Know you how long *I* have been in cloister?' she asked, with a smile, and I marvelled at her life-span, and was much comforted. For I already had, I think, an inkling of my own destiny, soft as thunder far away, but not yet insistent. She made many enquiries into my monetary affairs, how much had been my dower, how long was I at the Yorkshire house? And made a little note upon the book she carried, and then fixed me with her blue eyes and asked with startling suddenness:

'What happened on May Eve, at Grafton? Tell me again.'

I squirmed through the nasty moonlight of that night, and she made me repeat little bits, now and again whispering Our Lady's name as protection for us both. She would have it, exactly what they did, and more important, what was said. It was no trouble to recall, being burned into my mind.

'The Duchess said that men were fickle, and all was written,' I told her.

' "Forget not the other"? Is that right?'

I nodded.

'What other?' she asked.

'I know not, but when Elysande recounted my words to the Queen, she went white as death and said, "Jesu, mercy".'

The Mother said slowly: 'At no time did they mention Lord Talbot's daughter, Eleanor Butler?'

I shook my head, and dared to ask her why.

'There was a young man once, a chantry-priest, who came to me for confession,' she said, and stopped abruptly. She laid her hand on mine.

'Listen,' she said. 'No living soul shall hear of this from me. But I charge you, dame, never to speak of it again. For I know, soon or late, men will die by these words.'

There was a heavy silence, broken by a light tap on the door. The young nun entered, with Katherine, and all my fears fled away.

'The little one eats hearty, Mother,' said the sister, smiling. This brought me to another dilemma. Even as the Mother who, like so many, could not resist Katherine, took her on her knee, I said haltingly:

'I know we have but forty days' Sanctuary.' And then; 'Oh God, where then?'

'*Carpe diem*,' she answered. 'Live for the day.'

'We have . . .' I began.

'No money,' she said crisply. 'Yea, you roared it in your fever. Think you that after *an hundred* and forty days I would cast you off? We have but eight nuns left. This House is failing fast. But we are frugal, not like this Johanna of whom you speak. Can your presence bring us to ruin?' She looked at Katherine, then at me. 'Certes, mayhap. For never did I see two such great, lusty giants!'

The young nun grinned broadly, with fair white teeth. I lifted Katherine into the bed beside me. I heard the Vespers bell, so unlike the sour note once tolled by Edyth. The Mother bade me good-night. I kissed the plain jewel on her finger. She would have to do penance for speaking after the Hour.

'St Catherine keep you both,' she said. 'Tomorrow, you shall write to Richard of Gloucester.'

She left me, her last words robbing me of sleep. How, in the Name of God, could I write to him. I pictured the Lady Anne, cool and proud and angry, and a rift yawning between them because of me. I saw his anguished, outcast look, the same that he had worn at court, when none save I loved him. I drew Katherine close, and prepared for a night of wakefulness. But I slept instantly. And a dream came, the first of many I was to know at Leicester. Safety and comfort have sometimes an odd effect. When the body is easy, with no hazard threatening, the mind gains full play. Warm and safe, I slept.

I dreamed that he and I were together again, that we stood in the pleasaunce at Greenwich and kissed each other, softly, while from very near the sound of the mallets in the forbidden game of closh mingled with guilty laughter.

Substitute order for confusion, industry for sloth, the whole being salted with piety and peace: this was Leicester, just as I remembered it. But it was sad to think that Edyth, lately entombed by charitable monks at Nottingham, had bought back my childhood with her life. The Mother ordered a Requiem Mass for her; I thought it the fairest I had ever heard, and I had heard plenty in my time. There may have been only ten of us in the Chapel, but the singing was like a crystal flood, and all tender purity. Everything was as I remembered. The stolid pillars fanned upwards to heaven still, each buttress a sweep of fading gold, while all above was starred and pointed and vaulted with blue. And, running the length of the clerestory, their stone necks stretched out into the chancel, were the faces that had once cheered my terror. Ten years ago, while Queen Margaret ravaged the realm and we prayed, I had sought comfort in those faces. The laughing monk, the scowling demon, the rude, winking friar. The devout monk, extending his tongue for the Host. The weeping monk, the drunken monk, the falcon, the red-bearded lion. The four Apostles, and, in the farthest corner, a face which we had always suspected belonged to the mason himself, with a complacent expression and a tasselled hat.

That day, the Mother and I broke enclosure for a while. She rode ahead on her grey ambler; I followed upon a mule. Behind came Dame Ursula, her face as dear and familiar as any of the gargoyles. I say this without offence—each time I looked back she bowed and dimpled, mouthing how fortunate that I should have come home. I knew that never again in my life should I be completely happy, but this did not make me any less glad of this loving welcome. I was exceeding glad to see Dame Ursula again; it was she who had taught me to sew. There were no men in our House. Dame Lucy acted as precentrix. Wisely, the Mother did not permit that the two other serving priests should live on the premises, for all that they were both aged men. We passed through the Lodge and out on to Swine Market. A little way up the cobbled street to the north stood the Market Cross. The Castle reared up in the west, its ramparts already falling into ruin. Across the river, robed figures moved like busy birds among the fields of St Mary. They were our nuns, tossing a constant rain of oats into each raw furrow.

'We did our ploughing straightway after Candlemas,' said the Mother proudly. 'Soon we'll put in the barley. And if our peas are as good as last year, I'll be content.'

We ambled on towards the South Gate. Through a gap in the houses I saw the watermill, turning unhurriedly, and behind, the West Field, fallow this year. Eastward lay St Margaret's Fields, quartered by etch and tilth grain, and, swivelling my gaze still further, I caught a glimpse of the Abbey and its meadows, dotted with the shapes of toiling monks.

Leicester lay under a spring sun, lulled by the constant bubble of the Soar. The townsfolk made way for the Mother. Most of the women gave her obeisance, some men pulled off their caps, and one ran beside her a few paces, begging her prayers to St Bride for his sick cow. Yet there were looks, not quite hostile, but rather of affront. They reckoned she should stay in cloister, and I would have thought likewise, only I knew she must have a good reason, as ever, for riding out, and when she alighted outside a flimsy hovel, I guessed this was it. Just before the door, half off its hinge, swung open under her touch, she said to me:

'You said that you had suffered. Come.'

There must have been eight or nine children, the youngest about three years old. They crowded round their mother, and she herself was like some horrible parody of the female form. Dull sunken eyes watched us incuriously out of a white, turnip face. Her gross body strained at a ragged shift, the front of which was covered with filth and great patches of dried blood. Her bare legs and feet were crusted with the dirt of years. Around her the children shrank and jostled, half-naked, corpse-thin. Bloated lice, visible even from the doorway, tracked placidly amid their hair. The youngest child broke from its mother and crawled towards me.

From the far corner came a terrible stench. A man lay there, so skeletal and still I thought him dead. Suddenly the straw sleeping-pallet heaved, and disgorged a great rat, which ran, with an obscene slithering, into the wall. Bile rose unheralded into my mouth. The Mother closed the door carefully behind us. In the half-dark, the stink grew hotter and more vile. She touched the woman's hand in greeting, she bent, O God! she actually *kissed* the scabrous face of one of the children before passing on to where the sick man lay.

'*Domine vobiscum*,' she said calmly. Emotionless, she stripped the solitary rag from his belly. From it, a growth the size of my own head rose like a strange purple fruit. The Mother laid salve on a cloth, and bent closer. At that moment a convulsion seized the patient; he vomited, while at the same time black blood spumed from his bowels, some of it splattering on the Mother's habit. The odour of rotting entrails mingled with the already deathly stench in the room.

I had a bit of dried lavender, and thrust it into my nostrils, ny own stomach a nauseous knot. The Mother turned and saw me, and there was something in her face that made me wish I had kept still. All she said, however, was:

'If I had but known of him earlier! As it is, the poison has

501

devoured his bowel. This is tincture of ragwort—the lime it contains is a boon against the canker. And I swear by goose-grass—the wondrous aparine. But both have failed. Nay, my son,' as he moaned and twisted. 'Lie quiet.'

The woman's turnip face dissolved in grief. 'Lord, Lord!' she blubbered. 'What shall become of our children?'

The smallest had its filthy hand upon my shoe. Running sores ringed its mouth, it stank like plague.

'I will take your eldest into our House,' said the Mother, not looking up. She had a basin of rose-water and was sponging the dirt and vomit from the dying face.

'In charity,' she added, as the woman broke into a gobbling paean of gratitude. A pale boy of about ten was pushed forward, and stood staring blankly at the Mother.

'In charity,' she said again. She was looking at me, very hard. 'Would it not be kindness to wash that little maid?'

The dirty child still clutched my foot. Its skin was like a toad's, its head alive.

'Did the court spoil you so?' She threw a faggot at a peering rat. It fled into the straw. I leaned halfway to the child. I could not touch it.

'Think!' said the Mother, in a terrible voice. 'If it were Katherine! Think! If it were Christ Jesus!'

I washed the child. I stripped her rags and scoured her with lye soap. The lice, frightened, leaped to find a richer host in me, and set to feasting. And I know now of course that the child was in truth Christ, as are all like her, yet I can also see how easy it is to turn one's face away, as do many, and I nearly did. By the time I had finished, the Mother was hearing Confession from the sick man. I therefore sat with the others by the door, and washed the hands and face of the eldest boy, Giles, also, as he was to come with us. And from his incoherent, faltering whispers I knew that here we had another Edyth. Remembering Edyth, I was glad.

Later, I sat opposite the Mother in her private room. The parchment lay blank under my hand for half an hour. I put forward every argument that I knew, but when she spoke of Katherine's birthright I felt myself weaken. It was not an easy thing to explain, none the less. I could never discourse with a living soul on what I felt, or my fears for his happiness with the Lady Anne. She asked me, did I want Kate to grow up poor and needy? I shuddered, remembering the hovel we had just left. Why should the Lady Anne be vexed, over something that was long finished and done? The parchment cracked sharply in my fingers. For it was far from finished to me. The Mother told me: like her name-Saint, Anne was a full gracious lady. Take John. Of him she was passing fond; she had him to stay with her at Middleham. As he was of Richard's blood, so was he dear.

And who was John? She told me. Men were men; it had been a long exile. A woman of Flanders, they said. It was worse than hearing of his marriage from Patch. I had never known true jealousy. I welcomed the lice that writhed and itched in my flesh. I would have welcomed a burning brand thrust into my bosom. Anything, to divert this shaming, crippling stroke.

Had they been dancing? Or had he been in one of his sober, melancholy humours? Had she . . . comforted him right well, with Venus riding high? A Flemish doxy; they used them in the Southwark stews. How readily she ran to him! Yea, she would run to him, lecherous and black-eyed and bold; if she were not a woman of stone, she would run to him. I had no claim, no more than did this Flemish harlot. Yet it was a part of his life in which I had no sharing; there lay the fury, the sadness. Yet, strangest of all, my love renewed, redoubled.

'He will honour John; he will see him well endowed.'

She dropped the pen between my fingers.

'Men grow fond of their daughters,' she said.

So, at last I wrote to Richard, formally at the Mother's dictation, and not as I had planned, and it was sealed with both my seal and the convent's. And I did not dream that night, for I did not sleep.

It was not finished and done for me.

Is there, I wonder, a force which moulds our destiny? Something apart from the God of Truth, or the Lord of Evil, an entity less positive than either power; something which can throw a whim, like a dice, into the unwarned mind, then sit back, waiting? A whim? A hankering, to be assuaged in free will, or, as freely denied, and one which, if acted upon, will often profit least the actor; at least three times in my life it has come upon me. I need not have spoken to Elysande that far-off day, when the windblown hawks hung on blue haze. Yet I did, and gained for myself great trouble. I could have rested the night, without Newark: I struggled on, and Edyth died. And there was no real cause for me to go to Walsingham, in the spring of Kate's fourth year. But go I did, and ran from joy, unknowing.

'Pilgrimages cost money,' the Mother said before I left, then closed up her lips tight, as if she wished the words back. For she had forgotten for an instant, as I often did myself, that now I *had* money, plenty of it, that Kate was dressed in warm murrey edged with miniver, that there were two new shorthorns in our meadow, and that the food I took no longer choked me with kindness.

I do not know how she recovered part of my corrody from the Yorkshire House; all I know is that she brought it to me one day with as much of a smile of triumph as her meekness would permit; nor do I know by whose hand she transmitted my letter to Middleham. As always, I was content to suffer her good judgment. But I felt differently when the answer came from Richard. I wanted to know everything: the unseen bearer's name, the date of carrying, and I could scarcely touch the parchment that had my name, and Kate's, upon it; the letter, for the most foolish reason, brought grief. It was not written in his beloved, familiar hand. His secretary, Kendall, said the Mother, was a discreet, loyal man. It made no difference. No difference at all.

'A reward' the bill concerning me was called. There was unmeant irony in that term. The Mother had no need to tell me this was the usual designation for such favours. But I had loved him, loved him, and that love needed no reward. The grants to Kate were less impersonal. Here, he acknowledged her wholeheartedly; there were even the words 'gladness' and 'affection' in Kendall's neat round hand. There was mention of a good marriage for her when the time was full. He wrote that she should stay at Leicester for the nonce. He acclaimed her as his daughter, a Plantagenet, niece of the King himself. He commended her to the Father of all.

And at no place in the letter, turn it this way and that as I would, did he speak of coming to see her. Of course, he would be very busy. Lord of the North. He would be far too busy for that.

I became a little embittered. Was that why I went to Walsingham? I chose Walsingham rather than Canterbury or any of the seventy other shrines in Norfolk because I remembered he had called there once, before he came to me at Fotheringhay. I would kneel where he had knelt. I went like a great lady, on a tall grey mare hired from the best stable in Leicester—dressed in satin lined with squirrel fur and a cloak of fine green wool caught with a silver brooch. The people turned to gawp at me. One of our ancient chaplains acted as my squire, poor Giles my page. He, who had never been more than half a league outside Leicester, hung midway 'twixt fear and excitement, a dribble of saliva running down a chin already rounder through the Mother's cherishing.

I prayed full heartily at Walsingham. I spoke to Our Lady herself, asking her to intercede for Adelysia, to take her quickly from Purgatory, so that she should be young and fair once more in Paradise; and for Edyth, for whom there would surely be no Purgatory; for my mother, my father, and for the cleansing of Giles's mind. Giles had had a seizing on the road. As my chaplain held him in the hedge-bottom he jerked and foamed with the strength of seven devils. After, he was mild as ever. That did not make the chaplain love this show of heresy any the more.

The roads were flooded with travellers. And a great crowd at Walsingham; many nobles, mingling with the cheapjacks, the minstrels and the myriad, crawling beggars, lacking eyes, limbs, their faces festooned with suppuration, their wavering cries rising over the drone of prayer that wafted from the church. The taverns were bloated with the spring influx of pilgrims, and there was much drunkenness. In all the confusion I found what I wanted. I had longed to repay the Mother in some way for all her love and kindliness; two cows and my board were not enough. In one of the shrines I was shown a phial of the Virgin's Milk; I touched it, knew it to be truth. Did I imagine the glow that rose from that little gourd? I have seen other lights, other stars. If so, the price of my fancy was not cheap. The chaplain hissed as I counted money out. Had he known I carried so much, he would not have come, for fear of being murdered on the road.

Thus was my state as I returned from Walsingham: lightened by prayer, and almost happy, and longing to see the Mother's face when she received my gift. She would say little, I knew, but I would be able to mark her secret delight by perchance a movement of her hand; I only wished I could have brought her a vision of the Virgin, but I was plainly unworthy and I would not lie, though I knew that many did. Giles had a fit outside Leicester, at the North Gate, holding us up; I was impatient, I wanted to see Katherine, and I had two cards of French silk for Dame Ursula, my only real extravagance, for her use on the frontal at which she was working. Green satin it was, powdered with silver roses. So it was to Ursula that I first flew, bursting into the room where her work was spread out over her knees and falling on the floor, a swathe of shining green like grass where lovers lie. I ran and kissed her seared old face.

'Dame, dame, it's good to see you!' I cried, as if I had been away for a twelvemonth. 'And where's my daughter? And how's the Mother? Wait till you see what I have for her, something beyond price, yet I priced it, *and* bought it, and . . .'

She was shaking her bowed head, joy and exasperation mingled, striking a finger on her lips again and again. I laughed out loud, for once wishing that the lax law of the Yorkshire House obtained in Leicester. She could not speak; it was not yet the Hour. Her seamed eyes played and twinkled upon mine, she held both my hands hard in hers. Then I realized that she, too, had something to tell that was well-nigh killing her with its importance. At times I thought that she would burst. She sucked in her lips as if they were two demons to be crushed. She swelled with frustration; she ran up and down the room. She pointed at me, stabbing the air, she drew a figure on the table, the hour when she could speak. She patted the head of an invisible child, and my gladness ran away like a cold stream.

'Katherine,' I whispered. Something amiss had come to Kate. 'Oh God, she's sick!' I cried, and Ursula went Nay, Nay, with her head. I caught her hands, hurting her, and she snatched away from me, parodying a horseman, held up three fingers, three times, in honour of the Trinity? Nay, nay, nine horsemen, she pointed at the ceiling—horsemen in Heaven? Speak, Ursula! This cursed waiting for the Hour!

The finger pointed skywards again. High, merciful Saints, how high! 'You have flown exceeding high, and may God have mercy.' Mercy on me, indeed, against those ancient words. Horsemen. Of high rank? And her head going yea, yea, wimple all askew, and the satin slithering plop! off the table, marsh-green beneath our feet.

'Lords, Ursula?'

One finger raised. On it I could see the needle-marks, like holes in a pepper-pot.

'One lord, Ursula? Here, in Leicester?'

The hands became birds in flight.

'Gone?'

Yea, yea, yea. Say nay, Ursula, for if my mind has read your head and fingers aright, I cannot bear it. One lord, of high rank, with eight in his train. Who, Ursula? She was sewing frantically, at a little end of cloth. Though she had been at work on the frontal for years, none could sew faster than Ursula when she chose. Silver thread she used, with no heed of the waste. A great lord in truth. The needle caught fire. A silver shape grew, was burnt into the green, into my heart. After a moment or two she held it up, a perfect piece of threadwork, small and snarling and terrible, the emblem of my love and grief, the Boar.

'Gloucester, my lord of Gloucester.'

And the wimple going yea, yea, and the stabbing finger at my breast, and the clever fingers miming: he was here, and you were not. He looked for you, and you were gone. He came to see you—he saw you not. Ah, how did he look, dumb Ursula? What colour his eyes this day? What colour his thought? Sad-coloured, like mine?

'He looked well,' the Mother said slowly. 'I have seen him before. Once. But I had forgotten he was such a fair young knight.'

I could not ask her what clothes he wore, if he were still as courteous, kind and stern of mien, if he smiled that smile which was worth a thousand weeks of dolorousness. I could not ask the Mother these things; they were of the earth. I could hardly speak. She did all the talking. I listened avidly, desperately. Richard had been and I not there to greet him. What was she saying? Talk, Mother, so I may blot it out.

'I am pleased with you,' she said. Wretchedly, I thought she alluded to my gift. ' 'Tis naught,' I said.

Is there a force, I wonder, that by our own hand kills our joy? I think, nay, know there is.

'You nursed the widow at West Gate right well,' she continued. 'You brought comfort to her spirit. And your hand is skilled with medicines.'

She had been a dreadful woman. Kidney stones. Only the saxifrage root had broken down the evil, and she had cursed me for my pains. The Mother was speaking. Her words made nonsense. Richard had been, and found me missing. The Mother would like to see me professed. I knew it. I knew also she would not speak of it until I did. And the townsfolk thought she carried Christian charity too far. Richard had been, and had ridden away.

'It is not nunly to leave cloister, even to visit the sick,' I said, all in misery, and was appalled at myself. I had criticized her, for the first time ever. O holy God! Richard had been, and I not there to meet him.

'This is a dying House,' she said softly. 'Like so many others. Corruption and poverty are consuming our Order. 'Tis not like two hundred years ago, an era of saints. Therefore we must do what we can. If nuns can break enclosure to dance and drink, why should we not do likewise, to succour the sick, the dying, the oppressed?'

The Compline bell rang. Richard had been and I had not seen him.

Confiteor Deo omnipotenti, beatae Mariae semper Virgine; was he disappointed? I could get naught from Katherine, save that a dark man, in fine robes, had set her on his knee. She had sung to him. *Ideo precor beatam Mariam semper Virginem, beatum Michaelum Archangelum*, he had kissed her, he would have kissed me, in greeting and farewell, a courtly token, what would his eyes have said? . . . all the saints, and you, Father, to pray to the Lord our God for me. 'Tis naught to him. 'Tis naught. The Mother wishes me to be professed. But will he come to me again? Will he?

The Mother took down an old book from her shelf, the Mother knew all of my sorrow. The candles burned up steadfast and white in the spring dusk. Outside a blackbird sang, hesitantly sweet, sang of *his* departure.

'He came,' I said. 'While I was wasting prayers at Walsingham.'

'Are prayers ever wasted?' the Mother asked.

'He came!' I cried. My voice was an echoing wail of despair. It frightened me. The blackbird flew away. Will he come to me again? Ever? Never? The old rhyming words, so loosely used in poem and ballad. The saddest words in the whole word. The Mother handed me the open book.

'This is for you,' she said. 'Remember this life is a transient thing. All joy, all sorrow, are as naught beyond the grave.'

Are they? Are they, in truth? If I had only seen him, not to speak, even, just in the distance, to brand his image fresh upon my mind, a buckler against the dead past, the dying future. Is it truly sin, to know such love, such longing? Passions older than the tide, and the moon that moves it. My love, my love, it is long since I lay, love-locked, in your arms! The Mother would have me professed. In charity. For my soul's good. How can I, with these worldly thoughts? Then I read the prayer, and the sea of my trouble was engulfed in a far wider ocean, deeper than I had ever imagined . . .

'O sweet Jesu, the son of God, the endless sweetness of heaven and of earth and of all the world, be in my heart, in my mind, in my wit, in my will, now and ever more. Amen.'

But I loved him. Naught would change that, ever.

'Jesu mercy, Jesu gramercy, Jesu for thy mercy, Jesu as I trust to thy mercy, Jesu as thou art full of mercy, Jesu have mercy on me and all mankind redeemed with thy precious blood. Jesu. Amen.'

'There lies comfort,' said the Mother softly.

But not yet, not yet. Not for such as I, who found his presence in the same house an utter joy, his absence an affliction past bearing. Not with this hair, which armed me brown and gold, which he had loved and found so pleasant, which fell about me like a shroud.

I wrote in my book, the book I should not have at all. I keep it behind a loose stone under my window, the same window where Robin came each dawn to kiss and sing. I often wonder if that bird loved me for myself or for the crumbs I gave him.

I have said that the middle years are somewhat veiled. Therein, events were like an arrow's passage through the air, a swan's skimming flight across a lake; the air, the water, opens and closes, and all is as before. So were my years, passing without a ripple, a rustle, a sigh, not sad, not happy those days; flat and tranquil only, after Katherine went away.

In my secret book I wrote rarely, with only a little guilt at heart, for it seemed meet to mark the times thus, and I know that others have written—there was an Abbess, during the era of saints, too, who made a treatise on Fishing. Nobody held her to scorn for it; in fact they hailed her wisdom kindly.

Since Katherine went, I felt the need to do it. Even if it had been a great sin. Write, I mean. In this book, which I must burn before I die.

The blossom is out. Our orchard groans with all that pink and white. Katherine was good, courageous; she seems older than her six years. On the hour of None they came for her, we were both in church and they waited. She cut some blossom for me, pink and white. The weight of it was terrible in my arms when she had gone. John Skelton it was, come at my lord's command, and who better to carry a child through paths unknown? I would have liked to talk with him about the old times; he once told me of Richard's own flight, my poor little lord, fevered and raving aboard the night boat for Burgundy. But John Skelton did not know me; why should he? Years have passed since he called me fair, at Grafton; he was the first ever to call me fair.

Kate's sojourn here is ended. She is to live in one of Richard's northern castles. Sir Robert Brackenbury's young daughter shall be her companion, and under the protection of my sweet lord her father, how can she go amiss?

She will be a great lady, but our House will lack her laughter.

This evening the Mother sent for me again. She never presses me, but I know her heart. It would please her greatly were I to be professed. She fears the jeopardy of my soul. Never was woman so kind in all this world.

I combed my hair for an hour before going to my empty bed. It served to stop me thinking of Kate upon the Fosse Way. I still have a glass, it shows my hair, so bright and sheen.

John Skelton mentioned husbands. For me! It would seem that Richard is worried—a husband! I fear I laughed. I said, let them all come.

Richard's son does well. Edward, Anne's boy. Skelton says he is his father's joy and pride, loved beyond measure. I know all about love.

This day parted Katherine and I, the Feast of St Barnabas, in the fifteenth year of King Edward's reign.

Tomorrow belongs to St Giles. I asked the boy what he would like for a present, but he did not understand. He is a good boy; today he worked like two men in the hayfield. Ursula and I went down to help. We have six hirelings this year, and the sheaves were stacked by nightfall. The stubble is full of larks now, gleaning. Giles caught one. He didn't kill it, just sat holding it in his hands. Ursula and I took our dinner by the barn, and I sewed. She still gets cross with me if I make the lozenges too wide. When I told her it was a blood-band for the Mother she made me unpick it all and start anew. She herself has begun again on the frontal—the colours displeased her, the reds were too bright. Irreverent, she called them. Would that I had her patience!

The Mother is pale today. I fear she bleeds herself too much. Some days ago I brought her a fine dish of Warden pears. Then this woman, sick of the bloody flux, came knocking at our gate. She begged the Mother's skill. The latter made a cordial of those pears, which I hoped she herself would enjoy. It stopped the flow within hours. The woman scarcely thanked her. I thought her even contemptuous but it may have been my fancy. Sometimes I mislike these people of Leicester.

No word from Katherine. I shall not write first. She must stand alone, but it is hard. Three months now, without her.

Warden pears are ruled by Venus. They denote affection, content. They are also good for rheumatism. The Mother does not know what I suffer in that direction, or she would cosset me, and I am bound to myself to change. I think I am no longer such a faintheart, puling wretch.

I am not changed in other ways, though. When that time comes this hand will have lost its power to write. The dreams are still as fierce, there was another last night. Some are almost like visions, clearer than truth. They stay with me for hours. That is why, all this day, the hayfield shone like beaten brass and Ursula's face wavered in the smoke of my desire.

The Hour was pleasant tonight. The Mother told me more of the *Mirror of Our Lady*. The nuns of Syon showed her that book, years past. She knows it from end to end. There is much in it, she says, for the ghostly comfort and profit of my soul. I saw her Bible. I have never seen an English Bible before, did not even know she had one. Some would think it Lollardy—that word makes me tremble. Yet she said calmly it is necessary to read thus, if only to aid our translation of the Vulgate. Sometimes I fear for her deeply. She is like one born out of her time. But Lord Jesu, how good!

He is well. One of the hirelings knows a kinsman of Sir Francis Lovell. Second and third hand this news may be, but it tells me that Richard spends most of his time fighting the Scots. He's not wounded. He is well.

Still she does not press me. I told her this night: wait till the husbands have come, then I'll decide! We both laughed. But already I know the answer.

How should I marry, who have no heart?

Hard weather, for St Cecilia. The Mother makes me, Lucy and Ursula drink a posset of honey and cinnamon every night. I have finished my new flannel shift just in time, and breeches of the same for Giles. I helped him put them on—his fingers are useless for laces and delicate things. I know what it is to be cold in winter; his face is chap-covered where the spit runs down. He cannot keep a closed mouth; he talks well to me, most of it nonsense but with such a charming air. He it was who let in the first of my suitors. Mary have mercy!

Sir S. was tall. My head came up to his padded elbow. He was direct, too, put his cards squarely down, and told me his estate was not all it should be, that he badly needed a moneyed spouse and further, one who could grace his table, engage his friends and enemies alike in blithe, strategic talk, sing and play while he laboured to mend his dwindling affairs, a mistress who could make a good dinner out of slender means. There was one lord, whose favour he lusted to obtain. Woman could often succeed where man might fail. I asked him, did he know that I had borne a child? and he said he hoped I would do for him the same, strong sons to lengthen his line, not daughters, as maids were a veritable plague to dower and marry, whereupon I said, yea, behold one! at which his watery, white face reddened. We were just sitting looking at each other, he drumming on the table, his countenance unstable as water, and uneasy, when Giles, who had been told to stay without, rushed in, bearing in his hands a half-frozen robin; I put my arm about him, the better to hear his slavering tale, and the bird, like an ice-lump, in my bosom. When I looked again, the chair opposite was empty.

Lord, I could laugh! Not only at poor Sir S., halfway to London now, thinking that Giles is mine! but at Sir J., a clown in truth and far less honest. He flung himself at my feet. All the furniture shook. He likened me to Diana, said that my eyes struck him with bolts of madness, and that he would have none other but me. Then he found himself fixed, being not so young as he himself had thought, and portly. I had to raise him from the floor. I tugged and heaved; he clutched me with hands covered in reddish hair, and well-nigh brought me down too, and my hennin fell off and was crushed under his rolling, which angered me, for it was new that day . . .

Robin is thawed, and sleeps, with but a little quivering, in a casket on my sill. His feathers are soft, his face warm and bright.

I will have *him* for my lover.

A letter from Katherine! My Katherine, how I miss you. That little bill, with its sprawling capitals, brought it right home. It is dated from Sheriff Hutton, 'a windy place' she calls it. She and Brackenbury's daughter will soon be moving—she is not sure where, but it will be farther north. Middleham, perchance? She says his Grace her father called to see her, on the way to London, before Christmas. Merciful God, she says 'he was not in good heart.'

I wish she would not tell me this. Now I worry and wonder, wishing beyond this world to comfort him. Are my prayers enough? The prayers of a sinful woman are less effective than those of a nun. I was ever his true beadswoman, as well as his fleshly leman. If he came to me sad, he left me smiling. Always. Even the night when Warwick, and George, laughed at him.

George will laugh no more. This day we heard that he was dead. A strange mystery. They say that he drowned himself in wine, but in the Tower. The Mother had this news, privately, from London. She seemed at pains to discuss it with me. Always she harks back to the night at Grafton Regis. I try to give her pleasant answer, but it is something which I would forget. Whichever way I reply, she frowns.

She is pleased with my Shrove-cakes, though. You need new cheese, ground fine in a mortar, with eggs beaten to thistledown, and coloured rich with saffron, baked in coffins of pastry, not too long; I sprinkled nutmeg. They broke in the fingers.

Robin takes food from my lips. Faithful unto death—he has proved it. The first day I let him fly I thought never to see him again, but he came back calling at my window in the morning, and has remained ever since. Now spring is coming, he's a lusty lover. His little beak is like a tiny sword at my mouth. Shameless, singing Robin!

Yesterday I went to nurse a lad with rotten lungs. Rosepetal jelly. Only the red rose will do. Therefore I have no faith in it, so surely am I wedded to the House of York! Giles came with me. He is strong as a bull. He picked up the youth, and a tall fellow he was, in his arms for me to make his bed. Coming through Swine Market a man tried to fondle me and Giles knocked him down. I hate the hands of men.

So he was not in good heart. Lord Jesu give him joy again. Whatever the reason, let him not be sad.

Written on St Cuthbert of Lindisfarne, the seventeenth year of Edward's reign.

Could I pray better for you, love, were I a nun?

'It can't be vanity!' said the Mother.

She had known my heart; the moment had come. Our

bench by the dovecote was the only cool place. Beyond the circle of dark shadow where we sat, Robin strutted with the plump grey doves, jostling fearlessly for their grain. Now and then one would peck at him, angered by his lewd courage, but he merely tripped his fluttering dance to safety. Across the glaring, sun-white yard, a brindled cat was watching, a strange, meagre beast.

'Is that Willowkin?' asked the Mother, shading her eyes. 'Nay, it's too scrawny.' Willow, our own cat, was lazy and too old to menace Robin, who often sat impertinently upon his head. I threw a pebble. The strange cat rose noiselessly in a pouring leap over the high wall and disappeared. For a shameful moment I wished I were that cat. The Mother had a dispensation to talk with me outside the Hour, and here was I, wasting time. She stretched her fingers out to Robin. He put his head on one side and watched her, motionless.

'Play no games with that one, Robin,' she said.

I looked down at my hands. Burnt almost black by the summer's fieldwork, there were callouses on the palms, the nails were short and ragged.

'Mother, it's not vanity.'

'Do not fear accidia, either,' she murmured. 'You would find only deepest joy. I warrant it. I would give my life to see your peace. Your soul at anchor.'

And I wanted it too. Sweet Jesu in my heart, my mind, my wit, my will, for ever. Yet I knew in this there could be no compromise; while my spirit still roved the moors, or was sad with him in London—there could be no division. For he had come to me once, and he might come to me again. Would he? Ever? Never? Robin hopped on my thumb. I rubbed my cheek against his fluffy poll.

The Mother, watching, knew my every thought.

'He will not come again,' she said softly. 'He dotes upon his wife. That broken reed, that sweet, ailing woman, Anne.'

I did not know that she ailed. But she would have the best physicians, second only to the King. Whatever her malady, they would set it right. Or would they? If the sickness were deep-rooted, the bad humours firmly in the ascendancy . . . Oh God! what thoughts!

The Mother seized my changing face between her hands.

'Fight it,' she said sternly. 'This is not you, but the Devil himself. He will not come.'

But the dreams said otherwise, the dreams in which I never saw his face, heard only his whispering voice in the dark, felt his hands among the lustrous toils of my hair. If he should come, and find a shaven head, a habit . . .

'How say you this, Mother?' I asked, rough with longing. 'Have you read it in the stars? Are you a prophet?'

For a long space she was quiet. 'I am not of the Wise, nor would I wish to be,' she answered finally. 'Neither do I intend to embark upon a disputation. Yet, you wag your hypotheses before me, and for your good, I'll answer them. If he should come, yea, *if*, and seek your comfort . . .'

'All that he ever sought!' I cried.

'There are better balms than kisses,' she said. 'Services that only a woman of God can perform. Sweet charity, a Mass, the Sacrament. Have I not said that this life is a transient thing?'

The sheen on the white pavement hurt my eyes. There was the smell of thunder inside my head. Even as I looked, a cloud blotted the sun, and to the west an artery of light hung twitching on the air.

'Do I speak the truth?' asked the Mother.

I could not deny her, or what was right. Robin was eating the crumbs from the doves' table. The Duchess of Bedford had said it. All is written, long ago. Crumbs would be my portion. I stood up.

'Forgive me, Mother,' I whispered, bending for her embrace. The only time she kissed me in the future would be in church, the unfleshly salutation of the *Pax*.

'At least,' I said, 'I shall be able to sign my name on the letter of profession. Not a great untidy X. I'll serve you well, Mother . . .'

'Pride!' She held up a finger, but she laughed, and I also. I could laugh, for now the dreams were surely ended, and I needed a jest against that fact.

But that night of all nights, he came to me. I ran towards him, across the green lawns of Eltham, through the little stone archway, where God knows how many lovers had breathed one breath. He had his back to me. He wore a sky-coloured doublet, long boots of light doeskin. My feet made no sound—I fancied that I flew, caught up in the longing to join with him in love, to live and die with him, to rise one spirit . . . his in heart and thought, in the heat of the sun with the crying birds lifting in dreadful joy.

He turned. I saw his eyes, his mouth. He smiled, held out both hands. This time, I would never let him go. I flung myself, wanton, holy, wanton, upon his breast. I called his name, and my voice became a bell.

I woke, and there was only the voice of Prime, and the

hurrying nuns in the stone passage without, and the selfless kiss of Peace.

Written on the Beheading of St John Baptist. I took my Vigil yesterday. A long night. Now I find my wrists and elbows swollen, shiny red, as if they had been tied. I must embrace the pain. Today is a Fast, but later I will infuse the White Bryony, peerless against jointgripings. Last night the church seemed very large. Midnight dwarfed the candles, and in all four corners there seemed to be wraiths, rising whitely. Between the prayers and chanting the silence was immense.

I am learning. All I can about being a nun. My own ignorance haunts me. Only lately did I learn that Dame Johanna tricked me—she could not have taken Kate! Under this land's law a maiden is not recognized as professed until she is twelve. What a fool I was! The *Mirror of Our Lady* holds some sad tales. One little nun, yet a child, died and came again to her sisters, to be purged of the sin of whispering in church. If this be so, those at the Yorkshire House will spend half eternity before the altar! I must not judge, I shall learn my fill. I could now apply myself to the duty of any of these: Treasuress, Precentrix, Sacrist, Fratress, Almoness, Chambress, Cellaress. I could lighten Ursula's load. For in truth we are so small that the above are but courtesies; jills-of-all-trades, each of us helps the other.

I have this book. Old Ursula has a secret too. 'One lock,' she said guiltily, and tucked it in her purse. After her busy clipping my head felt like a puffball in the wind, light and cool and fragile. She stared down at the brightness that lapped her ankles. I thought she looked sad. I did not look at all.

I wonder if she will weave it in with her embroidery. Not on the frontal, of course, but in some little personal thing. Anyhow she has one lock of my hair.

Martinmas. A terrible screaming from the byre, where Giles is slaughtering. For all his baby's mind, he can turn his hand to anything. He tells me he has awful dreams, but I cannot define their sense. Strange he should come to *me* with dreams. He is killing the great hog we had sent us lately. It was a heriot—the dead man owed tithes, and the Bishop thought kindly of us. We shall be set up for the winter—it must be salted down immediately. Giles has been promised the pig's bladder to play with. He loves football, for all King Edward has forbidden it.

The King is not here to see him play.

No news of the other.

And K. writes infrequently, from a place called Barnard Castle. All her letters to the Mother now, and I can only answer her under the common seal.

Robin is still cross with me. He pecks at my wimple, sits on my shoulder with most lewd looks into my face. He does not understand the wimple—at first he tried to pull it off. The band is tight above my eyes, and the barbe presses on my throat.

Blessed be God.

The Sixth after Trinity, and a day in truth.

K. came, unheralded. Barnard Castle is being cleansed and they have stayed in London. Sir Rbt Brackenbury's daughter was with her, but I had eyes only for K. She was so gorgeous, blue and silver; she even had a sparrowhawk on her wrist. I noticed her purse worked with the device and a belt of the same. Though she gave me a good devotion I fancied there was something imperious about her—captivating, but dangerous. She is ten years old now; no husband yet, I asked, and she laughed.

She tells me she has seen King Edward. She was most unflattering about his looks—what she said I dare not write, but he cannot surely have put on all that royal flesh! Though it *is* nineteen years since he first wore the crown. Long may he reign.

She spoke of the other. He remains north. The sparrowhawk was from him. I had to shut Robin in a cupboard while I caressed it.

We heard Mass together. In the dusk, her face was like a flower.

Jesu preserve the King, and all those of the blood.

I thought I should not have time to write it. All day we have been besought. There was a courier at the North Gate before sun-up, beating with the flat of his sword. The bells go on and on. Some town folk have bought candles to place on our altar. A ceaseless Requiem tolls, backed by those thin voices, rising higher and higher, like a spool of silk drawn up to the sky.

For King Edward is dead.

The Mother swooned during the Gradual. I think she is not very well. She said some strange things this day. According to her it will be a bad day for England. She says if the Woodvilles gain power there will be many wives widowed. Like the old days, the bad times. I must cosset her. And it will be a Fast tomorrow, for Edward's soul. It is not like her to have this melancholy.

Written April, in the first year of King Edward Fifth's reign.

St Dunstan of Canterbury. The sun shines through a fine rainspray. The old pear tree has bloomed early and hangs over the garden wall like a tired man longing to sit down. Robin sings from a cluster of blossom; the garden is fair. In this light rain the gillies and scented stocks shimmer like some beautifully illuminated page, red and yellow and gold. A growth of speedwell is pushing through the moss right under my window, and a lilac bush comes into flower.

Some of these flourishing herbs spread everywhere. Even unto the cloister where our long-dead sisters lie. Some of those stones are very old, too old, I think, to be bothered by the rude ground-ivy. Gill-go-over-the-ground, they sell it in Swine Market. Gill tea is very good. Bind-weed and periwinkle tangle up the garden. I do not seem to have the time to dig them out; anyway they have a prettiness all their own, so let them multiply, all the more for our simple-store.

I have been thinking of him riding down from Middleham for the funeral, the coronation. Someone said that King Edward was chested already, but this I cannot believe. They would not be so hasty. I wonder how the child king will be. It's an ordeal for so young a knave. But he will be beside him, so what shall he fear? He will be there to escort Edward at his coronation, being the nearest of the blood. I hear there is quarrelling among the monks our neighbours. Sister Lucy even believes they draw lots for who shall attend the Abbey at Westminster. Foolish. It all depends on which has the Bishop's ear.

I feel better these days. With summer ahead, my joints seem eased.

God will give Edward grace to rule wisely. After the Picquigny scandal, we cannot afford another war. I do not expect the King of France wants one either. Here am I scratching of politics, I who know naught of them. But Edward is full young; he will need advisers. But why does the Mother say the day is bad? Surely the Woodvilles—

Ursula almost caught me just now, writing. I wonder of late whether I should confess it to my holy father? But is it really such a great sin? The Mother says if you need to ask this question, then it is sin; where such doubt is, there sin is also. She is still unwell, and last week actually took to her bed for a couple of hours. What she said privily to me made me sore uneasy. She cannot mean *me* to . . . She cannot mean what I think. For she will live, many years. God grant it.

St Alban's Day, and a strange letter from Katherine. A rider passed through their dwelling. Says that Richard has sent for tall fellows in harness, a desperate, urgent matter. It's like her, of course, to skim the top off the news and leave you guessing, though it may be she knows no more than this. Men, to cherish the young King? But there will be a host of Palace guards. I know.

The Mother is stronger. I got her to leave off the bleeding for a while, and made her take the wine of the valley lily. It made her heart beat good and fast. While she was reading K's letter she waxed yellowish and murmured to herself, I was really frightened, I know the lily is so dangerous, and thought I had made the dose too rare. She said, 'Ah, treachery!' She mentioned, yet again, Grafton Regis. I gave her but cursory answer—I only want her well again.

I do not wish to think that we are a dying House. But even my money does not stretch as far as I would like, and we are hard worked. Ursula has started, once more, on the frontal. It must be right, she says, to God's glory. I offered to help her with it. She was quite wroth. She is getting old. So low does she bend, her wimple makes a little dark cave for her work. I suppose in her mind's eye she sees it finished, glowing on the altar with two fat candles and the Holy Gospel snug atop. Her life's ambition, already, in fantasy, fair and fine.

Why should he write in desperation?

It is hearsay, anyway.

K. must have it wrong.

I am still stunned half-silly, I can scarcely write.

Richard Plantagenet is King, by grace of God.

And by an old stroke of destiny, but even to me, this could

never have been presaged. Now I know that this kingship was implicit in that night at Grafton Regis. Now and now only.

The ungodly, May Day marrying.

Now I know who 'the other' was.

Alas, poor Eleanor Butler! Among all the rejoicing and speculation, I'll make for her a special novena, share the dead sorrows of Edward's rightful Queen. How could he have been so cruel? He was out of his mind.

It's past and done, poor Eleanor.

For all the music in the psalter cannot house my jubilation. My hand shakes, I've spilled the ink. Robin's tracking feet make the page look like a spiderweb. *Gloria in Excelsis Deo.*

Written Nat. J. Baptista, the first year of King Richard the Third.

May the King live for ever.

Vivat Rex! Vivat Rex!

I knew that by now he would have forgotten my existence, but I still dreamed, waking and sleeping, amid repenting. And he came, not as I had forecast, but upon his royal progress. Leicester had already learned how he refused the money offered him by other towns; they shouted their anticipation all the louder for it. They garlanded the streets, twined roses in the bush that hangs above the taverns. They cleansed the streets, at long last removing the rotting corpse of a cat from Town Ditch. Men went anxiously to see if Leicester Castle was habitable, while the Mayor preened himself and swept out halls. And they were ready.

I knew he would not look upon my countenance again. He would pass distantly with his vast train of knights and noblemen, his heralds and pursuivants. I did not for one moment think that he would visit our House, but I played with a fancy; I starched my wimple with arrowroot and laid my habit nightly among woodruff and rosemary, and lodged him as splendidly as we could afford, and saw him enter the church to prostrate himself before the altar, dignified and aloof, fittingly devout and earnest, with only the vague knowledge that behind him knelt a cluster of robed women and around him soared the high holy voices that he loved.

He came to Leicester and again I missed seeing him. Not even in the distance, which was all I had wished. And this time, as I had been so prepared for disappointment, the hurt was less. All I saw was a host of people beneath the jostling sway of the standards, the crowd breaking free of the cordon of King's men and bailiffs and running with cheers; a splash of a gold pennon, the flash of a trumpet, a glimpsed knot of heralds shouldering aside a monk of St Mary's, so that he rolled against an alehouse door and through it, and there remained. I saw all this in one instant's peering through the outer gate, until the Mother sent for me. We were to have a guest from the royal entourage, and I must wait upon her. A lady renowned for piety and learning; I grew quite nervous.

When the page announced Lady Stanley it meant naught to me. I knew her as Lady Margaret Beaufort. I remembered her cursing me once for standing in her way. Her tight face was the same, with its prim mouth and narrow eyes, her stature scarcely higher than a dwarf's. She had her chaplain, Reynold Bray, with her, and made straight for the church. The richness of her gown took all colour from its furnishings. She prayed lustily and long. '*Judica me Deus, et discerne causam meam.*' Outside the streets grew quiet. But later, as I took our last flagon of Rhenish into the parlour, the King's train must again have appeared in public view, for another great bursting cheer arose, and swarmed through the open window on a hot breeze.

'By St Edmund! All this accursed pomp!'

I heard her distinctly, as I balanced the salver on my knee and fumbled the latch. Perchance she is weary, I thought. I went in and asked her, kneeling, had she a headache? Would she prefer a little violet cordial instead of wine? She answered tartly that she had her own physicians, and I felt my face scarlet for a moment. But she spoke kindly to me in the next breath, saying certes, the progress was exhausting work, but she already felt much refreshed. Then she prayed again, for hours, and after Compline sat reading aloud from a monstrous book of philosophy in the Greek.

So I missed seeing him for the second time, and could only remember him as before—sitting across the hearth from me, young and hurt, and ruefully smiling—or raising his hand in farewell, after a strange, glad, unhappy night.

Do I love him more, now he is King? I would love him were he King or beggar. The heart is no heretic. He is he, and I love him.

So wrote I, in my book.

Little do I know, for here all knowledge of the world seems slight. We are encased in our bubble. The days go on, a chaplet of constant, timeless prayer. Yet I imagine we know more news than most. The Mother seems *au fait* with London life, she it was who told me Hastings was dead. And Buckingham, whom last I saw gaily bending the knee to King Edward one Christmas, surrounded by Woodville wives. And gorgeous Anthony Woodville, who frightened me sore. Richard Haute too—him I do not remember.

And Dickon Grey, with whom I once played Hoodman Blind.

I might have wept for that one, remembering him as a little, wanton, naked boy—but the tear scalded my eyes, as if to direct their penance for a fleeting disloyalty.

For these men would have killed the King. It is but lately I realize his double vulnerability. All Kings have enemies, and he is gentler than Edward. Five men dead, the Mother says. In lieu of five thousand.

Winter comes soon. The Mother bade us all give thanks. According to her we have just escaped a war. We sang a good *Deo gratias*. That Tudor will never invade again. Not after this latest, black-advised impertinence. One could almost laugh at him sparring for Richard's crown. It is easy to forget that Lady Margaret is his mother. The next time, if she visits, I shall feel disinclined to serve her. Yet it's duty, charity, to pray for her soul when she wishes it. And as the King still cherishes her at court, then so shall I.

For his wisdom was ever my wisdom, his way, my way.

Half a year since my last notation. Robin sits by me—the chaplain remarked the other day what a hardy bird he is. I had him the month of my profession and he is still chirpy and hale. I say it is my care of him in the winter. He is a housebird—sleeps nightlong in my closet on straw and feathers. Sin, to cherish him so. But at least he does not come jargoning into church to upset the others. So he's an unholy, churchless fellow.

Lord! it seems that everything becomes a paradox, if you look at it long enough.

The *Ancren Rule* was writ primarily for female hermits but there's a deal of sense in it. It says you should not overdo the bleeding. In one of my disputations with the Mother I brought this up, and she was bound to smile, while chiding me. Now I know for certain—she would like me to take office when she is gone. I just said 'Domine, non sum dignus' very loudly in church in response to the priest, and she looked at me while the candles flickered unsteadily. I *am* unworthy, in truth.

K's last letter from Barnard made me blush. The Mother read out loud three phrases describing the joys, her new gowns, and the glamour of a recent joust. She is nearly fourteen, and no talk of a husband. I pray St Catherine she leads a proper life. It is a real little court they have up there, and I know the temptations.

His favourite saint is Ninian. This is news to me. His maxim was: 'Even the highest shall learn from the lowest.' One of the stalls at Middleham belongs to him who evangelized the Picts a thousand years ago. The Mother talked of the old custom of drawing straws for a saint to worship for one's own. I said I'd choose Ninian, and she told me of the nun who once drew Jude the Obscure, was vexed and threw him behind the altar chest. He visited her that night, striking her with palsy. Apparently you cannot choose what you most desire.

After I closed my book and hid it again, I sat thinking about the nun who had the visitation from St Jude. I could imagine it very clearly. The Saint's sad, militant face, possibly ringed with an angry nimbus of light, the powerful anger striking through the blackness of the dorter and across the woman's bed. These thoughts led on to others of similar aspect. Before my lifetime, a nun, dying, had seen the Blessed Virgin herself. She came to bear her up, they said the perfume of roses lingered long after in the infirmary. And Ursula's aunt had seen a fiend. He had waited for her when she went to bed, gibbering and frowning, and she had marched up to him, dealing him such a buffet on the ear that he howled for mercy, changed into a black dog and leaped through the window. I had not thought of these tales for years, but on this night they kept me awake.

I lay, and the moon peeped in on me. When I began to shiver, I wondered if in some way I had offended a saint, so said a few Aves with my beads under the clothes. But even the angelic salutation did not halt the feeling of melancholy, vague at first, which grew and enveloped me, worse than accidia, worse than the pain of a bad conscience, inexplicable, powerful, and terrifying. I thought that someone was standing against the window, very still. I dared not breathe or move. Once I would have leaped up and earned a penance by breaking silence, but this was no longer my way. Also I had no cause. No fiend attacked *me*. Only fear, the fear of fear itself, and a great sadness, of the same breed that had surged over me when I looked on Nottingham.

The shadow, if there ever was a shadow, was gone from the window. Only a cloud remained that stood across the moon, behind the dappled pear tree that waved in the April night wind. And sorrow, deep and heavy, not for myself. A visitation it was in truth, by that which was not seen, not evil, but dolorous beyond all thought.

Now I know. I hardly needed the telling, by town crier or herald, that some dreadful calamity had overtaken him.

His little son is dead.

They say he is nigh demented, by reason of his sudden grief.

Yesterday we rang the bell merrily for St George of England. Today, another Requiem bears the blossom down.

Whom shall it toll for next, I wonder?

My sisters looked oddly at me for days. They reckoned I knew of the Prince's passing before anyone. My face told it, they said.

Of course it's true, and this frightens me. Yet can I help it if his sorrow is ever my sorrow, his breath my life?

I shall write no more this day.

Then came Katherine, soon after Christmas, taller than I, her waist no rounder, I swear, than the fine festive candle we had lit to Christ's Mother. I watched her arrive, on a grey palfrey whose outline shimmered like a ghost horse in the lightly falling snow. She laughed, dismounting; one of her women chided her gently for laughing so loud within holy walls. When she knelt before me, with eyes bird-bright, the imprisoned smile still quivered on her mouth, she was lovely, fair. In her rich furs she was like a lissom animal. Her hood was forest green, her nut-brown hair silk to the touch.

'Kate, you're a song,' I said, utterly foolish. The slender, snow-damp face smiled against mine. I drew her down beside me on a chest in the parlour. To London she had been, for Christmas. She burst into a recital; the court revels from end to end, from the entry of the Boy-Bishop to the dwarfs riding their mules around the Great Hall. She told it all to me, who needed no telling. She coloured an old picture.

'Mother, the cook made a great pie! When the carver

opened it, a lot of frogs jumped out. There must have been a score of them, all the ladies screamed. One of the frogs leaped into Lady Grey's soup, and splashed her gown. She was furious.'

'Where did you stay?'

If at Greenwich, she would have roamed those same passages, mounted those old, broad stairs. Yet she, the King's daughter, would have walked in the light.

'Crosby's Place,' she replied. For the first time I noticed the ring on her finger, a large beryl set in gold. Crosby's Place, the tallest building in London. Was it still? My memory lurched with the sway of a crowded litter, the Duchess of Bedford's dog yapped around my feet, someone pointed out the sights to me, a bumpkin. Seventeen years ago, and I with a light heart. Then I had not known a man, this man now King, who owned Crosby's Place, had entered neither Heaven nor Hell. Kate was watching me. Probably I seemed stern, musing thus.

'King Richard sent for me, and for John of Gloucester. To pleasure us for Christmas,' she explained. Instantly I was hungry, longing.

'How did he look?'

'As a King looks,' she answered, then shot me a sideways glance, mischievous and at the same time well pleased, as if she were bringing me a piece of sewing, or writing, for approval. 'I am betrothed.'

With difficulty I tore my mind from the King.

'His name is Lord Herbert. William.'

'The Earl of Huntingdon?' I asked. She nodded, came close to my ear to whisper.

'And Mother, he is *young!* Handsome . . .' Her manner grew frivolous. 'We had thought he might be bald or squint. At Barnard we used to play for hours at guessing what my husband would be like! Ned and Dickon had a wager . . .'

'Dickon? Ned?' I asked sharply. She was laughing, she was fair, like a pretty, purring kitten. I had a sudden awful fear that she might have been foolish. With these unknown, teasing names.

'I trust you've comported yourself virtuously, Katherine, in the north,' I said severely, yet thinking Lord! how pompous! 'There are temptations in a household where young women and henchmen are thrust together . . .'

I might not have spoken. The flood of her talk went on.

'Yea, the Earl is handsome, and pleasant. And the King has settled a thousand marks a year upon us to start with, and he will send letters patent for at least another hundred pounds when we are wed. I had a private audience with him, in the State Chamber.'

All her laughter suddenly vanished. She twisted the beryl ring nervously. I looked at her, the long, odd-shaped eyes, and the hands like his, that moved like his, and I said, very quietly, for I wanted to hear, so much:

'What was his dress?'

'Black,' she said, and without warning, burst out crying and cast herself into my arms. 'His face was so sorrowful. So weary. He kissed me, his lips were cold. He seems . . . near death.'

I shook her, gave her harsh words. God forgive me.

'Don't say that! D'you want to put a curse upon his Grace?'

'Ah, never, never, but the Queen is sick of lung fever and I thought he may have taken it from her. He looks as if he never sleeps. I did not know he was . . . so old.'

A pain gripped my heart. 'He is but thirty-two,' I said, without emotion.

She was quiet, shaking her downcast head like an old woman. After a time I asked: 'Did he speak of the Queen?'

'He spoke only of me. He said how glad he was I am his daughter, and that once he had a little son, whom God took from him. Ah, Mother!' She raised eyes black with tears. 'He's a good man, good and gentle. And Ned and Dickon hate him so. When I return to Barnard they will call him names.'

I grew wrath with these unknown pages, who made rude wagers over Kate's betrothed, who spoke against the King.

'Who *are* these knaves?' I asked, angrily. 'Have naught to do with them. I forbid it.'

Now she looked mutinous. 'I'm teaching them to dance!' she expostulated. 'They are fond of me, really. Dickon is naughty, Ned often sick—but they both call me fair.'

Her pouting mouth unnerved me. King Edward's blood, I thought. As well as mine, and Richard's. The late King's lustful ardour, that seething itch. How much of it in Katherine? Holy God! next thing and Kate, royal maid or no, will be with child, not by Earl Huntingdon but one of these young rogues.

'Give me your word you'll have no more ado with them,' I said wildly. Rainbow-humoured, she was laughing again.

'But Mother, they *are* my cousins!' she cried. 'And if Dickon is sometimes rude, Ned is as courtly, in truth, as King Edward his late father would have been, had he not been drunken when I saw him last. Sweet Jesu! Mother, there's no harm . . .'

Then she stopped. Stopped dead. Every particle of colour fled her face, so that the hand she lifted to her mouth looked golden against that sudden whiteness. Truly I thought she was taken with catalepsy, possessed. I sat frozen in horror. We stared at each other like fools.

'What's the matter?' I whispered.

She said in an anguished voice: 'I have broken a promise, a promise made not seven days ago. I should have my tongue cut out.'

It was half an hour before I could get it from her. And when all was told, it seemed very little. What if the royal bastards *were* at Barnard Castle? But she would not be quenched, she would keep repeating: 'None must know, none must know. I promised King Richard. I swore on oath.' At the last, she dragged me into the church, and, frantic, ran searching the most sacred object so that I too should swear. Had I not been grieved for her guilt I might have felt annoyed. For any secret of Richard's I, above all, would hold most dear, whatever the reason. But she was not to know this, and eventually she had me kneel with my hands clasped on the phial of Virgin's Milk and swear before God never to tell the whereabouts of King Edward's sons.

Then we pleasured ourselves. I took her to see Ursula, who let her put a stitch in the frontal. That meant that all of us had at one time had a hand in it. It was a marvellous piece of work already; Ursula raised her head long enough to say that she hoped to have it ready by the Annunciation, then immediately fell to unpicking the last spray of roses, and Katherine and I went away shaking our heads. Robin came, and Kate played with him. The brindled cat, still clinging round our house for scraps, sat in the snow and watched, malevolently, its tail draggled with wet, a lousy, unkempt intruder. I hope and pray that Katherine was happy that day. Had I but known she was to be part of the long pattern—Adelysia, Edyth, even the old ballad-maker, for everything I touched must die—I would have given her soft, kind words and kisses every hour. Had I but known I would never again set eyes upon her, that she would be dead within the year of a foul wasting sickness that naught could stay, I would have laid down my own life to halt her passing. Sweet Katherine. If you watch over me, pray. Give me the strength to finish this tale, and, if it is sad, remember, there is truth in sadness, joy being but an illusion.

When she had gone, my thoughts returned to the King. I thought: Let him come to me, as I have dreamed it, saying: 'My son is dead, my wife also. Give me your smile, your joyful words, your welcoming hand.' And, though I could only offer him a psalm, a candle, the sound of sombre music, both he and I would be assuaged. That he should come again, I prayed it.

And my prayers were answered: in blood and fire and tears. *'Miseratur vestri omnipotens Deus, et dismissis peccatis vestris, perducat vos ad vitam aeternam.'*

Ursula squinted up from the frontal. Though by now she was almost blind, she had an eye at the end of each clever finger.

'Can you make it out? Is it clear, and fair, and true?'

Softly I read it. 'May almighty God have mercy upon you' (in purple) 'Forgive you your sins' A silver cross, and then the green, colour of hope: 'and bring you to life ever lasting.' Another cross, and then the royal Rose.

High above Ursula's cell, thunder shivered the skies. The seeing hands clasped my own.

'Tell me,' she said, a little querulously. ' 'Tis good? Are the colours too bright?'

'It's a masterwork,' I answered. Thank God, Dame, that you have lived to finish it. I swear you would have returned yearly, from your heavenly reward, had it been left undone. I said none of this.

'That is well,' she nodded. 'Now, I must make alteration. The border troubles me. The stitches seem lumpy and coarse. Hand me the gold, Sister.'

'Sweet Dame, sweet Ursula,' I said, doing as I was asked, 'leave it now, I beg you. You cannot better it. We must go. The Prioress has ordered that we pray. The Great Intercession . . .'

'Are we to be invaded?' she asked, calmly threading. 'I heard that the King is coming, in arms. Thank Christ I am too old to be afraid.' Her needle began to swoop and flash. 'It must be to the glory of God,' she said, for the thousandth time.

'Yea, it almost looks as if we shall be in the heart of the battle,' I said. She must have heard the tremor in my voice, though she could not know its true cause. He was coming. Even now, he rode to Leicester. Ursula sang half of a short psalm, bent low again, and went on sewing. I walked among her silks and tapestry frames, while the fitful August sun pried through the high window. I imagined all that Ursula could not.

The villagers were arming. From the south-west of Leicester, men marched to his standard. From Stoke Golding, Earl Shilton and Stapleton, from the hamlets of Kirkby Mallory, Atterton and Fenny Drayton they came. A few of them had knocked last night upon our gate for a blessing, strong, rustic men, soft-spoken, coarse-tongued, shuffling their thonged feet awkwardly up the nave. The King was coming to Leicester. Tomorrow, the day after, they were not sure. Little villages, known to us over the years for their poverty, their surly, crying needs, yielded up their men. Northeasterly marched the yeomen of Glenfield, Desford, Kirby Muxloe and Newbold Verdon. And from farther west they came, grim, patient and hastily equipped, the men of Atherstone, Maxstoke, Stone, Stanton, Sapcote and Appleby Magna. We had nursed and confessed them, these men of Leicester, over the long years, and now they crowded through Swine Market to the Cross, and down to the sign of the White Boar where the King would surely lie, tomorrow or the next day, before his triumph, his great campaign and acquittal, his vengeance and the wreaking of his might.

I had completed five days of the novena I was making for him, so I went into the church and stayed there to augment it after the others had gone. For the first time the words came haltingly, some I even had to grope for. There was too much distraction. Sounds drifted from the distant street, men's voices, the occasional trundle of wheels. I closed my eyes and pictures formed out of my blindness. I saw the men, the arms-cart, the plodding mule. One of the marchers played a little experimental riff on a drum. A great deep-throated roar of laughter sounded, as if they were going to a cockfight rather than to battle.

A female voice shrilled unintelligibly. More laughter. The camp-followers had come already. I wondered about men's lust, the strange potency that grips each soldier in the last hours before death, the weird need to perpetuate, in the jaws of extinction, his fleshly image . . . God! what thoughts! in the midst of my most special novena. I finished my broken prayer, flushed with shame, projecting the Cross into my mind. A face rose and blocked it out. Narrow, poised, with a sharp, inward-looking cleverness, it stared from behind my closed lids. There were demons in me, surely. Why, when my thoughts should be of God and the King, should she arise, little Lady Margaret Beaufort? I crossed myself and she faded, did Lady Stanley, who even now must hang her head, do penance for being mother to the enemy. Or would she, instead, seek comfort in old books of learning, tomorrow, or the next day, with her Henry justly slain?

I knew that Richard cherished her still. He would; it was ever his way.

I got up and went outside. By the pear tree, Robin provoked the brindled cat, with fluttering runs and leaping. Giles was there too, long-shadowed, simpering with excitement.

'Why aren't you at work?' I asked.

He was a great lummox. With sparkling baby-face, he pointed towards the dove-cote. On the bench beneath sat a man, a dark-jowled stranger, holding a harp.

'Pretty!' said Giles.

The man rose unhurriedly. His eye mocked us both.

'Good day, Sister!' he said, pulling off his cap. 'Your knave kindly gave me water. Playing to an army is thirsty work.'

All this came forth in a bastard accent. Another French import, I thought. Soon we shall have no good English minstrels left. On sight I disliked him.

'You've had your water? Then go.'

'Without payment?' he asked, with a smile, and stripping eyes. 'By St Denis, Sister, I thought the English gave *rien* away! I'm fortunate indeed. What shall I sing for you?'

'This is a holy house,' I said coldly. 'We need no bawdry.'

'Not even a psalm?' he answered softly and, with a still softer chord, began.

> *'Agnus Dei*
> *Qui tollis peccata mundi*
> *Miserere nobis*
> *Dona nobis pacem.'*

I admitted the music's beauty. He said quickly: 'My skill is much praised. Your Bishop Morton 'ad me sing for him. An whole hour.'

'Certes, you do well.'

'You know the Bishop of Ely?' he asked, eyes half-closed against the sun. 'One more song, then, Sister. Something to make you remember how life was before you took your vows.'

'No more,' I said.

'But *oui!*'—brows lifted. 'A song in English. 'Twas penned by Robert Cornysh—all admire 'im.'

He sang, warming my stale nunly blood. I did not like the words, but he was a craftsman.

'Adieu! adieu! my heart is lust,
Adieu, my joy and my solace,
In dubil sorrow complain I must
Until I die. Alas! Alas!'

'So we are having a little war tomorrow,' he said gaily, as I sat silent. 'The King comes to Leicester.'

'Have you seen him?' I think I would probably have asked the Devil himself. Out of the corner of my eye I glimpsed Robin, strutting around the cat, who lay jadedly licking a paw.

'I 'ave seen the King's bed,' he answered. 'They were carrying it into the Inn. He takes it with 'im wherever he goes. 'Im, I have not seen.'

He slung his harp and sauntered towards the outer gate. One hand on the latch, he said:

'The King sleeps badly, you know. *As well 'e might!*'

At that instant, the cat sprang. There was a flurry of feathers, a thin stream of blood upon the ground. Too late, I ran to Robin. The brave, silly bird had played his last, teasing game. Bright-breasted, he lay dying in my palm. So still, so pretty. Giles snatched up the snarling cat and broke its neck.

After a long time I said: 'Come, Giles, into the street.'

To see his standard, that was all I wished. Or his face among the banners? I thought: Richard, Richard, can my eyes support it? Or shall I, coward, run with turned-down face to cloister, rather than wake that joy and grief at sight of *your* eyes, risk hearing that voice and falling again into the abyss of love?

I felt faint as ever I did when I was a young maid. Down the road towards us came two heralds, and I heard those words again, which might as well be shaped in this wise: your heart is coming, your life is swelling, all the joy you had in this world rides towards you; for these men, whose faces I never even saw, doffed their caps within the shadow of our house and murmured:

'The King comes to Leicester.'

I had seen his standard, it was enough. We turned back towards the house. Giles made a little bubbling noise. 'What did they say?' he wanted to know.

'King Richard is coming,' I said, and began an Ave, my fingers slipping moistly.

'King Richard,' Giles, the popinjay. Repeat the last phrase spoken, as if to lock it in the mind, but alas, poor Giles, there was a little door at the nether end of his head and in a trice he would forget.

'King Richard.' Giles, of the wanton tongue. He was fumbling for something deep within the recesses of his mind, furrowing his brow, gasping and spluttering, all the while tugging at my sleeve, so I looked with a smile of encouragement at the bursting lips, the bubble of intelligence that would never be born.

Lightly I smoothed his eyes. 'Yea, our King,' I said. 'Perchance, if you go down to the market, you will see him.'

I was unready for his look of terror. 'Nay!' he cried, and twisted out and away, gathering himself to run. He pushed me back through the wicket, slammed the door and leaned against it, panting. And because I knew myself called to spend most of my life among idiots and the afflicted, I spoke him kind, while he blubbered palely as he did at nights when his dreams came upon him.

'Do you not want to see our King?' I asked gently, and it was as if the little door in this poor idiot's mind were half-open for words came tumbling out and his spittle streaked the front of my habit as he buried his face against me, and I knelt with him, trying to string the senseless beads of thought together. I felt the fear in him, like a sharp heartbeat. All he would do was wag his tow-head back and forth, shivering and sobbing, and I grew uneasy that if he were to suffer such fits more often and the Bishop saw him in one, he would once more be put through the torment of exorcism, tied foaming to the rood-screen in the nave, for they were doughty demons, these, and loath to leave their gentle host. I started to shush and chide him, while he whimpered of murder.

'And who is murdered then, chuck?'

It was best this way, as with his nightmares, to go along with the story until it unfolded in splutter and moan and was forgotten.

'The little King—' this came out well—'and his brother. In great London Tower.'

'You have never seen the Tower,' I said, laughing. 'And there's no little King. Only King Richard. He comes to deliver us from our enemies.'

What was he saying, this idiot boy?

'King Richard . . . did have them done to death. King Herod. Jesu, Jesu! King Herod is coming!' and he fell lower still, wormlike, his arms about my knees.

'God help you, child.' My lips were stiff. 'What's this talk?'

'The man said . . .' he blubbered.

'What man?'

He was crooning a little song, vaguely familiar, about love and joy and regret, a French air.

'Who spoke of King Herod?'

A fresh fit of shivering. A peeping eye, wet with witless tears. A smile to chill the blood with its empty charm.

'The man who played the harp,' he drooled. 'He did gi' me this . . . to buy suckets with.' He displayed a mark, a whole mark. A generous minstrel.

'And what said he of the King?'

The smile went again under a fear-cloud. He put his lips close to my face.

'He is a murderer,' Giles said, very clearly. 'The harp-man did gi' me a penny. Look! Pretty!' and he held it up, so it winked in the sun.

I had not finished the novena, so many things unfinished, I thought, lying stretched on the stones, pressing my hands over my ears so that I should not hear the royal army riding by. Hour after hour the vast train had clattered through Leicester to the field of battle, with fife and drum and chafing, creaking leather, out over the bridge westward. The calm church enfolded me as the last hoofbeats died and the trumpet faded on the light wind. Spots of thundery rain smacked against the window. The coloured saints darkened at a passing cloud. But beneath the phial of Virgin's Milk my candle burned with a steady flame.

Behind my closed lids, he sat opposite me and stretched his legs in the hearth. His eyes caught the firelight. They were so dark and intense they were almost frightening, until I took the courage to look deeply, *past* the eyes themselves, as it were, and catch at their spark, which was no more than a lonely kindness, a fragile hunger. Wisdom and sorrow to make him old beyond his years lay in that look. The essence of those eyes was pain. In church I thought of him lovingly, and my sin fled suddenly away. For had I not seen Christ, at the Mystery Play, chide those who would have stoned an adulteress? I remember Christ laughing to see them shrink and hide their own shame. He had a lovely laugh. I thought, in church, with love upon the King: I shall love Him until I die. We shall grow old together, leagues distant, rank and station apart. Though we shall never meet again, I, a nun, will love Him with my last breath, my heart's blood.

'Jesu! you are fair!' he whispered, and the altar candles wavered, merged in points of light. 'My maid, my maid, my true, good maid,' he murmured, and I felt the stone beneath my body grow fluid and warm like molten gold, like the fruit of the Philosopher's Stone, with which foolish Edward Plantagenet had once toyed; like the sap of the lily, the scent of the rose. And, call me by my name, sweet heart. Richard, my lord, my love, my heart was sad because I needed you, I said, and somewhere outside the church an anxious, rusty voice called me, and there was the floor chill beneath my hands, the candles flickering coldly, and sunlight looking gently in, the brief storm over.

'Are you sick?' Dame Lucy asked. She had with her a boy who had been crying. She touched my cheek with a worried finger. 'You are so pale.'

I recognized the youth, he was the son of the woman who lived at West Gate, the troublesome hussy who had been stricken with the kidneys.

'What's to do, Frank?' I asked, still dazed and in a dream. I had been in the fire, and burning. Slowly my visions ebbed away.

'Tis my mother, passing sick,' he gulped. 'Please come, Sister. Make her well again.'

'At this time!' cried Lucy, scandalized. 'Have sense, knave. There's soldiers on the road. Don't you know we are at war?' She pressed my hand. 'Are you well?' she whispered. 'You have been in the church all night. We heard Prime in the Mother's Chapel. We would not disturb you, as it was a novena. But you must eat, or you'll swoon.'

I smiled. 'All night?' I asked. Poor kind Lucy was wandering, but I would leave her her fancies.

'I'll go, if the Mother says I may.'

'The Mother is abed, too weak to rise this morning,' she muttered. 'And you, Frank, you've earned us all a penance! I should not speak. And the battle has begun. They camped last night around Market Bosworth, and fired the first shots an hour after Prime. Sister, don't go out today! You might be . . .'

Ravished, she was about to say, hence her rosy cheek. Again, I smiled. I had stolen a look into Katherine's mirror, the last time she came. Only a blind man would rape me now.

'I'll get my medicines,' I said.

The juice of stitchwort, those white delicate flowers with their golden anthers—a sunbeam in a jar. Saxifrage, the plant with which the Romans broke down rocks. And cherry, to

534

give the woman tranquil sleep. I went with Frank into the bright day. One or two windows trembled on their catches as we passed through Leicester, but the streets were very quiet.

'My uncle rides today,' Frank said, his lips quivering. 'And glad to go,' he said. 'That Henry Tudor came up by Earl Shilton and brought his men right through Brocky Fields. He ruined our corn.'

When I arrived, the woman had already passed two stones. I bled and physicked her and made her easy. Then, because she thought she was dying, I heard her confession—a neighbour cheated some months ago, an afternoon's whoring at the tavern, a blow, a blasphemy. She coughed of sundries, while Frank sat on the step outside, disconsolately picking his nose and staring at the empty street.

'Jesu be thanked for a little peace,' she said, after the absolution. 'All yesterday the army plagued my rest. Very fine they looked, going by'—with a leer. 'The King too, with his golden crown. His horse nigh threw him on the bridge, they say. What a pother! I'm a sick woman.' As if the battle should have been postponed, to her comfort. Her light eyes held mine contemptuously. I remember that woman well. She was part of the day.

'They fight for England,' I said. I dismissed that about the bridge as gossip. He was a consummate horseman.

'Pah!' She nipped off a flea between her breasts. 'Who cares? One King's the same as any other. What if they should lose? 'Tis naught to me.'

'God be with you.' It was hard to say. Rising, I instructed her which draughts to take, and she watched me, then said without warning: 'Good to be out, eh, Sister? There's still some lusty fellows in the ale-house with more sense than to march Bosworth way. Tell 'em in cloister that I kept you . . .'

'You've kept me all morning.' Have charity, I told myself. 'I've missed three Offices through your sickness, which I trust is mending.'

She opened her lips and Lord knows what give they would have uttered, when suddenly afar off, and nearing every moment, came a sound like a gale rattling window-panes, a heavy, urgent noise, the angry sound of horses hard-ridden under mail. Outside the open door and past it in a trice, a score of riders flashed by, so fast it was impossible to read their colours. We heard them roaring up through West Gate and on into the town, clashing and slithering on the cobbles. They screamed inaudible tidings, and were gone. Frank rushed in, his face alight.

'It's all over,' he cried.

The woman raised herself in bed to peer through the window. Now other sounds grew out of the distance, more galloping, shouting, the shrill neigh of a horse. There was a smell of metal and drifting dust. 'So soon?' she marvelled. 'Better be off, Sister. No place for you in the midst of a victorious army!'

I stepped outside. (No place for you, sweet heart. Among the rude soldiers and the harlots. So he had said, that night.) On the horizon I saw a surge of movement, shaping into an advance, filling the road. 'Let Frank go with you!' she called, but I shook my head, I clove to the ditch and bent low as the coloured host bore down with blinding sunlight on their mail. And blood too, I saw, as they came jostling nearly on top of me, blood spraying from a stirruped foot, from a half-severed hand at which the owner clutched while he rode, and grinned like a nightmare. Stinging clods of dirt flew up and choked my eyes. Foam from the horses, smelling of grass and blood, splashed my habit. The men were shouting, laughing, wild with war and life. As if they had drunk deep, they yelled, they sang.

'Cleave to the Crown though it hang on a bush!'

One of the horsemen pulled up in my path. His horse's hooves reared overhead. I slid into the ditch.

'Yea! yea! The King said that! The King said that, when all was done!' In the wake of their passing I stood to pray, for the King victorious. Along the road behind, more men advanced. I went to meet them. I went, willingly, towards outrageous grief, arms raised to clasp insanity. O Jesu! God! What was it that I saw!

This band came slowly, in formation. A column of mailed riders and infantry on either side of the road, flanked a mass that wavered and plunged as it came closer, of men whose feet dragged in the dirt, unarmed men in chains, men who staggered, and bled, and wept. At the core of the melee was a horseman, bent double as if mortally hurt. From his lax hand trailed the rein of a small beast, and across the beast's back hung a thing, swaying. At first glance it looked like a tapestry all red and white, bright white patterned with red, and above it a standard blew, a tattered strip of silk borne by the wounded knight who rode ahead. Arching over the mule was a forest of halberds. One of the outriders nudged his mount into a trot, leaned down and smote the mule upon the rump and it pricked forward, so that the dangling burden hung heavy and jostled and would have fallen had it not been held fast with thongs, and the felon's rope which clasped its neck under the tossing black hair. For it was a man, had been a man, once, and the ragged standard overhead, the arms of England, the lilies specked and spotted with blood, the leopards almost torn in two . . .

They were coming faster. They would ride me down. Would to God they had. For it was a man, and, as I knelt, the bloody, naked body, the swinging head, cast low like that of a slaughtered sheep, came close to mine, and I saw the face which for seventeen years had been held in my heart.

Others have told me how I got up and ran behind, crying out, and that the Tudor's men mocked me. That I ran alongside and fell upon my face, and got up, and fell again and again, until my robe was dabbled with blood and mire from the trail of his passage, caked dark with the blood of his wounds, and that I called him, most piteously, and sought ever and anon to touch his dangling hands, or a strand of his hair. And that as we came through into Leicester the people, crowding out of the houses, jeered at me and sang: 'A nun, a nun! Behind the traitor see her run!' But some there were that crossed themselves, and turned pale at what was reckoned after to be a wondrous sight, and some there were that swore and turned indoors again. But I saw none of this, neither did I properly hear the deep, swelling chant that came from the throats of Henry Tudor's mercenaries, those well-schooled agents of death, shame and defilement, the chanting that grew as we approached Bow Bridge, that little bridge, so small and stonily narrow. And I knew in my heart that there was no room for all that host to pass without injury to my lord, for 'tis true I thought him badly hurt but still alive, and screamed for them to halt, my scream lost in the clamour of the crowd, the roar of 'Murderer! Murderer! Murderer!' and the stinging rain of flints from a group of corner-boys who revelled in the show.

They surged on to the bridge, packed tight, the horses struggling in fear. The mule, now nearly dropping from weariness among the foaming destriers, the steel-clad thighs, its flanks sodden with bloody sweat, staggered against the side of the bridge. The King's head was crushed upon the stone. I heard the sound of rending bone, saw the bright new hurt done to that head which once did lie so sweetly in my lap. And I went mad.

All this is many years ago, now I may speak of it, whereas before, a certain noise or sight would have me raving in an instant, self-imprisoned in a closet for days on end, until the racking grief ebbed enough for me to walk again, and pray again, and take my meat once more.

They sent Giles out to find me, which he did, standing in the market-place. He said that I was singing, but that's a lie. He carried me home in his arms, with many a backward look. I reckon he came knowing that King Herod, dead, could do him no harm. Though I saw no more that day, I know that they laid Richard on a hurdle in the market-place, naked in death with eyes upturned to the circling kites and four of Henry's men standing yawning around him, on guard over the evidence of his destruction; and that the obedient townsfolk came to spit upon him and to gape at a proclamation that the Tudor had made to the effect that he, Henry, was King, and had been King by right of conquest from the day before the battle. So that there, stiff mortal clay, lay tyrant and usurper, traitor and renegade, Richard Plantagenet, who had dared ride against the King. Richard Plantagenet, whose soul I loved, whose child I bore.

Being then so devoid of sight and thought, I believed that he still lived, and had escaped. This I believed for three days while my mind went away—that he had gone overseas, to Flanders, mayhap, like when he was a young child, and that the corpse lying in Leicester Market had naught to do with him.

With the three days' dying, he came to me at last.

On the fourth day the Mother rose from her sick-bed and came to me. Her words were merely a formless babble of sound. All I could hear was the bell tolling, one thick stroke upon another, more regular, but almost in time with, my own heart beat. It rang on every hour for some little time, and the intervals of quiet were terrible to hear. They could not stop us ringing the bell, I told her, and she looked at me troublously, and brought me Clary wine. I knew it was Clary, I remembered the taste well, and I laughed in the Mother's face, which was ghostly and dewed with sickness and said: 'But I am not with child!'—meaning the Clary—a dreadful thing to say in truth, but she stroked me and murmured: 'Nay, my daughter,' and asked me to help her in a task and look for Giles. There was I, spilling the Clary, the madness potion, and trying, with a swollen bitten tongue, to explain that I

538

had sent Giles to the chandlers, with all the money I could lay hands on. Giles was not back yet, I said, the Tudor's men had caught him and he lay stripped stark dead down in the Market.

A little man stood behind the Mother; he had a leather bag with him and eyes that roamed uneasily about, up and down the nave as if he counted the gargoyles, the weeping monk, the holy monk, the mason and the lion; and his feet moved up and down too, first one and then the other, as if he was afraid the stone faces might come down and get him, or as if he was anxious to be up and doing at whatever craft was his.

Everyone was there except Ursula, and Lucy begged the Mother to rest, but the latter raised hands leaf-thin and said: 'Dame, our King is dead,' and Lucy bowed and started on her beads, which she had not left off telling for the three days, good Lucy. At this I marvelled, for King Edward had been dead many years.

Another man came to stand beside the Mother; I thought him at first one of the Abbey priests, for he had a black cloak wrapped all about him with the cowl pulled deep over his face so that only his lips were visible, moving in a whisper at the Mother's ear. They murmured together for a long while. Their whispering washed up over the carved columns and shivered goldly upon the altar-cross. Then I saw the Mother nodding, nodding, and heard her say: 'Yea, gladly. It shall all be done, when the boy comes back,' and I started to cry like a child, thinking in some way she was wroth with me for sending Giles out for so many candles. They went away, then. When he brought them to me there must have been an hundred, heavy as a sheaf of May-blossom, whiter than almond's milk. I tried to stay Giles but he ran off, saying that they wanted him, the Mother and a man, because he was so tall and strong.

I lit the candles one by one. I ranked them like soldiers all the way along the altar steps, and was glad that the evening outside was thunderous dull, for thus their light was unchallenged and fell, soft as silk, in a spreading stain from the altar to the tiles, to the edge of the misericords, crept softly up the walls and painted each gargoyle with soft light, so that each one had a shadow like a round black beard, wavering infinitesimally. All the way down the nave bloomed my petals of light, tier upon tier, echoing each other, my sacred fires, burning. At last there came calmness.

The garden was full of birds, singing. To the outer gate I went, and drew it wide. And waited. And knew. The little man with the leather bag stood beside me, chattering. 'Your Reverend Prioress is a passing noble lady,' he would say. Then: 'The streets are quieter now. The people have gone to their homes. Yea, they've all gone home.' Over and over he said the same thing, and fidgeted, and looked up and down, for fiends. 'She ought not to have gone out,' he would say, 'But the streets are much quieter. Yea, that's right.'

'What have you in your bag?' I said, watching the road.

'Why, Sister, thread and needles.'

'Then you must see Dame Ursula,' I said.

'I'm not selling.' He shifted his feet. A crazy man.

Together we watched the street. And soon they appeared in the dusky distance, and there was a light about them that was not earthly, and the dust that rose about them seemed silver and gold and hung like St Elmo's fire, a shining mist. Although when I glanced again at the needleseller whose wares were not for sale, he had it too.

Giles plodded on one side of the mule, the tall cloaked stranger on the other. Behind them walked the Prioress, holding up her cross.

' 'Tis scandal and shame,' said the needle-man. 'You'd have thought King Henry could have had him decently entombed. We couldn't leave him lying there, could we?'

They were coming. 'But the Abbey monks were afraid,' he said. 'Certes, I admire the Mother's charity. In truth, I do.'

They had reached the gate. I watched Giles move to the mule's offside, lifting strong arms. The swirling cloak of the stranger hid them from my sight.

I pushed the wicket wider still, so my lord should come to no harm.

They were bringing him in, and he was dead. None could have taken those blows, and lived. He was dead, and I loved him. He was dead, dead, my heart, my life, my lord, my love, my King. My love had come to me at last. My love was dead.

'Lay his Grace in church,' the Mother said. She wept. She said softly: 'Holy Jesu! this is an awful day!'

They had brought a catafalque and, lapped in light, he lay upon it. Someone had thrown a coarse cloth over him, covering him to the throat. Deftly the little man removed it, and became a craftsman. He opened his bag, drew out a shining spool, and threaded needles, clicking his tongue as if what he saw were a bad piece of work, something botched and untidy that he must right. Giles stood gaping near and listened to soft explanations, a bad business this, deep wounds, see, boy,

540

yonder was a knifethrust, this a pike, the arm is broken here, the bone protrudes, and by my faith, they hone their axes sharp these days—see how it let his blood! I kept them from his face, they took one look at mine, and went on, murmuring: right through the lungs here, lad, well, lookee! the sword broke in him here, and shame, shame! all this done after death. Pass me my fluid, knave, don't spill. This is for the embalming.

I kept them from his face. I looked on it again, my candles licked it gold. I took a cloth with water from a ewer and washed his face gently as he lay upon the bier, and he was dead, with his fine-boned countenance cloven and gashed by a dozen horrid wounds, and his long dark hair heavy with blood, and his eyes not yet at peace, for they were half open. So I it was who closed those eyes that stared deathward into betrayal, and I signed his brow with the Cross, and dared not kiss him, for he was the King, so instead I washed his feet and let them have his face, to make it fair again.

I thought of the old story Patch was wont to tell, of the woman who had loved Owen Tudor, who cleansed his face and combed his hair and set an hundred candles burning around him, and she too was a woman whom no one knew but who was thought a crazy woman, and now the cursed Tudor had slain my lord. And as all his sorrow was ever my sorrow, so did I die with him that day. Although I still walk and breathe and sometimes smile, I have no heart . . .

Men came to kneel by me, first one, cloaked like the stranger, then another still clad in harness and with a neck wound from which the red oozed wearily, then four or five together. One of these wore a hermit's robe, carelessly donned, with the strength of his mail winking beneath it. They say that the church filled up from porch to rood-screen with men who entered like ghosts and wept like babes. There were running feet and a voice that burst through the whispering silence with 'My Lord! My Lord Lovell!'—crying that they were hanging the prisoners and fugitives in Leicester Market and Lovell must fly at once, and for answer came only the deep, dreadful sound of men's grief; the hasty feet clattered nearer and stopped short, the voice said: 'Ah, Dickon!' as a child might wail in the night, then swore like a man in the face of murder. And the church was filled with love and hate and vengeance, and a heaviness that one could touch with the hand. Over all came the sweet blossomy smell of the candles, and the Tansy, with which my sisters anointed the hurt men. That wondrous wound herb, that false, pretentious herb, which, like all the flowers of this world, could not stay death.

His despair was my despair, his ruin my ruin. I died, and there was none to bury me.

Then suddenly Ursula came, hurrying, hobbling in, smiling joyfully, with her eyes blinking like a mole in the light. Unseeing and heedless of the silent work, the sadness, or the Mother's prone, praying form beneath the candles, she came, while the ranks of mourning men parted for her. It was days since she had left her cell. In her arms she carried a sheaf of satin riches, green as love, each shining rose perfect and proper, each spray a living frond, each colour a jewel, with the stern words of the Absolution limned like lustrous soldiers round the edge.

'I'll make penance the rest of my days,' she said in a joyous whisper. 'I've missed Mass, I've missed Confession. But, oh Lord, Sister! 'Tis finished! Is't not fair?'

She came close, blind to the grief, or the figure on the bier. 'And for you, child, see!' with a daring, naughty look. 'So small, and in *his* honour too!'

She had fashioned a silver Boar in each corner.

'Ursula,' I said. 'Ursula.'

She did not hear me. She was looking at his body, his murdered naked body, so white, so still.

'Ah!' she said, with deep compassion. 'Ah, the poor young knight!'

And she unfurled the beautiful frontal, like a banner. It was heavy, but with one movement of her old arms she threw it out upon the air, so that it caught and glowed in the light, green, the colour of hope, with its roses like stars, its crosses of flame, and the eternal words of the Absolution tall and clear. And it fell, as she had intended, upon the body of Richard, and he lay beneath it, lapped in green fire, and was magnificent.

Today, once more, I am forced to remember. It is All Souls' Day, and a lady sits by his grave. As she has come purposely to see us, I cannot refuse her.

It is sixteen years since we buried him, here in our own cloister, among the crumbling tombs of sisters long-departed, some of whom even lived in the era of saints. I think they might be pleased to know that such a one lay among them.

While the hangings went on outside, we sang the solemn

Dirige and *Placebo*. Our voices stretched to Heaven, while the low sad note of the men was like the buzzing of bees whose summer is over. The whole community kept vigil that night, and in the morning we fashioned a Mass for him as glorious as Ursula's gift. He had no money, so the Mother gave the Mass penny for him, that he should rest in Christ, in a place of cool repose, of light, and peace, and we prayed also for the brave men who had fought beside him and those who at that moment died by the rope, through that very bravery. Sir Francis Lovell escaped, and a man of York, John Sponer, who stayed behind to talk to us, only got away by the hairs of his head. He spoke of vengeance. Meanwhile, he said, he would show to the people of York what a great mischief had been done through treachery, that the Devil was surely let loose, and, in tears, said he wished his was not the task.

'It will bring them much sorrow,' he said.

My companion stirs. She is incredibly old, this lady, but her wits are still as undulled as the carvings on the Mother's tomb, against which she leans. Dame Lucy is Prioress now.

'That was exactly what was written,' she murmurs. 'In York Civic Records they noted it down. "Our good King Richard, late mercifully reigning over us. He was piteously slain and murdered, to the great heaviness of this city." '

I should not sit down on damp October days. Here am I, striving to rise, one would think I was the octogenarian, yet she sees my infirmity and gives me a most kind hand. Holding mine, she asks me something, fittingly whispered. 'Is it true?'

'Yea.' I can smile into her pretty, wrinkled face. 'A daughter. She died.'

My Katherine. There are days when I am certain it was better so and this is one of them, for I have heard fresh lies about her father, and though the oath I gave her kept me silent once, now it is too late.

But my guest's face becomes sorry, thoughtful.

'I had hoped at least one of his children lived,' she says. 'Especially after the business with John o' Gloucester, which was one of the most heinous acts ever wrought. You know why Henry had him killed?'

Nodding, I say: 'For having treasonable correspondence with Ireland.'

Years ago, the heralds had bawled it in Swine Market, lest any be in doubt.

'One letter,' says my lady, angry and sad. 'About hawks

and fishing and a new doublet. And to a kinsman of mine, too. It makes me feel to blame. Cursed be the King.'

I feel a tremor of life. I will offer her refreshment, later, and we will use her last words for a toast.

'There was no harm in John.'

'Yea!' she answers. 'But he lost his life. Because he was a King's son!'

I think of John sadly. I was once jealous of his mother. So was I jealous of this gentle lady, standing with her hand in my twisted claw. I think of John. And young Warwick. And Warbeck. Warbeck of Barnard Castle. Richard the Fourth, silenced for ever. But the brief fire dies and Katherine of Desmond is looking down, face quiet and tender, concealing all the things of which we need not speak. The talk that still goes on, unfought, for there is none to fight it.

'Jesu preserve thee, Richard,' she says, softly. Then: 'Why, the weeds grow on his grave!'

It's true. They break through even the cloister wall and come up in between the stones. Nasty, trailing, tangling things, they wrap themselves around his rest, and the ivy is the worst of all. As soon as I strip its horny tendrils down, a fresh growth seeds itself. But while I have the power I must combat it, for it rots the fabric and the roots go deep. For all it symbolizes Fidelity, it clings like a slander.

Soon my lady of Desmond and I will go inside to pray, and take wine, and then she will leave. I shall write of her coming in my book, which I must burn before I die. I can smile at that! It should have been burned sixteen years ago.

'Tis no heresy to love, and be mad.

For I have known death, and am risen, not to glory but to a plain of calm shadows. What I have told my lady today is all like something read in an old romance, and there is no movement in me, not even of sadness. And I construe this, for I can do no other, as the sure and true manifestation of mercy, contained in a special prayer whose touchstone of worth I have but lately learned to value.

Then may that mercy be in my heart, my mind, my wit, my will, for ever and sustain me. Through the last stages of this old complaint called life.

HERE ENDS THE NUN'S TALE
AND THAT OF THE MAIDEN